D0991242

Admiralty

Volume Four

The Collected Short Works of Poul Anderson

Edited by Rick Katze

NESFA Press

Post Office Box 809
Framingham, MA 01701
www.nesfa.org/press
2011

© 2011 by the Trigonier Trust

© 2011 by David G. Hartwell

© 1957, 1983 by Poul Anderson and Gordon R. Dickson
"The Adventure of the Misplaced Hound"

"Editor's Introduction" © 2011 by Rick Katze

Dust jacket illustration © 2011 by John Picacio

Dust jacket design © 2011 by Alice N. S. Lewis

All rights reserved.

No part of this book may be reproduced in any form or by any electronic, magical or mechanical means, including information storage and retrieval, without
permission in writing from the publisher, except by a reviewer, who may quote
brief passages in a review.

FIRST EDITION, February 2011

ISBN-10: 1-886778-94-9
ISBN-13: 978-1-886778-94-8

Publication History

"Poul Anderson" by David G. Hartwell is original to this volume.

"Admiralty" first appeared in *The Magazine of Fantasy & Science Fiction*, May 1963.

"The Adventure of the Misplaced Hound" by Poul Anderson and Gordon R. Dickson first appeared in *Universe Science Fiction,* December 1953.

"Delenda Est" first appeared in *The Magazine of Fantasy & Science Fiction*, December 1955.

"The Pugilist" first appeared in *The Magazine of Fantasy & Science Fiction*, November 1973.

"Inside Straight" first appeared in *The Magazine of Fantasy & Science Fiction*, August 1955.

"Lodestar" first appeared in *The John W Campbell Memorial Anthology*, Random House, 1973.

"The Bitter Bread" first appeared in *Analog Science Fiction / Science Fact,* December 1975.

"Gypsy" first appeared in *Astounding Science Fiction,* January *1950.*

"Marius" first appeared in *Astounding Science Fiction,* March 1957.

"Home", originally published under the title of "The Disinherited", first appeared in *Orbit 1*, Berkley Publishing Corporation, 1966.

"Quixote and the Windmill" first appeared in *Astounding Science Fiction,* November 1950.

"Black Bodies", a revised version of "Physicist's Lament", first published in 1992.

"Kyrie" first appeared in *The Farthest Reaches*, Pocket Books, 1968.

"The Problem of Pain" first appeared in *The Magazine of Fantasy & Science Fiction*, February 1973.

"Holmgang", originally published until the title of "Out of the Iron Womb", first appeared in *Planet Stories,* Summer 1955.

"Goat Song" first appeared in *The Magazine of Fantasy & Science Fiction*, February 1972.

"The Barrier Moment" first appeared in *Astounding Science Fiction (Analog Science Fact & Fiction),* March 1960.

"The Star Beast" first appeared in *Super Science Stories*, September 1950.

"Eutopia" first appeared in *Dangerous Visions*, Doubleday and Co. 1967.

"Eutopia (afterword) first appeared in *Past Times* TOR Books, 1984.

"Horse Trader" first appeared in *Galaxy Science Fiction,* March 1953.

"Murphy's Hall" first appeared in *Infinity Two*, Lancer Books 1971.

"Sister Planet" first appeared in *Satellite Science Fiction*, May 1959.

"Among Thieves" first appeared in *Astounding Science Fiction,* June 1957.

"Operation Changeling" first appeared in *The Magazine of Fantasy & Science Fiction*, May-June 1969.

Contents

Admiralty

EDITOR'S INTRODUCTION

This is volume 4 in a series collecting Poul Anderson's short fiction. I had originally planned for 6 volumes encompassing about 1.5 million words. I already have a list of stories for volume 5 with a significant additional number of stories which will form the basis for volume 6. Since Anderson's short fiction totals over 4 million words, I now expect that the series will be at least 7 volumes.

Some stories are a piece of a larger history. Some are stand-alone. These volumes are not intended to include complete series in a single volume. Nor are they published in any internal chronological order. For the most part, except for a few changes in the words used by Poul Anderson in later versions of the stories, I have tried to use the original magazine version.

As such, you will find stories of time travel, fantasy, the near future, and the far future which showcase Anderson's talent.

Manse Everard, David Falkyn, and Nicholas van Rijn are represented in this volume. In addition to the characters previously listed, Volume 5 is planned to include a Dominic Flandry story.

At the time that some of these stories were written, the events described in them were still possible. "The Pugilist" is a story about the future which will not happen. It is well-written and quite logical assuming that certain things happened in the 20th Century which, fortunately, did not happen.

While we now know that the physical attributes of the Venus as described in "Sister Planet" are not possible, this should not interfere with the reading of the story.

Poul Anderson was a devoted fan of Sherlock Holmes. Previous volumes have included a Sherlockian story. This volume is no different. See "The Adventure of the Misplaced Hound", cowritten with Gordon R. Dickson.

Sit back, open the book and read. And enjoy reading stories by a master craftsman who gave us so many good stories.

Rick Katze
Framingham, MA
October 2010

POUL ANDERSON

BY DAVID G. HARTWELL

Poul Anderson's "The Saturn Game" won both the Hugo and Nebula Awards for best novella in 1982, a choice therefore of both readers and writers. It is a story of men and women who have traveled far, some of whom out of boredom and lack of useful work have allowed themselves too much involvement in fantasy role-playing—they have turned away from real nature into the realms of the imagination. Then the natural universe confronts them with great beauty and great danger. And, enchanted by the beauty, they blind themselves to the danger. Time and again they fail to hear the voice of reason and so their flaw is sad and frustrating, if not tragic. Certainly it is deadly. And it is not theirs alone, for there are other groups of gamers exploring elsewhere perhaps in similar danger.

This is an allegory for our time as well as theirs, I think, calling out for psychological strength and balance in the face of the seduction of beguiling entertainments, in order that we might survive and achieve our goals. It is a sad story, in a way, but a wonderful story too, and filled with strange and compelling landscapes that have the virtue of reality. In it, Anderson uses both a fantasy style, a poetic language of allusion and metric rhythms, and a science fiction style, colloquial and clear, perhaps a bit hard-boiled in this case for contrast. The voice of reason is, in the end more powerful, but only just. There are many moments throughout the story when we feel, with the characters, that fantasy will get us through the worst moments, and this is perhaps Anderson's greatest achievement, and the root source of the story's emotional impact: that it does not, though often we want it to, and that SF triumphs over fantasy.

Poul Anderson, one of the Grand Masters of Science Fiction who lent particular honor to that title, died at the end of July 2001. He was a gentleman, a gentle wit, and a professional writer of astonishing competence, varied talents and interests, and a thoughtful and underappreciated stylist.

Poul Anderson's first published SF story was in Astounding, 1947. His first novel, *Vault of the Ages*, was published in 1952 and I read it in seventh grade, a year or so later, already familiar with Anderson's early short fiction. I thought it was a neat and engaging story then and still do. I began to follow his fiction, seek out his stories, and continue to do so to this day. I remember finally tracking down a hardcover of *The Broken Sword*, his rich, intriguing fantasy novel after several more years, (I didn't live near a bookstore 'til then) and being even more impressed. I still consider it one of the best fantasy novels of the 20th century. By the end of the 1950s he was one of my favorite SF writers. It was a particular pleasure to grow up and become, on several occasions between 1970 and the end of his life, his editor. I bought his books every chance I got, nearly everywhere I worked as an editor, for 30 years.

I thought so highly of his writings and his authorial persona that I was initially surprised, and I admit a little disappointed upon first meeting him to find he mostly wanted to talk about contracts and the mechanics of publishing. This was 1972 and I was a young consulting editor who had bought, or participated in buying, a five-book package of new novels from him. I remember him sitting there on the sofa at LACon 3 in the SFWA suite calmly talking business while Philip K. Dick convinced a young woman in a belly-dancing outfit to lie down on the carpet to demonstrate how she could move a quarter from her tummy into her navel by muscular control. I has mistakenly assumed that he would be personally flamboyant and dominate the room, as he so often dominated the issues of magazines in which his stories appeared.

Poul Anderson spent his early years as a writer in Minnesota, with his friends Gordon R. Dickson and Clifford D. Simak; later in the 1950s, he moved to California (the Bay Area, where he lived for the rest of his life) and become friends with Frank Herbert and Jack Vance as well. The three of them and their families all lived together on a houseboat one summer. I have heard stories about that summer from all of them. He was married to the poet and writer Karen Anderson, a famous beauty in her day—with whom he has also collaborated—and their daughter, Astrid, is married to Greg Bear. To the readers and writers who grew up reading his work he was something of a heroic figure, a living giant of the SF field.

And he was a big man, a sailor of small boats in his day (Jerry Pournelle used Poul the sailor as the model for the central character of one of his Wade Curtis paperback thrillers), stronger even than he looked, but also a talented poet. There was something of the Melancholy Dane about him, but also something of the Viking adventurer out for fun and profit. He used to go out and fight as a swordsman in mock battles put on by the Society for Creative Anachronism. I never saw it, but I heard he was a formidable opponent.

He never let his math skills from his undergraduate degree in physics rust, and was known to do appropriate calculations in designing the planetary and other settings of his fictions. I was pleased and somewhat awestruck to see that side of him in person, over dinner, as he enumerated—as he was calculating them in his head—many details of the nature of a world he might consider writing about, derived on the spot from the nature of its orbit and sun. First the science, then the fiction.

He was a popular guest at science fiction conventions around the world and an enthusiastic attendee. You might not have recognized him at first, because he was just as likely to be sitting in a corner drinking a beer and talking to someone about contractual terms, or politics, in later years as he moved somewhat to the right (somewhat in the manner of Robert A. Heinlein, who was his model early on). He didn't want to be taken to dinner in Berkeley, which he referred to as The People's Republic of Berkeley. But ask him a question and you would recognize in the response as wise and sharp a mind behind the answer as was behind the writing.

During the fifties and the following four decades he produced a long string of fine SF and fantasy adventure stories and novels. "He is perhaps sf's most prolific writer of any consistent quality," said *The Encyclopedia of Science Fiction*. I concur. The extraordinary thing is that he continued to write so well, given that he wrote so much. James Blish, in the 1950s, called him "the continuing explosion." I can't think of an Anderson book or story I couldn't recommend for reading pleasure.

His devotion both to science and to fiction made him one of the most admired and popular living SF writers. He continued the hard SF mode of Robert A. Heinlein and John W. Campbell, the Golden Age tradition that has yielded a high proportion of the classics of the field. It is also the tradition of Rudyard Kipling, and H.G. Wells, of Robert Louis Stevenson and Jack London. His best SF novels include *Brain Wave*, *The Enemy Stars*, *The High Crusade*, *Tau Zero*, and *The Boat of a Million Years*, and recently *Genesis*—and perhaps a dozen more. He won the Hugo Award for short fiction seven times. Of his many excellent collections, *All One Universe* is perhaps most revealing of the man, since it contains not only first class SF stories but also several fine essays and extensive story notes by Anderson, who has been notably reticent in his other books.

He also wrote an impressive body of fantasy fiction, most notably *The Broken Sword*, *Three Hearts and Three Lions*, *A Midsummer Tempest*, the novels of Ys, in collaboration with Karen, and the stories that make up *Operation Chaos*. He wrote mysteries for a while in the late fifties and early sixties, good ones, and was a Baker Street Irregular.

Anderson was a Romantic and a rugged individualist, with an affection for pastoral landscapes worthy of Wordsworth or Shelley, unusual in one who writes with such devotion about science, technology, and space travel. The only comparison that comes to mind is Arthur C. Clarke, for instance Clarke's poetic description of earthrise as seen on the moon, in *Earthlight*. Look, for instance, at the opening paragraphs of his famous story, "The Queen of Air and Darkness," for as lovely and precise a description of a field of flowers as you could find in SF—but they are alien flowers and the description serves to establish differences from our world as well as to give sensuous details and establish a mood. Not enough has been said about his command of technique and stylistic excellences as a writer, but I regard him as one of the premier masters of setting ever in the SF field. Whether he is being vivid and imaginative, as in the example above, or vivid and realistically true to known scientific facts and images, as in his depictions of distant astronomical vistas in *Tau Zero* or "Kyrie," Anderson is precise and sensitive to sensuous detail.

His heroes are heroic and strong in the slightly tragic vein of 19th century Romanticism—often they have suffered some earlier emotional wound—but blended in is a practical streak, an allegiance to reason and to knowledge that is a hallmark of hard science fiction characters, that Heinlein and Campbell tradition referred to above. You know a fair amount about what they are feeling, but what really matters is what they do, regardless of how they feel.

Anderson respects the military virtues of courage, loyalty, honor and sacrifice, and often subjects his characters to situations of extreme hardship, allowing them to show these virtues. But he usually doesn't write about battle. In fact, his characters are businessmen (such as series of books and stories about the wily trader Nicholas van Rijn) as often as soldiers (such as the Dominic Flandry series). In "The Saturn Game," as in *Tau Zero*, they are scientists, multiple specialists. In *The Boat of a Million Years*, they are immortals living throughout human history, from the distant past into the far future, not necessarily above average in intelligence or emotional maturity—though the necessities of survival through the calamities of history have weeded out the weaker ones, and even some of the stronger.

Instead, again in the hard SF tradition, he most often wrote about strong men and women pitted against the challenge of survival in the face of the natural universe. Some of them die. But Anderson was optimist enough to see beyond the dark times into both a landscape, sometimes a starscape, and a future of wonders—for the survivors. Anderson's future is not for the lazy or the stay-at-homes. He was fairly gloomy about current social trends, big government, repression of the individual, so he catapulted his characters into a future of new frontiers, making them face love and death in vividly imagined and depicted environments far from home. I recall the power and beauty and pathos of his fine black hole story, "Kyrie," the wit of *The Man Who Counts* (*The War of the Wing Men*) the good humor of "A Bicycle Built for Brew," the enormous scope and amazing compression of "Memorial." His range was impressive.

When Anderson died, I wrote a piece that said that the loss of a writer and a man of his stature to the community that is the SF field is incalculable, but enormous. He has left a body of work as a model to other writers, but the constant challenge of his presence to advance the tradition of rational wonder and to use the Romantic literary tradition's arsenal of styles and techniques to underpin the realism of the scientific ideas is irreplaceable.

David G. Hartwell
Pleasantville, NY

ADMIRALTY

Consider his problem. The Phoenix region lay a hundred and fifty-odd light-years from Sol. The only human settlement in it was the French colony planet New Europe, circling the sun Aurore. Alerion had seized this and was rapidly building orbital defenses which would make it impregnable. Gunnar Heim had one ship. *Fox II* was, indeed, a cruiser, her gravitrons capable of fantastic acceleration, her automated armament able to curtain her in laser energy and nuclear hellfire while directing a fatal slash through an enemy's similar defense. But she was alone, a privateer commissioned on a technicality. Her men had signed on less for loot than for the sake of striking at man's old foe. However, she could only resupply by selling her captures. Thus every Aleriona vessel she took drained her strength. The prize crews could not return and rendezvous, when *Fox* depended for survival on unpredictable motion through immensity. No news came from home. And that, slowly, wore down men's spirits.

The prisoners he interviewed continued to tell Heim that Earth had not moved, that the World Federation Navy was still merely glaring at Alerion's, out on the Marches. He believed them. As the months passed, his own hope faded.

Yet he was doing tremendous damage. Aurore was not so close to The Eith either. The occupiers of New Europe sat at the end of a long supply line; and they could not spare much bottom for this garrison, when Earth's superior force *might* strike. Heim had not killed anybody—he was proud of that—but he had sent valuable personnel off to internment; he had grabbed ships and material that were sorely missed; he tied up an unholy number of warcraft on convoy duty and the hunt for him. In the end, Alerion sent one of the best naval minds it had, to deal with the situation. The newcomer started arming unescorted cargo carriers.

Fox encountered only one such Q-boat. Had the human crew been less carefully picked and trained, it could have been the end of her. As it was, she reacted smoothly to the surprise, warded off everything that was cast, and laid the enemy under her guns. *Meroeth's* captain surrendered.

In a way, though, he had accomplished his purpose. None realized it, but Gunnar Heim's raiding was at an end.

-1-

Joy filled the ship, where she lay far outsystem with her captive. This was more than another success. There had been humans aboard *Meroeth,* who were now set free.

The mess seethed with men. Only twenty-five privateers remained, and a dozen New Europeans, in a room that had once held a hundred; but they seemed to overflow it, shouting, singing, clashing their glasses, until the bulkheads trembled. Endre Vadasz—wanderfooted troubadour of space, sworn brother to his captain—leaped onto a table. His slim body poised while his fingers flew across the guitar strings. More and more of the French began to sing with him:

> *C'est une fleur, fleur de prairie,*
> *C'est une belle Rose de Provence—*

At first Heim was laughing too loudly at Jean Irribarne's last joke to hear. Then the music grew, and it took him. He remembered a certain night in Bonne Chance. Suddenly he was there again. Roofs peaked around the garden, black under the stars, but the yellow light from windows joined the light of Diane rising full. A small wind rustled the shrubs, to mingle scents of rose and lily with unnamed pungencies from native blooms. Madelon's hand was trusting in his. Gravel scrunched beneath their feet as they walked toward the summerhouse. And somewhere someone was playing a tape, this very song drifted down the warm air, earthy and loving.

> —*Sa jolie taille ronde et gracieuse*
> *Comme une vague souple et mysterieuse.*

His eyes stung. He shook his head harshly.

Irribarne gave him a close look. The New European was medium tall, spare of build, dark-haired, long-headed, and clean-featured. He still wore the garments in which he had been captured, green tunic and trousers, soft boots, beret tucked in scaly leather belt, the uniform of a planetary constabulary turned maquisard. Lieutenant's bars gleamed on his shoulders.

"*Pourquoi cette tristesse soudaine?*"

"Eh?" Heim blinked. Between the racket in here, the rustiness of his French, and the fact that New Europe was well on the way to evolving its own dialect, he didn't understand.

"You show at once the trouble," Irribarne said. Enough English speakers visited his planet, in the lost days, that town dwellers usually had some command of their language.

"Oh...nothing. A memory. I spent several grand leaves on New Europe, when I was a Navy man. But that was—Judas, that was twenty-one years ago.

"And so you think of aliens that slither through streets made empty of men. How they move softly, like hunting panthers!" Irribarne scowled into his glass and drained it in a convulsive gesture. "Or perhaps you remember a girl, and wonder if she is dead or else hiding in the forests. *Hein?*"

"Let's get refills," said Heim brusquely.

Irribarne laid a hand on his arm. "*Un moment, s'il vous plaît.* The population of the whole planet is only five hundred thousand. The city people, that you would meet, they are much less. Perhaps I know."

"Madelon Dubois?"

"From Bonne Chance in origin? Her father a doctor? But yes! She married my own brother Pierre. They live, what last I heard."

Darkness passed before Heim. "*Gud ske lov,*" he breathed: as close to a prayer as he had come since childhood.

Irribarne considered him. The captain was a huge man, two meters in height, blocky of shoulders and face, roan-haired, eyes wintry blue; but on this instant he looked curiously helpless. "Ah, this matters to you. Come, shall we not speak alone?"

"All right. Thanks." Heim led the way to his cabin. When he shut the door, the noise of song and belling chords was chopped off as if they had entered another universe.

Irribarne sat down and glanced about the neat, compact room, the books, a model of a warship, pictures of a woman and a girl. "*Votre famille?*" he asked.

"Yes. My wife's dead, though. Daughter's with her grandfather on Earth." Heim took his glance away from Lisa's image. At fourteen, she might have changed unrecognizably by the time he got back. If he ever did. He offered one of his few remaining cigars and began to stuff a pipe for himself. His fingers were not absolutely steady. "How is your own family?"

"Well, thank you. Of course, that was a pair of weeks ago, when my force was captured." Irribarne got his cigar going and leaned back with a luxurious sigh. Heim stayed on his feet.

"How'd that happen, anyway? We've had no real chance to talk."

"Bad luck, I hope. We set out to blow up a uranium mine on the Cote Notre Dame that the Aleriona were exploiting. We found a sport submarine, for we know that the one thing those damned dryworlders do not have is submarine detection equipment. But the mine was better guarded than we expected. When we surfaced to go ashore at night, a shell hit. Chemical explosive only, or I would not sit here. Their troopers had, as you say, the drop when we swam to land. There was talk about shooting us for an example, or what is worse to squeeze information from us. But the new high commander heard and forbid. Instead, we were going to Alerion. They spoke about prisoner exchange."

"I see."

"But you make stalls. It is news of Madelon you wish, no?"

"Hell, I hate to get personal—Okay. We were in love, when I had a long leave on New Europe. Very innocent affair, I assure you. So damned innocent, in fact, that I shied away a bit and—Anyhow, next time I came back she'd moved."

"Indeed so. To Chateau de St. Jacques. I thought always Pierre got her...on the rebound? Now and then she has laughed about the big *Norwegien* when she was a girl. Such laughter, half happy, half sad, one always makes of young memories." Irribarne's gaze grew stiff. "Pierre is a good husband. They have four children."

Heim flushed. "Don't misunderstand me," he said around his pipe. "I couldn't have married better than I did either. It was just—she was in trouble, and I hoped I could help. Old friendship, nothing else."

He didn't believe he was lying. He had organized this expedition out of a conviction that Earth must strike back now, rather than wait for the enemy's strength to grow. A few other thoughts had crossed his mind, but they were not unduly painful to bury. The more so, he admitted, when he knew that Jocelyn Lawrie was waiting for him; and she was a fine, handsome, altogether satisfying woman, no longer young, of course, but then neither was he. Or Madelon.

"You have that from us all," Irribarne said heartily. "Now tell me more before we return to the festival. Why are you here in only one ship? When does the Navy come?"

God help me, Heim thought, *I wanted to spare them till tomorrow.*

"I don't know," he said.

"Nom d'un chien!" Irribarne sat bolt upright. "What is it that you say?"

Slowly, Heim dragged the tale from himself: how an honest wish for peace had been tangled with cowardice and the will to believe until most of Earth's powerful refused to credit the plain evidence of Alerion's intention to drive man out of space. After the clash at New Europe, the Federation fell over itself in eagerness to accept an offer of negotiation. One ranking delegate, Admiral Cynbe ru Taren himself, had privately admitted to Heim that his government only planned to consolidate its gains before making the next move; but whom could Gunnar Heim, the despised extremist warmonger, get to believe that? Endre Vadasz bummed his way home with an eyewitness account of what had really happened—and heard his proofs dismissed as fraudulent. Most of those who sat in the seats of the mighty were so afraid of war that they must believe Alerion spoke truly in claiming that New Europe had been accidentally depopulated in the course of a naval incident that got out of hand. They concluded that no planet of corpses was worth the lives that revenge would cost and that nothing mattered except to reduce tension; they set out to negotiate a settlement that would give the whole Phoenix to Alerion.

France, almost alone in her anger, showed Parliament that willy-nilly, according to law Earth was at war; and France gave Heim letters of marque and Heim got away before he could be stopped. But no further action followed, the Deepspace Fleet lay chained and muzzled while Parliament wrangled, quite possibly nothing except *Fox's* buccaneering prevented a resumption of those talks which to Alerion were only a more effective kind of war.

"Mais...mais...mais...vous—cette astronef—" Irribarne checked his stutter, caught breath, and said carefully, "This ship has ranged in the Auroran System. Have you, yourself, taken no proof we live?"

"I tried," Heim said. Back and forth he paced, smoke fuming, heels banging, big useless hands clasped behind his back till the nails stood white. "The prisoners that went home with my prizes, they could have been interrogated. Not easily; Aleriona don't respond like humans; but somebody could've ripped the truth from them! I guess nobody did.

"I also made a pass by New Europe. Not hard to do, if you're quick. Most of their defense satellites still aren't equipped, and we detected no warships too close to outrun. So I got photographs, nice clear ones, showing plainly that only Coeur d'Yvonne was destroyed, that there never had been a firestorm across Garance. Sent them back to Earth. I suppose they convinced some people, but evidently not the right ones. Don't forget, by now a lot of political careers are bound up with the peace issue. And even a man who might confess he was wrong and resign, if it only involved himself, will hesitate to drag his party down with him.

"Oh, I'm sure sentiment has moved in our favor. It'd already begun to do so when I left. Not long after, at Staurn for munitions, I met some latecomers from Earth. They told me the will to fight was becoming respectable. But that was four months ago!"

He shifted his pipe, stopped his feet, and went on more evenly: "I can guess what the next line of argument has been for the appeasement faction. 'Yes, yes,' they say, 'maybe the New Europeans still are alive. So isn't the most important thing to rescue them? We won't do that by war. Alerion can wipe them out any time she chooses. We have to trade their planet for their lives.' That's probably being said in Parliament tonight."

Irribarne's chin sank on his breast. *"Un demi million d'hommes,"* he mumbled. Abruptly: "But they will die all the same. Can one not see that? We have only a few more weeks."

"What?" Heim bellowed. His heart jolted him. "Is the enemy fixing to burn you out?"

That could be done quite easily, he knew in horror. *A thousand or so megatons exploded at satellite height on a clear day will set a good part of a continent afire. Madelon!*

"No, no," the colonist said. "They need for themselves the resources of the planet, in fortifying the system. A continental firestorm or a radioactive poisoning, that would make large trouble for them too. But the vitamin C."

Piece by piece, the story came out. Never doubting Earth would hurry to their aid, the seaboard folk of Pays d'Espoir refused to surrender and fled inland, to the mountains and forests of the Haute Garance. That nearly unmapped wilderness was as rich in game and edible vegetation as North America before the white man. With a high technology and no population pressure, the people were wealthy; hardly a one did not own hunting, fishing, and camping gear, as well as a flyer capable of going anywhere. Given a little camouflage and caution, fifty thousand scattered lodges and summer cottages were much too many for the Aleriona to find. On the rare occasions when it did happen, one could resort to tent or cave or lean-to.

Portable chargers, equally able to use sunlight, wind, or running water, were also standard outdoor equipment, that kept up power cells. Ordinary miniature transceivers maintained a communications net. It did the enemy scant good to monitor. He had come with people that knew French, but his own ossified culture had not allowed for provincial dialect, *Louchebeme,* or Basque. The boldest men organized raids on him, the rest stayed hidden.

With little axial tilt, New Europe enjoys a mild and rainy winter in the temperate zone, even at fairly high altitudes. It seemed that the humans could hold out indefinitely.

But they were not, after all, on Earth. Life had arisen and evolved separately here, through two or three billion years. Similar conditions led to similar chemistry. Most of what a man needed he could get from native organisms. But similarity is not identity. Some things were lacking on New Europe, notably vitamin C. The escapers had packed along a supply of pills. Now the store was very low. Alerion held the farmlands where Terrestrial plants grew, the towns where the biochemical factories stood.

Scurvy is a slow killer, working its way through gums, muscles, digestion, blood, bones. Most often the victim dies of something else which he no longer has the strength to resist. But one way or another, he dies.

"And they know it," Irribarne grated. "Those devils, they know our human weakness. They need only wait." He lifted one fist. "Has Earth forgotten?"

"No," Heim said. "It'd be bound to occur to somebody. But Earth's so confused…"

"Let us go there," Irribarne said. "I myself, all my men, we are witnesses. Can we not shame them till they move?"

"I don't know," Heim said in wretchedness. "We can try, of course. But— maybe I'm being paranoid—but I can still imagine the arguments. 'Nothing except negotiation can save you. Alerion will not negotiate unless we make prompt concessions.'"

"I know damn well that once inside the Solar System, *Fox* won't be allowed to leave again. The law, you see; only units under the Peace Authority can have nuclear weapons, or even weapon launchers, there. And we do. Our possession is legal now, on a technicality, but it won't be when we enter Federation space."

"Can you not dismantle your armament?"

"That'd take weeks. It's been integrated with the ship. And—what difference? I tell you, your appearance on Earth might cost us the war. And *that* would set Alerion up to prepare the next aggression." Heim thought of Madelon. "Or so I believe. Could be wrong, I suppose."

"No, you are right," Irribarne said dully.

"It might be the only way out. Surrender."

"There must be another! I will not be so fanatic that women and children surely die. But a risk of death, against the chance to keep our homes, yes, that is something we all accepted when we went into the *maquis.*"

Heim sat down, knocked out his pipe, and turned it over and over in his hands while he stared at the model of his first command. Inexplicably his emotions began to shift. He felt less heavy, there was a stirring in him, he groped through blackness toward some vague, strengthening glimmer.

"Look," he said, "let's try to reason this through. *Fox* is keeping the war alive by refusing to quit. As long as we're out here fighting, the people at home who think like us can argue that Alerion is being whittled down at no cost to the taxpayer. And, *ja,* they can beat the propaganda drums, make big fat heroes of us, stir the old tribal emotions. They haven't the political pull to make the Authority order the Navy to move; but they have enough to keep us from being recalled. I deduce this from the simple facts that the Navy has not moved and we have not been recalled.

"Obviously that's an unstable situation. It's only kept going this long, I'm sure, because France tied Parliament in legal knots as to whether or not there really was a war on. The deadlock will be resolved one way or another pretty soon. We want to tilt the balance our way.

"Okay, one approach is for you people to let it be known you are alive—let it be known beyond any possible doubt—and also make it plain you are not going to surrender. You'll die before you give in. The way to do that is…let me think, let me think…yes. We've got *Meroeth.* With some repairs, she can make the passage; or else we can make another capture. We stay here, though, ourselves. What we send is—not a handful of men—a hundred women and children." Heim's palm cracked against his knee. "There's an emotional appeal for you!"

Irribarne's eyes widened until they were rimmed with white. *"Comment?* You are crazy? You cannot land on Europe Neuve."

"The space defenses aren't ready yet."

"But…no, they do have some detector satellites, and warcraft in orbit, and—"

"Oh, it's chancy," Heim agreed. He had no real sense of that. Every doubt was smothered in upsurging excitement. "We'll leave *Fox* in space, with most of your men aboard. If we fail, she can snatch another prize and send your men back in that. But I think I have a way to get *Meroeth* down, and up again, and stay in touch meanwhile. We'll need some computer work to make sure, but I think it might pan out. If not, well, you can show me how to be a guerrilla."

"Ah." Irribarne drew deeply on his cigar. "May I ask if this idea would seem so attractive, did it not offer a way to see Madelon?"

Heim gaped at him.

"Pardon," Irribarne blurted. "That was not badly meant. Old friendship, as you said. I like a loyal man." He extended his hand.

Heim took it and rose. "Come on," he said rather wildly. "We can't do anything till tomorrow. Let's get back to the party."

-2-

Elsewhere *Fox* plunged dark, every engine stilled, nothing but the minimum of life support equipment in operation, toward the far side of the moon Diane. It was not garrisoned, and a diameter of 1275 kilometers makes a broad shield. Even so, the tender that went from her carried brave men. They might have been spotted by some prowling Aleriona warcraft, especially in the moments when they crammed on deceleration to make a landing. Once down on that rough, airless surface, they moved their boat into an extinct fumarole for concealment, donned space gear, and struck out afoot. Their trip around to the planet-facing hemisphere was a miniature epic; let it only be said that they completed their errand and got back. Rendezvous with the ship was much too risky to attempt. They settled in the boat and waited.

Not long after, a giant meteorite or dwarf asteroid struck New Europe, burning a hole across the night sky and crashing in the Ocean du Destin a few hundred kilometers east of the Garance coast. Atmospherics howled in every Aleriona detector.

They faded; alerted flyers returned to berth; the night stillness resumed.

For all but the men aboard *Meroeth*.

When the fifty thousand tons to which she was grappled hit the outermost fringes of air, she let go and dropped behind. But she could not retreat far. Too many kilometers per second of velocity must be shed in too few kilometers of distance, before ablation devoured her. That meant a burst of drive forces, a blast of energies from a powerplant strained to its ultimate. The enemy's orbital detection system was still inadequate; but it existed in part, and there were also instruments on the ground. Nothing could hide this advent—except the running, growing storm in the immediate neighborhood of a meteorite.

Radar would not pierce the ions which roiled at the stone's face and streamed back aft. Optical and infrared pickups were blinded. Neutrino or gravitronic detectors aimed and tuned with precision might have registered something which was not of local origin. But who would look for a ship in the midst of so much fury? Air impact alone, at that speed, would break her hull into a thousand flinders, which friction would then turn into shooting stars.

Unless she followed exactly behind the meteorite, using its mass for a bumper and heat shield, its flaming tail for a cloak.

No autopilot was ever built for that task. Gunnar Heim must do it. If he veered from his narrow slot of partial vacuum, he would die too quickly to know he was dead. For gauge he had only the incandescence outside, instrument readings, and whatever intuition was bestowed by experience. For guide he had a computation of where he ought to be, at what velocity, at every given moment, unreeling on tape before his eyes. He merged himself with the ship, his hands made a blur on the console, he did not notice the waves of heat, the buffetings and bellowings of turbulence, save as a thunderstorm deep in his body.

His cosmos shrank to a fire-streak, his reason for being to the need of holding this clumsy mass nose-on to the descent pattern. He became a robot, executing orders written for it by whirling electrons.

No: he was more. The feedback of data through senses, judgment, will, made the whole operation possible. But none of that took place on a conscious level. There wasn't time!

That was as well. Live flesh could not have met those demands for more than a few seconds. The meteorite, slowed only a little by the air wall through which it plunged, outraced the spaceship and hit the sea—still with such force that water had no chance to splash but actually shattered. *Meroeth* was as yet several kilometers aloft, her own speed reduced to something that metal could tolerate. The pattern tape said CUT and Heim slammed down a switch. The engine roar whirred into silence.

He checked his instruments. "All's well," he said. His voice sounded strange in his ears, only slowly did he come back to himself, as if he had run away from his soul and it must now catch up. "We're under the Bonne Chance horizon, headed southwest on just about the trajectory we were trying for."

"Whoo-oo-oo," said Vadasz in a weak tone. His hair was plastered lank to the thin high-cheeked face, his garments drenched.

"Bridge to engine room," Heim said. "Report."

"All in order, sir," came the voice of Diego Gonzales. "Shall I turn on the coolers?"

"Well, do you like this furnace?" grumbled Jean Irribarne. Heat radiated from every bulkhead.

"Go on," Heim decided. "If anyone's close enough to detect the anomaly, we've had it anyway." He kept eyes on the console before him, but jerked a thumb at Vadasz. "Radar registering?"

"No," said the Hungarian. "We appear to be quite private."

Those were the only men aboard. No more were needed for a successful landing; and in case of failure, Heim did not want to lose lives essential to *Fox*. Gonzales was a good third engineer; Vadasz had been a fairly competent steward, and as a minstrel had a lot to do with keeping morale high. Still, the ship could manage without them. One colonist sufficed to guide *Meroeth,* and Irribarne had pulled rank to win that dangerous honor. The rest must bring their story to Earth, should the present scheme miscarry. As for Heim himself—First Officer David Penoyer had protested and been overruled. Penoyer could serve quite well as captain. He had never understood, though, why Heim insisted on going down.

Madelon—

No, no, ridiculous. Maybe it's true that you never really fall out of love with anyone; but new loves do come, and while his wife lived he had rarely thought about New Europe. For that matter, his reunion with Jocelyn Lawrie had driven most else out of his mind. For a while.

No doubt he'd only been so keyed up about Madelon because of…he wasn't sure what. A silly scramble after his lost youth, probably. She was middle-aged now, placidly married, according to her brother-in-law she had put on weight. He wanted to see her again, of course, but he need only instruct *Meroeth*'s pilot to make sure she was among the evacuees.

No. That won't do. Too many unforeseen things could happen. I've got to be in the nucleus, personally.

A new sound filled the hull, the keening of sundered air, deepening toward a hollow boom, as the ship dropped below sonic speed. Heim looked out the forward viewport. The ocean reached vast beneath, phosphor-tinged waves and a shadow at the horizon that must be one of the Iles des Reves. He applied the least bit of thrust to keep in a stable glide.

This was not the ideal approach to Haute Garance. But while meteorites are plentiful, his had had too many requirements to meet. It must be large, yet not too large to nudge into the right orbit in a reasonable time; the point at which *Fox* grappled and towed must be fairly near the planet but not dangerously near; the path after release must look natural; it must terminate in an uninhabited region, at night. You couldn't scout the Auroran System forever, only until a halfway acceptable chunk of rock was found. Meanwhile *Meroeth* could be reconverted: lights, temperature, air systems adjusted for human comfort, the interior stripped of plants and less understandable Aleriona symbols, the controls ripped out and a Terrestrial version installed. The bridge had a plundered look. Heim thought, briefly and irrationally, how this—far more than any attack—would have struck his old antagonist Cynbe with horror and wrath.

Onward the ship fell, slower and lower until the sea appeared to rise and lick at her. Vadasz probed the sky with his instruments, awkwardly—he had gotten hasty training—and intently. His lips were half parted, as if to cry, "Fire!" to Irribarne in the single manned gun turret. But he found only night, unhurried winds and strange constellations.

It would not have been possible to travel thus far, undetected, across a civilization. But New Europe has 72 percent of Earth's surface area; it is an entire world. Coeur d'Yvonne had been almost the only outpost on any other continent than Pays d'Espoir, and that city was annihilated. The Aleriona occupied Garance, where the mines and machines were: a mere fringe on hugeness. Otherwise they must rely on scattered detector stations, roving flyers, and the still incomplete satellite system. His arrival being unknown to them, the odds favored Heim.

Nonetheless...careful, careful.

He started the engines again. At low power, *Meroeth* lumbered across the Golfe des Dragons. Diane hove into view, nearly full. The moon was smaller than Luna seen from Earth—22 minutes angular diameter—and less bright, but still a blue-marked tawny cornucopia that scattered metal shards across the water.

Then the mainland rose, hills and woods climbing swiftly toward snowpeaks. Irribarne left his gun and got on the radio in a harsh clatter of Basque. It wouldn't do to have the French shoot when they saw the great Aleriona craft. Or, more likely, run and hide. The wilderness concealed an entire headquarters base.

The land beneath grew ever more rugged. Rivers ran from the snows, leaped down cliffs, foamed into steep valleys and were lost to sight among the groves. A bird flock rose in alarm when the ship passed over, there must be a million pairs of wings, blotting out half the sky. Vadasz whistled in awe. "*Isten irgalmazzon!* I wondered how long the people could stay hidden, even alive, in the bush. But three times their number could do it."

"Yeh," Heim grunted. "Except for one thing."

Lac aux Nuages appeared, a wide wan sheet among darkling trees, remotely encircled by mountains whose glaciers gleamed beneath the moon. Irribarne relayed instructions. Heim found the indicated spot, just off the north shore, and lowered ship. The concealing waters closed over him. He heard girders groan a little, felt an indescribable soft resistance go through the frame to himself, eased off power and let the hull settle in ooze. When he cut the interior gee-field, he discovered the deck was canted.

His heart thuttered, but he could only find flat words: "Let's get ashore." Even in seven-tenths of Terrestrial gravity, it was a somewhat comical effort to reach the emergency escape lock without falling. When the four men were crowded inside, clothes bundled on their necks, he dogged the inner door and cranked open the outer one. Water poured icily through. He kicked to the surface and swam as fast as possible toward land. Moonlight glimmered on the guns of the men who stood there waiting for him.

-3-

The tent was big. The trees that surrounded it were taller yet. At the top of red-brown trunks, they fountained in branches whose leaves overarched and hid the pavilion under cool sun-flecked shadows. Their foliage was that greenish gold hue the native "grasses" shared, to give the Garance country its name. Wind rustled them. Through the open flap, Heim could look down archways of forest to the lake. It glittered unrestfully, outward past the edge of vision. Except for some wooded islands, the only land seen in that direction was the white-crowned sierra. Blue with distance, the peaks jagged into a deep blue sky.

Aurore was not long up. The eastern mountains were still in a dusk, the western ones still faintly flushed. They would remain so for a while; New Europe takes more than 75 hours to complete a rotation. The sun did not look much different from Earth's, about the same apparent size, a little less brilliant, its color more orange than yellow. Heim had found Vadasz in the dews at dawn, watching the light play in the mists that streamed over the lake, altogether speechless.

That time was ended. Colonel Robert de Vigny, once constabulary commandant, now beret-crowned king of the *maquis,* bridged his fingers, leaned stiffly across his desk, and said, "So. You have made the situation clear, and we seem to have threshed out a plan of action. Let me review what was decided."

Heim could just follow the swift, crisp French: "Your privateer has found a way to lie undetected in this vicinity, and you can summon her by that most admirable means you have invented. We have the big transport *Meroeth.* We will put some two hundred women and children aboard her, with supplies, to bring Earth a direct appeal that Earth may find hard to resist. They can flit in by ones and twos during the next few days, while my men run an underwater loading tube to an airlock.

"Meanwhile, we in the forest must live. So I will establish radio contact with the Aleriona and ask for a parley. They will doubtless agree, especially since their new chief of naval operations seems to be a rather decent fellow. I daresay they will receive our representatives already tomorrow.

"We shall try to reach an agreement that will leave us free. Cessation of guerrilla raids in exchange for vitamins—yes, they should think that is to their advantage, for they will count on dealing with us after the space fortifications are complete. You, Captain Heim, with your professional eye, and Monsieur Vadasz, with your poet's grasp of nonhuman psychology, will be with our delegation in the guise of ordinary colonists. Perhaps you can gather some useful intelligence.

"Whatever the result, our representatives will return here.

"Then you summon *Fox*. She makes a covering raid while *Meroeth* gets aloft, and convoys her to the necessary distance from Aurore where her Mach engines can start her off faster than light.

"After that, if we are provided with the capsules, you continue your warfare in space. If we are not, and if *Fox* cannot help us steal them by providing air cover, I will call the enemy again and offer him an end to your privateering on condition he supply us. This he is virtually sure to accept. So…at large cost or small, we will have gained time, during which we hope Earth will come to help. Have I stated matters correctly?"

Heim nodded and got out his pipe. De Vigny's nostrils dilated. "Tobacco?" the New European breathed. "One had almost forgotten."

Heim chuckled and threw the pouch onto the desk. De Vigny picked up a bell and rang it. An aide-de-camp materialized in the tent entrance, saluting. "Find me a pipe," de Vigny said. "And, if the captain does not object, you may find one for yourself too."

"At once, my colonel!" The aide dematerialized.

"Well." De Vigny unbent a trifle. "Thanks are a poor thing, Monsieur. What can New Europe *do* for you?"

Heim grew conscious of Vadasz's half-jocose, half-sympathetic regard, blushed, and said roughly, "I have an old friend on this planet, who's now Jean Irribarne's sister-in-law. See to it that she and her family are among the evacuees."

"Pierre will not go when other men stay," the Basque said gently.

"But they shall most certainly come here if you wish," de Vigny said. He rang for another aide. "Lieutenant Irribarne, why do you not go with Major Legrand to my own flyer? It has a set which can call to anywhere in the Haute Garance. If you will tell the operator where they are, your kin—" When that was done, he said to Heim and Vadasz, "I shall be most busy today, it is plain. But let us relax until after lunch. We have many stories to trade."

And so they did.

When at last de Vigny must dismiss them, Heim and Vadasz were somewhat at loose ends. There was little to see. Though quite a few men were camped around the lake, the shelters were scattered and hidden, the activity unobtrusive. Now and then a flyer came by, as often as not weaving between tree trunks under the concealing foliage. Small radars sat in camouflage, watching for the unlikely appearance of an Aleriona vessel. The engineers could not install their tube to the ship before night, unless one of the frequent fogs rose to cover their work. Men sat about yarning, gambling, doing minor chores. All were eager to talk with the Earthlings, but the Earthlings soon wearied of repeating themselves. Toward noon, a degree of physical tiredness set in as well. They had been up for a good eighteen hours.

Vadasz yawned. "Let us go back to our tent," he suggested. "This planet has such an inconvenient rotation. You must sleep away a third of the daylight and be awake two-thirds of the night. But at the tent I have a flask of brandy, and—"

They were not far from it then, were crossing a meadow where flame-colored blossoms nodded in the golden grass. Jean Irribarne stepped from under the trees. "Ah," he hailed, *"vous voilà.* I have looked for you."

"What about?" Heim asked.

The lieutenant beamed. "Your friends are here." He turned and called, "'Allo-o-o!"

They came out into the open, six of them. The blood left Heim's heart and flooded back. He stood in a sunlit darkness that whirled.

She approached him timidly. Camp clothes, faded and shapeless, had today been exchanged for a dress brought along to the woods and somehow preserved. It fluttered light and white around her long-legged slenderness. Aurore had bleached the primly braided brown hair until it was paler than her skin; but still it shone, and one lock blew free above the heartshaped face.

"Madelon," he croaked.

"Gunnar." The handsome plumpish woman took both his hands. *"C'est si bon te voir encore. Bienvenu."*

"A nej—" The breath rasped into him. He pulled back his shoulders. "I was surprised," he said limpingly. "Your daughter looks so much like you."

"Pardon?" The woman struggled with long-unused English.

Her husband, an older and heavier version of Jean, interpreted while he shook Heim's hand. Madelon laughed. *"Oui, oui, tout le monde le dit. Quand j'étais jeune, peut-être. Danielle, je voudrais que tu fasses la connaissance de mon vieil ami Gunnar Heim."*

"Je suis très honorée, Monsieur." She could scarcely be heard above the wind as it tossed the leaves and made light and shadow dance behind her. The fingers were small and cool in Heim's, quickly withdrawn.

In some vague fashion he met teen-age Jacques, Cecile, and Yves. Madelon talked a lot, without much but friendly banalities coming through the translations of the Irribarne brothers. All the while Danielle stood quiet. But at parting, with promises of a real get-together after sleep, she smiled at him.

Heim and Vadasz watched them leave, before going on themselves. When the forest had closed upon her, the minstrel whistled. "Is that indeed the image of your one-time sweetheart, yonder girl?" he asked.

"More or less," Heim said, hardly aware that he talked to anyone else. "There must be differences, I suppose. Memory plays tricks."

"Still, one can see what you meant by—Forgive me, Gunnar, but may I advise that you be careful? There are so many years to stumble across."

"Good Lord!" Heim exploded angrily. "What do you take me for? I was startled, nothing else."

"Well, if you are certain...You see, I would not wish to—"

"Shut up. Let's find that brandy." Heim led the way with tremendous strides.

-4-

Day crept toward evening. But life kept its own pace, which can be a fast one in time of war. At sunset Heim found himself on a ness jutting into the lake, alone with Danielle.

He was not sure how. There had been the reunion and a meal as festive as could be managed, in the lean-to erected near the Irribarne flyer. Champagne, which he had taken care to stow aboard *Meroeth,* flowed freely. Stiffness dissolved in it. Presently they sprawled on the grass, Vadasz's guitar rang and most voices joined his. But Heim and Madelon kept somewhat apart, struggling to talk, and her oldest daughter sat quietly by.

They could not speak much of what had once been. Heim did not regret that, and doubted Madelon did. Meeting again like this, they saw how widely their ways had parted; now only a look, a smile, a bit of laughter could cross the distance between. She was an utterly good person, he thought, but she was not Connie or even Jocelyn. And, for that matter, he was not Pierre.

So they contented themselves with trading years. Hers had been mild until the Aleriona came. Pierre, the engineer, built dikes and power stations while she built their lives. Thus Heim found himself relating the most. It came natural to make the story colorful.

His eyes kept drifting toward Danielle.

Finally—this was where the real confusion began as to what had happened—the party showed signs of breaking up. He wasn't sleepy himself, though the wine bubbled in his head, and his body demanded exercise. He said something about taking a stroll. Had he invited the girl along, or had she asked to come, or had Madelon, chuckling low in the way he remembered, sent them off together with a remark about his needing a guide? Everybody had spoken, but between his bad French and hammering pulse he wasn't sure who had said what. He did recall that the mother had given them a little push toward the deeper forest, one hand to each.

Song followed them awhile. (*"Aupres de ma blonde, qu'il fait bon, fait bon, fait bon—"*) but by the time they reached the lake-shore they heard simply a lap-lap of wavelets, rustle of leaves, flute of a bird. Aurore was going down behind the western peaks, which stood black against a cloud bank all fire and gold. The same long light made a molten bridge on the water, from the sun toward him and her. But eastward fog was rolling, slow as the sunset, a topaz wall that at the top broke into banners of dandelion yellow in a sky still clear with day. The breeze cooled his skin.

He saw her clasp arms together. *"Avez-vous froid, Mademoiselle?"* he asked, much afraid they would have to go back. She smiled even before he took off his cloak, probably at what he was doing to her language. He threw it over her shoulders. When his hands brushed along her neck, he felt his sinews go taut and withdrew in a hurry.

"Thank you." She had a voice too light for English or Norwegian, which turned French into song. "But will you not be cold?"

"No. I am fine." (Damn! Did *fin* have the meaning he wanted?) "I am—" He scratched around for words. "Too old and hairy to feel the weather."

"You are not old, Monsieur Captain," she said gravely.

"Ha!" He crammed fists into pockets. "What age have you? Nineteen? I have a daughter that which she—I have a daughter a few years less."

"Well—" She laid a finger along her jaw. He thought wildly what a delicate line that bone made, over the small chin to a gentle mouth; and, yes, her nose tipped gaily upward, with some freckles dusted across the bridge. "I know you are my mother's age. But you do not look it, and what you have done is more than any young man could."

"Thanks. Thanks. Nothing."

"Mother was so excited when she heard," Danielle said. "I think Father got a little jealous. But now he likes you."

"Your father is a good man." It was infuriating to be confined to this first-grade vocabulary.

"May I ask you something, Monsieur?"

"Ask me anybody." The one rebellious lock of hair had gotten free again.

"I have heard that we who go to Earth do so to appeal for help. Do you really think we will matter that much?"

"Well, uh, well, we had a necessity to come here. That is to say, we have now made established communication from your people to mine in space. So we can also take people like you away."

A crease of puzzlement flitted between her brows. "But they have spoken of how difficult it was to get so big a ship down without being seen. Could you not better have taken a little one?"

"You are very clever, Mademoiselle, but—" Before he could construct a cover-up, she touched his arm (how lightly!) and said:

"You came as you did, risking your life, for Mother's sake. Is that not so?"

"Uh, uh, well, naturally I thought over her. We are old friends."

She smiled. "Old sweethearts, I have heard. Not all the knights are dead, Captain. I sat with you today, instead of joining in the music, because you were so beautiful to watch."

His heart sprang until he realized she had been using the second person plural. He hoped the sunset light covered the hue his face must have. "Mademoiselle," he said, "your mother and I are friends. Only friends."

"Oh, but of course. I understand. Still, it was so good of you, everything you have done for us." The evening star kindled above her head. "And now you will take us to Earth. I have dreamed about such a trip since I was a baby."

There was an obvious opening to say that she was more likely to make Earth sit up and beg than vice versa, but he could only hulk over her, trying to find a graceful way of putting it. She sighed and looked past him.

"Your men too, they are knights," she said. "They have not even your reason to fight for New Europe. Except perhaps Monsieur Vadasz?"

"No, Endre has no one here," Heim said. "He is a troubadour."

"He sings so wonderfully," Danielle murmured. "I was listening all the time. He is a Hungarian?"

"By birth. Now he has no home." *Endre, you're a right buck, but this is getting to be too much about you.* "I have—have—When you to arrive on Earth, you and your family use my home. I come when I can and take you in my ship."

She clapped her hands. "Oh, wonderful!" she caroled. "Your daughter and I, we shall become such good friends. And afterward, a voyage on a warship—What songs of victory we will sing, homeward bound!"

"Well—um—We return to camp now? Soon is dark." Under the circumstances, one had better be as elaborately gentlemanly as possible.

Danielle drew the cloak tight around her. "Yes, if you wish." He wasn't sure whether that showed reluctance or not. But as she started walking immediately, he made no comment, and they spoke little en route.

The party was indeed tapering off. Heim's and Danielle's return touched off a round of goodnights. When she gave him back his cloak, he dared squeeze her hand. Vadasz kissed it, with a flourish.

On their way back through leafy blue twilight, the minstrel said, "Ah, you are the lucky one still."

"What do you mean?" Heim snapped.

"Taking the fair maiden off that way. What else?"

"For God's sake!" Heim growled. "We just wanted to stretch our legs. I don't have to rob cradles yet."

"Are you quite honest, Gunnar?—No, wait, please don't tie me in a knot. At least, not in a granny knot. It is only that Mlle. Irribarne is attractive. Do you mind if I see her?"

"What the blaze have I got to say about that?" Heim retorted out of his anger. "But listen, she's the daughter of a friend of mine, and these colonial French have a medieval notion of what's proper. Follow me?"

"Indeed. No more need be said." Vadasz whistled merrily the rest of the way. Once in his sleeping bag, he drowsed off at once. Heim had a good deal more trouble doing so.

Perhaps for that reason, he woke late and found himself alone in the tent. Probably Diego was helping de Vigny's sappers and Endre had wandered off—wherever. It was not practical for guerrillas to keep a regular mess, and the camp-stove, under a single dim light, showed that breakfast had been prepared. Heim fixed his own, coffee, wildfowl, and a defrosted chunk of the old and truly French bread which is not for tender gums. Afterward he washed, depilated the stubble on his face, shrugged into some clothes and went outside.

No word for me, evidently. If any comes, it'll keep. I feel restless. How about a swim? He grabbed a towel and started off.

Diane was up. Such light as came through the leaves made the forest a shifting bewilderment of black and white, where his flashbeam bobbed lonely. The air had warmed and cleared. He heard summery noises, whistles, chirps, croaks, flutters, none of them quite like home. When he emerged on the shore, the lake was a somehow bright sable, each little wave tipped with moonfire. The snow-peaks stood hoar beneath a universe of stars. He remembered the time on Staurn when he had tried to pick out Achernar; tonight he could do so with surety, for it burned great in this sky. His triumph, just about when Danielle was being born—*"Vous n'etes pas vieux, Monsieur le Capitaine."*

He stripped, left the beam on to mark the spot, and waded out. The water was cold, but he needed less willpower than usual to take the plunge when it was waist deep. For a time he threshed about, warming himself, then struck out with long quiet strokes. Moonlight rippled in his wake. The fluid slid over his skin like a girl's fingers.

Things are looking up, he thought with a growing gladness. *We really do have a good chance to rescue this planet. And if part of the price is that I stop raiding—why, I'll be on Earth too.*

Did it sing within him, or had a bird called from the nest ahead?

No. Birds don't chord on twelve strings. Heim grinned and swam forward as softly as he was able. Endre's adrenal glands would benefit from a clammy hand laid on him from behind and a shouted "Boo!"

The song grew stronger.

> *Röslein, Röslein, Röslein rot,*
> *Röslein auf der Heiden.*

As it ended, Heim saw Vadasz seated on a log, silhouetted against the sky. He was not alone.

Her voice came clear through the night. *"Oh, c'est beau. Je n'aurais jamais cru que les allemands pouvaient avoir une telle sensibilite."*

Vadasz laughed. *"Vous savez, Goethe vecut il y a long-temps. Mais pourquoi rappeler de vieilles haines pendant une si belle nuit? Nous sommes ici pour admirer, parler, et chanter, n'est-ce pas?"*

Briefly, blindingly, Heim remembered himself with Jocelyn Lawrie, that time not long ago when they met again after years—and she told him that for her those had been years wasted—and her tone was like Danielle's now—

"Chantez encore, je vous en prie."

The strings rang very softly, made themselves a part of night and woods and water. Vadasz's words twined among them. Danielle sighed and leaned a bit closer.

Heim swam away.

No, he told himself, and once more: *No. Endre isn't being a bastard. He asked me.*

The grip on his throat did not loosen. He ended his quietness and churned the water with steamboat violence. *He's young. I could have been her father. But I junked the chance.*

No. I'm being ridiculous. I had you, Connie, while you lived.

Ved Gud—Ilis brain went in rage to the tongue of his childhood. *By God, if he does anything—! I'm not too old to break a man's neck.*

What the hell business is it of mine? I've got Jocelyn!...

He stormed ashore and abraded himself dry. Clothes on, he stumbled through the woods. There was a bottle in the tent, not quite empty.

A man waited for him. He recognized one of de Vigny's aides. "Well?"

The officer sketched a salute. "I 'ave a message for you, Monsieur. The colonel 'as contact the enemy. They receive a delegation in Bonne Chance after day 'as break."

"Okay. Goodnight."

"But, Monsieur—"

"I know. We have to confer. Well, I'll come when I can. We've plenty of time. It's going to be a long night." Heim brushed past the aide and closed his tent flap.

-5-

Below, the Carsac Valley rolled broad and rich. Farmsteads could be seen, villages, an occasional factory surrounded by gardens—but nowhere man, the land was empty, livestock run wild, weeds reclaiming the fields. Among them flowed the river, metal-bright in the early sun.

When he looked out the viewports of the flyer where he sat, Heim saw his escort, four Aleriona military vehicles. The intricate, gaily colored patterns painted on them did not soften their barracuda outlines. Guns held aim on the unarmed New European. *We could change from delegates to prisoners in half a second,* he thought, and reached for his pipe.

"Pardon." Lieutenant Colonel Charles Navarre, head of the eight-man negotiation team, tapped his shoulder. "Best lock that away, Monsieur. We have not had tobacco in the *maquis* for one long time."

"Damn! You're right. Sorry." Heim got up and stuck his smoking materials in a locker.

"They are no fools, them." Navarre regarded the big man carefully. "Soon we land. Is anything else wrong with you, Captain Alphonse Lafayette?"

"No, I'm sure not," Heim said in English. "But let's go down the list. My uniform's obviously thrown together, but that's natural for a guerrilla. I don't look like a typical colonist, but they probably won't notice, and if they do it won't surprise them."

"Comment?" asked another officer.

"Didn't you know?" Heim said. "Aleriona are bred into standardized types. From their viewpoint, humans are so wildly variable that a difference in size and coloring is trivial. Nor have they got enough familiarity with French to detect my accent, as long as I keep my mouth shut most of the time. Which'll be easy enough, since I'm only coming along in the hope of picking up a little naval intelligence."

"Yes, yes," Navarre said impatiently. "But be most careful about it." He leaned toward Vadasz, who had a seat in the rear. "You too, Lieutenant Gaston Girard."

"On the contrary," the minstrel said, "I have to burble and chatter and perhaps irritate them somewhat. There is no other way to probe the mood of non-humans. But have no fear. This was all thought about. I am only a junior officer, not worth much caution on their part." He smiled tentatively at Heim. "You can vouch for how good I am at being worthless, no, Gunnar?"

Heim grunted. Pain and puzzlement flickered across the Magyar's features. When first his friend turned cold to him, he had put it down to a passing bad mood. Now, as Heim's distantness persisted, there was no chance—in this crowded, thrumming cabin—to ask what had gone wrong.

The captain could almost read those thoughts. He gusted out a breath and returned to his own seat forward. *I'm being stupid and petty and a son of a bitch in general,* he knew. *But I can't forget Danielle, this sunrise with the fog drops like jewels in her hair, and the look she gave him when we said goodbye. Wasn't I the one who'd earned it?*

He was quite glad when the flyer started down.

Through magnification before it dropped under the horizon, he saw that Bonne Chance had grown some in twenty years. But it was still a small city, nestled on the land's seaward shoulder: a city of soft-hued stucco walls and red tile roofs, of narrow ambling streets, suspension bridges across the Carsac, a market square where the cathedral fronted on outdoor stalls and outdoor cafes, docks crowded with watercraft, and everywhere trees, Earth's green chestnut and poplar mingled with golden bellefleur and gracis. The bay danced and dazzled, the countryside rolled ablaze with wildflowers, enclosing the town exactly as they had done when he wandered hand in hand with Madelon.

Only…the ways were choked with dead leaves; houses stared blank and blind; boats moldered in the harbor; machines rusted silent; the belfry rooks were dead or fled and a fauquette cruised the sky on lean wings, searching for prey. The last human thing that stirred was the aerospace port, twenty kilometers inland.

And those were not men or men's devices bustling over its concrete. The airships bringing cargo had been designed by no Terrestrial engineer. The factories they served were windowless prolate domes, eerily graceful for all that they were hastily assembled prefabs. Conveyors, trucks, lifts were manmade, but the controls had been rebuilt for hands of another shape and minds trained to another concept of number. Barracks surrounded the field, hundreds of buildings reaching over the hills; from above, they looked like open-petaled bronze flowers. Missiles stood tall among them, waiting to pounce. Auxiliary spacecraft clustered in the open. One was an armed pursuer, whose snout reached as high as the cathedral cross.

"It must belong to a capital ship in planetary orbit," Heim decided. "And if that's the only such, the other warships must be out on patrol."

"I do not see how you can use the information," Navarre said. "A single spacecraft of the line gives total air superiority when there is nothing against it but flyers. And our flyers are not even military."

"Still, it's helpful to see what you're up against. You're sure their whole power is concentrated here?"

"Yes, quite sure. This area has most of our industrial facilities. There are garrisons elsewhere, at certain mines and plants, as well as at observation posts. But our scouts have reported those are negligible in themselves."

"So…I'd guess, then, knowing how much crowding Aleriona will tolerate—let me think—I'd estimate their number at around 50,000. Surely the military doesn't amount to more than a fifth of that. They don't need more defense. Upper-type workers—what we'd call managers, engineers, and so forth—are capable of fighting but aren't trained for it. The lower-type majority have had combativeness bred out. So we've really only got 10,000 Aleriona to worry about. How many men could you field?"

"Easily a hundred thousand—who would be destroyed the moment they ventured out of the forests."

"I know. A rifle isn't much use when you face heavy ground and air weapons." Heim grimaced.

The flyer touched concrete at the designated point and halted. Its escort remained hovering. Navarre stood up. *"Sortons,"* he said curtly, and led the way out the door.

Twenty Aleriona of the warrior class waited in file. Their lean, forward-slanting, long-tailed forms were less graceful than those of the master breed; their fur lacked the silvery sparkle, the fair hair did not flow loose but was braided under the conical helmets, the almost-human faces were handsome rather than possessing the disturbing muliebrile beauty of an overlord. The long sunrays turned their scaly garments almost incandescent.

They did not draw the crooked swords at their belts nor point guns at the newcomers; they might have been statues. Their officer stepped forward, making the intricate gesture that signified respect. He was taller than his followers, though still below average human height.

"Well are you come," he sang in fairly good French. "Wish you rest or refreshment?"

"No, thank you," Navarre said, slowly so the alien could follow his dialect. Against the fluid motion that confronted him, his stiffness looked merely lumpy. "We are prepared to commence discussions at once."

"Yet first ought you be shown your quarters. Nigh to the high masters of the Garden of War is prepared a place as best we might." The officer trilled an order. Several low-class workers appeared. They did not conform at all to Earth's picture of Aleriona—their black-clad bodies were too heavy, features too coarse, hair too short, fur too dull, and there was nothing about them of that inborn unconscious arrogance which marked the leader types. Yet they were not servile, nor were they stupid. A million years of history, its only real change the glacial movement toward an ever more unified society, had fitted their very genes for this part. If the officer was a panther and his soldiers watchdogs, these were mettlesome horses.

In his role as aide, Vadasz showed them the party's baggage. They fetched it out, the officer whistled a note, the troopers fell in around the humans and started off across the field. There was no marching; but the bodies rippled together like parts of one organism. Aurore struck the contact lenses which protected them from its light and turned their eyes to rubies.

Heim's own eyes shifted back and forth as he walked. Not many other soldiers were in evidence. Some must be off duty, performing one of those enigmatic rites that were communion, conversation, sport, and prayer to an Aleriona below the fifth level of mastery. Others would be at the missile sites or on air patrol. Workers and supervisors swarmed about, unloading cargo, fetching metal from a smelter or circuit parts from a factory to another place where it would enter some orbital weapon. Their machines whirred, clanked, rumbled. Nonetheless, to a man the silence was terrifying. No shouts, no talk, no jokes or curses were heard: only an occasional melodic command, a thin weaving of taped orchestral music, the *pad-pad* of a thousand soft feet.

Vadasz showed his teeth in a grin of sorts. *"Ils considerent la vie tres serieuse-ment,"* he murmured to Navarre. *"Je parierais qu'ils ne font jamais de plaisanteries douteuses."*

Did the enemy officer cast him a look of—incomprehension? *"Taisez vousz",* Navarre said.

But Vadasz was probably right, Heim reflected. Humor springs from a certain inward distortion. To that great oneness which was the Aleriona soul, it seemed impossible: literally unthinkable.

Except…yes, the delegates to Earth, most especially Admiral Cynbe, had shown flashes of a bleak wit. But they belonged to the ultimate master class. It suggested a difference from the rest of their species which—He dismissed specu-lation and went back to observing as much detail as he could.

The walk ended at a building some hundred meters from the edge of the field. Its exterior was no different from the other multiple curved structures surround-ing it. Inside, though, the rooms had clearly been stripped, the walls were raw plastic and floors stained where the soil of flowerbeds had been removed. Furni-ture, a bath cubicle, Terrestrial-type lights, plundered from houses, were arranged with a geometric precision which the Aleriona doubtless believed was pleasing to men. "Hither shall food and drink be brought you," the officer sang. "Have you wish to go elsewhere, those guards that stand outside will accompany."

"I see no communicator," Navarre said.

"None there is. With the wilderness dwellers make you no secret discourse. Within camp, your guards bear messages. Now must we open your holders-of-things and make search upon your persons."

Navarre reddened. "What? Monsieur, that violates every rule of parley."

"Here the rule is of the Great Society. Wish you not thus, yourselves you may backtake to the mountains." It was hard to tell whether or not that lilting voice held insult, but Heim didn't think so. The officer was stating a fact.

"Very well," Navarre spat. "We submit under protest, and this shall be held to your account when Earth has defeated you."

The Aleriona didn't bother to reply. Yet the frisking was oddly like a series of caresses.

No contraband was found, there not being any. Most of the colonists were surprised when the officer told them, "Wish you thus, go we this now to seek the Intellect Masters." Heim, recalling past encounters, was not. The Aleriona overlords had always been more flexible than their human counterparts. With so rigid a civilization at their beck, they could afford it.

"Ah…just who are they?" Navarre temporized.

"The *imbiac* of planetary and space defense are they, with below them the prime engineering operator. And then have they repositories of information and advice," the officer replied. "Is not for you a similarity?"

"I speak for the constabulary government of New Europe," Navarre said. "These gentlemen are my own experts, advisors, and assistants. But whatever I agree to must be ratified by my superiors."

Again the girlish face, incongruous on that animal body, showed a brief loosening that might betoken perplexity. "Come you?" the song wavered.

"Why not?" Navarre said. "Please gather your papers, Messieurs." His heels clacked on the way out.

Heim and Vadasz got to the door simultaneously. The minstrel bowed. "After you, my dear Alphonse," he said. The other man hesitated, unwilling: But no, you had to maintain morale. He bowed back: "After *you,* my dear Gaston." They kept it up for several seconds.

"Make you some ritual?" the officer asked.

"A most ancient one." Vadasz sauntered off side by side with him.

"Never knew I such grew in your race," the officer admitted.

"Well, now, let me tell you—" Vadasz started an energetic argument. *He's doing his job right well,* Heim conceded grudgingly.

Not wanting to keep the Magyar in his consciousness, he looked straight ahead at the building they were approaching. In contrast to the rest, it lifted in a single high curve, topped with a symbol resembling an Old Chinese ideogram. The walls were not blank bronze, but scored with microgrooves that turned them shiftingly, bewilderingly iridescent. He saw now that this was the source of the music, on a scale unimagined by men, that breathed across the port.

No sentries were visible. An Aleriona had nothing to fear from his underlings. The wall dilated to admit those who neared, and closed behind them.

There was no decompression chamber. The occupiers must find it easier to adapt themselves, perhaps with the help of drugs, to the heavy wet atmosphere of this planet. A hall sloped upward, dimly seen in the dull red light from a paraboloidal ceiling. The floor was carpeted with living, downy turf, the walls with phosphorescent vines and flowers that swayed, slowly keeping time to the music, and drenched the air with their odors. The humans drew closer together, as if for comfort. Ghost silent, ghost shadowy, they went with their guards to the council chamber.

It soared in a vault whose top was hidden by dusk, but where artificial stars glittered wintry keen. The interior was a vague, moving labyrinth of trellises, bushes, and bowers. Light came, only from a fountain at the center, whose crimson-glowing waters leaped five meters out of a bowl carved like an open mouth, cascaded down again and filled every corner of the jungle with their clear splash and gurgle. Walking around it, Heim thought he heard wings rustle in the murk overhead.

The conqueror lords stood balanced on tails and clawed feet, waiting. There were half a dozen all told. None wore any special insignia of rank, but the light flickered lovingly over metal-mesh garments, lustrous hair and silver-sparked white fur. The angelic faces were in repose, the emerald eyes altogether steady.

To them the officer genuflected and the soldiers dipped their rifles. A few words were sung. The guards stepped back into darkness and the humans stood alone.

One Aleriona master arched his back and hissed. Almost instantly, his startlement passed. He trod forward so that his countenance came into plain view. Laughter belled from him, low and warm.

"Thus, Captain Gunnar Heim," he crooned in English. "Strangeness, how we must ever meet. Remember you not Cynbe ru Taren?"

-6-

So shattered was Heim's universe that he was only dimly aware of what happened. Through the red gloom, trillings went among the Aleriona. One bristled and cried an order to the guards. Cynbe countermanded it with an imperious gesture. Above the racket of his pulse, Heim heard the admiral murmur: "You would they destroy on this now, but such must not become. Truth, there can be no release; truth alike, you are war's honored prisoners." And there were more songs, and at last the humans were marched back to their quarters. But Heim remained.

Cynbe dismissed his fellow chieftains and all but four guards. By then the sweat was drying on the man's skin, his heartbeat slowed, the first total despair thrust down beneath an iron watchfulness. He folded his arms and waited.

The Aleriona lord prowled to the fountain, which silhouetted him as if against liquid flames. For a while he played with a blossoming vine. The sole noises were music, water, and unseen circling wings. It was long before he intoned, softly and not looking at the man:

"Hither fared I to have in charge the hunt for you the hunter. Glad was my hope that we might meet in space and love each the other with guns. Why came you to this dull soil?"

"Do you expect me to tell you?"

Heim rasped.

"We are kinfolk, you and I. Sorrow, that I must wordbreak and keep you captive. Although your presence betokens this was never meant for a real parley."

"It was, however. I just happened to come along. You've no right to hold the New Europeans, at least."

"Let us not lawsplit. We two rear above such. Release I the others, home take they word to your warship. Then may she well strike. And we have only my cruiser *Jubalcho* to meet her. While she knows not what has happened to you her soul, *Fox II* abides. Thus gain I time to recall my deep-scattered strength."

The breath hissed between Heim's teeth. Cynbe swung about. His eyes probed like fire weapons. "What bethink you?"

"Nothing!" Heim barked frantically.

It raced within him: *He believes I took* Fox *down. Well, that's natural. Not knowing about our meteorite gimmick, he'd assume that only a very small or a very fast craft could sneak past his guard. And why should I come in a tender?* Fox *on the surface could do terrific damage, missile this base and strike at his flagship from a toadhole position.*

I don't know what good it is having him misinformed but—play by ear, boy, play by ear. You haven't got anything left except your rusty old wits.

Cynbe studied him a while. "Not long dare I wait to act," he mused. "And far are my ships."

Heim forced a jeering note: "The practical limit of a maser beam is about twenty million kilometers. After that, if nothing else, the position error for a ship gets too big. And there's no way to lock onto an accelerating vessel till she's so close that you might as well use an ordinary 'caster. Her coordinates change too fast, with too many unpredictables like meteorite dodging. So how many units have you got on known orbits within twenty million kilometers?"

"Insult me not," Cynbe asked quietly. He stalked to the wall, brushed aside a curtain of flowers and punched the keys of an infotrieve. It chattered and extruded a printout. He brooded over the symbols. "*Inisant* the cruiser and *Savaidh* the lancer can we reach. All ignorant must the others wheel their way, until one by one they return on slow schedule and find only battle's ashes."

"What are the factors for those two?" Heim inquired. Mostly he was holding at bay the blood-colored stillness. It jarred him—not too much to jam the numbers into his memory—when Cynbe read off in English the orbital elements and present positions.

"Hence have I sent my race-brothers to summon them," the Aleriona went on. At highest acceleration positive and negative, *Savaidh* takes orbit around Europe Neuve in eighteen hours, *Inisant* in twenty-three. I think not the Foxfolk will dread for you thus soon. With three warcraft aloft, this entire planet do we scan. Let your ship make the least of little moves, and destruction shall thunder upon her unstoppable. Although truth, when ready for smiting we shall send detector craft all places and seek her lair."

His tone had not been one of threat. It grew still milder: "This do I tell you in my thin hoping you yield her. Gallant was that ship, unfitting her death where the stars cannot see."

Heim pinched his lips together and shook his head.

"What may I offer you for surrender," Cynbe asked in sadness, "unless maychance you will take my love?"

"What the devil!" Heim exclaimed.

"We are so much alone, you and I," Cynbe sang. For the first time scorn touched his voice, as he jerked his tail in the direction of the warriors who stood, blank-faced and uncomprehending, half hidden in the twilight. "Think you I am kin to that?"

He glided closer. The illumination played over shining locks and disconcertingly fair countenance. His great eyes lingered on the man. "Old is Alerion," he chanted, "old, old. Long-lived are the red dwarf stars, and late appears life in so feeble a radiance. Once we had come to being, our species, on a planet of seas vanished, rivers shrunk to trickles in desert, a world niggard of air, water, metal, life—uncountable ages lingered we in savagehood. Ah, slow was the machine with coming to us. What you did in centuries, we did in tens upon thousands of years; and when it was done, a million years a-fled, one society alone endured, swallowed every other, and the machine's might gave it upon us a grip not to be broken. Starward fared the Wanderers, vast-minded the Intellects, yet were but ripples over the still deep of a civilization eternity-rooted. Earth lives for goals, Alerion for changelessness. Understand you that, Gunnar Heim? Feel you how ultimate the winter you are?"

"I—you mean—" Cynbe's fingers stroked like a breath across the human's wrist. He felt the hair stir beneath them, and groped for a handhold in a world suddenly tilting. "Well, uh, it's been theorized. That is, some people believe you're just reacting because we threaten your stability. But it doesn't make sense. We could reach an accommodation, if all you want is to be let alone. You're trying to hound us out of space."

"Thus must we. Sense, reason, logic, are what save instruments of most ancient instinct? If races less powerful than we change, that makes nothing more than pullulation among insects. But you, you come in ten or twenty thousand years, one flick of time, come from the caves, bear weapons to shake planets as is borne a stone war-ax, you beswarm these stars and your dreams reach at the whole cosmos. *That* can we not endure! Instinct feels doom in this becoming one mere little enclave, given over helpless to the wild mercy of those who bestride the galaxy. Would you, could you trust a race grown strong that feeds on living brains? No more is Alerion able to trust a race without bounds to its hope. Back to your own planets must you be cast, maychance back to your caves or your dust."

Heim shook the soft touch loose, clenched his fists and growled: "You admit this, and still talk about being friends?"

Cynbe confronted him squarely, but sang with less than steadiness: "Until now said I 'we' for all Alerion. Sure is that not truth. For when first plain was your menace, plain too was that those bred stiff-minded, each for a one element of the Great Society, must go down before you who are not bound and fear not newness. Mine was the master type created that it might think and act as humans and so overmatch them." His hands smote together. "Lonely, lonely!"

Heim looked upon him in his beauty and desolation, and found no words.

Fiercely the Aleriona asked: "Guess you not how I must feel alone, I who think more Earthman than any save those few created like me? Know you not that glory there was to be on Earth, to lock with minds that had also no horizon, drown in your books and music and too much alive eye-arts? Barren are we, the Intellect Masters of the Garden of War; none may descend from us for troubling of Alcrion's peace; yet were we given the forces of life, that our will and fury rear tall as yours, and when we meet, those forces bind us through rites they knew who stood at Thermopylae. But…when you seized me, Gunnar Heim, that once you ransomed your daughter with me…afterward saw I that too was a rite."

Heim took a backward step. Coldness ran down his spine and out into every nerve end.

Cynbe laughed. The sound was glorious to hear. "Let me not frighten you, *Star Fox* captain. I offer only that which you will take." Very gently: "Friendship? Talk? Together-faring? I ask you never betrayal of your people. Well might I order a wresting from you of your knowledge and plans, but never. Think you are a war captive, and no harm that you share an awareness with your captor, who would be your friend."

My God, it leaped in Heim. The sounds about him came through as if across a barrier of great distance or of fever. *Give me some time and…and I could use him.*

"Recall," Cynbe urged, "my might on Alerion stands high. Well can I some-day make a wall for the race that bred you, and so spare them that which is extinction."

No! Sheer reflex. *I can't. I can't.*

Cynbe held out one hand. "Clasp this, as once you did," he begged. "Give me oath you will seek no escape nor warning to your breedmates. Then no guard shall there be for you; freely as myself shall you betread our camps and ships."

"No!" Heim roared aloud.

Cynbe recoiled. His teeth gleamed forth. "Little the honor you show to me," he whispered.

"I can't give you a parole," Heim said. *Whatever you do, don't turn him flat against you. There may be a chance here somewhere. Better dead, trying for a break, than—*Something flashed across his brain. It was gone before he knew what it was. His consciousness twisted about and went in a pursuit that made the sweat and heart-banging take over his body again.

Somehow, though every muscle was tight and the room had taken on an aspect of nightmare, he said dryly: "What'd be the use? I credit you with not being an idiot. You'd have an eye kept on me—now wouldn't you?"

Where a man might have been angered, Cynbe relaxed and chuckled. "Truth, at the least until *Fox II* be slain. Although afterward, when better we know each the other—"

Heim captured the thought that had run from him. Recognizing it was like a blow. He couldn't stop to weigh chances, they were probably altogether forlorn and he would probably get himself killed. *Let's try the thing out, at least. There's no commitment right away. If it's obviously not going* to *work, then I just won't make the attempt.*

He ran a dry tongue over dry lips, husked, and said, "I couldn't give you a parole anyway, at any time. You don't really think like a human, Cynbe, or you'd know why."

Membranes dimmed those eyes. The golden head drooped. "But always in your history was honor and admiration among enemies," the music protested.

"Oh, yes, that. Look, I'm glad to shake your hand." Oddly, it was no lie, and when the four slim fingers coiled around his, Helm did not let go at once, "But I can't surrender to you, even verbally," he said. "I guess my own instincts won't let me."

"No, now, often have men—"

"I tell you, this isn't something that can be put in words. I can't really feel what you said, about humans being naturally horrible to Aleriona. No more can you feel what I'm getting at. But you did give me some rough idea. Maybe. I could give you an idea of…well, what it's like to be a man whose people have lost their homes."

"I listen."

"But I'd have to show you. The symbols, the—You haven't any religion as humans understand it, you Aleriona, have you? That's one item among many. If I showed you some things you could see and touch, and tried to explain what they stand for, maybe—Well, how about it? Shall we take a run to Bonne Chance?"

Cynbe withdrew a step. Abruptly he had gone catlike.

Heim mocked him with a chopping gesture. "Oh, so you're scared I'll try some stunt? Bring guards, of course. Or don't bother, if you don't dare." He half turned. "I'd better get back to my own sort."

"You play on me," Cynbe cried.

"Nah. I say to hell with you, nothing else. The trouble is, you don't know what you've done on this planet. You aren't capable of knowing."

"Arvan!" Heim wasn't sure how much was wrath in that explosion and how much was something else. "I take your challenge. Go we this now."

A wave of weakness passed through Heim. *Whew! So I did read his psychology right. Endre couldn't do better.* The added thought came with returning strength. "Good," he accepted shakily. "Because I am anxious for you to realize as much as possible. As you yourself said, you could be a powerful influence for helping Earth, if the war goes against us. Or if your side loses—that could happen, you know; our Navy's superior to yours, if only we can muster the guts to use it—in that case, I'd have some voice in what's to be done about Alerion. Let's take Vadasz along. You remember him, I'm sure."

"Ye-e-es. Him did I gain tell in your party, though scant seemed he to matter. Why wish you him?"

"He's better with words than I am, He could probably make it clearer to you." *He speaks German, and I do a little. Cynbe knows English, French, doubtless some Spanish—but German?*

The admiral shrugged and gave an order. One soldier saluted and went out ahead of the others, who accompanied the leaders—

—down the hall, into the morning, across the field to a military flyer. Cynbe stopped once, that he might slip contacts over eyeballs evolved beneath a red coal of a sun.

Vadasz waited with his guards. He looked small, hunched and defeated. "Gunnar," he said dully, "what's this?"

Heim explained. For a moment the Hungarian was puzzled. Then hope lit in his visage. "Whatever your idea is, Gunnar, I am with you," he said, and masked out expression.

Half a dozen troopers took places at the rear of the vehicle. Cynbe assumed the controls. "Put us down in the square," Heim suggested, "and we'll stroll around."

"Strange are your ways," Cynbe cantillated. "We thought you were probed and understood, your weakness and shortsightedness in our hands, but then *Fox II* departed. And now—"

"Your problem is, sir, that Aleriona of any given class, except no doubt your own, are stereotypes," Vadasz said. "Every human is a law to himself."

Cynbe made no reply. The flyer took off.

It landed minutes later. The party debarked.

Silence dwelt under an enormous sky. Fallen leaves covered the pavement and overflowed a dry fountain. A storm had battered the market booths, toppled cafe tables and chairs, ripped the gay little umbrellas. Only the cathedral rose firm. Cynbe moved toward it. "No," Heim said, "let's make that the end of the tour."

He started in the direction of the river. Rubbish rustled from his boots, echoes flung emptily back from walls. "Can't you see what's wrong?" he asked. "Men lived here."

"Hence-driven are they," Cynbe answered. "Terrible to me Aleriona is an empty city. And yet, Gunnar Heim, was this a…a dayfly. Have you such rage that the less than a century is forsaken?"

"It was going to grow," Vadasz said.

Cynbe made an ugly face.

A small huddle of bones lay on the sidewalk. Heim pointed. 'That was somebody's pet dog," he said. "It wondered where its gods had gone, and waited for them, and finally starved to death. Your doing."

"Flesh do you eat," Cynbe retorted.

A door creaked, swinging back and forth in the breeze off the water. Most of the house's furniture could still be seen inside, dusty and rain-beaten. Near the threshold sprawled the remnants of a rag doll. Heim felt tears bite his eyes.

Cynbe touched his hand. "Well remember I what are your children to you," he crooned.

Heim continued with long strides. "Humans live mostly for their children," Vadasz said.

The riparian esplanade came in sight. Beyond its rail, the Carsac ran wide and murmurous toward the bay. Sunlight flared off that surface, a trumpet call made visible.

Now! Heim thought. The blood roared in him. "One of our poets said what I mean," he spoke slowly. *"Wenn wir sind an der Fluss gekommen, und im Falls wir die Möglichkeit sehen, dann werden wir ausspringen und nach dem Hafen Schwimmen."*

He dared not look to see how Vadasz reacted. Dimly he heard Cynbe ask, in a bemused way, "What token those words?"

With absolute coolness, Vadasz told him, "Man who is man does not surrender the hope of his loins unless manhood has died within."

Good lad! Heim cheered. But most of his consciousness crawled with the guns at his back.

They started west along the embankment. "Still apprehend I not," Cynbe sang. "Also Aleriona make their lives for those lives that are to come. What difference?"

Heim didn't believe he could hide his purpose much longer. So let it be this moment that he acted—the chance did not look too bad—let him at worst be shattered into darkness and the end of fear.

He stopped and leaned on the rail. "The difference," he said, "you can find in the same man's words. *Ich werde diesen Wesen in das Wasser sturzen. Dann springen wir beide.* It's, uh, it's hard to translate. But look down here."

Vadasz joined them. Glee quirked his lips, a tiny bit, but he declared gravely: "The poem comes from a saying of Heraclitus. 'No man bathes twice in the same river.'"

"That have I read." Cynbe shuddered. "Seldom was thus dreadful a thought."

"You see?" Heim laid a hand on his shoulder and urged him forward, until he also stood bent over the rail. His gaze was forced to the flowing surface, and held there as if hypnotized. "Here's a basic human symbol for you," Heim said. "A river, bound to the sea, bound to flood a whole countryside if you dam it. Motion, power, destiny, time itself."

"Had we known such on Alerion—" Cynbe whispered. "Our world raised naked rock."

Heim closed fingers on his neck. The man's free hand slapped down on the rail. A surge of arm and shoulder cast him and Cynbe across. They struck the current together.

-7-

His boots dragged him under. Letting the Aleriona go, he writhed about and clawed at the fastenings. The light changed from green to brown and then was gone. Water poured past, a cool and heavy force that tumbled him over and over. One off—two off—he struck upward with arms and legs. His lungs felt near bursting. Puff by grudged puff, he let out air. His mind began to wobble. *Here goes,* he thought, *a breath or a firebeam.* He stuck out as little of his face as he could, gasped, saw only the embankment, and went below again to swim.

Thrice more he did likewise, before he guessed he had come far enough to risk looking for Vadasz. He shook the wetness from hair and eyes and continued in an Australian crawl. Above the tinted concrete that enclosed the river, trees trapped sunlight in green and gold. A few roofpeaks showed, otherwise his ceiling was the sky, infinitely blue.

Before long Vadasz's head popped into sight. Heim waved at him and threshed on until he was under a bridge. It gave some protection from searchers. He grabbed a pier and trod water. The minstrel caught up and panted.

"*Karhoztatas,* Gunnar, you go as if the devil himself were after you!"

"Isn't he? Though it helps a lot that the Aleriona don't see so well here. Contacts stop down the brightness for them, but Aurore doesn't emit as much of the near infrared that they're most sensitive to as The Eith does." Heim found it calming to speak academically. It changed him from a hunted animal to a military tactician. "Just the same, we'd better stay down as much as we can. And stay separate, too. You know the old Quai des Coquillages—it's still there? Okay. I'll meet you underneath it. If one of us waits an hour, let him assume the other bought a farm."

Since Vadasz looked more exhausted than himself, Heim started first. He didn't hurry, mostly he let the current bear him along, and reached the river-mouth in good shape: so good that the sheer wonder of his escape got to him.

He spent his time beneath the dock simply admiring light-sparkles on water, the rake of masts, the fluid chill enclosing his skin, the roughness of the bollard he held, the chuckle against hulls and their many vivid colors. His mood had just begun to ravel away in worry *(Damn, I should've told Endre what I know)* when the Magyar arrived.

"Will they not seek us here first?" Vadasz asked.

"M-m, I doubt it," Heim said. "Don't forget, they're from a dry planet. The idea of using water for anything but drinking doesn't come natural to them; you notice they've left all these facilities untouched, though coastwise transport would be a handy supplement to their air freighters. Their first assumption ought to be that we went ashore as soon as we could and holed up in town. Still, we want to get out of here as fast as possible, so let's find a boat in working order."

"There you must choose. I am a landlubber by heritage."

"Well, I never got along with horses, so honors are even." Helm risked climbing onto the wharf for an overview. He picked a good-looking pleasure craft, a submersible hydrofoil, and trotted to her. Once below, she'd be undetectable by any equipment the Aleriona had.

"Can we get inside?" the minstrel asked from the water.

"*Ja,* she's not locked. Yachtsmen trust each other." Heim unslipped the lines, pulled the canopy back, and extended an arm to help Vadasz up on deck. They tumbled into the cabin and closed the glasite. "Now, you check the radio while I have a look at the engine."

A year's neglect had not much hurt the vessel. In fact, the sun had charged her accumulators to maximum. Her bottom was foul, but that could be lived with. Excitement surged in Heim. "My original idea was to find a communicator somewhere in town, get word to camp, and then skulk about hoping we wouldn't be tracked down and wouldn't starve," he said. "But now—hell, we might get back in person! It'll at least be harder for the enemy to pick up our message and send a rover bomb after the source, if we're at sea. Let's go."

The motor chugged. The boat slid from land. Vadasz peered anxiously out the dome. "Why are they not after us in full cry?"

"I told you how come. They haven't yet guessed we'd try this way. Also, they must be disorganized as a bawdyhouse on Monday morning, after what I did to Cynbe." Nonetheless, Heim was glad to leave obstacles behind and submerge. He went to the greatest admissible depth, set the pilot for a southeasterly course, and began peeling off his wet clothes.

Vadasz regarded him with awe. "Gunnar," he said, in a tone suggesting he was not far from tears, "I will make a ballad about this, and it will not be good enough, but still they will sing it a thousand years hence. Because your name will live that long."

"Aw, shucks, Endre. Don't make my ears burn."

"No, I must say what's true. However did you conceive it?"

Heim turned up the heater to dry himself. The ocean around—murky green, with now and then a curiously shaped fish darting by—would dissipate infrared radiation. He had an enormous sense of homecoming, as if again he were a boy on the seas of Gea. For the time being, it overrode everything else. The frailty and incompleteness of his triumph could be seen later; let him now savor it.

"I didn't," he confessed. "The idea sort of grew. Cynbe was eager to…be friends or whatever. I talked him into visiting Bonne Chance, in the hope something might turn up that I could use for a break. It occurred to me that probably none of his gang could swim, so the riverside looked like the best place. I asked to have you along because we could use German under their noses. Also, having two of us doubled the odds that one would get away."

Vadasz's deference cracked in a grin. "That was the most awful *Schweindeutsch* I have yet heard. You are no linguist."

Memory struck at Heim. "No," he said harshly. Trying to keep his happiness a while, he went on fast: "We were there when I thought if I could pitch Cynbe in the drink, his guards would go all out to save him, rather than run along the bank shooting at us. If you can't swim yourself, you've got a tough job rescuing another non-swimmer."

"Do you think he drowned?"

"Well, one can always hope," Heim said, less callously than he sounded. "I wouldn't be surprised if they lost at least a couple of warriors fishing him out. But we've likely not seen the last of him. Even if he did drown, they can probably get him to a revival machine before brain decay sets in.—Still, while he's out of commission, things are apt to be rather muddled for the enemy. Not that the organization can't operate smoothly without him. But for a while it'll lack direction, as far as you and I are concerned, anyhow. That's the time we'll use to put well out to sea and call de Vigny."

"Why…yes, surely they can send a fast flyer to our rescue." Vadasz leaned back with a cat-outside-canary smile. "La belle Danielle is going to see me even before she expected. Dare I say, before she hoped?"

Anger sheeted in Heim. "Dog your hatch, you clotbrain!" he snarled. "This is no picnic. We'll be lucky to head off disaster."

"What—what—" Color left Vadasz's cheeks. He winced away from the big man. "Gunnar, did I say—"

"Listen." Heim slammed a fist on the arm of his seat. "Our amateur try at espionage blew up the whole shebang. Have you forgotten the mission was to negotiate terms to keep our people from starving? That's been dimmed. Maybe something can be done later, but right now we're only concerned with staying alive. Our plan for evacuating refugees is out the airlock too. Cynbe jumped to the conclusion that *Fox* herself is on this planet. He's recalled a lancer and a cruiser to supplement his flagship. Between them, those three can detect *Meroeth* raising mass, and clobber her. It won't do us any good to leave her doggo, either. They'll have air patrols with high-gain detectors sweeping the whole planet. So there goes de Vigny's nice hidey-hole at Lac aux Nuages. For that matter, with three ships this close to her position, *Fox* herself is in mortal danger.

"You blithering, self-centered rockhead! Did you think I was risking death just so we could escape? What the muck have we got to do with anything? Our people have got to be warned!"

With a growl, he turned to the inertial navigator panel. No, they weren't very far out yet. But maybe he should surface anyway, take his chances, to cry what he knew at this instant.

The boat pulsed around him. The heater whirred and threw waves of warmth across his hide. There was a smell of oil in the air. Outside the ports, vision was quickly blocked—as he had been blocked, thwarted, resisted and evaded at every turn. "Those ships will be here inside an Earth day," he said. "*Fox* better make for outer space, the rest of us for the woods."

"Gunnar—" Vadasz began.

"Oh, be quiet!"

The minstrel flushed and raised his voice. "No. I don't know what I have done to be insulted by you, and if you haven't the decency to tell me, that must be your affair. But I have something to tell you, Captain. We can't contact *Fox* in time."

"Huh?" Heim whirled.

"Think for a moment. Diego has his big maser set erected near the lake. But morning is well along, and Diane is nearly full. It set for the Haute Garance hours ago. It won't rise again for, I guess, thirty hours."

"Satan…i…helvede," Heim choked. Strength drained from him. He felt the ache in his flesh and knew he had begun to grow old.

After a time in which he merely stared, Vadasz said to him, timidly: "You are too much a man to let this beat you. If you think it so important, well, perhaps we can get *Meroeth* aloft. Her own communicator can reach the moon. The enemy satellites will detect her, and the cruiser close in. But she is lost anyway, you inform me, and she can surrender. We only need three or four men to do it. I will be one of them."

Lightning-struck, Heim sprang to his feet. His head bashed the canopy. He looked up and saw a circle of sunlight, blinding on the ocean surface, above him.

"Are you hurt?" Vadasz asked.

"By heaven—and hell—and everything in between." Heim offered his hand. "Endre, I've been worse than a bastard. I've been a middle-aged adolescent. Will you forgive me?"

Vadasz gripped hard. Perception flickered in his eyes. "Oh, so," he murmured. "The young lady…Gunnar, she's nothing to me. Mere pleasant company. I thought you felt the same."

"I doubt that you do," Heim grunted. "Never mind. We've bigger game to hunt. Look, I happen to know what the orbits and starting positions of those ships were. Cynbe saw no reason not to tell me when I asked—I suppose unconsciously I was going on the old military principle of grabbing every piece of data that comes by, whether or not you think you'll ever use it. Well I also know their classes, which means I know their capabilities. From that, we can pretty well compute their trajectories. They can be pinpointed at any given time—close enough for combat purposes, but not close enough for their ground base to beam them any warning. Okay, so that's one advantage we've got, however small. What else?"

He began to pace, two steps to the cabin's end, two steps back, fist beating palm and jaw muscles standing in knots. Vadasz drew himself aside. Once more the cat's grin touched his mouth. He knew Gunnar Heim in that mood.

"Listen." The captain hammered out the scheme as he spoke. *"Meroeth*'s a big transport. So she's got powerful engines. In spite of her size and clumsiness, she can move like a hellbat when empty. She can't escape three ships on patrol orbit. But at the moment there's only one, Cynbe's personal *Jubalcho*. I don't know her orbit, but the probabilities favor her being well away at any given time that *Meroeth* lifts. She could pursue, sure, and get so close that *Meroeth* can't outrun a missile. But she ain't gonna—I hope—because Cynbe knows that wherever I am, *Fox* isn't likely very distant, and he's got to protect his base against *Fox* till his reinforcements arrive. Or if the distance is great enough, he'll assume the transport *is* our cruiser, and take no chances!

"So…okay…given good piloting, *Meroeth* has an excellent probability of making a clean getaway. She can flash a message to *Fox*. But then—what? If *Fox* only takes us aboard, we're back exactly where we started. No, we're worse off, because the New Europeans have run low on morale and losing their contact with us could well push them right into quitting the fight. So—wait—let me think—Yes!" Heim bellowed. "Why not? Endre, we'll go for broke!"

The minstrel shouted his answer.

Heim reined in his own eagerness. "The faster we move, the better," he said. "We'll call HQ at the lake immediately. Do you know Basque, or any other language the Aleriona don't that somebody on de Vigny's staff does?"

"I fear not. And a broadcast, such as we must make, will doubtless be monitored. I can use *Louchebeme*, if that will help."

"It might, though they're probably on to it by now…Hm. We'll frame something equivocal, as far as the enemy's concerned. He needn't know it's us calling from a sub. Let him assume it's a *maquisard* in a flyer. We can identify ourselves by references to incidents in camp.

"We'll tell de Vigny to start lightening the spaceship as much as possible. No harm in that, since the Aleriona know we do have a ship on the planet. It'll confirm for them that she must be in the Haute Garance, but that's the first place they'd look anyhow." Heim tugged his chin. "Now…unfortunately, I can't send any more than that without tipping my hand. We'll have to deliver the real message in person. So we'll submerge right after you finish calling and head for a rendezvous point where a flyer is to pick us up. How can we identify that, and not have the enemy there with a brass band and the keys to the city?"

"Hm-m-m. Let me see a map." Vadasz unrolled a chart from the pilot's drawer. "Our radius is not large, if we are to be met soon. *Ergo*—Yes. I will tell them…so-and-so many kilometers due east of a place—" he blushed, pointing to Fleurville, a ways inland and down the Cote Notre Dame—"where Danielle Irribarne told Endre Vadasz there is a grotto they should visit. That was shortly before moonset. We, um, sat on a platform high in a tree and—"

Heim ignored the hurt and laughed. "Okay, lover boy. Let me compute where we can be in that coordinate system."

Vadasz frowned. "We make risks, acting in this haste," he said. "First we surface, or at least lie awash, and broadcast a strong signal so near the enemy base."

"It won't take long. We'll be down again before they can send a flyer. I admit one might be passing right over us this minute, but probably not."

"Still, a New European vessel has to meet us. No matter if it goes fast and takes the long way around over a big empty land, it is in daylight and skirting a dragon's nest. And likewise for the return trip with us."

"I know." Heim didn't look up from the chart on his knees. "We could do it safer by taking more time. But then we'd be too late for anything. We're stuck in this orbit, Endre, no matter how close we have to skim the sun."

-8-

"Bridge to stations, report."

"Engine okay," said Diego Gonzales.

"Radio and main radar okay," said Endre Vadasz.

"Gun Turret One okay and hungry," said Jean Irribarne. The colonists in the other emplacements added a wolfish chorus.

Easy, lads, Heim thought. *If we have to try those popguns on a real, functioning warship, we're dead.* "Stand by to lift," he called. Clumsy in his spacesuit, he moved hands across the board.

The lake frothed. Waves swept up its beaches. A sighing went among the trees, and *Meroeth* rose from below. Briefly her great form blotted out the sun, where it crawled toward noon, and animals fled down wilderness trails. Then, with steadily mounting velocity, she flung skyward. The cloven air made a continuous thunderclap. Danielle and Madelon Irribarne put hands to tormented ears. When the shape was gone from sight, they returned to each other's arms.

"Radar, report!" Heim called through drone and shiver.

"Negative," Vadasz said.

Higher and higher the ship climbed. The world below dwindled, humped into a curve, turned fleecy with clouds and blue with oceans. The sky went dark, the stars blazed forth.

"Signal received on the common band," Vadasz said. "They must have spotted us. Shall I answer?"

"Hell, no," Heim said. "All I want is her position and vector."

The hollow volume of *Meroeth* trapped sound, bounced echoes about, until a booming rolled from stem to stern and port to starboard. It throbbed in Heim's skull. His open faceplate rattled.

"Can't find her," Vadasz told him. "She must be far off."

But she found us. Well, she has professional detector operators. I've got to make do with whatever was in camp. No time to recruit better-trained people.

We should be so distant that she'd have to chase us for some ways to get inside the velocity differential of her missiles. And she should decide her duty is to stay put. If I've guessed wrong on either of those, we've hoisted our last glass. Heim tasted blood, hot and bitter, and realized he had caught his tongue between his teeth. He swore, wiped his face, and drove the ship.

Outward and outward. New Europe grew smaller among the crowding suns. Diane rose slowly to view. "Captain to radio room. Forget about everything else. Lock that maser and cut me in on the circuit." Heim reached for racked instruments and navigational tables. "I'll have the figures for you by the time you're warmed up."

If we aren't destroyed first. Please…let me live that long. I don't ask for more. Please, Fox *has got to be told.* He reeled off a string of numbers.

In his shack, among banked meters that stared at him like troll eyes, Vadasz punched keys. He was no expert, but the comsystem computer had been preprogrammed for him; he need merely feed in the data and punch the directive "Now." A turret opened to airlessness. A transceiver thrust its skeletal head out for a look at the universe. A tight beam of coherent radio waves speared from it.

There were uncertainties. Diane was orbiting approximately 200,000 kilometers on the other side of New Europe, and *Meroeth* was widening that gulf with ever-increasing speed. But the computer and the engine it controlled were sophisticated; the beam had enough dispersion to cover a fairly large circle by the time it reached the target area; it had enough total energy that its amplitude then was still above noise level.

Small, bestrewn with meteoric dust, in appearance another boulder among thousands on the slope of a certain crater wall, an instrument planted by the men from the boat sat waiting. The signal arrived. The instrument—an ordinary microwave relay, such as every spaceship carries by the score, with a solar battery—amplified the signal and bounced it in another tight beam to another object high on a jagged peak. That one addressed its next fellow; and so on around the jagged desert face of the moon. Not many passings were needed. The man's-height horizon on Diane is about three kilometers, much greater from a mountaintop, and the last relay only had to be a little ways into that hemisphere which never sees New Europe.

Thence the beam leaped skyward. Some 29,000 kilometers from the center of Diane, to *Fox II.* The problem had been: how could a spaceship lurk near a hostile planet from which detectors probed and around which warcraft spun? If she went free-fall, every system throttled down to the bare minimum, her neutrino emission would not register above the cosmic background. But optical, infrared, and radar eyes would still be sure to find her. Unless she interposed the moon between herself and the planet…No. She dared not land and sit there naked to anyone who chanced close when the far hemisphere was daylit. She could not assume an orbit around the satellite, for she would move into view. She could not assume a concentric orbit around New Europe itself, for she would revolve more slowly and thus drop from behind her shield—

Or would she?"

Not necessarily! In any two-body system there are two Lagrangian points where the secondary's gravitation combines with the primary's in such a way that a small object put there will remain in place, on a straight line between the larger bodies. It is not stable; eventually the object will be perturbed out of its resting spot; but "eventually" is remote in biological time. *Fox* put herself in the more distant Lagrangian point and orbited in the moon-disc's effortless concealment.

The maneuver had never been tried before. But then, no one had ever before needed to have a warship on call, unbeknownst to an enemy who occupied the ground where he himself meant to be. Heim thought it would become a textbook classic, if he lived to brag about it.

"*Meroeth* to *Fox II*," he intoned. "*Meroeth* to *Fox II*. Now hear this and record. Record. Captain Heim to Acting Captain Penoyer, stand by for orders."

There could be no reply, except to Lac aux Nuages. The system, simple and hastily built, had been conceived in the belief that he would summon his men from there. If anything was heisenberg at the other end, he wouldn't know till too late. He spoke into darkness.

"Because of unexpected developments, we've been forced to lift directly, without passengers. It doesn't seem as if we're being pursued. But we have extremely important intelligence, and on that basis a new plan.

"First: we know there is only one capital ship in orbit around New Europe. All but two others are scattered beyond recall, and not due back for quite some time. The sentry vessel is the enemy flagship *Jubalcho,* a cruiser. I don't know the exact class—see if you can find her in Jane's—but she's doubtless only somewhat superior to *Fox.*

"Second: the enemy learned we were on the planet and recalled the two vessels in reach. They are presently accelerating toward New Europe. The first should already have commenced deceleration. That is the lancer *Savaidh.* The other is the cruiser *Inisant.* Check them out too; but I think they are ordinary Aleriona ships of their respective classes. The ballistic data are approximately as follows—" He recited the figures.

"Now, third: the enemy probably believes *Meroeth* is *Fox.* We scrambled with so much distance between that contrary identification would have been difficult or impossible, and also we took him by surprise. So I think that as far as he knows, *Fox* is getting away while the getting is good. But he cannot communicate with the other ships till they are near the planet, and he doubtless wants them on hand anyway.

"Accordingly we have a chance to take them piecemeal. Now hear this. Pay no attention to the lancer. *Meroeth* can deal with her; or if I fail she's no major threat to you. Moreover, nuclear explosions in space would be detected and alert the enemy. Stay put, *Fox,* and plot an interception for *Inisant.* She won't be looking for you. Relative velocity will be high. If you play your cards right, you have an excellent probability of putting a missile in her while warding off anything she has time to throw.

"After that, come get me. My calculated position and orbit will be approximately as follows." Again a string of numbers. "If I'm a casualty, proceed at discretion. But bear in mind that New Europe will be guarded by only one cruiser!"

Heim sucked air into his lungs. It was hot and had an electric smell. "Repeating message," he said. And at the end of the third time: "The primary relay point seems to be going under Diane's horizon, on our present course. I'll have to sign off. Gunnar Heim to Dave Penoyer and the men of *Fox II*—good hunting. Over and out."

Then he sat in his seat, looked to the stars in the direction of Sol, and wondered how Lisa his daughter was doing.

Increment by increment, *Meroeth* piled on velocity. It didn't seem long—though much desultory conversation had passed through the intercom—before the moment came to reverse and slow down. They mustn't have a suspicious vector when they encountered *Savaidh*.

Heim went to the saloon for a snack. He found Vadasz there, with a short redhaired colonist who slurped at his cup as if he had newly come off a Martian desert. *"Ah, mon Capitaine,"* the latter said cheerily, *"je n'avais pas bu de café depuis un sacré long temps. Merci beaucoup!"*

"You may not thank me in a while," Heim said.

Vadasz cocked his head. "You shouldn't look so grim, Gun—sir," he chided. "Everybody else is downright cocky."

"Tired, I guess." Heim slumped onto the Aleriona settle.

"I'll fix you up. A *grand Danois* of a sandwich, hm?" Vadasz bounced out. When he returned with the food, he had his guitar slung over his back. He sat down on the table, swinging his legs, and began to chord and sing:

> *There was a rich man and he lived in Jerusalem.*
> *Glory, hallelujah, hi-ro-de-rung!*—

The memory came back. A grin tugged at Heim's lips. Presently he was beating time; toward the end, he joined in the choruses. *That's the way! Who says we can't take them?* He returned to the bridge with a stride of youth.

And time fled. And battle stations were sounded. And *Savaidh* appeared in the viewports.

The hands that had built her were not human. But the tool was for the same job, under the same laws of physics, as Earth's own lancers. Small, slim, leopard-spotted for camouflage and thermal control, leopard deadly and beautiful, the ship was so much like his old *Star Fox* that Heim's hand paused. *Is it right to kill her this way? A legitimate ruse of war. Yes.* He punched the intercom. "Bridge to radio. Bridge to radio. Begin distress signal."

Meroeth spoke, not in any voice but in the wailing radio pattern which Naval Intelligence had long known was regulation for Alerion. Surely the lancer captain (was this his first command?) ordered an attempt at communication. There was no reply. The gap closed. Relative speed was slight by spaceship standards; but *Savaidh* grew swiftly before Heim's eyes.

Unwarned, the Aleriona had no reason to doubt this was one of their own vessels. The transport was headed toward the Mach limit; not directly for The Eith, but then, none of them did lest the raider from Earth be able to predict their courses. Something had gone wrong. Her communications must be out.

Probably her radio officer had cobbled together a set barely able to cry, "SOS!" The trouble was clearly not with her engines, since she was under power. What, then? Breakdown of radiation screening? Air renewal? Thermostats? Interior gee field? There were so many possibilities. Life was so terribly frail, here where life was never meant to be.

Or…since the probability of her passing near the warship by chance, in astronomical immensity, was vanishingly small…did she bear an urgent message? Something that, for some reason, could not be transmitted in the normal way? The shadow of *Fox II* lay long and cold across Alerion.

"Close spacesuits," Heim ordered. "Stand by." He clashed his own faceplate shut and lost himself in the task of piloting. Two horrors nibbled at the edge of consciousness. The lesser one, because least likely, was that the other captain would grow suspicious and have him blasted. The worst was that *Savaidh* would continue her rush to Cynbe's help. He could not match accelerations with a lancer.

Needles wavered before his eyes. Radar—vectors—impulse—*Savaidh* swung about and maneuvered for rendezvous.

Heim cut drive to a whisper. Now the ships were on nearly parallel tracks, the lancer decelerating heavily while the transport ran almost free. Now they were motionless with respect to each other, with a kilometer of vacuum between. Now the lancer moved with infinite delicacy toward the larger vessel.

Now Heim rammed down an emergency lever. At full sidewise thrust, *Meroeth* hurtled to her destiny.

There was no time to dodge, no time to shoot. The ships crashed together. That shock roared through plates and ribs, ripped metal apart, hurled unharnessed Aleriona to their decks or against their bulkheads with bone-cracking violence.

A spaceship is not thickly armored, even for war. She can withstand the impact of micrometeorites; the larger stones, which are rare, she can detect and escape; nothing can protect from nuclear weapons, when once they have struck home. *Meroeth's* impact speed was not great, but her mass was. Through and through *Savaidh* she sheared. Her own hull gave way. Air puffed out in a frosty cloud, quickly lost to the light-years. Torn frameworks wrapped about each other. Locked in a stag's embrace, the ruined ships tumbled on a lunatic orbit. Aurore flared radiance across their guts; the stars looked on without pity.

"Prepare to repel boarders!"

Heim didn't know if his cry had been transmitted through his helmet jack to the others. Likely not. Circuits were ripped asunder. The fusion reaction in the power generator had guttered out. Darkness, weightlessness, airlessness flowed through the ship. It didn't matter. His men knew what to do. He undid his harness by feel and groped aft to the gun turret he had chosen for himself.

Most of the Aleriona crew must be dead. Some might survive, in spacesuits or sealed compartments. If they could find a gun still workable and bring it to bear, they'd shoot. Otherwise they'd try for hand-to-hand combat. Untrained for space, the New Europeans couldn't withstand that.

The controls of Heim's laser had their own built-in illumination. Wheels, levers, indicators glowed like watchfires. He peered along the barrel, out the cracked glasite, past wreckage where shadows slid weirdly as the system rotated; he suppressed the slight nausea due Coriolis force, forgot the frosty glory of constellations, and looked for his enemy.

It came to him, a flicker across tautness, that he had brought yet another tactic to space warfare: ramming. But that wasn't new. It went back ages, to when men first adventured past sight of land. *Olaf Tryggvason, on the blood-reddened deck of the* Long Serpent.

No. To hell with that. His business was here and now: to stay alive till *Fox* picked him up. Which wouldn't be for a long time.

A weapon spat. He saw only the reflection of its beam off steel, and squinted till the dazzle passed. *One for our side. I hope.* A heavy vibration passed through the hull and his body. An explosion? He wasn't sure. The Aleriona might be wild enough to annihilate him, along with themselves, by touching off a nuclear warhead. The chances were against it, since they'd need tools that would be hard to find in that mess out yonder. But—

Well, war was mostly waiting.

A spacesuited figure crawled over a girder. The silhouette was black and unhuman against the stars, save where sunlight made a halo on the helmet. One survivor, at least, bravely striving to—Heim got him in the sights and fired. Vapor rushed from the pierced body. It drifted off into space. "I hated to do that," Heim muttered to the dead one. "But you could have been carrying something nasty, you know."

His shot had given him away. A beam probed at his turret. He crouched behind the shield. Intolerable brightness gnawed centimeters away from him. Then more bolts struck. The enemy laser winked out. "Good man!" Heim gasped. "Whoever you are!"

The fight did not last long. No doubt the Aleriona, if any were left, had decided to hole up and see what happened. But it was necessary to remain on guard.

In the dreamlike state of free fall, muscles did not protest confinement. Heim let his thoughts drift where they would. Earth, Lisa, Jocelyn…New Europe, Danielle…there really wasn't much in a man's life that mattered. But those few things mattered terribly.

Hours passed.

It was anticlimax when *Fox's* lean shape closed in. Not that Heim didn't cheer—so she had won!—but rendezvous was tricky; and then he had to make his way through darkness and ruin until he found an exit; and then signal with his helmet radio to bring a tender into safe jumping distance; and then come aboard and get a shot to counteract the effects of the radiation he had taken while unscreened in space; and then transfer to the cruiser—

The shouts and backslappings, bear hugs and bear dances, seemed unreal in his weariness. Not even his victory felt important. He was mainly pleased that a good dozen Aleriona were alive and had surrendered. "You took *Inisant?*" he asked Penoyer.

"Oh, my, yes. Wizard cum spiff! One pass, and she was a cloud of isotopes. What next, sir?"

"Well—" Heim rubbed sandy eyes. "Your barrage will have been detected from New Europe. Now, when *Inisant* is overdue, the enemy must realize who lost. He may have guessed you went after *Savaidh* next, and be attempting an interception. But it's most likely that he's stayed pretty close to base. Even if he hasn't, he'll surely come back there. Do you think we can beat *Jubalcho?*"

Penoyer scowled. "That's a pitchup, sir. According to available data, she has more teeth, though we've more acceleration. I've computed several tactical patterns which give us about an even chance. But should we risk it?"

"I think so," Heim said. "If we get smeared, well, let's admit that our side won't have lost much. On the other hand, if we win we've got New Europe."

"Sir?"

"Sure. There are no other defenses worth mentioning. We can knock out their ground-based missiles from space. Then we give air support to the colonists, who're already preparing a march on the seaboard. You know as well as I do, no atmospheric flyer ever made has a fish's chance on Friday against a nuclear-armed spaceship. If the Aleriona don't surrender, we'll simply swat them out of the sky, and then go to work on their ground troops. But I expect they will give in. They're not stupid. And...then we've got hostages."

"But—the rest of their fleet—"

"Uh-huh. One by one, over a period of weeks or months, they'll come in. *Fox* should be able to bushwhack them. Also, we'll have the New Europeans hard at work, finishing the space defenses. Evidently there isn't much left to do there. Once that job's completed, the planet's nearly impregnable, whatever happens to us.

"Somewhere along the line, probably rather soon, another transport ship will come in, all unsuspecting. We'll nobble her and send off a load of New Europeans as originally planned. When Earth hears they're not only not dead, not only at the point of defeat, but standing space siege and doing a crackling hell of a job at it...why, if Earth doesn't move then, I resign from the human race."

Heim straightened. "I'm no damned hero, Dave." he finished. "Mainly I want to get home to the pipe and slippers. But don't you think a chance like this is worth taking?"

Penoyer's nostrils flared. "By...by Jove," he stammered, *"Yes."*

"Very good. Make course for New Europe and call me if anything happens."

Heim stumbled to his cabin and toppled into sleep.

Vadasz's hand shook him awake. "Gunnar! Contact's made—with *Jubalcho*— we'll rendezvous inside half an hour."

Nothing remained of tiredness, fear, doubt, nor even anger. Heim went to the bridge with more life running through his veins than ever since Connie departed. Stars filled the viewports, so big and bright in the crystal dark that it seemed he could reach out and touch them. The ship murmured and pulsed. His men stood by their weapons; he could almost sense their oneness with him and with her. He took his place of command, and it was utterly right that Cynbe's voice should ring from the speaker.

"*Star Fox* captain, greet I you again? Mightily have we striven. You refuse not battle this now?"

"No," said Heim. "We're coming in. Try and stop us."

The laughter of unfallen Lucifer replied. "Truth. And I thank you, my brother. Let come what that time-flow brings that you are terrible enough to live with…I thank you for this day."

"Goodbye," Heim said, and thought, a little surprised, *Why, that means "God be with you."*

"Captain of mine," Cynbe sang, "fare you well."

The radio beams cut out. Dark and silent, the two ships moved toward their meeting place.

-9-

A hundred kilometers north of Bonne Chance, on a high and lovely headland where meadows and woods ran wind-rippled down to the sea, was a house which had been made a gift of honor.

Rear Admiral Moshe Peretz, commanding blastship *Jupiter*, Deepspace Fleet of Earth's World Federation, set his borrowed flyer down on the landing strip and went out. A fresh breeze swayed the nearby garden, clouds scudded white, sunlight speared between them to dance on a restless ocean. He walked slowly, a short man, very erect in his uniform, with combat ribbons on his breast that freed him to admire a view or a blossom.

Gunnar Heim came out to welcome him, also in uniform: but his was different, gray tunic, a red stripe down the trousers, a *fleur-de-lys* on the collar. He towered over his guest, bent down a face that had known much sun of late, grinned in delight and engulfed the other man's hand in one huge paw. "Hey, Moshe, it's good to see you again! How many years?"

"Hello," Peretz said.

Heim released him, stung and surprised. "Uh…anything wrong?"

"I am all right, thank you. This is a nice home you have."

"Well, I like it. Want to see the grounds before we go in?"

"If you wish."

Heim stood for a moment before he sighed and said, "Okay, Moshe. Obviously you accepted my dinner invitation for more reasons than to jaw with your old Academy classmate. Want to discuss 'em now? There'll be some others coming pretty soon."

Peretz regarded him closely, out of brown eyes that were also pained, and said, "Yes, let us get it over with."

They started walking across the lawn. "Look at the matter from my side," Peretz said. "Thanks to you, Earth went into action. We beat the Aleriona decisively in the Marches, and now they have sued for peace. Wonderful. I was proud to know you. I pulled every wire in sight so that I could command the ship that went officially to see how New Europe is doing, how Earth can help reconstruct, what sort of memorial we should raise for the dead of both planets—because victory was not cheap."

"Haven't your men been well treated?" Heim asked.

"Yes, certainly." Peretz sliced the air with his hand, as if chopping at a neck. "Every liberty party has been wined and dined till it could hardly stagger back to the tender. But…I issued those passes most reluctantly, only because I did not want to make a bad situation worse. After all—when we find this planet ringed with defense machines—machines which are not going to be decommissioned—when a ship of the World Federation is told how near she may come—what do you expect a Navy man to think?"

Heim bit his lip. "*Ja.* That was a mistake, ordering you around. I argued against it in council, but they outvoted me. I give you my oath no insult was intended, not by anyone. The majority feeling was simply that we'd better express our sovereignty at the outset. Once the precedent has been accepted, we'll relax."

"But *why?*" His rage flickered to death, leaving Peretz no more than hurt and bewildered. "This fantastic declaration of independence…what kind of armed forces have you? Your fleet can't amount to more than your own old privateer and perhaps a few Aleriona prizes. Otherwise there is just the constabulary. What strength can half a million people muster?"

"Are you threatening us, Moshe?" Heim asked gently.

"What?" Peretz jarred to a stop and gaped. "What do you mean?"

"Is Earth going to reconquer us? You could, of course. It'd be bloody and expensive, but you could."

"No—no—did the occupation drive everyone here paranoid?"

Heim shook his head. "On the contrary, we rely on Earth's good will and sense. We expect you to protest, but we know you won't use force. Not when your planet and ours have shed blood together."

"But…see here. If you want national status, well, that concerns mainly yourselves and the French government. But you say you are leaving the whole Federation!"

"We are," Heim answered. "Juridically, at least. We hope to make mutually beneficial treaties with Earth as a whole, and we'll always stand in a special relationship to France. In fact, President de Vigny thinks France won't object at all, will let us go with her blessings."

"M-m-m…I am afraid he is right," said Peretz grimly. He began walking again, stiff-gaited. "France is still rather cool toward the. Federation. She won't leave it herself, but she will be glad to have you do so for her, as long as French interests are not damaged."

"She'll get over her grudge," Heim predicted.

"Yes, in time. Did you break loose for the same cause?"

Heim shrugged. "To a certain extent, no doubt. The Conference of Chateau de St. Jacques was one monstrous emotional scene, believe me. The plebiscite was overwhelmingly in favor of independence. But there were better reasons than a feeling of having been let down in an hour of need. Those are the ones that'll last."

"De Vigny tried to convince me," Peretz snorted.

"Well, let me try in less elegant language. What is the Federation? Something holy, or an instrument for a purpose? We think it's a plain old instrument, and that it can't serve its purpose out here."

"Gunnar, Gunnar, have you forgotten all history? Do you know what a breakup would mean?"

"War," Heim nodded. "But the Federation isn't going to die. With all its faults, it's proved itself too good for Earth to scrap. Earth's a single planet, though. You can orbit it in ninety minutes. The nations have got to unify, or they'll kill each other." His gaze swept the horizon. "Here we have more room."

"But—"

"The universe is too big for any one pattern. No man can understand or control it, let alone a government. The proof is right at hand. We had to trick and tease and browbeat the Federation into doing what we could see, with our own eyes, was necessary—because it didn't see. It wasn't able to see. If a man is going to live throughout the galaxy, he's got to be free to take his own roads, the ones his direct experience shows him are best for *his* circumstances. And that way, won't the race realize all its potential? Is there any other way we can, than by trying everything out, everywhere?" Heim clapped Peretz's back. "I know. You're afraid of interstellar wars in the future, if planets are sovereign. Don't worry. It's ridiculous. What do entire, self-sufficient, isolated worlds have to fight about?"

"We just finished an interstellar war," Peretz said.

"Uh-huh. What brought it on? Somebody who wasn't willing to let the human race develop as it should. Moshe, instead of trying to freeze ourselves into one shape, instead of staying small because we're scared of losing control, let's work out something different. Let's find how many kinds of society, human and non-human, can get along without a policeman's gun pointed at them. I don't think there is any limit."

"Well—" Peretz shook his head. "Maybe. I hope you are right. Because you have committed us, blast you." He spoke without animosity.

After a minute: "I must confess I felt better when President de Vigny apologized officially for keeping our ship at arm's length."

"You have my personal apologies," Heim said low.

"All right!" Peretz thrust out his hand, features crinkled with abrupt laughter. "Accepted and forgotten, you damned old squarehead."

His trouble lifted from Heim, too. "Great!" he exclaimed. "Come on inside and we'll buckle down to getting drunk. Lord, how much yarning we've got to catch up on!"

They entered the living room and settled themselves. A maid curtsied. "What'll you have?" Heim asked. "Some items of food are still in short supply, and of course machinery's scarce, which is why I employ so many live servants. But these Frenchmen built big wine cellars."

"Brandy and soda, thanks," Peretz said.

"Me too. We *are* out of Scotch on New Europe. Uh…will there be cargoes from Earth soon?"

Peretz nodded. "Some are already on the way. Parliament will scream when I report what you have done, and there will be talk of an embargo, but you know that won't come to anything. If we aren't going to fight, to hold you against your will, it is senseless to antagonize you with annoyances."

"Which bears out what I said."

Heim put the drink orders into French.

"Please, don't argue any more. I told you I have accepted your *fait accompli.*" Peretz leaned forward. "But may I ask something, Gunnar? I see why New Europe did what it did. But you yourself—You could have come home, been a world hero, and a billionaire with your prize money. Instead you take citizenship here—well, blaze, they are nice people, but they aren't yours!"

"They are now," Heim said quietly.

He took out his pipe and tamped it full. His words ran on, almost of themselves:

"Mixed motives, as usual. I had to stay till the war was over. There was a lot of fighting, and afterward somebody must mount guard. And…well…I'd been lonely on Earth. Here I found a common purpose with a lot of absolutely first-class men. And a whole new world, elbow room, infinite possibilities. It dawned on me one day, when I was feeling homesick—what was I homesick for? To go back and rot among my dollars?

"So now, instead, I'm New Europe's minister of space and the navy. We're short of hands, training, equipment, everything; you name it and we probably haven't got it. But I can see us grow, day by day. And that's my doing!"

He struck fire and puffed. "Not that I intend to stay in government any longer than necessary," he went on. "I want to experiment with pelagic farming; and prospect the other planets and asteroids in this system; and start a merchant spaceship yard; and—shucks, I can't begin to tell you how much there is. I can't wait to become a private citizen again."

"But you do wait," Peretz said. Heim looked out a window at sea and sun and sky. "Well," he said, "it's worth some sacrifice. There's more involved than this world. We're laying the foundations of—" he hunted for words—"admiralty. Man's, throughout the universe."

The maid came in with her tray. Heim welcomed her not only for refreshment, but as an excuse to change the subject. He wasn't much of a talker on serious matters. A man did what he must; that sufficed.

The girl ducked her head. *"Un voleur s'approche, Monsieur,"* she reported.

"Good," Heim said. "That'll be Endre Vadasz and his wife. You'll like them, Moshe. These days he's giving his Magyar genes full rein on a 10,000 hectare ranch in the Bordes Valley—but he's still one solar flare of a singer. You may already have heard his ballad about Admiral Cynbe."

"No. About who?"

A brief bleakness crossed Heim's eyes. "I'll tell you later. Someone Endre and I both thought should be remembered." He raised his glass. *"Skaal."*

"Shalom."

Both men got up when the Vadaszes entered. *"Bienvenu,"* Heim said, shook his friend's hand with gladness and kissed Danielle's. By now he'd learned how to do that with authority.

It was a surprise, he thought as he looked at her, how fast a certain wound was healing. Life isn't a fairy tale; the knight who kills the dragon doesn't necessarily get the princess. So what? Who'd want to live in a cosmos less rich and various than the real one? You commanded yourself as you did a ship—with discipline, reasonableness, and spirit—and thus you came to port. By the time he fulfilled his promise to stand godfather to her firstborn, why, his feelings toward her would be downright avuncular.

No, he realized with a sudden quickening of blood, it wouldn't even take that long. The war was over. He could send for Lisa. He had little doubt that Jocelyn would come along.

THE ADVENTURE OF THE MISPLACED HOUND

Whitcomb Geoffrey was the very model of a modern major operative. Medium tall, stockily muscular, with cold gray eyes in a massively chiseled, expressionless face, he was quietly dressed in purple breeches and a crimson tunic whose slight bulge showed that he carried a Holman ray-thrower. His voice was crisp and hard as he said: "Under the laws of the Inter-being League, you are required to give every assistance to a field agent of the Interstellar Bureau of Investigation. Me."

Alexander Jones settled his lean length more comfortably behind the desk. His office seemed to crackle with Geoffrey's dynamic personality; he felt sure that the agent was inwardly scorning its easygoing sloppiness. "All right," he said. "But what brings you to Toka? This is still a backward planet, you know. Hasn't got very much to do with spatial traffic." Remembering the Space Patrol episode, he shuddered slightly and crossed his fingers.

"That's what you think!" snapped Geoffrey. "Let me explain."

"Certainly, if you wish," said Alex blandly.

"Thanks, I will," said the other man. He caught himself, bit his lip, and glared. It was plain that he thought Alex much too young for the exalted position of plenipotentiary. And in fact Alex's age was still, after nearly ten years in this job, well below the average for a ranking CDS official.

After a moment, Geoffrey went on: "The largest problem the IBI faces is interstellar dope smuggling, and the most dangerous gang in that business is—or was—operated by a group of renegade ppussjans from Ximba. Ever seen one, or a picture? They're small, slim fellows, cyno-centauroid type: four legs and two arms, spent years trying to track down this particular bunch of dream peddlers. We finally located their headquarters and got most of them. It was on a planet of Yamatsu's Star, about six light-years from here. But the leader, known as Number Ten—"

"Why not Number One?" asked Alex.

"Ppussjans count rank from the bottom up. Ten escaped, and has since been resuming his activities on a smaller scale, building up the ring again. We've *got* to catch him, or we'll soon be right back where we started.

"Casting around in this neighborhood with tracer beams, we caught a space-ship with a ppussjan and a load of nixl weed. The ppussjan confessed what he knew, which wasn't much, but still important. Ten himself is hiding out alone

56

here on Toka—he picked it because it's backward and thinly populated. He's growing the weed and giving it to his confederates, who land here secretly at night. When the hunt for him has died down, he'll leave Toka, and space is so big that we might never catch him again."

"Well," said Alex, "didn't your prisoner tell you just where Ten is hiding?"

"No. He never saw his boss. He merely landed at a certain desolate spot on a large island and picked up the weed, which had been left there for him. Ten could be anywhere on the island. He doesn't have a boat of his own, so we can't track him down with metal detectors; and he's much too canny to come near a spaceship, if we should go to the rendezvous and wait for him."

"I see," said Alex. "And nixl is deadly stuff, isn't it? Hm-m-m. You have the coordinates of this rendezvous?"

He pushed a buzzer. A Hoka servant entered, in white robes, a turban, and a crimson cummerbund, to bow low and ask: "What does the sahib wish?"

"Bring me the big map of Toka, Rajat Singh," said Alex. "He's been reading Kipling," said Alex apologetically. It did not seem to clear away his guest's puzzlement.

The coordinates intersected on a large island off the main continent. "Hm," said Alex, "England. Devonshire, to be precise."

"Huh?" Geoffrey pulled his jaw up with a click. An IBI agent is never surprised. "You and I will go there at once," he said firmly. "Remember your duty, Jones!"

"Oh, all right. I'll go. But you understand," added the younger man diffidently, "there may be a little trouble with the Hokas themselves."

Geoffrey was amused. "We're used to that in the IBI," he said. "We're well-trained not to step on native toes."

Alex coughed, embarrassed. "Well, it's not exactly that—" he stumbled. "You see…well, it may be the other way around."

A frown darkened Geoffrey's brow. "They may hamper us, you mean?" he clipped. "Your function is to keep the natives non-hostile, Jones."

"No," said Alex unhappily. "What I'm afraid of is that the Hokas may try to help us. Believe me, Geoffrey, you've no idea of what can happen when Hokas take it into their heads to be helpful."

Geoffrey cleared his throat. He was obviously wondering whether or not to report Alex as incompetent. "All right," he said. "We'll divide up the work between us. I'll let you do all the native handling, and you let me do the detecting."

"Good enough," said Alex, but he still looked doubtful.

The green land swept away beneath them as they flew toward England in the plenipotentiary's runabout. Geoffrey was scowling. "It's urgent," he said. "When the spaceship we captured fails to show up with its cargo, the gang will know something's gone wrong and send a boat to pick up Ten. At least one of them must know exactly where on the island he's hiding. They'll have an excellent chance of sneaking him past any blockade we can set up." He took out a cigarette and puffed nervously. "Tell me, why is the place called England?"

"Well—" Alex drew a long breath. "Out of maybe a quarter million known intelligent species, the Hokas are unique. Only in the last few years have we really begun to probe their psychology. They're highly intelligent, unbelievably quick to learn, ebullient by nature…and fantastically literal-minded. They have difficulty distinguishing fact from fiction, and since fiction is so much more colorful, they don't usually bother. Oh, my servant back at the office doesn't consciously believe he's a mysterious East Indian; but his subconscious has gone overboard for the role, and he can easily rationalize anything that conflicts with his wacky assumptions." Alex frowned, in search of words. "The closest analogy I can make is that the Hokas are somewhat like small human children, plus having the physical and intellectual capabilities of human adults. It's a formidable combination."

"All right," said Geoffrey. "What's this got to do with England?"

"Well, we're still not sure just what is the best starting point for the development of civilization among the Hokas. How big a forward step should the present generation be asked to take? More important, what socio-economic forms are best adapted to their temperaments and so on? Among other experiments, about ten years ago the cultural mission decided to try a Victorian English setup, and chose this island for the scene of it. Our robofacs quickly produced steam engines, machine tools, and so on for them…of course, we omitted the more brutal features of the actual Victorian world. The Hokas quickly carried on from the start we'd given them. They consumed mountains of Victorian literature—"

"I see," nodded Geoffrey.

"You begin to see," said Alex a little grimly. "It's more complicated than that. When a Hoka starts out to imitate something, there are no half measures about it. For instance, the first place we're going to get the hunt organized is called London, and the office we'll contact is called Scotland Yard, and—well, I hope you can understand a nineteenth-century English accent, because that's all you'll hear."

Geoffrey gave a low whistle. "They're that serious about it, eh?"

"If not more so," said Alex. "Actually, the society in question has, as far as I know, succeeded very well—so well that, being busy elsewhere, I haven't had a chance to keep up with events in England. I've no idea what that Hoka logic will have done to the original concepts by now. Frankly, I'm scared!"

Geoffrey looked at him curiously and wondered whether the plenipotentiary might not perhaps be a little off-balance on the subject of his wards.

From the air, London was a large collection of peak-roofed buildings, split by winding cobbled streets, on the estuary of a broad river that could only be the Thames. Alex noticed that it was being remodeled to a Victorian pattern: Buckingham Palace, Parliament, and the Tower were already erected, and St. Paul's was halfway finished. An appropriate fog was darkening the streets, so that gas lamps had to be lit. He found Scotland Yard on his map and landed in the court, between big stone buildings. As he and Geoffrey climbed out, a Hoka bobby complete with blue uniform and bulging helmet saluted them with great deference.

"'Umans!" he exclaimed. "H'I sye, sir, this must be a right big case, eh what? Are you working for 'Er Majesty, h'if h'I might myke so bold as ter awsk?"

"Well," said Alex, "not exactly." The thought of a Hoka Queen Victoria was somewhat appalling. "We want to see the chief inspector."

"Yes, sir!" said the teddy bear. "H'Inspector Lestrade is right down the 'all, sir, first door to yer left."

"Lestrade," murmured Geoffrey. "Where've I heard that name before?"

They mounted the steps and went down a gloomy corridor lit by flaring gas jets. The office door indicated had a sign on it in large letters:

FIRST BUNGLER

"Oh no!" said Alex under his breath.

He opened the door. A small Hoka in a wing-collared suit and ridiculously large horn-rimmed spectacles got up from behind the desk.

"The plenipotentiary!" he exclaimed in delight. "And another human! What is it, gentlemen? Has—" He paused, looked in sudden fright around the office, and lowered his voice to a whisper. "Has Professor Moriarty broken loose again?"

Alex introduced Geoffrey. They sat down and explained the situation. Geoffrey wound up with: "So I want you to organize your—CID, I imagine you call it—and help me track down this alien."

Lestrade shook his head sadly. "Sorry, gentlemen," he said. "We can't do that."

"Can't do it?" echoed Alex, shocked. "Why not?"

"It wouldn't do any good," said Lestrade, gloomily. "We wouldn't find anything. No, sir, in a case as serious as this, there's only one man who can lay such an arch-criminal by the heels. I refer, of course, to Mr. Sherlock Holmes."

"Oh, NO!" said Alex.

"I beg your pardon?" asked Lestrade.

"Nothing," said Alex, feverishly wiping his brow. "Look here—Lestrade—Mr. Geoffrey here is a representative of the most effective police force in the Galaxy. He—"

"Come now, sir," said Lestrade, with a pitying smile. "You surely don't pretend that he is the equal of Sherlock Holmes. Come, come, now!"

Geoffrey cleared his throat angrily, but Alex kicked his foot. It was highly illegal to interfere with an established cultural pattern, except by subtler means than argument. Geoffrey caught on and nodded as if it hurt him. "Of course," he said in a strangled voice. "I would be the last to compare myself with Mr. Holmes."

"Fine," said Lestrade, rubbing his stubby hands together. "Fine. I'll take you around to his apartment, gentlemen, and we can lay the problem before him. I trust he will find it interesting."

"So do I," said Alex, hollowly.

A hansom cab was clopping down the foggy streets and Lestrade hailed it. They got in, though Geoffrey cast a dubious look at the beaked, dinosaurian reptile which the Hokas called a horse, and went rapidly through the tangled lanes.

Hokas were abroad on foot, the males mostly in frock coats and top hats, carrying tightly rolled umbrellas, the females in long dresses; but now and then a bobby, a red-coated soldier, or a kilted member of a Highland regiment could be seen. Geoffrey's lips moved silently.

Alex was beginning to catch on. Naturally, the literature given these—Englishmen—must have included the works of A. Conan Doyle, and he could see where the romantic Hoka nature would have gone wild over Sherlock Holmes. So they had to interpret everything literally; but who had they picked to be Holmes?

"It isn't easy being in the CID, gentlemen," said Lestrade. "We haven't much of a name hereabouts, y'know. Of course, Mr. Holmes always gives us the credit, but somehow word gets around." A tear trickled down his furry cheek.

They stopped before an apartment building in Baker Street and entered the hallway. A plump elderly female met them. "Good afternoon, Mrs. Hudson," said Lestrade. "Is Mr. Holmes in?"

"Indeed he is, sir," said Mrs. Hudson. "Go right up." Her awed eyes followed the humans as they mounted the stairs.

Through the door of 221-B came a horrible wail. Alex froze, ice running along his spine, and Geoffrey cursed and pulled out his raythrower. The scream sawed up an incredible scale, swooped down again, and died in a choked quivering. Geoffrey burst into the room, halted, and glared around.

The place was a mess. By the light of a fire burning in the hearth, Alex could see papers heaped to the ceiling, a dagger stuck in the mantel, a rack of test tubes and bottles, and a "V.R." punched in the wall with bullets. It was hard to say whether the chemical reek or the tobacco smoke was worse. A Hoka in dressing gown and slippers put down his violin and looked at them in surprise. Then he beamed and came forward to extend his hand.

"Mr. Jones!" he said. "This is a real pleasure. Do come in."

"Uh—that noise—" Geoffrey looked nervously around the room.

"Oh, that," said the Hoka, modestly. "I was just trying out a little piece of my own. Concerto in Very Flat for violin and cymbals. Somewhat experimental, don't y'know."

Alex studied the great detective. Holmes looked about like any other Hoka—perhaps he was a trifle leaner, though still portly by human standards. "Ah, Lestrade," he said. "And Watson—do you mind if I call you Watson, Mr. Jones? It seems more natural."

"Oh, not at all," said Alex, weakly. He thought the real Watson—no, dammit, the Hoka Watson!—must be somewhere else; and the natives' one-track minds—

"But we are ignoring our guest here, whom I perceive to be in Mr. Lestrade's branch of the profession," said Holmes, laying down his violin and taking out a big-bowled pipe.

IBI men do not start; but Geoffrey came as close to it as one of his bureau's operatives had ever done. He had no particular intention of maintaining an incognito, but no officer of the law likes to feel that his profession is written large upon him. "How do you know that?" he demanded.

Holmes' black nose bobbed. "Very simple, my dear sir," he said. "Humans are a great rarity here in London. When one arrives, thus, with the estimable Lestrade for company, the conclusion that the problem is one for the police and that you yourself, my dear sir, are in some way connected with the detection of criminals, becomes a very probable one. I am thinking of writing another little monograph—But sit down, gentlemen, sit down, and let me hear what this is all about."

Recovering what dignity they could, Alex and Geoffrey took the indicated chairs. Holmes himself dropped into an armchair so overstuffed that he almost disappeared from sight. The two humans found themselves confronting a short pair of legs beyond which a button nose twinkled and a pipe fumed.

"First," said Alex, pulling himself together, "let me introduce Mr.—"

"Tut-tut, Watson," said Holmes. "No need. I know the estimable Mr. Gregson by reputation, if not by sight."

"Geoffrey, dammit!" shouted the IBI man.

Holmes smiled gently. "Well, sir, if you wish to use an alias, there is no harm done. But between us, we may as well relax, eh?"

"H-h-how," stammered Alex, "do you know that he's named Gregson?"

"My dear Watson," said Holmes, "since he is a police officer, and Lestrade is already well known to me, who else could he be? I have heard excellent things of you, Mr. Gregson. If you continue to apply my methods, you will go far."

"Thank you," snarled Geoffrey.

Holmes made a bridge of his fingers. "Well, Mr. Gregson," he said, "let me hear your problem. And you, Watson, will no doubt want to take notes. You will find pencil and paper on the mantel."

Gritting his teeth, Alex got them while Geoffrey launched into the story, interrupted only briefly by Holmes' "Are you getting all this down, Watson?" or occasions when the great detective paused to repeat slowly something he himself had interjected so that Alex could copy it word for word.

When Geoffrey had finished, Holmes sat silent for a while, puffing on his pipe. "I must admit," he said finally, "that the case has its interesting aspects. I confess to being puzzled by the curious matter of the Hound."

"But I didn't mention any hound," said Geoffrey numbly.

"That is the curious matter," replied Holmes. "The area in which you believe this criminal to be hiding is Baskerville territory, and you didn't mention a Hound once." He sighed and turned to the Scotland Yard Hoka. "Well, Lestrade," he went on, "I imagine we'd all better go down to Devonshire and you can arrange there for the search Gregson desires. I believe we can catch the 8:05 out of Paddington tomorrow morning."

"Oh, no," said Geoffrey, recovering some of his briskness. "We can fly down tonight."

Lestrade was shocked. "But I say," he exclaimed. "That just isn't done."

"Nonsense, Lestrade," said Holmes.

"Yes, Mr. Holmes," said Lestrade, meekly.

———

The village of St. Vitus-Where-He-Danced was a dozen thatch-roofed houses and shops, a church, a tavern, set down in the middle of rolling gray-green moors. Not far away, Alex could see a clump of trees which he was told surrounded Baskerville Hall. The inn had a big signboard announcing "The George and Dragon," with a picture of a Hoka in armor spearing some obscure monster. Entering the low-ceilinged tap-room, Alex's party were met by an overawed landlord and shown to clean, quiet rooms whose only drawback was the fact that the beds were built for one-meter Hokas.

By then it was night. Holmes was outside somewhere, bustling around and talking to the villagers, and Lestrade went directly to bed; but Alex and Geoffrey came back downstairs to the taproom. It was full of a noisy crowd of Hoka farmers and tradesmen, some talking in their squeaky voices, some playing darts, some clustering around the two humans. A square, elderly native introduced as Farmer Toowey joined them at their table.

"Ah, lad," he said, "it be terrible what yeou zee on the moor o' nights." And he buried his nose in the pint mug which should have held beer but, true to an older tradition, brimmed with the fiery liquor this high-capacity race had drunk from time immemorial. Alex, warned by past experience, sipped more cautiously at his pint; but Geoffrey was sitting with a half-empty mug and a somewhat wild look in his eyes.

"You mean the Hound?" asked Alex.

"I du," said Farmer Toowey. "Black, 'tis, an' bigger nor any bullock. And they girt teeth! One chomp and yeou'm gone."

"Is that what happened to Sir Henry Baskerville?" queried Alex. "Nobody seems to know where he's been for a long time."

"Swall'd um whole," said Toowey, darkly, finishing his pint and calling for another one. "Ah, poor Sir Henry! He was a good man, he was. When we were giving out new names, like the human book taught us, he screamed and fought, for he knew there was a curse on the Baskervilles, but—"

"The dialect's slipping, Toowey," said another Hoka.

"I be zorry," said Toowey. "I be oold, and times I forget masel'."

Privately, Alex wondered what the real Devonshire had been like. The Hokas must have made this one up out of whole cloth.

Sherlock Holmes entered in high spirits and sat down with them. His beady black eyes glittered. "The game is afoot, Watson!" he said. "The Hound has been doing business as usual. Strange forms seen on the moors of late— I daresay it's our criminal, and we shall soon lay him by the heels."

"Ridic'lous," mumbled Geoffrey. "Ain't—isn't any Hound. We're affer dope smuggler, not some son of—YOWP!" A badly thrown dart whizzed by his ear.

"Do you have to do that?" he quavered.

"Ah, they William," chuckled Toowey. "Ee's a fair killer, un is."

Another dart zoomed over Geoffrey's head and stuck in the wall. The IBI man choked and slid under the table—whether for refuge or sleep, Alex didn't know.

"Tomorrow," said Holmes, "I shall measure this tavern. I always measure," he added in explanation. "Even when there seems to be no point in it."

The landlord's voice boomed over the racket. "Closing time, gentlemen. It is time!"

The door flew open and banged to again. A Hoka stood there, breathing hard. He was unusually fat, and completely muffled in a long black coat; his face seemed curiously expressionless, though his voice was shrill with panic.

"Sir Henry!" cried the landlord. "Yeou'm back, squire!"

"The Hound," wailed Baskerville. "The Hound is after me!"

"Yeou've na cause tu fee-ar naow, Sir Henry," said Farmer Toowey. "'Tis Sheer-lock Holmes unself coom own to track yan brute."

Baskerville shrank against the wall. "Holmes?" he whispered.

"And a man from the IBI," said Alex. "But we're really after a criminal lurking on the moors—"

Geoffrey lifted a tousled head over the table. "Isn't no Hound," he said. "I'm affer uh dirty ppussjan, I am. Isn't no Hound nowheres."

Baskerville leaped. "It's at the door!" he shrieked, wildly. Plunging across the room, he went through the window in a crash of glass.

"Quick, Watson!" Holmes sprang up, pulling out his archaic revolver. "We'll see if there is a Hound or not!" He shoved through the panicky crowd and flung the door open.

The thing that crouched there, dimly seen by the firelight spilling out into darkness, was long and low and black, the body a vague shadow, a fearsome head dripping cold fire and snarling stiffly. It growled and took a step forward.

"Here naow!" The landlord plunged ahead, too outraged to be frightened. "Yeou can't coom in here. 'Tis closing time!" He thrust the Hound back with his foot and slammed the door.

"After him, Watson!" yelled Holmes. "Quick, Gregson!"

"Eek," said Geoffrey.

He must be too drunk to move, Alex thought. Alex himself had consumed just enough to dash after Holmes. They stood in the entrance, peering into darkness.

"Gone," said the human.

"We'll track him down!" Holmes paused to light his bull's-eye lantern, button his long coat, and jam his deerstalker cap more firmly down over his ears. "Follow me."

No one else stirred as Holmes and Alex went out into the night. It was pitchy outside. The Hokas had better night vision than humans and Holmes' furry hand closed on Alex's to lead him. "Confound these cobblestones!" said the detective. "No tracks whatsoever. Well, come along." They trotted from the village.

"Where are we going?" asked Alex.

"Out by the path to Baskerville Hall," replied Holmes sharply. "You would hardly expect to find the Hound anyplace else, would you, Watson?"

Properly rebuked, Alex lapsed into silence, which he didn't have the courage to break until, after what seemed an endless time, they came to a halt. "Where are we now?" he inquired of the night.

"About midway between the village and the Hall," replied the voice of Holmes, from near the level of Alex's waist. "Compose yourself, Watson, and wait while I examine the area for clues." Alex felt his hand released and heard the sound of Holmes moving away and rustling about on the ground. "Aha!"

"Find something?" asked the human, looking nervously around him.

"Indeed I have, Watson," answered Holmes. "A seafaring man with red hair and a peg leg has recently passed by here on his way to drown a sackful of kittens."

Alex blinked. "What?"

"A seafaring man—" Holmes began again, patiently.

"But—" stammered Alex. "But how can you tell that?"

"Childishly simple, my dear Watson," said Holmes. The light pointed to the ground. "Do you see this small chip of wood?"

"Y-yes, I guess so."

"By its grain and seasoning, and the type of wear it has had, it is obviously a piece which has broken off a peg leg. A touch of tar upon it shows that it belongs to a seafaring man. But what would a seafaring man be doing on the moors at night?"

"That's what I'd like to know," said Alex.

"We may take it," Holmes went on, "that only some unusual reason could force him out with the Hound running loose. But when we realize that he is a redheaded man with a terrific temper and a sackful of kittens with which he is totally unable to put up for another minute, it becomes obvious that he has sallied forth in a fit of exasperation to drown them."

Alex's brain, already spinning somewhat dizzily under the effect of the Hoka liquor, clutched frantically at this explanation, in an attempt to sort it out. But it seemed to slip through his fingers.

"What's all that got to do with the Hound, or the criminal we're after?" he asked weakly.

"Nothing, Watson," reproved Holmes sternly. "Why should it have?"

Baffled, Alex gave up.

Holmes poked around for a few more minutes, then spoke again. "If the Hound is truly dangerous, it should be sidling around to overwhelm us in the darkness. It should be along very shortly. Hah!" he rubbed his hands together. "Excellent!"

"I suppose it is," said Alex, feebly.

"You stay here, Watson," said Holmes, "and I will move on down the path a ways. If you see the creature, whistle." His lantern went out and the sound of his footsteps moved away.

Time seemed to stretch on interminably. Alex stood alone in the darkness, with the chill of the moor creeping into his bones as the liquor died within him, and wondered why he had ever let himself in for this in the first place. What would Tanni say? What earthly use would he be even if the Hound should appear? With his merely human night vision, he could let the beast stroll past within arm's reach and never know it. Of course, he could probably hear it...

Come to think of it, what kind of noise would a monster make when walking? Would it be a pad-pad, or a sort of shuffle-shuffle-shuffle like the sound on the path to his left?

The sound—*Yipe!*

The night was suddenly shattered. An enormous section of the blackness reared up and smashed into him with the solidity and impact of a brick wall. He went spinning down into the star-streaked oblivion of unconsciousness.

When he opened his eyes again, it was to sunlight streaming through the leaded windows of his room. His head was pounding, and he remembered some fantastic nightmare in which—hah!

Relief washing over him, he sank back into bed. Of course. He must have gotten roaring drunk last night and dreamt the whole weird business. His head was splitting. He put his hands up to it.

They touched a thick bandage.

Alex sat up as if pulled on a string. The two chairs which had been arranged to extend the bed for him went clattering to the floor. "Holmes!" he shouted. "Geoffrey!"

His door opened and the individuals in question entered, followed by Farmer Toowey. Holmes was fully dressed, fuming away on his pipe; Geoffrey looked red-eyed and haggard. "What happened?" asked Alex, wildly.

"You didn't whistle," said Holmes reproachfully.

"Aye, that yeou di'n't," put in the farmer. "When they boor yeou in, tha face were white nor a sheet, laike. Fair horrible it were, the look on tha face, lad."

"Then it wasn't a dream!" said Alex, shuddering.

"I—er—I saw you go out after the monster," said Geoffrey, looking guilty. "I tried to follow you, but I couldn't get moving for some reason." He felt gingerly of his own head.

"I saw a black shape attack you, Watson," added Holmes. "I think it was the Hound, even though that luminous face wasn't there. I shot at it but missed, and it fled over the moors. I couldn't pursue it with you lying there, so I carried you back. It's late afternoon now—you slept well, Watson!"

"It must have been the ppussjan," said Geoffrey with something of his old manner. "We're going to scour the moors for him today."

"No, Gregson," said Holmes. "I am convinced it was the Hound."

"Bah!" said Geoffrey. "That thing last night was only—was only—well, it was not a ppussjan. Some local animal, no doubt."

"Aye," nodded Farmer Toowey. "The Hound un were, that."

"Not the Hound!" yelled Geoffrey. "The ppussjan, do you hear? The Hound is pure superstition. There isn't any such animal."

Holmes wagged his finger. "Temper, temper, Gregson," he said.

"And stop calling me Gregson!" Geoffrey clutched his temples. "Oh, my head—!"

"My dear young friend," said Holmes patiently, "it will repay you to study my methods if you wish to advance in your profession. While you and Lestrade were out organizing a futile search party, I was studying the terrain and gathering clues. A clue is the detective's best friend, Gregson. I have five hundred measurements, six plaster casts of footprints, several threads torn from Sir Henry's coat by a splinter last night, and numerous other items. At a conservative estimate, I have gathered five pounds of clues."

"Listen." Geoffrey spoke with dreadful preciseness. "We're here to track down a dope smuggler, Holmes. A desperate criminal. We are not interested in country superstitions."

"I am, Gregson," smiled Holmes.

With an inarticulate snarl, Geoffrey turned and whirled out of the room. He was shaking. Holmes looked after him and tut-tutted. Then, turning: "Well, Watson, how do you feel now?"

Alex got carefully out of bed. "Not too bad," he admitted. "I've got a thumping headache, but an athetrine tablet will take care of it."

"Oh, that reminds me—" While Alex dressed, Holmes took a small flat case out of his pocket. When Alex looked that way again, Holmes was injecting himself with a hypodermic syringe.

"Hey!" cried the human. "What's that?"

"Morphine, Watson," said Holmes. "A seven percent solution. It stimulates the mind, I've found."

"Morphine!" Alex cried. Here was an IBI man currently present for the purpose of running down a dope smuggler and one of his Hokas had just produced— "OH, NO!"

Holmes leaned over and whispered in some embarrassment: "Well, actually, Watson, you're right. It's really just distilled water. I've written off for morphine several times, but they never send me any. So—well, one has one's position to keep up, you know."

"Oh," Alex feebly mopped his brow. "Of course." While he stowed away a man-sized dinner, Holmes climbed up on the roof and lowered himself down the chimney in search of possible clues. He emerged black but cheerful. "Nothing, Watson," he reported. "But we must be thorough." Then, briskly: "Now come. We've work to do."

"Where?" asked Alex. "With the search party?'

"Oh, no. They will only alarm some harmless wild animals, I fear. We are going exploring elsewhere. Farmer Toowey here has kindly agreed to assist us."

"S'archin', laike," nodded the old Hoka.

As they emerged into the sunlight, Alex saw the search party, a hundred or so local yokels who had gathered under Lestrade's direction with clubs, pitchforks and flails to beat the bush for the Hound—or for the ppussjan, if it came to that. One enthusiastic farmer drove a huge "horse"-drawn reaping machine.

Geoffrey was scurrying up and down the line, screaming as he tried to bring some order into it. Alex felt sorry for him.

They struck out down the path across the moor. "First we're off to Baskerville Hall," said Holmes. "There's something deucedly odd about Sir Henry Baskerville. He disappears for weeks, and then reappears last night, terrified by his ancestral curse, only to dash out onto the very moor which it is prowling. Where has he been in the interim, Watson? Where is he now?"

"Hm—yes," agreed Alex. "This Hound business and the ppussjan—do you think that there could be some connection between the two?"

"Never reason before you have all the facts, Watson," said Holmes. "It is the cardinal sin of all young police officers such as our impetuous friend Gregson."

Alex couldn't help agreeing. Geoffrey was so intent on his main assignment that he just didn't take time to consider the environment; to him, this planet was only a backdrop for his search. Of course, he was probably a cool head ordinarily, but Sherlock Holmes could unseat anyone's sanity.

Alex remembered that he was unarmed. Geoffrey had a raythrower, but this party only had Holmes' revolver and Toowey's gnarled staff. He gulped and tried to dismiss thoughts of the thing that had slugged him last night. "A nice day," he remarked to Holmes.

"It is, is it not? However," said Holmes, brightening up, "some of the most bloodcurdling crimes have been committed on fine days. There was, for example, the Case of the Dismembered Bishop—I don't believe I have ever told you about it, Watson. Do you have your notebook to hand?"

"Why, no," said Alex, somewhat startled.

"A pity," said Holmes. "I could have told you not only about the Dismembered Bishop, but about the Leaping Caterpillar, the Strange Case of the Case of Scotch, and the Great Ghastly Case—all very interesting problems. How is your memory?" he asked suddenly.

"Why—good, I guess," said Alex.

"Then I will tell you about the Case of the Leaping Caterpillar, which is the shortest of the lot," commenced Holmes. "It was considerably before your time, Watson. I was just beginning to attract attention with my work; and one day there was a knock on the door and in came the strangest—"

"Here be Baskerville Hall, laike," said Farmer Toowey.

An imposing Tudoresque pile loomed behind its screen of trees. They went up to the door and knocked. It opened and a corpulent Hoka in butler's black regarded them with frosty eyes. "Tradesmen's entrance in the rear," he said.

"Hey!" cried Alex.

The butler took cognizance of his humanness and became respectful. "I beg your pardon, sir," he said. "I am somewhat near-sighted and— I am sorry, sir, but Sir Henry is not at home."

"Where is he, then?" asked Holmes, sharply.

"In his grave, sir," said the butler, sepulchrally.

"Huh?" said Alex.

"His grave?" barked Holmes. "Quick, man! Where is he buried?"

"In the belly of the Hound, sir. If you will pardon the expression."

"Aye, aye," nodded Farmer Toowey. "Yan Hound, ee be a hungry un, ee be."

A few questions elicited the information that Sir Henry, a bachelor, had disappeared one day several weeks ago while walking on the moors, and had not been heard from since. The butler was surprised to learn that he had been seen only last night, and brightened visibly. "I hope he comes back soon, sir," he said. "I wish to give notice. Much as I admire Sir Henry, I cannot continue to serve an employer who may at any moment be devoured by monsters."

"Well," said Holmes, pulling out a tape measure, "to work, Watson."

"Oh, no, you don't!" This time Alex asserted himself. He couldn't see waiting around all night while Holmes measured this monstrosity of a mansion. "We've got a ppussjan to catch, remember?"

"Just a little measurement," begged Holmes.

"No!"

"Not even one?"

"All right." Jones relented at the wistful tone. "Just one."

Holmes beamed and, with a few deft motions, measured the butler.

"I must say, Watson, that you can be quite tyrannical at times," he said. Then, returning to Hoka normal: "Still, without my Boswell, where would I be?" He set off at a brisk trot, his furry legs twinkling in the late sunlight. Alex and Toowey stretched themselves to catch up.

They were well out on the moor again when the detective stopped and, his nose twitching with eagerness, leaned over a small bush from which one broken limb trailed on the ground. "What's that?" asked Alex.

"A broken bush, Watson," said Holmes snappishly. "Surely even you can see that."

"I know. But what about it?"

"Come, Watson," said Holmes, sternly. "Does not this broken bush convey some message to you? You know my methods. Apply them."

Alex felt a sudden wave of sympathy for the original Dr. Watson. Up until now he had never realized the devilish cruelty inherent in that simple command to apply the Holmesian methods. Apply them—how?

He stared fiercely at the bush, which continued to ignore him, without being able to deduce more than that it was (a) a bush and (b) broken. "Uh—a high wind?" he asked hesitantly.

"Ridiculous, Watson," retorted Holmes. "The broken limb is green; doubtless it was snapped last night by something large passing by in haste. Yes, Watson, this confirms my suspicions. The Hound has passed this way on its way to its lair, and the branch points us the direction."

"They be tu Grimpen Mire, a be," said Farmer Toowey dubiously. "Yan mire be impassable, un be."

"Obviously it is not, if the Hound is there," said Holmes. "Where it can go, we can follow. Come, Watson!" And he trotted off, his small body bristling with excitement.

They went through the brush for some minutes until they came to a wide boggy stretch with a large signboard in front of it.

GRIMPEN MIRE
FOUR MILES SQUARE
DANGER!!!!!!

"Watch closely, Watson," said Holmes. "The creature has obviously leaped from tussock to tussock. We will follow his path, watching for trampled grass or broken twigs. Now, then!" And bounding past the boundary sign, Holmes landed on a little patch of turf, from which he immediately soared to another one.

Alex hesitated, gulped, and followed him. It was not easy to progress in jumps of a meter or more, and Holmes, bouncing from spot to spot, soon pulled away. Farmer Toowey cursed and grunted behind Alex. "Eigh, ma oold boons can't tyke the leaping na moor, they can't," he muttered when they paused to rest. "If we'd knowed the Mire were tu be zo much swink, we'd never a builted un, book or no book."

"You made it yourselves?" asked Alex. "It's artificial?'

"Aye, lad, that un be. 'Twas in the book, Grimpen Mire, an' un swall'd many a man doon, un did. Many brave hee-arts lie asleep in un deep." He added apologetically: "Ow-ers be no zo grimly, though un tried hard. Ow-ers, yeou oonly get tha feet muddy, a-crossing o't. Zo we stay well away fran it, yeou understand."

Alex sighed.

The sun was almost under the hills now, and long shadows swept down the moor. Alex looked back, but could not make out any sign of Hall, village, or search party. A lonesome spot—not exactly the best place to meet a demoniac Hound, or even a ppussjan. Glancing ahead, he could not discern Holmes either, and he put on more speed.

An island—more accurately, a large hill—rose above the quaking mud. Alex and Toowey reached it with a final leap. They broke through a wall of trees and brush screening its stony crest. Here grew a wide thick patch of purple flowers. Alex halted, looked at them, and muttered an oath. He'd seen those blossoms depicted often enough in news articles.

"Nixl weed," he said. "So this is the ppussjan hideout!"

Dusk came swiftly as the sun disappeared. Alex remembered again that he was unarmed and strained wildly through the gathering dimness. "Holmes!" he called. "Holmes! I say, where are you, old fellow?" He snapped his fingers and swore. *Damn! Now I'm doing it!*

A roar came from beyond the hilltop. Jones leaped back. A tree stabbed him with a sharp branch. Whirling around, he struck out at the assailant. "Ouch!" he yelled. "Heavens to Betsy!" he added, though not in precisely those words.

The roar lifted again, a bass bellow that rumbled down to a savage snarling. Alex clutched at Farmer Toowey's smock. "What's that?" he gasped. "What's happening to Holmes?"

"Might be Hound's got un," offered Toowey, stolidly. "We hears un eatin', laike."

Alex dismissed the bloodthirsty notion with a frantic gesture. "Don't be ridiculous," he said.

"Ridiculous I may be," said Toowey stubbornly, "but they girt Hound be hungry, for zartin sure."

Alex's fear-tautened ears caught a new sound—footsteps from over the hill. "It's—coming this way," he hissed.

Toowey muttered something that sounded like "dessert."

Setting his teeth, Alex plunged forward. He topped the hill and sprang, striking a small solid body and crashing to earth. "I say, Watson," came Holmes' dry, testy voice, "this really won't do at all. I have told you a hundred times that such impetuosity ruins more good police officers than any other fault in the catalogue."

"Holmes!" Alex picked himself up, breathing hard. "My God, Holmes, it's you! But that other noise—the bellowing—?"

"That," said Holmes, "was Sir Henry Baskerville when I took the gag out of his mouth. Now come along, gentlemen, and see what I have found."

Alex and Toowey followed him through the nixl patch and down the rocky slope beyond it. Holmes drew aside a bush and revealed a yawning blackness. "I thought the Hound would shelter in a burrow," he said, "and assumed he would camouflage its entrance. So I merely checked the bushes. Do come in, Watson, and relax."

Alex crawled after Holmes. The tunnel widened into an artificial cave, about two meters high and three square, lined with a spray-plastic—not too bad a place. By the vague light of Holmes' bull's-eye, Alex saw a small cot, a cookstove, a radio transceiver, and a few luxuries. The latter, apparently, included a middle-aged Hoka in the tattered remnants of a once-fine tweed suit. He had been fat, from the way his skin hung about him, but was woefully thin and dirty now. It hadn't hurt his voice, though—he was still swearing in a loud bass unusual for the species, as he stripped the last of his bonds from him.

"Damned impertinence," he said. "Man isn't even safe on his own grounds any more. And the rascal had the infernal nerve to take over the family legend—*my* ancestral curse, dammit!"

"Calm down, Sir Henry," said Holmes. "You're safe now."

"I'm going to write to my M.P.," mumbled the real Baskerville. "I'll tell him a thing or two, I will. There'll be questions asked in the House of Commons, egad!"

Alex sat down on the cot and peered through the gloom. "What happened to you, Sir Henry?" he asked.

"Damned monster accosted me right on my own moor," said the Hoka, indignantly. "Drew a gun on me, he did. Forced me into his noisome hole. Had the unmitigated gall to take a mask of my face. Since then he's kept me on bread and water. Not even fresh bread, by Godfrey! It—it isn't British! I've been tied up in this hole for weeks. The only exercise I got was harvesting his blinking weed for him. When he went away, he'd tie me up and gag me—" Sir Henry drew an outraged breath. "So help me, he gagged me *with my own school tie!*"

"Kept as slave and possibly hostage," commented Holmes. "Hm. Yes, we're dealing with a desperate fellow. But Watson, see here what I have to show you." He reached into a box and pulled out a limp, black object with an air of triumph. "What do you think of this, Watson?"

Alex stretched it out: a plastimask of a fanged monstrous head, grinning like a toothpaste ad. When he held it in shadow, he saw the luminous spots on it. The Hound's head!

"Holmes!" he cried. "The Hound is the—the—"

"Ppussjan," supplied Holmes.

"How do you do?" said a new voice, politely.

Whirling around, Holmes, Alex, Toowey, and Sir Henry managed, in the narrow space, to tie themselves in knots. When they had gotten untangled, they looked down the barrel of a raythrower. Behind it was a figure muffled shapelessly in a great, trailing black coat, but with the head of Sir Henry above it.

"Number Ten!" gulped Alex.

"Exactly," said the ppussjan. His voice had a Hoka squeakiness, but the tone was cold. "Fortunately, I got back from scouting around before you could lay an ambush for me. It was pathetic, watching that search party. The last I saw of them, they were headed for Northumberland."

"They'll find you," said Alex, with a dry voice. "You don't dare hurt us."

"Don't I?" asked the ppussjan, brightly.

"I zuppoze yeou du, at that," said Toowey.

Alex realized sickly that if the ppussjan's hideout had been good up to now, it would probably be good until his gang arrived to rescue him. In any case, he, Alexander Braithwaite Jones, wouldn't be around to see.

But that was impossible. Such things didn't happen to him. He was League plenipotentiary to Toka, not a character in some improbable melodrama, waiting to be shot. He—

A sudden wild thought tossed out of his spinning brain: "Look here, Ten, if you ray us you'll sear all your equipment here too." He had to try again; no audible sounds had come out the first time.

"Why, thanks," said the ppussjan. "I'll set the gun to narrow-beam." Its muzzle never wavered as he adjusted the focusing stud. "Now," he asked, "have you any prayers to say?"

"I—" Toowey licked his lips. "Wull yeou alloo me to zay one poem all't' way through? It have given me gree-at coomfort, it have."

"Go ahead, then."

"By the shores of Gitchee Gumee—"

Alex knelt too—and one long human leg reached out and his foot crashed down on Holmes' lantern. His own body followed, hugging the floor as total darkness whelmed the cave. The raybeam sizzled over him—but, being narrow, missed and splatted the farther wall.

"Yoiks!" shouted Sir Henry, throwing himself at the invisible ppussjan. He tripped over Alex and went rolling to the floor. Alex got out from underneath, clutched at something, and slugged hard. The other slugged back.

"Take that!" roared Alex. "And that!"

"Oh, no!" said Sherlock Holmes in the darkness. "Not again, Watson!"

They whirled, colliding with each other, and groped toward the sounds of fighting. Alex clutched at an arm. "Friend or ppussjan?" he bellowed.

A raybeam scorched by him for answer. He fell to the floor, grabbing for the ppussjan's skinny legs.

Holmes climbed over him to attack the enemy. The ppussjan fired once more, wildly, then Holmes got his gun hand and clung. Farmer Toowey yelled a Hoka battle cry, whirled his staff over his head, and clubbed Sir Henry.

Holmes wrenched the ppussjan's raythrower loose. It clattered to the floor. The ppussjan twisted in Alex's grasp, pulling his leg free. Alex got hold of his coat. The ppussjan slipped out of it and went skidding across the floor, fumbling for the gun. Alex fought the heavy coat for some seconds before realizing that it was empty.

Holmes was there at the same time as Number Ten, snatching the raythrower from the ppussjan's grasp. Ten clawed out, caught a smooth solid object falling from Holmes' pocket, and snarled in triumph. Backing away, he collided with Alex. "Oops, sorry," said Alex, and went on groping around the floor.

The ppussjan found the light switch and snapped it. The radiance caught a tangle of three Hokas and one human. He pointed his weapon. "All right!" he screeched. "I've got you now!"

"Give that back!" said Holmes indignantly, drawing his revolver.

The ppussjan looked down at his own hand. It was clutching Sherlock Holmes' pipe.

Whitcomb Geoffrey staggered into the George and Dragon and grabbed the wall for support. He was gaunt and unshaven. His clothes were in rags. His hair was full of burrs. His shoes were full of mud. Every now and then he twitched, and his lips moved. A night and half a day trying to superintend a Hoka search party was too much for any man, even an IBI man.

Alexander Jones, Sherlock Holmes, Farmer Toowey, and Sir Henry Baskerville looked sympathetically up from the high tea which the landlord was serving them. The ppussjan looked up too, but with less amiability. His vulpine face sported a large black eye, and his four-legged body was lashed to a chair with Sir Henry's old school tie. His wrists were bound with Sir Henry's regimental colors.

"I say, Gregson, you've had rather a thin time of it, haven't you?" asked Holmes. "Do come have a spot of tea."

"Whee-ar's the s'arch party, lad?" asked Farmer Toowey.

"When I left them," said Geoffrey, dully, "they were resisting arrest at Potteringham Castle. The earl objected to their dragging his duckpond."

"Wull, wull, lad, the-all ull be back soon, laike," said Toowey, gently.

Geoffrey's bloodshot eyes fell on Number Ten. He was too tired to say more than: "So you got him after all."

"Oh, yes," said Alex. "Want to take him back to Headquarters?"

With the first real spirit he had shown since he had come in, Geoffrey sighed. "Take him back?" he breathed. "I can actually leave this planet?"

He collapsed into a chair. Sherlock Holmes refilled his pipe and leaned his short furry form back into his own seat.

"This has been an interesting little case," he said. "In some ways it reminds me of the Adventure of the Two Fried Eggs, and I think, my dear Watson, that it may be of some small value to your little chronicles. Have you your notebook ready?...Good. For your benefit, Gregson, I shall explain my deductions, for you are in many ways a promising man who could profit by instruction."

Geoffrey's lips started moving again.

"I have already explained the discrepancies of Sir Henry's appearance in the tavern," went on Holmes implacably. "I also thought that the recent renewed activity of the Hound, which time-wise fitted in so well with the ppussjan's arrival, might well be traceable to our criminal. Indeed, he probably picked this hideout because it did have such a legend. If the natives were frightened of the Hound, you see, they would be less likely to venture abroad and interfere with Number Ten's activities; and anything they did notice would be attributed to the Hound and dismissed by those outsiders who did not take the superstition seriously. Sir Henry's disappearance was, of course, part of this program of terrorization; but also, the ppussjan needed a Hoka face. He would have to appear in the local villages from time to time, you see, to purchase food and to find out whether or not he was being hunted by your bureau, Gregson. Watson has been good enough to explain to me the process by which your civilization can cast a mask in spray-plastic. The ppussjan's overcoat is an ingenious, adaptable garment; by a quick adjustment, it can be made to seem either like the body of a monster, or, if he walks on his hind legs, the covering of a somewhat stout Hoka. Thus, the ppussjan could be himself, or Sir Henry Baskerville, or the Hound of the Baskervilles, just as it suited him."

"Clever fella," murmured Sir Henry. "But dashed impudent, don't y'know. That sort of thing just isn't done. It isn't playing the game."

"The ppussjan must have picked up a rumor about our descent," continued Holmes. "An aircraft makes quite a local sensation. He had to investigate and see if flyers were after him and, if so, how hot they might be on his trail. He broke into the tavern in the Sir Henry disguise, learned enough for his purposes, and went out the window. Then he appeared again in the Hound form. This was an attempt to divert our attention from himself and send us scampering off after a non-existent Hound—as, indeed, Lestrade's search party was primarily doing when last heard from. When we pursued him that night, he tried to do away with the good Watson, but fortunately I drove him off in time. Thereafter he skulked about, spying on the search party, until finally he returned to his lair. But I was already there, waiting to trap him."

That, thought Alex, was glossing the facts a trifle. However—

Holmes elevated his black nose in the air and blew a huge cloud of nonchalant smoke. "And so," he said smugly, "ends the Adventure of the Misplaced Hound."

Alex looked at him. Damn it—the worst of the business was that Holmes was right. He'd been right all along. In his own Hoka fashion, he had done a truly magnificent job of detection. Honesty swept Alex off his and he spoke without thinking.

"Holmes—by the Lord Harry, Holmes," he said, "this—this is sheer genius."

No sooner were the words out of his lips than he realized what he had done. But it was too late now—too late to avoid the answer that Holmes must inevitably give. Alex clutched his hands together and braced his tired body, resolved to see the thing through like a man. Sherlock Holmes smiled, took his pipe from between his teeth, and opened his mouth. Through a great, thundering mist, Alexander Jones heard THE WORDS.

"Not at all. *Elementary, my dear Watson!*"

DELENDA EST

The hunting is good in Europe twenty thousand years ago, and the winter sports are unexcelled anywhen. So the Time Patrol, always solicitous for its highly trained personnel, maintains a lodge in the Pleistocene Pyrenees.

Manse Everard stood on a glassed-in verandah and looked across ice-blue distances toward the northern slopes where the mountains fell off into woodland, marsh, and tundra. His big body was clad in loose green trousers and tunic of twenty-third century insulsynth, boots handmade by a nineteenth-century French-Canadian; he smoked a foul old briar of indeterminate origin. There was a vague restlessness about him, and he ignored the noise from within, where half a dozen agents were drinking and talking and playing the piano.

A Cro-Magnon guide went by across the snow-covered yard, a tall handsome fellow dressed rather like an Eskimo (why had romance never credited paleolithic man with enough sense to wear jacket, pants, and footgear in a glacial period?), his face painted, one of the steel knives he had earned at his belt. The Patrol could act quite freely, this far back in time; there was no danger of upsetting the past, for the metal would rust away and the strangers be forgotten in a few centuries. The main nuisance was that female agents from the more libertine periods upstairs were always having affairs with the native hunters.

Piet Van Sarawak (Dutch-Indonesian-Venusian, early twenty-fourth A.D.), a slim, dark young man whose looks and technique gave the guides some stiff competition, joined Everard. They stood for a moment in companionable silence. He was also Unattached, on call to help out in any milieu, and had worked with the American before. They had taken their first vacation together.

He spoke first, in Temporal. "I hear they've spotted a few mammoths near Toulouse." The city would not be built for a long while yet, but habit was powerful.

"I've bagged one," said Everard impatiently. "I've also been skiing and mountain-climbing and watched the native dances."

Van Sarawak nodded, took out a cigarette, and puffed it into lighting. The bones stood out in his lean brown face as he sucked the smoke inward. "A pleasant loafing spell, this," he agreed, "but after a bit the outdoor life begins to pall."

There were still two weeks left of their furlough. In theory, since he could return almost to the moment of departure, an agent could take indefinite vacations; but actually he was supposed to devote a certain percentage of his probable lifetime to the job. (They never told you when you were scheduled to die, and you had better sense than to try finding out for yourself. It wouldn't have been certain anyhow, time being mutable. One perquisite of an agent's office was the Danellian longevity treatment.)

"What I would enjoy," continued Van Sarawak, "is some bright lights, music, girls who've never heard of time travel—"

"Done!" said Everard.

"Augustan Rome?" asked the other eagerly. "I've never been there. I could get a hypno on language and customs here."

Everard shook his head. "It's overrated. Unless we want to go 'way upstairs, the most glorious decadence available is right in my own milieu. New York, say…If you know the right phone numbers, and I do."

Van Sarawak chuckled. "I know a few places in my own sector," he replied, "but by and large, a pioneer society has little use for the finer arts of amusement. Very good, let's be off to New York, in—when?"

"Make it 1960. That was the last time I was there, in my public *persona*, before coming here-now."

They grinned at each other and went off to pack. Everard had foresightedly brought along some midtwentieth garments in his friend's size.

Throwing clothes and razor into a small suitcase, the American wondered if he could keep up with Van Sarawak. He had never been a high-powered roisterer, and wouldn't have known how to buckle a swash anywhere in space-time. A good book, a bull session, a case of beer—that was about his speed. But even the soberest men must kick over the traces occasionally.

Or a little more than that, if he was an Unattached agent of the Time Patrol; if his job with the Engineering Studies Company was only a blind for his wanderings and warrings through all history; if he had seen that history rewritten in minor things—not by God, which would have been endurable, but by mortal and fallible men—for even the Danellians were somewhat less than God; if he was forever haunted by the possibility of a major change, such that he and his entire world would never have existed at all…Everard's battered, homely face screwed into a grimace. He ran a hand through his stiff brown hair, as if to brush the idea away. Useless to think about. Language and logic broke down in the face of the paradox. Better to relax at such moments as he could.

He picked up the suitcase and went to join Piet Van Sarawak.

Their little two-place antigravity scooter waited on its skids in the garage. You wouldn't believe, to look at it, that the controls could be set for any place on Earth and any moment of time. But an airplane is wonderful too, or a ship, or a fire.

Auprés de ma blonde
Qu'il fait bon, fait bon, fait bon,

Auprés de ma blonde
Qu'il fait bon dormir!

Van Sarawak sang it aloud, his breath steaming from him in the frosty air as he hopped onto the rear saddle. He'd picked up the song once when accompanying the army of Louis XIV. Everard laughed. "Down, boy!"

"Oh, come, now," warbled the younger man. "It is a beautiful continuum, a merry and gorgeous cosmos. Hurry up this machine."

Everard was not so sure; he had seen enough human misery in all the ages. You got case-hardened after a while, but down underneath, when a peasant stared at you with sick brutalized eyes, or a soldier screamed with a pike through him, or a city went up in radioactive flame, something wept. He could understand the fanatics who had tried to change events. It was only that their work was so unlikely to make anything better…

He set the controls for the Engineering Studies warehouse, a good confidential place to emerge. Thereafter they'd go to his apartment, and then the fun could start.

"I trust you've said good-bye to all your lady friends here," Everard remarked.

"Oh, most gallantly, I assure you. Come along there. You're as slow as molasses on Pluto. For your information, this vehicle does not have to be rowed home."

Everard shrugged and threw the main switch. The garage blinked out of sight.

-2-

For a moment, shock held them unstirring.

The scene registered in bits and pieces. They had materialized a few inches above ground level—the scooter was designed never to come out inside a solid object and since that was unexpected, they hit the pavement with a teeth-rattling bump. They were in some kind of square. Nearby a fountain jetted, its stone basin carved with intertwining vines. Around the plaza, streets led off between squarish buildings six to ten stories high, of brick or concrete, wildly painted and ornamented. There were automobiles, big clumsy-looking things of no recognizable type, and a crowd of people.

"Jumping gods!" Everard glared at the meters. The scooter had landed them in lower Manhattan, 23 October 1960, at 11:30 A.M. and the spatial coordinates of the warehouse. But there was a blustery wind throwing dust and soot in his face, the smell of chimneys, and…

Van Sarawak's sonic stunner jumped into his fist. The crowd was milling away from them, shouting in some babble they couldn't understand. It was a mixed lot: tall, fair roundheads, with a great deal of red hair; a number of Amerinds; half-breeds in all combinations. The men wore loose colorful blouses, tartan kilts, a sort of Scotch bonnet, shoes and knee-length stockings. Their hair was long and many favored drooping mustaches. The women had full skirts reaching to the ankles and tresses coiled under hooded cloaks. Both sexes went in for massive bracelets and necklaces.

"What happened?" whispered the Venusian. "Where are we?"

Everard sat rigid. His mind clicked over, whirling through all the eras he had known or read about. Industrial culture—those looked like steam cars, but why the sharp prows and figurehead?—-coal-burning—postnuclear Reconstruction? No, they hadn't worn kilts then, and they had spoken English…

It didn't fit. There was no such milieu recorded.

"We're getting out of here!"

His hands were on the controls when the large man jumped him. They went over on the pavement in a rage of fists and feet. Van Sarawak fired and sent someone else down unconscious; then he was seized from behind. The mob piled on top of them both, and things became hazy.

Everard had a confused impression of men in shining coppery breastplates and helmets, who shoved a billy-swinging way through the riot. He was fished out and supported in his grogginess while handcuffs were snapped on his wrists. Then he and Van Sarawak were searched and hustled off to a big enclosed vehicle. The Black Maria is much the same in all times.

He didn't come back to full consciousness until they were in a damp and chilly cell with an iron-barred door.

"Name of a flame!" The Venusian slumped on a wooden cot and put his face in his hands.

Everard stood at the door, looking out. All he could see was a narrow concrete hall and the cell across it. The map of Ireland stared cheerfully through those bars and called something unintelligible.

"What's going on?" Van Sarawak's slim body shuddered.

"I don't know," said Everard very slowly. "I just don't know. That machine was supposed to be foolproof, but maybe we're bigger fools than they allowed for."

"There's no such place as this," said Van Sarawak desperately. "A dream?" He pinched himself and managed a rueful smile. His lip was cut and swelling, and he had the start of a gorgeous shiner. "Logically, my friend, a pinch is no test of reality, but it has a certain reassuring effect."

"I wish it didn't," said Everard.

He grabbed the bars so hard they rattled. "Could the controls have been askew, in spite of everything? Is there any city, anywhere on Earth—because I'm damned sure this is Earth, at least—any city, however obscure, which was ever like this?"

"Not to my knowledge."

Everard hung on to his sanity and rallied all the mental training the Patrol had ever given him. That included total recall; and he had studied history, even the history of ages he had never seen, with a thoroughness that should have earned him several Ph.D.'s.

"No," he said at last. "Kilted brachycephalic whites, mixed up with Indians and using steam-driven automobiles, haven't happened."

"Coordinator Stantel V," said Van Sarawak faintly. "In the thirty-eighth century. The Great Experimenter—colonies reproducing past societies—"

"Not any like this," said Everard.

The truth was growing in him, and he would have traded his soul for things to be otherwise. It took all the strength he had to keep from screaming and bashing his brains out against the wall.

"We'll have to see," he said in a flat tone.

A policeman (Everard assumed they were in the hands of the law) brought them a meal and tried to talk to them. Van Sarawak said the language sounded Celtic, but he couldn't make out more than a few words. The meal wasn't bad.

Toward evening, they were led off to a washroom and got cleaned up under official guns. Everard studied the weapons: eight-shot revolvers and long-barreled rifles. There were gas lights, whose brackets repeated the motif of wreathing vines and snakes. The facilities and firearms, as well as the smell, suggested a technology roughly equivalent to the earlier nineteenth century.

On the way back he spied a couple of signs on the walls. The script was obviously Semitic, but though Van Sarawak had some knowledge of Hebrew through dealing with the Israeli colonies on Venus, he couldn't read it.

Locked in again, they saw the other prisoners led off to do their own washing: a surprisingly merry crowd of bums, toughs, and drunks. "Seems we get special treatment," remarked Van Sarawak.

"Hardly astonishing," said Everard. "What would you do with total strangers who appeared out of nowhere and had unheard-of weapons?"

Van Sarawak's face turned to him with an unwonted grimness. "Are you thinking what I'm thinking?" he asked.

"Probably."

The Venusian's mouth twisted, and horror rode his voice: "Another time line. Somebody *has* managed to change history."

Everard nodded.

They spent an unhappy night. It would have been a boon to sleep, but the other cells were too noisy. Discipline seemed to be lax here. Also, there were bedbugs.

After a bleary breakfast, Everard and Van Sarawak were allowed to wash again and shave with safety razors not unlike the familiar type. Then a ten-man guard marched them into an office and planted itself around the walls.

They sat down before a desk and waited. The furniture was as disquietingly half-homelike, half-alien, as everything else. It was some time before the big wheels showed up. They were two: a white-haired, ruddy-cheeked man in cuirass and green tunic, presumably the chief of police, and a lean, hard-faced half-breed, gray-haired but black-mustached, wearing a blue tunic, a tam-o'-shanter, and on his left breast a golden bull's head which seemed an insigne of rank. He would have had a certain aquiline dignity had it not been for the thin hairy legs beneath his kilt. He was followed by two younger men, armed and uniformed much like himself, who took up their places behind him as he sat down.

Everard leaned over and whispered: 'The military, I'll bet. We seem to be of interest."

Van Sarawak nodded sickly.

The police chief cleared his throat with conscious importance and said something to the—general? The latter answered impatiently, and addressed himself to the prisoners. He barked his words out with a clarity that helped Everard get the phonemes, but with a manner that was not exactly reassuring.

Somewhere along the line, communication would have to be established. Everard pointed to himself. "Manse Everard," he said. Van Sarawak followed the lead and introduced himself similarly.

The general started and went into a huddle with the chief. Turning back, he snapped, "*Yrn Cimberland?*"

Then: "*Gothland? Svea? Nairoin Teutonach?*"

"Those names—if they are names—they sound Germanic, don't they?" muttered Van Sarawak.

"So do our names, come to think of it," answered Everard tautly. "Maybe they think we're Germans." To the general: "*Sprechen sie Deutsch?*" Blankness rewarded him. "*Taler ni svensk? Nederlands? Dansk? Parlez-vous francais?* Goddammit, *¿habla usted español?*"

The police chief cleared his throat again and pointed to himself. "Cadwallader Mac Barca," he said. The general hight Cynyth ap Ceorn. Or so, at least, Everard's Anglo-Saxon mind interpreted the noises picked up by his ears.

"Celtic, all right," he said. Sweat prickled under his arms. "But just to make sure…" He pointed inquiringly at a few other men, being rewarded with monikers like Hamilcar ap Angus, Asshur yr Cathlan, and Finn O'Carthia. "No… there's a distinct Semitic element here too. That fits in with their alphabet."

Van Sarawak wet his lips. "Try classical languages," he urged harshly. "Maybe we can find out where this history went insane."

"*Loquerisne latine?*" That drew a blank. "*'Aἑἁíβæåéò?*"

General ap Ceorn jerked, blew out his mustache, and narrowed his eyes. "*Hellenach?*" he demanded. "*Yrn Parthia?*"

Everard shook his head. "They've at least heard of Greek," he said slowly. He tried a few more words, but no one knew the tongue.

Ap Ceorn growled something to one of his men, who bowed and went out. There was a long silence.

Everard found himself losing personal fear. He was in a bad spot, yes, and might not live very long; but whatever happened to him was ludicrously unimportant compared to what had been done to the entire world.

God in Heaven! To the universe!

He couldn't grasp it. Sharp in his mind rose the land he knew, broad plains and tall mountains and prideful cities. There was the grave image of his father, and yet he remembered being a small child and lifted up skyward while his father laughed beneath him. And his mother…they had a good life together, those two.

There had been a girl he knew in college, the sweetest little wench a man would ever have been privileged to walk in the rain with; and Bernie Aaronson, the nights of beer and smoke and talk; Phil Brackney, who had picked him out of the mud in France when machine guns were raking a ruined field; Charlie and Mary Whitcomb, high tea and a low cannel fire in Victoria's London; Keith and Cynthia Denison in their chrome-plated eyrie above New York; Jack Sandoval among tawny Arizona crags; a dog he had once had; the austere cantos of Dante and the ringing thunder of Shakespeare; the glory which was York Minster and the Golden Gate Bridge—Christ, a man's life, and the lives of who knew how many billions of human creatures, toiling and enduring and laughing and going down into dust to make room for their sons…It had never been.

He shook his head, dazed with grief, and sat devoid of real understanding.

The soldier came back with a map and spread it out on the desk. Ap Ceorn gestured curtly, and Everard and Van Sarawak bent over it.

Yes, Earth, a Mercator projection, though eidetic memory showed that the mapping was rather crude. The continents and islands were there in bright colors, but the nations were something else.

"Can you read those names, Van?"

"I can make a guess on the basis of the Hebraic alphabet," said the Venusian. He began to read out the words. Ap Ceorn grunted and corrected him.

North America down to about Colombia was Ynys yr Afallon, seemingly one country divided into states. South America was a big realm, Huy Braseal and some smaller countries whose names looked Indian. Australasia, Indonesia, Borneo, Burma, eastern India and a good deal of the Pacific belonged to Hinduraj. Afghanistan and the rest of India were Punjab. Han included China, Korea, Japan, and eastern Siberia. Littorn owned the rest of Russia and reached well into Europe. The British Isles were Brittys, France and the Low Countries were Gallis, the Iberian peninsula was Celtan. Central Europe and the Balkans were divided into many small nations, some of which had Hunnish-looking names. Switzerland and Austria made up Helveti; Italy was Cimberland; the Scandinavian peninsula was split down the middle, Svea in the north and Gothland in the south. North Africa looked like a confederacy, reaching from Senegal to Suez and nearly to the equator under the name of Carthagalann; the southern part of the continent was partitioned among minor sovereignties, many of which had purely African titles. The Near East held Parthia and Arabia.

Van Sarawak looked up. He had tears in his eyes.

Ap Ceorn snarled a question and waved his finger about. He wanted to know where they were from.

Everard shrugged and pointed skyward. The one thing he could not admit was the truth. He and Van Sarawak had agreed to claim they were from another planet, since this world hardly had space travel.

Ap Ceorn spoke to the chief, who nodded and replied. The prisoners were returned to their cell.

-3-

"A nd now what?" Van Sarawak slumped on his cot and stared at the floor.

"We play along," said Everard grayly. "We do anything to get at our scooter and escape. Once we're free, we can take stock."

"But what happened?"

"I don't know, I tell you! Offhand, it looks as if something upset the Graeco-Romans and the Celts took over, but I couldn't say what it was." Everard prowled the room. A bitter determination was growing in him.

"Remember your basic theory," he said. "Events are the result of a complex. There are no single causes. That's why it's so hard to change history. If I went back to, say, the Middle Ages, and shot one of FDR's Dutch forebears, he'd still be born in the late nineteenth century—because he and his genes resulted from the entire world of his ancestors, and there'd have been compensation. But every so often, a really key event does occur. Some one happening is a nexus of so many world lines that its outcome is decisive for the whole future.

"Somehow, for some reason, somebody has ripped up one of those events, back in the past."

"No more Hesperus City," mumbled Van Sarawak. "No more sitting by the canals in the blue twilight, no more Aphrodite vintages, no more—did you know I had a sister on Venus?"

"Shut up!" Everard almost shouted it. "I know. To hell with that. What counts is what we can do.

"Look," he went on after a moment, "the Patrol and the Danellians are wiped out. (Don't ask me why they weren't always wiped out; why this is the first time we came back from the far past to find a changed future. I don't understand the mutable-time paradoxes. We just did, that's all.) But anyhow, such of the Patrol offices and resorts as antedate the switch point won't have been affected. There must be a few hundred agents we can rally."

"If we can get back to them."

"We can then find that key event and stop whatever interference there was with it. We've got to!"

"A pleasant thought. But…"

Feet tramped outside. A key clicked in the lock. The prisoners backed away. Then, all at once, Van Sarawak was bowing and beaming and spilling gallantries. Even Everard had to gape.

The girl who entered in front of three soldiers was a knockout. She was tall, with a sweep of rusty-red hair past her shoulders to the slim waist; her eyes were green and alight, her face came from all the Irish colleens who had ever lived; the long white dress was snug around a figure meant to stand on the walls of Troy. Everard noticed vaguely that this time-line used cosmetics, but she had small need of them. He paid no attention to the gold and amber of her jewelry, or to the guns behind her.

She smiled, a little timidly, and spoke: "Can you understand me? It was thought you might know Greek."

Her language was Classical rather than modern. Everard, who had once had a job in Alexandrine times, could follow it through her accent if he paid close heed—which was inevitable anyway

"Indeed I do," he replied, his words stumbling over each other in their haste to get out.

"What are you snakkering?" demanded Van Sarawak.

"Ancient Greek," said Everard.

"It would be," mourned the Venusian. His despair seemed to have vanished, and his eyes bugged.

Everard introduced himself and his companion. The girl said her name was Deirdre Mac Morn. "Oh, no," groaned Van Sarawak. 'This is too much. Manse, teach me Greek. Fast."

"Shut up," said Everard. "This is serious business."

"Well, but can't I have some of the business?"

Everard ignored him and invited the girl to sit down. He joined her on a cot, while the other Patrolman hovered unhappily by. The guards kept their weapons ready.

"Is Greek still a living language?" asked Everard.

"Only in Parthia, and there it is most corrupt," said Deirdre. "I am a Classical scholar, among other things. *Saorann* ap Ceorn is my uncle, so he asked me to see if I could talk with you. Not many in Afallon know the Attic tongue."

"Well"—Everard suppressed a silly grin—"I am most grateful to your uncle."

Her eyes rested gravely on him. "Where are you from? And how does it happen that you speak only Greek, of all known languages?"

"I speak Latin, too."

"Latin?" She frowned in thought. "Oh, the Roman speech, was it not? I am afraid you will find no one who knows much about it"

"Greek will do," said Everard firmly.

"But you have not told whence you came," she insisted.

Everard shrugged. "We've not been treated very politely," he hinted.

"I'm sorry." It seemed genuine. "But our people are so excitable. Especially now, with the international situation what it is. And when you two appeared out of thin air…"

That had an unpleasantly familiar ring. "What do you mean?" he inquired.

"Surely you know. With Huy Braseal and Hinduraj about to go to war, and all of us wondering what will happen…It is not easy to be a small power."

"A small power? But I saw a map. Afallon looked big enough to me."

"We wore ourselves out two hundred years ago, in the great war with Littorn. Now none of our confederated states can agree on a single policy." Deirdre looked directly into his eyes. "What is this ignorance of yours?"

Everard swallowed and said, "We're from another world."

"What?"

"Yes. A planet (no, that means 'wanderer')…an orb encircling Sirius. That's our name for a certain star."

"But—what do you mean? A world attendant on a star? I cannot understand you."

"Don't you know? A star is a sun like…"

Deirdre shrank back and made a sign with her finger. "The Great Baal aid us," she whispered. "Either you are mad or…The stars are mounted in a crystal sphere."

Oh, no!

"What of the wandering stars you can see?" asked Everard slowly. "Mars and Venus and—"

"I know not those names. If you mean Moloch, Ashtoreth, and the rest, of course they are worlds like stars attendant on the sun like our own. One holds the spirits of the dead, one is the home of witches, one…"

All this and steam cars too. Everard smiled shakily. "If you'll not believe me, then what do you think I am?"

Deirdre regarded him with large eyes. "I think you must be sorcerers," she said.

There was no answer to that. Everard asked a few weak questions, but learned little more than that this city was Catuvellaunan, a trading and manufacturing center. Deirdre estimated its population at two million, and that of all Afallon at fifty million, but wasn't sure. They didn't take censuses here.

The Patrolmen's fate was equally undetermined. Their scooter and other possessions had been sequestered by the military, but no one dared monkey with the stuff, and treatment of the owners was being hotly debated. Everard got the impression that all government, including the leadership of the armed forces, was rather a sloppy process of individualistic wrangling. Afallon itself was the loosest of confederacies, built out of former nations—Brittic colonies and Indians who had adopted European culture—all jealous of their rights. The old Mayan Empire, destroyed in a war with Texas (Tehannach) and annexed, had not forgotten its time of glory, and sent the most rambunctious delegates of all to the Council of Suffetes.

The Mayans wanted to make an alliance with Huy Braseal, perhaps out of friendship for fellow Indians. The West Coast states, fearful of Hinduraj, were toadies of the Southeast Asian empire. The Middle West (of course) was isolationist; the Eastern States were torn every which way, but inclined to follow the lead of Brittys.

When he gathered that slavery existed here, though not on racial lines, Everard wondered briefly and wildly if the time changers might not have been Dixiecrats.

Enough! He had his own neck, and Van's, to think about. "We are from Sirius," he declared loftily. "Your ideas about the stars are mistaken. We came as peaceful explorers, and if we are molested, there will be others of our kind to take vengeance."

Deirdre looked so unhappy that he felt conscience-stricken. "Will they spare the children?" she begged. "The children had nothing to do with it." Everard could imagine the vision in her head, small crying captives led off to the slave markets of a world of witches.

"There need be no trouble at all if we are released and our property returned," he said.

"I shall speak to my uncle," she promised, "but even if I can sway him, he is only one man on the Council. The thought of what your weapons could mean if we had them has driven men mad."

She rose. Everard clasped both her hands—they lay warm and soft in his—and smiled crookedly at her. "Buck up, kid," he said in English. She shivered, pulled free of him, and made the hex sign again.

"Well," demanded Van Sarawak when they were alone "what did you find out?" After being told, he stroked his chin and murmured. "That was one glorious little collection of sinusoids. There could be worse worlds than this."

"Or better," said Everard roughly. "They don't have atomic bombs, but neither do they have penicillin, I'll bet. Our job is not to play God."

"No. No, I suppose not." The Venusian sighed.

-4-

They spent a restless day. Night had fallen when lanterns glimmered in the corridor and a military guard unlocked the cell. The prisoners were led silently to a rear exit where two automobiles waited; they were put into one, and the whole troop drove off.

Catuvellaunan did not have outdoor lighting, and there wasn't much night traffic. Somehow that made the sprawling city unreal in the dark. Everard paid attention to the mechanics of his car. Steam-powered, as he had guessed, burning powdered coal; rubber-tired wheels; a sleek body with a sharp nose and serpent figurehead; the whole simple to operate and honestly built, but not too well designed. Apparently this world had gradually developed a rule-of-thumb engineering, but no systematic science worth talking about.

They crossed a clumsy iron bridge to Long Island, here also a residential section for the well-to-do. Despite the dimness of oil-lamp headlights, their speed was high. Twice they came near having an accident: no traffic signals, and seemingly no drivers who did not hold caution in contempt.

Government and traffic…hm. It all looked French, somehow ignoring those rare interludes when France got a Henry of Navarre or a Charles de Gaulle. And even in Everard's own twentieth century, France was largely Celtic. He was no respecter of windy theories about inborn racial traits, but there was something to be said for traditions so ancient as to be unconscious and ineradicable. A Western world in which the Celts had become dominant, the Germanic peoples reduced to a few small outposts…Yes, look at the Ireland of home; or recall how tribal politics had queered Vercingetorix's revolt…But what about Littorn? Wait a minute! In *his* early Middle Ages, Lithuania had been a powerful state; it had held off Germans, Poles, and Russians alike for a long time, and hadn't even taken Christianity till the fifteenth century. Without German competition, Lithuania might very well have advanced eastward…

In spite of the Celtic political instability, this was a world of large states, fewer separate nations than Everard's. That argued an older society. If his own Western civilization had developed out of the decaying Roman Empire about, say, A.D. 600, the Celts in this world must have taken over earlier than that.

Everard was beginning to realize what had happened to Rome, but reserved his conclusions for the time being.

The cars drew up before an ornamental gate set in a long stone wall. The drivers talked with two armed guards wearing the livery of a private estate and the thin steel collars of slaves. The gate was opened and the cars went along a graveled driveway between lawns and trees. At the far end, almost on the beach, stood a house. Everard and Van Sarawak were gestured out and led toward it.

It was a rambling wooden structure. Gas lamps on the porch showed it painted in gaudy stripes; the gables and beam ends were carved into dragon heads. Close by he heard the sea, and there was enough light from a sinking crescent moon for Everard to make out a ship standing in close: presumably a freighter, with a tall smokestack and a figurehead.

The windows glowed yellow. A slave butler admitted the party. The interior was paneled in dark wood, also carved, the floors thickly carpeted. At the end of the hall was a living room with overstuffed furniture, several paintings in a stiff conventionalized style, and a merry blaze in an enormous stone fireplace.

Saorann ap Ceorn sat in one chair, Deirdre in another. She laid aside a book as they entered and rose, smiling. The officer puffed a cigar and glowered. Some words were swapped, and the guards disappeared. The butler fetched in wine on a tray, and Deirdre invited the Patrolmen to sit down.

Everard sipped from his glass—the wine was an excellent burgundy—and asked bluntly, "Why are we here?"

Deirdre dazzled him with a smile. "Surely you find it more pleasant than the jail."

"Of course. As well as more ornamental. But I still want to know. Are we being released?"

"You are…" She hunted for a diplomatic answer, but there seemed to be too much frankness in her. "You are welcome here, but may not leave the estate. We hope you can be persuaded to help us. You would be richly rewarded."

"Help? How?"

"By showing our artisans and druids how to make more weapons and magical carts like your own."

Everard sighed. It was no use trying to explain. They didn't have the tools to make the tools to make what was needed, but how could he get that across to a folk who believed in witchcraft?

"Is this your uncle's home?" he asked.

"No, my own," said Deirdre. "I am the only child of my parents, who were wealthy nobles. They died last year."

Ap Ceorn clipped out several words. Deirdre translated with a worried frown: "The tale of your advent is known to all Catuvellaunan by now; and that includes the foreign spies. We hope you can remain hidden from them here."

Everard, remembering the pranks Axis and Allies had played in little neutral nations like Portugal, shivered. Men made desperate by approaching war would not likely be as courteous as the Afallonians.

"What is this conflict going to be about?" he inquired.

"The control of the Icenian Ocean, of course. In particular, certain rich islands we call Ynys yr Lyonnach." Deirdre got up in a single flowing movement and pointed out Hawaii on a globe. "You see," she went on earnestly, "as I told you, Littorn and the western alliance—including us—wore each other out fighting. The great powers today, expanding, quarreling, are Huy Braseal and Hinduraj. Their conflict sucks in the lesser nations, for the clash is not only between ambitions, but between systems: the monarchy of Hinduraj against the sun-worshipping theocracy of Huy Braseal."

"What is your religion, if I may ask?"

Deirdre blinked. The question seemed almost meaningless to her. "The more educated people think that there is a Great Baal who made all the lesser gods," she answered at last, slowly. "But naturally, we maintain the ancient cults, and pay respect to the more powerful foreign gods too, such as Littorn's Perkunas and Czernebog, Wotan Ammon of Cimberland, Brahma, the Sun…Best not to chance their anger."

"I see."

Ap Ceorn offered cigars and matches. Van Sarawak inhaled and said querulously, "Damn it, this would have to be a time line where they don't speak any language I know." He brightened. "But I'm pretty quick to learn, even without hypno. I'll get Deirdre to teach me."

"You and me both," said Everard in haste. "But listen, Van." He reported what he had learned.

"Hm." The younger man rubbed his chin. "Not so good, eh? Of course, if they'd just let us aboard our scooter, we could make an easy getaway. Why not play along with them?"

"They're not such fools," answered Everard. "They may believe in magic, but not in undiluted altruism."

"Funny they should be so backward intellectually, and still have combustion engines."

"No. It's quite understandable. That's why I asked about their religion. It's always been purely pagan; even Judaism seems to have disappeared, and Buddhism hasn't been very influential. As Whitehead pointed out, the medieval idea of one almighty God was important to the growth of science, by inculcating the notion of lawfulness in nature. And Lewis Mumford added that the early monasteries were probably responsible for the mechanical clock—a very basic invention—because of having regular hours for prayer. Clocks seem to have come late in this world." Everard smiled wryly, a shield against the sadness within. "Odd to talk like this. Whitehead and Mumford never lived."

"Nevertheless—"

"Just a minute." Everard turned to Deirdre. "When was Afallon discovered?"

"By white men? In the year 4827."

"Um…when does your reckoning start from?"

Deirdre seemed immune to further startlement. "The creation of the world. At least, the date some philosophers have given. That is 5964 years ago."

Which agreed with Bishop Usher's famous 4004 B.C., perhaps by sheer coincidence—but still, there was definitely a Semitic element in this culture. The creation story in Genesis was of Babylonian origin too.

"And when was steam (*pneuma*) first used to drive engines?" he asked.

"About a thousand years ago. The great druid Boroihme O'Fiona—"

"Never mind." Everard smoked his cigar and mulled his thoughts for a while before looking back at Van Sarawak.

"I'm beginning to get the picture," he said. 'The Gauls were anything but the barbarians most people think. They'd learned a lot from Phoenician traders and Greek colonists, as well as from the Etruscans in cisalpine Gaul. A very energetic and enterprising race. The Romans, on the other hand, were a stolid lot, with few intellectual interests. There was little technological progress in our world till the Dark Ages, when the Empire had been swept out of the way.

"In *this* history, the Romans vanished early. So, I'm pretty sure, did the Jews. My guess is, without the balance-of-power effect of Rome, the Syrians did suppress the Maccabees; it was a near thing even in our history. Judaism disappeared and therefore Christianity never came into existence. But anyhow, with Rome removed, the Gauls got the supremacy. They started exploring, building better ships, discovering America in the ninth century. But they weren't so far ahead of the Indians that those couldn't catch up…could even be stimulated to build empires of their own, like Huy Braseal today. In the eleventh century, the Celts began tinkering with steam engines. They seem to have gotten gunpowder too, maybe from China, and to have made several other inventions. But it's all been cut-and-try, with no basis of real science."

Van Sarawak nodded. "I suppose you're right. But what did happen to Rome?"

"I don't know. Yet. But our key point is back there somewhere."

Everard returned his attention to Deirdre. "This may surprise you," he said smoothly. "Our people visited this world about twenty-five hundred years ago. That's why I speak Greek but don't know what has occurred since. I would like to find out from you; I take it you're quite a scholar."

She flushed and lowered long dark lashes such as few redheads possess. "I will be glad to help as much as I can." With a sudden appeal: "But will you help us in return?"

"I don't know," said Everard heavily. "I'd like to. But I don't know if we can."

Because after all, my job is to condemn you and your entire world to death.

-5-

When Everard was shown to his room, he discovered that local hospitality was more than generous. He was too tired and depressed to take advantage of it…but at least, he thought on the edge of sleep, Van's slave girl wouldn't be disappointed.

They got up early here. From his upstairs window, Everard saw guards pacing the beach, but they didn't detract from the morning's freshness. He came down with Van Sarawak to breakfast, where bacon and eggs, toast and coffee added the last touch of dream. Ap Ceorn had gone back to town to confer, said Deirdre; she herself had put wistfulness aside and chattered gaily of trivia. Everard learned that she belonged to an amateur dramatic group which sometimes gave Classical Greek plays in the original: hence her fluency. She liked to ride, hunt, sail, swim—"And shall we?" she asked.

"Huh?"

"Swim, of course." Deirdre sprang from her chair on the lawn, where they had been sitting under flame-colored leaves, and whirled innocently out of her clothes. Everard thought he heard a dull clunk as Van Sarawak's jaw hit the ground.

"Come!" she laughed. "Last one in is a Sassenach!"

She was already tumbling in the gray surf when Everard and Van Sarawak shuddered their way down to the beach. The Venusian groaned. "I come from a warm planet. My ancestors were Indonesians. Tropical birds."

"There were some Dutchmen too, weren't there?" Everard grinned.

"They had the sense to move to Indonesia."

"All right, stay ashore."

"Hell! If she can do it, I can!" Van Sarawak put a toe in the water and groaned again.

Everard summoned up all the control he had ever learned and ran in. Deirdre threw water at him. He plunged, got hold of a slender leg, and pulled her under. They frolicked about for several minutes before running back to the house for a hot shower. Van Sarawak followed in a blue haze.

"Speak about Tantalus," he mumbled. "The most beautiful girl in the whole continuum, and I can't talk to her and she's half polar bear."

Toweled dry and dressed in the local garb by slaves, Everard returned to stand before the living-room fire. "What pattern is this?" he asked, pointing to the tartan of his kilt.

Deirdre lifted her ruddy head. "My own clan's," she answered. "An honored guest is always taken as a clan member during his stay, even if a blood feud is going on." She smiled shyly. "And there is none between us, Manslach."

It cast him back into bleakness. He remembered what his purpose was.

"I'd like to ask you about history," he said. "It is a special interest of mine."

She nodded, adjusted a gold fillet in her hair, and got a book from a crowded shelf. "This is the best world history, I think. I can look up any details you might wish to know."

And tell me what I must do to destroy you.

Everard sat down with her on a couch. The butler wheeled in lunch. He ate moodily, untasting.

To follow up his hunch—"Did Rome and Carthage ever fight a war?"

"Yes. Two, in fact. They were allied at first, against Epirus, but fell out. Rome won the first war and tried to restrict Carthaginian enterprise." Her clean profile bent over the pages, like a studious child's. "The second war broke out twenty-three years later, and lasted…hmm…eleven years all told, though the last three were only a mopping up after Hannibal had taken and burned Rome."

Ah-hah! Somehow, Everard did not feel happy at his success.

The Second Punic War (they called it the Roman War here)—or, rather, some crucial incident thereof—was the turning point. But partly out of curiosity, partly because he feared to tip his hand, Everard did not at once try to identify the deviation. He'd first have to get straight in his mind what had actually happened, anyway. (No…what had not happened. The reality was here, warm and breathing beside him; he was the ghost.)

"So what came next?" he asked tonelessly.

"The Carthaginian empire came to include Hispania, southern Gaul, and the toe of Italy," she said. "The rest of Italy was impotent and chaotic, after the Roman confederacy had been broken up. But the Carthaginian government was too venal to remain strong. Hannibal himself was assassinated by men who thought his honesty stood in their way. Meanwhile, Syria and Parthia fought for the eastern Mediterranean, with Parthia winning and thus coming under still greater Hellenic influence than before.

"About a hundred years after the Roman Wars, some Germanic tribes overran Italy." (That would be the Cimbri with their allies the Teutones and Ambrones, whom Marius had stopped in Everard's world.) "Their destructive path through Gaul had set the Celts moving too, eventually into Hispania and North Africa as Carthage declined. And from Carthage the Gauls learned much.

"A long period of wars followed, during which Parthia waned and the Celtic states grew. The Huns broke the Germans in middle Europe, but were in turn defeated by Parthia; so the Gauls moved in and the only Germans left were in Italy and Hyperborea." (That must be the Scandinavian peninsula.) "As ships improved, trade grew up with the Far East, both from Arabia and directly around Africa." (In Everard's history, Julius Caesar had been astonished to find the Veneti building better vessels than any in the Mediterranean.) "The Celtanians discovered southern Afallon, which they thought was an island—hence the 'Ynys'—but they were thrown out by the Mayans. The Brittic colonies farther north did survive, though, and eventually won their independence.

"Meanwhile Littorn was growing apace. It swallowed up most of Europe for a while. The western end of the continent only regained its freedom as part of the peace settlement after the Hundred Years' War I've told you about. The Asian countries have shaken off their exhausted European masters and modernized themselves, while the Western Nations have declined in their turn." Deirdre looked up from the book, which she had been skimming as she talked. "But this is only the barest outline, Manslach. Shall I go on?"

Everard shook his head. "No thanks." After a moment; "You are very honest about your own country."

Deirdre said roughly, "Most of us won't admit it, but I think it best to look truth in the eyes."

With a surge of eagerness: "But tell me of your own world. This is a marvel past belief."

Everard sighed, switched off his conscience, and began lying.

The raid took place that afternoon.

Van Sarawak had recovered his poise and was busily learning the Afallonian language from Deirdre. They walked through the garden hand in hand, stopping to name objects and act out verbs. Everard followed, wondering vaguely if he was a third wheel or not, most of him bent to the problem of how to get at the scooter.

Bright sunlight spilled from a pale cloudless sky. A maple was a shout of scarlet, a drift of yellow leaves scudded across the grass. An elderly slave was raking the yard in a leisurely fashion, a young-looking guard of Indian race lounged with his rifle slung on one shoulder, a pair of wolfhounds dozed under a hedge. It was a peaceful scene; hard to believe that men prepared murder beyond these walls.

But man was man in any history This culture might not have the ruthless will and sophisticated cruelty of Western civilization; in fact, in some ways it looked strangely innocent. Still, that wasn't for lack of trying. And in this world, a genuine science might never emerge, man might repeat endlessly the cycle of war, empire, collapse, and war. In Everard's future, the race had finally broken out of it.

For what? He could not honestly say that this continuum was worse or better than his own. It was different, that was all. And didn't these people have as much right to their existence as—as his own, who were damned to nullity if he failed?

He knotted his fists. The issue was too big. No man should have to decide something like this.

At the showdown, he knew, no abstract sense of duty would compel him, but the little things and the little folk he remembered.

They rounded the house and Deirdre pointed to the sea. "*Awarkinn*," she said. Her loose hair burned in the wind.

"Now does that mean 'ocean' or 'Atlantic' or 'water'?" laughed Van Sarawak. "Let's go see." He led her toward the beach.

Everard trailed. A kind of steam launch, long and fast, was skipping over the waves, a mile or two offshore. Gulls trailed it in a snowstorm of wings. He thought that if he'd been in charge, a Navy ship would have been on picket out there.

Did he even have to decide anything? There were other Patrolmen in the pre-Roman past. They'd return to their respective eras and...

Everard stiffened. A chill ran down his back and congealed in his belly.

They'd return, and see what had happened, and try to correct the trouble. If any of them succeeded, this world would blink out of spacetime, and he would go with it.

Deirdre paused. Everard, standing in a sweat, hardly noticed what she was staring at, till she cried out and pointed. Then he joined her and squinted across the sea.

The launch was standing in close, its high stack fuming smoke and sparks, the gilt snake figurehead agleam. He could see the forms of men aboard, and something white with wings...It rose from the poop deck and trailed at the end of a rope, mounting. A glider! Celtic aeronautics had gotten that far, at least.

"Pretty," said Van Sarawak. "I suppose they have balloons, too."

The glider cast its tow and swooped inward. One of the guards on the beach shouted. The rest pelted from behind the house. Sunlight flashed off their guns. The launch headed straight for the shore. The glider landed, plowing a furrow in the beach.

An officer yelled and waved the Patrolmen back. Everard had a glimpse of Deirdre's face, white and uncomprehending. Then a turret on the glider swiveled—a detached part of his mind guessed it was manually operated—and a light cannon spoke.

Everard hit the dirt. Van Sarawak followed, dragging the girl with him. Grapeshot plowed hideously through the Afallonian soldiers.

There followed a spiteful crack of guns. Men sprang from the aircraft, dark-faced men in turbans and sarongs. *Hinduraj!* thought Everard. They traded shots with the surviving guards, who rallied about their captain.

The officer roared and led a charge. Everard look up from the sand to see him almost upon the glider's crew. Van Sarawak leaped to his feet. Everard rolled over, caught him by the ankle, and pulled him down before he could join the fight.

"Let me *go!*" The Venusian writhed, sobbing. The dead and wounded left by the cannon sprawled nightmare red. The racket of battle seemed to fill the sky.

"No, you bloody fool! It's us they're after, and that wild Irishman's done the worst thing he could have—" A fresh outburst yanked Everard's attention elsewhere.

The launch, shallow-draft and screw-propelled, had run up into the shallows and was retching armed men. Too late the Afallonians realized that they had discharged their weapons and were now being attacked from the rear.

"Come on!" Everard hauled Deirdre and Van Sarawak to their feet. "We've got to get out of here—get to the neighbors..."

A detachment from the boat saw him and veered. He felt rather than heard the flat smack of a bullet into soil, as he reached the lawn. Slaves screamed hysterically inside the house. The two wolfhounds attacked the invaders and were gunned down.

Crouched, zigzag, that was the way: over the wall and out onto the road! Everard might have made it, but Deirdre stumbled and fell. Van Sarawak halted to guard her. Everard stopped also, and then it was too late. They were covered.

The leader of the dark men snapped something at the girl. She sat up, giving him a defiant answer. He laughed shortly and jerked his thumb at the launch.

"What do they want?" asked Everard in Greek.

"You." She looked at him with horror. "You two—" The officer spoke again. "And me to translate…No!"

She twisted in the hands that had closed on her arms, got partly free and clawed at a face. Everard's fist traveled in a short arc that ended in a squashing of nose. It was too good to last. A clubbed rifle descended on his head, and he was only dimly aware of being frog-marched off to the launch.

-6-

The crew left the glider behind, shoved their boat into deeper water, and revved it up. They left all the guardsmen slain or disabled, but took their own casualties along.

Everard sat on a bench on the plunging deck and stared with slowly clearing eyes as the shoreline dwindled. Deirdre wept on Van Sarawak's shoulder, and the Venusian tried to console her. A chill noisy wind flung spindrift in their faces.

When two white men emerged from the deckhouse, Everard's mind was jarred back into motion. Not Asians after all. Europeans! And now when he looked closely, he saw the rest of the crew also had Caucasian features. The brown complexions were merely greasepaint.

He stood up and regarded his new owners warily. One was a portly, middle-aged man of average height, in a red silk blouse and baggy white trousers and a sort of astrakhan hat; he was clean-shaven and his dark hair was twisted into a queue. The other was somewhat younger, a shaggy blond giant in a tunic sewn with copper links, legginged breeches, a leather cloak, and a purely ornamental horned helmet. Both wore revolvers at their belts and were treated deferentially by the sailors.

"What the devil?" Everard looked around once more. They were already out of sight of land, and bending north. The hull quivered with the haste of the engine, spray sheeted when the bows hit a wave.

The older man spoke first in Afallonian. Everard shrugged. Then the bearded Nordic tried, first in a completely unrecognizable dialect but afterward: "*Taelan thu Cimbric?*"

Everard, who knew several Germanic languages, took a chance, while Van Sarawak pricked up his Dutch ears. Deirdre huddled back, wide-eyed, too bewildered to move.

"*Ja,*" said Everard, "*ein wenig.*" When Goldilocks looked uncertain, he amended it: "A little."

"*Ah, aen litt. Gode!*" The big man rubbed his hands. "*Ik hait Boierik Wulfilasson ok main gefreond heer erran Boleslav Arkonsky.*"

It was no language Everard had ever heard of—couldn't even be the original Cimbric, after all these centuries—but the Patrolman could follow it reasonably well. The trouble came in speaking; he couldn't predict how it had evolved.

"What the hell erran thu maching, anyway?" he blustered. "Ik bin aen man auf Sirius—the stern Sirius, mit planeten ok all. Set uns gebach or willen be der Teufel to pay!"

Boierik Wulfilasson looked pained and suggested that the discussion be continued inside, with the young lady for interpreter. He led the way back into the deckhouse, which turned out to include a small but comfortably furnished saloon. The door remained open with an armed guard looking in and more on call.

Boleslav Arkonsky said something in Afallonian to Deirdre. She nodded, and he gave her a glass of wine. It seemed to steady her, but she spoke to Everard in a thin voice.

"We've been captured, Manslach. Their spies found out where you were kept. Another group is supposed to steal your traveling machine. They know where that is, too."

"So I imagined," replied Everard. "But who in Baal's name are they?"

Boierik guffawed at the question and expounded lengthily on his own cleverness. The idea was to make the Suffetes of Afallon think Hinduraj was responsible. Actually, the secret alliance of Littorn and Cimberland had built up quite an effective spy service. They were now bound for the Littornian embassy's summer retreat on Ynys Llangollen (Nantucket), where the wizards would be induced to explain their spells and a surprise prepared for the great powers.

"And if we don't do this?"

Deirdre translated Arkonsky's answer word for word: "I regret the consequences to you. We are civilized men, and will pay well in gold and honor for your free cooperation. If that is withheld, we will get your forced cooperation. The existence of our countries is at stake."

Everard looked closely at them. Boierik seemed embarrassed and unhappy, the boastful glee evaporated from him. Boleslav Arkonsky drummed on the tabletop, his lips compressed but a certain appeal in his eyes. *Don't make us do this. We have to live with ourselves.*

They were probably husbands and fathers, they must enjoy a mug of beer and a friendly game of dice as well as the next man, maybe Boierik bred horses in Italy and Arkonsky was a rose fancier on the Baltic shores. But none of this would do their captives a bit of good, when the almighty Nation locked horns with its kin.

Everard paused to admire the sheer artistry of this operation, and then began wondering what to do. The launch was fast, but would need something like twenty hours to reach Nantucket, as he remembered the trip. There was that much time, at least.

"We are weary," he said in English. "May we not rest awhile?"

"*Ja deedly,*" said Boierik with a clumsy graciousness. "*Ok wir skallen gode gefreonds bin, ni?*"

Sunset smoldered in the west. Deirdre and Van Sarawak stood at the rail, looking across a gray waste of waters. Three crewmen, their makeup and costumes removed, poised alert and weaponed on the poop; a man steered by compass; Boierik and Everard paced the quarterdeck. All wore heavy clothes against the wind.

Everard was getting some proficiency in the Cimbrian language; his tongue still limped, but he could make himself understood. Mostly, though, he let Boierik do the talking.

"So you are from the stars'? These matters I do not understand. I am a simple man. Had I my way, I would manage my Tuscan estate in peace and let the world rave as it will. But we of the Folk have our obligations." The Teutonics seemed to have replaced the Latins altogether in Italy, as the English had done the Britons in Everard's world.

"I know how you feel," said the Patrolman. "Strange that so many should fight when so few want to."

"Oh, but this is necessary." A near whine. "Carthagalann stole Egypt, our rightful possession."

"*Italia irredenta*," murmured Everard.

"Hunh?"

"Never mind. So you Cimbri are allied with Littorn, and hope to grab off Europe and Africa while the big powers are fighting in the East."

"Not at all!" said Boierik indignantly. "We are merely asserting our rightful and historic territorial claims. Why, the king himself said…" And so on and so on.

Everard braced himself against the roll of the deck. "Seems to me you treat us wizards rather hard," he remarked. "Beware lest we get really angered at you."

"All of us are protected against curses and shapings."

"Well—"

"I wish you would help us freely. I will he happy to demonstrate to you the justice of our cause, if you have a few hours to spare."

Everard shook his head, walked off and stopped by Deirdre. Her face was a blur in the thickening dusk, but he caught a forlorn fury in her voice: "I hope you told him what to do with his plans, Manslach."

"No," said Everard heavily. "We are going to help them."

She stood as if struck.

"What are you saying, Manse?" asked Van Sarawak. Everard told him.

"No!" said the Venusian.

"Yes," said Everard.

"By God, no! I'll—"

Everard grabbed his arm and said coldly: "Be quiet. I know what I'm doing. We can't take sides in this world: we're against everybody, and you'd better realize it. The only thing to do is play along with these fellows for a while. And don't tell that to Deirdre."

Van Sarawak bent his head for a moment, thinking. "All right," he said dully.

-7-

The Littornian resort was on the southern shore of Nantucket, near a fishing village but walled off from it. The embassy had built in the style of its homeland: long, timber houses with roofs arched like a cat's back, a main hall and its outbuildings enclosing a flagged courtyard. Everard finished a night's sleep and a breakfast which Deirdre's eyes had made miserable by standing on deck as they came in to the private pier. Another, bigger launch was already there, and the grounds swarmed with hard-looking men. Arkonsky's excitement flared up as he said in Afallonian: "I see the magic engine has been brought. We can go right to work."

When Boierik interpreted, Everard felt his heart slam. The guests, as the Cimbrian insisted on calling them, were led into an outsize room where Arkonsky bowed the knee to an idol with four faces, that Svantevit which the Danes had chopped up for firewood in the other history. A fire burned on the hearth against the autumn chill, and guards were posted around the walls. Everard had eyes only for the scooter, where it stood gleaming on the floor.

"I hear the fight was hard in Catuvellaunan to gain this thing," remarked Boierik. "Many were killed; but our gang got away without being followed." He touched a handlebar gingerly. "And this wain can truly appear anywhere its rider wishes, out of thin air?"

"Yes," said Everard.

Deirdre gave him a look of scorn such as he had rarely known. She stood haughtily away from him and Van Sarawak.

Arkonsky spoke to her, something he wanted translated. She spat at his feet. Boierik sighed and gave the word to Everard:

"We wish the engine demonstrated. You and I will go for a ride on it. I warn you, I will have a revolver at your back. You will tell me in advance everything you mean to do, and if aught untoward happens, I will shoot. Your friends will remain here as hostages, also to be shot on the first suspicion. But I'm sure," he added, "that we will all be good friends."

Everard nodded. Tautness thrummed in him; his palms felt cold and wet. "First I must say a spell," he answered.

His eyes flickered. One glance memorized the spatial reading of the position meters and the time reading of the clock on the scooter. Another look showed Van Sarawak seated on a bench, under Arkonsky's drawn pistol and the rifles of the guards. Deirdre sat down too, stiffly, as far from him as she could get. Everard made a close estimate of the bench's position relative to the scooter's, lifted his arms, and chanted in Temporal:

"Van, I'm going to try to pull you out of here. Stay exactly where you are now, repeat, exactly. I'll pick you up on the fly. If all goes well, that'll happen about one minute after I blink off with our hairy comrade."

The Venusian sat wooden-faced, but a thin beading of sweat sprang out on his forehead.

"Very good," said Everard in his pidgin Cimbric. "Mount on the rear saddle, Boierik, and we'll put this magic horse through her paces."

The blond man nodded and obeyed. As Everard took the front seat, he felt a gun muzzle held shakily against his back. "Tell Arkonsky we'll be back in half an hour," he instructed. They had approximately the same time units here as in his world, both descended from the Babylonian. When that had been taken care of,

Everard said, "The first thing we will do is appear in midair over the ocean and hover."

"F-f-fine," said Boierik. He didn't sound very convinced.

Everard set the space controls for ten miles east and a thousand feet up, and threw the main switch.

They sat like witches astride a broom, looking down on greenish-gray immensity and the distant blur which was land. The wind was high, it caught at them and Everard gripped tight with his knees. He heard Boierik's oath and smiled stiffly.

"Well," he asked, "how do you like this?"

"Why…it's wonderful." As he grew accustomed to the idea, the Cimbrian gathered enthusiasm. "Balloons are as nothing beside it. With machines like this, we can soar above enemy cities and rain fire down on them."

Somehow, that made Everard feel better about what he was going to do.

"Now we will fly ahead," he announced, and sent the scooter gliding through the air. Boierik whooped exultantly. "And now we will make the instantaneous jump to your homeland."

Everard threw the maneuver switch. The scooter looped the loop and dropped at a three-gee acceleration.

Forewarned, the Patrolman could still barely hang on. He never knew whether the curve or the dive had thrown Boierik. He only got a moment's glimpse of the man, plunging down through windy spaces to the sea, and wished he hadn't.

For a little while, then, Everard hung above the waves. His first reaction was a shudder. Suppose Boierik had had time to shoot? His second was a thick guilt. Both he dismissed, and concentrated on the problem of rescuing Van Sarawak.

He set the space verniers for one foot in front of the prisoners' bench, the time unit for one minute after he had departed. His right hand he kept by the controls—he'd have to work fast—and his left free.

Hang on to your hats, fellas. Here we go again.

The machine flashed into existence almost in front of Van Sarawak. Everard clutched the Venusian's tunic and hauled him close, inside the spatiotemporal drive field, even as his right hand spun the time dial back and snapped down the main switch.

A bullet caromed off metal. Everard had a moment's glimpse of Arkonsky shouting. And then it was all gone and they were on a grassy hill sloping down to the beach. It was two thousand years ago.

He collapsed shivering over the handlebars.

A cry brought him back to awareness. He twisted around to look at Van Sarawak where the Venusian sprawled on the hillside. One arm was still around Deirdre's waist.

The wind lulled, and the sea rolled in to a broad white strand, and clouds walked high in heaven.

"Can't say I blame you, Van." Everard paced before the scooter and looked at the ground, "But it does complicate matters."

"What was I supposed to do?" the other man asked on a raw note. "Leave her there for those bastards to kill—or to be snuffed out with her entire universe?"

"Remember, we're conditioned. Without authorization, we couldn't tell her the truth even if we wanted to. And I, for one, don't want to."

Everard glanced at the girl. She stood breathing heavily, but with a dawn in her eyes. The wind ruffled her hair and the long thin dress.

She shook her head, as if to clear it of nightmare, ran over and clasped their hands. "Forgive me, Manslach," she breathed. "I should have known you'd not betray us."

She kissed them both. Van Sarawak responded as eagerly as expected, but Everard couldn't bring himself to. He would have remembered Judas.

"Where are we?" she continued. "It looks almost like Llangollen, but no dwellers. Have you taken us to the Happy Isles?" She spun on one foot and danced among summer flowers. "Can we rest here a while before returning home?"

Everard drew a long breath. "I've bad news for you, Deirdre," he said.

She grew silent. He saw her gather herself.

"We can't go back."

She waited mutely.

"The…the spells I had to use, to save our lives—I had no choice. But those spells debar us from returning home."

"There is no hope?" He could barely hear her.

His eyes stung. "No," he said.

She turned and walked away. Van Sarawak moved to follow her but thought better of it and sat down beside Everard. "What'd you tell her?" he asked.

Everard repeated his words. "It seems the best compromise," he finished. "I can't send her back to what's waiting for this world."

"No." Van Sarawak sat quiet for a while, staring across the sea. Then: "What year is this? About the time of Christ? Then we're still upstairs of the turning point."

"Yeh. And we still have to find out what it was."

"Let's go back to some Patrol office in the farther past. We can recruit help there."

"Maybe." Everard lay down in the grass and regarded the sky. Reaction overwhelmed him. "I think I can locate the key event right here, though, with Deirdre's help. Wake me when she comes back."

She returned dry-eyed, though one could see she had wept. When Everard asked if she would assist in his own mission, she nodded, "Of course. My life is yours who saved it."

After getting you into the mess in the first place. Everard said carefully: "All I want from you is some information. Do you know about…about putting people to sleep, a sleep in which they may believe anything they're told?"

She nodded doubtfully. "I've seen medical druids do that."

"It won't harm you. I only wish to make you sleep so you can remember everything you know, things you believe forgotten. It won't take long."

Her trustfulness was hard for him to endure. Using Patrol techniques, he put her in a hypnotic state of total recall and dredged out all she had ever heard or read about the Second Punic War. That added up to enough for his purposes.

Roman interferences with Carthaginian enterprise south of the Ebro, in direct violation of treaty, had been the final goading. In 219 B.C. Hannibal Barca, governor of Carthaginian Spain, laid siege to Saguntum. After eight months he took it, and thus provoked his long-planned war with Rome. At the beginning of May, 218, he crossed the Pyrenees with 90,000 infantry, 12,000 cavalry, and 37 elephants, marched through Gaul, and went over the Alps. His losses en route were gruesome: only 20,000 foot and 6,000 horse reached Italy late in the year. Nevertheless, near the Ticinus River he met and broke a superior Roman force. In the course of the following year, he fought several bloodily victorious battles and advanced into Apulia and Campania.

The Apulians, Lucanians, Bruttians, and Samnites went over to his side. Quintus Fabius Maximus fought a grim guerrilla war, which laid Italy waste and decided nothing. But meanwhile Hasdrubal Barca was organizing Spain, and in 211 he arrived with reinforcements. In 210 Hannibal took and burned Rome, and by 207 the last cities of the confederacy had surrendered to him.

"That's it," said Everard. He stroked the coppery mane of the girl lying beside him. "Go to sleep now. Sleep well and wake up glad of heart."

"What'd she tell you?" asked Van Sarawak.

"A lot of detail," said Everard. The whole story had required more than an hour. "The important thing is this: her knowledge of those times is good, but she never mentioned the Scipios."

"The who's?"

"Publius Cornelius Scipio commanded the Roman army at Ticinus. He was beaten there all right, in our world. But later he had the intelligence to turn westward and gnaw away the Carthaginian base in Spain. It ended with Hannibal being effectively cut off in Italy, and what little Iberian help could be sent him was annihilated. Scipio's son of the same name also held a high command, and was the man who finally whipped Hannibal at Zama; that's Scipio Africanus the Elder.

"Father and son were by far the best leaders Rome had. But Deirdre never heard of them."

"So…" Van Sarawak stared eastward across the sea, where Gauls and Cimbri and Parthians were ramping through the shattered Classical world. "What happened to them in this time line?"

"My own total recall tells me that both the Scipios were at Ticinus, and very nearly killed. The son saved his father's life during the retreat, which I imagine was more like a stampede. One gets you ten that in this history the Scipios died there."

"Somebody must have knocked them off," said Van Sarawak. His voice tightened. "Some time traveler. It could only have been that."

"Well, it seems probable, anyhow. We'll see." Everard looked away from Deirdre's slumbrous face. "We'll see."

-8-

A t the Pleistocene resort—half an hour after having left it for New York—the Patrolmen put the girl in charge of a sympathetic Greek-speaking matron and summoned their colleagues. Then the message capsules began jumping through spacetime.

All offices prior to 218 B.C.—the closest was Alexandria, 250-230—were "still" there, with two hundred or so agents altogether. Written contact with the future was confirmed to be impossible, and a few short jaunts upstairs clinched the proof. A worried conference met at the Academy, back in the Oligocene Period. Unattached agents ranked those with steady assignments, but not each other; on the basis of his own experience, Everard found himself the chairman of a committee of top-bracket officers.

That was a frustrating job. These men and women had leaped centuries and wielded the weapons of gods. But they were still human, with all the ingrained orneriness of their race.

Everyone agreed that the damage would have to be repaired. But there was fear for those agents who had gone ahead into time before being warned, as Everard himself had done. If they weren't back when history was realtered, they would never be seen again. Everard deputized parties to attempt rescue, but doubted there'd be much success. He warned them sternly to return within a day, local time, or face the consequences.

A man from the Scientific Renaissance had another point to make. Granted, the survivors' plain duty was to restore the "original" time track. But they had a duty to knowledge as well. Here was a unique chance to study a whole new phase of humankind. Several years' anthropological work should be done before—Everard slapped him down with difficulty. There weren't so many Patrolmen left that they could take the risk.

Study groups had to determine the exact moment and circumstances of the change. The wrangling over methods went on interminably. Everard glared out the window, into the prehuman night, and wondered if the sabertooths weren't doing a better job after all than their simian successors.

When he had finally gotten his various gangs dispatched, he broke out a bottle and got drunk with Van Sarawak.

Reconvening next day, the steering committee heard from its deputies, who had run up a total of years in the future. A dozen Patrolmen had been rescued from more or less ignominious situations; another score would simply have to be written off. The spy group's report was more interesting. It seemed that two Helvetian mercenaries had joined Hannibal in the Alps and won his confidence. After the war, they had risen to high positions in Carthage. Under the names of Phrontes and Himilco, they had practically run the government, engineered Hannibal's murder, and set new records for luxurious living. One of the Patrolmen had seen their homes and the men themselves. "A lot of improvements that hadn't been thought of in Classical times. The fellows looked to me like Neldorians, two-hundred-fifth millennium."

Everard nodded. That was an age of bandits who had "already" given the Patrol a lot of work. "I think we've settled the matter," he said. "It makes no difference whether they were with Hannibal before Ticinus or not. We'd have hell's own time arresting them in the Alps without such a fuss that we'd change the future ourselves. What counts is that they seem to have rubbed out the Scipios, and that's the point we'll have to strike at."

A nineteenth-century Britisher, competent but with elements of Colonel Blimp, unrolled a map and discoursed on his aerial observations of the battle. He'd used an infrared telescope to look through low clouds. "And here the Romans stood—"

"I know," said Everard. "A thin red line. The moment when they took flight is the critical one, but the confusion then also gives us our chance. Okay, we'll want to surround the battlefield unobtrusively, but I don't think we can get away with more than two agents actually on the scene. The baddies are going to be alert, you know, looking for possible counterinterference. The Alexandria office can supply Van and me with costumes."

"I say," exclaimed the Englishman, "I thought I'd have the privilege."

"No. Sorry." Everard smiled with one corner of his mouth. "No privilege, anyway. Just risking your neck, in order to negate a world full of people like yourself."

"But dash it all—"

Everard rose. "I've got to go," he said flatly. "I don't know why, but I've got to."

Van Sarawak nodded.

They left their scooter in a clump of trees and started across the field.

Around the horizon and up in the sky waited a hundred armed Patrolmen, but that was small consolation here among spears and arrows. Lowering clouds hurried before a cold whistling wind, there was a spatter of rain; sunny Italy was enjoying its late fall.

The cuirass was heavy on Everard's shoulders as he trotted across blood-slippery mud. He had helmet, greaves, a Roman shield on his left arm and a sword at his waist; but his right hand gripped a stunner. Van Sarawak loped behind, similarly equipped, eyes shifting under the wind-ruffled officer's plume.

Trumpets howled and drums stuttered. It was all but lost among the yells of men and tramp of feet, screaming riderless horses and whining arrows. Only a few captains and scouts were still mounted; as often before stirrups were invented, what started to be a cavalry battle had become entirely a fight on foot after the lancers fell off their mounts. The Carthaginians were pressing in, hammering edged metal against the buckling Roman lines. Here and there the struggle was already breaking up into small knots, where men cursed and cut at strangers.

The combat had passed over this area already. Death lay around Everard. He hurried behind the Roman force, toward the distant gleam of the eagles. Across helmets and corpses, he made out a banner that fluttered triumphant red and purple. And there, looming monstrous against the gray sky, lifting their trunks and bawling, came a squad of elephants.

War was always the same: not a neat affair of lines across maps, nor a hallooing gallantry, but men who gasped and sweated and bled in bewilderment.

A slight, dark-faced youth squirmed nearby, trying feebly to pull out the javelin which had pierced his stomach. He was a slinger from Carthage, but the burly Italian peasant who sat next to him, staring without belief at the stump of an arm, paid no attention.

A flight of crows hovered overhead, riding the wind and waiting.

"This way," muttered Everard. "Hurry up, for God's sake! That line's going to break any minute."

The breath was raw in his throat as he jogged toward the standards of the Republic. It came to him that he'd always rather wished Hannibal had won. There was something repellent about the frigid, unimaginative greed of Rome. And here he was, trying to save the city. Well-a-day, life was often an odd business.

It was some consolation that Scipio Africanus was one of the few decent men left after the war.

Screaming and clangor lifted, and the Italians reeled back. Everard saw something like a wave smashed against a rock. But it was the rock which advanced, crying out and stabbing, stabbing.

He began to run. A legionary went past, howling his panic. A grizzled Roman veteran spat on the ground, braced his feet, and stood where he was till they cut him down. Hannibal's elephants squealed and blundered about. The ranks of Carthage held firm, advancing to an inhuman pulse of drums.

Up ahead, now! Everard saw men on horseback, Roman officers. They held the eagles aloft and shouted, but nobody could hear them above the din.

A small group of legionaries trotted past. Their leader hailed the Patrolmen: "Over here! We'll give 'em a fight, by the belly of Venus!"

Everard shook his head and continued. The Roman snarled and sprang at him. "Come here, you cowardly..." A stun beam cut off his words. He crashed into the muck. His men shuddered, someone wailed, and the party broke into flight.

The Carthaginians were very near, shield to shield and swords running red. Everard could see a scar livid on the cheek of one man, the great hook nose of another. A hurled spear clanged off his helmet. He lowered his head and ran.

A combat loomed before him. He tried to go around, and tripped on a gashed corpse. A Roman stumbled over him in turn. Van Sarawak cursed and dragged him clear. A sword furrowed the Venusian's arm.

Beyond, Scipio's men were surrounded and battling without hope. Everard halted, sucked air into starved lungs, and looked into the thin rain. Armor gleamed wetly as a troop of Roman horsemen galloped closer, with mud up to their mounts' noses. That must be the son, Scipio Africanus to be, hastening to rescue his father. The hoofbeats made thunder in the earth.

"Over there!"

Van Sarawak cried out and pointed. Everard crouched where he was, rain dripping off his helmet and down his face. From another direction, a Carthaginian party was riding toward the battle around the eagles. And at their head were two men with the height and craggy features of Neldor. They wore G.I. armor, but each of them held a slim-barreled gun.

"This way!" Everard spun on his heel and dashed toward them. The leather in his cuirass creaked as he ran.

The Patrolmen were close to the Carthaginians before they were seen. Then a horseman called the warning. Two crazy Romans! Everard saw how he grinned in his beard. One of the Neldorians raised his blast rifle.

Everard flopped on his stomach. The vicious blue-white beam sizzled where he had been. He snapped a shot, and one of the African horses went over in a roar of metal. Van Sarawak stood his ground and fired steadily. Two, three, four—and there went a Neldorian, down in the mud!

Men hewed at each other around the Scipios. The Neldorians' escort yelled with terror. They must have had the blaster demonstrated beforehand, but these invisible blows were something else. They bolted. The second of the bandits got his horse under control and turned to follow.

"Take care of the one you potted, Van," gasped Everard. "Drag him off the battlefield—we'll want to question—" He himself scrambled to his feet and made for a riderless horse. He was in the saddle and after the Neldorian before he was fully aware of it.

Behind him, Publius Cornelius Scipio and his son fought clear and joined their retreating army.

Everard fled through chaos. He urged speed from his mount, but was content to pursue. Once they had gotten out of sight, a scooter could swoop down and make short work of his quarry.

The same thought must have occurred to the time rover. He reined in and took aim. Everard saw the blinding flash and felt his cheek sting with a near miss. He set his pistol to wide beam and rode in shooting.

Another firebolt took his horse full in the breast. The animal toppled and Everard went out of the saddle. Trained reflexes softened the fall. He bounced to his feet and lurched toward his enemy. The stunner was gone, fallen into the mud, no time to look for it. Never mind, it could be salvaged later, if he lived. The widened beam had found its mark; it wasn't strong enough at such dilution to knock a man out, but the Neldorian had dropped his blaster and the horse stood swaying with closed eyes.

Rain beat in Everard's face. He slogged up to the mount. The Neldorian jumped to earth and drew a sword. Everard's own blade rasped forward.

"As you will," he said in Latin. "One of us will not leave this field."

-9-

The moon rose over mountains and turned the snow to a sudden wan glitter. Far in the north, a glacier threw back the light, and a wolf howled. The Cro-Magnons chanted in their cave, the noise drifted faintly through to the verandah.

Deirdre stood in darkness, looking out. Moonlight dappled her face and caught a gleam of tears. She started as Everard and Van Sarawak came up behind her.

"Are you back so soon?" she asked. "You only came here and left me this morning."

"It didn't take long," said Van Sarawak. He had gotten a hypno in Attic Greek.

"I hope—" she tried to smile—"I hope you have finished your task and can rest from your labors."

"Yes," said Everard, "we finished it."

They stood side by side for a while, looking out on a world of winter.

"Is it true what you said, that I can never go home?" Deirdre spoke gently.

"I'm afraid so. The spells..." Everard swapped a glance with Van Sarawak.

They had official permission to tell the girl as much as they wished and take her wherever they thought she could live best. Van Sarawak maintained that would be Venus in his century, and Everard was too tired to argue.

Deirdre drew a long breath. "So be it," she said. "I'll not waste of life lamenting. But the Baal grant that they have it well, my people at home."

"I'm sure they will," said Everard.

Suddenly he could do no more. He only wanted to sleep. Let Van Sarawak say what had to be said, and reap whatever rewards there might be.

He nodded at his companion. "I'm turning in," he declared. "Carry on, Van."

The Venusian took the girl's arm. Everard went slowly back to his room.

THE PUGILIST

They hadn't risked putting me in the base hospital or any other regular medical facility. Besides, the operation was very simple. Needed beforehand: a knife, an anesthetic, and a supply of coagulant and enzyme to promote healing inside a week. Needed afterward: drugs and skillful talking to, till I got over being dangerous to myself or my surroundings. The windows of my room were barred; I was brought soft plastic utensils with my meals; my clothes were pajamas and paper slippers; and two husky men sat in the hall near my open door. Probably I was also monitored on closed-circuit TV.

There was stuff to read, especially magazines which carried stories about the regeneration center in Moscow. Those articles bore down on the work being still largely experimental. A structure as complicated as a hand, a leg, or an eye wouldn't yet grow back right, though surgery helped. However, results were excellent with the more basic tissues and organs. I saw pics of a girl whose original liver got mercury poisoned, a man who'd had most of his skin burned off in an accident, beaming from the pages as good as new, or so the text claimed.

Mannix must have gone to some trouble to find those issues. The latest was from months ago. You didn't see much now that wasn't related to the war.

Near the end of that week my male nurse gave me a letter from Bonnie. It was addressed to me right here, John Reed AFB, Willits, California 95491, in her own slanty-rounded handwriting, and according to the postmark—when I remembered to check that several hours later—had doubtless been mailed from our place, not 30 kilometers away. The envelope was stamped EXAMINED, but I didn't think the letter had been dictated. It was too her. About how the kids and the roses were doing, and the co-op where she worked was hoping the Recreation Bureau would okay its employees vacationing at Lake Pillsbury this year, and hamburger had been available day before yesterday, and she'd spent three hours with her grandmother's old cookbook deciding how to fix it, "and if only you'd been across the table, you and your funny slow smile; oh, do finish soon, Jim-Jim, and c'mon home!"

I read slowly, the first few times. My hands shook so much. Later I crawled into bed and pulled the sheet over my face against bugeyes.

Mannix arrived next morning. He's small and chipper, always in the neatest of civies, his round red face always amiable—almost always—under a fluff of white hair. "Well, how are you, Colonel Dowling?" he exclaimed as he bounced in. The door didn't close behind him at once. My guards would watch awhile. I stand 190 cm in my bare feet and black belt.

I didn't rise from my armchair, though. Wasn't sure I could. It was as if that scalpel had, actually, teased the bones out of me. Windows stood open to a cool breeze and a bright sky. Beyond the neat buildings and electric fence of the base I could see hills green with forest roll up and up toward the blueness of the Sierra. It felt like painted scenery. Bonnie acts in civic theater.

Mannix settled on the edge of my bed. "Dr. Arneson tells me you can be discharged anytime, fit for any duty," he said. "Congratulations."

"Yeah," I managed to say, though I could hear how feeble the sarcasm was. "You'll send me right back to my office."

"Or to your family? You have a charming wife."

I stirred and made a noise. The guard in the entrance looked uneasy and dropped a hand to his stunner. Mannix lifted a palm. "If you please," he chirped. "I'm not baiting you. Your case presents certain difficulties. As you well know."

I'd imagined I was, not calm, but numb. I was wrong. Blackness took me in a wave that roared. "Why, why, why?" I felt rip my throat. "Why not just shoot me and be done?"

Mannix waited till I sank back. The wind whined in and out of me. Sweat plastered the pajamas to my skin. It reeked.

He offered me a cigarette. At first I ignored him, then accepted both it and the flare of his lighter, and dragged my lungs full of acridness. Mannix said mildly, "The surgical procedure was necessary, Colonel. You were told that. Diagnosis showed cancer."

"The f-f-f—the hell it did," I croaked.

"I believe the removed part is still in alcohol in the laboratory," Mannix said. "Would you like to see it?"

I touched the hot end of the cigarette to the back of my hand. "No," I answered.

"And," Mannix said, "regeneration is possible."

"In Moscow."

"True, the Lomonosov Institute has the world's only such capability to date. I daresay you've been reading about that." He nodded at the gay-colored covers on the end table. "The idea was to give you hope. Still…you are an intelligent, technically educated man. You realize it isn't simple to make the adult DNA repeat what it did in the fetus, and not repeat identically, either. Not only are chemicals, catalysts, synthevirus required; the whole process must be monitored and computer-controlled. No wonder they concentrate on research and save clinical treatment for the most urgent cases." He paused. "Or the most deserving."

"I saw this coming," I mumbled.

Mannix shrugged. "Well, when you are charged with treasonable conspiracy against the People's Republic of the United States—" That was one phrase he had to roll out in full, every time.

"You haven't proved anything," I said mechanically.

"The fact of your immunity to the usual interrogation techniques is, shall we say, indicative," He grew arch again, "Consider your own self-interest. Let the war in the Soviet Union break into uncontrolled violence, and where is Moscow? Where's the Institute? The matter is quite vital, Colonel."

"What can I do?" I asked out of hollowness.

Mannix chuckled. "Depends on what you know, what you are. Tell me and we'll lay plans. Eh?" He cocked his head. Bonnie, who knew him merely as a political officer, to be invited to dinner now and then on that account, liked him. She said he ought to play the reformed Scrooge, except he'd be no good as the earlier, capitalist Scrooge, before the Spirits of the New Year visited him.

"I've been studying your file personally," he went on. "And I'm blessed if I can see why you should have gotten involved in this unsavory business. A fine young man who's galloped through his promotions at the rate you have. It's not as if your background held anything un-American. How did you ever get sucked in?"

He bore down a little on the word "sucked." That broke me.

I'd never guessed how delicious it is to let go, to admit—fully admit and take into you—the fact that you're whipped. It was like, well, like the nightly surrender to Bonnie. I wanted to laugh and cry and kiss the old man's hands. Instead, stupidly, all I could say was. "I don't know."

The answer must lie deep in my past.

I was a country boy, raised in the backwoods of Georgia, red earth, gaunt murky-green pines, cardinals and mockingbirds, and a secret fishing hole. The government had tried to modernize our area before I was born, but it didn't lend itself to collectives. So mostly we were allowed to keep our small farms, stores, sawmills, and repair shops on leasehold. The schools got taped lectures on history, ideology, and the rest. However, this isn't the same as having trained political educators in the flesh. Likewise, our local scoutmaster was lax about everything except woodcraft. And while my grandfather mumbled a little about damn niggers everywhere like nothing since Reconstruction, he used to play poker with black Sheriff Jackson. Sometimes he, Granddad, that is, would take on a bit too much moon and rant about how poor, decent Joe Jackson was being used. My parents saw to it that no outsiders heard him.

All in all, we lived in a pretty archaic fashion. I understand the section has since been brought up to date.

Now patriotism is as Southern as hominy grits. They have trouble realizing this further north. They harp on the Confederate Rebellion, though actually—as our teachers explained to us—folk in those days were resisting Yankee capitalism, and the slaveholders were a minority who milked the common man's love for his land. True, when the People's Republic was proclaimed, there was some hothead talk, even some shooting. But there was never any need for the heavy concentration of marshals and deputies they sent down to our states. Damn it, we still belonged.

We were the topmost rejoicers when word came: the Treaty of Berlin was amended; the United States could maintain armed forces; well above police level and was welcomed to the solid front of peace-loving nations against the Sino-Japanese revisionists.

Grandad turned into a wild man in a stiff jacket. He'd fought for the imperialist régime once, when it tried to suppress the Mekong Revolution, though he never said a lot about that. Who would? (I suppose Dad was lucky, just ten years old at the time of the Sacred War, which thus to him was like a hurricane or some other natural spasm. Of course, the hungry years afterward stunted his growth.) "This's the first step!" Granddad cried to us. "The first step back! You hear?" He stood outdoors waving his cane, autumn sumac a shout of red behind him, and the wind shouted too;, till I imagined old bugles blowing again at Valley Forge and Shiloh and Omaha Beach. Maybe that was when I first thought I might make the army a career.

A year later, units of the new service held maneuvers beneath Stone Mountain. Granddad had been tirelessly reading and watching news, writing letters, making phone calls from the village booth, keeping in touch. Hence he knew about the event well in advance, knew the public would be invited to watch from certain areas, and saved his money and his travel allowance till he could not only go himself but take me along.

And it was exciting, oh, yes, really beautiful when the troops went by in ground-effect carriers like magic boats, the dinosaur tanks rumbled past, the superjets screamed low overhead, while the Star and Stripes waved before those riders carved in the face of the mountain.

Except—the artillery opened up. Granddad and I were quite a ways off; the guns were toys in our eyes; we'd see a needle-thin flash, a puff where the shell exploded; long, long afterward, distance-shrunken thunder reached us. The monument was slow to crumble away. That night, in the tourist dorm, I heard a speech about how destroying that symbol of oppression marked the dawn of our glorious new day. I didn't pay much attention. I kept seeing Granddad, there under the Georgia sky, suddenly withered and old.

Nobody proposed I go home to Bonnie. Least of all myself. Whether or not I could have made an excuse for...not revealing to her what had happened...I couldn't have endured it. I did say, over and over, that she had no idea I was in the Stephen Decatur Society. This was true. Not that she would have betrayed me had she known, Bonnie whose heart was as bright as her hair. I was already too far in to back out when first we met, too weak and selfish to run from her; but I was never guilty of giving her guilty knowledge.

"She and your children must have had indications," Mannix murmured. "If only subliminal. They might be in need of correctional instruction."

I whimpered before him. There are camps and camps, of course, but La Pasionara is the usual one for West Coast offenders. I've met a few of the few who've been released from it. They are terribly obedient, hard-working, and close-mouthed. Most lack teeth. Rumor says conditions can make young girls go directly from puberty to menopause. I have a daughter.

Mannix smiled. "At ease. Jim. Your family's departure would tip off the Society."

I blubbered my thanks.

"And, to be sure, you may be granted a chance to win pardon, if we can find a proper way," he soothed me. "Suggestions?"

"I, I, I can tell you…what I know—"

"An unimaginative minimum. Let us explore you for a start. Maybe we'll hit on a unique deed you can do." Mannix drummed his desktop.

We had moved to his office, which was lush enough that the portraits of Lenin and the President looked startlingly austere. I sat snug and warm in a water chair, cigarettes, coffee, brandy to hand, nobody before me or behind me except this kindly white-haired man and his recorder. But I was still gulping, sniffing, choking, and shivering, still too dazed to think. My lips tingled and my body felt slack and heavy.

"What brought you into the gang, Jim?" he asked as if in simple curiosity.

I gaped at him. I'd told him I didn't know. But maybe I did. Slowly I groped around in my head. The roots of everything go back to before you were born.

I'd inquired about the origins of the organization, in my early days with it. Nobody knew much except that it hadn't been important before Sotomayor took the leadership—whoever, wherever he was. Until him, it was a spontaneous thing.

Probably it hadn't begun right after the Sacred War. Americans had done little except pick up pieces, those first years. They were too stunned when the Soviet missiles knocked out their second-strike capability and all at once their cities were hostages for the good behavior of their politicians and submarines. They were too relieved when no occupation followed, aside from inspectors and White House advisors who made sure the treaty limitations on armaments were observed. (Oh, several generals and the like were hanged as war criminals.) True, the Soviets had taken a beating from what U.S. nukes did get through, sufficient that they couldn't control China or, later, a China-sponsored Japanese S.S.R. The leniency shown Americans was not the less welcome for being due to a shortage of troops.

Oath-brothers had told me how they were attracted by the mutterings of friends, and presently recruited, after Moscow informed Washington that John Halpern would be an unacceptable candidate for President in the next election. Others joined in reaction against a collectivist sentiment whose growth was hothouse-forced by government, schools, and universities.

I remember how Granddad growled on a day when we were alone in the woods and I'd asked him about that period:

"The old order was blamed for the war and war's consequences, Jimmy. Militarists, capitalists, imperialists, racists, bourgeoisie. Nobody heard any different any more. Those who'd've argued weren't gettin' published or on the air, nothin'." He drew on his pipe. Muscles bunched in the angle of his jaw. "Yeah, everybody was bein' blamed—except the liberals who'd worked to lower our guard so their snug dreams wouldn't be interrupted, the conservatives who helped 'em so's to save a few wretched tax dollars, the radicals who disrupted the country, the copouts who lifted no finger—" The bit snapped between his teeth. We stooped for the bowl and squinted at it ruefully while his heel ground out the scattered ashes. At last he sighed. "Don't forget what I've told you, Jimmy. But bury it deep, like a seed."

I can't say if he was correct. My life was not his. I wasn't born when the Constitutional Convention proclaimed the People's Republic. Nor did I ever take a strong interest in politics.

In fact, my recruitment was glacier gradual. In West Point I discovered step by step that my best friends were those who wanted us to become a first-class power again, not conquer anybody else, merely cut the Russian apron strings…Clandestine bitching sessions, winked at by our officers, slowly turned into clandestine meetings which hinted at eventual action. An illegal newsletter circulated…After graduation and assignment, I did trivial favors, covering up for this or that comrade who might otherwise be in trouble, supplying bits of classified information to fellows who said they were blocked from what they needed by stupid bureaucrats, hearing till I believed it that the proscribed and abhorred Stephen Decatur Society was not counterrevolutionary, not fascist, simply patriotic and misunderstood…

The final commitment to something like that is when you make an excuse to disappear for a month—in any case, a backpacking trip with a couple of guys, though my C.O. warned me that asocial furloughs might hurt my career—and you get flitted to an unspecified place where they induct you. One of the psychotechs there explained that the treatment, drugs, sleep deprivation, shock conditioning, meant more than installing a set of reflexes. Those guarantee you can't be made to blab involuntarily, under serum or torture. But the suffering has a positive effect too: it's a rite of passage. Afterward you can't likely be bribed either.

Likely. The figures may change on a man's price tag, but he never loses it.

I don't yet know how I was detected. A Decaturist courier had cautioned my cell about microminiature listeners which can be slipped a man in his food, operate off body heat, and take days to be eliminated. With my work load, both official on account of the crisis and after hours in preparing for our coup, I must have gotten careless.

Presumably, though, I was caught by luck rather than suspicion, in a spot check. If the political police had identified any fair-sized number of conspirators, Mannix wouldn't be as anxious to use me as he was.

Jarred, I realized I hadn't responded to his last inquiry. "Sir," I begged, "honest, I'm no traitor. I wish our country had more voice in its own affairs. Nothing else."

"A Titoist." Recognizing my glance of dull surprise at the new word, he waved it off. "Never mind. I forgot they've re-improved the history text since I was young. Let's stick to practical matters, then."

"I, I can…identify for you—those in my cell." Jack, whose wife was pregnant; Bill who never spared everyday helpfulness; Tim…"B-but there must be others on the base and in the area, and, well, some of them must know *I* belong."

"Right." Mannix nodded. "We'll stay our hand as regards those you have met. Mustn't alert the organization. It does seem to be efficient. That devil Sotomayor—Well. Let's get on."

He was patient. Hours went by before I could talk coherently.

At that time he had occasion to turn harsh. Leaning across his desk he snapped: "You considered yourself a patriot. Nevertheless you plotted mutiny."

I cringed. "No, sir. Really. I mean, the idea was—was—"

"Was what?" In his apple face stood the eyes of Old Scrooge.

"Sir, when civil war breaks out in the Motherland—those Vasiliev and Kunin factions—"

"Party versus army."

"What?" I don't know why I tried to argue. "Sir, last I heard, Vasiliev's got everything west of the, uh, Yenisei…millions of men under arms, effective control of West Europe—"

"You do not understand how to interpret events. The essential struggle is between those who are loyal to the principles of the party, and those who would substitute military dictatorship." His finger jabbed. "Like you, Dowling."

We had told each other in our secret meetings, we Decatur folk, better government by colonels than commissioners.

"No, sir, no, sir," I protested. "Look, I'm only a soldier. But I see…I smell the factions here too…the air's rotten with plotting…and what about in Washington? I mean, do we *know* what orders we'll get, any day now? And what is the situation in Siberia?"

"You have repeatedly been informed, the front is stabilized and relatively quiet."

My wits weren't so shorted out that I hinted the official media might ever shade the truth. I did reply: "Sir, I'm a missileman. In the, uh, the opinion of every colleague I've talked with—most of them loyal, I'm certain—what stability the front has got is due to the fact both sides have ample rockets, lasers, the works. If they both cut loose, there'd be mutual wipeout. Unless we Americans—We hold the balance." Breath shuddered into me. "Who's going to order our birds targeted where?"

Mannix sat for a while that grew very quiet. I sat listening to my heart stutter. Weariness filled me like water a sponge. I wanted to crawl off and curl up in darkness, alone, more than I wanted Bonnie or my children or tomorrow's sunrise or that which had been taken from me. But I had to keep answering.

At last he asked, softly, almost mildly, "Is this your honest evaluation? Is this why you were in a conspiracy to seize control of the big weapons?"

"Yes, sir." A vacuum passed through me. I shook myself free of it. "Yes, sir. I think my belief—the belief of most men involved—is, uh, if a, uh, a responsible group, led by experts, takes over the missile bases for the time being…those birds

won't get misused. Like by, say, the wrong side in Washington pulling a coup—"
I jerked my head upright.

"Your superiors in the cabal have claimed to you that the object is to keep the
birds in their nests, keep America out of the war," Mannix said. "How do you
know they've told you the truth?"

I thought I did. Did I? Was I? Big soft waves came rolling.

"Jim," Mannix said earnestly, "they've tricked you through your whole adult
life. Nevertheless, what we've learned shows me you're important to them. You're
slated for commander here at Reed, once the mutiny begins. I wouldn't be surprised but what they've been grooming you for years, and that's how come your
rapid rise in the service. Clues there—But as for now, you must have ways to get
in touch with higher echelons."

"Uh-huh," I said. "Uh-huh. Uh-huh."

Mannix grew genial. "Let's discuss that, shall we?"

I don't remember being conducted to bed. What stands before me is how I woke,
gasping for air, nothing in my eyes except night and nothing in the hand that
grabbed at my groin.

I rolled over on my belly, clutched the pillow and crammed it into my mouth.
Bonnie, Bonnie, I said, they've left me this one way back to you. I pledge allegiance to you, Bonnie, and to the Chuck and Joanlet you have mothered, and
screw the rest of the world!

("Even for a man in his thirties," said a hundred teachers, intellectuals, officials, entertainers out of my years, "or even for an adolescent, romantic atavism is
downright unpatriotic. The most important thing in man's existence is his duty
to the people and the molding of their future." The echoes went on and on.)

I've been a rat, I said to my three, to risk—and lose—the few things which
counted, all of which were ours. Bonnie, it's no excuse for my staying with the
Decaturists, that I'd see you turn white at this restriction or that command to
volunteer service or yonder midnight vanishing of a neighbor. No excuse, nothing but a rationalization. I've led us down my rathole, and now my duty is to get
us out, in whatever way I am able.

("There should be little bloodshed," the liaison man told our cell; we were
not shown his face. "The war is expected to remain stalemated for the several
weeks we need. When the moment is right, our folk will rise, disarm and expel
everybody who isn't with us, and dig in. We can hope to seize most of the rocket
bases. Given the quick retargetability of every modern bird, we will then be in
a position to hit any point on Earth and practically anything in orbit. However,
we won't. The threat—plus the short-range weapons—should protect us from
counterattack. We will sit tight and thus realize our objective: to keep the blood
of possibly millions off American hands, while giving America the self-determination that once was hers.")

Turn the Decaturists over to the Communists. Let all the ists kill each other
off and leave human beings in peace.

("My friend, my friend," Mannix sighed, "you cannot be naive enough to suppose the Asians have no hand in this. You yourself, I find, were involved in our rocket-scattering of munitions across the rebellious parts of India. Should they not make use of trouble in our coalition? Have they not been advising, subsidizing, equipping, infiltrating the upper leadership of your oh-so-patriotic Decatur Society? Let the Soviet Union ruin itself—which is the likeliest outcome if America doesn't intervene—let that happen, and, yes, America could probably become the boss of the Western Hemisphere. But we're not equipped to conquer the Eastern. You're aware of that. The gooks would inherit. The Russians may gripe you. You may consider our native leaders their puppets. But at least they're white; at least they share a tradition with us. Why, they helped us back on our feet, Jim, after the war. They let us rearm, they aided it, precisely so we could cover each other's backs, they in the Old World, we in the New…Can you prove your Society isn't a Jappochink tool?")

No, but I can prove we have rockets here so we'll draw some of the Jappochink fire in the event of a big war.—They're working on suicide regardless of what I do, Bonnie. America would already have declared for one splinter or the other, if America weren't likewise divided. Remember your Shakespeare? Well, Caesar has conquered the available world and is dead; Anthony and Octavian are disputing his loot. What paralyzes America is—has to be—a silent struggle in Washington. Maybe not altogether silent; I get word of troop movements, "military exercises" under separate commands, throughout the Atlantic states…Where can we hide, Bonnie?

("We have reason to believe," said the political lecturer to us at assembly, "that the conflict was instigated, to a considerable degree at least, by *agents provacateurs* of the Asian deviationists, who spent the past twenty years or more posing as Soviet citizens and worming their way close to the top. With our whole hearts we trust the dispute can be settled peacefully. Failing that, gentlemen, your duty will be to strike as ordered by your government, to end this war before irrevocable damage has been done the Motherland.")

There is no place to hide, Bonnie Brighteyes. Nor can we bravely join the side of the angels. There are no angels either.

("Yeah, sure, I've heard the same," said Jack who belonged to my cell. "If we grab those bases and refuse to join this fight, peace'll have to be negotiated, lives and cultural treasures 'ull be spared, the balance of power 'ull be preserved, yeah, yeah.—Think, man. What do you suppose Sotomayor and the rest really want? Isn't it for the war to grow hot—incandescent? Never mind who tries the first strike. The Kuninists might, thinking they'd better take advantage of a U.S. junta fairly sympathetic to them before it's overthrown. Or the Visilievists might, they being party types who can't well afford a compromise. Either way, no matter who comes out on top, the Soviets overnight turn themselves into the junior member of our partnership. Then *we* tell *them* what to do for a change.")

Not that I am altogether cynical, Bonnie. I don't choose to believe we've brought Chuck and Joan into a world of sheer wolves and jackals—when you've said you wish for a couple more children. No, I've simply changed my mind, simply had demonstrated to me that our best chance—mankind's best chance—lies with the legitimate government of the United States as established by the People's Constitutional Convention.

Next day Mannix turned me over to his interrogation specialists, who asked me more questions than I'd known I had answers for. A trankstim pill kept me alert but unemotional, as if I were operating myself by remote control.

Among other items, I showed them how a Decaturist who had access to the right equipment made contact with fellows elsewhere, whom he'd probably never met, or with higher-ups whom he definitely hadn't. The method had been considered by political police technicians, but they'd failed to devise any means of coping.

Problem: How do you maintain a network of illicit communications?

In practice you mostly use the old-fashioned mail drop. It's unfeasible to read the entire mails. The authorities must settle for watching the correspondence of suspicious individuals, and these may have ways of posting and collecting letters unobserved.

Yet sometimes you need to send a message fast.

The telephone's no good, of course, since computers became able to monitor every conversation continuously. However those same machines, or their cousins, can be your carriers.

Remember, we have millions of computers around these days, nationally interconnected. They do drudge work like record keeping and billing; they operate automated plants; they calculate for governmental planners and R & D workers; they integrate organizations; they keep day-by-day track of each citizen; etc., etc. Still more than in the case of the mails, the volume of data transmissions would swamp human overseers.

Give suitable codes, programmers and other technicians can send practically anything practically anywhere. The printout is just another string of numbers to those who can't read it. Once it has been read, the card is recycled and the electronic traces are wiped as per routine. That message leaves the office in a single skull.

Naturally, you save this capability for your highest priority calls. I'd used it a few times, attracting no attention, since my job on base frequently required me to prepare or receive top-secret calculations.

I couldn't give Mannix's men any code except the latest that had been given me. Every such message was re-encoded en route, according to self-changing programs buried deep down in the banks of the machines concerned. I could, though, put him in touch with somebody close to Sotomayor. Or, rather, I could put myself in touch.

What would happen thereafter was uncertain. We couldn't develop an exact plan. My directive was to do my best, and if my best was good enough, I'd be pardoned and rewarded.

I was rehearsed in my cover story till I was letter perfect, and given a few items like phone numbers to learn. Simulators and reinforcement techniques made this quick.

Perhaps my oath-brothers would cut my throat immediately, as a regrettable precaution. That didn't seem to matter. The drug left me no particular emotion except a desire to get the business done.

At a minimum, I was sure to be interrogated, strip-searched, encephalo-grammed, X-rayed, checked for metal and radioactivity. Perhaps blood, saliva, urine, and spinal fluid would be sampled. Agents have used pharmaceuticals and implants for too many years.

Nevertheless Mannix's outfit had a weapon prepared for me. It was not one the army had been told about. I wondered what else the political police labs were working on. I also wondered if various prominent men, who might have been awkward to denounce, had really died of strokes or heart attacks.

"I can't tell you details," said a technician. "With your education, you can figure out the general idea for yourself. It's a micro version of the fission gun, enclosed in lead to baffle detectors. You squeeze—you'll be shown how—and the system opens; a radioactive bombards another material which releases neutrons which touch off the fissionable atoms in one of ten successive chambers."

Despite my chemical coolness, awe drew a whistle from me. Given the right isotopes, configurations, and shielding, critical mass gets down to grams, and you can direct the energy through a minilaser. I'd known that. In this system, the lower limit must be milligrams; and the efficiency must approach one hundred percent, if you could operate it right out of your own body.

Still— "You do have components that'll register if I'm checked very closely," I said.

The technician grinned. "I doubt you will be, where we have in mind. They'll load you tomorrow morning."

Because I'd need practice in the weapon, I wasn't drugged then. I'd expected to be embarrassed. But when I entered an instrument-crammed concrete room after being unable to eat breakfast, I suddenly began shaking.

Two P. P. men I hadn't met before waited for me. One wore a lab coat, one a medic's tunic. My escort said, "Dowling," closed the door and left me alone with them.

Lab Coat was thin, bald, and sourpussed. "Okay, peel down and let's get started," he snapped.

Medic, who was a fattish blond, laughed—giggled, I thought in a gust of wanting to kill him. "Short arm inspection," he said.

Bonnie, I reminded myself, and dropped my clothes on a chair. Their eyes went to my crotch. Mine couldn't. I bit jaws and fists together and stared at the wall beyond them.

Medic sat down. "Over here," he ordered. I obeyed, stood before him, felt him finger what was left. "Ah," he chuckled. "Balls but no musket, eh?"

"Shut up, funny man," Lab Coat said and handed him a pair of calipers. I felt him measure the stump.

"They should've left more," Lab Coat complained. "At least two centimeters more."

"This glue could stick it straight onto his bellybutton," Medic said.

"Yeah, but the gadgets aren't rechargeable," Lab Coat retorted. "He'll go through four or five today before the final one, and nothing but elastic collars holding 'em in place. What a clot of a time I'll have fitting *them*." He shuffled over to a workbench and got busy.

"Take a look at your new tool," Medic invited me. "Generous, eh? Be the envy of the neighborhood. And what a jolt for your wife."

The wave was red, not black, and tasted of blood. I lunged, laid fingers around his throat, and bawled—I can't remember—maybe, "Be quiet, you filthy fairy, before I kill you!"

He squealed, then gurgled. I shook him till his teeth rattled. Lab Coat came on the run. "Stop that!" he barked. "Stop or I'll call a guard!"

I let go, sank down on the floor—its chill flowed into my buttocks, up my spine, out along my rib cage—and struggled not to weep.

"You bastard," Medic chattered. "I'm gonna file charges, I am."

"You are not. Another peep and I'll report you." Lab Coat hunkered beside me, laid an arm around my shoulder, and said, "I understand, Dowling. It was heroic of you to volunteer. You'll get the real thing back when you're finished. Never forget that."

Volunteer?

Laughter exploded. I whooped, I howled, I rolled around and beat my fists on the concrete, my muscles ached from laughing when finally I won back to silence.

After that, and a short rest, I was calm—cold, even—and functioned well. My aim improved fast, till I could hole the center circle at every shot.

"You've ten charges," Lab Coat reminded me. "No more. The beam being narrow, the head's your best target. If the apparatus gets detected after all, or if you're in Dutch for some other reason and your ammo won't last, press inward from the end—like this—and it'll self-destruct. You'll be blown apart and escape a bad time. Understand? Repeat."

He didn't bother bidding me good-by at the end of the session. (Medic was too sulky for words.) No doubt he'd figured what sympathy to administer earlier. Efficiency is the P.P. ideal. Mannix, or somebody, must have ordered my gun prepared almost at the moment I was arrested, or likelier before.

My escort had waited, stolid, throughout those hours. Though I recognized it was a practical matter of security, I felt hand-lickingly grateful to Mannix that this fellow—that very few people—knew what I was.

The day after. I placed my call to the Decaturists. It was brief. I had news of supreme importance—the fact I'd vanished for almost a month made this plausible—and would stand by for transportation at such-and-such different rendezvous, such-and-such different times.

Just before the first of these, I swallowed a stim with a hint of trank, in one of those capsules which attach to the stomach wall and spend the next three hundred hours dissolving. No one expected I'd need more time before the metabolic price had to be paid. A blood test would show its presence, but if I was carrying a vital message, would I not have sneaked me a supercharger?

I was not met, and went back to my room and waited. A side effect, when every cell worked at peak, was longing for Bonnie. Nothing sentimental; I loved her, I wanted her, I had to keep thrusting away memories of eyes, lips, breasts beneath my hand till my hand traveled downward…In the course of hours, I learned how to be a machine.

They came for me at the second spot on my list, a trifle past midnight. The place was a bar in a village of shops and rec centers near the base. It wasn't the sleek, state-owned New West, where I'd be recognized by officers, engineers, and party functionaries who could afford to patronize. This was a dim and dingy shack, run by a couple of workers on their own time, at the tough end of town. Music, mostly dirty songs, blared from a taper, ear-hurtingly loud, and the booze was rotgut served in glasses which seldom got washed. Nevertheless I had to push through the crowd and, practically, the smoke—pot as well as tobacco. The air smelled of sweat.

You see more of this kind of thing every year. I imagine the government only deplores the trend officially. People need some unorganized pleasure. Or, as the old joke goes, "What is the stage between socialism and communism called? Alcoholism."

A girl in a skimpy dress made me a business offer. She wasn't bad-looking, in a sleazy fashion, and last month I'd merely have said no, thanks. As it was, the drug in me didn't stop me from screaming, "Get away, you whore!" Scared, she backed off, and I drew looks from the men around. In cheap civies, I was supposed to be inconspicuous. Jim Dowling, officer, rocketeer, triple agent, boy wonder, ha! I elbowed my way onward to the bar. Two quick shots eased my shakes, and the racket around forgot me.

I'd almost decided to leave when a finger tapped my arm. A completely forgettable little man stood there. "Excuse me," he said. "Aren't you Sam Chalmers?"

"Uh, no, I'm his brother Roy." Beneath the once more cold surface, my pulse knocked harder.

"Well, well," he said. "Your father's told me a lot about you both. My name's Ralph Wagner."

"Yes, he's mentioned you. Glad to meet you, Comrade Wagner."

We shook hands and ad-libbed conversation a while. The countersigns we'd used were doubtless obsolete; but he'd allowed for my having been out of touch. Presently we left.

A car bearing Department of Security insignia was perched on the curb. Two much larger men, uniformed, waited inside. We joined them, the blowers whirred, and we were off. One man touched a button. A steel plate slid down and cut us three in the rear seat off from the driver. The windows I could see turned opaque. I had no need to know where we were bound. I did estimate our acceleration and thus our cruising speed. About 300 K.P.H. Going some, even for a Security vehicle!

From what Granddad had told me, this would have been lunacy before the war. Automobiles were so thick then that often they could barely crawl along. Among my earliest memories is that the government was still congratulating itself on having solved that problem.

Wind hooted around the shell. A slight vibration thrummed through my bones. The overhead light was singularly bleak. The big man on my left and the small man on my right crowded me.

"Okay," said the big man, "what happened?"

"I'll handle this," said he who named himself Wagner. The bruiser snapped his mouth shut and settled back. He was probably the one who'd kill me if that was deemed needful, but he was not the boss.

"We've been alarmed about you." Wagner spoke as gently as Mannix. In an acid way I liked the fact that he didn't smile.

I attempted humor in my loneliness: "I'd be alarmed if you hadn't been."

"Well?"

"I was called in for top-secret conferences. They've flitted me in and out-to Europe and back-under maximum security."

The big man formed an oath. Wagner waited. "They've gotten wind of our project," I said.

"I don't know of any other vanishments than yours,"

Wagner answered, flat-voiced.

"Would you?" I challenged. He shrugged. "Perhaps not."

"Actually," I continued, "I wasn't told about arrests and there may have been none. What they discussed was the Society, the Asians—they have a fixed idea the Peking-Tokyo Axis has taken over the Society—and what they called 'open indications.' The legal or semilegal talk you hear about 'socialist lawfulness,' 'American socialism,' and the rest. Roger Mannix—he turns out to be high in the P.P., by the way, and a shrewd man; I recommend we try to knock him off—Mannix takes these signs more seriously than I'd imagined anybody in the government did." I cleared my throat. "Details at your convenience. The upshot is, the authorities decided there is a definite risk of a cabal seizing the rocket bases. Never mind whether they have the data to make that a completely logical conclusion. What counts is that it *is* their conclusion."

"And right, God damn it, right," muttered the big man. He slammed a fist on his knee.

"What do they propose to do?" Wagner asked, as if I'd revealed the government was considering a reduced egg ration.

"That was a…tough question." I stared at the blank, enclosing panel. "They dare not shut down the installations, under guard of P.P., who don't know a mass ratio from a hole in the ground. Nor dare they purge the personnel, hoping to be left with loyal skeleton crews—because they aren't yet sure who those crews had better be loyal to. Oh, I saw generals and commissioners scuttling around like toads in a chamber pot, believe me." Now I turned my head to confront his eyes. "And believe me," I added, "we were lucky they happened to include one Decatur man."

Again, under the tranquilization and the stimulation (how keenly I saw the wrinkles around his mouth, heard cleft air brawl, felt the shiver of speed, snuffed stale bodies, registered the prickle of hairs and sweat glands, the tightened belly muscles and selfseizing guts beneath!), fear fluttered in me, and under the fear I was hollow. The man on whom I had turned my back could put a gun muzzle at the base of my skull.

Wagner nodded. "Yes-s-s."

Though it was too early to allow myself relief, I saw I'd passed the first watchdog. The Society might have been keeping such close surveillance that Wagner would know there had in fact been no mysterious travels of assorted missilemen.

This wasn't plausible, Mannix had declared. The Society was limited in what it could do. Watching every nonmember's every movement was ridiculous.

"Have they reached a decision?" Wagner asked.

"Yes." No matter how level I tried to keep it, my voice seemed to shiver the bones in my head. "American personnel will be replaced by foreigners till the crisis is past. I suppose you know West Europe has a good many competent rocketeers. In civilian jobs, of course; still, they could handle a military assignment. And they'd be docile, regardless of who gave orders. The Spanish and French especially, considering how the purges went through those countries. In short, they'd not be players in the game, just parts of the machinery."

My whetted ears heard him let out a breath. "When?"

"Not certain. A move of that kind needs study and planning beforehand. A couple, three weeks? My word is that we'd better compress our own timetable."

"Indeed. Indeed." Wagner bayoneted me with his stare. "If you are correct."

"You mean if I'm telling the truth," I said on his behalf.

"You understand, Colonel Dowling, you'll have to be quizzed and examined. And we'll meet an ironic obstacle in your conditioning against involuntary betrayal of secrets."

"Eventually you'd better go ahead and trust me…after all these years."

"I think that will be decided on the top level."

They took me to a well-equipped room somewhere and put me through the works. They were no more unkind than necessary, but extremely thorough. Never mind details of those ten or fifteen hours. The thoroughness was not quite sufficient. My immunity and my story held up. The physical checks showed nothing suspicious. Mannix had said, "I expect an inhibition too deep for consciousness will prevent the idea from occurring to them." I'd agreed. The reality was what had overrun me.

Afterward I was given a meal and—since I'd freely admitted being full of stim—some hours under a sleep inducer. It didn't prevent dreams which I still shiver to recall. But when I was allowed to wake. I felt rested and ready for action.

Whether I'd get any was an interesting question. Mannix's hope was that I'd be taken to see persons high in the outfit, from whom I might obtain information on plans and membership. But maybe I'd be sent straight home. My yarn declared that, after the bout of talks was over, I'd requested a few days' leave, hinting to my superiors that I had a girlfriend out of town.

My guards, two young men now grown affable, couldn't guess what the outcome would be. We started a poker game but eventually found ourselves talking. These were full-time undergrounders. I asked what made them abandon their original identities. The first said, "Oh, I got caught strewing pamphlets and had to run. What brought me into the Society to start with was…well, one damn thing after another, like when I was a miner and they boosted our quota too high for us to maintain safety structures and a cave-in killed a buddy of mine."

The second, more bookish, said thoughtfully, "I believe in God."

I raised my brows. "Really? Well, you're not forbidden to go to church. You might not get a good job, positively never a clearance, but—"

"That's not the point. I've heard a lot of preachers in a lot of different places. They're all windup toys of the state. The Social Gospel, you know—no, I guess you don't."

Wagner arrived soon afterward. His surface calm was like dacron crackling in a wind. "Word's come, Dowling," he announced. "They want to interview you, ask your opinions, your impressions, you having been our sole man on the spot."

I rose. "They?"

"The main leadership. Sotomayor himself, and his chief administrators. Here." Wagner handed me a wallet. "Your new ID card, travel permit, ration tab, the works, including a couple of family snapshots. Learn it. We leave in an hour."

I scarcely heard the latter part. Alfredo Sotomayor! The half-legendary president of the whole Society!

I'd wondered plenty about him. Little was known. His face was a fixture on post office walls, wanted for a variety of capital crimes, armed and dangerous. The text barely hinted at his political significance. Evidently the government didn't wish to arouse curiosity. The story told me, while I was in the long process of joining, was that he'd been a firebrand in his youth, an icily brilliant organizer in middle life, and in his old age was a scholar and philosopher, at work on a proposal for establishing a "free country," whatever that meant. Interested, I'd asked for some of his writings. They were denied me. Possession was dangerous. Why risk a useful man unnecessarily?

I was to meet rebellious Lucifer, whom I would be serving yet had not the political police laid hand on me and mine.

Not that those fingers had closed on Bonnie or the kids. They would if I didn't undo my own rebelliousness. Camp La Pasionara…What was Sotomayor to me?

How could I believe a spig bandit had any real interest in America, except to plunder her? I had *not* been shown those writings.

"You feel well, Jim?" asked the man who believed in God. "You look kind of pale."

"Yeah, I'm okay," I mumbled. "Better sit down, though, and learn my new name."

A fake Security car, windows blanked, could bring me to an expendable hidey-hole like this, off in a lonely section of hills. The method was too showy for a meeting which included brains, heart, and maybe spinal cord of Decatur. Wagner and I would use public transportation.

We walked to the nearest depot, a few kilometers off. I'd have enjoyed the sunlight, woods, peace asparkle with bird song, if Bonnie had been my companion (and I whole, I whole). As was, neither of us spoke. At the newsstand I bought a magazine and read about official plans for my future while the train was an hour late. It lost another hour, for some unexplained reason, en route. About par for the course. Several times the coach rattled to the sonic booms of military jets. Again, nothing unusual, especially in time of crisis. The People's Republic keeps abundant warcraft.

Our destination was Oakland. We arrived at 2000, when the factories were letting out, and joined the pedestrian swarm. I don't like city dwellers. They smell sour and look grubby. Well, that's not their fault; if soap and hot water are in short supply, people crowded together will not be clean. But their grayness goes deeper than their skins—except in ethnic districts, of course, which hold more life but which you'd better visit in armed groups.

Wagner and I found a restaurant and made the conversation of two petty production managers on a business trip. I flatter myself that I gave a good performance. Concentrating on it took my mind off the food and service.

Afterward we saw a movie, an insipidity about boy on vacation volunteer meets girl on collective. When it and the political reel had been endured, meeting time was upon us. We hadn't been stopped to show our papers, and surely any plain-clothes man running a random surveillance had lost interest in us. A street car groaned us to a surprisingly swank part of town, and the house to which we walked was a big old mansion in big old grounds full of the night breath of roses.

"Isn't this too conspicuous?" I wondered.

"Ever tried being inconspicuous in a tenement?" Wagner responded. "The poor may hate the civil police, but the prospect of reward money makes them eyes and ears for the P. P."

He hesitated. "Since you could check it out later anyway," he said, "I may as well tell you we're at the home of Lorenzo Berg, commissioner of electric power for northern California. He's been one of us since his national service days."

I barely maintained my steady pace. This fact alone would buy me back my life.

A prominent man is a watched man. Berg's task in the Society had been to build, over the years, the image of a competent bureaucrat, who had no further ambitions and therefore was no potential menace to anybody, but who amused himself by throwing little parties where skewball intellectuals would gather to discuss the theory of chess or the origin of *Australopithecus*. Most of these affairs were genuine. For the few that weren't, he had the craft to nullify the bugs in his house and later play tapes for them which had been supplied him. Of course, a mobile tapper could have registered what was actually said—he dared not screen the place—but the P.P. had more to do than make anything but spot checks on a harmless eccentric.

Thus Berg could provide a scene for occasional important Society meetings. He could temporarily shelter fugitives. He could maintain for this area that vastly underrated tool, a reference library; who'd look past the covers of his many books and microreels? Doubtless his services went further, but never into foolish flamboyancies.

I don't recall him except as a blur. He played his role that well, even that night among those men. Or was he his role? You needn't be a burning-eyed visionary to live by a cause.

A couple like that were on hand. They must have been able in their fields. But one spoke of his specialty, massive sabotage, too lovingly for me. My missiles were counterforce weapons, not botulin mists released among women and children. Another, who was a black, dwelt on Russian racism. I'm sure his citations were accurate, of how the composition of the Politburo has never since the beginning reflected the nationalities in the Soviet Union. Yet what had that to do with us and why did his eyes dwell so broodingly on the whites in the room?

The remaining half dozen were entirely businesslike in their various ways, except Sotomayor, who gave me a courteous greeting and then sat quietly and listened. They were ordinary Americans, which is to say a mixed lot, a second black man, a Jew to judge by the nose (it flitted across my mind how our schools keep teaching that the People's Republic has abolished the prejudices of the imperialist era, which are described in detail), a Japanese-descended woman, the rest of them like me…except, again, Sotomayor, who I think was almost pure Indio. His features were rather long and lean for that, but he had the cheekbones, the enduringly healthy brown skin, dark eyes altogether alive under straight white hair, flared nostrils and sensitive mouth. He dressed elegantly, and sat and stood as erect as a candle.

I repeated my story, was asked intelligent questions, and carried everything off well. Maybe I was helped by Bonnie having told me a lot about theater and persuading me to take occasional bit parts. The hours ticked by. Finally, around 0100, Sotomayor stirred and said in his soft but youthful voice: "Gentlemen, I think perhaps we have done enough for the present, and it might arouse curiosity if the living room lights shone very late on a midweek night. Please think about this matter as carefully as it deserves. You will be notified as to time and place of our next meeting."

All but one being from out of town, they would sleep here. Berg led them off to their cots. Sotomayor said he would guide me. Smiling, as we started up a grand staircase the Socialist Functionalist critics would never allow to be built today, he took my arm and suggested a nightcap.

He rated not a shakedown but a suite cleared for his use.

Although a widower, Berg maintained a large household. Four grown sons pleaded the apartment shortage as a reason for living here with their families and so preventing the mansion's conversion to an ordinary tenement. They and the wives the Society had chosen for them had long since been instructed to stay completely passive, except for keeping their kids from overhearing anything, and to know nothing of Society affairs.

Given that population under this roof, plus a habit of inviting visiting colleagues to bunk with him, plus always offering overnight accommodations when parties got wet, Berg found that guests of his drew no undue notice.

All in all, I'd entered quite a nest. And the king hornet was bowing me through his door.

The room around me was softly lit, well furnished, dominated by books and a picture window. The latter overlooked a sweep of city—lanes of street lamps cut through humpbacked darknesses of buildings—and the Bay and a deeper spark-speckled shadow which was San Francisco. A nearly full moon bridged the waters with frailty. I wondered if men would ever get back yonder. The requirements of defense against the revisionists—

Why in the name of madness was I thinking about that?

Sotomayor closed the door and went to a table whereon stood a bottle, a carafe of water, and an ice bucket which must be an heirloom. "Please be seated, Colonel Dowling," he said. "I have only this to offer you, but it is genuinely from Scotland. You need a drink, I'm sure, tense as you are."

"D-does it show that much?" Hearing the idiocy of the question, I hauled myself to full awareness. Tomorrow morning, when the group dispersed, Wagner would conduct me home and I would report to Mannix. My job was to stay alive until then.

"No surprise." He busied himself. "In fact, your conduct has been remarkable throughout. I'm grateful for more than your service, tremendous though that may turn out to be. I'm joyful to know we have a man like you. The kind is rare and precious."

I sat down and told myself over and over that he was my enemy. "You, uh, you overrate me, sir."

"No. I have been in this business too long to cherish illusions. Men are limited creatures at best. This may perhaps make their striving correspondingly more noble, but the limitations remain. When a strong, sharp tool comes to hand, we cherish it."

He handed me my drink, took a chair opposite me, and sipped at his own. I could barely meet those eyes, however gentle they seemed. Mine stung. I took a long gulp and blurted the first words that it occurred to me might stave off silence: "Why, being in the Society is such a risk, sir, would anybody join who's not, well, unusual?"

"Yes, in certain cases, through force of circumstance. We have taken in criminals—murderers, thieves—when they looked potentially useful."

After a moment of stillness, he added slowly: "In fact, revolutionaries, be they Decaturists or members of other outfits or isolated in their private angers—revolutionaries have always had motivations as various as their humanity. Some are idealists; yet let us admit that some of the ideals are nasty, like racism. Some want revenge for harm done them or theirs by officials who may have been sadistic or corrupt but often were merely incompetent or overzealous, in a system which allows the citizen no appeal. Some hope for money or power or fame under a new dispensation. Some are old-fashioned patriots who want us out of the empire. Am I right that you fall in that category. Colonel Dowling?"

"Yes," I said, "you were."

Sotomayor's gaze went into me and beyond me. "One reason I want to know you better," he said, "is that I think you can be educated to a higher ideal."

I discovered, with a sort of happiness, that I was interested enough to take my mind off the fact I was drinking the liquor of a man who believed I was his friend and a man. "To your own purposes, sir?" I asked. "You know, I never have been told what you yourself are after."

"On as motley a collection as our members are, the effect of an official doctrine would be disruptive. Nor is any required. The history of Communist movements in the last century gives ample proof. I've dug into history, you realize. The franker material is hard to find, after periodic purges of the libraries. But it's difficult to eliminate a book totally. The printing press is a more powerful weapon than any gun—for us or for our masters." Sotomayor smiled and sighed. "I ramble. Getting old. Still, I have spent these last years of mine trying to understand what we are doing, in the hope we can do what is right."

"And what are your conclusions, sir?"

"Let us imagine our takeover plan succeeds," he answered. "We hold the rocket bases. Given those, I assure you there are enough members and sympathizers in the rest of the armed services and in civilian life that, while there will doubtless be some shooting, the government will topple and we will take over the nation."

The drink slopped in my hand. Sweat prickled forth on my skin and ran down my ribs.

Sotomayor nodded. "Yes, we are that far along," he said. "After many years and many human sacrifices, we are finally prepared. The war has given us the opportunity to use what we built."

Surely, I thought wildly, the P.P., military intelligence, high party officials, surely they knew something of the sort was in the wind. You can't altogether conceal a trend of such magnitude.

Evidently they did not suspect how far along it was.

Or…wait…you didn't need an enormous number of would-be rebels in the officer corps. You really only needed access to the dossiers and psychographs kept on everybody. Then in-depth studies would give you a good notion of how the different key men would react.

"Let us assume, then, a junta," Sotomayor was saying. "It cannot, must not be for more than the duration of the emergency. Civilian government must be restored and made firm. But *what* government? That is the problem I have been working on."

"And?" I responded in my daze.

"Have you ever read the original Constitution of the United States? The one drawn in Philadelphia in 1786?"

"Why…well, no. What for?"

"It may be found in scholarly works. A document so widely disseminated cannot be gotten rid of in 30 or 40 years. Though if the present system endures, I do not give the old Constitution another 50." Sotomayor leaned forward. Beneath his softness, intensity mounted. "What were you taught about it in school?"

"Oh…well, uh, let me think…Codification of the law for the bourgeoisie of the cities and the slaveowners of the South…Modified as capitalism evolved into imperialism."

"Read it sometime." A thin finger pointed at a shelf.

"Take it to bed with you. It's quite brief."

After a moment: "Its history is long, though, Colonel Dowling, and complicated, and not always pleasant—especially toward the end, when the original concept had largely been lost sight of. Yet it was the most profoundly revolutionary thing set down on paper since the New Testament."

"Huh?"

He smiled again. "Read it, I say, and compare today's version, and look up certain thinkers who are mentioned in footnotes if at all—Hobbes, Locke, Hamilton, Burke, and the rest. Then do your own thinking. That won't be easy. Some of the finest minds which ever existed spent centuries groping toward the idea— that law should be a contract the people make among each other, and that every man has absolute rights, which protect him in making his private destiny and may never be taken from him."

His smile had dissolved. I have seldom heard a bleaker tone: "Think how radical that is. Too radical, perhaps. The world found it easier to bring back overlords, compulsory belief, and neolithic god-kings."

"W-would you…revive the old government?"

"Not precisely. The country and its people are too changed from what they were. I think, however, we could bring back Jefferson's original idea. We could write a basic law which does not compromise with the state, and hope that in time the people will again understand."

He had spoken as if at a sacrament. Abruptly he shook himself, laughed a little, and raised his glass. "Well!" he said. "You didn't come here for a lecture. *A vuestra salud.*"

My hand still shook when I drank with him.

"We'd better discuss your personal plans," he suggested. "I know you've had a hatful of business lately, but none of us dare stay longer than overnight here. Where might you like to go?"

"Sir?" I didn't grasp his meaning at once. Drug or no, my brain was turning slowly under its burdens. "Why…home. Back to base. Where else?"

"Oh, no. Can't be. I said you have proved you are not a man we want to risk."

"Bu-but…if I don't go back, it's a giveaway!"

"No fears. We have experts at this sort of thing. You will be provided unquestionable reasons why your leave should be extended. A nervous collapse, maybe, plausible in view of the recent strains on you, and fakeable to fool any military medic into prescribing a rest cure. Why, your family can probably join you at some pleasant spot." Sotomayor chuckled. "Oh, you'll work hard. We want you in consultation, and between times I want to educate you. We'll try to arrange a suitable replacement at Reed. But one missile base is actually less important than the duties I have in mind for you,"

I dropped my glass. The room whirled. Through a blur I saw Sotomayor jump up and bend over me, heard his voice: "What's the matter? Are you sick?"

Yes, I was. From a blow to the…the belly.

I rallied, and knew I might argue for being returned home, and knew it would be no use. Fending off his anxious hands, I got to my feet. "Exhaustion, I guess," I slurred. "Be okay in a minute. Which way's uh bathroom ?"

"Here." He took my arm again.

When the door had closed on him, I stood in tiled sterility and confronted my face. But adrenalin pumped through me, and Mannix's chemicals were still there. Everything Mannix had done was still there.

If I stalled until too late…the Lomonosov Institute might or might not survive. If it did, I might or might not be admitted. If it didn't, something equivalent might or might not be built elsewhere in some latter year. I might or might not get the benefit thereof, before I was too old.

Meanwhile Bonnie—and my duty was not, not to anybody's vague dream—and I had barely a minute to decide—and it would take longer than that to change my most recent programming—

Act! yelled the chemicals.

I zipped down my pants, took my gun in my right hand, and opened the door.

Sotomayor had waited outside. At his back I saw the main room, water, moon, stars. Astonishment smashed his dignity. "Dowling, *¿esta usted loco?* What the flaming hell—?"

Each word I spoke made me more sure, more efficient. "This is a weapon. Stand back."

Instead, he approached. I remembered he had been in single combats and remained vigorous and leathery. I aimed past him and squeezed as I had been taught. The flash of light burned a hole through carpet and floorboards at his feet. Smoke spurted from the pockmark. It smelled harsh.

Sotomayor halted, knees bent, hands cocked. Once, hunting in the piny woods of my boyhood, we'd cornered a bobcat. It had stood the way he did, teeth peeled but body crouched moveless, watching every instant for a chance to break free.

I nodded. "Yeah," I said. "A zap gun. Sorry, I've changed teams."

He didn't stir, didn't speak, until he forced me to add: "Back. To yonder phone I see. I've got a call to make." My lips twitched sideways. "I can't very well do otherwise, can I?"

"Has that thing—" he whispered, "has that thing been substituted for the original?"

"Yes," I said. "Forget your *machismo.* I've got the glands."

"Pugilist," he breathed, almost wonderingly. Faintly through the blood-filled stiffness of me, I felt surprise. "What?"

"The ancient Romans often did the same to their pugilists," he said in monotone. "Slaves who boxed in the arenas, iron on their fists. The man kept his physical strength, you see, but his bitterness made him fight without fear or pity…Yes. Pavlov and those who used Pavlov's discoveries frequently got good reconditioning results from castration. Such a fundamental shock. This is more efficient. Yes."

Fury leaped in me. "Shut your mouth! They'll grow me back what I've lost. I love my wife."

Sotomayor shook his head. "Love is a convenient instrument for the almighty state, no?"

He had no right to look that scornful, like some aristocrat. History had dismissed them, the damned feudal oppressors; and when the men in this house were seized, and the information, his own castle would crash down.

He made a move. I leveled my weapon. His right hand simply gestured, touching brow, lips, breast, left and right shoulders. "Move!" I ordered.

He did—straight at me, shouting loud enough to wake the dead in Philadelphia.

I fired into his mouth. His head disintegrated. A cooked eyeball rolled out. But he had such speed that his corpse knocked me over.

I tore free of the embrace of those arms, spat out his blood, and leaped to lock the hall door. Knocking began a minute afterward, and the cry, "What's wrong? Let me in!"

"Everything's all right," I told the panel. "Comrade Sotomayor slipped and nearly fell. I caught him."

"Why's he silent? Let us in!"

I'd expected nothing different and was already dragging furniture in front of the door. Blows and kicks, clamor and curses waxed beyond. I scuttled to the telephone—sure, they provided this headquarters well—and punched the number Mannix had given me. An impulse would go directly to a computer which would trace the line and dispatch an emergency squad here. Five minutes?

They threw themselves at the door, thud, thud, thud. That isn't as easy as the shows pretend. It would go down before long, though. I used bed, chairs, and tables to barricade the bathroom door. I chinked my fortress with books and placed myself behind, leaving a loophole.

When they burst through, I shot and I shot and I shot. I grew hoarse from yelling. The air grew sharp with ozone and thick with cooked meat.

Two dead, several wounded, the attackers retreated. It had dawned on them that I must have summoned help and they'd better get out.

The choppers descended as they reached the street.

My rescuers of the civil police hadn't been told anything, merely given a Condition A order to raid a place. So I must be held with the other survivors to wait for higher authority. Since the matter was obviously important, this house was the jail which would preserve the most discretion.

But they had no reason to doubt my statement that I was a political agent. I'd better be confined respectfully. The captain offered me my pick of rooms and was surprised when I asked for Sotomayor's if the mess there had been cleaned up.

Among other features, it was the farthest away from everybody else, the farthest above the land.

Also, it had that bottle. I could drink if not sleep. When that didn't lift my postcombat sadness, I started thumbing through books. There was nothing else to do in the night silence.

I read: We hold these Truths to be self-evident, that all Men are created equal, that they are endowed by their Creator with certain unalienable Rights, that among these are Life, Liberty, and the Pursuit of Happiness—That to secure these Rights, Governments are instituted among Men, deriving their just Powers from the Consent of the Governed, that whenever any Form of Government becomes destructive of those Ends, it is the Right of the People to alter or to abolish it, and to institute new Government, laying its Foundation on such Principles, and organizing its Powers in such Form, as to them shall seem most likely to effect their Safety and Happiness.

I read: We the People of the United States…secure the Blessings of Liberty to ourselves and our Posterity…

I read: Congress shall make no law respecting an establishment of religion, or prohibiting the free exercise thereof; or abridging the freedom of speech, or of the press; or the right of the people peacefully to assemble, and to petition the Government for a redress of grievances.

I read: The powers not delegated to the United States by the Constitution, nor prohibited by it to the States, are reserved to the States respectively, or to the people.

I read: "I have sworn upon the altar of God eternal hostility toward every form of tyranny over the mind of man."

I read: "In giving freedom to the slave, we assure freedom to the free,—honourable alike in what we give and what we preserve."

I read: But they shall sit every man under his vine and under his fig tree; and none shall make them afraid…

When Mannix arrived—in person—he blamed my sobbing on sheer weariness. He may have been right.

Oh, yes, he kept his promise. My part in this affair could not be completely shielded from suspicion among what rebels escaped the roundup. A marked man, I had my best chance in transferring to the technical branch of the political police. They reward good service.

So, after our internal crisis was over and the threat of our rockets made the Kunin faction quit, with gratifyingly little damage done the Motherland, I went to Moscow and returned whole.

Only it's no good with Bonnie, I'm no good at all.

INSIDE STRAIGHT

In the main, sociodynamic theory predicted quite accurately the effects of the secondary drive. It foresaw that once cheap interstellar transportation was available, there would be considerable emigration from the Solar System—men looking for a fresh start, malcontents of all kinds, "peculiar people" desiring to maintain their form of life without interference. It also predicted that these colonies would in turn spawn colonies, again of unsatisfied minority groups, until this part of the Galaxy was sprinkled with human settled planets; and that in their relative isolation, these politically independent worlds would develop some very odd societies.

However, the economic bias of the Renascence period, and the fact that war was a discarded institution in the Solar System, led these same predictors into errors of detail. It was felt that, since planets useful to man are normally separated by scores of light-years, and since any planet colonized on a high technological level would be quite self-sufficient, there would be little intercourse and no strife between these settlements. In their own reasonableness, the Renascence intellectuals overlooked the fact that man as a whole is not a rational animal, and that exploration and war do not always have economic causes.

—Simon Vardis
A Short History of Pre-Commonwealth Politics
Reel I, Frame 617

They did not build high on New Hermes. There was plenty of room, and the few cities sprawled across many square kilometers in a complex of low, softly tinted domes and cylindroids. Parks spread green wherever you looked, each breeze woke a thousand bell-trees into a rush of chiming, flowers and the bright-winged summerflits ran wildly colored beneath a serene blue sky. The planetary capital, Arkinshaw, had the same leisurely old-fashioned look as the other towns Ganch had seen; only down by the docks was there a fevered energy and a brawling life.

The restaurant Wayland had taken him to was incredibly archaic; it even had live service. When they had finished a subtly prepared lunch, the waiter strolled to their table. "Was there anything else, sir?" he asked.

"I thank you, no," said Wayland. He was a small, lithe man with close-cropped gray-shot hair and a brown nutcracker face in which lay startlingly bright blue eyes. On him, the local dress—a knee-length plaid tunic, green buskins, and yellow mantle—looked good…*which was more than you could say for most of them*, reflected Ganch.

The waiter produced a tray. There was no bill on it, as Ganch had expected, but a pair of dice. *Oh, no!* he thought. *By the Principle, no! Not this again!*

Wayland rattled the cubes in his hand, muttering an incantation. They flipped on the table, eight spots looked up. "Fortune seems to favor you, sir," said the waiter.

"May she smile on a more worthy son," replied Wayland. Ganch noted with disgust that the planet's urbanity-imperative extended even to servants. The waiter shook the dice and threw.

"Snake eyes," he smiled. "Congratulations, sir. I trust you enjoyed the meal."

"Yes, indeed," said Wayland, rising. "My compliments to the chef, and you and he are invited to my next poker game. I'll have an announcement about it on the telescreens."

He and the waiter exchanged bows and compliments. Then Wayland left, ushering Ganch through the door and out onto the slidewalk. They found seats and let it carry them toward the waterfront, which Ganch had expressed a desire to see.

"Ah—" Ganch cleared his throat. "How was that done?"

"Eh?" Wayland blinked. "Don't you even have dice on Dromm?"

"Oh, yes. But I mean the principle of payment for the meal."

"I shook him. Double or nothing. I won."

Ganch shook his head. He was a tall, muscular man in a skin-tight black uniform. That and the scarlet eyes in his long bony face (not albinism, but healthy mutation) marked him as belonging to the Great Cadre of Dromm.

"But then the restaurant loses money," he said.

"This time, yes," nodded Wayland. "It evens out in the course of a day—just as all our commerce evens out, so that in the long run everybody earns his rightful wage or profit."

"But suppose one—ah—cheats?"

Surprisingly, Wayland reddened, and looked around. When he spoke again, it was in a low voice: "Don't ever use that word, sir, I beg of you. I realize the mores are different on your planet, but here there is one unforgiveable, utterly obscene sin, and it's the one you just mentioned." He sat back, breathing heavily for a while, then seemed to cool off and proffered cigars. Ganch declined—tobacco did not grow on Dromm—but Wayland puffed his own into lighting with obvious enjoyment.

"As a matter of fact," he said presently, "our whole social conditioning is such as to preclude the possibility of…unfairness. You realize how thoroughly an imperative can be inculcated with modern psychopediatrics. It's a matter of course that all equipment, from dice and coins to the most elaborate Stellarium set, is periodically checked by a Games Engineer."

"I see," said Ganch doubtfully. He looked around as the slidewalk carried him on. It was a pleasant, sunny day, like most on New Hermes. Only to be expected on a world with two small continents, all the rest of the land split into a multitude of islands. The people he saw had a relaxed appearance—the men in their tunics and mantles, women in their loose filmy gowns, the children in little or nothing. A race of sybarites; they had had it too easy here, and degenerated.

Sharply he remembered Dromm, its gaunt glacial peaks and wind-scoured deserts, storm and darkness, galloping down from the poles, the huge iron cubicles of cities and the obedient gray-clad masses that filled them. That world had brought forth the Great Cadre, and tempered them in struggle and heartbreak, and given them power first over a people and then over a planet and then over two systems.

Eventually…who knew? The Galaxy?

"I am interested in your history," he said, recalling himself. "Just how was New Hermes settled?"

"The usual process," shrugged Wayland. "Our folk came from Caledonia, which had been settled from Old Hermes, whose people were from Earth. A puritanical gang got into control and started making all kinds of senseless restrictions on natural impulses. Finally a small group, our ancestors, could take no more, and went off looking for a planet of their own. That was about three hundred years ago. They went far, into this spiral arm which was then completely unexplored, in the hope of being left alone; and that hope has been realized. To this day, except for a couple of minor wars, we've had only casual visitors like yourself."

Casual! A grim amusement twisted Ganch's mouth upward.

To cover it, he asked: "But surely you've had your difficulties? It cannot have been simply a matter of landing here and founding your cities."

"Oh, no, of course not. The usual pioneer troubles—unknown diseases, wild animals, storms, a strange ecology. There were some hard times before the machines were constructed. Now, of course, we have it pretty good. There are fifty million of us, and space for many more; but we're in no hurry to expand the population. We like elbow room."

Ganch frowned until he had deduced the meaning of that last phrase. They spoke Anglic here, as on Dromm and most colonies, but naturally an individual dialect had evolved.

Excitement gripped him. Fifty million! There were two hundred million people on Dromm, and conquered Thanit added half again as many.

Of course, said his military training, sheer numbers meant little. Automatized equipment made all but the most highly skilled officers and technicians irrelevant. War between systems involved sending a space fleet, which met and beat the enemy fleet in a series of engagements; bases on planets had to be manned, and sometimes taken by ground forces, but the fighting was normally remote from the worlds concerned. Once the enemy navy was broken, its home had to capitulate or be sterilized by bombardment from the skies.

Still…New Hermes should be an even easier prey than Thanit had been.

"Haven't you taken any precautions against…hostiles?" he asked, mostly because the question fitted his assumed character.

"Oh, yes, to be sure," said Wayland. "We maintain a navy and marine corps; matter of fact, I'm in the Naval Intelligence Reserve myself, captain's rank. We had to fight a couple of small wars in the previous century, once with the Corridans—nonhumans out for loot—and once with Oberkassel, whose people were on a religious-fanatic kick. We won them both without much trouble." He added modestly: "But of course, sir, neither planet was very intelligently guided."

Ganch suppressed a desire to ask for figures on naval strength. This guileless dice-thrower might well spout them on request, but—

The slide walk had reached the waterfront by now, and they got off. Here the sea glistened blue, streaked with white foam, and the harbor was crowded with shipping. There were not only flying boats, but big watercraft moored to the ferroconcrete piers. Machines were loading and unloading in a whirl of bright steel arms, warehouses gaped for the planet's wealth, the air was rich with oil and spices. A babbling confusion of humanity surfed around Ganch and broke on his eardrums in a roar.

Wayland pointed unobtrusively here and there, his voice almost lost in the din: "See, we have quite a cultural variety of our own. That tall blond man in the fur coat is from Norrin, he must have brought in a load of pelts. The little dark fellow in the sarong is a spice trader from the Radiant Islands. The Mongoloid wearing a robe is clear from the Ivory Gate, probably with handicrafts to exchange for our timber. And—"

They were interrupted by a young woman, a very good-looking young woman with long black hair and a tilt-nosed freckled face. She wore a light blue uniform jacket with a lieutenant's twin comets on the shoulders, as well as a short loose-woven skirt revealing slim brown legs. "Will! Where have you been?"

"Showing the distinguished guest of our government around," said Wayland formally. "The Prime Selector himself appointed me to that pleasant task. Ganch, may I have the honor of presenting my niece, Lieutenant Christabel Hesty of the New Hermesian Navy? Lieutenant Hesty, this gentleman hight Ganch, from Dromm. It's a planet lying about fifty light-years from us, a very fine place I'm sure. They are making a much-overdue ethnographic survey of this Galactic region, and Ganch is taking notes on us."

"Honored, sir." She bowed and shook hands with herself in the manner of Arkinshaw. "We've heard of Dromm. There have been visitors thence in the past several years. I trust you are enjoying your stay?"

Ganch saluted stiffly, as was prescribed for the Great Cadre. "Thank you, very much." He was a little shocked at such blatant sexual egalitarianism, but reflected that it might be turned to advantage.

"Will, you're just the man I want to see." Lieutenant Hesty's voice bubbled over. "I came down to wager on a cargo from Thorncroft and you—"

"Ah, yes. I'll be glad to help you, though of course the requirements of my guild are—"

"You'll get your commission." She made a face at him and turned laughing to Ganch. "Perhaps you didn't know, sir, my uncle is a Tipster?"

"No, I didn't," said the Dromman. "What profession is that?"

"Probability analyst. It takes years and years of training. When you want to make an important wager, you call in a Tipster." She tugged at Wayland's sleeve. "Come on, the trading will start any minute."

"Do you mind, sir?" asked Wayland.

"Not at all," said Ganch. "I would be very interested. Your economic system is unique." *And*, he added, *the most inefficient I have yet heard of.*

They entered a building which proved to be a single great room. In the center was a long table, around which crowded a colorful throng of men and women. There was an outsize electronic device of some kind at the end, with a tall rangy man in kilt and beryllium-copper breastplate at the controls. Wayland stood aside, his face taking on an odd withdrawn look.

"How does this work?" asked Ganch—*sotto voce*, for the crowd did not look as if it wanted its concentration disturbed.

"The croupier there is the trader from Thorncroft," whispered Christabel Hesty. This close, with her head just beneath his chin, Ganch could smell the faint sun-warmed perfume of her hair. It stirred a wistfulness in him, buried ancestral memories of summer meadows on Earth. He choked off the emotion and listened to her words.

"He's brought in a load of refined thorium, immensely valuable. He puts that up as his share, and those who wish to trade get into the game with shares of what they have—they cover him, just as in craps, though they're playing Orthotron now. The game is a complex one, I see a lot of Tipsters around...yes, and the man in the green robe is a Games Engineer, umpire and technician. I'm afraid you wouldn't understand the rules at once, but perhaps you would like to make side bets?"

"No, thank you," said Ganch. "I am content to observe."

He soon found out that Lieutenant Hesty had not exaggerated the complications. Orthotron seemed to be a remote descendant of roulette such as they had played on Thanit before the war, but the random-pulse tubes shifted the probabilities continuously, and the rules themselves changed as the game went on. When the scoreboard on the machine flashed, chips to the tune of millions of credits clattered from hand to hand. Ganch found it hard to believe that anyone could even learn the system, let alone become so expert in it as to make a profession of giving advice. A Tipster would have to allow for the presence of other Tipsters, and—

His respect for Wayland went up. The little man must have put a lightning-fast mind through years of the most rigorous training; and there must be a highly developed paramathematical theory behind it all. If that intelligence and energy had gone into something useful, military technics for instance—

But it hadn't, and New Hermes lay green and sunny, wide open for the first determined foe.

Ganch grew aware of tension. It was not overtly expressed, but faces tightened, changed color, pupils narrowed and pulses beat in temples until he could almost feel the emotion, crackling like lightning in the room. Now and then Wayland spoke quietly to his niece, and she laid her bets accordingly.

It was with an effort that she pulled herself away, with two hours lost and a few hundred credits gained. Only courtesy to the guest made her do it. Her hair was damply plastered to her forehead, and she went out with a stiff-legged gait which only slowly loosened.

Wayland accepted his commission and laughed a little shakily. "I earn my living, sir!" he said. "It's brutal on the nerves."

"How long will they play?" asked Ganch.

"Till the trader is cleaned out or has won so much that no one can match him. In this case, I'd estimate about thirty hours."

"Continuous? How can the nervous system endure it—not to mention the feet?"

"It's hard," admitted Christabel Hesty, seeming to wake from a troubled dream. Her eyes burned. "But exciting! There's nothing in the Galaxy quite like that suspense. You lose yourself in it."

"And, of course," said Wayland mildly, "man adapts to any cultural pattern. We'd find it difficult to live as you do on Dromm."

No doubt, thought Ganch sardonically. *But you are going to learn how!*

On an isolated planet like this, an outworlder was always a figure of romance. In spite of manners which must seem crude here, Ganch had only to suggest an evening out for Christabel Hesty to leap at the offer.

He simply changed to another uniform, but she appeared in a topless gown of deep-blue silkite, her dark hair sprinkled with tiny points of light, and made his heart stumble. He reminded himself that women were breeders, nothing else. But Principle! How dull they were on Dromm!"

His object was to gain information, but he decided he might as well enjoy his work.

They took an elevated way to the Stellar House, Arkinshaw's only skyscraper, and had cocktails in a clear-domed roof garden with sunset rioting around them. A gentle music, some ancient waltz from Earth herself, lilted in the air, and the gaily clad diners talked in low voices and clinked glasses and laughed softly.

Lieutenant Hesty raised her glass to his. "Your luck, sir," she pledged him. Then, smiling: "Shall we lower guard?"

"I beg your pardon?"

"My apologies. I forgot you are a stranger, sir. The proposal was to relax formality for this evening."

"By all means," said Ganch. He tried to smile in turn. "Though I fear my class is always rather stiff."

Her long, soot-black eyelashes fluttered. "Then I hight Chris tonight," she said, "And your first name...?"

"My class does not use them. I am simply Ganch, with various identifying symbols attached."

"We meet some strange outworlders," she said frankly, "but in truth, you Drommans seem the most exotic of all."

"And New Hermes gives us that impression," he chuckled.

"We know so little about you—there have been only a few explorers and traders, and now you. Is your mission official?"

"Everything on Dromm is official," said Ganch, veraciously enough. "I am only an ethnographer making a detailed study of your folkways." And that was a lie.

"Excuse my saying so, I shouldn't criticize another civilization, but isn't it terribly dull having all one's life regulated by the State?"

"It is…" Ganch hunted for words. "Secure," he finished earnestly. "Ordered. One knows where one stands."

"A pity you had that war with Thanit. They seemed such nice people, those who visited here."

"We had no choice," answered Ganch with the smoothness of rote. "An irresponsible, aggressive government attacked us." She did not ask for details, and he supposed it was the usual thing: interest in other people's fate obeys an inverse-square law, and 50 light-years is a gulf of distance no man can really imagine.

In point of fact, he told himself with the bitter honesty of his race, Thanit had sought peace up to the last moment; Dromm's ultimatum had demanded impossible concessions, and Thanit had had no choice but to fight a hopeless battle. Her conquest had been well-planned, the armored legions of Dromm had romped over her and now she was being digested by the State.

Chris frowned, a shadow on the wide clear brow. "I find it hard to see why they would make war—why anyone would," she murmured. "Isn't there enough on any planet to content its people? And if by chance they should be unhappy, there are always new worlds."

"Well," shrugged Ganch, "you should know why. You're in the Navy yourself, aren't you, and New Hermes has fought a couple of times."

"Only in self-defense," she said.

"Naturally, we now mount guard on our defeated enemies, even 70 years later, just to be sure they don't try again. As for me, I have a very peaceful desk job in the statistics branch, correlating data."

Ganch felt a thrumming within himself. He could hardly have asked for better luck. Precise information on the armament of New Hermes was just what Dromm lacked. If he could bring it back to old wan Halsker—it would mean a directorship, at least!

And afterward, when a new conquest was to be administered and made over… His ruby eyes studied Chris from beneath drooping lids. A territorial governor had certain perquisites of office.

"I suppose there are many poor twisted people in the universe," went on the girl. "Like those Oberkassel priests, with their weird doctrine they wanted to force on all mankind. It's hard to believe intolerance exists, but alien planets have done strange things to human minds."

There was a veiling in her own violent gaze as she looked at him. She must want to know his own soul, what it was that drove the Great Cadre and why anyone should enjoy having power over other men. He could have told her a great deal—the cruel wintry planet, the generations-long war against the unhuman Ixlatt who made sport of torturing prisoners, then war between factions that split men, war against the red-eyed mutants, whipped-up xenophobia, pogroms, concentration camps...Ganch's grandfather had died in one.

But the mutation was more than an accidental mark, it was in the nervous system, a steel answer to a pitiless environment. A man of the Great Cadre simply did not know fear on the conscious level. Danger lashed him to alertness, but there was no fright to cloud his thoughts. And, by genetics or merely as the result of persecution, he had a will to power which only death could stop. The Great Cadre had subdued a hundred times their numbers, and made them into brain-channeled tools of the State, simply by being braver and more able in war. And Dromm was not enough, not when each darkness brought a mockery of unconquered stars out overhead.

A philosopher from distant Archbishop, where they went in for imaginative speculation, had visited Dromm a decade ago. His remark still lay in Ganch's mind, and stung: "Unjust treatment is apt to produce paranoia in the victim. Your racc has outlived its oppressors, but not the reflexes they built into your society. You'll never rest till all the universe is enslaved, for your canalized nervous systems make you incapable of regarding anyone else as anything but a dangerous enemy."

The philosopher had not gone home alive, but his words remained; Ganch had tried to forget them, and could not.

Enough! His mind had completed its track in the blink of an eye, and now he remembered that the girl expected an answer. He sipped his cocktail and spoke thoughtfully:

"Yes, these special groups, isolated on their own special planets, have developed in many peculiar ways. New Hermes, for instance, if you will pardon my saying so."

Chris raised level brows. "Of course, this is my home and I'm used to it, Ganch," she replied, "but I fail to see anything which would surprise an outsider very much. We live quietly, for the most part, with a loose parliamentary government to run planetary affairs. The necessities of life are produced free for all by the automatic factories; to avoid the annoyance of regulations, we leave everything else to private enterprise, subject only to the reasonable restrictions of the Conservation Authority and a fair-practices act. We don't need more government than that, because the educational system instills respect for the rights and dignity of others and we have no ambitious public-works projects.

"You might say our whole culture is founded merely on a principle of live and let live."

She stroked her chin, man-fashion. "Of course, we have police and courts. And we discourage a concentration of power, political or economic, but that's only to preserve individual liberty. Our economic system helps; it's hard to build up a gigantic business when one game may wipe it out."

"Now there," said Ganch, "you strike the oddity. This passion for gambling. How does it arise?"

"Oh…I wouldn't call it a passion. It's merely one way of pricing goods and services, just as haggling is on Kwan-Yin, and socialism on Arjay, and supply-demand on Alexander."

"But how did it originate?"

Chris lifted smooth bare shoulders and smiled. "Ask the historians, not me. I suppose our ancestors, reacting from the Caledonian puritanism, were apt to glorify all vices and practice them to excess. Gambling was the only one which didn't taper off as a more balanced society evolved. It came to be a custom. Gradually it superseded the traditional methods of exchange.

"It doesn't make any difference, you see; being honest gambling, it comes out even. Win one, lose one…that's almost the motto of our folk. To be sure, in games of skill like poker, a good player will come out ahead in the long run; but any society gives an advantage to certain talents. On Alexander, most of the money and prestige flow to the successful entrepreneur. On Einstein, the scientists are the rich and honored leaders. On Hellas, it's male prowess and female beauty. On Arjay, it's the political spellbinder. On Dromm, I suppose, the soldier is on top. With us, it's the shrewd gambler.

"The important thing," she finished gravely, "is not who gets the most, but whether everyone gets enough."

"But that is what makes me wonder," said Ganch. "This trader we saw today, for instance. Suppose he loses everything?"

"It would be a blow, of course. But he wouldn't starve, because the necessities are free anyway; and he'll have enough sense—he'll have learned in the primaries—to keep a small emergency reserve to start over with. We have very few paupers."

"Your financial structure must be most complicated."

"It is," she said wryly. "We've had to develop a tremendous theoretical science and a great number of highly trained men to handle it. That game today was childish compared with what goes on in, say, the securities exchange. I don't pretend to understand what happens there. I'm content to turn a wheel for my monthly pay, and if I win to go out and see if I can't make a little more."

"And you *enjoy* this—insecurity?"

"Why, yes. As I imagine you enjoy war, and an engineer enjoys building a spaceship, and—" Chris looked at the table. "It's always hard and risky settling a new planet, even one as Earth-like as ours. Our ancestors got a taste for excitement. When there was no more to be had in subduing nature, they transferred the desire to—Ah, here come the *hors d'oeuvres*."

Ganch ate a stately succession of courses with pleasure. He was not good at small talk, but Chris made such eager conversation that it was simple to lead her:

the details of her life and work, little insignificant items but they clicked together. By the coffee and liqueur, Ganch knew where the military microfiles of New Hermes were kept and was fairly sure he knew how to get at them.

Afterward they danced. Ganch had never done it before, but his natural coordination soon fitted him into the rhythm. There was a curious bittersweet savor to holding the girl in his arms...dearest enemy. He wondered if he should try to make love to her. An infatuated female officer would be useful—

No. In such matters, she was the sophisticate and he the bumbling yokel. Coldly, though not without, regret, he dismissed the idea.

They sat at a poker table for a while, where the management put up chips to the value of their bill. Ganch was completely outclassed; he learned the game readily enough, but his excellent analytical mind simply could not match the Hermesians. It was almost as if they knew what cards he held. He lost heavily, but Chris made up for it and when they quit they only had to pay half what they owed.

They hired an aircar, and for a while its gravity drive lifted them noiselessly into a night-blue sky, under a flooding moon and a myriad stars and the great milky sprawl of the Galaxy. Beneath them, a broken bridge of moonlight shuddered across the darkened sea, and they heard the far, faint crying of birds.

When he let Chris off at her apartment, Ganch wanted to stay. It was a wrenching to say goodnight and turn back to his own hotel. He stamped out the wish with a bleak will and bent his mind elsewhere. There was work to do.

Dromm was nothing if not thorough. Her agents had been on New Hermes for ten years now, mostly posing as natives of unsuspicious planets like Guise and Anubis. Enough had been learned to earmark this world for conquest after Thanit, and to layout the basic military campaign.

The Hermesians were not really naive. They had their own spies and counterspies. Customs inspection was careful. But each Dromman visitor had brought a few plausible objects with him—a personal teleset, a depilator, a sample of small nuclear-powered tools for sale—nothing to cause remark; and those objects had stayed behind, in care of a supposed immigrant from Kwan-Yin who lived in Arkinshaw. This man had refashioned them into as efficient a set of machinery for breaking and entering as existed anywhere in the known Galaxy.

Ganch was quite sure Wayland had a tail on him. It was an elementary precaution. But a Field Intelligence officer of Dromm had ways to shake a tail off without its appearing more than accidental. Ganch went out the following afternoon, having notified Wayland that he did not need a guide: he only wanted to stroll around and look at things for himself. After wandering a bit, he went into a pleasure house. It was a holiday, Discovery Day, and Arkinshaw swarmed with a merry crowd; in the jam-packed house, Ganch slipped quietly into a washroom cubicle.

His shadows would most likely watch all exits; and they wouldn't be surprised if he stayed inside for many hours. The hetaerae of New Hermes were famous.

Alone, Ganch slipped out of his uniform and stuffed it down the rubbish disintegrator. Beneath it he wore the loose blue coat and trousers of a Kwan-Yin colonist. A life-mask over his head, a complete alteration of posture and gait…it was another man who stepped into the hall and sauntered out the main door as if his amusements were completed. He went quite openly to Fraybiner's house; what was more natural than that some home-planet relative of Tao Chung should pay a call?

When they were alone, Fraybiner let out a long breath. "By the Principle, it's good to be with a man again!" he said. "If you knew how sick I am of these chattering decadents—"

"Enough!" snapped Ganch. "I am here on business. Operation Lift."

Fraybiner's surgically slanted and darkened eyes widened. "So it's finally coming off?" he murmured. "I was beginning to wonder."

"If I get away with it," said Ganch grimly. "Even if I don't, it doesn't matter. Exact knowledge of the enemy's strength will be valuable, but we have enough information already to launch the war."

Fraybiner began operating concealed studs. A false wall slid aside to reveal a large safe, on which he got to work. "How will you take it home?" he asked. "When they find their files looted, they won't let anyone leave the planet without a thorough search."

Ganch didn't reply; Fraybiner had no business knowing. Actually, the files were going to be destroyed, once read, and their contents go home in Ganch's eidetic memory. But that versatile ethnographer did not plan to leave for some weeks yet: no use causing unnecessary suspicion. When he finally did—a surprise attack on all the Hermesian bases would immobilize them at one swoop.

He smiled to himself. Even knowing they were to be attacked, their whole planet fully alerted, the Hermesians were finished. It was well-established that their fleet had less than half the strength of Dromm's, and not a single Supernova-class dreadnaught. Ganch's information would be extremely helpful, but it was by no means vital.

Except, of course, to Ganch Z-17837-JX-39. But death was a threat he treated with the contempt it deserved.

Fraybiner had gotten the safe open, and a dull metal gleam of instruments and weapons lay before their gaze. Ganch inspected each item carefully while the other jittered with impatience. Finally he donned the flying combat armor and hung the implements at its belt. By that time, the sun was down and the stars out.

Chris had said the Naval HQ building was deserted at night except for its guards. Previous spies had learned where these were posted. "Very well," said Ganch. "I'm on my way. I won't see you again, and advise you to move elsewhere soon. If the natives turn out to be stubborn, we'll have to destroy this city."

Fraybiner nodded, and activated the ceiling door. Ganch went up on his gravity beams and out into the sky. The city was a jeweled spiderweb beneath him, and fireworks burst with great soft explosions of color. His outfit was a nonreflecting dull black, and there was only a whisper of air to betray his flight.

The HQ building, broad and low, rested on a greensward several kilometers from Arkinshaw. Ganch approached its slumbering dark mass, carefully, taking his time. A bare meter's advance, an instrument reading…yes, they had a radio-alarm field set up. He neutralized it with his heterodyning unit, flew another cautious meter, stopped to readjust the neutralization. The moon was down, but he wished the stars weren't so bright.

It was past midnight when he lay in the shrubbery surrounding a rear entrance. A pair of sentries, armed and helmeted, tramped almost by his nose, crossing paths in front of the door. He waited, learning the pattern of their march.

When his tactics were fully planned, he rose as one marine came by and let the fellow have a sonic stun-beam. Too low-powered to trip an alarm, it was close-range and to the base of the neck. Ganch caught the body as it fell, let it down, and picked up the same measured tread.

He felt no conscious tension as he neared the other man, though a sharp glance through darkness would end the ruse, but his muscles gathered themselves. He was almost abreast of the Hermesian when he saw the figure recoil in alarm. His stunner went off again. It was a bad shot; the sentry lurched but retained a wavering consciousness. Ganch sprang on him, one tigerish bound, a squeezed trigger, and he lowered the marine as gently as a woman might her lover.

For a moment he stood looking down on the slack face. A youngster, hardly out of his teens, there was something strangely innocent about him as he slept. About this whole world. They were too kind here, they didn't belong in a universe of wolves.

He had no doubt they would fight bravely and skillfully. Dromm would have to pay for her conquest. But the age of heroes was past. War was not an art, it was a science, and a set of giant computers coldly chewing an involved symbolism told ships and men what to do. Given equal courage and equally intelligent leadership, it was merely a heartless arithmetic that the numerically superior fleet would win.

No time to lose! He spun on his heel and crouched over the door. His instruments traced out its circuits, a diamond drill bit into plastic, a wire shorted a current…the door opened for him and he went into a hollow darkness of corridors.

Lightly, even in the clumsy armor, he made his way toward the main file room. Once he stopped, his instruments sensed a black-light barrier and it took him a quarter of an hour to neutralize it. But then he was in among the cabinets.

They were not locked, and his thin flash beam picked out the categories held in each drawer. Swiftly, then, he took the spools relating to ships, bases, armament, disposition…he ignored the codes, which would be changed anyway when the burglary was discovered. The entire set went into one small pouch such as the men of Kwan-Yin carried, and he had a microreader at the hotel.

The lights went on.

Before his eyes had adjusted to that sudden blaze, before he was consciously aware of action, Ganch's drilled reflexes had gone to work. His faceplate clashed down, gauntlets snapped shut around his hands, and a Mark IV blaster was at his shoulder even as he whirled to meet the intruders.

There were a score of them, and their gay holiday attire was somehow nightmarish behind the weapons they carried. Wayland was in the lead, harshness on his face, and Christabel at his back. The rest Ganch did not recognize, they must be naval officers but—He crouched, covering them, a robot figure cased in a centimeter of imperviousness.

"So." Wayland spoke it quietly, a flat tone across the enormous silence. "I wondered—Ganch, I suppose."

The Dromman did not answer.

There was a thin fine singing as his helmet absorbed the stun beam Chris was aiming at it.

"When my men reported you had been ten hours in the joyhouse, I thought it best to check up: first your quarters and then—" Wayland paused. "I didn't think you'd penetrate this far. But it could only be you, Ganch, so you may as well surrender."

The spy shook his head, futile gesture inside that metal box he wore. "No. It is you who are trapped," he answered steadily. "I can blast you all before your beams work through my armor…Don't move!"

"You wouldn't escape," said Wayland. "The fight would trip alarms bringing the whole Fort Canfield garrison down on you." Sweat beaded his forehead. Perhaps he thought of his niece and the gun which could make her a blackened husk; but his own small-bore flamer held firm.

"This means war," said Chris. "We've wondered about Dromm for a long time. Now we know." Tears glimmered in her eyes. "And it's so senseless!"

Ganch laughed without much humor. "Impasse," he said. "I can kill all of you, but that would bring my own death. Be sure, though, that the failure of my mission will make little difference."

Wayland stood brooding for a while. "You're congenitally unafraid to die," he said at last. "The rest of us prefer to live, but will die if we must. So any decision must be made with a view to planetary advantage."

Ganch's heart sprang within his ribs. He had lost, unless—

He still had an even chance.

"You're a race of gamblers," he said. "Will you gamble now?"

"Not with our planet," said Chris.

"Let me finish! I propose we toss a coin, shake dice, whatever you like that distributes the probabilities evenly. If I win, I go free with what I've taken here—you furnish me safe-conduct and transportation home. You'll still have the knowledge that Dromm is going to attack, and some time to prepare. If you win, I surrender and cooperate with you. I have valuable information, and you can drug me to make sure I don't lie."

"No!" shouted one of the officers.

"Wait. Let me think…I have to make an estimate." Wayland lowered his gun and stood with half-shut eyes. He looked as he had down in the traders' hall, and Ganch, remembered uneasily that Wayland was a gambling analyst.

But there was little to lose. If he won, he went home with his booty; if he lost—he knew how to will his heart to stop beating.

Wayland looked up. There was a fever-gleam in his eyes. "Yes," he said.

The others did not question him. They must be used to following a Tipster's advice blindly. But one of them asked how Ganch could be trusted. "I'll lay down my blaster when you produce the selection device," said the Dromman. "All the worlds know you do not cheat."

Chris reached into her pouched belt and drew out a deck of cards. Wordlessly, she shuffled them and gave them to her uncle. The spy put his gun on the floor. He half expected the others to rush him, but they stood where they were.

Wayland's hands shook as he cut the deck. He smiled crookedly. "One-eyed jack," he whispered. "Hard to beat."

He shuffled the cards again and held them out to Ganch. The armored fingers were clumsy, but they opened the deck.

It was the king of spades.

Stars blazed in a raw naked blackness. The engines which had eaten light-years were pulsing now on primary drive, gravities, accelerating toward the red sun which lay three astronomical units ahead.

Ganch thought that the space distortions of the drive beams were lighting the fleet up like a nova for the Hermesian detectors. But you couldn't fight a battle at trans-light speeds, and their present objective was to seek the enemy out and destroy him.

Overcommandant wan Halsker peered into the viewscreens of the dreadnaught. There was something avid in his long gaunt face, but he spoke levelly: "I find it hard to believe. They actually gave you a speedster and let you go."

"I expected treachery myself, sir," answered Ganch deferentially. Despite promotion, he was still only the chief intelligence officer attached to Task Force One. "Surely, with their whole civilization at stake, any rational people would have—But their mores are unique. They always pay their gambling debts."

It was very quiet, down here in the bowels of the Supernova ship. A ring of technicians sat before their instruments, watching the dials unblinkingly. Wan Halsker's eyes never left the simulacrum of space in his screens, though all he saw was stars. There was too much emptiness around to show the 500 ships of his command, spread in careful formation through some billions of cubic kilometers.

A light glowed, and a technician said dully: "Contact made. *Turolin* engaging estimated five Meteor-class enemy vessels."

Wan Halsker allowed himself a snort. "Insects! Don't break formation; let the *Turolin* swat them as she proceeds."

Ganch sat waiting, rehearsing in his mind the principles of modern warfare. The gravity drive had radically changed them in the last few centuries. A forward vector could be killed almost instantaneously, a new direction taken as fast, while internal pseudograv fields compensated for accelerations which would otherwise have crumpled a man. A fight in space was not unlike one in air, with this difference: that the velocities used were too high, the distances too great, the units involved too many, for a human brain to grasp. It had to be done by machine.

Subspace quivered with coded messages, the ships' own electronic minds transmitting information back to the prime computers on Dromm—the computers which laid out not only the overall strategy, but the tactics of every major engagement. A man could not follow that esoteric mathematics, he could only obey the monster he had built.

No change of orders came, a few torpedo ships were unimportant, and Task Force One continued.

Astran was a clinker, an airless valueless planet of a waning red dwarf star, but it housed a key base of the Hermesian Navy. With Astran reduced, wan Halsker's command could safely go on to rendezvous with six other fleets that had been taking care of their own assignments; the whole group would then continue to New Hermes herself, and just let the enemy dare try to stop them!

Such, in broad outline, was the plan; but only a hundred computers, each filling a large building, could handle all the details of strategy, tactics, and logistics.

Ganch had an uneasy feeling of being a very small cog in a very large machine. He didn't matter; the commandant didn't; the ship, the fleet, the gray mass of commoners didn't; only the Cadre, and above them the almighty State, had a real existence.

The Hermesians would need a lot of taming before they learned to think that way.

Now fire was exploding out in space, great guns cutting loose as the outnumbered force sought the invaders. Ganch felt a shuddering when the Supernova's own armament spoke. The ship's computer, her brain, flashed and chattered, the enormous vessel leaped on her gravity beams, ducking, dodging, spouting flame and hot metal. Stars spun on the screen in a lunatic dance. Ten thousand men aboard the ship had suddenly become robots feeding her guns.

"Compartment Seven hit...sealed off."

"Hit made on enemy Star-class, damage looks light."

"Number Forty-two gun out of action. Residual radioactivity...compartment sealed off."

Men died, scorched and burned, air sucked from their lungs as the armored walls peeled away, listening to the clack of radiation counters as leaden bulkheads locked them away like lepers. The Supernova trembled with each hit. Ganch heard steel shriek not far away and braced his body for death.

Wan Halsker sat impassively, hands folded on his lap, watching the screens and the dials. There was nothing he could do; the ship fought herself, men were too slow. But he nodded after a while, a dark satisfaction in his eyes.

"We're sustaining damage," he said, "but no more than expected." He stared at a slim small crescent in the screen. "There's the planet. We're working in...we'll be in bombardment range soon."

The ships' individual computers made their decisions on the basis of information received; but they were constantly sending a digest of the facts back to their electronic masters on Dromm. So far no tactical change had been ordered, but—

Ganch frowned at the visual tank which gave a crude approximation of the reality ramping around him. The little red specks were his own ships, the green ones such of the enemy as had been spotted. It seemed to him that too many red lights had stopped twinkling, and that the Hermesian fireflies were driving a wedge into the formation. But there was nothing he could do.

A bell clanged. Change of orders! *Turolin* to withdraw three megakilometers toward Polaris, *Colfin* to swing around toward enemy Constellation Number Four, *Hardes* to—Watching the tank in a hypnotized way, Ganch decided vaguely it must be some attempt at a flanking movement. But there was a Hermesian squadron out there!

Well…

The battle snarled its way across vacuum. It was many hours before the Dromman computers gave up and flashed the command: Break contact, retreat in formation to Neering Base.

They had been outmaneuvered. Incredibly, New Hermes' machines had outthought Dromm's and the battle was lost.

Wayland entered the mapping room with a jaunty step that belied the haggardness in his face. Christabel Hesty looked up from her task of directing the integrators and cried aloud: "Will! I didn't expect you back so soon!"

"I thumbed a ride home with a courier ship," said Wayland. "Three months' leave. By that time the war will be over, so—" He sat down on her desk, swinging his short legs, and got out an old and incredibly foul pipe. "I'm just as glad, to tell the truth. Planetarism is all right in its place, but war's an ugly business."

There was something haunted in his eyes. A Hermesian withstood the military life better than most; he was used not only to moments of nerve-ripping suspense but to long and patient waiting. Wayland, though, had during the past year seen too many ships blown up, too many men dead or screaming with their wounds. His hands shook a little as he tamped the pipe full.

"Luck be praised you're alive!"

"It hasn't been easy on you either, has it? Chained to a desk like this. Here, sit back and take a few minutes off, the war can wait." Wayland kindled his tobacco and blew rich clouds. "But at least it never got close to our home, and our losses have been even lighter than expected."

"If you get occupation duty—"

"I'm afraid I will."

"Well; I want to come too. I've never been off this planet; it's disgraceful."

"Dromm is a pretty dreary place, I warn you. But Thanit is close by, of course—it used to be a gay world, it will be again, and every Hermesian will be Luck incarnate to them. Sure, I'll wangle an assignment for you."

Chris frowned. "Only three months to go, though? It's hard to believe."

"Two and a half is the official estimate. Look here." Wayland stumped over to the three-dimensional sector map, which was there only for the enlightenment of humans. The military computers dealt strictly in lists of numbers.

"See, we whipped them at the Cold Stars, and now a feint of ours is drawing what's left of them into Ransome's Nebula."

"Ransome's—oh, you mean the Queen of Clubs? Mmm-hm. And what's going to happen to them there?"

"Tch, tch. Official secrets, my dear inquisitive nieceling. But just imagine what *could* happen to a fleet concentrated in a mess of nebular dust that blocks their detectors!"

Wayland did not see Ganch again until he was stationed on Dromm. There he grumbled long and loudly about the climate, the food, and the tedious necessity of making sure that a subjugated enemy stayed subjugated. He looked forward to his next furlough on Thanit, and still more to rotation home in six months. Chris, being younger, enjoyed herself. They had no mountains on New Hermes, and she was going to climb Hell's Peak with Commander Gallery. About half a dozen other young officers would be jealously present, so her uncle felt she would be adequately chaperoned.

They were working together in the political office, interviewing Cadre men and disposing of their cases. Wayland was not sympathetic toward the prisoners. But when Ganch was led in, he felt a certain kinship and even smiled.

"Sit down," he invited. "Take it easy. I don't bite."

Ganch slumped into a chair before the desk and looked at the floor. He seemed as shattered as the rest of his class. *They weren't really tough,* thought Wayland; *they couldn't stand defeat, most of them suicided rather than undergo psychorevision.*

"Didn't expect to see you again," he said. "I understood you were on combat duty, and—um—"

"I know," said Ganch lifelessly. "Our combat units averaged ninety per cent casualties, toward the end." In a rush of bitterness: "I wish I had been one of them."

"Take it easy," repeated Wayland. "We Hermesians aren't vindictive. Your planet will never have armed forces again—it'll join Corrid and Oberkassel as a protectorate of ours—but once we've straightened you out you'll be free to live as you please."

"Free!" mumbled Ganch.

He lifted tortured red eyes to the face before him, but shifted from its wintry smile to Chris. She had some warmth for him, at least.

"How did you do it?" he whispered. "I still don't understand. I thought you must have some new kind of computer, but our intelligence swore you didn't… and we outnumbered you, and there was all that information you let me take home, and—"

"We're gamblers," said the girl soberly.

"Yes, but—"

"Look at it this way," she went on. "War is a science, based on a complex paramathematical theory. All maneuvers and engagements are ordered with a view to gaining the maximum advantage for one's own side, in the light of known information. But of course, *all* the information is never available, so intelligent guesswork has to fill in the gaps.

"Well, a system exists for making such guesses and for deciding what move has the maximum probability of success. It applies to games, business, war—all competitive enterprises. It's called games theory."

"I—" Ganch's jaw dropped. He snapped it shut again and said desperately: "But that's elementary! It's been known for centuries."

"Of course," nodded Chris. "But New Hermes has based her whole economy on gambling—on probabilities, on games of skill where no player has all the information. Don't you see, it would make our entire intellectual interest turn toward games theory. And in fact we had to have a higher development of such knowledge, and a large class of men skilled in using it, or we could not maintain as complex a civilization as we do.

"No other planet has a comparable body of knowledge. And, while we haven't kept it secret, no other planet has men able to use that knowledge on its highest levels.

"Just take that night we caught you in the file room. If we cut cards with you, there was a fifty-fifty chance you'd go free. Will here had to estimate whether the overall probabilities justified the gamble. Because he decided they did, we three are alive today."

"But I *did* bring that material home!" cried Ganch.

"Yes," said the girl. "And the fact you had it was merely another item for our strategic computers to take into account. Indeed, it helped us: it was definite information about what you knew, and your actions became all the more predictable."

Laughter, gentle and unmocking, lay in her throat. "Never draw to an inside straight," she said. "And never play with a man who knows enough not to, when you don't."

Ganch sagged further down in his chair. He felt sick. He went through Wayland's questioning in a mechanical fashion, and heard sentence pronounced, and left under guard...

As he stumbled out, he heard Wayland say thoughtfully: "Three gets you four he suicides rather than take psychorevision."

"You're covered!" said Christabel.

LODESTAR

Lightning reached. David Falkayn heard the crack of torn air and gulped a rainy reek of ozone. His cheek stung from the near miss. In his eyes, spots of blue-white dazzle danced across night.

"Get aboard, you two," Adzel said. "I'll hold them." Crouched, Falkayn peered after a target for his own blaster. He saw shadows move beneath strange constellations—that, and flames which tinged upward-roiling smoke on the far side of the spacefield, where the League outpost was burning. Shrieks resounded. "No, you start," he rasped. "I'm armed, you're not."

The Wodenite's bass remained steady but an earthquake rumble entered it. "No more death. A single death would have been too much, of folk outraged in their own homes. David, Chee: *go.*"

Half-dragon, half-centaur, four and a half meters from snout to tailtip, he moved toward the unseen natives. Firelight framed the hedge of bony plates along his back, glimmered off scales and belly-scutes.

Chee Lan tugged at Falkayn's trousers. "Come on," she spat. "No stopping that hairy-brain when he wambles off on an idealism binge. He won't board before us, and they'll kill him if we don't move fast." A sneer: "I'll lead the way, if that'll make you feel more heroic."

Her small, white-furred form shot from the hauler behind which they had taken refuge. (No use trying to get that machine aloft. The primitives had planned their attack shrewdly, must have hoarded stolen explosives as well as guns for years, till they could demolish everything round the base at the same moment as they fell upon the headquarters complex.) Its mask-markings obscured her blunt-muzzled face in the shuddering red light; but her bottled-up tail stood all too clear.

A Tamethan saw. On long thin legs, beak agape in a war-yell, he sped to catch her. His weapon was merely a spear. Sick-hearted, Falkayn took aim. Then Chee darted between those legs, tumbled the autochthon on his tochis and bounded onward.

Hurry! Falkayn told himself. Battle ramped around Adzel. The Wodenite could take a certain number of slugs and blaster bolts without permanent damage, he knew, but not many…and those mighty arms were pulling their punches. Keeping to shadow as well as might be, the human followed Chee Lan.

Their ship loomed ahead, invulnerable to the attackers. Her gangway was descending. So the Cynthlan had entered audio range, had called an order to the main computer...*Why didn't we tell Muddlehead to use initiative in case of trouble?* groaned Falkayn's mind. *Why didn't we at least carry radios to call for its help? Are we due for retirement? A sloppy trade pioneer is a dead trade pioneer.*

A turret gun flashed and boomed. Chee must have ordered that. It was a warning shot, sent skyward, but terrifying. The man gusted relief. His rangy body sped upramp, stopped at the open airlock, and turned to peer back. Combat seemed to have frozen. And, yes, here Adzel came, limping, trailing blood, but alive. Falkayn wanted to hug his old friend and weep.

No. First we haul mass out of here. He entered the ship. Adzel's hoofs boomed on the gangway. It retracted, the airlock closed, gravity drive purred, and *Muddlin' Through* ascended to heaven.

Gathered on the bridge, her crew stared at a downward-viewing screen. The fires had become sparks, the spacefield a scar, in an illimitable night. Far off a river cut through jungle, shining by starlight like a drawn sword.

Falkayn ran fingers through his sandy hair. "We, uh, well, do you think we can rescue any survivors?" he asked.

"I doubt there are any by now," Adzel said. "We barely escaped because we have learned, over years, to meet emergencies as a team."

"And if there are," Chee added, "who cares?" Adzel looked reproof at her. She bristled her whiskers. "We saw how those slimesouls were treating the aborigines."

"I feel sure much of the offense was caused simply by ignorance of basic psychology and mores."

"That's no excuse, as you flapping well know. They should've taken the trouble to learn such things. But no, the companies couldn't wait for that. They sent their bespattered factors and field agents right in, who promptly set up a little dunghill of an empire—*Ya-pu-yeh!*" In Chee's home language that was a shocking obscenity, even for her.

Falkayn's shoulders slumped. "I'm inclined to agree," he said. "Besides, we mustn't take risks. We've got to make a report."

"Why?" Adzel asked. "Our own employer was not involved."

"No, thanks be. I'd hate to feel I must quit...This is League business, however. The mutual-assistance rule—"

"And so League warcraft come and bomb some poor little villages?" Adzel's tail drummed on the deck.

"With our testimony, we can hope not. The Council verdict ought to be, those klongs fell flat on their own deeds." Falkayn sighed. "I wish we'd been around here longer, making a regular investigation, instead of just chancing by and deciding to take a few days off on a pleasant planet." He straightened. "Well. To space, Muddlehead, and to—m-m-m, nearest major League base—Irumclaw."

"And you come along to sickbay and let me dress those wounds, you overgrown bulligator," Chee snapped at the Wodenite, "before you've utterly ruined this carpet, drooling blood on it."

Falkayn himself sought a washroom, a change of clothes, his pipe and tobacco, a stiff drink. Continuing to the saloon, he settled down and tried to ease away his trouble. In a viewscreen, the world dwindled which men had named Tametha—arbitrarily, from a native word in a single locality, which they'd doubtless gotten wrong anyway. Already it had shrunk in his vision to a ball, swirled blue and white: a body as big and fair as ever Earth was, four or five billion years in the making, uncounted swarms of unknown life forms, sentiences and civilizations, histories and mysteries, become a marble in a game…or a set of entries in a set of data banks, for profit or loss, in a few cities a hundred or more light-years remote.

He thought: *This isn't the first time I've seen undying wrong done. Is it really happening oftener and oftener, or am I just getting more aware of it as I age? At thirty-three, I begin to feel old.*

Chee entered, jumped onto the seat beside him, and reported Adzel was resting. "You do need that drink, don't you?" she observed. Falkayn made no reply. She inserted a mildly narcotic cigarette in an interminable ivory holder and puffed it to ignition.

"Yes," she said, "I get irritated likewise, no end, whenever something like this befouls creation."

"I'm coming to think the matter is worse, more fundamental, than a collection of episodes." Falkayn spoke wearily. "The Polesotechnic League began as a mutual-benefit association of companies, true; but the idea was also to keep competition within decent bounds. That's breaking down, that second aspect. How long till the first does too?"

"What would you prefer to free enterprise? The Terran Empire, maybe?"

"Well, you being a pure carnivore, and coming besides from a trading culture that was quick to modernize—exploitation doesn't touch you straight on the nerves, Chee. But Adzel—he doesn't say much, you know him but I've become certain it's a bitterness to him, more and more as time slides by, that nobody will help his people advance…because they haven't anything that anybody wants enough to pay the price of advancement. And—well, I hardly dare guess how many others. Entire worldsful of beings who look at yonder stars till it aches in them, and know that except for a few lucky individuals none of them will ever get out there, nor will their descendants have any real say about the future, no, will instead remain nothing but potential victims—"

Seeking distraction, Falkayn raised screen magnification and swept the scanner around jewel-blazing blackness. When he stopped for another pull at his glass, the view happened to include the enigmatic glow of the Crab Nebula.

"Take that sentimentalism and stuff it back where it came from," Chee suggested. "The new-discovered species will simply have to accumulate capital. Yours did. Mine did soon after. We can't give a free ride to the whole universe."

"N-no. Yet you know yourself—be honest—how quick somebody already established would be to take away that bit of capital, whether by market manipulations or by thinly disguised piracy. Tametha's a minor example. All that those tribesbeings wanted was to trade directly with Over-the-Mountains." Falkayn's fist clamped hard around his pipe. "I tell you, lass, the heart is going out of the

League, in the sense of ordinary compassion and helpfulness. How long till the heart goes out in the sense of its own survivability? Civilization *needs* more than the few monopolists we've got."

The Cynthian twitched her ears, quite slowly, and exhaled smoke whose sweetness blent with the acridity of the man's tobacco. Her eyes glowed through it, emerald-hard. "I sort of agree. At least, I'd enjoy listening to the hot air hiss out of certain bellies. How though Davy? How?"

"Old Nick—he's a single member of the Council, I realize—"

"Our dear employer keeps his hirelings fairly moral, but strictly on the principle of running a taut ship. He told me that himself once, and added, 'Never mind what the ship is taught, ho, ho, ho!' No, you won't make an idealist of Nicholas van Rijn. Not without transmuting every atom in his fat body."

Falkayn let out a tired chuckle. "A new isotope. Van Rijn-235, no, likelier Vr-235,000—"

And then his glance passed over the Nebula, and as if it had spoken to him across more than a thousand parsecs, he fell silent and grew tense where he sat.

This happened shortly after the Satan episode, when the owner of Solar Spice & Liquors had found it needful once more to leave the comforts of the Commonwealth, risk his thick neck on a cheerless world, and finally make a month-long voyage in a ship which had run out of beer. Returned home, he swore by all that was holy and much that was not: Never again!

Nor, for most of the following decade, had he any reason to break his vow. His business was burgeoning, thanks to excellently chosen personnel in established trade sites and to pioneers like the *Muddlin' Through* team who kept finding him profitable new lands. Besides, he had maneuvered himself into the overlordship of Satan. A sunless wandering planet, newly thawed out by a brush with a giant star, made a near-ideal site for the manufacture of odd isotopes on a scale commensurate with present-day demand. Such industry wasn't his cup of tea "or," he declared, "my glass Genever that molasses-on-Pluto-footed butler is supposed to bring me before I crumble away from thirst." Therefore van Rijn granted franchises, on terms calculated to be an ångstrom short of impossibly extortionate.

Many persons wondered, often in colorful language, why he didn't retire and drink himself into a grave they would be glad to provide, outsize though it must be. When van Rijn heard about these remarks, he would grin and look still harder for a price he could jack up or a competitor he could undercut. Nevertheless, compared to earlier years, this was for him a leisured period. When at last word got around that he meant to take Coya Conyon, his favorite granddaughter, on an extended cruise aboard his yacht—and not a single mistress along for him—hope grew that he was slowing down to a halt.

I can't say I like most of those money-machine merchant princes, Coya reflected, several weeks after leaving Earth; *but I really wouldn't want to give them heart attacks by telling them we're now on a nonhuman vessel, equipped in curious ways but unmistakably battle-ready, bound into a region that nobody is known to have explored.*

She stood before a viewport set in a corridor. A ship built by men would not have carried that extravagance; but to Ythrians, sky dwellers, ample outlook is a necessity of sanity. The air she breathed was a little thinner than at Terrestrial sea level; odors included the slight smokiness of their bodies. A ventilator murmured not only with draft but with a barely heard rustle, the distance-muffled sound of wingbeats from crewfolk off duty cavorting in an enormous hold intended for it. At 0.75 standard weight she still—after this long a trip—felt exhilaratingly light.

She was not presently conscious of that. At first she had reveled in adventure. Everything was an excitement; every day offered a million discoveries to be made. She didn't mind being the sole human aboard besides her grandfather. He was fun in his bearish fashion: had been as far back as she could remember, when he would roll roaring into her parents' home, toss her to the ceiling, half-bury her under presents from a score of planets, tell her extravagant stories and take her out on a sailboat or to a live performance or, later on, around most of the Solar System…Anyhow, to make Ythrian friends, to discover a little of how their psyches worked and how one differed from another, to trade music, memories, and myths, watch their aerial dances and show them some ballet, that was an exploration in itself.

Today, however—They were apparently nearing the goal for which they had been running in a search helix, whatever it was. Van Rijn remained boisterous; but he would tell her nothing. Nor did the Ythrians know what was sought, except for Hirharouk, and he had passed on no other information than that all were to hold themselves prepared for emergencies cosmic or warlike. A species whose ancestors had lived like eagles could take this more easily than men. Even so, tension had mounted till she could smell it.

Her gaze sought outward. As an astrophysicist and a fairly frequent tourist, she had spent a total of years in space during the twenty-five she had been in the universe. She could identify the brightest individual stars amidst that radiant swarm, lacy and lethal loveliness of shining nebulae, argent torrent of Milky Way, remote glimmer of sister galaxies. And still size and silence, unknownness and unknowability, struck against her as much as when she first fared forth.

Secrets eternal…why, of course. They had run at a good pseudovelocity for close to a month, starting at Ythri's sun (which lies 278 light-years from Sol in the direction of Lupus) and aiming at the Deneb sector. That put them, oh, say a hundred parsecs from Earth. Glib calculation. Yet they had reached parts which no record said anyone had ever done more than pass through, in all the centuries since men got a hyperdrive. The planetary systems here had not been catalogued, let alone visited, let alone understood. Space is that big, that full of worlds.

Coya shivered, though the air was warm enough. *You're yonder somewhere, David,* she thought, *if you haven't met the inevitable final surprise. Have you gotten my message? Did it have any meaning to you?*

She could do nothing except give her letter to another trade pioneer whom she trusted. He was bound for the same general region as Falkayn had said *Muddlin' Through* would next go questing in. The crews maintained rendezvous stations. In one such turbulent place he might get news of Falkayn's team. Or he could deposit the letter there to be called for.

Guilt nagged her, as it had throughout this journey. A betrayal of her grandfather—No! Fresh anger flared. *If he's not brewing something bad, what possible harm can it do him that David knows what little I knew before we left—which is scarcely more than the old devil has let me know to this hour?*

And he did speak of hazards. I did have to force him into taking me along (because the matter seemed to concern you, David, oh, David). If we meet trouble, and suddenly you arrive—

Stop romancing, Coya told herself. *You're a grown girl now.* She found she could control her thoughts, somewhat, but not the tingle through her blood.

She stood tall, slender almost to boyishness, clad in plain black tunic, slacks, and sandals. Straight dark hair, shoulder-length, framed an oval face with a snub nose, mouth a trifle too wide but eyes remarkably big and gold-flecked green. Her skin was very white. It was rather freakish how genes had recombined to forget nearly every trace of her ancestry—van Rijn's Dutch and Malay; the Mexican and Chinese of a woman who bore him a girlchild and with whom he had remained on the same amicable terms afterward as, somehow, he did with most former loves; the Scots (from Hermes, David's home planet) plus a dash of African (via a planet called Nyanza) in that Malcolm Conyon who settled down on Earth and married Beatriz Yeo.

Restless, Coya's mind skimmed over the fact. Her lips could not help quirking. *In short, I'm a typical modern human.* The amusement died. *Yes, also in my life. My grandfather's generation seldom bothered to get married. My father's did. And mine, why, we're reviving patrilineal surnames.*

A whistle snapped off her thinking. Her heart lurched until she identified the signal. "All hands alert."

That meant something had been detected. Maybe not the goal; maybe just a potential hazard, like a meteoroid swarm. In uncharted space, you traveled warily, and van Rijn kept a candle lit before his little Martian sandroot statuette of St. Dismas.

A moment longer, Coya confronted the death and glory beyond the ship. Then, fists knotted, she strode aft. She was her grandfather's granddaughter.

"Lucifer and leprosy!" bellowed Nicholas van Rijn. "You have maybe spotted what we maybe are after, at extreme range of your instruments tuned sensitive like an artist what specializes in painting pansies, a thing we cannot reach in enough hours to eat three good rijstaffels, and you have the bladder to tell me I got to armor me and stand around crisp saying, 'Aye-yi-yi, sir'?" Sprawled in a lounger, he waved a two-liter tankard of beer he clutched in his hairy left paw. The right held a churchwarden pipe, which had filled his stateroom with blue reek.

Hirharouk of the Wryfields Choth, captain of the chartered ranger *Gaiian* (=*Dewfall*), gave him look for look. The Ythrian's eyes were large and golden, the man's small and black and crowding his great hook nose; neither pair gave way, and Hirharouk's answer held an iron quietness: "No. I propose that you stop guzzling alcohol. You do have drugs to induce sobriety, but they may show side effects when quick decision is needed."

While his Anglic was fluent, he used a vocalizer to convert the sounds he could make into clearly human tones. The Ythrian voice is beautifully ringing but less flexible than man's. Was it to gibe or be friendly that van Rijn responded in pretty fair Planha? "Be not perturbed. I am hardened, which is why my vices cost me a fortune. Moreover, a body my size has corresponding capacity." He slapped the paunch beneath his snuff-stained blouse and gaudy sarong. The rest of him was huge in proportion. "This is my way of resting in advance of trouble, even as you would soar aloft and contemplate."

Hirharouk eased and fluted his equivalent of a laugh. "As you wish. I daresay you would not have survived to this date, all the sworn foes you must have, did you not know what you do."

Van Rijn tossed back his sloping brow. Long swarthy ringlets in the style of his youth, except for their greasiness, swirled around the jewels in his earlobes; his chins quivered beneath waxed mustaches and goatee; a bare splay foot smote the densely carpeted deck. "You mistake me," he boomed, reverting to his private version of Anglic. "You cut me to the quiche. Do you suppose I, poor old lonely sinner, *ja,* but still a Christian man with a soul full of hope, do you suppose *I* ever went after anything but peace—as many peaces as I could get? No, no, what I did, I was pushed into, self-defense against sons of mothers, greedy rascals who I may forgive though God cannot, who begrudge me what tiny profit I need so I not become a charge on a state that is only good for grinding up taxpayers any-way. Me, I am like gentle St. Francis, I go around ripping off olive branches and covering stormy seas with oil slicks and watering troubled fish."

He stuck his tankard under a spout at his elbow for a refill. Hirharouk observed him. And Coya, entering the disordered luxury of the stateroom, paused to regard them both.

She was fond of van Rijn. Her doubts about this expedition, the message she had felt she must try to send to David Falkayn, had been a sharp blade in her. Nonetheless she admitted the Ythrian was infinitely more sightly. Handsomer than her too, she felt, or David himself. That was especially true in flight; yet, slow and awkward though they were aground, the Ythrians remained magnificent to see, and not only because of the born hunter's inborn pride.

Hirharouk stood some 150 centimeters tall. What he stood on was his wings, which spanned five and a half meters when unfolded. Turned downward, they spread claws at the angle which made a kind of foot; the backward-sweeping alatan surface could be used for extra support. What had been legs and talons, geological epochs ago, were arms and three-fingered two-thumbed hands. The skin on those was amber-colored. The rest of him wore shimmering bronze feath-ers, save where these became black-edged white on crest and on fan-shared tail. His body looked avian, stiff behind its jutting keelbone. But he was no bird. He had not been hatched. His head, raised on a powerful neck, had no beak: rather, a streamlined muzzle, nostrils at the tip, below them a mouth whose lips seemed oddly delicate against the keen fangs.

And the splendor of these people goes beyond the sunlight on them when they ride the wind, Coya thought. *David frets about the races that aren't getting a chance. Well, Ythri was primitive when the Grand Survey found it. The Ythrians studied Technic civilization, and neither licked its boots nor let it overwhelm them, but took what they wanted from it and made themselves a power in our corner of the galaxy. True, this was before that civilization was itself overwhelmed by* laissez-faire *capitalism—*

She blinked. Unlike her, the merchant kept his quarters at Earth-standard illumination; and Quetlan is yellower than Sol. He was used to abrupt transitions. She coughed in the tobacco haze. The two males grew aware of her.

"Ah, my sweet bellybird," van Rijn greeted, a habit he had not shaken from the days of her babyhood. "Come in. Flop yourself." A gesture of his pipe gave a choice of an extra lounger, a desk chair, an emperor-size bed, a sofa between the liquor cabinet and the bookshelf, or the deck. "What you want? Beer, gin, whisky, cognac, vodka, arrack, akvavit, half-dozen kinds wine and liqueur, ansa, totipot, slumthunder, maryjane, ops, galt, Xanadu radium, or maybe—" he winced "—a soft drink? A soft, flabby drink?"

"Coffee will do, thanks." Coya drew breath and courage. "*Gunung Tuan,* I've got to talk with you."

"*Ja,* I outspected you would. Why I not told you more before is because—oh, I wanted you should enjoy your trip, not brood like a hummingbird on ostrich eggs."

Coya was unsure whether Hirharouk spoke in tact or truth: "Freeman van Rijn, I came to discuss our situation. Now I return to the bridge. For honor and life…*khr-r-r,* I mean please…hold ready for planlaying as information lengthens." He lifted an arm. "Free lady Conyon, hail and fare you well."

He walked from them. When he entered the bare corridor, his claws clicked. He stopped and did a handstand. His wings spread as wide as possible in that space, preventing the door from closing till he was gone, exposing and opening the gill-like slits below them. He worked the wings, forcing those antlibranchs to operate like bellows. They were part of the "supercharger" system which enabled a creature his size to fly under basically terrestroid conditions. Coya did not know whether he was oxygenating his bloodstream to energize himself for command, or was flushing out human stench.

He departed. She stood alone before her grandfather.

"Do sit, sprawl, hunker, or how you can best relax," the man urged. "I would soon have asked you should come. Time is to make a clean breast, except mine is too shaggy and you do not take off your tunic." His sigh turned into a belch. "A shame. Customs has changed. Not that I would lech in your case, no, I got incest repellent. But the sight is nice."

She reddened and signalled the coffeemaker. Van Rijn clicked his tongue. "And you don't smoke neither," he said. "Ah, they don't put the kind of stuff in youngsters like when I was your age."

"A few of us try to exercise some forethought as well as our consciences," Coya snapped. After a pause: "I'm sorry. Didn't mean to sound self-righteous."

"But you did. I wonder, has David Falkayn influenced you that way, or you him?—Ho-ho, a spectroscope would think your face was receding at speed of light!" Van Rijn wagged his pipestem. "Be careful. He's a good boy, him, except he's not a boy no more. Could well be, without knowing it, he got somewhere a daughter old as you."

"We're friends," Coya said half-furiously. She sat down on the edge of the spare lounger, ignored its attempts to match her contours, twined fingers between knees, and glared into his twinkle. "What the chaos do you expect my state of mind to be, when you wouldn't tell me what we're heading for?"

"You did not have to come along. You shoved in on me, armored in black mail."

Coya did not deny the amiably made statement. She had threatened to reveal the knowledge she had gained at his request, and thereby give his rivals the same clues. He hadn't been too hard to persuade; after warning her of possible danger, he growled that he would be needing an astrophysicist and might as well keep things in the family.

I hope, God, how I hope he believes my motive was a hankering for adventure as I told him! He ought to believe it, and flatter himself I've inherited a lot of his instincts…No, he can't have guessed my real reason was the fear that David is involved in a wrong way. If he knew that, he need only have told me, "Blab and be damned," and I'd have had to stay home, silent. As is…David, in me you have here an advocate, whatever you may have done.

"I could understand your keeping me ignorant while we were on the yacht," she counterattacked. "No matter how carefully picked the crew, one of them might have been a commercial or government spy and might have managed to eavesdrop, But when, when in the Quetlan System we transferred to this vessel, and the yacht proceeded as if we were still aboard, and won't make any port for weeks—why didn't you speak?"

"Maybe I wanted you should for punishment be like a Yiddish brothel."

"What?"

"Jews in your own stew. Haw, haw, haw!" She didn't smile. Van Rijn continued: "Mainly, here again I could not be full-up sure of the crew. Ythrians is fearless and I suppose more honest by nature than men. But that is saying microbial little, *nie?* Here too we might have been overheard and—Well, Hirharouk agreed, he could not either absolute predict how certain of them would react. He tried but was not able to recruit everybody from his own choth." The Planha word designated a basic social unit, more than a tribe, less than a nation, with cultural and religious dimensions corresponding to nothing human. "Some, even, is from different societies and belong to no choths at alles. Ythrians got as much variation as the Commonwealth—no, more, because they not had time yet for technology to make them into homogeneouses."

The coffeemaker chimed. Coya, rose, tapped a cup, sat back down, and sipped. The warmth and fragrance were a point of comfort in an infinite space.

"We had a long trek ahead of us," the merchant proceeded, "and a lot of casting about, before we found what it *might* be we are looking for. Meanwhiles

Hirharouk, and me as best I was able, sounded out those crewbeings not from Wryfields, got to understand them a weenie bit and—Hokay, he thinks we can trust them regardless how the truth shapes up or ships out. And now, like you know, we have detected an object which would well be the simple, easy, small dissolution to the riddle."

"What's small about a supernova'!" Coya challenged. "Even an extinct one?"

"When people ask me how I like being old as I am," van Rijn said circuitously, "I tell them, 'Not bad when I consider the alternative.' Bellybird, the alternative here would make the Shenn affair look like a game of peggletymum."

Coya came near spilling her coffee. She had been adolescent when the sensation exploded: that the Polesotechnic League had been infiltrated by agents of a nonhuman species, dwelling beyond the regions which Technic civilization dominated and bitterly hostile to it; that war had barely been averted; that the principal rescuers were her grandfather and the crew of a ship named *Muddlin' Through*. On that day David Falkayn was unknowingly promoted to god (j.g.). She wondered if he knew it yet, or knew that their occasional outings together after she matured had added humanness without reducing that earlier rank.

Van Rijn squinted at her. "You guessed we was hunting for a supernova remnant?" he probed.

She achieved a dry tone: "Since you had me investigate the problem, and soon thereafter announced your plans for a 'vacation trip,' the inference was fairly obvious."

"Any notion why I should want a white dwarf or a black hole instead of a nice glass red wine?"

Her pulse knocked. "Yes, I think I've reasoned it out."

And I think David may have done so before either of us, almost ten years ago. When you, Grandfather, asked me to use in secret—

—the data banks and computers at Luna Astrocenter, where she worked, he had given a typically cryptic reason. "Could be this leads to a nice gob of profit nobody else's nose should root around in because mine is plenty big enough." She didn't blame him for being close-mouthed, then. The League's self-regulation was breaking down, competition grew ever more literally cutthroat, and governments snarled not only at the capitalists but at each other. The Pax Mercatoria was drawing to an end and, while she had never wholly approved of it, she sometimes dreaded the future.

The task he set her was sufficiently interesting to blot out her fears. However unimaginably violent, the suicides of giant suns by supernova bursts, which may outshine a hundred billion living stars, are not rare cosmic events. The remains, in varying stages of decay—white dwarfs, neutron stars, in certain cases those eldritch not-quite-things known as black holes—are estimated to number fifty million in our galaxy alone. But its arms spiral across a hundred thousand light-years. In this raw immensity, the prospects of finding by chance a body the size of a smallish planet or less, radiating corpse-feebly if at all, are negligible.

(The analogy with biological death and decomposition is not morbid. Those lay the foundation for new life and further evolution. Supernovae, hurling atoms together in fusing fury, casting them forth into space as their own final gasps, have given us all the heavier elements, some of them vital, in our worlds and our bodies.)

No one hitherto had—openly—attempted a more subtle search. The scientists had too much else to do, as discovery exploded outward. Persons who wished to study supernova processes saw a larger variety of known cases than could be dealt with in lifetimes. Epsilon Aurigae, Sirius B, and Valenderay were simply among the most famous examples.

Coya in Astrocenter had at her beck every fact which Technic civilization had ever gathered about the stellar part of the universe. From the known distribution of former supernovae, together with data on other star types, dust, gas, radiation, magnetism, present location and concentrations, the time derivatives of these quantities: using well-established theories of galactic development, it is possible to compute with reasonable probability the distribution of undiscovered dark giants within a radius of a few hundred parsecs.

The problem is far more complex than that, of course; and the best of self-programming computers still needs a highly skilled sophont riding close herd on it, if anything is to be accomplished. Nor will the answers be absolute, even within that comparatively tiny sphere to which their validity is limited. The most you can learn is the likelihood (not the certainty) of a given type of object existing within such-and-such a distance of yourself, and the likeliest (not the indubitable) direction. To phrase it more accurately, you get a hierarchy of decreasingly probable solutions.

This suffices. If you have the patience, and money, to search on a path defined by the equations, you *will* in time find the kind of body you are interested in.

Coya had taken for granted that no one before van Rijn had been that interested. But the completeness of Astrocenter's electronic records extended to noting who had run which program when. The purpose was to avoid duplication of effort, in an era when nobody could keep up with the literature in the smallest specialty. Out of habit rather than logic, Coya called for this information and—

—*I found out that ten years earlier, David wanted to know precisely what you, Grandfather, now did. But he never told you, nor said where he and his partners went afterward, or anything.* Pain: *Nor has he told me. And I have not told you. Instead, I made you take me along; and before leaving, I sent David a letter saying everything I knew and suspected.*

Resolution: *All right, Nick van Rijn! You keep complaining about how moralistic my generation is. Let's see how you like getting some cards off the bottom of the deck!*

Yet she could not hate an old man who loved her.

"What do you mean by your 'alternative'?" she whispered.

"Why, simple." He shrugged like a mountain sending off an avalanche. "If we do not find a retired supernova, being used in a way as original as spinning the peach basket, then we are up against a civilization outside ours, infiltrating ours, same as the Shenna did—except this one got technology would make ours let go in its diapers and scream, 'Papa, Papa, in the closet is a boogeyman!'" Unaccustomed grimness descended on him. "I think, in that case, really is a boogeyman, too."

Chill entered her guts. "Supermetals?"

"What else?" He took a gulp of beer. "Ha, you is guessed what got me started was Supermetals?"

She finished her coffee and set the cup on a table. It rattled loud through a stretching silence. "Yes," she said at length, flat-voiced. "You've given me a lot of hours to puzzle over what this expedition is for."

"A jigsaw puzzle it is indeed, girl, and us sitting with bottoms snuggled in front of the jigsaw."

"In view of the very, very special kind of supernova-and-companion you thought might be somewhere not too far from Sol, and wanted me to compute about—in view of that, and of what Supermetals is doing, sure, I've arrived at a guess."

"Has you likewise taken into account the fact Supermetals is not just secretive about everything like is its right, but refuses to join the League?"

"That's also its right."

"Truly true. Nonetheleast, the advantages of belonging is maybe not what they used to was; but they do outweigh what small surrender of anatomy is required."

"You mean autonomy, don't you?'

"I suppose. Must be I was thinking of women. A stern chaste is a long chaste… But you never got impure thoughts." Van Rijn had the tact not to look at her while he rambled, and to become serious again immediately: "You better hope, you heathen, and I better pray, the supermetals what the agents of Supermetals is peddling do not come out of a furnace run by anybody except God Himself."

The primordial element, with which creation presumably began, is hydrogen-1, a single proton accompanied by a single electron. To this day, it comprises the overwhelming bulk of matter in the universe. Vast masses of it condensed into globes, which grew hot enough from that infall to light thermonuclear fires. Atoms melted together, forming higher elements. Novae, supernovae—and, less picturesquely but more importantly, smaller suns shedding gas in their red giant phase—spread these through space, to enter into later generations of stars. Thus came planets, life, and awareness.

Throughout the periodic table, many isotopes are radioactive. From polonium (number 84) on, none are stable. Protons packed together in that quantity generate forces of repulsion with which the forces of attraction cannot forever cope. Sooner or later, these atoms will break up. The probability of disintegration—in effect, the half-life—depends on the particular structure. In general, though, the higher the atomic number the lower the stability.

Early researchers thought the natural series ended at uranium. If further elements had once existed, they had long since perished. Neptunium, plutonium, and the rest must be made artificially. Later, traces of them were found in nature: but merely traces, and only of nuclei whose atomic numbers were below 100. The creation of new substances grew progressively more difficult, because of proton repulsion, and less rewarding, because of vanishingly brief existence, as atomic number increased. Few people expected a figure as high as 120 would ever be reached.

Well, few people expected gravity control or faster-than-light travel, either. The universe is rather bigger and more complicated than any given set of brains. Already in those days, an astonishing truth was soon revealed. Beyond a certain point, nuclei become *more* stable. The periodic table contains an "island of stability," bounded on the near side by ghostly short-lived isotopes like those of 112 and 113, on the far side by the still more speedily fragmenting 123, 124…etc.… on to the next "island" which theory says could exist but practice has not reached save on the most infinitesimal scale.

The first is amply hard to attain. There are no easy intermediate stages, like the neptunium which is a stage between uranium and plutonium. Beyond 100, a half-life of a few hours is Methuselan; most are measured in seconds or less. You build your nuclei by main force, slamming particles into atoms too hard for them to rebound—though not so hard that the targets shatter.

To make a few micrograms of, say element 114, eka-platinum, was a laboratory triumph. Aside from knowledge gained, it had no industrial meaning.

Engineers grew wistful about that. The proper isotope of eka-platinum will not endure forever; yet its half-life is around a quarter million years, abundant for mortal purposes, a radioactivity too weak to demand special precautions. It is lustrous white, dense (31.7), of high melting point (ca. 4700°C.*),* nontoxic, hard and tough and resistant. You can only get it into solution by grinding it to dust, then treating it with H_2F_2 and fluorine gas, under pressure at 250°.

It can alloy to produce metals with a range of properties an engineer would scarcely dare daydream about. Or, pure, used as a catalyst, it can become a veritable Philosopher's Stone. Its neighbors on the island are still more fascinating.

When Satan was discovered, talk arose of large-scale manufacture. Calculations soon damped it. The mills which were being designed would use rivers and seas and an entire atmosphere for cooling, whole continents for dumping wastes, in producing special isotopes by the ton. But these isotopes would all belong to elements below 100. Not even on Satan could modern technology handle the energies involved in creating, within reasonable time, a ton of eka-platinum; and supposing this were somehow possible, the cost would remain out of anybody's reach.

The engineers sighed…until a new company appeared, offering supermetals by the ingot or the shipload, at prices high but economic. The source of supply was not revealed. Governments and the Council of the League remembered the Shenna.

To them, a Cynthian named Tso Yu explained blandly that the organization for which she spoke had developed a new process which it chose not to patent but to keep proprietary. Obviously, she said, new laws of nature had been discovered first; but Supermetals felt no obligation to publish for the benefit of science. Let science do its own sweating. Nor did her company wish to join the League, or put itself under any government. If some did not grant it license to operate in their territories, why, there was no lack of others who would.

In the three years since, engineers had begun doing things and building devices which were to bring about the same kind of revolution as did the transistor, the fusion converter, or the neg-gravity generator. Meanwhile a horde of investigators, public and private, went quietly frantic.

The crews who delivered the cargoes and the agents who sold them were a mixed lot, albeit of known species. A high proportion were from backward worlds like Diomedes, Woden, or Ikrananka; some originated in neglected colonies like Lochlann (human) or Catawrayannis (Cynthian). This was understandable. Beings to whom Supermetals had given an education and a chance to better themselves and help out their folk at home would be especially loyal to it. Enough employees hailed from sophisticated milieus to deal on equal terms with League executives.

This did not appear to be a Shenn situation. Whenever an individual's past life could be traced, it proved normal, up to the point when Supermetals engaged him (her, it, yx…)—and was not really abnormal now. Asked point blank, the being would say he didn't know himself where the factory was or how it functioned or who the ultimate owners were. He was merely doing a well-paid job for a good, *simpático* outfit. The evidence bore him out.

("I suspect, me, some detecting was done by kidnaps, drugs, and afterward murder," van Rijn said bleakly. "I would never allow that, but fact is, a few Supermetals people have disappeared. And…as youngsters like you, Coya, get more prudish, the companies and governments get more brutish." She answered: "The second is part of the reason for the first.")

Scoutships trailed the carriers and learned that they always rendezvoused with smaller craft, built for speed and agility. Three or four of these would unload into a merchantman, then dash off in unpredictable directions, using every evasive maneuver in the book and a few that the League had thought were its own secrets. They did not stop dodging until their instruments confirmed that they had shaken their shadowers.

Politicians and capitalists alike organized expensive attempts to duplicate the discoveries of whoever was behind Supermetals. Thus far, progress was nil. A body of opinion grew, that that order of capabilities belonged to a society as far ahead of the Technic as the latter was ahead of the neolithic. Then why this quiet invasion?

"I'm surprised nobody but you has thought of the supernova alternative," Coya said.

"Well, it *has* barely been three years," van Rijn answered. "And the business began small. It is still not big. Nothing flashy-splashy: some kilotons arriving annually, of stuff what is useful and will get more useful after more is learned about the properties. Meanwhiles, everybody got lots else to think about, the usual skulduggeries and unknowns and whatnots. Finalwise remember, I am pustulent—*dood en ondergang,* this Anglic!—I am postulating something which astronomically is hyperimprobable. If you asked a colleague offhand, his first response would be that it isn't possible. His second would be, if he is a sensible man, How would you like to come to his place for a drink?" He knocked the dottle from his pipe. "No doubt somebody more will eventual think of it too, and sic a computer onto the problem of: Is this sort of thing possible, and if so, where might we find one?"

He stroked his goatee. "Howsomever," he continued musingly, I think a good whiles must pass before the idea does occur. You see, the ordinary being does not care. He buys from what is on the market without wondering where it come from or what it means. Besides, Supermetals has not gone after publicity, it uses direct contacts and what officials are concerned about Supermetals has been happy to avoid publicity themselves. A big harroo might too easy get out of control, lose them votes or profits or something."

"Nevertheless," Coya said, "a number of bright minds are worrying; and the number grows as the amount of supermetals brought in does."

"*Ja.* Except who wears those minds? Near-as-damn all is corporation executives, politicians, laboratory scientists, military officers, and—now I will have to wash my mouth out with Genever—bureaucrats. In shorts, they is planetlubbers: When they cross space, they go by cozy passenger ships, to cities where everything is known except where is a restaurant fit to eat in that don't charge as if the dessert was eka-platinum à la mode.

"Me, my first jobs was on prospecting voyages. And I traveled plenty after I founded Solar, troublepotshooting on the frontier and beyond in my own personals. I know—every genuine spaceman knows down in his marrow like no deskman ever can—-how God always makes surprises on us so we don't get too proud, or maybe just for fun. To me it came natural to ask myself: What joke might God have played on the theorists this time?"

"I hope it is only a joke," Coya said.

The star remained a titan in mass. In dimensions, it was hardly larger than Earth, and shrinking still, megayear by megayear, until at last light itself could no longer escape and there would be in the universe one more point of elemental blackness and strangeness. That process was scarcely started—Coya estimated the explosion had occurred some 500 millennia ago—and the giant-become-dwarf radiated dimly in the visible spectrum, luridly in the X-ray and gamma bands. That is, each square centimeter emitted a gale of hard quanta; but so small was the area in interstellar space that the total was a mere spark, undetectable unless you came within a few parsecs.

Standing in the observation turret, staring into a viewscreen set for maximum photoamplification, she discerned a wan-white speck amidst stars which thronged the sky and, themselves made to seem extra brilliant, hurt her eyes. She looked away, toward the instruments around her which were avidly gathering data. The ship whispered and pulsed, no longer under hyperdrive but accelerating on negagravity thrust.

Hirharouk's voice blew cool out of the intercom, from the navigation bridge where he was: "The existence of a companion is now confirmed. We will need a long baseline to establish its position, but preliminary indications are of a radius vector between forty and fifty a.u."

Coya marveled at a detection system which could identify the light-bending due to a substellar object at that distance. Any observatory would covet such equipment. Her thought went to van Rijn: *If you paid what it cost,* Gunung Tuan, *you were smelling big money.*

"So far?" came her grandfather's words. "By damn, a chilly ways out, enough to freeze your astronomy off."

"It had to be," she said. "This was an A-zero: radiation equal to a hundred Sols. Closer in, even a superjovian would have been cooked down to the bare metal—as happened when the sun detonated."

"*Ja,* I knows, I knows, my dear. I only did not foresee things here was on quite this big a scale…Well, we can't spend weeks at sublight. Go hyper, Hirharouk, first to get your baseline sights, next to come near the planet."

"Hyperdrive, this deep in a gravitational well?" Coya exclaimed.

"Is hokay if you got good engines well tuned, and you bet ours is tuned like a late Beethoven quartet. Music, maestro!"

Coya shook her head before she prepared to continue gathering information under the new conditions of travel.

Again *Dewfall* ran on gravs. Van Rijn agreed that trying to pass within visual range of the ultimate goal, faster than light, when to them it was still little more than a mystery wrapped in conjectures, would be a needlessly expensive form of suicide.

Standing on the command bridge between him and Hirharouk, Coya stared at the meters and displays filling an entire bulkhead, as if they could tell more than the heavens in the screens. And they could, they could, but they were not the Earth-built devices she had been using; they were Ythrian and she did not know how to read them.

Poised on his perch, crested carnivore head lifted against the Milky Way, Hirharouk said: "Data are pouring in as we approach. We should make optical pickup in less than an hour."

"Hum-hum, better call battle stations," the man proposed.

"This crew needs scant notice. Let them slake any soulthirst they feel. God may smite some of us this day." Through the intercom keened a melody, plangent strings and thuttering drums and shrilling pipes, like nothing Earth had brought forth but still speaking to Coya of hunters high among their winds.

Terror stabbed her. "You can't expect to fight!" she cried.

"Oh, an ordinary business precaution," van Rijn smiled.

"No! We mustn't!"

"Why not, if they are here and do rumblefumbles at us?"

She opened her lips, pulled them shut again, and stood in anguish. *I can't tell you why not. How can I tell you these may be David's people?*

"At least we are sure that Supermetals is not a *whinna* for an alien society," Hirharouk said. Coya remembered vaguely, through the racket in her temples, a demonstration of the *whinna* during her groundside visit to Ythri. It was a kind of veil, used by some to camouflage themselves, to resemble floating mists in the eyes of unflying prey; and this practical use had led to a form of dream-lovely airborne dance; and—*And here I was caught in the wonder of what we have found, a thing which must be almost unique even in this galaxy full of miracles…and everything's gotten tangled and ugly and, and, David, what can we do?*

She heard van Rijn: "Well, we are not total-sure. Could be our finding is accidental; or maybe the planet is not like we suppose. We got to check on that, and hope the check don't bounce back in our snoots."

"Nuclear engines are in operation around our quarry," Hirharouk said. "Neutrinos show it. What else would they belong to save a working base and spacecraft?"

Van Rijn clasped hands over rump and paced, slap-slap-slap over the bare deck. "What can we try and predict in advance? Forewarned is forearmed, they say, and the four arms I want right now is a knife, a blaster, a machine gun, and a rover missile, nothing fancy, maybe a megaton."

"The mass of the planet—" Hirharouk consulted a readout. The figure he gave corresponded approximately to Saturn.

"No bigger?" asked van Rijn, surprised.

"Originally, yes." Coya heard herself say. The scientist in her was what spoke, while her heart threshed about like any animal netted by a stooping Ythrian. "A gas giant, barely substellar. The supernova blew most of that away—you can hardly say it boiled the gases off; we have no words for what happened—and nothing was left except a core of nickel-iron and heavier elements."

She halted, noticed Hirharouk's yellow gaze intent on her, and realized the skipper must know rather little of the theory behind this venture. To him she had not been repeating banalities. And he was interested. If she could please him by explaining in simple terms, then maybe later—

She addressed him: "Of course, when the pressure of the outer layers was removed, that core must have exploded into new allotropes, a convulsion which flung away the last atmosphere and maybe a lot of solid matter. Better keep a sharp lookout for meteoroids."

"That is automatic," he assured her. "My wonder is why a planet should exist. I was taught that giant stars, able to become supernovae, do not have them."

"Well, they is still scratching their brains to account for Betelgeuse," van Rijn remarked.

"In this case," Coya told the Ythrian, "the explanation comes easier. True, the extremely massive suns do not in general allow planetary systems to condense around them. The parameters aren't right. However, you know giants can be partners in multiple star systems, and sometimes the difference between partners is quite large. So, after I was alerted to the idea that it might happen, and wrote a program which investigated the possibility in detail, I learned that, yes, under special conditions, a double can form in which one member is a large sun and one a superjovian planet. When I extrapolated backward things like the motion of dust and gas, changes in galactic magnetism, et cetera—it turned out that such a pair could exist in this neighborhood."

Her glance crossed the merchant's craggy features. *You found a clue in the appearance of the supermetals,* she thought. *David got the idea all by himself.* The lean snubnosed face, the Vega-blue eyes came between her and the old man.

Of course, David may not have been involved. This could be a coincidence. Please, God of my grandfather Whom I don't believe in, please make it a coincidence. Make those ships ahead of us belong not to harmless miners but to the great and terrible Elder Race.

She knew the prayer would not be granted. And neither van Rijn nor Hirharouk assumed that the miners were necessarily harmless.

She talked fast, to stave off silence: "I daresay you've heard this before, Captain, but you may like to have me recapitulate in a few words. When a supernova erupts, it floods out neutrons in quantities that I, I can put a number to, perhaps, but I cannot comprehend. In a full range of energies, too, and the same for other kinds of particles and quanta—Do you see? Any possible reaction *must* happen.

"Of course, the starting materials available, the reaction rates, the yields, every quantity differs from case to case. The big nuclei which get formed, like the actinides are a very small percentage of the total. The supermetals are far less. They scatter so thinly into space that they're effectively lost. No detectable amount enters into the formation of a star or planet afterward.

"Except—here—here was a companion, a planet-sized companion, turned into a bare metallic globe. I wouldn't try to guess how many quintillion tons of blasted-out incandescent gases washed across it. Some of those alloyed with the molten surface, maybe some plated out—and the supermetals, with their high condensation temperatures, were favored.

"A minute fraction of the total was supermetals, yes, and a minute fraction of that was captured by the planet, also yes. But this amounted to—how much?—billions of tons? Not hard to extract from combination by modern methods; and a part may actually be lying around pure. It's radioactive; one must be careful, especially of the shorter-lived products, and a lot has decayed away by now. Still, what's left is more than our puny civilization can ever consume. It took a genius to think this might be!"

She grew aware of van Rijn's eyes upon her. He had stopped pacing and stood troll-burly, tugging his beard.

A whistle rescued her. Planha words struck from the intercom. Hirharouk's feathers rippled in a series of expressions she could not read; his tautness was unmistakable.

She drew near to the man's bulk. "What next?" she whispered. "Can you follow what they're saying?"

"*Ja,* pretty well; anyhow, better than I can follow words in an opera. Detectors show three ships leaving planetary orbit on an intercept course. The rest stay behind. No doubt those is the working vessels. What they send to us is their men-of-war."

Seen under full screen magnification, the supermetal world showed still less against the constellations than had the now invisible supernova corpse—a ball, dimly reflecting star-glow, its edge sharp athwart distant brightnesses. And yet, Coya thought: a world.

It could not be a smooth sphere. There must be uplands, lowlands, flatlands, depths, ranges and ravines, cliffs whose gloom was flecked with gold, plains where mercury glaciers glimmered; there must be internal heat, shudders in the steel soil, volcanoes spouting forth flame and radioactive ash; eternally barren, it must nonetheless mumble with a life of its own.

Had David Falkayn trod those lands? He would have, she knew, merrily swearing because beyond the ship's generated field he and his space gear weighed five or six times what they ought, and no matter the multitudinous death traps which a place so uncanny must hold in every shadow. Naturally, those shadows had to be searched out; whoever would mine the metals had first to spend years, and doubtless lives, in exploring, and studying, and the development and testing and redevelopment of machinery…but that wouldn't concern David. He was a charger, not a plowhorse. Having made his discovery, told chosen beings about it, perhaps helped them raise the initial funds and recruit members of races which could better stand high weight than men can—having done that, he'd depart on a new adventure, or stop off in the Solar Commonwealth and take Coya Conyon out dancing.

"Iyan wherill-ll cha quellan."

The words, and Hirharouk's response, yanked her back to this instant. "What?"

"Shush." Van Rijn, head cocked, waved her to silence. "By damn, this sounds spiky. I should tell you, Shushkebab."

Hirharouk related: "Instruments show one of the three vessels is almost equal to ours. Its attendants are less, but in a formation to let them take full advantage of their firepower. If that is in proportion to size, which I see no reason to doubt, we are outgunned. Nor do they act as if they simply hope to frighten us off. That formation and its paths are well calculated to bar our escape spaceward."

"Can you give me details—? No, wait." Van Rijn swung on Coya. "Bellybird, you took a stonkerish lot of readings on the sun, and right here is an input-output panel you can switch to the computer system you was using. I also ordered, when I chartered the ship, should be a program for instant translation between Anglic language, Arabic numerals, metric units whatever else kinds of ics is useful—translations back and forth between those and the Planha sort. Think you could quick-like do some figuring for us?" He clapped her shoulder, nearly felling her. "I know you can." His voice dropped. "I remember your grandmother."

Her mouth was dry, her palms were wet, it thudded in her ears. She thought of David Falkayn and said. "Yes. What do you want?"

"Mainly the pattern of the gravitational field, and what phenomena we can expect at the different levels of intensity. Plus radiation, electromagnetics, anything else you got time to program for. But we is fairly well protected against those, so don't worry if you don't get a chance to go into details there. Nor don't let outside talkings distract you—Whoops!" Hirharouk was receiving a fresh report. "Speak of the devil and he gives you horns."

The other commander had obviously sent a call on a standard band, which had been accepted. As the image screen awoke, Coya felt hammerstruck. *Adzel!*

No...no...the head belonged to a Wodenite, but not the dear dragon who had given her rides on his back when she was little and had tried in his earnest, tolerant fashion to explain his Buddhism to her when she grew older Behind the being she made out a raven-faced Ikranankan and a human in the garb of a colony she couldn't identify.

His rubbery lips shaped good Anglic, a basso which went through her bones: "Greeting. Commodore Nadi speaks."

Van Rijn thrust his nose toward the scanner. "Whose commodore?" he demanded like a gravel hauler dumping its load.

For a second, Nadi was shaken. He rallied and spoke firmly: *"Kho,* I know who you are, Freeman van Rijn. "What an unexpected honor, that you should personally visit our enterprise."

"Which is Supermetals, *nie?"*

"It would be impolite to suggest you had failed to reach that conclusion."

Van Rijn signalled Coya behind his back. She flung herself at the chair before the computer terminal. Hirharouk perched imperturbable, slowly fanning his wings. The Ythrian music had ended. She heard a rustle and whisper through the intercom, along the hurtling hull.

Words continued. Her work was standardized enough that she could follow them.

"Well, you see, Commodore, there I sat, not got much to do no more, lonely old man like I am except when a girl goes wheedle-wheedle at me, plenty time for thinking, which is not fun like drinking but you can do it alone and it is easier on the kidneys and the hangovers next day are not too much worse. I thought, if the supermetals is not made by an industrial process we don't understand, must be they was made by a natural one, maybe one we do know a little about. That would have to be a supernova. Except a supernova blows everything out into space, and the supermetals is so small, proportional, that they get lost. Unless the supernova had a companion what could catch them?"

"Freeman, pray accept my admiration. Does your perspicacity extend to deducing who is behind our undertaking?"

"Ja, I can say, bold and bald, who you undertakers are. A consortium of itsy-bitsy operators, most from poor or primitive societies, pooling what capital they can scrape together. You got to keep the secret, because if they know about this hoard you found, the powerful outfits will horn themselves in and you out; and what chance you get afterward, in courts they can buyout of petty cash? No, you will keep this hidden long as you possible can. In the end, somebody is bound to repeat my sherlockery. But give you several more years, and you will have pumped gigacredits clear profit out of here. You may actual have got so rich you can defend your property."

Coya could all but see the toilers in their darkness—in orbital stations; aboard spacecraft; down on the graveyard surface, where robots dug ores and ran refineries, and sentient beings stood their watches under the murk and chill and weight and radiation and millionfold perils of Eka-World...

Nadi, slow and soft: "That is why we have these fighting ships, Freeman and Captain."

"You do not suppose," van Rijn retorted cheerily, "I would come this far in my own precious blubber and forget to leave behind a message they will scan if I am not home in time to race for the Micronesia Cup?"

"As a matter of fact, Freeman, I suppose precisely that. The potential gains here are sufficient to justify virtually any risk, whether the game be played for money or...something else." Pause. "If you have indeed left a message, you will possess hostage value. Your rivals may be happy to see you a captive, but you have allies and employees who will exert influence. My sincere apologies, Freeman, Captain, everyone aboard your vessel. We will try to make your detention pleasant."

Van Rijn's bellow quivered in the framework. "*Wat drommel?* You sit smooth and calm like buttered granite and say you will make us prisoners?"

"You may not leave. If you try, we will regretfully open fire."

"You are getting on top of yourself. I warn you, always she finds nothing except an empty larder, Old Mother Hubris."

"Freeman, please consider. We noted your hyperdrive vibrations and made ready. You cannot get past us to spaceward. Positions and vectors guarantee that one of our vessels will be able to close in, engage, and keep you busy until the other two arrive." Reluctantly, van Rijn nodded. Nadi continued: "True, you can double back toward the sun. Evidently you can use hyperdrive closer to it than most. But you cannot go in that direction at anywhere near top pseudospeed without certain destruction. We, proceeding circuitously, but therefore able to go a great deal faster, will keep ahead of you. We will calculate the conoid in which your possible paths spaceward lie, and again take a formation you cannot evade."

"You is real anxious we should taste your homebrew, ha?"

"Freeman, I beg you, yield at once. I promise fair treatment—if feasible, compensation—and while you are among us, I will explain why we of Supermetals have no choice."

"Hirharouk," van Rijn said, "maybe you can talk at this slagbrain." He stamped out of scanner reach. The Ythrian threw him a dubious glance but entered into debate with the Wodenite. Van Rijn hulked over Coya where she sat. "How you coming?" he whispered, no louder than a Force Five wind.

She gestured at the summary projected on a screen. Her computations were of a kind she often handled. The result were shown in such terms as diagrams and equations of equipotential surfaces, familiar to a space captain. Van Rijn read them and nodded. "We got enough information to set out on," he decided. "The rest you can figure while we go."

Shocked, she gaped at him. "What? Go? But we're caught!"

"He thinks that. Me, I figured whoever squats on a treasure chest will keep guards, and the guards will not be glimmerwits but smart, trained oscos, in spite of what I called the Commodore. They might well cook for us a cake like what wc is now baked in. Ergo, I made a surprise recipe for them." Van Rijn's regard turned grave. "It was for use only if we found we was sailing through dire straits. The surprise may turn around and bite us. Then we is dead. But better dead than losing years in the nicest jail, *nie?*" (And she could not speak to him of David.) "I said this trip might be dangerous." Enormous and feather-gentle, a hand stroked down her hair. "I is very sorry, Beatriz, Ramona." The names he murmured were of her mother and grandmother.

Whirling, he returned to Hirharouk, who matched pride against Nadi's patience, and uttered a few rapid-fire Planha words. The Ythrian gave instant assent. Suddenly Coya knew why the man had chosen a ship of that planet. Hirharouk continued his argument. Van Rijn went to the main command panel, snapped forth orders, and took charge of *Dewfall*.

At top acceleration, she sprang back toward the sun.

Of that passage, Coya afterward remembered little. First she glimpsed the flashes when nuclear warheads drove at her, and awaited death. But van Rijn and Hirharouk had adjusted well their vector relative to the enemy's. During an hour of negagrav flight, no missile could gather sufficient relative velocity to get past defensive fire; and that was what made those flames in heaven.

Then it became halfway safe to go hyper. That must be at a slower pace than in the emptiness between stars; but within an hour, the fleeing craft neared the dwarf. There, as gravitation intensified, she had to resume normal state.

Instead of swinging wide, she opened full thrust almost straight toward the disc.

Coya was too busy to notice much of what happened around her. She must calculate, counsel, hang into her seat harness as forces tore at her which were too huge for the compensator fields. She saw the undead supernova grow in the viewscreens till its baneful radiance filled them; she heard the ribs of the vessel groan and felt them shudder beneath stress; she watched the tale of the radiation meters mounting and knew how close she came to a dose whose ravages medicine could not heal; she heard orders bawled by van Rijn, fluted by Hirharouk, and whistling replies and storm of wingbeats, always triumphant though *Dewfall* flew between the teeth of destruction. But mainly she was part of the machinery.

And the hours passed and the hours passed.

They could not have done what they did without advance preparation. Van Rijn had foreseen the contingency and ordered computations made whose results were in the data banks. Her job was to insert numbers and functions corresponding to the reality on hand, and get answers by which he and Hirharouk might steer. The work killed her, crowded out terror and sometimes the memory of David.

Appalled, Nadi watched his quarry vanish off his telltales. He had followed on hyperdrive as close as he dared, and afterward at sublight closer than he ought to have dared. But for him was no possibility of plunging in a hairpin hyperbola around yonder incandescence. In all the years he had been stationed here, not he nor his fellows had imagined anyone would ever venture near the roiling remnant of a sun which had once burned brighter than its whole galaxy. Thus there were no precalculations in storage, nor days granted him to program them on a larger device than a ship might carry.

Radiation was not the barrier. It was easy to figure how narrow an approach a crew could endure behind a given amount of armor. But a mass of half a dozen Sols, pressed into the volume of an Earth, has stupendous gravitational power; the warped space around makes the laws of nature take on an eerie aspect. Moreover, a dwarf star spins at a fantastic rate: which generates relativistic forces. Describable only if you have determined the precise quantities involved. And pulsations, normally found nowhere outside the atomic nucleus, reach across a million or more kilometers—

After the Ythrian craft whipped around the globe into weirdness, Nadi had no way of knowing what she did, how she moved. He could not foretell where she would be when she again became detectable. And thus he could plan no interception pattern.

He could do nothing but hope she would never reappear. A ship flying so close, not simply orbiting but flying, would be seized, torn apart, and hauled into the star, unless the pilot and his computers knew exactly what they did.

Or almost exactly. That was a crazily chancy ride. When Coya could glance from her desk, she saw blaze in the screens, Hirharouk clutching his perch with both hands while his wings thundered and he yelled for joy, van Rijn on his knees in prayer. Then they ran into a meteoroid swarm (she supposed) which rebounded off their shield-fields and sent them careening off trajectory; and the man shook his fist, commenced on a mighty oath, glimpsed her and turned it into a Biblical "Damask rose and shittah tree!" Later, when something else went wrong—some interaction with a plasma cloud—he came to her, bent over and kissed her brow.

They won past reef and riptide, lined out for deep space, switched back into hyperdrive and ran on homeward.

Coincidences do happen. The life would be freakish which held none of them.

Muddlin' Through, bound for Eka-World in response to Coya's letter, passed within detection range of *Dewfall,* made contact, and laid alongside. The pioneers boarded.

This was less than a day after the brush with oblivion. And under no circumstances do Ythrians go in for tumultuous greetings. Apart from Hirharouk, who felt he must represent his choth, the crew stayed at rest. Coya, roused by van Rijn, swallowed a stimpill, dressed, and hastened to the flying hold—the sole chamber aboard which would comfortably accommodate Adzel. In its echoing dim space she threw her arms partway around him, took Chee Lan into her embrace, kissed David Falkayn and wept and kissed him and kissed him.

Van Rijn cleared his throat. "A-hem!" he grumbled. "Also bgr-rrm. I been sitting here hours on end, till my end is sore, wondering when everybody elses would come awake and make celebrations by me; and I get word about you three mosquito-ears is coming in, and by my own self I hustle stuff for a party." He waved at the table he had laid, bottles and glasses, platesful of breads, cheeses, sausage, lox, caviar, kanuba, from somewhere a vaseful of flowers. Mozart lilted in the background. "Well, ha, poets tell us love is enduring, but I tell us good food is not, so we take our funs in the right order, *nie?*"

Formerly Falkayn would have laughed and tossed off the first icy muglet of akvavit; he would have followed it with a beer chaser and an invitation to Coya that they see what they could dance to this music. Now she felt sinews tighten in the fingers that enclosed hers; across her shoulder he said carefully: "Sir, before we relax, could you let me know what's happened to you?"

Van Rijn got busy with a cigar. Coya looked a plea at Adzel, stroked Chee's fur where the Cynthian crouched on a chair, and found no voice. Hirharouk told the story in a few sharp words.

"A-a-ah," Falkayn breathed. "Judas priest. Coya, they ran you that close to that hellkettle—" His right hand let go of hers to clasp her waist. She felt the grip tremble and grew dizzy with joy.

"Well," van Rijn huffed. "I didn't want she should come, my dear tender little bellybird, *ja,* tender like tool steel—"

Coya had a sense of being put behind Falkayn, as a man puts a woman when menace draws near. "Sir," he said most levelly, "I know, or can guess, about that. We can discuss it later if you want. What I'd like to know immediately, please, is what you propose to do about the Supermetals consortium."

Van Rijn kindled his cigar and twirled a mustache.

"You understand," he said, "I am not angry if they keep things under the posies. By damn, though, they tried to make me a prisoner or else shoot me to bits of lard what would go into the next generation of planets. And Coya, too, Davy boy, don't forget Coya, except she would make those planets prettier. For that, they going to pay."

"What have you in mind?"

"Oh…a cut. Not the most unkindest, neither. Maybe like ten percent of gross."

The creases deepened which a hundred suns had weathered into Falkayn's countenance. "Sir, you don't need the money. You stopped needing more money a long while back. To you it's nothing but a counter in a game. Maybe, for you, the only game in town. Those beings aft of us, however—they are not playing."

"What do they do, then?"

Surprisingly, Hirharouk spoke. "Freeman, you know the answer. They seek to win that which will let their peoples fly free." Standing on his wings, he could not spread gold-bronze plumes; but his head rose high. "In the end, God the Hunter strikes every being and everything which beings have made. Upon your way of life I see His shadow. Let the new come to birth in peace."

From Falkayn's hands, Coya begged: *"Gunung Tuan,* all you have to do is do nothing. Say nothing. You've won your victory. Tell them that's enough for you, that you too are their friend."

She had often watched van Rijn turn red—never before white. His shout came ragged: *"Ja! Ja!* Friend! So nice, so kind, maybe so farsighted—Who, what I thought of like a son, broke his oath of fealty to me? Who broke kinship?"

He suspected. Coya realized sickly, *but he wouldn't admit it to himself till this minute, when I let out the truth.* She held Falkayn sufficiently hard for everyone to see.

Chee Lan arched her back. Adzel grew altogether still.

Falkayn forgot Coya—she could feel how he did—and looked straight at his chief while he said, word by word like blows of a hammer: "Do you want a response? I deem best we let what is past stay dead."

Their gazes drew apart. Falkayn's dropped to Coya.

The merchant watched them standing together for a soundless minute. And upon him were the eyes of Adzel, Chee, and Hirharouk the sky dweller.

He shook his head. "Hokay," said Nicholas van Rijn, well-nigh too low to hear. "I keep my mouth shut. Always. Now can we sit down and have our party for making you welcome?" He moved to pour from a bottle; and Coya saw that he was indeed old.

THE BITTER BREAD

Seven years have gone since last we on Earth had news of *Uriel* in heaven, and I do not think we ever shall again. Whether they died or triumphed or their wild hunt still runs between the stars, yon crew has eternally left us. Should they after all return, it will surely be only briefly, with word and image for mankind and maybe, maybe a smile recorded for me.

That smile must then travel here, first in a shipboard tape, then in a code beamed through the sky, the censor, the global comweb to my house on Hoy. I shall never more see space. Three years ago the directors required me to retire. I am not unhappy. Steep red and yellow cliffs, sea green in sunlight or gray under clouds until it breaks in whiteness and thunder, gulls riding a cold loud wind, inland the heather and a few gnarly trees across hills where sheep still graze, a hamlet of rough and gentle Orkney folk an hour's walk away, my cat, my books, my rememberings—these things are good. They are well worth being often chilled, damp, a wee bit hungry. It may even be for the best that the weather seldom gives me a clear look at the stars.

Also, eccentric though I was to spend my savings on this place, rather than enter a Church lodge for senior spacemen, nobody will trouble to come here and examine my scribblings. Are they found after I am dead, they should not hurt my sons in their own careers. For one thing, I have always been openly kittle. The Protectorate must needs allow, yes, expect a measure of oddness among its top-rank technos. Of course, my papers would be deemed subversive and whiffed. So I put them each night in a box under a flagstone I have loosened, wondering if some archeologist someday may read them…and smile?

In the main, though, you archeologist, I write for myself, to bring back years and loves: today, Daphne.

When she sought me out, I had lately been appointed head of the *Uriel* relief mission. To organize this, I had taken an office in New Jerusalem, high up in Armstrong Center where my view swept across city roofs and towers, on over the Cimarron to the wheat-bronze Kansas plain beyond. That day was hard, hot, cloudless. The cross on the topmost spire of the Supreme Church blazed as if its gold had gone incandescent, and flitfighters on guard above the armored bulk of the Capitol gleamed like dragonflies. Though the room was air-conditioned,

171

I could almost feel the weather beyond my window, a seethe or crackle amongst steady murmurs of traffic.

My intercom announced, "Mrs. Asklund, sir." I muttered a heartfelt "Damn!" and laid down the manifest I'd been working on. I'd forgotten that, somehow, the wife of *Uriel*'s navigator had obtained a personal appointment. Hadn't I over-much to do, in ghastly short time, without soothing distraught females? Eido-phone conversations with two other crewmen's wives had been difficult—when at least they were accepting God's will in Christian fortitude, and wanted only to ask about sending messages or gifts to the men they would never remeet in this life. "Aweel, remind her I've but a few minutes to spill, and let her in," I ordered.

Then Daphne came through the door, and everything was suddenly a bright surprise.

She was tall. A gown of standard dark modesty did not hide a fine figure. The skirt swished around her ankles with the sea-wind vigor of her stride. Green-eyed, curve-nosed, full-mouthed, framed in coils of mahogany hair, her face wasn't pretty, it was beautiful. I saw there not sorrow but determination. When she stopped before my desk, folded her hands and bowed her head above them to me, the salutation had scant meekness. Yet her voice was low and mild, the English bearing a slight accent: "Captain Sinclair, I am Daphne Asklund. You are kind to receive me."

We both knew I did so because she had pulled wires. However, I could say no less than, "Please sit down, sister. I'd call this a pleasure were the occasion not sad. How can I be of help to you?"

She settled herself and spent a few seconds studying my grizzle-topped lanki-ness, almost like a friendly challenge, before she curved her lips upward a very little and answered, "You can hear me out, sir. What I'll propose isn't quite as fantastic as it will sound."

"The whole business is fantastic." I leaned back in my own chair and reached for my pipe. "Uh, I do sympathize. I'm affected too. Matthew King was my class-mate at the Academy, and we were always close friends afterward."

"But you don't know Valdemar?"

"Your husband? Not really, I fear. The Astronautic Corps is small enough that we have occasionally been at the same conference or the same refresher training session; but it's big enough that we didn't get truly acquainted. He did...does impress me well, Mrs. Asklund."

"*Uriel*'s skipper is your friend. Its navigator is my husband. I hope you can imagine the difference," she said: no hint of self-pity, simply remarking on a fact.

I am not sure why, already then, I let go my reserve and told her, "Yes. My wife died only last year."

Her look softened. "I'm sorry. My apologies. Captain Sinclair. I've been too snarled in my personal troubles to—Well." She straightened. "Val is not departed, though. He...they all face years, decades of...endless trial." Exile, imprisoned in a metal shell ahurtle among the stars—perhaps at last madness, murder, horror beyond guessing, till a lone man squatted among dead bones—she did not mention these things either.

I gathered myself to speak bluntly. "We'll do what we can for them. That's the duty I'm on, and you will forgive me if it leaves scant attention to spare for anybody Earthbound. I—I am told clergy are counseling the wives to—Well, they expect the Pastorate will soon permit, aye, encourage dissolution of any unions involved, and the ladies be free to remarry. Has not your minister spoken to you of this?"

She met my plainness with hers. "No. I am not a Christian. My maiden name was Greenbaum."

"What?"

"I'm not a good Jewess either, I admit. Haven't been to temple in years—that would have handicapped Val too much, professionally—but I could never bring myself to convert. Nor did he want me to." She left tacit the obvious, that his faith was probably mostly on his lips. Reading history, I have seen how tolerance has grown in the World Protectorate since its early days after the Armageddon War. But the time will be long yet before a professed non-Christian, not to mention an outright unbeliever, gets a spaceman's berth.

Daphne Asklund's background did help explain why her husband was aboard *Uriel*. The Corps doesn't exactly have a policy of giving its deviant members the most hazardous assignments. But they tend to volunteer for these, in the hope of advancement despite their social disadvantages or for deeper personality reasons. And then the tendency is to choose them from among qualified applicants, in compassion or a silent hope they may be more original and resourceful than average, or (I suppose) now and again a less honorable motive. Matt King, for instance, when young and foolish, had fathered a bastard. Or—I, commanding the relief mission, did not belong to the Absolute Christian Church but to a remnant of the old Kirk of Scotland; and kinfolk of mine, before I was born, were involved in the European Insurrection.

"Well," I said. "Well." My pipe and tobacco busied my hands. "Best we come to business. What do you want of me that lower echelons can't arrange for you? And why this visit, instead of a message or a phone call?"

"Only you can give me what I am after," she replied, "and you would not do it for a stranger. I don't expect you to say yes the first time."

You take for granted there will be more times, I thought. "Go on."

She drew breath. "Let me first describe myself. I hold full North American citizenship"—which had opened the ears of men who could grant access to me, a client national—"but was born and raised in Caribbea. My father was stationed there as an engineer for the Oceanic Power Authority. I grew up swimming, diving, sailing, hiking; or we'd hop to the Andes and mountaineer. I still do such things—did, with Val. My father got me entry to the University of Mexico, where I took a degree in microbiotics. Afterward I was an assistant to Sancho Dominguez—yes, I helped him develop his improvements in balanced life-support systems for spacecraft. That was how I met Val. He was on the team that tested them, and came to the laboratory for conferences. After we married, I had to resign my job—you know how spacemen get moved around, also on Earth—but Dr. Dominguez keeps me on retainer as a consultant and has called me in on several problems. That's the main reason we put off having children, social stigma be damned."

An oath on a woman's tongue seemed not altogether wrong; when tears glimmered forth on her eyelashes. Did the golden cross throw too harsh a light, or had she all at once felt that now they would have no children ever? She blinked, lifted her head, and went on defiantly:

"A peculiar life, hasn't it been? Almost like a female's before Armageddon." She flushed, though her tone stayed crisp. "Except for their moral looseness, of course. But please understand, sir—check me out later on—in spite of my sex, I'm athletic, used to handling emergencies, scientifically skilled, a specialist in the very thing your expedition is chiefly concerned with—

"Captain Sinclair, I want to go along."

It happened that our propaganda department had completed the official film on this task, and screened it that afternoon for me and my staff prior to release. I invited Daphne to join us. "Frankly, the reaction of a wife may show us changes we ought to make," I said. Hesitating: "You may prefer to wait, and watch at home when it's 'cast. They've doubtless included shots of your husband."

"Could I wish not to see those?" she answered.

On our way to the auditorium, I explained the need for a dramatic presentation. Spiritual relations were no great problem. The Church could scarcely object to an errand of mercy. A few canons had expressed fear that men spending a lifetime shipbound, no chaplain among them, might fall into despair, curse God, yes, commit the sin against nature. But unless we let them starve, or slaughtered them, that risk must be taken. And in truth, the temptation was their opportunity: to smite Satan, bear witness, win sainthood.

As for temporal authorities, the Protector himself had approved our undertaking. He had more interest in science than Enoch IV before him or, for that matter, David III today. Out of disaster we could pluck a farther-ranging exploration of the galaxy than anyone had awaited for generations. We might even find that long-sought dream, New Eden, the planet so like a virgin Earth that full-scale colonization is possible. Rumors reaching me said some of the Council had warned against that. Start men moving freely outward, and what heresies, what libertinisms and rebellions, might they soon spawn? However, at present the opposition didn't appear too strong.

The public was what we must convince, at any rate a sufficient minority. "Every special interest protests resources going to space research instead of it," I remarked. "You can't imagine the pressure. I didn't myself, in spite of being in the Corps, until I got this administrative post. The journalistic media don't report major disputes. That doesn't mean they don't exist."

"But if our rulers—" Hastily: "If most of the government endorses what we do, who cares about mobs?" she asked. I was to learn that she didn't lack charity for the humble of Earth, save when they threatened her man. And then her anger blasted mainly at their ignorance. ("Can't they *listen*? Why, just what's been learned out there about repairing radiation damage should have each soul of the millions that crater dust has blown across, down on his knees in thanks.")

I shrugged. "The Protectorate is only total in theory. In practice, it rests as much on being the compromise maker, the broker, between nations, races, classes, faiths, as it does on military force."

"Faiths?" she half scoffed. "When it keeps an established Church?"

"Och, wait, sister. You're educated, you know the Articles. The Absolute Christian Church is recognized as advisory to the government, no more. Membership in it can't be compelled. If nothing else, that would be politically impossible. Think of your own case."

"Ye-e-es. Still, you're aware what communicancy means in practice. And everything the Church calls a sin, the Protectorate has made universally illegal, under stiff penalties."

I stared. "Do you object? Besides murder and theft—Well, would you want lads and lasses free to fornicate? Your husband free to commit adultery? Or…forgive me…under his present circumstances, worse?"

Her nostrils flared. "He never would!"

"There, you see, the thought makes you indignant. Doesn't that prove you share the same moral code?"

"True," she sighed. "Mosaic principles. As internalized in me as in anybody, no doubt. I simply wonder if God wants us to shove them on others at gunpoint. Wasn't righteousness more meaningful before Armageddon, in those parts of the world where people were let choose for themselves? Where they could individually seek the truth, make their lives as they saw fit, why, it sounds trivial, but when women in particular could wear whatever they liked—Oh, never mind. Here we are, aren't we?"

I was relieved. We had been alone in the corridor, she hadn't spoken loudly, and hers weren't forbidden questions. But if a zealot had overheard, an embarrassing scene would have followed. Her chance of joining my expedition would have dropped to zero. I wasn't sure why I feared that, when I had insisted the idea was impossible.

Though the auditorium was uncrowded, Daphne sat next to me. As the room went dark and the showing started, she caught my hand and did not let go.

Our proppas had used minimum fake effects, where necessary to bridge gaps. They had ample real data to work with. Men aboard the associated vessels, *Abdiel*, *Raphael*, and *Zephon*, had taken excellent shots both before and after the catastrophe. In *Uriel* they kept cameras going too, and later transmitted what these recorded. Aimed almost at random, the lenses were cruelly honest. Our producers had not much more to do than choose sequences and add occasional explanatory narration.

I see, hear, all but feel and taste and smell the story around me now.

A thousand light-years hence, stars throng blackness, jewel-hued, icy sharp, marshalled in alien constellations. The galactic band and the clouds that cleave its silver are less changed to sight—except dead ahead, where a haze grows as the ships near, until it fills a quarter of heaven. White and flame-blue at its heart, the nebula roils outward to edges which are a lacework formed of molten rainbows.

Instruments take over, seeing and projecting what vision cannot. In the middle of that majestic chaos, two things which have been suns whirl crazily about each other. One, hardly bigger than Earth although more massive than Sol, has no light of its own, but flings back the fury of its huge companion's death. There are no words to tell of this. And yet the image is a ghost, a mathematical construct. Men who looked straight upon the reality would die before they knew they had been blinded.

Narrator: "Here crews have stood watch and watch for a score of years, ever since astronomers predicted that the blue giant would soon explode. Here was our chance to observe a supernova close at hand. Who could tell what we might learn? And what about its companion, a neutron star orbiting almost in contact? How was this possible? It must once have undergone the same throes, perhaps even more violent. But an outburst like that should drive the members of a pair apart, not together.

"We think probably there was a third member, also a giant, which blew up at about the same former time. Itself escaping, it took such a path that the second body was drawn close in toward the still steadily shining first. Friction with expelled gases must have helped shorten the orbit.

"Our investigators have searched for that third object. Its remnants cannot have traveled far, in cosmic terms. But they must be very feebly shining, or altogether dark, collapsed into a ball the size of a planet. We have not found them. God made the universe too big; let us put down our pride."

The tone cools: "Now that the last of the trio has erupted, the system is indeed breaking apart. Losing immense quantities of mass, the supernova must spiral away from the neutron star, and vice versa, to conserve angular momentum. But friction, again, hinders this retreat. It had scarcely begun when *Uriel* arrived, to relieve *Zophiel* on the regular three-month rotation plan.

"Certain persons question the sense of traveling a light-millennium, weeks at top quasispeed, for so short a season of duty. But we have no choice. The radiation around a recent supernova is too intense. Even under superdrive, a ship gets some of it, and a percentage of that comes through the heaviest shielding. Nor can the crew make accurate studies, entirely while moving faster than light. Much of their work must be done in normal state, at true velocity. Of course, then they extend magnetohydrodynamic fields well beyond the hull, control a plasma cloud, and enjoy quite effective protection. But no protection is perfect, unless it be divine. In view of probable cumulative dosage, the rule has been that three months is the maximum safe exposure time.

"In *Uriel*'s case, the period was greatly lessened."

The screen has been carrying diagrams and cartoons to clarify this physics for the layman. Next leaps forth a view from the observation bridge of a craft already on station, yes, I glimpse an officer whom I recognize, Ludwig Taube, aboard *Abdiel*. Cameras always record arrivals, to have information should misfortune occur. The scanning is Solward, whence the newcomer is expected. Those who wait will get no advance warning—what signal could outpace light?—but they have no reason to think King is off schedule, give or take a few hours. And, in a corner of the screen, see! The lean shape flashes into sight, into existence within the framework of relativity. It drifts off scene. Tracking, the camera catches and centers it. Stars appear to stream past; *Uriel* is moving swiftly across their field. Those in a cone ahead of the vessel show a flicker, their light rippled by its thrust drive as it decelerates. Taube's words: "What a hellbat of an intrinsic. I wonder why."

More drawings and narration explain: "—conservation of energy. A ship about to enter superdrive has a certain definite velocity—speed and direction—with respect to any other given object in the universe, including its destination. Crossing space with inertia nullified does not change that velocity, nor do gravitational wells affect it significantly…as a rule. In ordinary procedure, we try to match this so-called intrinsic to the intrinsic of the target, as closely as feasible, before staring the nonrelativistic part of our journey. Else we might have to spend too much fuel at the far end of the trip, where it can't readily be replaced. Not even the tanks of a fusion engine can carry enough for more than about five thousand kilometers per second of delta-V—that is, total velocity changes, both speedups and slowdowns, added together in the course of a mission…" Old hat. I noticed acutely how warm and tightly gripping was Daphne's hand.

Switch back to intership transmission. Matt King's blocky face appears, reporting to over-commander Cauldwell aboard *Zephon*. "Sorry about our excess V. I thought I had our vector well calculated."

"Don't fret," his superior smiles. "You're within acceptable limits—barely, but nevertheless within, praise God. Given the uncertainty and variability of parameters, you've done OK."

Jump to a date weeks later, Cauldwell before the board of inquiry on Earth. His features are worn and strained, a tic plagues his mouth, he speaks roughly: "Gentlemen, the guilt is mine. I should have weighed the possibility that the trouble was due to a fault developing within *Uriel*, worsening till a breakdown must occur."

"But nothing ominous had registered on their gauges en route, had it?" says the presiding officer. I know him. He is a man who, in the fear of the Lord, strives to be just. "We realize how intricate a thing a spaceship is. The least carelessness in maintenance can plant the seed of a terrible surprise."

"Father, forgive me," Cauldwell groans toward the infinite. "I should have thought seriously about that and ordered them straight home."

"Thus canceling their scientific projects: forever, because the stellar system would not have remained long in that particular state," declares the president. "No, Admiral, your decision was correct. Note well that King did not request an abort, nor any of his men. Our task is to track down whatever technician homeside was negligent, and find out what he did wrong." Pause. "The Pastorate will set his penance."

Narrator: "Seven men aboard *Uriel*—"

Singly, they go past us. Captain Matthew King, commanding. Lieutenant Commander Valdemar Asklund, navigator and first officer. Lieutenant Jesse

Smith, chief engineer. Lieutenant Blaise Policard, second engineer and supervisor of life-support systems. That is all the crew which one of our marvelous wanderers needs, and each has been taught in addition how to assist the scientists. Those are not members of the Corps, though naturally in fine physical shape and sent through basic astronautical training. Nikolai Vissarionovich Kuzmin has planned especially to study nuclear reactions as they gutter out in the bared kernel of the ruptured star, Ioannes Venizelos gas and radiation dynamics in the nebula, Sugiyama Kito the gravity waves as configurations change. We see their lives, wives, parents, children—

Daphne, and I because of her, saw Valdemar Asklund as if he were alone.

He is a tall young man, lean, blond, narrow-faced, crinkly-eyed, readily smiling. His grays always seem the least bit rumpled, tunic open at the throat and bare of the ribbon to which he is entitled for his role in the daring rescue of *Michael*. His English carries the rise and fall of surf against the cliffs of that fjord where he was born. He was an indifferent student and barely got accepted into the Corps, but thereafter did brilliantly. Yet he is no spacegoing machine. He loves what remains of Earth's outdoors; he reads widely, with a special fondness for the comedies of Aristophanes, Shakespeare, Holberg, and Yarbro; he paints, plays chess and tennis, can cook a tasty meal or mix a powerful drink (that's a minor point against him, of course), is a genial host and sought-after guest; influenced by his wife, he is deep into the music of Beethoven and has been learning the piano; he has likewise been pondering and quoting old American writings like the Declaration of Independence (good), though he omits the Churchly glosses upon them (bad); he keeps a seemingly unlimited supply of jokes for both stag gatherings and polite company; the more I see, the better I like him. And...those glimpses of him and Daphne which the filmmakers were able to dig out of this newsfile or that private album...appearances, frolics, the little possessions which turned their series of apartments into a single home—how happy they made each other!

Return our scene to space. Vessels extrude gang tubes, men cross between and cheerily fraternize, the chaplain aboard *Zephon* holds a special service for these seven who have gone weeks without hearing the Word from an ordained mouth. But time is fleeting. Captains and scientists confer. The four vessels will proceed in formation to the fringes of the nebula. Thence *Uriel* will plunge further, to conduct its first set of planned experiments.

The little fleet glides on superdrive to the initial goal. The three which will wait there, making different observations as they free-float in normal state, are sufficiently distant from the core—a quarter light-year—that their hulls and low-intensity MHD fields guard personnel from harm. Fading fast as it expands, today the burst sun gives them hardly more heat and X-rays than they would get in the orbit of Venus; the blast of leptons has already gone past this region, the baryons and ions have not yet reached it, the thin light-haze around is mainly due to excited interstellar gas.

Uriel leaves them. The recorded transmission includes sight of Asklund at his work. He reads off a string of figures, then abruptly grins, his head haloed in stars, waves, calls, "So long and cheerio."

Daphne's nails bit blood out of my hand. I did not stir.

Briefly back under superdrive, *Uriel* slips close, close to the inferno before reverting to normal state, visibility, vulnerability. From protector nozzles gushes a cloud of plasma, which a heightened field wraps around the hull like a faintly shimmering cocoon. This will ward off not only the hurricane of charged particles, but the lethal photons…most of them. Should the dose aboard approach a safe limit, the ship will flee, faster than light.

These events must be shown in reconstruction. No outside lens, were any that close, could have spied a work of man against the nebular blaze. No message beam, were any receiver that close, could have pierced the wild electricity around. What we see is an impressionistic view, the craft large till it suddenly whirls off, dwindles to sight, vanishes amidst fire. Next, as if given the eyes of angels, we see the greater globe white-hot and still collapsing, the lesser burnt-out and compressed though now ashimmer, whipping in seconds through their orbit. And we see a dot which images *Uriel*. That dot plunges in.

Closeups: Needles abruptly aswoop across dials, numbers in screens changing too fast to follow, frantic chatter of printout; afterward men, whose resoluteness is a cage for horror.

Narrator: "Without warning, power failed. Engineers Smith and Policard could barely squeeze out the ergs to maintain radiation shielding. Nothing could be spared for either thrust or superdrive. The collapse of the MHD field for half an instant would mean death. There was nothing to do but work— find the cause of the trouble and make repairs—while *Uriel*, helpless, was hauled in like a comet by the gravity of two suns both heavier than Sol itself.

"The orbit had been established beforehand, to swing safely wide of the hot companion, slightly nearer the cold. Nobody had expected to continue in the path for long—certainly not till it almost grazed the sun-clinker. But this is what happened."

A scarlet thread grows behind the dot, marking its track through space. At first, time on the screen is compressed. *Uriel* had a high intrinsic in the direction of the double, whose mass accelerated it ever more furiously. Nevertheless the ship took days, terrible days to reach apastron.

Later, time is necessarily stretched. For close in, speed increases, increases, increases, dizzily beyond what the simple attraction of matter for matter can wreak. *Uriel* sweeps around the side of the neutron star opposite the late supernova, a moment in shadow which saves the men, since radiation is forcing itself past their screens in such amounts that every danger signal shrills. Acceleration climbs to better than half a million gees, five hundred kilometers per second per second. Thus the ship departs spaceward in the wink of a quantum, too swiftly for its re-exposure to the starblast to kill. The acceleration tumbles down again; but by then, *Uriel* is coursing on the heels of light.

Narrator: "Bodies as massive as these two, spinning as fast, generate forces according to the laws of general relativity which act like a kind of negative gravity. That is what seized our unhappy men. They felt no drag, no pressure; they were in free fall throughout, and did not come within the effective tidal action zone.

But their intrinsic mounted to more than fifty times what their thrust drive could possibly shed before fuel was exhausted. They were, they are trapped in the speed they have gained."

I meant to write down everything we saw, the pictures taken on board, the forlorn gallantry of men who toiled, suffered, prayed, endured, never really expecting survival nor, maybe, really wanting it. But I cannot.

I will merely write of scenes toward the end, that Daphne and I watched while she wept, my arm around her. The faulty powerplant has been repaired. The medication against radiation exposure is taking effect. The interior of the ship is cool again, scorch and sweat are gone from the air, pseudogravity generators once more provide stable weight, guardian fields scoop interstellar gas aside in an invisible bow wave so that rays no longer seethe through bodies; and a great silence has fallen.

In awe, the seven stand on their observation bridge. Lengths are shrunken, masses swollen, time dilated. Doppler shift has muffled nearly all stars fore and aft, though a few glint wanly still. Aberration has turned the rest into a single eldritch constellation girdling enormous night.

By no other light than that, Captain King leads his men in thanksgiving. "The heavens declare the glory of God: and the firmament sheweth his handy-work... For I will consider thy heavens, even the works of thy fingers: the moon and the stars, which thou has ordained. What is man, that thou art mindful of him: and the son of man, that thou visitest him?"

But Asklund stands erect, looking outward as if into the face of a foe.

Afterward they resume stations, start the superdrive; automatic optical compensators give them an illusion of being back in a familiar universe; they run toward rendezvous with their fellows.

Narrator: "In the inertialess condition, a difference of intrinsic does not manifest itself. Taking due precautions, crews from the spared vessels boarded *Uriel*, offered consolation, taped messages to bring home."

Some words are stammered, some stilted, some tearful. Asklund smiles almost wryly into the camera, though tenderness dwells in his voice: "—Daphne, darling, do you remember that old, old ballad I translated for you, about the dead knight who returns to his sweetheart? Do you remember what he tells her?"

> *For every time you're weeping*
> *And sad your mood,*
> *Then is my coffin filled inside*
> *With clotted blood...*

> *But every time you're singing*
> *And have no grief,*
> *Then is my coffin filled inside*
> *With rose and leaf...*

"Please give me that gift. Live. Let me know and be glad that you're happy. Because I'll be alive myself, don't forget. This is no coffin. We can have good and useful lives, if people will help. If you will help, Daphne, by not mourning but living—" There is a little more.

Narrator: "*Uriel* stayed on cruise while the men recovered fully from their ordeal. Meanwhile the Astronautic Corps debated what is best for them. A plan is ready, a mission in progress."

Daphne swallowed hard before she whispered in my ear: "And Sinclair, I'm going too!"

Not till she returned from training did I learn, in part, how she got her way. The recommendation she magicked out of me was not enough, however hard I wrangled.

Director Jarvis: "Nonsense. The trouble and expense of teaching a one-shot rookie, when we've got career men? And a woman? Great Scott, just imagine the plumbing problems!"

Secretary Wardour: "Well, yes, it wouldn't hurt the Corps to perform a well-publicized act of compassion. But what kind of mercy is this, letting them meet for a couple of weeks in a crowded hull, her spacesuit always between them?"

Pastor Benson: "Propriety first. It would be extremely difficult, at best, for a sole woman to travel and work among men, in close quarters, without occasionally revealing what should not be revealed. Morality second. She could not help arousing lust. Oh, I realize nothing untoward would happen. But minds would stray from godliness—from concentration on temporal duties also, perhaps, in that dangerous environment. Religion third but foremost. Might not the unexpected, stunning sight of her, an attractive female, briefly among men condemned to lifelong celibacy—not only her husband but the whole seven, young and virile—might that not weaken their resolve to accept the will of God? Might the memory not haunt them until at last they despair of his grace and fall into the Devil's claws?"

I was astounded when the OK came through. But I had been too busy to see much of Daphne or hear her schemes. And she was promptly whisked off to Luna base for two intensive months, while the load on me redoubled. You don't casually gather a crew, hop into a craft, and take off for the deeps. Look what happened to *Uriel*, where everybody supposed that everything had been checked out. The operation which I headed involved more unknowns yet.

Maybe you, archeologist, wonder why. In your ultrasophisticated astronautics (if God has not closed down technological civilization, lest we make an idol of material progress) what could be simpler than to lay alongside, both vessels in superdrive, and transfer cargo? Why, you may know how to kill such speed and let its victims rejoin the human race.

But we—Well, *Uriel* already had systems for recycling air and water. However, they were not completely adequate. Nobody had expected them to be in continuous use for half a century. They would degrade, poisonous organics would accumulate, unless we added refinements and ancilliaries. And we couldn't simply plug in the new stuff. We had to do considerable rebuilding. Likewise, the ship had carried six months' worth of food. We would install closed-ecology units that would feed the men indefinitely, indeed yield a large surplus. But this too we couldn't merely dump aboard. It must be integrated with everything else. For a single example of our needful planning, remember that health and sanity required we leave the crew reasonable elbow room.

And while we labored, we must take elaborate precautions to assure no substantial number of atoms from *Uriel* got aboard our own ship. A few nanograms would destroy us, the moment we reverted to normal state and they took off at their light-like intrinsic velocity. There wouldn't be an explosion unless the mass was really gross, up in the milligrams or whatever. But from end to end of our hull would go a fatal wave of radiation.

Obviously, *Uriel* can never leave the inertialess state. It must always keep moving at a quasispeed which outruns light—a modern incarnation of that eerie ancient legend, the Flying Dutchman. (What did its crew ever do, to merit their damnation?) Even if we invented a means to slow it, it would first have to enter normal state—would it not?—and our gift of supplies and machinery would annihilate it in a brief brilliance that might rival a nova.

Fortunately, fuel is no problem. The demands of life support are modest, those of keeping an inertialess body moving are less. Tanks topped off by us ought to serve for more years of exploration than those men have left in their bodies.

You may not believe me, in your hypothetical age of universal enlightenment, but fools have actually asked why *Uriel* didn't backtrack, once its superdrive was operational again, and let the double star undo what was wrought. Evidently, for them the narration was futile when explaining that a velocity is a direction as well as a speed. And, to be sure, Asklund calculated that at the rate yon companions are moving apart, already then they could no longer accelerate an infalling object in anything near the fashion they handled him.

Less crackpot was the suggestion that the ship find a safe, solitary and cold neutron star, go normal near its surface, and let gravity act as a brake, repeating this process until the intrinsic was down to a reasonable figure. But doubtless you need not do the arithmetic to estimate how many passes this would require. The limited food stocks would be exhausted years before an end was in sight.

Another double of precisely the right characteristics, or any of several more exotic and hypothetical things, could reverse the effect, yes. While we have not publicized the fact, *Uriel* spent what months were possible on minimum rations, before reserves got hopelessly low, seeking just such a deliverance. The hunt was foredoomed, of course. Recall the sheer size of space, and guess at the probabilities. Then think what spirit was in those men, that they tried.

Further search is pointless. The equipment of survival, which we have given our comrades, has a differential intrinsic of almost three hundred thousand kilometers per second: to the best of our present-day knowledge and imagination, irrevocable.

Why is my dictascribe trudging through elementary physics? Don't I want to remember how Daphne came back to me?

She protested the two-week furlough granted our crew before departure. They were edging starvation in that ship. I told her the custom was vital. We dared not go to space tired, tense, unrefreshed by our loves. We would meet our deadline, which King and Cauldwell had determined between them a thousand light-years from home. Let her not fear.

"Yes, I've been told," she said. "I'm sorry I grew impatient."

"You have a downright duty to enjoy yourself." I wagged a finger at her. "Where will you go, if I may ask?"

"Well," she said, "my parents have passed away, I haven't anybody close, I'd like to, oh, bid Earth good-bye. Luna was magnificent but stark. Doesn't the Corps maintain a wilderness resort?"

"Aye," I answered, and changed my mind about visiting my sons.

Autumn descends early upon the Grand Tetons. Except for the lodge staff, we had this part of them to ourselves. During the days we tramped their trails, canoed on their lakes, dared their glaciers, found nooks of sunlit warmth and sat down to wonder at their birds, beasts, trees, and distances. Evenings we attacked dinner, surprised at how often we japed and laughed; afterward we took our ease before a stone fireplace, in dimness that burning pine logs made flickery fragrant, and talked more seriously, traded memories, thoughts, and—shyly at first—dreams.

I will sketch a single hour, soon after we arrived. We left in the morning for a hike to the peak above. Our path took us through a wood where leaves glowed in crystalline sunlight, scarlet maple, golden birch, fallow aspen. Between their slim trunks we saw how the mountain slanted toward a dale where a brook went rushing, and how on the far side the range lifted anew in white and violet purity. The sky was like sapphire. The air was chill in our nostrils, smoky when we breathed out, sweetened by faint odors of soil and damp and life. Sometimes a raven went "Gruk!" or a squirrel streaked up a bole and chattered at us; twice a flock of geese passed overhead, their calls drifting down; else our footfalls resounded through holy quietness.

We stopped a while to rest. The ground was soft beneath us. Daphne sat looking outward, arms clasped around knees, cheeks flushed from our climb. The warmth of her went over me in a wave. Her hair, tumbling from a headband and across her shoulders, shimmered as bronze does, or heavy silk.

She said at last, low, maybe to herself, "Val spoke of this country a lot. We were going to pay a visit together. But something always made us postpone. We didn't really understand that we weren't immortal. So now it seems we never will come."

"You will," I promised.

"I…won't be able to. I'm temporarily associated, not actually in the Corps."

"I can bring guests."

She turned her head and gave me a grave smile. "Thank you, Alec. You're kinder to me than is right. But no. I've seen what it costs, and won't have that sort of money."

"Eh?" I was startled, having read the dossier on her which Personnel compiled. "I thought your parents left you quite well off."

"They did. Everything's gone for a bribe, though."

"What?"

She chuckled. "Poor shockable Alec! Nobody told you? Oh, not strictly a bribe. I informed the Pastorate that if it would approve my going in your gang, and pressure an acceptance through secular channels, I'd donate my inheritance to the Church. I dropped a strong hint that otherwise I'd endow a synagogue. They huffed and puffed, but in the end—" She shrugged. "I'll spare you the list of my other blackmails, browbeatings, bluffs, and deceits."

"Lass, lass," I whispered, "how can it mean that much to you, squinting at him through a helmet visor?"

"It does."

I gathered courage to say, "He himself begged you to put him behind you."

She looked back toward the snowpeaks. "I don't think I can. 'In plenty and in want; in joy and in sorrow; in sickness and in health; as long as we both shall live.'" Her hands, groping about, closed on a fallen dry branch. "I… suppose… I'm more of a monogamist…in my way…than he is." The noise was startlingly loud when the branch snapped. "But he does love me!"

A deer bounded into sight. Our gaze followed, enchanted. "He loves Earth also," she ended, "and he's been forever shut away. Shouldn't I bring him what touch—what remembrance I can?"

To hurt him the worse? Have you thought how selfish you maybe are? I barely halted my tongue, and hunched appalled. What good would lie in lashing out at her craziness? The fault was mine. I should have stood on my veto at the beginning. Now we were locked in. She was precision-fitted for a crucial role. Quite rightly, the directors would not allow me to substitute her backup for any reason less than a medical emergency. Nor would she ever forgive me.

Whereas—Very well, keep silence, let her get that adieu out of her system. Afterward—

"You find this a bonny land, do you not?" I asked rhetorically.

She nodded. "I'll never forget," she murmured.

"You need not hanker," I told her. "When we return to Earth—" My heart slammed. "We can come here. Whenever we're both free. No matter money. I draw a good wage, and nobody depends on me anymore."

"Oh, Alec!" For an instant I glimpsed tears. For another instant her arms were around me, her face buried in my shoulder. Then she leaped up. "C'mon, lazy-legs!" she cried, and we were on our way again.

We made rendezvous beyond Mars, where *Uriel* had lately been flying a prearranged exact circle. Knowing position and quasispeed of the exiles, my instruments, automatons, and I brought *Gabriel* carefully closing in. When the two counterinertial fields, extending a few kilometers beyond either hull, began to mesh, I saw ghostlike waverings across the Milky Way. As we neared, our objective solidified. Having reached the same phase, an optic screen showed it not far off, as real among the stars as we were…or as unreal, in this mass-annulled condition we shared.

"Synchronism achieved," I mumbled into the intercom, and sank back in my pilot chair. The process had been slow, trying, dangerous because of the short range within which mutual detection was possible; inside our fields, we still had inertia with respect to each other if not to the outside cosmos, and a collision could wreck us both. I smelled the sweat rank on me, heard breath and pulse rattle, felt the separate stiffnesses and aches in a body no longer young.

"How are they?" rang Daphne's voice. "May we see?"

I decided I wasn't ready for the boneyard yet, and switched the telereceivers aft into the visual compensator circuit. A buzz of excited talk reached me vaguely, from my men. They were five altogether besides her, excellent fellows, who had treated her with awkward chivalry while we rehearsed and at last ran outward from Earth orbit. I wish them well. But none of them especially matters.

"Maintain stations," I ordered. "I'll try for contact." Right off, I saw my mistake. "I'll make contact," I amended. They must not be dead or insane over there! My fingers stumbled across the com panel. "*Gabriel* to *Uriel*, come in."

"*Uriel* to *Gabriel*." The screen flashed color. Matt King stared forth. His eyes and cheeks were sunken back among the bones of his face, and he spoke in a hoarse whisper; but he was clean, closely groomed, crisply uniformed. My worst fears drained out of me. "Welcome, welcome." He managed a shaky smile. "You're skippering the mission, are you, Alexander Sinclair, you old rascal? What a pleasant surprise."

"How is everybody?" I barked.

"Basically healthy, praise God. Weak but functional, and we got out of the habit of hunger six months ago. Morale is, um, not bad. We do hope you've brought steaks and champagne! When do you expect you can board?"

"We need rest, and I want a complete final checkout of every system…Let's say in twenty-four hours. I'm sorry it cannot be sooner. Uh, I wonder if Valdemar Asklund could come to your pickup?"

"Why, well, yes, if you wish."

"Will you report to the command bridge?" I said into the intercom. No reason to state who.

She arrived just as Asklund's hollowed-out countenance appeared. Through a minute or more, they were dumb. I might not leave my post until relieved by Roberts, my first officer; but I glowered at the optic screens. In one of them, its radiance stopped down for the sake of my vision, the sun looked shrunken and cold; in another, Earth shone deep blue, loveliest of the stars and somehow more distant-seeming than any else; in the rest gleamed inhuman hordes and the immensities between.

Finally I heard Asklund sigh, "Daphne, why?"

"To be with you," she wept.

"When we can't even touch? I…we're going away as soon as—Oh, my dearest, I worked for weeks on a message to record for you, and now—no words—" I heard him weep too.

Presently she said, "I'll be busy, you realize. I'm responsible for the core parts of your food-cycling equipment. But you can assist me, and—and Captain Sinclair did promise we'd have chances, a compartment where we're by ourselves, or a private line—"

To talk.

We used no gang tube. A handful of air molecules, diffusing from *Uriel* to *Gabriel*, would bring the same doom on us. Instead, we kept the ships as far apart as synchronicity allowed, and jetted across in spacesuits which we wore during an entire shift. This handicapped us infernally. Sheer bulk got in its own way. Gloved fingers, being clumsy, must often operate specially designed manipulators. Speech was via sonic amplifiers, likewise a nuisance. But there was no help for it; and, to be sure, as we instructed them in the requirements, our outcast comrades became quite skillful teammates. Returning to our vessel to eat and sleep, we paused outside the entry lock and practiced elaborate rotations and contortions while an infrared beam boiled off whatever atoms might cling to our suits, and well-nigh baked us. Those were the more obvious, physical discomforts.

And they were not what made us long to finish and be gone. No, it was what *Uriel*'s men said, generally with Spartan mildness, and their eyes upon us, and the way they handled the letters, pictures, tapes, mementos we brought them.

I remember a talk out of many which King and I had. We were off duty, seated in our cabins, using an exclusive frequency. This is standard on spacecraft, whose captains may have to reach a grim decision. We let Daphne and her husband into these cubicles at a regular hour out of the twenty-four.

King poured whiskey from a bottle, my smuggled gift, raised the tumbler, and toasted. "Here's to our noble selves." I responded in kind. He didn't show it, really—indeed, having begun to flesh out since we brought abundant food, he looked better than erstwhile—but he had let himself become a trifle drunk.

"Or skoal, my navigator would say," he added.

I let the drink glow down my throat. The leastmost cheer felt large. What had I around me? Three meters by two of room, gray-painted metal, bunk, locker, chair, desk, reference works, Bible, a file of favorite books and a microreader for them, a small musical library and player, a harmonica that I occasionally tootled on, pipes and tobacco, photographs of Meg who was dead and our sons who were grown—that, and starriness outside.

But I could go walk on planets of yon suns, including a planet named Earth.

"Your pronunciation is wrong, Matt," I tried to laugh.

"How do you know?" he bridled. A ventilator muttered around his words.

"Well, ah, Daphne Asklund told me I had it wrong, and taught me a closer approximation." I took a second swallow, much sooner than I had intended.

He peered at me. "Why did she make you bring her?"

"What? Why did I? I've explained. She told you herself. She saw how to join her husband this brief while—unless when you return to the Solar System—and since she could in fact carry her share of the load, I had no heart to refuse her."

The image of his head shook from side to side in the cramped screen. "Don't evade my question, Alec. It wasn't about your motive—that's pathetically obvious—but hers. Nobody who wasn't...terrifyingly...strong and clearheaded could have swung what she did. I know how these things work as well as you do; I can make the same estimate of the barriers she had to break down, the powerful men she had to outface and outsmart. Such a person doesn't do such a thing for an orgy of sentimentalism that can only agonize her man. Then *why?*"

"Who knows what drives a soul?" I counterattacked. "Do you understand yours? I don't mine. How is Asklund taking it?"

"How does he strike you? I've been meaning to get your outside opinion, Alec, to check my impression. We'll spend the rest of our mutual life together; I'd better have an accurate judgment of him."

I needn't stop to ponder, having done that in uncounted wakeful nightwatch hours. "He was knocked off his orbit at first, I'd say. But he appears to have recovered fast. I don't see him much, you ken, and almost always in public, at work. He's calm, competent—rather withdrawn, I think. They both are."

"He wears a stout mask." The lines deepened around King's mouth. "I gauge him as being under the tightest, breaking-point control."

"Is that uncanny?"

"No, I suppose not. My other men—she's causing them trouble too, not as intense but nevertheless trouble."

"Psychological disturbance was foreseen and allowed for. Still, what is she to them? A bulgy suit like everybody's from *Gabriel*. A face in the visor, a voice out of a speaker, aye, those are female. But men throughout history, in military units or monasteries, have seen more of women, and not been tantalized beyond endurance."

"Soldiers expected to get home; monks expected to keep vows they'd made. We're neither. Already Blai—an astronaut has admitted to me being in love with her. I myself—" King tossed off a mouthful and quirked a smile. "Oh, we'll get over our emotions, our itch, that is. But frankly, I'm thankful this will soon end. Please don't let her join in the next rendezvous."

Wordlessness hummed between us.

"Have you decided where you will go first?" I blurted. We'd brought a bundle of recommendations from different scientists, but the *Uriel* crew had taken no opportunity thus far to study these. King had mentioned how, in the months of their hunt for a savior star, they discussed every imaginable possibility and contingency. What else was there for them?

And what else had they to do in the years that remained, but range the galaxy, and, from time to time, bring us tales of their discoveries? A radio capsule, shot free of the counterinertial field, could summon our people to a meeting. Though we dared not accept any physical record, we could make copies.

But we could merely request and recommend, never command. They were untouchable.

"A shakedown cruise," he answered. "To the Orion Nebula. You know what a lot of unsolved puzzles it holds, and…we'd like to see new suns being formed. Then, when we're reasonably sure of our ship and ourselves—the long jump. Clear to galactic center."

I was not altogether surprised. Nevertheless—"Already?" For that would be a voyage of years; and opinion continues divided as to whether, beyond the vast dust clouds which hide it from our probings, the heart of the Milky Way is a hell of radiation or—

"The Elders," he capped my thought.

Surely we are not the solitary species who fare between the stars. God is too generous for that. Far out in this fringe of a spiral arm, barely starting to fumble around off our home shores, we must be like cavemen on a raft, compared to races ahead of us which, maybe, are not burdened by original sin, not plagued by the Devil or a myriad lunacies. Half our astronomers think the middle regions are clear, the suns close together but old and benign, the likeliest hearths of beings whose recorded history runs for multiple millions of years—

—and who might even know how to lift the curse off *Uriel*.

"What have we to lose?" King said.

To that same room came Daphne, at the close of our mission.

When I heard her knock, I soared from the chair where I had been grinding at return-trip calculations, hit my knee on the desk, and in the pain swore at myself for a lubberly old gowk. Aloud, I called, "Enter." She came through in her pride and gentleness, and I forgot about hurting.

"The captain summoned me," she uttered formally. Her eyes were the green of Earth's living seas.

"Aye. Please shut the door. Sit down." I gestured her to the chair. As she brushed past, touching me, I scented her warmth afresh, after these many days in spacesuits or a crowded mess or a bunk alone. When she was seated, her gaze must travel too far to meet mine. So I perched on a corner of my desk, swung the foot that was free of the deck, and speculated at the back of my mind whether this made me seem younger.

Did she, regardless, bear dread behind her face? I studied closely. She blinked, drew a long breath, then eased back and smiled. "Everything I've worked on checks out swab-O," she said. "And my fellows tell me they're satisfied."

I nodded, while fighting my throat.

"What can I do further?" she asked, neither wondering nor defying but quietly helping me along.

"You—" I tried again. "You are in a, an unco situation, lass. I couldna but see—Well, tomorrow mornwatch we go to *Uriel* for…we canna call't a celebration—a speech or twa—and—"

She said (how kindly!), "You wonder if Val and I have any special last request, don't you, Alec?"

"I've seen your glove seek him."

She laid her hand across mine where it clenched the desk edge. Is not a woman's hand twice beautiful on the knobbly hairy paw of a man? "If we could go off by ourselves, to Matt King's cabin or wherever, a while, we'd be grateful."

"You know you can that," I snapped after air. "Why I called you here…I'm not quite sure. I thought, 'twill be a hard farewell. And he, Val, he does trust you'll build a life of your own afterward. I want you to, to know you have a friend here who cares for you very much, Daphne. How can I be of service?"

"Oh, Alec, Alec." Suddenly she kissed me, and fled crying.

At last I slept.

We would have been mad to leave *Gabriel* long unattended, on automatics. Nor could anybody stand much ceremony. But rightness required that, together, we see directly through our visors our comrades for whom we had toiled and clasp them good-bye in our armored arms, and wish them godspeed till death or a miracle delivered them.

Crossing over, I flew as near as might be to Daphne. She was half a shadow, half a shimmer, amidst the stars and silence around. I heard naught save a radio hiss in my earphones, a thrum of thrust, my heart knocking. At breakfast, some of us had been boisterous and some bleak; she had been unreadable; now none talked. Did we feel guilt, that soon we would know blueness, clouds, rain, leaves in the wind? Myself, did I do wrong to hope?

The sternest realism I could muster warned she would remarry, if she did, for convenience and companionship. Well, I dared not want more.

My boots thudded on *Uriel's* hull.

We cycled through the lock. At the inner valve waited Matthew King, Jesse Smith, Blaise Policard, Nikolai Kuzmin, Ioannes Venizelos, Sugiyama Kito, Valdemar Asklund. No longer grimy in coveralls, no longer starved, and no longer looking forward to human advent, they stood in dress uniforms as if on parade; and I saw that these brave, decent men were unsure how they might comfort us.

"Welcome," King said. Walking down the corridor, he took me around the waist. After half a second I was ashamed that I was shocked. He did have woman-less years before him, but I was his old friend, and muffled away from the very air he breathed, and due to depart in an hour. Next I noticed that, while Daphne and Asklund were side by side, they had not embraced as they did when first she boarded. Their faces were as shut as her helmet.

What had she told him, in the privacies we gave them?

Though we fourteen had fractional room to move around in the mess, we quickly took places at its table. By prearrangement, *Uriel's* crew had set out glasses and the last bottle of champagne. They would drink for both and we, homeward bound after this was done, would pray for both.

King stood up, klinged thumbnail on goblet, and said: "Mrs. Asklund and gentlemen, we cannot reckon or repay what we owe you. I speak less of your help which will let us live on—that was rendered in the tradition of the Corps—than of your spirit, your generosity—"

I, rising to respond, said: "Brothers, forgive a, a wee bit of dramatics. From your wives, children, parents, your kin and closest well-wishers on Earth, we brought what they gave us to bring you. But we held back one small thing for each till now, whatever they felt would be extra special—"

We tried together to stay calm, and even I hardly saw the Asklunds excuse themselves and leave.

"—we will never forget," I was saying; "mankind will never forget," when they made re-entry, bare hand in hand. She wore her undergarb, and carried high her head and the unbound ruddy hair.

I am a starship captain, therefore disciplined into command of myself. I roared the chaos around the table back to order. Matt King came to my help. Daphne and Valdemar waited calmly.

Jezebel, harlot of outlaws, wandering Jewess—what pain did the curses give her, give them, when *Uriel* returned for the first and last time to report wonders? What freedom have they found to keep them away ever since, if death does not? And what interior victory, readiness of both to give ungrudging love, must he and she have won before at last, in sight of us all, she kissed her man full upon the mouth?

GYPSY

From afar, I caught a glimpse of the *Traveler* as my boat swung toward the planet. The great spaceship looked like a toy at that distance, a frail bubble of metal and air and energy against the enormous background of space. I thought of the machines within her, humming and whirring and clicking very faintly as they pursued their unending round of services, making that long hull into a living world—the hull that was now empty of life—and I had a sudden odd feeling of sympathy. As if she were alive, I felt that the *Traveler* was lonely.

The planet swelled before me, a shining blue shield blazoned with clouds and continents, rolling against a limitless dark and the bitterly burning stars. Harbor, we had named that world, the harbor at the end of our long journey, and there were few lovelier names. Harbor, haven, rest and peace and a sky overhead as roof against the naked blaze of space. It was good to get home.

I searched the heavens for another glimpse of the *Traveler*, but I couldn't find her tiny form in that thronging wilderness of stars. No matter, she was still on her orbit about Harbor, moored to the planet, perhaps forever. I concentrated on bringing the spaceboat down.

Atmosphere whistled about the hull. After a month in the gloom and poisonous cold of the fifth planet, alone among utterly unhuman natives, I was usually on fire to get home and brought my craft down with a recklessness that overloaded the gravity beams. But this time I went a little more carefully, telling myself that I'd rather be late for supper than not arrive at all. Or perhaps it was that brief chance vision of the *Traveler* which made me suddenly thoughtful. After all, we had had some good times aboard her.

I sent the boat slanting toward the peninsula in the north temperate zone on which most of us were settled. The outraged air screamed behind me as I slammed down on the hard-packed earth that served us for a landing field. There were a few warehouses and service shops around it, long low buildings of the heavy timbers used by most of the colonists, and a couple of private homes a kilometer or so away. But otherwise only long grass rustled in the wind, gardens and wild groves, sunlight streaming out of a high blue sky. When I stepped from the boat, the fresh vivid scent of the land fairly leaped to meet me. I could hear the sea growling beyond the horizon.

Tokogama was on duty at the field. He was sitting on the porch of the office, smoking his pipe and watching the clouds sail by overhead, but he greeted me with the undemonstrative cordiality of old friends who know each other too well to need many words.

"So that's the portmaster," I said. "Soft touch. All you have to do is puff that vile-smelling thing and say hello to me."

"That's all," he admitted cheerfully. "I am retained only for my uncommonly high ornamental value."

It was, approximately, true. Our aircraft used the field with no formality, and we only kept this one space vessel in operation. The portmaster was on hand simply to oversee servicing and in the unlikely case of some emergency or dispute. But none of the colony's few public posts—captain, communications officer, and the rest—required much effort in as simple a society as ours, and they were filled as spare-time occupations by anyone who wanted them. There was no compensation except getting first turn at using the machinery for farming or heavy construction which we owned in common.

"How was the trip?" asked Tokogama.

"Pretty good," I said. "I gave them our machines and they filled my holds with their ores and alloys. And I managed to take a few more notes on their habits, and establish a few more code symbols for communication."

"Which is a very notable brick added to the walls of science, but in view of the fact that you're the only one who ever goes there it really makes no odds." Tokogama's dark eyes regarded me curiously. "Why do you keep on making those trips out there, Erling? Quite a few of the other boys wouldn't mind visiting Five once in a while. Will and Ivan both mentioned it to me last week."

"I'm no hog," I said. "If either of them, or anyone else, wants a turn at the trading job, let 'em learn space piloting and they can go. But meanwhile—I like the work. You know that I was one of those who voted to continue the search for Earth."

Tokogama nodded. "So you were. But that was three years ago. Even you must have grown some roots here."

"Oh, I have," I laughed. "Which reminds me I'm hungry, and judging by the sun it's the local dinner time. So I'll get on home, if Alanna knows I'm back."

"She can't help it," he smiled. "The whole continent knows when you're back, the way you rip the atmosphere coming in. That home cooking must have a powerful magnetic attraction."

"A steak aroma of about fifty thousand gauss—" I turned to go, calling over my shoulder: "Why don't you come to dinner tomorrow evening? I'll invite the other boys and we'll have an old-fashioned hot air session."

"I was sort of hinting in that direction," said Tokogama.

I got my carplane out of the hangar and took off with a whisper of air and a hum of grav-beam generators. But I flew low over the woods and meadows, dawdling along at fifty kilometers an hour and looking across the landscape. It lay quietly in the evening, almost empty of man, a green fair breadth of land veined with bright rivers. The westering sun touched each leaf and grass blade with molten gold, an aureate glow which seemed to fill the cool air like a tangible presence, and I could hear the chirp and chatter of the great bird flocks as they settled down in the trees. Yes—it was good to get home.

My own house stood at the very edge of the sea, on a sandy bluff sloping down to the water. The windy trees which grew about it almost hid the little stone and timber structure, but its lawns and gardens reached far, and beyond them were the fields from which we got our food. Down by the beach stood the boathouse and the little dock I had made, and I knew our sailboat lay waiting there for me to take her out. I felt an almost physical hunger for the sea again, the mighty surge of waves out to the wild horizon, the keen salt wind and the crying white birds. After a month in the sterile tanked air of the spaceboat, it was like being born again.

I set the plane down before the house and got out. Two small bodies fairly exploded against me—Einar and Mike. I walked into the house with my sons riding my shoulders.

Alanna stood in the doorway waiting for me. She was tall, almost as tall as I, and slim and red-haired and the most beautiful woman in the universe. We didn't say much—it was unnecessary, and we were otherwise occupied for the next few minutes.

And afterward I sat before a leaping fire where the little flames danced and chuckled and cast a wavering ruddy glow over the room, and the wind whistled outside and rattled the door, and the sea roared on the nighted beach, and I told them of my fabulous space voyage, which had been hard and monotonous and lonely but was a glamorous adventure at home. The boys' eyes never stirred from my face as I talked, I could feel the eagerness that blazed from them. The gaunt sun-seared crags of One, the misty jungles of Two, the mountains and deserts of Four, the great civilization of Five, the bitter desolation of the outer worlds—and beyond those the stars. But we were home now, we sat in a warm dry house and heard the wind singing outside.

I was happy, in a quiet way that had somehow lost the exuberance of my earlier returns. Content, maybe.

Oh, well, I thought. These trips to the fifth world were becoming routine, just as life on Harbor, now that our colony was established and our automatic and semiautomatic machines running smoothly, had quieted down from the first great riot of work and danger and work again. That was progress, that was what we had striven for, to remove want and woe and the knife-edged uncertainty which had haunted our days. We had arrived, we had graduated into a solid assurance and a comfort which still held enough unsureness and challenge to keep us from getting sluggish. Grown men don't risk their necks climbing the uppermost branches of trees, the way children do; they walk on the ground, and when they have to rise they do so safely and comfortably, in a carplane.

"What's the matter, Erling?" asked Alanna.

"Why—nothing." I started out of my reverie, suddenly aware that the children were in bed and the night near its middle. "Nothing at all. I was just sitting thinking. A little tired, I guess. Let's turn in."

"You're a poor liar, Erling," she said softly. "What were you really thinking about?"

"Nothing," I insisted. "That is, well, I saw the old *Traveler* as I was coming down today. It just put me in mind of old times."

"It would," she said. And suddenly she sighed. I looked at her in some alarm, but she was smiling again. "You're right, it is late, and we'd better go to bed."

I took the boys out in the sailboat the next day. Alanna stayed home on the excuse that she had to prepare dinner, though I knew of her theory that the proper psychodevelopment of children required a balance of paternal and maternal influence. Since I was away so much of the time, out in space or with one of the exploring parties which were slowly mapping our planet, she made me occupy the center of the screen whenever I was home.

Einar, who was nine years old and getting interested in the microbooks we had from the *Traveler*—and so, ultimately, from Earth—looked at her and said: "Back at Sol you wouldn't have to make food, Mother. You'd just set the au…autochef, and come out with us."

"I like to cook," she smiled. "I suppose we could make autochefs, now that the more important semirobot machinery has been produced, but it'd take a lot of fun out of life for me."

Her eyes went past the house, down to the beach and out over the restless sun-sparked water. The sea breeze ruffled her red hair, it was like a flame in the cool shade of the trees. "I think they must miss a lot in the Solar System," she said. "They have so much there that, somehow, they can't have what we've got—room to move about, lands that never saw a man before, the fun of making something ourselves."

"You might like it if you went there," I said. "After all, sweetheart, however wisely we may talk about Sol, we know it only by hearsay."

"I know I like what we have here," she answered. I thought there was a faint note of defiance in her voice. "If Sol is just a legend, I can't be sure I'd like the reality. Certainly it could be no better than Harbor."

"All redheads are chauvinists," I laughed, turning down toward the beach.

"All Swedes make unfounded generalizations," she replied cheerfully. "I should'a known better than to marry a Thorkild."

"Fortunately, Mrs. Thorkild, you didn't." I bowed.

The boys and I got out the sailboat. There was a spanking breeze, and in minutes we were scudding northward, along the woods and fields and tumbling surf of the coast.

"We should put a motor on the *Naughty Nancy*, Dad," said Einar. "Suppose this wind don't hold."

"I like to sail," I said. "The chance of having to man the sweeps is part of the fun."

"Me too," said Mike, a little ambiguously.

"Do they have sailboats on Earth?" asked Einar.

"They must," I said, "since I designed the *Nancy* after a book about them. But I don't think it'd ever be quite the same, Einar. The sea must always be full of boats, most of them powered, and there'd be aircraft overhead and some sort of building wherever you made landfall. You wouldn't have the sea to yourself."

"Then why'd you want to keep looking for Earth when ever'body else wanted to stay here?" he challenged.

A nine-year-old can ask some remarkably disconcerting questions. I said slowly: "I wasn't the only one who voted to keep on searching. And—well, I admitted it at the time, it wasn't Earth but the search itself that I wanted. I liked to find new planets. But we've got a good home now, Einar, here on Harbor."

"I still don't understand how they ever lost Earth," he said.

"Nobody does," I said. "The *Traveler* was carrying a load of colonists to Alpha Centauri—that was a star close to Sol—and men had found the hyperdrive only a few years before and reached the nearer stars. Anyway, something happened. There was a great explosion in the engines, and we found ourselves somewhere else in the galaxy, thousands of light-years from home. We don't know how far from home, since we've never been able to find Sol again. But after repairing the ship, we spent more than twenty years looking. We never found home." I added quickly, "Until we decided to settle on Harbor. That was our home."

"I mean, how'd the ship get thrown so far off?"

I shrugged. The principles of the hyperdrive are difficult enough, involving as they do the concept of multiple dimensions and of discontinuous psi functions. No one on the ship—and everyone with a knowledge of physics had twisted his brains over the problem—had been able to figure out what catastrophe it was that had annihilated space-time for her. Speculation had involved space warps—whatever that term means, points of infinite discontinuity, undimensional fields, and Cosmos knows what else. Could we find what had happened, and purposefully control the phenomenon which had seized us by some blind accident, the galaxy would be ours. Meanwhile, we were limited to pseudovelocities of a couple of hundred lights, and interstellar space mocked us with vastness.

But how explain that to a nine-year-old? I said only: "If I knew that, I'd be wiser than anyone else, Einar. Which I'm not."

"I wanna go swimming," said Mike.

"Sure," I said. "That was our idea, wasn't it? We'll drop anchor in the next bay—"

"I wanna go swimming in Spacecamp Cove."

I tried to hedge, but Einar was all over me, too. It was only a few kilometers farther up the coast, and its broad sheltered expanse, its wide sandy beach, and the forest immediately behind, made it ideal for such an expedition. And after all, I had nothing against it.

Nothing—except the lure of the place.

I sighed and surrendered. Spacecamp Cove it was.

We had a good time there, swimming and picnicking, playing ball and loafing in the sand and swimming some more. It was good to lie in the sun again, with a cool wet wind blowing in from the sea and talking in the trees. And to the boys, the glamour of it was a sort of crown on the day.

But I had to fight the romance. I wasn't a child any more, playing at spacemen and aliens, I was the grown man with some responsibilities. The community of the *Traveler* had voted by an overwhelming majority to settle on Harbor, and that was that.

And here, half hidden by long grass, half buried in the blowing sand, were the unmistakable signs of what we had left.

There wasn't much. A few plasticontainers for food, a couple of broken tools of curious shape, some scattered engine parts. Just enough to indicate that a while ago—ten years ago, perhaps—a party of spacemen had landed here, camped for a while, made some repairs, and resumed their journey.

They weren't from the fifth planet. Those natives had never left their world, and even with the technological impetus we were giving them in exchange for their metals they weren't ever likely to, the pressures they needed to live were too great. They weren't from Sol, or even some colony world—not only were the remains totally unlike our equipment, but the news of a planet like Harbor, almost a duplicate of Earth but without a native intelligent race, would have brought settlers here in swarms. So—somewhere in the galaxy, someone else had mastered the hyperdrive and was exploring space.

As we had been doing—

I did my best to be cheerful all the way home, and think I succeeded on the surface. And that in spite of Einar's wildly romantic gabble about the unknown campers. But I couldn't help remembering—

In twenty years of spacing, you can see a lot of worlds, and you can have a lot of experience. We had been gods of a sort, flitting from star to star, exploring, trading, learning, now and again mixing into the destinies of the natives. We had fought and striven, suffered and laughed and stood silent in wonder. For most of us, the dreadful hunger for home, the weariness of the hopeless quest, had shadowed that panorama of worlds which reeled through my mind. But—before Cosmos, I had loved every minute of it!

I fell into unrelieved moodiness as soon as we had stowed the *Naughty Nancy* in our boathouse. The boys ran ahead of me toward the house, but I followed slowly. Alanna met me at the door.

"Better wash up right away," she said. "The company will be here any minute."

"Uh-huh."

She looked at me, for a very long moment, and laid her hand on my arm. In the long dazzling rays of the westering sun, her eyes were brighter than I had seen them before. I wondered if tears were not wavering just behind them.

"You were at Spacecamp Cove," she said quietly.

"The boys wanted to go there," I answered. "It's a good place."

"Erling—" She paused. I stood looking at her, thinking how beautiful she was. I remembered the way she had looked on Hralfar, the first time I kissed her. We had wandered a ways from the camp of the detail exploring that frosty little world and negotiating with its natives for supplies. The sky had been dark overhead, with a shrunken sun casting its thin pale light on the blue-shadowed snow. It was quiet, breathlessly quiet, the air was like sharp fire in our nostrils and her hair, the only color in that white horizon, seemed to crackle with frost. That was quite a long time ago, but nothing had changed between us since.

"Yes?" I prompted her. "Yes, what is it?"

Her voice came quickly, very low so the boys wouldn't hear: "Erling, are you really happy here?"

"Why"—I felt an almost physical shock of surprise—"of course I am, dear. That's a silly question."

"Or a silly answer?" She smiled, with closed lips. "We did have some good times on the *Traveler*. Even those who grumbled loudest at the time admit that, now when they've got a little perspective on the voyage and have forgotten something of the overcrowding and danger and weariness. But you—I sometimes think the *Traveler* was your life, Erling."

"I liked the ship, of course." I had a somewhat desperate sense of defending myself. "After all, I was born and raised on her. I never really knew anything else. Our planetary visits were so short, and most of the worlds so unterrestrial. You liked it too."

"Oh, sure, it was fun to go batting around the galaxy, never knowing what might wait at the next sun. But a woman wants a home. And—Erling, plenty of others your age, who also had never known anything else, hated it."

"I was lucky. As an officer, I had better quarters, more privacy. And, well, that 'something hid behind the ranges' maybe meant more to me than to most others. But—good Cosmos, Alanna! you don't think that now—"

"I don't think anything, Erling. But on the ship you weren't so absentminded, so apt to fall into daydreams. You didn't sit around the place all day, you were always working on something…" She bit her lip. "Don't misunderstand, Erling. I have no doubt you keep telling yourself how happy you are. You could go to your cremation, here on Harbor, thinking you'd had a rather good life. But—I sometimes wonder!"

"Now look—" I began.

"No, no, nothing more out of you. Get inside and wash up, the company'll be coming in half a minute."

I went, with my head in a whirl. Mechanically, I scrubbed myself and changed into evening blouse and slacks. When I came out of the bedroom, the first of the guests were already waiting.

MacTeague Angus was there, the old first mate of the *Traveler* and captain in the short time between Kane's death and our settling on Harbor. So was my brother Thorkild Gustav, with whom I had little in common except a mutual liking. Tokogama Hideyoshi, Petroff Ivan, Ortega Manuel, and a couple of others showed up a few minutes later. Alanna took charge of their wives and children, and I mixed drinks all around.

For a while the talk was of local matters. We were scattered over quite a wide area, and had as yet not produced enough telescreens for every house, so that communication was limited to direct personal travel by plane. A hailstorm on Gustav's farm, a minor breakdown in the vehicle factory superintended by

Ortega, Petroff's project of a fleet of semirobot fishing boats—small gossip. Presently dinner was served.

Gustav was rapturous over the steak. "What is it?" he asked.

"Some local animal I shot the other day," I said. "Ungulate, reddish-brown, broad flat horns."

"Oh, yes. Hm-m-m—I'll have to try domesticating some. I've had pretty good luck with those glug-gugs."

"Huh?" Petroff stared at him.

"Another local species," laughed Gustav. "I had to call them something, and they make that kind of noise."

"The *Traveler* was never like this," said Ortega, helping himself to another piece of meat.

"I never thought the food was bad," I said.

"No, we had the hydroponic vegetables and fruits, and the synthetic meats, as well as what we picked up on different planets," admitted Ortega. "But it wasn't this good, ever. Hydroponics somehow don't have the flavor of Earth-grown stuff."

"That's your imagination," said Petroff. "I can prove—"

"I don't care what you can prove, the facts remain." Ortega glanced at me. "But there were compensations."

"Not enough," muttered Gustav. "I've got room to move, here on Harbor."

"You're being unjust to the *Traveler*," I said. "She was only meant to carry about fifty people for a short voyage at that. When she lost her way for twenty years, and a whole new generation got jammed in with their parents, it's no wonder she grew crowded. Actually, her minimum crew is ten or so. Thirty people—fifteen couples, say, plus their kids—could travel in her in ease and comfort, with private apartments for all."

"And still…still, for over twenty years, we fought and suffered and stood the monotony and the hopelessness—to find Earth." Tokogama's voice was musing, a little awed. "When all the time, on any of a hundred uninhabited terrestroid planets, we could have had—this."

"For at least half that time," pointed out MacTeague, "we were simply looking for the right part of the galaxy. We knew Sol wasn't anywhere near, so we had no hopes to be crushed, but we thought as soon as the constellations began to look fairly familiar we'd be quickly able to find home." He shrugged. "But space is simply too big, and our astrogational tables have so little information. Star travel was still in its infancy when we left Sol.

"An error of, say, one percent could throw us light-years off in the course of several hundred parsecs. And the galaxy is lousy with G0-type suns, which are statistically almost certain to have neighbors sufficiently like Sol's to fool an unsure observer. If our tables had given positions relative to, say, S Doradus, we could have found home easily enough. But they used Sirius for their bright-star point—and we couldn't find Sirius in that swarm of stars! We just had to hop from star to star which might be Sol—and find it wasn't, and go on, with the sickening fear that maybe we were getting farther away all the time, maybe Sol lay just off the bows, obscured by a dark nebula. In the end—we gave it up as a bad job."

"There's more to it than that," said Tokogama. "We realized all that, you know. But there was Captain Kane and his tremendous personality, his driving will to success, and we'd all come to rely more or less blindly on him. As long as he lived, nobody quite believed in the possibility of failure. When he died, everything seemed to collapse at once."

I nodded grimly, remembering those terrible days that followed—Seymour's mutinous attempt to seize power, bringing home to us just how sick and weary we all were; the arrival at this star which might have solved it all, might have given us a happy ending, if it had been Sol; the rest on Harbor, a rest which became a permanent stay—

"Something else kept us going all those years, too," said Ortega quietly. "There was an element among the younger generation which liked to wander. The vote to stay here wasn't unanimous."

"I know," said MacTeague. His level gaze rested thoughtfully on me. "I often wonder, Erling, why some of you don't borrow the ship and visit the nearer stars, just to see what's there."

"Wouldn't do any good," I said tonelessly. "It'd just make our feet itch worse than ever—and there'd always be stars beyond those."

"But why—" Gustav fumbled for words. "Why would anyone *want* to go— stargazing that way? I…well, I've got my feet on ground now, my own ground, my own home…it's growing, I'm building and planting and seeing it come to reality before my own eyes, and it'll be there for my children and their children. There's air and wind and rain, sunlight, the sea, the woods and mountains—Cosmos! Who wants more? Who wants to trade it for sitting in a sterile metal tank, riding from star to star, homeless, hopeless?"

"Nobody," I said hastily. "I was just trying—"

"The most pointless existence—simply to be a…a spectator in the universe!"

"Not exactly," said Tokogama. "There was plenty we did, if you insist that somebody must do something. We brought some benefits of human civilization to quite a number of places. We did some extensive star-mapping, if we ever see Earthmen again they'll find our tables useful, and our observations within different systems. We…well, we were wanderers, but so what? Do you blame a bird for not having hoofs?"

"The birds have hoofs now," I said. "They're walking on the ground. And"—I flashed a glance at Alanna—"they like it."

The conversation was getting a little too hot. I steered it into safer channels until we adjourned to the living room. Over coffee and tobacco it came back.

We began reminiscing about the old days, planets we had seen, deeds we had done. Worlds and suns and moons, whirling through a raw dark emptiness afire with stars, were in our talk—strange races, foreign cities, lonely magnificence of mountains and plains and seas, the giant universe opening before us. Oh, by all the gods, we had fared far!

We had seen the blue hell-flames leaping over the naked peaks of a planet whose great sun almost filled its sky. We had sailed with a gang of happy pirates over a sea red as new-spilled blood toward the grotesque towers of a fortress older than their history. We had seen the rich color and flashing metal of a tournament on Drangor and the steely immensity of the continental cities on Alkan. We had talked philosophy with a gross wallowing cephalopod on one world and been shot at by the inhumanly beautiful natives of another. We had come as gods to a planet to lift its barbaric natives from the grip of a plague that scythed them down and we had come as humble students to the ancient laboratories and libraries of the next. We had come near perishing in a methane storm on a planet far from its sun and felt then how dear life is. We had lain on the beaches of the paradise world Luanha and let the sea sing us to sleep. We had ridden centauroids who conversed with us as they went to the aerial city of their winged enemies—

More than the wildly romantic adventures—which, after all, had been pretty dirty and bloody affairs at the time—we loved to remember the worlds themselves: a fiery sunset on the snowfields of Hralfar; a great brown river flowing through the rain forest which covered Atlang; a painted desert on Thyvari; the mighty disk of New Jupiter swelling before our bows; the cold and vastness and cruelty and emptiness and awe and wonder of open space itself. And, in our small clique of frank tramps, there had been the comradeship of the road, the calm unspoken knowledge of having friends who would stand firm—a feeling of *belonging*, such as men like Gustav had achieved only since coming here, and which we seemed to have lost.

Lost—yes, why not admit it? We didn't see each other very often any more, we were too scattered, too busy. And the talk of the others was just a little bit boring.

Well, it couldn't be helped—

It was late that night when the party broke up. Alanna and I saw the guests out to their planes. When the last vehicle had whispered into the sky, we stood for a while looking around us. The night was very still and cool, with a high starry sky in which the moon of Harbor was rising. Its light glittered on the dew under our feet, danced restlessly on the sea, threw a dim silver veil on the dreaming land—our land.

I looked down at Alanna. She was staring over the darkened view, staring as if she had never seen it before—or never would again. The moonlight was tangled like frost in her hair. *What if I never see open space again? What if I sit here till I die? This is worth it.*

She spoke at last, very slowly, as if she had to shape each word separately: "I'm beginning to realize it. Yes, I'm quite sure."

"Sure of what?" I asked.

"Don't play dumb. You know what I mean. You and Manuel and Ivan and Hideyoshi and the others who were here—except Angus and Gus, of course. And quite a few more. You don't belong here. None of you."

"How—so?"

"Look, a man who had been born and raised in a city, and had a successful life in it, couldn't be expected to take to the country all of a sudden. Maybe never. Put him among peasants, and he'd go around all the rest of his life wondering vaguely why he wasn't honestly happy."

"We—Now don't start that again, sweetheart," I begged.

"Why not? Somebody's got to. After all, Erling, this is a peasantry we've got, growing up on Harbor. More or less mechanized, to be sure, but still rooted to the soil, close to it, with the peasant strength and solidity and the peasant's provincial outlook. Why, if a ship from Earth landed tomorrow, I don't think twenty people would leave with it.

"But you, Erling, you and your friends—you grew up in the ship, and you made a successful adaptation to it. You spent your formative years wandering. By now—you're cosmopolites. For you, a mountain range will always be more than it really is, because of what's behind it. One horizon isn't enough, you've got to have many, as many as there are in the universe.

"Find Earth? Why, you yourself admitted you don't care whether Earth is ever found. You only want the search.

"You're a gypsy, Erling. And no gypsy could ever be tied to one place."

I stood for a long while, alone with her in the cold calm moonlight, and said nothing. When I looked down at her, finally, she was trying not to cry, but her lip was trembling and the tears were bright in her eyes. Every word was wrenched out of me:

"You may be right, Alanna. I'm beginning to be horribly afraid you are. But what's to be done about it?"

"Done?" She laughed, a strangely desolate laugh. "Why, it's a very simple problem. The answer is circling right there up in the sky. Get a crew who feel the way you do, and take the *Traveler*. Go roaming—forever!"

"But…you? You, the kids, the place here…you—"

"Don't you see?" Her laughter rang louder now, echoing faintly in the light night. "Don't you see? I want to go, too!" She almost fell into my arms. "I want to go, too!"

There is no reason to record the long arguments, grudging acceptances, slow preparations. In the end we won. Sixteen men and their wives, with half a dozen children, were wild to leave.

That summer blazed up into fall, winter came, spring, and summer again, while we made ready. Our last year on Harbor. And I had never realized how much I loved the planet. Almost, I gave up.

But space, free space, the open universe and the ship come alive again—!

We left the colony a complete set of plans, in the unlikely event that they should ever want to build a starship of their own, and a couple of spaceboats and duplicates of all the important automatic machinery carried by the *Traveler*. We would make astrogating tables, as our official purpose, and theoretically we might some day come back.

But we knew we never would. We would go traveling, and our children would carry the journey on after us, and their children after them, a whole new civilization growing up between the stars, rootless but tremendously alive. Those who wearied of it could always colonize a planet; we would be spreading mankind over the galaxy. When our descendants were many, they would build other ships until there was a fleet, a mobile city hurtling from sun to sun. It would be a culture to itself, drawing on the best which all races had to offer and spreading it over the worlds. It would be the bloodstream of the interstellar civilization which was slowly gestating in the universe.

As the days and months went by, my boys grew even more impatient to be off. I smiled a little. Right now, they only thought of the adventure of it, romantic planets and great deeds to be done. Well, there were such, they would have eventful lives, but they would soon learn that patience and steadfastness were needed, that there was toil and suffering and danger—and life!

Alanna—I was a little puzzled. She was very gay when I was around, merrier than I had ever seen her before. But she often went out for long walks, alone on the beach or in the sun-dappled woods, and she started a garden which she would never harvest. Well—so it went, and I was too busy with preparations to think much about it.

The end came, and we embarked on the long voyage, the voyage which has not ceased yet and, I hope, will never end. The night before, we had Angus and Gustav in for a farewell party, and it was a strange feeling to be saying good-bye knowing that we would never see them again, or hear from them. It was like dying.

But we were alone in the morning. We went out to our carplane, to fly to the landing field where the gypsies would meet. From there, a boat would take us to the *Traveler*. I still could not fully realize that I was captain—I, captain of the great ship which had been my world, it didn't seem real. I walked slowly, my head full of the sudden universe of responsibility.

Alanna touched my arm. "Look around, Erling," she whispered. "Look around at our land. You'll never see it again."

I shook myself out of my reverie and let my eyes sweep the horizon. It was early, the grass was still wet, flashing in the new sun. The sea danced and glittered beyond the rustling trees, crying its old song to the fair green land, and the wind that blew from it was keen and cold and pungent with life. The fields were stirring in the wind, a long ripple of grass, and high overhead a bird was singing.

"It's—very beautiful," I said.

"Yes." I could hardly hear her voice. "Yes, it is. Let's go, Erling."

We got into the carplane and slanted skyward. The boys crowded forward with me, staring ahead for the first glimpse of the landing field, not seeing the forests and meadows and shining rivers that slipped away beneath us.

Alanna sat behind me, looking down over the land. Her bright head was bent away so I couldn't see her face. I wondered what she was thinking, but somehow I didn't want to ask her.

MARIUS

It was raining again, with a bite in the air as the planet spun toward winter. They hadn't yet restored the street lights, and an early dusk seeped up between ruined walls and hid the tattered folk dwelling in caves grubbed out of rubble. Etienne Fourre, chief of the Maquisard Brotherhood and therefore representative of France in the Supreme Council of United Free Europe, stubbed his toe on a cobblestone. Pain struck through a worn-out boot, and he swore with tired expertness. The fifty guards ringing him in, hairy men in a patchwork of clothes—looted from the uniforms of a dozen armies, their own insignia merely a hand-sewn Tricolor brassard—tensed. It was an automatic reaction, the bristling of a wolf at any unawaited noise, long ago drilled into them.

"Eh, bien," said Fourre. "Perhaps Rouget de l'Isle stumbled on the same rock while composing the *'Marseillaise.'"*

One-eyed Astier shrugged, an almost invisible gesture in the murk. "When is the next grain shipment coming?" he asked. It was hard to think of anything but food above the noise of a growling belly, and the Liberators had shucked military formalities during the desperate years.

"Tomorrow, perhaps, or the next day, if the barges aren't waylaid by river pirates," said Fourre. "And I don't think they will be, this close to Strasbourg." He tried to smile. "Be of good cheer, my old. Next year there should be an ample harvest. The Americans are shipping us a new blight-preventive."

"Always next year," grumbled Astier. "Why don't they send us something to eat now?"

"The blights hit them, too. It is the best they can do for us. Had it not been for them, we would still be skulking in the woods sniping at Russians."

"We had a little something to do with winning."

"More than a little, thanks to Professor Valti. I do not think any of the free people could have won without all the others."

"If you call this victory." Astier's soured voice faded into silence. They were passing the broken cathedral, and it was known that childpacks often hid there. The little wild ones had sometimes attacked armed men with their jagged bottles and rusty bayonets. But fifty soldiers were too many, of course. Fourre thought he

203

heard a scuttering among the stones; but it might only have been the rats. Never had he dreamed there could be so many rats.

The thin sad rain blew into his face and weighted his beard. Night rolled out of the east, as if it were a message from Soviet lands plunged into chaos and murder. But we are rebuilding, he thought defensively; each week the authority of the Strasbourg Council reached a civilizing hand farther into the smashed lands of Europe. In ten years, five perhaps—automation was so fantastically productive, if only you could get hold of the machines in the first place—the men of the West would again be peaceful farmers and shopkeepers, their culture again a going concern.

If the multinational Councilors made the right decisions. And they had not been making them. Valti had finally convinced Fourre of that. Therefore, he walked through the rain, hugging an old bicycle poncho to his sleazy jacket, and men in barracks were quietly estimating how many jumps it would take to reach their racked weapons. It would be necessary to overpower those who did not agree.

A wry thought, that the ancient feudal principle of personal loyalty to a chief should have to be invoked to enforce the decrees of a new mathematics that only some thousand minds out of all the world understood. But you wouldn't expect the Norman peasant Astier or the Parisian Apache Renault to bend the scanty spare time of a year to learning the operations of symbolic sociology. You would merely say, "Come," and they would come because they loved you.

The streets resounded hollow under his feet. It was a world without logic, this one. Only the accidents of survival had made the village apothecary Etienne Fourre into the *de facto* commander of Free France. He could have wished those accidents had taken him and spared Jeanette, but at least he had two sons living, and some day, if they hadn't gotten too much radiation, there would be grandchildren. God was not altogether revengeful.

"There we are, up ahead," said Astier.

Fourre did not bother to reply. He had never been under the common human necessity of forever mouthing words.

Strasbourg was the seat of the Council because of its location and because it was not too badly hit. It had been a conventional battle with chemical explosives which rolled through it, eighteen months ago. The University had almost completely escaped destruction, so Jacques Reinach had his headquarters there. His men prowled about on guard; one wonders what Goethe would have thought, could he have returned to the scene of his student days. And yet it was men such as this, with dirty hands and clean weapons, who were civilization. It was their kind who had harried the wounded Russian colossus out of the West and who would restore law and liberty and wind-rippled fields of grain. Some day. Perhaps.

There was a machine-gun nest at the first check point. The sergeant in charge recognized Fourre and gave a sloppy salute. (Still, the fact that Reinach had extorted so much discipline from his horde spoke for the man's personality.) "Your escort must wait here, general," he said, half apologizing. "It is the new regulation."

"I know," said Fourre. Not all of his guards did, and there was a snarling which he shushed. "I have an appointment to see the Commandant."

"Yes, sir. Please stay to the lighted paths. Otherwise you might be shot by mistake for a looter."

Fourre nodded and walked through, onto the campus. His body wanted to get in out of the rain, but he went slowly, delaying the moment. Jacques Reinach was, after all, not only his countryman but his friend. He was nowhere near as close to, say, Helgesen of the Nordic Alliance, or the Italian Totti, or Rojansky of Poland, and he positively disliked the German Auerbach.

But Vaki's matrices were not concerned with a man's heart. They simply told you that given such-and-such conditions, this-and-that would probably happen. It was a cold knowledge to bear.

The Headquarters building was a loom of darkness, but a few windows glowed at him. Reinach had had an electric generator set up—and very rightly, of course, when his tired staff and his tired self must often work around the clock.

A sentry admitted Fourre to an outer office. There were half a dozen armed men picking their teeth in it and dicing for cartridges while a tubercular secretary coughed over files written on old laundry bills, flyleaves, any scrap of paper that came to hand. They all stood up, and Fourre told them he had an appointment with the Commandant, chairman of the Council.

"Yes, sir." The officer was still in his teens, fuzzy face already shriveled into old age, and spoke very bad French. "Just check your weapons with us and go on in."

Fourre unbuckled his guns, reflecting that this latest requirement, disarming commanders before they could see Chairman Reinach, was what had driven Alvarez into fury and the conspiracy. Yet the regulation was not unreasonable—Reinach must know of gathering opposition, and all the people had grown much too used to settling disputes with weapons. Ah, well, Alvarez was no philosopher but he was boss of the Iberian Irregulars and you had to use what human material was available.

The officer frisked him, and that was a wholly new indignity which heated Fourre's own skin. He choked his anger, thinking that Valti had predicted as much.

Down a corridor then, that smelled moldy in the autumnal dankness, and to a door where one more sentry was posted. Fourre nodded at him and opened the door.

"Good evening, Etienne. What can I do for you?"

The big blond man looked up from his desk and smiled. It was a curiously shy, almost a young smile, and something wrenched within Fourre.

This had been a professor's office, before the war. Dust was thick on the books that lined the walls. Really, they should take more care of books, even if it meant giving less attention to famine and plague and banditry.

There was a window closed at the rear, with a dark wash of rain flowing across miraculously intact glass. Reinach sat with a lamp by his side and his back to the night.

Fourre lowered himself, the visitor's chair creaked under a gaunt-fleshed but heavy-boned weight. "Can't you guess, Jacques?" he asked.

The handsome Alsatian face, one of the few clean-shaven faces left in the world, turned to study him for a while. "I wasn't sure you were against me, too," said Reinach. "Helgesen, Totti, Alexios...yes, that lot...but you? We have been friends for many years, Etienne. I didn't think you would turn on me."

"Not on you." Fourre sighed and wished for a cigarette, but tobacco was a remote memory. "Never you, Jacques. Only your policies. I am here, speaking for all of us—"

"Not quite all," said Reinach. His tone was quiet and unaccusing. "Only now do I realize how cleverly you maneuvered my firm supporters out of town. Brevoort flying off to Ukrainia to establish relations with the revolutionary government; Ferenczi down in Genoa to pick up those ships for our merchant marine; Janosek talked into leading an expedition against the bandits in Schleswig. Yes, yes, you plotted it carefully, didn't you? But what do you think they will have to say on their return?"

"They will accept a *fait accompli*, if they must," answered Fourre. "This generation has had a bellyful of war. But I said I was here to speak to you on behalf of my associates. It was hoped you would listen to reason from me, at least."

"If it is reason." Reinach leaned back in his chair, cat-comfortable, one palm resting on a revolver butt. "We have threshed out all the arguments in council. If you bring them up again..."

"...It is because I must." Fourre sat looking at the scarred bony hands in his lap. "After all, Jacques, we understand that the chairman of the Council must have supreme power for the duration of the emergency. We all agreed to give you the final word. But not the *only* word."

A paleness of anger flicked up in the blue eyes. "I have been maligned enough," said Reinach coldly. "They think I want to set myself up as a dictator. Etienne, after the Second War was over and you went off to become a snug civilian, why do you think I elected to make the Army my career? It was not because I had any taste for militarism. It was only that I foresaw our land would again be in danger, within my own lifetime, and I wanted to hold myself ready. Does that sound like...like some new kind of Hitler?"

"No, of course not, my friend. And when we chose you to lead our combined forces, we could not have chosen better. Without you—and Valti—there would still be war on the eastern front. We...I...we think of you as our deliverer, just as if we were the humblest peasant given back his own plot of earth. But you have not been *right*."

"We all make mistakes." Reinach actually smiled. "I admit my own. I bungled badly in cleaning out those communists at—"

Fourre shook his head, stubbornly. "You don't understand, Jacques. It isn't that kind of mistake I mean. Your great error is that you have not realized we are at peace. The war is over."

Reinach lifted a sardonic brow. "Not a barge goes up the Rhine, not a kilometer of railroad track is relaid, but we have to fight bandits, local war lords, half-crazed fanatics of a hundred new creeds. Does that sound like peacetime?"

"It is a difference of…of objectives," said Fourre. "And man is such an animal that it is the end, not the means, which makes the difference. War is morally simple: one purpose, to impose your will upon the enemy. Not to surrender to an inferior force. But a policeman? He is protecting an entire society of which the criminal is also a part. A politician? He has to make compromises, even with small groups and people he despises. You think like a soldier, Jacques, and we no longer want or need a soldier commanding us."

"Now you're quoting that senile fool Valti," snapped Reinach.

"If we hadn't had Professor Valti and his sociosymbolic logic to plan our strategy for us—we would still be locked with the Russians. There was no way for us to be liberated from the outside, this time. The Anglo-Saxon countries had too much to do in Asia, besides all their internal difficulties. We had to liberate ourselves, with ragged men and bicycle cavalry and aircraft patched together out of wrecks. If it weren't for Valti's plans—and, to be sure, your execution of them—we could never have done it." Fourre shook his head again. He would *not* get angry with Jacques. "I think such a record entitles the professor to respect."

"It did…then," said Reinach. His tone lifted and grew rapid. "But he's senile now, I tell you. Babbling of the future, of long-range trends—Can we eat the future? People are dying of plague and starvation and anarchy *now!*"

"He has convinced me," said Fourre. "I thought much the same way, too, a year ago. But he instructed me in the elements of his science, and he showed me the way we are heading. He is an old man, Eino Valti, but there is still a brain under that bald pate."

Reinach relaxed. A tolerant warmth played across his lips. "Very well, Etienne," he asked, "what way *are* we heading?"

Fourre looked past him, into night. "Toward war," he said, quite softly. "Another nuclear war, some fifty years hence. It isn't certain the human race itself can survive that."

Rain stammered on the windowpanes. It was falling hard now, and wind hooted in the empty streets. Fourre glanced at his watch. There wasn't much time left. He fingered the police whistle hung about his neck.

Reinach started. Then, gradually, he eased back. "If I thought that were true," he replied, "I would resign this minute."

"I know you would," mumbled Fourre. "That is what makes my task so hard for me."

"But it isn't true," said Reinach. His hand waved as if to brush away a nightmare. "If only because people have had such a grim lesson that—"

"People, in the mass, don't learn," Fourre told him. "The only way to prevent future wars is to set up a world-peace authority—to reconstitute the United Nations and give it some muscles. And Europe is crucial to that enterprise. North of the Himalayas and east of the Don there is nothing any more—howling cannibals. It will take too long to civilize them again. It is *we* who must speak for the whole Eurasian continent."

"Very good, very good," said Reinach impatiently. "Granted. But what am I doing that is so wrong?"

"A great many things, Jacques. I could give you a long list." Fourre's head turned, slowly, as if it creaked on its neckbones, and locked eyes with the man behind the desk. "It is one thing to improvise in wartime. But you are improvising the peace. You forced the decision to send only two men to represent all our nations at the conference planned in Rio. Why? Because we're short on transportation, clerical help, paper—even on decent clothes! The problem should have been studied. It may be all right to treat Europe as a unit—or it may not; perhaps this decision will only exacerbate nationalism. You made the decision in one minute when the question was raised, and you would not even hear debate."

"Of course not!" said Reinach harshly. "If you remember, that was the day we learned of the Neofascist coup in Corsica."

"Corsica could have waited a while. It would have been more difficult to win back, yes, if we hadn't struck at once—but this business of our UN representation could decide the entire future of—"

"I know, I know! Valti and his theory about the 'pivotal decision.' Bah!"

"The theory happens to work, my old."

"In its proper place. I'm a hard head, Etienne, I admit it." Reinach leaned across the desk, chuckling. "Don't you think the times demand a hard head? When hell is romping loose, it is no time to spin fine philosophies…or try to elect a parliament, which I understand is another of the postponements Dr. Valti holds against me."

"It is," said Fourre. "Do you like roses ?"

"Why, why…yes." Reinach blinked. "To look at, anyway." Wistfulness crossed his eyes. "Now that you mention it, it's been many years since I last saw a rose."

"But you don't like gardening. I remember that from…old days." The curious tenderness of man for man, which no one has ever quite understood, tugged at Fourre. He cast it aside, not daring to do otherwise, and said impersonally: "And you like democratic government, too, but were never interested in the grubby work of maintaining it. There is a time to plant seed? If we delay, it will be too late, strong-arm rule will have become too much of a habit."

"There is also a time to keep alive. Just to keep alive, nothing else."

"I know. Jacques, I can't accuse you of hard-heartedness. You are a sentimentalist: you see a child with belly bloated from hunger, a house marked with a cross to show that the Black Death has walked in—and you feel too much pity to be able to think. It is…Valti, myself, all of us…who are cold-blooded—who are prepared to sacrifice a few thousand more lives now, by neglecting the immediately necessary, for the sake of saving all humankind fifty years hence."

"You may be right," said Reinach. "About your cold souls, I mean." His voice was so low that the rain almost drowned it.

Fourre looked at his watch. Scant time remaining—this had been taking longer than expected. He said in a slurred, hurried tone: "What touched off this affair was the Papandrou business."

"I thought so," agreed Reinach evenly. "I don't like it either. I know as well as you do that Papandrou is a murderous crypto-communist scoundrel whose own people hate him. But curse it, man—don't you know rats do worse than steal food and gnaw the faces of sleeping children? Don't you know they spread plague? And Papandrou has offered us the services of the only efficient rat-exter-minating force in Eurasia. All he asks is that we recognize his Macedonian Free State and give him a seat on the Council."

"It is too much to pay," said Fourre. "In one or two years we can bring the rats under control ourselves."

"And meanwhile?"

"Meanwhile, we must hope that nobody we love is taken sick."

Reinach grinned without mirth. "It won't do," he said. "I can't agree to that. If Papandrou's squads help us, We can save a year of reconstruction, a hundred thousand lives—"

"And throw away lives by the hundred millions in the future!"

"Oh, come now! One little province like Macedonia?"

"One very big precedent," said Fourre. "We will not merely be conceding a petty war lord the right to his loot. We will be conceding"—he lifted hairy hands and counted off on the fingers—"the right of any dictatorship, anywhere, to exist at all—which might, if yielded, means war and war and war again; the fatally outmoded principle of unlimited national sovereignty; the friendship of an outraged Greece, which is sure to invoke that same principle in retaliation; the inevitable political repercussions throughout the Near East, which is already turbulent enough; therefore war between us and the Arabs, because we *must* have oil; a seat on the Council to a clever and ruthless man who frankly, Jacques, can think rings around you—*No!*"

"You are theorizing about tomorrow," said Reinach. "The rats are already here. What would you have me do instead?"

"Refuse the offer. Let me take a bicycle brigade down there. That will be enough to knock Papandrou to hell—unless we let him get too strong first."

Reinach shook his head, good-naturedly. "Who is the war monger now?" he laughed.

"I never denied there is still a great deal of fighting ahead of us," said Fourre. Sadness tinged his voice, he had seen too many men spilling their life blood on the ground. "I only want to be sure it will serve the final purpose—that there shall never again be a world war. That my children and grandchildren will not have to fight at all."

"And Valti's equations show the way to achieve that?" asked Reinach quietly.

"They do."

"I'm sorry, Etienne." Reinach shook his head. "I simply cannot believe it. Turning human society into a…what is it?…a potential field, and operating on it with symbolic logic—it's too remote. I am here, in the flesh—such of it as is left on our diet—not in a set of scribbles made by some gang of long-haired theorists."

"It was a similar gang which, well, discovered atomic energy," said Fourre. "Yes, Valti's science is young. But within its admitted limitations, *it works.* If you would only study it—"

"There's too much else to do." Reinach shrugged. A blankness seemed to draw across his face. "We've wasted too much time already. What is it you, your group of generals, wants me to do?"

Fourre gave it to him, as he knew his comrade would wish it, hard and straight like a bayonet thrust. "We ask for your resignation. Naturally, you'll keep a seat on the Council, but Professor Valti will assume the chairmanship and set about making the reforms we want. We will issue a formal promise to have a constitutional convention in the spring and dissolve the military government within one year."

Then he bent his head and looked at the time. There was a minute and a half remaining.

"No," said Reinach.

"But—"

"Be still!" The Alsatian stood up. The single lamp threw his shadow grotesque and enormous across the dusty books. "Do you think I didn't see this coming? Why do you imagine I only let one man at a time in here, and disarm him? The devil with your generals! The common people know me, they know I stand for them first—and hell take your misty futures! We'll meet the future when it comes!"

"That is what man has always done," said Fourre. He spoke like a beggar. "And that is why the race has always blundered from one catastrophe to the next. This may be our last chance to change the pattern."

Reinach began pacing, up and down behind the desk. "Do you think I like this miserable job?" he answered. "It simply happens that no one else can do it."

"So now you are the indispensable man," whispered Fourre, "I had hoped you would escape that."

"Go on home, Etienne." Reinach halted, and there was kindness returning to him. "Go back and tell them I won't hold this against them personally. You had a right to make your demand. Well, it has been made and refused." He nodded to himself, thoughtfully, "There will have to be some changes in our organization, though. I don't want to be a dictator, but—"

Zero hour. Fourre felt very tired.

He had been refused, and so he had not blown the whistle that would stop the rebels, and it was out of his hands now.

"Sit down," he said. "Sit down, Marius, and let us talk about old times for a while."

Reinach looked surprised. "Marius? What do you mean?"

"Oh…it was an example from history which Professor Valti gave me." Fourre considered the floor. There was a cracked board by his left toe. Cracked and crazy, a tottering wreck of a civilization…how had the same race built Chartres and the hydrogen bomb?

His words dragged out of him: "In the second century before Christ, the Cimbri and their allies, Teutonic barbarians, came down out of the north. For a generation they wandered about, ripping Europe apart. They chopped up the Roman armies sent to stop them. Finally they invaded Italy. It did not look as if they could be halted before they took Rome itself. But there was one general by the name of Marius who rallied his men: He met the barbarians and annihilated them."

"Well…thank you." Reinach sat down, puzzled. "But—"

"Oh, never mind." Fourre's mouth twisted into a smile. "Let us take a few minutes free and just talk. Do you remember that night after the Second War, we were still just boys freshly out of the Maquis, and we tumbled around the streets of Paris and toasted the sunrise from Sacre Coeur?"

"Yes…to be sure. That was a wild night!" Reinach laughed. "How long ago it seems! What was your girl's name? I've forgotten."

"Marie. And you had Simone…a beautiful little baggage, Simone. I wonder whatever became of her?"

"I don't know. The last I heard—No. Remember how bewildered the waiter was when—"

A shot cracked through the rain, and then the wrathful clatter of machine guns awoke. Reinach was on his feet in one tiger bound, pistol in hand, crouched by the window. Fourre remained seated.

The noise lifted, louder and closer.

Reinach spun about and his gun muzzle glared emptily at Fourre.

"Yes, Jacques."

"Revolt!"

"We had to." Fourre discovered that he could again meet Reinach's eyes. "The situation was that crucial. If you had yielded…if you had even been willing to discuss the matter…I would have blown this whistle and nothing would have happened. Now it's too late, unless you want to surrender. If you do, our offer still stands. We still want you to work with us."

A grenade blasted somewhere nearby.

"You—"

"Go on and shoot. It doesn't matter very much."

"No—" The pistol wavered. "Not unless you—Stay where you are! Don't move!" The hand Reinach passed across his forehead shuddered. "You know how well this place is guarded. You know the people will rise to my side—"

"I think not. They worship you, yes, but they are tired and starved. Just in case, though, we staged this for the nighttime. By tomorrow morning it will all be over." Fourre spoke like a rusty machine. "The barracks have already been seized. Those more distant noises are the artillery being captured. The University is surrounded, and cannot stand against an attack."

"This building can!"

"So you won't give up, Jacques?"

"If I could do that," said Reinach, "I wouldn't be here tonight."

The window broke open. Reinach whirled. The man who was vaulting though shot first.

The guard outside the door looked in. His rifle was poised, but he died before he could use it. Then men with black clothes and blackened faces were swarming across the sill.

Fourre knelt beside Reinach. A bullet through the head—it had been quick, at least. But if it had struck farther down, perhaps Reinach's life could have been saved. Fourre wanted to weep, but he had forgotten how.

The big man who had killed Reinach ignored his commando to stoop over the body with Fourre. "I'm sorry, sir," he mumbled. It was hard to tell whom he was speaking to.

"Not your fault, Stefan." Fourre's tone jerked.

"We had to run through the shadows, up under the wall...I got a boost through this window—there wasn't time to take aim. I didn't even realize who it was till—"

"It's all right, I said. Go on, now, take charge of your party, get this building cleaned out. Once we hold it, the rest of his boys should give up pretty soon."

The big man nodded and went out into the corridor.

Fourre crouched by Jacques Reinach while a sleet of bullets drummed on the outer walls. His heard them only dimly. Most of him was wondering if perhaps *this* hadn't been the best ending. Now they could give their chief a funeral with full military honors, and later they would build a monument to the man who saved the West, and—

And it might not be quite that easy to bribe a ghost. But you had to try.

"I didn't tell you the rest of the story, Jacques," he said. His hands were like a stranger's, using his jacket to wipe up the blood, and his voice ran on of itself. "I wish I had...maybe you would have understood...and maybe not. Marius went into politics afterward, you see. He had all the prestige of his victory behind him, he was the most powerful man in Rome, but he did not understand politics. There followed a witch's dance of corruption, murder, and civil war...fifty years of it, the final extinction of the Republic. Caesarism only gave a name to what had already been done.

"I would like to think that I helped to spare Jacques Reinach the name of Marius."

Rain slanted in through the broken window. Fourre's hands reached out and closed the darkened eyes. He wondered if he would ever be able to close them within himself.

HOME

Like a bullet, but one that hunted its own target, the ferry left the mother ship and curved down from orbit. Stars crowded darkness, unwinking and wintry. Jacob Kahn's gaze went out the viewport over the pilot board, across thirty-three light-years to the spark which was Sol. Almost convulsively, he looked away again, seeking the clotted silver of the Milky Way and the sprawl of Sagittarius. There, behind dust clouds where new suns were being born, lay the galaxy's heart.

Once he had dreamed of voyaging there himself. But he had been a boy then, who stood on a rooftop and peered through city sky glow and city haze. Afterward the dream struck facts of distance, energy and economics. The wreck had not gone under in an instant. His sons, his grandsons—

No. Probably no man ever would.

Beside him, Bill Redfeather's craggy features scowled at instruments. "All systems check," he said.

"I should hope so." Kahn's mouth twitched.

Redfeather looked irritated. It was the pilot's, not the co-pilot's, responsibility to be sure they would not burn like a meteorite in the atmosphere of the planet.

Its night side swelled before them, a monstrous darkness when you remembered the lights of Earth, but rimmed to dayward with blue and rosy red. An ocean sheened, polished metal scutcheoned with a hurricane, and that was alien, too, no pelagicultural cover, no floating towns or crisscrossing transport webs. As he watched Kahn staring at it, Redfeather's mood turned gentle.

"You think too damn much, Jake."

"Well—" Kahn shrugged. "My last space trip."

"Nonsense. They'll need men yet on the Lunar run."

"A nice, safe shuttle." Kahn's Israeli accent turned harsher. "No, thank you. I will make a clean break and stay groundside. High time I began raising a family anyway."

The ferry was coming into daylight now. Groombridge 1830 rose blindingly over the curve of its innermost planet. Clouds drifted gold across plains and great wrinkled mountains.

"Think we can get in some hunting and such?" Redfeather asked eagerly. "I mean the real thing, not popping loose at a robot in an amusement park."

"No doubt," Kahn said. "We will have time. They can't pack up and leave on no more notice than our call after we entered orbit."

"Damned shame, to end the project," Redfeather said. "I hope they solved the rotation problem, anyhow."

"Which?"

"You know. With the tidal action this sun must exert, why does Mithras have only a sixty-hour day?"

"Oh, that. That was answered in the first decade the base was here. I have read old reports. A smaller liquid core makes for less isostatic friction. Other factors enter in, too, like the absence of a satellite. Trivial, compared to what they have been learning since. Imagine a biochemistry like Earth's, but with its own evolution, natives as intelligent as we are but not human, an entire *world*."

Kahn's fist smote the arm of his chair light-bodied under the low deceleration, bounced a little in his harness. "The Directorate is governed by idiots," he said roughly. "Terminating the whole interstellar program just because some cost-accountant machine says population has grown so large and resources so low that we can't afford to keep on learning. My God, we can't afford not to! Without new knowledge, what hope have we for changing matters?"

"Could be the Directors had that in mind also," Redfeather grunted.

Kahn gave the co-pilot a sharp glance. Sometimes Redfeather surprised him.

The houseboat came down the Benison River, past Riptide Straits, and there lay the Bay of Desire. The sun was westering, a huge red-gold ball that struck fire off the waters. Kilometers distant, on the opposite shore, the Princess reared her blue peak high over the clustered, climbing roofs of Withylet village; closer at hand, the sails of boats shone white as the wings of the sea whistlers cruising above them. The air was still warm, but through an open window David Thrailkill sensed a coolness in the breeze, and a smell of salt, off the Weatherwomb Ocean beyond the Door.

"Want to take the helm, dear?" he asked Leonie.

"Sure, if you'll mind Vivian," said his wife.

Thrailkill went aft across the cabin to get a bottle of beer from the cooler. The engine throb, louder there, did not sound quite right. Well, an overhaul was due, after so long a time upriver. He walked forward again, with his seven-year-old daughter in tow. (That would have been three years on Earth, an enchanting age.) Leonie chuckled at them as they went by.

Strongtail was on the porch, to savor the view. They were following the eastern bayshore. It rose as steeply as the other side, in hills that were green from winter rains but had begun to show a tinge of summer's tawniness. Flameflowers shouted color among pseudograsses and scattered boskets. Thrailkill lowered his lanky form into a chair, cocked feet on rail, and tilted the bottle. Cold pungency gurgled past his lips, like water cloven by the twin bows. "Ahhh!" he said. "I'm almost sorry to come home."

Vivian flitted in Strongtail's direction, several balls clutched to her chest. "Juggle?" she said.

"Indeed," said the Mithran.

The girl laughed for joy, and bounced around as much as the balls. Strongtail had uncommon skill in keeping things aloft and awhirl. His build helped, of course. The first expedition had compared the autochthones to kangaroos with bird heads and with arms as long as a gibbon's. But a man who had spent his life among them needed no chimeras. To Thrailkill, his friend's nude brown-furred small form was a unity, more graceful and in a way more beautiful than any human.

The slender beak remained open while Strongtail juggled, uttering those trills which men could not imitate without a vocalizer. "Yes, a pleasant adventure," he said, "Fortune is that we have ample excuse to repeat it."

"We sure do." Thrailkill's gaunt face cracked in a grin. "This is going to rock them back on their heels in Treequad. For nigh on two hundred and fifty years, we've been skiting across the world, and never dreamed about an altogether fantastic culture right up the Benison. *Won't* Painted Jaguar be surprised?"

He spoke English. After an Earth century of contact, the Mithrans around the Bay understood even if they were not able to voice the language. And naturally every human kid knew what the flutings of his playmates meant. You could not travel far, though, before you met strangeness—not surprising, on a planet whose most advanced civilization was pre-industrial and whose natives were nowhere given to exploration or empire building.

Sometimes Thrailkill got a bit exasperated with them. They were too damned gentle! Not that they were not vigorous, merry, and all that. You could not ask for a better companion than Strongtail. But he lacked ambition. He had helped build this boat, and gone xenologizing on it, for fun and to oblige his buddy. When the mores of the riparian tribes became evident in all their dazzling complexities, he had not seen why the humans got so excited; to him, it was merely an occasion for amusement.

"I do not grasp your last reference," said Strongtail.

"Hm? Painted Jaguar? An old story among my people." Thrailkill looked toward the sun, where it touched the haze around the Princess with amber. Earth's sun he had watched only on film, little and fierce and hasty in heaven. "I'm not sure I understand it myself, quite."

Point Desire hove in view, the closest thing to a city that the region possessed, several hundred houses with adobe walls and red tile roofs on a headland above the docks. A dozen or so boats were in, mainly trading ketches from the southern arm of the Bay.

"Anxious though I am to see my kindred," the Mithran said, "I think we would do wrong not to dine with Rich-In-Peace."

Thrailkill laughed. "Come off it, you hypocrite. You know damn well you want some of her cooking." He rubbed his chin. "As a matter of fact, so do I."

The houseboat rode on. When it passed another craft, Strongtail exchanged cheerful whistles. That the blocky structure moved without sails or oars was no longer a cause of wonder, and never had been very much. The people took for granted that humans made curious things.

"Indeed this has been a delightful journey," Strongtail said. "Morning mists rolling still and white, islands hidden among waterstalks, a fish line to trail aft, and at night our jesting in our own snug world…I would like a houseboat for myself."

"Why, you can use this one any time," Thrailkill said.

"I know. But so many kin and friends would wish to come with me, years must pass before they have each shared my pleasure. There should be at least one other houseboat."

"So make one. I'll help whenever I get a chance, and you can have a motor built in Treequad."

"For what fair value in exchange? I would have to work hard, to gather food or timber or whatever else the builder might wish." Strongtail relaxed. "No, too many other joys wait, ranging Hermit Woods, lazing on Broadstrands, making music under the stars. Or playing with your cub." He sent the balls through a series of leaps that made Vivian squeal.

The boat eased into a berth. There followed the routine of making fast, getting shipshape, packing the stuff that must go ashore. That went quickly, because several Mithrans stopped their dockside fishing to help. They seemed agitated about something, but would not say what. Presently everyone walked to the landward end of the dock. Planks boomed underfoot.

Rich-In-Peace's inn was not large, even by local standards. The few customers sat on their tails at the counter, which had been split from a single scarletwood log, and talked with more excitement than usual. Leonie let the door-screen fold behind her. "Hello," she called. "We're back for some of your delicious chowder."

"And beer," Strongtail reminded. "Never forget beer."

Rich-In-Peace bustled around the counter. Her big amber eyes glistened. The house fell silent; this was her place, she was entitled to break the news.

"You have not heard?" she caroled.

"No, our radio went out on the way back," Thrailkill replied. "What's happened?"

She spread her hands. They had three fingers apiece, at right angles to each other. "But so wonderful!" she exclaimed. "A ship has come from your country. They say you can go home." As if the implications had suddenly broken on her, she stopped. After a moment: "I hope you will want to come back and visit us."

She doesn't realize, flashed through the stupefaction in Thrailkill. He was only dimly aware of Leonie's tight grasp on his arm. *That's a one-way trip.*

Sunset smoldered away in bronze and gold. From the heights above Treequad, Kahn and Thrailkill could look past the now-purple hills that flanked the Door out to a glimpse of the Weatherwomb Ocean. The xenologist sighed. "I always wanted to build a real sea-going schooner and take her there," he said. "Coasting down to Gate-of-the-South—what a trip!"

"I am surprised that the natives have not done so," Kahn said. "They appear to have the capability, and it would be better for trade than those toilsome overland routes you mentioned."

I suggested that, and my father before me," Thrailkill answered. "But none of them cared to make the initial effort. Once we thought about doing it ourselves, to set an example. But we had a lot of other work, and too few of us.

"Well, if the natives are so shiftless, why do you care about improving their lot?"

Thrailkill bristled at the insult to his Mithrans, until he remembered that Kahn could not be expected to understand. "'Shiftless' is the wrong word," he said. "They work as hard as necessary. Their arts make everything of ours look sick. Let's just call them less adventurous than humans." His smile was wry. "Probably the real reason we've done so much here, and wanted to do so much more. Not for altruism, just for the hell of it."

The mirth departed from him. He looked from the Door, past the twinkling lanterns of Goodwort and Withylet which guarded it, back across the mercury sheet of the Bay, to Treequad at his feet.

"So I'm not going to build that schooner," he said, then added roughly, "Come on, we'd better return."

They started downhill, over a trail which wound among groves of tall sweet-scented sheathbud trees. Leaves rustled in the twilight, a flock of marsh birds winged homeward with remote trumpetings, insects chirred from the pseudo-grasses. Below, Treequad was a darkness filling the flatlands between hills and Bay. Lights could be seen from windows, and the Center tower was etched slim against the waters. But the impression was of openness and peace, with some underlying mystery to which men could not put a name.

"Why did you establish yourselves here, rather than at the town farther north?" Kahn asked. His voice seemed flat and loud, and the way he jumped from subject to subject was also an offense to serenity. Thrailkill did not mind, though. He had recognized his own sort of man in the dark, moody captain; that was why he had invited Kahn to stay with him and had taken his guest on this ramble.

Good Lord, what can he do but grab blindly at whatever he notices? He left Earth a generation ago, and even if he read everything we sent up till then, why, we never could transmit more than a fraction of what we saw and heard and did. He's got two and a half—well, an Earth century's worth of questions to ask.

Thrailkill glanced around. The eastern sky had turned plum color, where the first few stars shown. *We ourselves,* he thought, *have a thousand years'—ten thousand years' worth. But of course now those questions never will be asked.*

"Why Treequad?" he said slowly. "Well, they already had a College of Poets and Ceremonialists here—call it the equivalent of an intellectual community, though in human terms it isn't very. They made useful go-betweens for us, in dealing with less educated natives. And then, uh, Point Desire is a trading center, therefore especially worth studying. We didn't want to disturb conditions by plumping our own breed down right there."

"I see. That is also why you haven't expanded your numbers?"

"Partly. We'd like to. This continent, this whole planet is so underpopulated that— But a scientific base can't afford to grow. How would everyone be brought home again when it's terminated?"

Fiercely, he burst out, "Damn you on Earth! You're terminating us too soon!"

"I agree," Kahn said. "If it is any consolation, all the others are being ended too. They don't mind so greatly. This is the sole world we have found where men can live without carrying around an environmental shell."

"What? There must be more."

"Indeed. But how far have we ranged? Less than fifty light-years. And never visited half the stars in that radius. You don't know what a gigantic project it is, to push a ship close to the speed of light. Too gigantic. The whole effort is coming to an end, as Earth grows poor and weary. I doubt if it will ever be revived."

Thrailkill felt a chill. The idea had not occurred to him before in the excitement of meeting the ferriers, but—"What can we do when we get there?" he demanded. "We're not fitted for...for City life."

"Have no fears," Kahn said. "Universities, foundations, vision programs, any number of institutions will be delighted to have you. At least, that was so when I left, and society appears to have grown static. And you should have party conversation for the rest of your lives, about our adventures on Mithras."

"M-m-m, I s'pose." Thrailkill rehearsed some fragments of his personal years.

Adventure enough. When he and Tom Jackson and Gleam-Of-Wings climbed the Snowtoothe, white starkness overhead and the wind awhistle below them, the thunder and plumes of an avalanche across a valley, the huge furry beast that came from a cave and must be slain before it slew them. Or shooting the rapids on a river that tumbled down the Goldstream Hills, landing wet and cold at Volcano to boast over their liquor in the smoky-raftered taproom of Monstersbane Inn. Prowling the alleys and passing the lean temples of the Fivedom, and standing off a horde of the natives' half-intelligent, insensately ferocious cousins, in the stockade at Tearwort. Following the caravans through the Desolations, down to Gate-of-the-South, while drums beat unseen from dry hills, or simply this last trip, along the Benison through fogs and waterstalks, to those lands where the dwellers gave their lives to nothing but rites that made no sense and one dared not laugh. Indeed Earth offered nothing like that, and the vision-screen people would pay well for a taste of it to spice their fantasies.

Thrailkill remembered quieter times more clearly, and did not see how they could be told. The Inn of the Poetess, small and snug beneath the stormcloud mass of Demon Mountain. Firelight, songs, comradeship; shadows and sun-flecks and silence in Hermit Woods; sailing out to Fish Hound Island with Leonie on their wedding night, that the sunrise might find them alone on its crags (how very bright the stars had been, even little Sol was a beacon for them); afterward, building sand castles with Vivian on Broadstrands, while the surf rolled in from ten thousand kilometers of ocean. They used to end such a day by finding some odd eating place in Kings Point Station or Goodwort, and Vivian would fall asleep to the creak of the sweeps as their ferry plowed home across the water.

Well, those were private memories anyway.

He realized they had been walking for some time in silence. Only their foot-falls on the cobbles, now that they were back in town, or an occasional trill from the houses that bulked on either side, could be heard. Courtesy insisted he should make conversation with the vaguely visible shape on his right. "What will you do?" he asked. "After we return, I mean."

"I don't know," Kahn said. "Teach, perhaps."

"Something technical, no doubt."

"I could, if need be. Science and technology no longer change from genera-tion to generation. But I would prefer history. I have had considerable time to read history, in space."

"Really? I mean, the temporal contraction effect—"

"You forget that at one gravity acceleration, a ship needs a year to reach near-light speed, and another year to brake at the end. You passengers will be in sus-pended animation, but we of the crew must stand watch."

Kahn lit a cigarette. Earlier, Thrailkill had experimented with one, but tobacco made him ill, he found. He wondered for a moment if Earth's food had the savor of Mithras'. *Funny. I never appreciated kernelkraut or sour nuts or filet of crackler till now, when I'm about to lose them.*

The cigarette end brightened and faded, brightened and faded, like a tiny red watchlight in the gloaming. "After all," Kahn said, "I have seen many human events. I was born before the Directorate came to power. My father was a radia-tion technician in the Solar War. And, too, mine are an old people, who spent most of their existence on the receiving end of history. It is natural that I should be interested. You have been more fortunate."

"And the Mithrans are luckier yet, eh?"

"I don't know. Thus far, they are essentially a historyless race. Or are they? How can you tell? We look through our own eyes. To us, accomplishment equals exploitation of the world. Our purest science and art remain a sort of conquest. What might the Mithrans do yet, in Mithran terms?"

"Let us keep up the base," Thrailkill said, "and we'll keep on reporting what they do."

"That would be splendid," Kahn told him, "except for the fact that there will be no ships to take your descendants home. You have maintained yourselves as an enclave of a few hundred people for a century. You cannot do so forever. If noth-ing else, genetic drift in that small a population would destroy you."

They walked on unspeaking, till they reached the Center. It was a village within the village, clustered around the tower. Thence had sprung the maser beams, up through the sky to the relay satellite, and so to those on Earth who wondered what the universe was like. *No more,* Thrailkill thought. *Dust will gather, nightcats will nest in corroding instruments, legends will be muttered about the tall strangers who built and departed, and one century an earthquake will bring down this tower which talked across space, and the very myths will die.*

On the far side of the Mall, close to the clear plash of Louis' Fountain, they stopped. There lay Thrailkill's house, long and solid, made to endure. His grandfather had begun it, his father had completed it, he himself had wanted to add rooms but had no reason, for he would be allowed only two children. The windows were aglow, and he heard a symphony of Mithran voices.

"What the devil!" he exclaimed. "We've got company." He opened the door.

The fireplace danced with flames, against the evening cold. Their light shimmered off the beautiful grain of wainscoting, glowed on patterned rugs and the copper statue which owned one corner, and sheened along the fur of his friends. The room was full of them: Strongtail, Gleam-Of-Wings, Nightstar, Gift-Of-God, Dreamer, Elf-In-The-Forest, and more and more, all he had loved who could get here quickly enough. They sat grave on their tails, balancing cups of herb tea in their hands, while Leonie attended to the duties of a hostess

She stopped when Thrailkill and Kahn entered. "How late you are!" she said. "I was growing worried."

"No need," Thrailkill replied, largely for Kahn's benefit. "The last prowltiger hereabouts was shot five years ago." *I did that. Another adventure—hai, what a stalk through the folded hills! (The Mithrans didn't like it. They attached some kind of significance to the ugly brutes. But prowltigers never took a Mithran. When the Harris boy was killed, we stopped listening to objections. Our friends forgave us eventually.)* He looked around. "You honor this roof," he said with due formality. "Be welcome in good cheer."

Strongtail's music was a dirge. "Is the story true that you can never return?"

"Yes, I'm afraid so," Thrailkill said. Aside to Kahn: "They want us to stay. I'm not sure why. We haven't done anything in particular for them."

"But you tried," said Nightstar. "That was a large plenty, that you should care."

"And you were something to wonder at," Elf-In-The-Forest added.

"We have enjoyed you," Strongtail said. "Why must you go?"

"We took council," sang Gift-Of-God, "and came hither to ask from house to house that you remain."

"But we can't!" Leonie's voice cracked.

"Why can you not?" responded Dreamer.

It burst upon Thrailkill like a nova. He stood in the home of his fathers and shouted aloud: "Why not? We can!"

The meeting hall in Treequad was so big that the entire human population could gather within. Mounting the stage, Kahn looked between gaily muraled walls to the faces. The very graybeards, he thought, had an air of youth which did not exist for any age on Earth. Sun and wind had embraced them throughout their lives. They had had a planet to wander in, the like of which men had not owned since Columbus.

He turned to Thrailkill, who had accompanied him. "Is everybody here?"

Thrailkill's gaze swept the room. Sunlight streamed in the windows, to touch women's hair and men's eyes with ruddiness. A quiet had fallen, underscored by rustlings and shufflings. Somewhere a baby cried, but was quickly soothed.

"Yes," he said. "The last field expedition came in two hours ago, from the Ice-floe Dwellers." He scowled at Kahn. "I don't know why you want this assembly. Our minds are made up."

The spaceman consulted his watch. He had to stall for a bit. His men would not get down from orbit for some minutes yet, and then they must walk here. "I told you," he said. "I want to make a final appeal."

"We've heard your arguments," Thrailkill said.

"Not formally."

"Oh, all right." Thrailkill advanced to the lectern. The amplifiers boomed his words forth under the rafters.

"The meeting will please come to order," he said. "As you know, we're met for the purpose of officially ratifying the decision that we have reached. I daresay Captain Kahn will need such a recorded vote. First he'd like to address you." He bowed slightly to his guest and took a chair. Leonie was in the front row with Vivian; he winked at them.

Kahn leaned on the stand. His body felt heavy and tired. "Ladies and gentlemen," he said, "you have spent many hours this past night talking things over in private groups. Quite an exciting night, no? I have asked you to come here after sleeping on the question, because your choice should be made in a calmer mood, it being irrevocable.

"Hardly any of you have agreed to leave with us. I wonder if the majority have considered what their own desires mean. As was said long ago, *'Il faut vouloir les conséquences de ce que l'on veut.'*" Blankness met him, driving home how far these people had drifted from Earth. "I mean you must want the results of what you want. You are too few to maintain a culture at the modern level. True, your ancestors brought along the means to produce certain amenities, and you have a lot of information on microtape. But there are only so many heads among you, and each head can hold only so much. You are simply not going to have enough engineers, medical specialists, psychopediatricians, geneticists…every trained type necessary to operate a civilization, as opposed to a mere scientific base. Some of your children will die from causes that could have been prevented. Those who survive will mature ignorant of Earth's high heritage.

"A similar thing happened before, on the American frontier. But America was close to Europe. The new barbarism ended in a few generations, as contact strengthened. You will be alone, with no more than one thin thread of radio, a lifetime passing between message and answer. Do you want to sink back into a dark age?"

Someone called, "We've done okay so far." Others added remarks. Kahn was content to let them wrangle; thus he gained time, without drawing on his own thin resources. But Thrailkill hushed them and said:

"I believe we're aware of that problem, Captain. In fact, we've lived with it during the whole existence of this…colony." *There,* Kahn thought, *he had spoken the word.* "We haven't really been bothered. From what we hear about Earth, we've gained more than we've lost." Applause. "And now that you've made us realize this is our home, this is where we belong, why, we won't stay small. For purely genetic reasons we'll have to expand our population as fast as possible. My wife and I always did want a houseful of kids. Now we can have them." Cheering began. His reserve broke apart. "We'll build our own civilization! And someday we'll come back to you, as visitors. You're giving up the stars. We're not!"

They rose from their chairs and shouted.

Kahn let the noise surf around him. *Soon,* he begged. *Let it be soon.* Seeing that he remained where he was, the crowd grew gradually still. He waited till the last one had finished talking to his neighbor. Then the silence was so deep that he could hear the songbirds outside.

"Very well," he said in a dull tone. "But what is to become of the Mithrans?"

Thrailkill, who had also stayed on his feet, said rapidly, "You mentioned that to me before, Captain. I told you then and I tell you now, the planet has room for both races. We aren't going to turn on our friends."

"My mate Bill Redfeather is an Amerind," Kahn said. "Quite a few of his ancestors were friends to the white man. It didn't help them in the long run. I am a Jew myself, if you know what that means. My people spent the better part of two thousand years being alien. We remember in our bones how that was. Finally some started a country of their own. The Arabs who were there objected, and lived out the rest of their lives in refugee camps. Ask Muthaswamy, my chief engineer, to explain the history of Moslem and Hindu in India. Ask his assistant Ngola to tell you what happened when Europe entered Africa. And, as far as that goes, what happened when Europe left again. You cannot intermingle two cultures. One of them will devour the other. And already, this minute, yours is the more powerful."

They mumbled, down in the hall, and stared at him and did not understand. He sucked air into his lungs and tried anew:

"Yes, you don't intend to harm the Mithrans. Thus far there has been little conflict. But when your numbers grow, when you begin to rape the land for all the resources this hungry civilization needs, when mutual exasperation escalates into battle—can you speak for your children? Your grandchildren? Their grand-children, to the end of time? The people of Bach and Goethe brought forth Hitler. No, you don't know what I am talking about, do you?

"Well, let us suppose that man on this planet reverses his entire previous record and gives the natives some fairly decent reservations and does not take them away again. Still, how much hope have they of becoming anything but miserable parasites? They cannot become one with you. The surviving Amerinds could be assimilated, but they were human. Mithrans are not. They do not and cannot think like humans. But don't they have the right to live in their world as they wish, make their own works, hope their own hopes?

"You call this planet underpopulated. By your standards, that is correct. But not by the natives'. How many individuals per hectare do you expect an economy like theirs to support? Take away part of a continent and you murder that many unborn sentient beings. But you won't stop there. You will take the world, and so murder an entire way of existence. How do you know that way isn't better than ours? Certainly you have no right to deny the universe the chance that it is better."

They seethed and buzzed at his feet. Thrailkill, advanced, fists clenched, and said flatly, "Have you so little pride in being a man?"

"On the contrary," Kahn answered. "I have so much pride that I will not see my race guilty of the ultimate crime. We are not going to make anyone else pay for our mistakes. We are going home and see if we cannot amend them ourselves."

"So you say!" spat Thrailkill.

O God of mercy, send my men. Kahn looked into the eyes of the one whose salt he had eaten, and knew they would watch him for what remained of his life. And behind would gleam the Bay of Desire, and the Princess' peak holy against a smokeless heaven, and the Weatherwomb waiting for ships to sail west. "You will be heroes on Earth," he said. "And you will at least have memories. I—"

The communicator in his pocket buzzed *Ready*. He slapped it once: *Go ahead.*

Thunder crashed on the roof, shaking walls. A deep-toned whistle followed. Kahn sagged back against the lectern. That would be the warboat, with guns and nuclear bombs.

The door flew open. Redfeather entered, and a squad of armed men. The rest had surrounded the hall.

Kahn straightened. His voice was a stranger's, lost in the yells and oaths: "You are still citizens of the Directorate. As master of an official ship, I have discretionary police authority. Will or no, you shall come back with me."

He saw Leonie clutch her child to her. He ducked Thrailkill's roundhouse swing and stumbled off the stage, along the aisle toward his men. Hands grabbed at him. Redfeather fired a warning burst, and thereafter he walked alone. He breathed hard, but kept his face motionless. It would not do for him to weep. Not yet.

QUIXOTE AND THE WINDMILL

The first robot in the world came walking over green hills with sunlight aflash off his polished metal hide. He walked with a rippling grace that was almost feline, and his tread fell noiselessly—but you could feel the ground vibrate ever so faintly under the impact of that terrific mass, and the air held a subliminal quiver from the great engine that pulsed within him.

Him. You could not think of the robot as neuter. He had the brutal maleness of a naval rifle or a blast furnace. All the smooth silent elegance of perfect design and construction did not hide the weight and strength of a two and a half-meter height. His eyes glowed, as if with inner fires of smoldering atoms, they could see in any frequency range he selected, he could turn an X-ray beam on you and look you through and through with those terrible eyes. They had built him humanoid, but had had the good taste not to give him a face; there were the eyes, with their sockets for extra lenses when he needed microscopic or telescopic vision, and there were a few other small sensory and vocal orifices, but otherwise his head was a mask of shining metal. Humanoid, but not human—man's creation, but more than man—the first independent, volitional, nonspecialized machine—but they had dreamed of him, long ago, he had once been the jinni in the bottle or the Golem, Bacon's brazen head or Frankenstein's monster, the man-transcending creature who could serve or destroy with equal contemptuous ease.

He walked under a bright summer sky, over sunlit fields and through little groves that danced and whispered in the wind. The houses of men were scattered here and there, the houses which practically took care of themselves; over beyond the horizon was one of the giant, almost automatic food factories; a few self-piloting carplanes went quietly overhead. Humans were in sight, sun-browned men and their women and children going about their various errands with loose bright garments floating in the breeze. A few seemed to be at work, there was a colorist experimenting with a new chromatic harmony, a composer sitting on his verandah striking notes out of an omniplayer, a group of engineers in a transparent-walled laboratory testing some mechanisms. But with the standard work period what it was these days, most were engaged in recreation. A picnic, a dance under trees, a concert, a pair of lovers, a group of children in one of the immemorially ancient games of their age-group, an old man happily enhammocked with a book and a bottle of beer—the human race was taking it easy.

They saw the robot go by, and often a silence fell as his tremendous shadow slipped past. His electronic detectors sensed the eddying pulses that meant nervousness, a faint unease—oh, they trusted the cybernetics men, they didn't look for a devouring monster, but they wondered. They felt man's old unsureness of the alien and unknown, deep in their minds they wondered what the robot was about and what his new and invincible race might mean to Earth's dwellers—then, perhaps, as his gleaming height receded over the hills, they laughed and forgot him.

The robot went on.

There were not many customers in the Casanova at this hour. After sunset the tavern would fill up and the autodispensers would be kept busy, for it had a good live-talent show and television was becoming unfashionable. But at the moment only those who enjoyed a mid-afternoon glass, together with some serious drinkers, were present.

The building stood alone on a high wooded ridge, surrounded by its gardens and a good-sized parking lot. Its colonnaded exterior was long and low and gracious; inside it was cool and dim and fairly quiet; and the general air of decorum, due entirely to lack of patronage, would probably last till evening. The manager had gone off on his own business and the girls didn't find it worthwhile to be around till later, so the Casanova was wholly in the charge of its machines.

Two men were giving their autodispenser a good workout. It could hardly deliver one drink before a coin was given it for another. The smaller man was drinking whiskey and soda, the larger one stuck to the most potent available ale, and both were already thoroughly soused.

They sat in a corner booth from which they could look out the open door, but their attention was directed to the drinks. It was one of those curious barroom acquaintances which spring up between utterly diverse types. They would hardly remember each other the next day. But currently they were exchanging their troubles.

The little dark-haired fellow, Roger Brady, finished his drink and dialed for another. "Beatcha!" he said triumphantly.

"Gimme time," said the big redhead, Pete Borklin. "This stuff goes down slower."

Brady got out a cigarette. His fingers shook as he brought it to his mouth and puffed it into lighting. "Why can't that drink come right away?" he mumbled. "I resent a ten-second delay. Ten dry eternities! I demand instantaneously mixed drinks, delivered faster than light."

The glass arrived, and he raised it to his lips. "I am afraid," he said, with the careful precision of a very drunk man, "that I am going on a weeping jag. I would much prefer a fighting jag. But unfortunately there is nobody to fight."

"I'll fight you," offered Borklin. His huge fists closed.

"Nah—why? Wouldn't be a fight, anyway. You'd just mop me up. And why should we fight? We're both in the same boat."

"Yeah," Borklin looked at his fists. "Not much use, anyway," he said. "Somebody'd do a lot better job o' killing with an autogun than I could with—

these." He unclenched them, slowly, as if with an effort, and took another drag at his glass.

"What we want to do," said Brady, "is to fight a world. We want to blow up all Earth and scatter the pieces from here to Pluto. Only it wouldn't do any good, Pete. Some machine'd come along and put it back together again."

"I just wanna get drunk," said Borklin. "My wife left me. D'I tell you that? My wife left me."

"Yeah, you told me."

Borklin shook his heavy head, puzzled. "She said I was a drunk. I went to a doctor like she said, but it didn't help none. He said…I forget what he said. But I had to keep on drinking anyway. Wasn't anything else to do."

"I know. Psychiatry helps people solve problems. It's not being able to solve a problem that drives a man insane. But when the problem is inherently insoluble—what then? One can only drink, and try to forget."

"My wife wanted me to amount to something," said Borklin. "She wanted me to get a job. But what could I do? I tried. Honest, I tried. I tried for…well, I've been trying all my life, really. There just wasn't any work around. Not any I could do."

"Fortunately, the basic citizen's allowance is enough to get drunk on," said Brady. "Only the drinks don't arrive fast enough. I demand an instantaneous autodispenser."

Borklin dialed for another ale. He looked at his hands in a bewildered way. "I've always been strong," he said. "I know I'm not bright, but I'm strong, and I'm good at working with machines and all. But nobody would hire me." He spread his thick workman's fingers. "I was handy at home. We had a little place in Alaska, my dad didn't hold with too many gadgets, so I was handy around there. But he's dead now, the place is sold, what good are my hands?"

"The worker's paradise." Brady's thin lips twisted. "Since the end of the Transition, Earth has been Utopia. Machines do all the routine work, *all* of it, they produce so much that the basic necessities of life are free."

"The hell. They want money for everything."

"Not much. And you get your citizen's allowance, which is just a convenient way of making your needs free. When you want more money, for the luxuries, you work, as an engineer or scientist or musician or painter or tavern keeper or spaceman or…anything there's a demand for. You don't work too hard. Paradise!" Brady's shaking fingers spilled cigarette ash on the table. A little tube dipped down from the wall and sucked it up.

"I can't find work. They don't want me. Nowhere."

"Of course not. What earthly good is manual labor these days? Machines do it all. Oh, there are technicians to be sure, quite a lot of them—but they're all highly skilled men, years of training. The man who has nothing to offer but his strength and a little rule-of-thumb ingenuity doesn't get work. There *is* no place for him!" Brady took another swallow from his glass. "Human genius has eliminated the need for the workman. Now it only remains to eliminate the workman himself."

Borklin's fists closed again, dangerously. "Whattayuh mean?" he asked harshly. "Whattayuh mean, anyway?"

"Nothing personal. But you know it yourself. Your type no longer fits into human society. So the geneticists are gradually working it out of the race. The population is kept static, relatively small, and is slowly evolving toward a type which can adapt to the present en…environment. And that's not your type, Pete."

The big man's anger collapsed into futility. He stared emptily at his glass. "What to do?" he whispered. "What can I do?"

"Not a thing, Pete. Just drink, and try to forget your wife. Just drink."

"Mebbe they'll get out to the stars."

"Not in our lifetimes. And even then, they'll want to take their machines along. We still won't be any more useful. Drink up, old fellow. Be glad! You're living in Utopia!"

There was silence then, for a while. The day was bright outside. Brady was grateful for the obscurity of the tavern.

Borklin said at last: "What I can't figure is you. You look smart. You can fit in…can't you?"

Brady grinned humorlessly. "No, Pete. I had a job, yes. I was a mediocre servotechnician. The other day I couldn't take any more. I told the boss what to do with his servos, and I've been drinking ever since. I don't think I ever want to stop."

"But how come?"

"Dreary, routine—I hated it. I'd rather stay tight. I had psychiatric help too, of course, and it didn't do me any good. The same insoluble problem as yours, really."

"I don't get it."

"I'm a bright boy, Pete. Why hide it? My I.Q. puts me in the genius class. But—not quite bright enough." Brady fumbled for another coin. He could only find a bill, but the machine gave him change. "I want inshantaneous auto…or did I say that before? Never mind. It doesn't matter." He buried his face in his hands.

"How do you mean, not quite bright enough?" Borklin was insistent. He had a vague notion that a new slant on his own problem might conceivably help him see a solution. "That's what they told me, only politer. But you—"

"I'm too bright to be an ordinary technician. Not for long. And I have none of the artistic or literary talent which counts so highly nowadays. What I wanted was to be a mathematician. All my life I wanted to be a mathematician. And I worked at it. I studied. I learned all any human head could hold, and I know where to look up the rest." Brady grinned wearily. "So what's the upshot? The mathematical machines have taken over. Not only all routine computation—that's old—but even independent research. At a higher level than the human brain can operate.

"They still have humans working at it. Sure. They have men who outline the problems, control and check the machines, follow through all the steps—men who are the…the soul of the science, even today.

"*But*—only the top-flight geniuses. The really brilliant, original minds, with flashes of sheer inspiration. *They* are still needed. But the machines do all the rest."

Brady shrugged. "I'm not a first-rank genius, Pete. I can't do anything that an electronic brain can't do quicker and better. So I didn't get my job, either."

They sat quiet again. Then Borklin said, slowly: "At least you can get some fun. I don't like all these concerts and pictures and all that fancy stuff. I don't have more than drinking and women and maybe some stereofilm."

"I suppose you're right," said Brady indifferently. "But I'm not cut out to be a hedonist. Neither are you. We both *want* to work. We want to feel we have some importance and, value—we want to amount to something. Our friends…your wife…I had a girl once, Pete…we're expected to amount to something."

"Only there's nothing for us to do—"

A hard and dazzling sun-flash caught his eye. He looked out through the door, and jerked with a violence that upset his drink.

"Great universe!" he breathed. "Pete…Pete…look, it's the robot! *It's the robot!*"

"Huh?" Borklin twisted around, trying to focus his eyes out the door. "Whazzat?"

"The robot—you've heard of it, man." Brady's soddenness was gone in a sudden shivering intensity. His voice was like metal. "They built him three years ago at Cybernetics Lab. Manlike, with a volitional, non-specialized brain—manlike, but more than man!"

"Yeah…yeah, I heard." Borklin looked out and saw the great shining form striding across the gardens, bound on some unknown journey that took him past the tavern. "They were testing him. But he's been running around loose for a year or so now—Wonder where he's going?"

"I don't know." As if hypnotized, Brady looked after the mighty thing. "I don't know—" His voice trailed off, then suddenly he stood up and then lashed out: "But we'll find out! Come on, Pete!"

"Where…huh…why—" Borklin rose slowly, fumbling through his own bewilderment. "What do you mean?"

"Don't you see, don't you see? It's *the robot*—the man after man—all that man is, and how much more we don't even imagine. Pete, the machines have been replacing men, here, there, everywhere. This is the machine that will replace *man!*"

Borklin said nothing, but trailed out after Brady. The smaller man kept on talking, rapidly, bitterly: "Sure—why not? Man is simply flesh and blood. Humans are only human. They're not efficient enough for our shiny new world. Why not scrap the whole human race? How long till we have nothing but men of metal in a meaningless metal ant-heap?

"Come on, Pete. Man is going down into darkness. But we can go down fighting!"

Something of it penetrated Borklin's mind. He saw the towering machine ahead of him, and suddenly it was as if it embodied all which had broken him. The ultimate machine, the final arrogance of efficiency, remote and godlike and indifferent as it smashed him—suddenly he hated it with a violence that seemed to split his skull apart. He lumbered clumsily beside Brady and they caught up with the robot together.

"Turn around!" called Brady. "Turn around and fight!"

The robot paused. Brady picked up a stone and threw it. The rock bounced off the armor with a dull clang.

The robot faced about. Borklin ran at him, cursing. His heavy shoes kicked at the robot's ankle joints, his fists battered at the front. They left no trace.

"Stop that," said the robot. His voice had little tonal variation, but there was the resonance of a great bell in it. "Stop that. You will injure yourself."

Borklin retreated, gasping with the pain of bruised flesh and smothering impotence. Brady reeled about to stand before the robot. The alcohol was singing and buzzing in his head, but his voice came oddly clear.

"We can't hurt you," he said. "We're Don Quixote, tilting at windmills. But you wouldn't know about that. You wouldn't know about any of man's old dreams."

"I am unable to account for your present actions," said the robot. His eyes blazed with their deep fires, searching the men. Unconsciously, they shrank away a little.

"You are unhappy," decided the robot. "You have been drinking to escape your own unhappiness, and in your present intoxication you identify me with the causes of your misery."

"Why not?" flared Brady. "Aren't you? The machines are taking over all Earth with their smug efficiency, making man a parasite—and now you come, the ultimate machine, you're the one who's going to replace man himself."

"I have no belligerent intentions," said the robot. "You should know I was conditioned against any such tendencies, even while my brain was in process of construction." Something like a chuckle vibrated in the deep metal voice. "What reason do I have to fight anyone?"

"None," said Brady thinly. "None at all. You'll just take over, as more and more of you are made, as your emotionless power begins to—"

"Begins to what?" asked the robot. "And how do you know I am emotionless? Any psychologist will tell you that emotion, though not necessarily of the human type, is a basis of thought. What logical reason does a being have to think, to work, even to exist? It cannot rationalize its so doing, it simply does, because of its endocrine system, its power plant, whatever runs it…its emotions! And any mentality capable of self-consciousness will feel as wide a range of emotion as you—it will be as happy or as interested—or as miserable—as you!"

It was weird, even in a world used to machines that were all but alive, thus to stand and argue with a living mass of metal and plastic, vacuum and energy. The strangeness of it struck Brady, he realized just how drunk he was. But still he had to snarl his hatred and despair out, mouth any phrases at all just so they relieved some of the bursting tension within him.

"I don't care how you feel or don't feel," he said, stuttering a little now. "It's that you're the future, the meaningless future when all men are as useless as I am now, and I hate you for it and the worst of it is I can't kill you."

The robot stood like a burnished statue of some old and non-anthropomorphic god, motionless, but his voice shivered the quiet air: "Your case is fairly common. You have been relegated to obscurity by advanced technology. But do not identify yourself with all mankind. There will always be men who think and dream and sing and carry on all the race has ever loved. The future belongs to them, not to you—or to me.

"I am surprised that a man of your apparent intelligence does not realize my position. But—what earthly good is a robot? By the time science had advanced to the point where I could be built, there was no longer any reason for it. Think— you have a specialized machine to perform or help man perform every conceivable task. What possible use is there for a nonspecialized machine to do them all? Man himself fulfills that function, and the machines are no more than his tools. Does a housewife want a robot servant when she need only control the dozen machines which already do all the work? Why should a scientist want a robot that could, say, go into dangerous radioactive rooms when he has already installed automatic and remote-controlled apparatus which does everything there? And surely the artists and thinkers and policy-makers don't need robots, they are performing specifically human tasks, it will always be *man* who sets man's goals and dreams his dreams. The all-purpose machine is and forever will be—man himself.

"Man, I was made for purely scientific study. After a couple of years they had learned all there was to learn about me—and I had no other purpose! They let me become a harmless, aimless, meaningless wanderer, just so I could be doing something—and my life is estimated at five hundred years!

"I have no purpose. I have no real reason for existence. I have no companion, no place in human society, no use for my strength and my brain. Man, man, do you think *I* am happy?"

The robot turned to go. Brady was sitting on the grass, holding his head to keep it from whirling off into space, so he didn't see the giant metal god depart. But he caught the last words flung back, and somehow there was such a choking bitterness in the toneless brazen voice that he could never afterward forget them.

"Man, you are the lucky one. *You* can get drunk!"

BLACK BODIES

Black bodies give off radiation
And ought to continuously,
Black bodies give off radiation
But do it by Planck's theory.

    Bring back, bring back,
    Oh, bring back that old continuity,
    Bring back, bring back,
    Oh, bring back Clerk Maxwell to me!

Though now we have Schrödinger functions
Dividing up h by 2π,
That damned differential equation
Still has no solution for ψ.

    Bring back…

Well, Heisenberg came to the rescue,
Intending to make all secure;
What is the result of his efforts?
We are absolutely unsure.

    Bring back…

Dirac spoke of energy levels,
Both minus and plus. How droll!
And now, just because of his teachings,
We don't know our mass from a hole.

    Bring back…

231

The theory's complex and fragile,
And smells full of logical traps;
Whenever we open the catbox
Our wave functions promptly collapse.

> *Bring back, bring back,*
> *Oh, bring back that old continuity,*
> *Bring back, bring back,*
> *Oh, bring back Clerk Maxwell to me!*

(as expanded by Poul Anderson, March, 1992)[1]

---

1 The original title was "Physicist's Lament." Based on a discussion with Karen Anderson, the title was changed to "Black Bodies." This version is from Karen Anderson's records as expanded by Poul Anderson, March, 1992)

KYRIE

On a high peak in the Lunar Carpathians stands a convent of St. Martha of Bethany. The walls are native rock; they lift dark and cragged as the mountainside itself, into a sky that is always black. As you approach from Northpole, flitting low to keep the force screens along Route Plato between you and the meteoroidal rain, you see the cross which surmounts the tower, stark athwart Earth's blue disc. No bells resound from there—not in airlessness.

You may hear them inside at the canonical hours, and throughout the crypts below where machines toil to maintain a semblance of terrestrial environment. If you linger a while you will also hear them calling to requiem mass. For it has become a tradition that prayers be offered at St. Martha's for those who have perished in space; and they are more with every passing year.

This is not the work of the sisters. They minister to the sick, the needy, the crippled, the insane, all whom space has broken and cast back. Luna is full of such, exiles because they can no longer endure Earth's pull or because it is feared they may be incubating a plague from some unknown planet or because men are so busy with their frontiers that they have no time to spare for the failures. The sisters wear space suits as often as habits, are as likely to hold a medikit as a rosary.

But they are granted some time for contemplation. At night, when for half a month the sun's glare has departed, the chapel is unshuttered and stars look down through the glaze-dome to the candles. They do not wink and their light is winter cold. One of the nuns in particular is there as often as may be, praying for her own dead. And the abbess sees to it that she can be present when the yearly mass, that she endowed before she took her vows, is sung.

> *Requiem aeternam dona eis, Domine, et lux perpetua luceat eis.*
> *Kyrie eleison, Christe eleison, Kyrie eleison.*

The Supernova Sagittarii expedition comprised fifty human beings and a flame. It went the long way around from Earth orbit, stopping at Epsilon Lyrae to pick up its last member. Thence it approached its destination by stages.

This is the paradox: time and space are aspects of each other. The explosion was more than a hundred years past when noted by men on Lasthope. They were part

233

of a generations-long effort to fathom the civilization of creatures altogether unlike us; but one night they looked up and saw a light so brilliant it cast shadows.

That wave front would reach Earth several centuries hence. By then it would be so tenuous that nothing but another bright point would appear in the sky. Meanwhile, though, a ship overleaping the space through which light must creep could track the great star's death across time.

Suitably far off, instruments recorded what had been before the outburst, incandescence collapsing upon itself after the last nuclear fuel was burned out. A jump, and they saw what happened a century ago, convulsion, storm of quanta and neutrinos, radiation equal to the massed hundred billion suns of this galaxy.

It faded, leaving an emptiness in heaven, and the *Raven* moved closer. Fifty light-years—fifty years—inward, she studied a shrinking fieriness in the midst of a fog which shone like lightning.

Twenty-five years later the central globe had dwindled more, the nebula had expanded and dimmed. But because the distance was now so much less, everything seemed larger and brighter. The naked eye saw a dazzle too fierce to look straight at, making the constellations pale by contrast. Telescopes showed a blue-white spark in the heart of an opalescent cloud delicately filamented at the edges.

The *Raven* made ready for her final jump, to the immediate neighborhood of the supernova.

Captain Teodor Szili went on a last-minute inspection tour. The ship murmured around him, running at one gravity of acceleration to reach the desired intrinsic velocity. Power droned, regulators whickered, ventilation systems rustled. He felt the energies quiver in his bones. But metal surrounded him, blank and comfortless. Viewports gave on a dragon's hoard of stars, the ghostly arch of the Milky Way: on vacuum, cosmic rays, cold not far above absolute zero, distance beyond imagination to the nearest human hearthfire. He was about to take his people where none had ever been before, into conditions none was sure about, and that was a heavy burden on him.

He found Eloise Waggoner at her post, a cubbyhole with intercom connections directly to the command bridge. Music drew him, a triumphant serenity he did not recognize. Stopping in the doorway, he saw her seated with a small tape machine on the desk.

"What's this?" he demanded.

"Oh!" The woman (he could not think of her as a girl, though she was barely out of her teens) started. "I…I was waiting for the jump."

"You were to wait at the alert."

"What have I to do?" she answered less timidly than was her wont. "I mean, I'm not a crewman or a scientist."

"You are in the crew. Special communications technician."

"With Lucifer. And he likes the music. He says we come closer to oneness with it than in anything else he knows about us."

Szili arched his brows. "Oneness?"

A blush went up Eloise's thin cheeks. She stared at the deck and her hands twisted together. "Maybe that isn't the right word. Peace, harmony, unity… God?…I sense what he means, but we haven't any word that fits."

"Hm. Well, you are supposed to keep him happy." The skipper regarded her with a return of the distaste he had tried to suppress. She was a decent enough sort, he supposed, in her gauche and inhibited way; but her looks! Scrawny, big-footed, big-nosed, pop eyes, and stringy dust-colored hair—and, to be sure, telepaths always made him uncomfortable. She said she could only read Lucifer's mind, but was that true?

No. Don't think such things. Loneliness and otherness can come near breaking you out here, without adding suspicion of your fellows.

If Eloise Waggoner was really human. She must be some kind of mutant at the very least. Whoever could communicate thought to thought with a living vortex had to be.

"What are you playing, anyhow?" Szili asked.

"Bach. The *Third Brandenburg Concerto*. He, Lucifer, he doesn't care for the modern stuff. I don't either."

You wouldn't, Szili decided. Aloud: "Listen, we jump in half an hour. No telling what we'll emerge in. This is the first time anyone's been close to a recent supernova. We can only be certain of so much hard radiation that we'll be dead if the screenfields give way. Otherwise we've nothing to go on except theory. And a collapsing stellar core is so unlike anything anywhere else in the universe that I'm skeptical about how good the theory is. We can't sit daydreaming. We have to prepare."

"Yes, sir." Whispering, her voice lost its usual harshness.

He stared past her, past the ophidian eyes of meters and controls, as if he could penetrate the steel beyond and look straight into space. There, he knew, floated Lucifer.

The image grew in him: a fireball twenty meters across, shimmering white, red, gold, royal blue, flames dancing like Medusa locks, cometary tail burning for a hundred meters behind, a shiningness, a glory, a piece of hell. Not the least of what troubled him was the thought of that which paced his ship.

He hugged scientific explanations to his breast, though they were little better than guesses. In the multiple star system of Epsilon Aurigae, in the gas and energy pervading the space around, things took place which no laboratory could imitate. Ball lightning on a planet was perhaps analogous, as the formation of simple organic compounds in a primordial ocean is analogous to the life which finally evolves. In Epsilon Aurigae, magnetohydrodynamics had done what chemistry did on Earth. Stable plasma vortices had appeared, had grown, had added complexity, until after millions of years they became something you must needs call an organism. It was a form of ions, nuclei, and forcefields. It metabolized electrons, nucleons, X-rays; it maintained its configuration for a long lifetime; it reproduced; it thought.

But what did it think? The few telepaths who could communicate with the Aurigeans, who had first made humankind aware that the Aurigeans existed, never explained clearly. They were a queer lot themselves.

Wherefore Captain Szili said, "I want you to pass this on to him."

"Yes, sir." Eloise turned down the volume on her taper. Her eyes unfocused. Through her ears went words, and her brain (how efficient a transducer was it?) passed the meanings on out to him who loped alongside *Raven* on his own reaction drive.

"Listen, Lucifer. You have heard this often before, I know, but I want to be positive you understand in full. Your psychology must be very foreign to ours. Why did you agree to come with us? I don't know. Technician Waggoner said you were curious and adventurous. Is that the whole truth?

"No matter. In half an hour we jump. We'll come within five hundred million kilometers of the supernova. That's where your work begins. You can go where we dare not, observe what we can't, tell us more than our instruments would ever hint at. But first we have to verify we can stay in orbit around the star. This concerns you too. Dead men can't transport you home again.

"So. In order to enclose you within the jumpfield, without disrupting your body, we have to switch off the shield screens. We'll emerge in a lethal radiation zone. You must promptly retreat from the ship, because we'll start the screen generator up sixty seconds after transit. Then you must investigate the vicinity. The hazards to look for—" Szili listed them. "Those are only what we can foresee. Perhaps we'll hit other garbage we haven't predicted. If anything seems like a menace, return at once, warn us, and prepare for a jump back to here. Do you have that? Repeat."

Words jerked from Eloise. They were a correct recital; but how much was she leaving out?

"Very good." Szili hesitated. "Proceed with your concert if you like. But break it off at zero minus ten minutes and stand by."

"Yes, sir." She didn't look at him. She didn't appear to be looking anywhere in particular.

His footsteps clacked down the corridor and were lost.

—Why did he say the same things over? asked Lucifer.

"He is afraid," Eloise said.

—?—

"I guess you don't know about fear," she said.

—Can you show me?...No, do not. I sense it is hurtful. You must not be hurt.

"I can't be afraid anyway, when your mind is holding mine."

(Warmth filled her. Merriment was there, playing like little flames over the surface of Father-leading-her-by-the-hand-when-she-was-just-a-child-and-they-went-out-one-summer's-day-to-pick-wildflowers; over strength and gentleness and Bach and God.) Lucifer swept around the hull in an exuberant curve. Sparks danced in his wake.

—Think flowers again. Please.

She tried.

—They are like (image, as nearly as a human brain could grasp, of fountains blossoming with gamma-ray colors in the middle of light, everywhere light). But so tiny. So brief a sweetness.

"I don't understand how you can understand," she whispered.

—You understand for me. I did not have that kind of thing to love, before you came.

"But you have so much else. I try to share it, but I'm not made to realize what a star is."

—Nor I for planets. Yet ourselves may touch.

Her cheeks burned anew. The thought rolled on, interweaving its counterpoint to the marching music.—That is why I came, do you know? For you. I am fire and air. I had not tasted the coolness of water, the patience of earth, until you showed me. You are moonlight on an ocean.

"No, don't," she said. "Please."

Puzzlement:—Why not? Does joy hurt? Are you not used to it?

"I, I guess that's right." She flung her head back. "No! Be damned if I'll feel sorry for myself!"

—Why should you? Have we not all reality to be in, and is it not full of suns and songs?

"Yes. To you. Teach me."

—If you in turn will teach me—The thought broke off. A contact remained, unspeaking, such as she imagined must often prevail among lovers.

She glowered at Motilal Mazundar's chocolate face, where the physicist stood in the doorway. "What do you want?"

He was surprised. "Only to see if everything is well with you, Miss Waggoner."

She bit her lip. He had tried harder than most aboard to be kind to her.

"I'm sorry," she said. "I didn't mean to bark at you. Nerves."

"We are everyone on edge." He smiled. "Exciting though this venture is, it will be good to come home, correct?"

Home, she thought: four walls of an apartment above a banging city street. Books and television. She might present a paper at the next scientific meeting, but no one would invite her to the parties afterward.

Am I that horrible? she wondered. I know I'm not anything to look at, but I try to be nice and interesting. Maybe I try too hard.

—You do not with me, Lucifer said.

"You're different," she told him.

Mazundar blinked. "Beg pardon?"

"Nothing," she said in haste.

"I have wondered about an item," Mazundar said in an effort at conversation. "Presumably Lucifer will go quite near the supernova. Can you still maintain contact with him? The time dilation effect, will that not change the frequency of his thoughts too much?"

"What time dilation?" She forced a chuckle. "I'm no physicist. Only a little librarian who turned out to have a wild talent."

"You were not told? Why, I assumed everybody was. An intense gravitational field affects time just as a high velocity does. Roughly speaking, processes take place more slowly than they do in clear space. That is why light from a massive star is somewhat reddened. And our supernova core retains almost three solar masses. Furthermore, it has acquired such a density that its attraction at the surface is, ah, incredibly high. Thus by our clocks it will take infinite time to shrink to the Schwarzschild radius; but an observer on the star itself would experience this whole shrinkage in a fairly short period."

"Schwarzschild radius? Be so good as to explain." Eloise realized that Lucifer had spoken through her.

"If I can without mathematics. You see, this mass we are to study is so great and so concentrated that no force exceeds the gravitational. Nothing can counterbalance. Therefore the process will continue until no energy can escape. The star will have vanished out of the universe. In fact, theoretically the contraction will proceed to zero volume. Of course, as I said, that will take forever as far as we are concerned. And the theory neglects quantum-mechanical considerations which come into play toward the end. Those are still not very well understood. I hope, from this expedition, to acquire more knowledge." Mazundar shrugged. "At any rate, Miss Waggoner, I was wondering if the frequency shift involved would not prevent our friend from communicating with us when he is near the star."

"I doubt that." Still Lucifer spoke, she was his instrument and never had she known how good it was to be used by one who cared. "Telepathy is not a wave phenomenon. Since it transmits instantaneously, it cannot be. Nor does it appear limited by distance. Rather, it is a resonance. Being attuned, we two may well be able to continue thus across the entire breadth of the cosmos; and I am not aware of any material phenomenon which could interfere."

"I see." Mazundar gave her a long look. "Thank you," he said uncomfortably. "Ah...I must get to my own station. Good luck." He bustled off without stopping for an answer.

Eloise didn't notice. Her mind was become a torch and a song. "Lucifer!" she cried aloud. "Is that true?"

—I believe so. My entire people are telepaths, hence we have more knowledge of such matters than yours do. Our experience leads us to think there is no limit.

"You can always be with me? You always will?"

—If you so wish, I am gladdened.

The comet body curvetted and danced, the brain of fire laughed low.—Yes, Eloise, I would like very much to remain with you. No one else has ever—Joy. Joy. Joy.

They named you better than they knew, Lucifer, she wanted to say, and perhaps she did. They thought it was a joke; they thought by calling you after the devil they could make you safely small like themselves. But Lucifer isn't the devil's real name. It means only Light Bearer. One Latin prayer even addresses Christ as Lucifer. Forgive me, God, I can't help remembering that. Do You mind? He isn't Christian, but I think he doesn't need to be, I think he must never have felt sin, Lucifer, Lucifer.

She sent the music soaring for as long as she was permitted.

The ship jumped. In one shift of world line parameters she crossed twenty-five light-years to destruction.

Each knew it in his own way, save for Eloise who also lived it with Lucifer.

She felt the shock and heard the outraged metal scream, she smelled the ozone and scorch and tumbled through the infinite falling that is weightlessness. Dazed, she fumbled at the intercom. Words crackled through: "...unit blown...back EMF surge...how should I know how long to fix the blasted thing?...stand by, stand by..." Over all hooted the emergency siren.

Terror rose in her, until she gripped the crucifix around her neck and the mind of Lucifer. Then she laughed in the pride of his might.

He had whipped clear of the ship immediately on arrival. Now he floated in the same orbit. Everywhere around, the nebula filled space with unrestful rainbows. To him, *Raven* was not the metal cylinder which human eyes would have seen, but a lambence, the shield screen reflecting a whole spectrum. Ahead lay the supernova core, tiny at this remove but alight, alight.

—Have no fears (he caressed her). I comprehend. Turbulence is extensive, so soon after the detonation. We emerged in a region where the plasma is especially dense. Unprotected for the moment before the guardian field was reestablished, your main generator outside the hull was short-circuited. But you are safe. You can make repairs. And I, I am in an ocean of energy. Never was I so alive. Come, swim these tides with me.

Captain Szili's voice yanked her back. "Waggoner! Tell that Aurigean to get busy. We've spotted a radiation source on an intercept orbit, and it may be too much for our screen." He specified coordinates. "What *is* it?"

For the first time, Eloise felt alarm in Lucifer. He curved about and streaked from the ship.

Presently his thought came to her, no less vivid. She lacked words for the terrible splendor she viewed with him: a million-kilometer ball of ionized gas where luminance blazed and electric discharges leaped, booming through the haze around the star's exposed heart. The thing could not have made any sound, for space here was still almost a vacuum by Earth's parochial standards; but she heard it thunder, and felt the fury that spat from it.

She said for him: "A mass of expelled material. It must have lost radial velocity to friction and static gradients, been drawn into a cometary orbit, held together for a while by internal potentials. As if this sun were trying yet to bring planets to birth—"

"It'll strike us before we're in shape to accelerate," Szili said, "and overload our shield. If you know any prayers, use them."

"Lucifer!" she called; for she did not want to die, when he must remain.

—I think I can deflect it enough, he told her with a grimness she had not hitherto met in him.—My own fields, to mesh with its; and free energy to drink; and an unstable configuration; yes, perhaps I can help you. But help me, Eloise. Fight by my side.

His brightness moved toward the juggernaut shape.

She felt how its chaotic electromagnetism clawed at his. She felt him tossed and torn. The pain was hers. He battled to keep his own cohesion, and the combat was hers. They locked together, Aurigean and gas cloud. The forces that shaped him grappled as arms might; he poured power from his core, hauling that vast tenuous mass with him down the magnetic torrent which streamed from the sun; he gulped atoms and thrust them backward until the jet splashed across heaven.

She sat in her cubicle, lending him what will to live and prevail she could, and beat her fists bloody on the desk.

The hours brawled past.

In the end, she could scarcely catch the message that flickered out of his exhaustion:—Victory.

"Yours," she wept.

—Ours.

Through instruments, men saw the luminous death pass them by. A cheer lifted.

"Come back," Eloise begged.

—I cannot. I am too spent. We are merged, the cloud and I, and are tumbling in toward the star. (Like a hurt hand reaching forth to comfort her:) Do not be afraid for me. As we get closer, I will draw fresh strength from its glow, fresh substance from the nebula. I will need a while to spiral out against that pull. But how can I fail to come back to you, Eloise? Wait for me. Rest. Sleep.

Her shipmates led her to sickbay. Lucifer sent her dreams of fire flowers and mirth and the suns that were his home.

But she woke at last, screaming. The medic had to put her under heavy sedation.

He had not really understood what it would mean to confront something so violent that space and time themselves were twisted thereby.

His speed increased appallingly. That was in his own measure; from *Raven* they saw him fall through several days. The properties of matter were changed. He could not push hard enough or fast enough to escape.

Radiation, stripped nuclei, particles born and destroyed and born again, sleeted and shouted through him. His substance was peeled away, layer by layer. The supernova core was a white delirium before him. It shrank as he approached, ever smaller, denser, so brilliant that brilliance ceased to have meaning. Finally the gravitational forces laid their full grip upon him.

—Eloise! he shrieked in the agony of his disintegration.—Oh, Eloise, help me!

The star swallowed him up. He was stretched infinitely long, compressed infinitely thin, and vanished with it from existence.

The ship prowled the farther reaches. Much might yet be learned.

Captain Szili visited Eloise in sickbay. Physically she was recovering. "I'd call him a man," he declared through the machine mumble, "except that's not praise enough. We weren't even his kin, and he died to save us."

She regarded him from eyes more dry than seemed natural. He could just make out her answer. "He is a man. Doesn't he have an immortal soul too?"

"Well, uh, yes, if you believe in souls, yes, I'd agree." She shook her head. "But why can't he go to his rest?"

He glanced about for the medic and found they were alone in the narrow metal room. "What do you mean?" He made himself pat her hand. "I know, he was a good friend of yours. Still, his must have been a merciful death. Quick, clean; I wouldn't mind going out like that."

"For him…yes, I suppose so. It has to be. But—" She could not continue. Suddenly she covered her ears. "Stop! Please!"

Szili made soothing noises and left. In the corridor he encountered Mazundar. "How is she?" the physicist asked.

The captain scowled. "Not good. I hope she doesn't crack entirely before we can get her to a psychiatrist."

"Why, what is wrong?"

"She thinks she can hear him."

Mazundar smote fist into palm. "I hoped otherwise," he breathed.

Szili braced himself and waited.

"She does," Mazundar said. "Obviously she does."

"But that's impossible! He's dead!"

"Remember the time dilation," Mazundar replied. "He fell from the sky and perished swiftly, yes. But in supernova time. Not the same as ours. To us, the final stellar collapse takes an infinite number of years. And telepathy has no distance limits." The physicist started walking fast, away from that cabin. "He will always be with her."

THE PROBLEM OF PAIN

Maybe only a Christian can understand this story. In that case I don't qualify. But I do take an interest in religion, as part of being an amateur psychologist, and—for the grandeur of its language if nothing else—a Bible is among the reels that accompany me wherever I go. This was one reason Peter Berg told me what had happened in his past. He desperately needed to make sense of it, and no priest he'd talked to had quite laid his questions to rest. There was an outside chance that an outside viewpoint like mine would see what a man within the faith couldn't.

His other reason was simple loneliness. We were on Lucifer, as part of a study corporation. That world is well named. It will never be a real colony for any beings whose ancestors evolved amidst clean greenery. But it might be marginally habitable, and if so, its mineral wealth would be worth exploiting. Our job was to determine whether that was true. The gentlest-looking environment holds a thousand death traps until you have learned what the difficulties are and how to grip them. (Earth is no exception.) Sometimes you find problems which can't be solved economically, or can't be solved at all. Then you write off the area or the entire planet, and look for another.

We'd contracted to work three standard years on Lucifer. The pay was munificent, but presently we realized that no bank account could buy back one day we might have spent beneath a kindlier sun. It was a knowledge we carefully avoided discussing with teammates.

About midway through, Peter Berg and I were assigned to do an in-depth investigation of a unique cycle in the ecology of the northern middle latitudes. This meant that we settled down for weeks—which ran into months—in a sample region, well away from everybody else to minimize human disturbances. An occasional supply flitter gave us our only real contact; electronics were no proper substitute, especially when that hell-violent star was forever disrupting them.

Under such circumstances, you come to know your partner maybe better than you know yourself. Pete and I got along well. He's a big, sandy-haired, freckle-faced young man, altogether dependable, with enough kindliness, courtesy, and dignity that he need not make a show of them. Soft-spoken, he's a bit short in the humor department. Otherwise I recommend him as a companion. He has a lot to tell from his own wanderings, yet he'll listen with genuine interest to your memories and brags; he's well-read too, and a good cook when his turn comes; he plays chess at just about my level of skill.

I already knew he wasn't from Earth, had in fact never been there, but from Aeneas, nearly 200 light-years distant, more than 300 from Lucifer. And, while he'd gotten an education at the new little university in Nova Roma, he was raised in the outback. Besides, that town is only a far-off colonial capital. It helped explain his utter commitment to belief in a God who became flesh and died for love of man. Not that I scoff. When he said his prayers, night and morning in our one-room shelterdome, trustingly as a child, I didn't rag him nor he reproach me. Of course, over the weeks, we came more and more to talk about such matters.

At last he told me of that which haunted him.

We'd been out through the whole of one of Lucifer's long, long days; we'd toiled, we'd sweated, we'd itched and stunk and gotten grimy and staggered from weariness, we'd come near death once: and we'd found the uranium-concentrating root which was the key to the whole weirdness around us. We came back to base as day's fury was dying in the usual twilight gale; we washed, ate something, went to sleep with the hiss of storm-blown dust for a lullaby. Ten or twelve hours later we awoke and saw, through the vitryl panels, stars cold and crystalline beyond this thin air, auroras aflame, landscape hoar, and the twisted things we called trees all sheathed in glittering ice.

"Nothing we can do now till dawn," I said, "and we've earned a celebration." So we prepared a large meal, elaborate as possible—breakfast or supper, what relevance had that here? We drank wine in the course of it, and afterward much brandy while we sat, side by side in our loungers, watching the march of constellations which Earth or Aeneas never saw. And we talked. Finally we talked of God.

"—maybe you can give me an idea," Pete said. In the dim light, his face bore a struggle. He stared before him and knotted his fingers.

"M-m, I dunno," I said carefully. "To be honest, no offense meant, theological conundrums strike me as silly."

He gave me a direct blue look. His tone was soft: "That is, you feel the paradoxes don't arise if we don't insist on believing?"

"Yes. I respect your faith, Pete, but it's not mine. And if I did suppose a, well, a spiritual principle or something is behind the universe—" I gestured at the high and terrible sky "—in the name of reason, can we confine, can we understand whatever made *that*, in the bounds of one little dogma?"

"No. Agreed. How could finite minds grasp the infinite? We can see parts of it, though, that've been revealed to us." He drew breath. "Way back before space travel, the Church decided Jesus had come only to Earth, to man. If other intelligent races need salvation—and obviously a lot of them do!—God will have made His suitable arrangements for them. Sure. However, this does not mean Christianity is not true, or that certain different beliefs are not false."

"Like, say, polytheism, wherever you find it?"

"I think so. Besides, religions evolve. The primitive faiths see God, or the gods, as power; the higher ones see Him as justice; the highest see Him as love." Abruptly he fell silent. I saw his fist clench, until he grabbed up his glass and drained it and refilled it in nearly a single savage motion.

"I must believe that," he whispered.

I waited a few seconds, in Lucifer's crackling night stillness, before saying: "An experience made you wonder?"

"Made me...disturbed. Mind if I tell you?"

"Certainly not." I saw he was about to open himself; and I may be an unbeliever, but I know what is sacred.

"Happened about five years ago. I was on my first real job. So was the—" his voice stumbled the least bit—"the wife I had then. We were fresh out of school and apprenticeship, fresh into marriage." In an effort at detachment: "Our employers weren't human. They were Ythrians. Ever heard of them?"

I sought through my head. The worlds, races, beings are unknowably many, in this tiny corner of this one dust-mote galaxy which we have begun to explore a little. "Ythrians, Ythrians...wait. Do they fly?"

"Yes. Surely one of the most glorious sights in creation. Your Ythrian isn't as heavy as a man, of course; adults mass around twenty-five or thirty kilos—but his wingspan goes up to six meters, and when he soars with those feathers shining gold-brown in the light, or stoops in a crack of thunder and whistle of wind—"

"Hold on," I said. "I take it Ythri's a terrestroid planet?"

"Pretty much. Somewhat smaller and drier than Earth, somewhat thinner atmosphere—about like Aeneas, in fact, which it's not too far from as interstellar spaces go. You can live there without special protection. The biochemistry's quite similar to ours."

"Then how the devil can those creatures be that size? The wing loading's impossible, when you have only cell tissue to oxidize for power. They'd never get off the ground."

"Ah, but they have antlibranchs as well." Pete smiled, though it didn't go deep. "Those look like three gills, sort of, on either side, below the wings. They're actually more like bellows, pumped by the wing muscles. Extra oxygen is forced directly into the bloodstream during flight. A biological supercharger system."

"Well, I'll be a...never mind what." I considered, in delight, this new facet of nature's inventiveness. "Um-m-m...if they spend energy at that rate, they've got to have appetites to match."

"Right. They're carnivores. A number of them are still hunters. The advanced societies are based on ranching. In either case, obviously, it takes a lot of meat animals, a lot of square kilometers, to support one Ythrian. So they're fiercely territorial. They live in small groups—single families or extended households—which attack, with intent to kill, any uninvited outsider who doesn't obey an order to leave."

"And still they're civilized enough to hire humans for space exploration?"

"Uh-huh. Remember, being flyers, they've never needed to huddle in cities in order to have ready communication. They do keep a few towns, mining or manufacturing centers, but those are inhabited mostly by wing-clipped slaves. I'm glad to say that institution's dying out as they get modern machinery."

"By trade?" I guessed.

"Yes," Pete replied. "When the first Grand Survey discovered them, their most advanced culture was at an Iron Age level of technology; no industrial revolution, but plenty of sophisticated minds around, and subtle philosophies." He paused. "That's important to my question—that the Ythrians, at least of the Planha-speaking *choths*, are not barbarians and have not been for many centuries. They've had their equivalents of Socrates, Aristotle, Confucius, Galileo, yes, and their prophets and seers."

After another mute moment: "They realized early what the visitors from Earth implied, and set about attracting traders and teachers. Once they had some funds, they sent their promising young folk off-planet to study. I met several at my own university, which is why I got my job offer. By now they have a few spacecraft and native crews. But you'll understand, their technical people are spread thin, and in several branches of knowledge they have no experts. So they employ humans."

He went on to describe the typical Ythrian: warm-blooded, feathered like a golden eagle (though more intricately) save for a crest on the head, and yet not a bird. Instead of a beak, a blunt muzzle full of fangs juts before two great eyes. The female bears her young alive. While she does not nurse them, they have lips to suck the juices of meat and fruits, wherefore their speech is not hopelessly unlike man's. What were formerly the legs have evolved into arms bearing three taloned fingers, flanked by two thumbs, on each hand. Aground, the huge wings fold downward and, with the help of claws at the angles, give locomotion. That is slow and awkward—but aloft, ah!

"They become more alive, flying, than we ever do," Pete murmured. His gaze had lost itself in the shuddering auroras overhead. "They must: the metabolic rate they have then, and the space around them, speed, sky, a hundred winds to ride on and be kissed by…That's what made me think Enherrian, in particular, believed more keenly than I could hope to. I saw him and others dancing, high, high in the air, swoops, glides, hoverings, sunshine molten on their plumes; I asked what they did, and was told they were honoring God."

He sighed. "Or that's how I translated the Planha phrase, rightly or wrongly," he went on. "Olga and I had taken a cram course, and our Ythrian teammates all knew Anglic; but nobody's command of the foreign tongue was perfect. It couldn't be. Multiple billion years of separate existence, evolution, history—what a miracle that we could think as alike as we did!

"However, you could call Enherrian religious, same as you could call me that, and not be too grotesquely off the mark. The rest varied, just like humans. Some were also devout, some less, some agnostics or atheists; two were pagans, following the bloody rites of what was called the Old Faith. For that matter, my Olga—" the knuckles stood forth where he grasped his tumbler of brandy—"had tried, for my sake, to believe as I did, and couldn't.

"Well. The New Faith interested me more. It was new only by comparison—at least half as ancient as mine. I hoped for a chance to study it, to ask questions and compare ideas. I really knew nothing except that it was monotheistic, had sacraments and a theology though no official priesthood, upheld a high ethical and moral standard—for Ythrians, I mean. You can't expect a race which can only live by killing animals, and has an oestrous cycle, and is incapable by instinct of maintaining what we'd recognize as a true nation or government, and on and on—you can't expect them to resemble Christians much. God has given them a different message. I wished to know what. Surely we could learn from it." Again he paused. "After all...being a faith with a long tradition...and not static but seeking, a history of prophets and saints and believers...I thought it must know God is love. Now what form would God's love take to an Ythrian?"

He drank. I did too, before asking cautiously: "Uh, where was this expedition?"

Pete stirred in his lounger. "To a system about eighty light-years from Ythri's," he answered. "The original Survey crew had discovered a terrestroid planet there. They didn't bother to name it. Prospective colonists would choose their own name anyway. Those could be human or Ythrian, conceivably both—if the environment proved out.

"Offhand, the world—our group called it, unofficially, Gray, after that old captain—the world looked brilliantly promising. It's intermediate in size between Earth and Ythri, surface gravity 0.8 terrestrial; slightly more irradiation, from a somewhat yellower sun, than Earth gets, which simply makes it a little warmer; axial tilt, therefore seasonal variations, a bit less than terrestrial; length of year about three-quarters of ours, length of day a bit under half; one small, close-in, bright moon; biochemistry similar to ours—we could eat most native things, though we'd require imported crops and livestock to supplement the diet. All in all, seemingly well-nigh perfect."

"Rather remote to attract Earthlings at this early date," I remarked. "And from your description, the Ythrians won't be able to settle it for quite a while either."

"They think ahead," Pete responded. "Besides, they have scientific curiosity and, yes, in them perhaps even more than in the humans who went along, a spirit of adventure. Oh, it was a wonderful thing to be young in that band!"

He had not yet reached thirty, but somehow his cry was not funny.

He shook himself. "Well, we had to make sure," he said. "Besides planetology, ecology, chemistry, oceanography, meteorology, a million and a million mysteries to unravel for their own sakes—we must scout out the death traps, whatever those might be.

"At first everything went like Mary's smile on Christmas morning. The spaceship set us off—it couldn't be spared to linger in orbit—and we established base on the largest continent. Soon our hundred-odd dispersed across the globe, investigating this or that. Olga and I made part of a group on the southern shore, where a great gulf swarmed with life. A strong current ran eastward from there, eventually striking an archipelago which deflected it north. Flying over those waters, we spied immense, I mean immense, patches—no, floating islands—of vegetation, densely interwoven, grazed on by monstrous marine creatures, no doubt supporting any number of lesser plant and animal species.

"We wanted a close look. Our camp's sole aircraft wasn't good for that. Anyhow, it was already in demand for a dozen jobs. We had boats, though, and launched one. Our crew was Enherrian, his wife Whell, their grown children Rusa and Arrach, my beautiful new bride Olga, and me. We'd take three or four Gray days to reach the nearest atlantis weed, as Olga dubbed it. Then we'd be at least a week exploring before we turned back—a vacation, a lark, a joy."

He tossed off his drink and reached for the bottle. "You ran into grief," I prompted.

"No." He bent his lips upward, stiffly. "It ran into us. A hurricane. Unpredicted; we knew very little about that planet. Given the higher solar energy input and, especially, the rapid rotation, the storm was more violent than would've been possible on Earth. We could only run before it and pray.

"At least, I prayed, and imagined that Enherrian did."

Wind shrieked, hooted, yammered, hit flesh with fists and cold knives. Waves rumbled in that driven air, black and green and fang-white, fading from view as the sun sank behind the cloud-roil which hid it. Often a monster among them loomed castlelike over the gunwale. The boat slipped by, spilled into the troughs, rocked onto the crests and down again. Spindrift, icy, stinging, bitter on lips and tongue, made a fog across her length.

"We'll live if we can keep sea room," Enherrian had said when the fury first broke. "She's well-found. The engine capacitors have ample kilowatt-hours in them. Keep her bow on and we'll live."

But the currents had them now, where the mighty gulfstream met the outermost islands and its waters churned, recoiled, spun about and fought. Minute by minute, the riptides grew wilder. They made her yaw till she was broadside on and surges roared over her deck; they shocked her onto her beam ends, and the hull became a toning bell.

Pete, Olga, and Whell were in the cabin, trying to rest before their next watch. That was no longer possible. The Ythrian female locked hands and wing-claws around the net-covered framework wherein she had slept, hung on, and uttered nothing. In the wan glow of a single overhead fluoro, among thick restless shadows, her eyes gleamed topaz. They did not seem to look at the crampedness around—at what, then?

The humans had secured themselves by a line onto a lower bunk. They embraced, helping each other fight the leaps and swings which tried to smash them against the sides. Her fair hair on his shoulder was the last brightness in his cosmos. "I love you," she said, over and over, through hammerblows and groans. "Whatever happens, I love you, Pete, I thank you for what you've given me."

"And you," he would answer. *And You,* he would think. *Though You won't take her, not yet, will You? Me, yes, if that's Your will. But not Olga. It'd leave Your creation too dark.*

A wing smote the cabin door. Barely to be heard through the storm, an Ythrian voice—high, whistly, but resonant out of full lungs—shouted: "Come topside!"

Whell obeyed at once, the Bergs as fast as they could slip on life jackets. Having taken no personal grav units along, they couldn't fly free if they went overboard. Dusk raved around them. Pete could just see Rusa and Arrach in the stern, fighting the tiller. Enherrian stood before him and pointed forward. "Look," the captain said. Pete, who had no nictitating membranes, must shield eyes with fingers to peer athwart the hurricane. He saw a deeper darkness hump up from a wall of white; he heard surf crash.

"We can't pull free," Enherrian told him. "Between wind and current—too little power. We'll likely be wrecked. Make ready."

Olga's hand went briefly to her mouth. She huddled against Pete and might have whispered, "Oh, no." Then she straightened, swung back down into the cabin, braced herself as best she could, and started assembling the most vital things stored there. He saw that he loved her still more than he had known.

The same calm descended on him. Nobody had time to be afraid. He got busy too. The Ythrians could carry a limited weight of equipment and supplies, but sharply limited under these conditions. The humans, buoyed by their jackets, must carry most. They strapped it to their bodies.

When they re-emerged, the boat was in the shoals. Enherrian ordered them to take the rudder. His wife, son, and daughter stood around—on hands which clutched the rails with prey-snatching strength—and spread their wings to give a bit of shelter. The captain clung to the cabin top as lookout. His yelled commands reached the Bergs dim, tattered.

"Hard right!" Upward cataracts burst on a skerry to port. It glided past, was lost in murk. "Two points starboard—steady!" The hull slipped between a pair of rocks. Ahead was a narrow opening in the island's sheer black face. To a lagoon, to safety? Surf raged on either side of that gate, and everywhere else.

The passage was impossible. The boat struck, threw Olga off her feet and Arrach off her perch. Full reverse engine could not break loose. The deck canted. A billow and a billow smashed across.

Pete was in the water. It grabbed him, pulled him under, dragged him over a sharp bottom. He thought: *Into Your hands, God. Spare Olga, please, please*—and the sea spewed him back up for one gulp of air.

Wallowing in blindness, he tried to gauge how the breakers were acting, what he should do. If he could somehow belly-surf in, he might make it, he barely might...He was on the neck of a rushing giant, it climbed and climbed, it shoved him forward at what he knew was lunatic speed. He saw the reef on which it was about to smash him and knew he was dead.

Talons closed on his jacket. Air brawled beneath wings. The Ythrian could not raise him, but could draw him aside...the bare distance needed, and Pete went past the rock whereon his bones were to have been crushed, down into the smother and chaos beyond. The Ythrian didn't get free in time. He glimpsed the plumes go under, as he himself did. They never rose.

He beat on, and on, without end.

He floated in water merely choppy, swart palisades to right and left, a slope of beach ahead. He peered into the clamorous dark and found nothing. "Olga," he croaked. "Olga. Olga."

Wings shadowed him among the shadows. "Get ashore before an undertow eats you!" Enherrian whooped, and beat his way off in search.

Pete crawled to gritty sand, fell, and let annihilation have him. He wasn't unconscious long. When he revived, Rusa and Whell were beside him. Enherrian was further inland. The captain hauled on a line he had snubbed around a tree. Olga floated at the other end. She had no strength left, but he had passed a bight beneath her arms and she was alive.

At wolf-gray dawn the wind had fallen to gale force or maybe less, and the cliffs shielded lagoon and strand from it. Overhead it shrilled, and outside the breakers cannonaded, their rage aquiver through the island. Pete and Olga huddled together, a shared cloak across their shoulders. Enherrian busied himself checking the salvaged material. Whell sat on the hindbones of her wings and stared seaward. Moisture gleamed on her grizzled feathers like tears.

Rusa flew in from the reefs and landed. "No trace," he said. His voice was emptied by exhaustion. "Neither the boat nor Arrach." Through the rust in his own brain, Pete noticed the order of those words.

Nevertheless—he leaned toward the parents and brother of Arrach, who had been beautiful and merry and had sung to them by moonlight. "How can we say—?" he began, realized he didn't have Planha words, and tried in Anglic: "How can we say how sorry we both are?"

"No necessity," Rusa answered.

"She died saving me!"

"And what you were carrying, which we needed badly." Some energy returned to Rusa. He lifted his head and its crest. "She had deathpride, our lass."

Afterward Pete, in his search for meaning, would learn about that Ythrian concept. "Courage" is too simple and weak a translation. Certain Old Japanese words come closer, though they don't really bear the same value either.

Whell turned her hawk gaze full upon him. "Did you see anything of what happened in the water?" she asked. He was too unfamiliar with her folk to interpret the tone: today he thinks it was loving. He did know that, being creatures of seasonal rut, Ythrians are less sexually motivated than man is, but probably treasure their young even more. The strongest bond between male and female is children, who are what life is all about.

"No, I...I fear not," he stammered.

Enherrian reached out to lay claws, very gently and briefly, on his wife's back. "Be sure she fought well," he said. "She gave God honor." (Glory? Praise? Adoration? His due?)

Does he mean she prayed, made her confession, while she drowned? The question dragged itself through Pete's weariness and caused him to murmur: "She's in heaven now." Again he was forced to use Anglic words.

Enherrian gave him a look which he could have sworn was startled. "What do you say? Arrach is dead."

"Why, her...her spirit—"

"Will be remembered in pride." Enherrian resumed his work.

Olga said it for Pete: "So you don't believe the spirit outlives the body?"

"How could it?" Enherrian snapped. "Why should it?" His motions, his posture, the set of his plumage added: Leave me alone.

Pete thought: *Well, many faiths, including high ones, including some sects which call themselves Christian, deny immortality. How sorry I feel for these my friends, who don't know they will meet their beloved afresh!*

They will, regardless. It makes no sense that God, Who created what is because in His goodness he wished to share existence, would shape a soul only to break it and throw it away.

Never mind. The job on hand is to keep Olga alive, in her dear body. "Can I help?"

"Yes, check our medical kit," Enherrian said.

It had come through undamaged in its box. The items for human use—stimulants, sedatives, anesthetics, antitoxins, antibiotics, coagulants, healing promoters, et standard cetera—naturally outnumbered those for Ythrians. There hadn't been time to develop a large scientific pharmacopoeia for the latter species. True, certain materials work on both, as does the surgical and monitoring equipment. Pete distributed pills which took the pain out of bruises and scrapes, the heaviness out of muscles. Meanwhile Rusa collected wood, Whell started and tended a fire, Olga made breakfast. They had considerable food, mostly freeze-dried, gear to cook it, tools like knives and a hatchet, cord, cloth, flashbeams, two blasters and abundant recharges: what they required for survival.

"It may be insufficient," Enherrian said. "The portable radio transceiver went down with Arrach. The boat's transmitter couldn't punch a call through that storm, and now the boat's on the bottom—nothing to see from the air, scant metal to register on a detector."

"Oh, they'll check on us when the weather slacks off," Olga said. She caught Pete's hand in hers. He felt the warmth.

"If their flitter survived the hurricane, which I doubt," Enherrian stated. "I'm convinced the camp was also struck. We had built no shelter for the flitter, our people will have been too busy saving themselves to secure it, and I think that thin shell was tumbled about and broken. If I'm right, they'll have to call for an aircraft from elsewhere, which may not be available at once. In either case, we could be anywhere in a huge territory; and the expedition has no time or personnel for an indefinite search. They will seek us, aye; however, if we are not found before an arbitrary date—" A ripple passed over the feathers of face and neck; a human would have shrugged.

"What...can we do?" the girl asked.

"Clear a sizeable area in a plainly artificial pattern, or heap fuel for beacon fires should a flitter pass within sight—whichever is practicable. If nothing comes of that, we should consider building a raft or the like."

"Or modify a life jacket for me," Rusa suggested, "and I can try to fly to the mainland."

Enherrian nodded. "We must investigate the possibilities. First let's get a real rest."

The Ythrians were quickly asleep, squatted on their locked wing joints like idols of a forgotten people. Pete and Olga felt more excited and wandered a distance off, hand in hand.

Above the crag-enclosed beach, the island rose toward a crest which he estimated as three kilometers away. If it was in the middle, this was no large piece of real estate. Nor did he see adequate shelter. A mat of mossy, intensely green plants squeezed out any possibility of forest. A few trees stood isolated. Their branches tossed in the wind. He noticed particularly one atop a great outcrop nearby, gaunt brown trunk and thin leaf-fringed boughs that whipped insanely about. Blossoms, torn from vines, blew past, and they were gorgeous; but there would be naught to live on here, and he wasn't hopeful about learning, in time, how to catch Gray's equivalent of fish.

"Strange about them, isn't it?" Olga murmured.

"Eh?" He came, startled, out of his preoccupations.

She gestured at the Ythrians. "Them. The way they took poor Arrach's death."

"Well, you can't judge them by our standards. Maybe they feel grief less than we would, or maybe their culture demands stoicism." He looked at her and did not look away again. "To be frank, darling, I can't really mourn either. I'm too happy to have you back."

"And I you—oh, Pete, Pete, my only—"

They found a secret spot and made love. He saw nothing wrong in that. Do you ever in this life come closer to the wonder which is God?

Afterward they returned to their companions. Thus the clash of wings awoke them, hours later. They scrambled from their bedrolls and saw the Ythrians swing aloft.

The wind was strong and loud as yet, though easing off in fickleness, flaws, downdrafts, whirls, and eddies. Clouds were mostly gone. Those which remained raced gold and hot orange before a sun low in the west, across blue serenity. The lagoon glittered purple, the greensward lay aglow. It had warmed up till rich odors of growth, of flowers, blent with the sea salt.

And splendid in the sky danced Enherrian, Whell, and Rusa. They wheeled, soared, pounced, and rushed back into light which ran molten off their pinions. They chanted, and fragments blew down to the humans: *"High flew your spirit on many winds...be always remembered..."*

"What *is* that?" Olga breathed.

"Why, they—they—" The knowledge broke upon Pete. "They're holding a service for Arrach."

He knelt and said a prayer for her soul's repose. But he wondered if she, who had belonged to the air, would truly want rest. And his eyes could not leave her kindred.

Enherrian screamed a hunter's challenge and rushed down at the earth. He flung himself meteoric past the stone outcrop Pete had seen; for an instant the man gasped, believing he would be shattered; then he rose, triumphant.

He passed by the lean tree of thin branches. Gusts flailed them about. A nearly razor edge took off his left wing. Blood spurted; Ythrian blood is royal purple. Somehow Enherrian slewed around and made a crash landing on the bluff top, just beyond range of what has since been named the surgeon tree.

Pete yanked the medikit to him and ran. Olga wailed, briefly, and followed. When they reached the scene, they found that Whell and Rusa had pulled feathers from their breasts to try staunching the wound.

Evening, night, day, evening, night.

Enherrian sat before a campfire. Its light wavered, picked him red out of shadow and let him half-vanish again, save for the unblinking yellow eyes. His wife and son supported him. Stim, cell-freeze, and plasma surrogate had done their work, and he could speak in a weak roughness. The bandages on his stump were a nearly glaring white.

Around crowded shrubs which, by day, showed low and russet-leaved. They filled a hollow on the far side of the island, to which Enherrian had been carried on an improvised litter. Their odor was rank, in an atmosphere once more subtropically hot, and they clutched at feet with raking twigs. But this was the most sheltered spot his companions could find, and he might die in a new storm on the open beach.

He looked through smoke, at the Bergs, who sat as close together as they were able. He said—the surf growled faintly beneath his words, while never a leaf rustled in the breathless dark—"I have read that your people can make a lost part grow forth afresh."

Pete couldn't answer. He tried but couldn't. It was Olga who had the courage to say, "We can do it for ourselves. None except ourselves." She laid her head on her man's breast and wept.

Well, you need a lot of research to unravel a genetic code, a lot of development to make the molecules of heredity repeat what they did in the womb. Science hasn't had time yet for other races. It never will for all. They are too many.

"As I thought," Enherrian said. "Nor can a proper prosthesis be engineered in my lifetime. I have few years left; an Ythrian who cannot fly soon becomes sickly."

"Grav units—" Pete faltered.

The scorn in those eyes was like a blow. Dead metal to raise you, who have had wings?

Fierce and haughty though the Ythrian is, his quill-clipped slaves have never rebelled: for they are only half-alive. Imagine yourself, human male, castrated. Enherrian might flap his remaining wing and the stump to fill his blood with air; but he would have nothing he could do with that extra energy, it would turn inward and corrode his body, perhaps at last his mind.

For a second, Whell laid an arm around him.

"You will devise a signal tomorrow," Enherrian said, "and start work on it. Too much time has already been wasted."

Before they slept, Pete managed to draw Whell aside. "He needs constant care, you know," he whispered to her in the acrid booming gloom. "The drugs got him over the shock, but he can't tolerate more and he'll be very weak."

True, she said with feathers rather than voice. Aloud: "Olga shall nurse him. She cannot get around as easily as Rusa or me, and lacks your physical strength. Besides, she can prepare meals and the like for us."

Pete nodded absently. He had a dread to explain. "Uh...uh...do you think— well, I mean in your ethic, in the New Faith—might Enherrian put an end to himself?" And he wondered if God would really blame the captain.

Her wings and tail spread, her crest erected, she glared, "You say that of him?" she shrilled. Seeing his concern, she eased, even made a *krrr* noise which might answer to a chuckle. "No, no, he has his deathpride. He would never rob God of honor."

After survey and experiment, the decision was to hack a giant cross in the island turf. That growth couldn't be ignited, and what wood was burnable—deadfall— was too scant and stingy of smoke for a beacon.

The party had no spades; the vegetable mat was thick and tough; the toil became brutal. Pete, like Whell and Rusa, would return to camp and topple into sleep. He wouldn't rouse till morning, to gulp his food and plod off to labor. He grew gaunt, bearded, filthy, numb-brained, sore in every cell.

Thus he did not notice how Olga was waning. Enherrian was mending, some-what, under her care. She did her jobs, which were comparatively light, and would have been ashamed to complain of headaches, giddiness, diarrhea, and nausea. Doubtless she imagined she suffered merely from reaction to disaster, plus a sketchy and ill-balanced diet, plus heat and brilliant sun and—she'd cope.

The days were too short for work, the nights too short for sleep. Pete's terror was that he would see a flitter pass and vanish over the horizon before the Ythri-ans could hail it. Then they might try sending Rusa for help. But that was a long, tricky flight; and the gulf coast camp was due to be struck rather soon anyway.

Sometimes he wondered dimly how he and Olga might do if marooned on Gray. He kept enough wits to dismiss his fantasy for what it was. Take the simple fact that native life appeared to lack certain vitamins—

Then one darkness, perhaps a terrestrial week after the shipwreck, he was roused by her crying his name. He struggled to wakefulness. She lay beside him. Gray's moon was up, nearly full, swifter and brighter than Luna. Its glow drowned most of the stars, frosted the encroaching bushes, fell without pity to show him her fallen cheeks and rolling eyes. She shuddered in his arms; he heard her teeth clapping. "I'm cold, darling, I'm cold," she said in the subtropical sum-mer night. She vomited over him, and presently she was delirious.

The Ythrians gave what help they could, he what medicines he could. By sun-rise (an outrageousness of rose and gold and silver-blue, crossed by the jubilant wings of waterfowl) he knew she was dying.

He examined his own physical state, using a robot he discovered he had in his skull: yes, his wretchedness was due to more than overwork, he saw that now; he too had had the upset stomach and the occasional shivers, nothing like the disintegration which possessed Olga, nevertheless the same kind of thing. Yet the Ythrians stayed healthy. Did a local germ attack humans while finding the other race undevourable?

The rescuers, who came on the island two Gray days later, already had the answer. That genus of bushes is widespread on the planet. A party elsewhere, after getting sick and getting into safety suits, analyzed its vapors. They are a cumulative poison to man; they scarcely harm an Ythrian. The analysts named it the hell shrub.

Unfortunately, their report wasn't broadcast until after the boat left. Meanwhile Pete had been out in the field every day, while Olga spent her whole time in the hollow, over which the sun regularly created an inversion layer.

Whell and Rusa went grimly back to work. Pete had to get away. He wasn't sure of the reason, but he had to be alone when he screamed at heaven, "Why did You do this to her, why did You do it?" Enherrian could look after Olga, who had brought him back to a life he no longer wanted. Pete had stopped her babblings, writhings, and saw-toothed sounds of pain with a shot. She ought to sleep peacefully into that death which the monitor instruments said was, in the absence of hospital facilities, ineluctable.

He stumbled off to the heights. The sea reached calm, in a thousand hues of azure and green, around the living island, beneath the gentle sky. He knelt in all that emptiness and put his question.

After an hour he could say, "Your will be done" and return to camp.

Olga lay awake. "Pete, Pete!" she cried. Anguish distorted her voice till he couldn't recognize it; nor could he really see her in the yellowed sweating skin and lank hair drawn over a skeleton, or find her in the stench and the nails which flayed him as they clutched. "Where were you, hold me close, it hurts, how it hurts—"

He gave her a second injection, to small effect.

He knelt again, beside her. He has not told me what he said, or how. At last she grew quiet, gripped him hard and waited for the pain to end.

When she died, he says, it was like seeing a light blown out.

He laid her down, closed eyes and jaw, folded her hands. On mechanical feet he went to the pup tent which had been rigged for Enherrian. The cripple calmly awaited him. "She is fallen?" he asked.

Pete nodded.

"That is well," Enherrian said.

"It is not," Pete heard himself reply, harsh and remote. "She shouldn't have aroused. The drug should've—did you give her a stim shot? Did you bring her back to suffer?"

"What else?" said Enherrian, though he was unarmed and a blaster lay nearby for Pete to seize. *Not that I'll ease him out of his fate!* went through the man in a spasm. "I saw that you, distraught, had misgauged. You were gone and I unable to follow you. She might well die before your return."

Out of his void, Pete gaped into those eyes. "You mean," rattled from him, "you mean...she...mustn't?"

Enherrian crawled forth—he could only crawl, on his single wing—to take Pete's hands. "My friend," he said, his tone immeasurably compassionate, "I honored you both too much to deny her her deathpride."

Pete's chief awareness was of the cool sharp talons.

"Have I misunderstood?" asked Enherrian anxiously. "Did you not wish her to give God a battle?"

Even on Lucifer, the nights finally end. Dawn blazed on the tors when Pete finished his story.

I emptied the last few ccs into our glasses. We'd get no work done today. "Yeh," I said. "Cross-cultural semantics. Given the best will in the universe, two beings from different planets—or just different countries, often—take for granted they think alike; and the outcome can be tragic."

"I assumed that at first," Pete said. "I didn't need to forgive Enherrian—how could he know? For his part, he was puzzled when I buried my darling. On Ythri they cast them from a great height into wilderness. But neither race wants to watch the rotting of what was loved, so he did his lame best to help me."

He drank, looked as near the cruel bluish sun as he was able, and mumbled: "What I couldn't do was forgive God."

"The problem of evil," I said.

"Oh, no. I've studied these matters, these past years: read theology, argued with priests, the whole route. Why does God, if He is a loving and personal God, allow evil? Well, there's a perfectly good Christian answer to that. Man—intelligence everywhere—must have free will. Otherwise we're puppets and have no reason to exist. Free will necessarily includes the capability of doing wrong. We're here, in this cosmos during our lives, to learn how to be good of our unforced choice."

"I spoke illiterately," I apologized. "All that brandy. No, sure, your logic is right, regardless of whether I accept your premises or not. What I meant was: the problem of pain. Why does a merciful God permit undeserved agony? If He's omnipotent, He isn't compelled to.

"I'm not talking about the sensation which warns you to take your hand from the fire, anything useful like that. No, the random accident which wipes out a life...or a mind—" I drank. "What happened to Arrach, yes, and to Enherrian, and Olga, and you, and Whell. What happens when a disease hits, or those catastrophes we label acts of God. Or the slow decay of us if we grow very old. Every such horror. Never mind if science has licked some of them; we have enough left, and then there were our ancestors who endured them all.

"Why? What possible end is served? It's not adequate to declare we'll receive an unbounded reward after we die and therefore it makes no difference whether a life was gusty or grisly. That's no explanation.

"Is this the problem you're grappling with, Pete?"

"In a way." He nodded, cautiously, as if he were already his father's age. "At least, it's the start of the problem.

"You see, there I was, isolated among Ythrians. My fellow humans sympathized, but they had nothing to say that I didn't know already. The New Faith, however…Mind you, I wasn't about to convert. What I did hope for was an insight, a freshness, that'd help me make Christian sense of our losses. Enherrian was so sure, so learned, in his beliefs—

"We talked, and talked, and talked, while I was regaining my strength. He was as caught as me. Not that he couldn't fit our troubles into his scheme of things. That was easy. But it turned out that the New Faith has no satisfactory answer to the problem of *evil*. It says God allows wickedness so we may win honor by fighting for the right. Really, when you stop to think, that's weak, especially in carnivore Ythrian terms. Don't you agree?"

"You know them, I don't," I sighed. "You imply they have a better answer to the riddle of pain than your own religion does."

"It seems better." Desperation edged his slightly blurred tone:

"They're hunters, or were until lately. They see God like that, as the Hunter. Not the Torturer—you absolutely must understand this point—no, He rejoices in our happiness the way we might rejoice to see a game animal gamboling. Yet at last He comes after us. Our noblest moment is when we, knowing He is irresistible, give Him a good chase, a good fight.

"Then He wins honor. And some infinite end is furthered. (The same one as when my God is given praise? How can I tell?) We're dead, struck down, lingering at most a few years in the memories of those who escaped this time. And that's what we're here for. That's why God created the universe."

"And this belief is old," I said. "It doesn't belong just to a few cranks. No, it's been held for centuries by millions of sensitive, intelligent, educated beings. You can live by it, you can die by it. If it doesn't solve every paradox, it solves some that your faith won't, quite. This is your dilemma, true?"

He nodded again. "The priests have told me to deny a false creed and to acknowledge a mystery. Neither instruction feels right. Or am I asking too much?"

"I'm sorry, Pete," I said, altogether honestly. It hurt. "But how should I know? I looked into the abyss once, and saw nothing, and haven't looked since. You keep looking. Which of us is the braver?"

"Maybe you can find a text in Job. I don't know, I tell you, I don't know."

The sun lifted higher above the burning horizon.

HOLMGANG

-1-

The most dangerous is not the outlawed murderer, who only slays men, but the rebellious philosopher, for he destroys worlds.

Darkness and the chill glitter of stars, Bo Jonsson crouched on a whirling speck of stone and waited for the man who was coming to kill him.

There was no horizon. The flying mountain on which he stood was too small. At his back rose a cliff of jagged rock, losing its own blackness in the loom of shadows; its teeth ate raggedly across the Milky Way. Before him, a tumbled igneous wilderness slanted crazily off, with one long thin crag sticking into the sky like a grotesque bow-sprit.

There was no sound except the thudding of his own heart, the harsh rasp of his own breath, locked inside the stinking metal skin of his suit. Otherwise…no air, no heat, no water or life or work of man, only a granite nakedness spinning through space out beyond Mars.

Stooping, awkward in the clumsy armor, he put the transparent plastic of his helmet to the ground. Its cold bit at him even through the insulating material. He might be able to hear the footsteps of his murderer conducted through the ground.

Stillness answered him. He gulped a heavy lungful of tainted air and rose. The other might be miles away yet, or perhaps very close, catfooting too softly to set up vibrations. A man could do that when gravity was feeble enough.

The stars blazed with a cruel wintry brilliance, over him, around him, light-years to fall through emptiness before he reached one. He had been alone among them before; he had almost thought them friends. Sometimes, on a long watch, a man found himself talking to Vega or Spica or dear old Beetle Juice, murmuring what was in him as if the remote sun could understand. But they didn't care, he saw that now. To them, he did not exist, and they would shine carelessly long after he was gone into night.

He had never felt so alone as now, when another man was on the asteroid with him, hunting him down.

Bo Jonsson looked at the wrench in his hand. It was long and massive, it would have been heavy on Earth, but it was hardly enough to unscrew the stars and reset the machinery of a universe gone awry. He smiled stiffly at the thought.

257

He wanted to laugh too, but checked himself for fear he wouldn't be able to stop.

Let's face it, he told himself. *You're scared. You're scared sweatless.* He wondered if he had spoken it aloud.

There was plenty of room on the asteroid. At least two hundred square miles, probably more if you allowed for the rough surface. He could skulk around, hide…and suffocate when his tanked air gave out. He had to be a hunter, too, and track down the other man, before he died. And if he found his enemy, he would probably die anyway.

He looked about him. Nothing. No sound, no movement, nothing but the streaming of the constellations as the asteroid spun. Nothing had ever moved here, since the beginning of time when moltenness congealed into death. Not till men came and hunted each other.

Slowly he forced himself to move. The thrust of his foot sent him up, looping over the cliff to drift down like a dead leaf in Earth's October. Suit, equipment, and his own body, all together, weighed only a couple of pounds here. It was ghostly, this soundless progress over fields which had never known life. It was like being dead already.

Bo Jonsson's tongue was dry and thick in his mouth. He wanted to find his enemy and give up, buy existence at whatever price it would command. But he couldn't do that. Even if the other man let him do it, Which was doubtful, he couldn't. Johnny Malone was dead.

Maybe that was what had started it all—the death of Johnny Malone.

There are numerous reasons for basing on the Trojan asteroids, but the main one can be given in a single word: stability. They stay put in Jupiter's orbit, about sixty degrees ahead and behind, with only minor oscillations; spaceships need not waste fuel coming up to a body which has been perturbed a goodly distance from where it was supposed to be. The trailing group is the jumping-off place for trans-Jovian planets, the leading group for the inner worlds—that way, their own revolution about the sun gives the departing ship a welcome boost, while minimizing the effects of Jupiter's drag.

Moreover, being dense clusters, they have attracted swarms of miners, so that Achilles among the leaders and Patroclus in the trailers have a permanent boom town atmosphere. Even though a spaceship and equipment represent a large investment, this is one of the last strongholds of genuinely private enterprise; the prospector, the mine owner, the rockhound dreaming of the day when his stake is big enough for him to start out on his own—a race of individualists, rough and noisy and jealous, but living under iron rules of hospitality and rescue.

The Last Chance on Achilles has another name, which simply sticks an "r" in the official one; even for that planetoid, it is a rowdy bar where Guardsmen come in trios. But Johnny Malone liked it, and talked Bo Jonsson into going there for a final spree before checkoff and departure. "Nothing to compare," he insisted. "Every place else is getting too fantangling civilized, except Venus, and I don't enjoy Venus."

Johnny was from Luna City himself: a small, dark man with the quick nervous movements and clipped accent of that roaring commercial metropolis. He affected the latest styles, brilliant colors in the flowing tunic and slacks, a beret cocked on his sleek head. But somehow he didn't grate on Bo, they had been partners for several years now.

They pushed through a milling crowd at the bar, rockhounds who watched one of Archilles' three live ecdysiasts with hungry eyes, and by some miracle found an empty booth. Bo squeezed his bulk into one side of the cubicle while Johnny, squinting through a reeking smoke-haze, dialed drinks. Bo was larger and heavier than most spacemen—he'd never have gotten his certificate before the ion drive came in—and was usually content to let others talk while he listened. A placid blond giant, with amiable blue eyes in a battered brown face, he did not consider himself bright, and always wanted to learn.

Johnny gulped his drink and winced. "Whiskey, they call it yet! Water, synthetic alcohol, and a dash of caramel they have the gall to label whiskey and charge for!"

"Everything's expensive here," said Bo mildly. "That's why so few rockhounds get rich. They make a lot of money, but they have to spend it just as fast to stay alive."

"Yeh…yeh…wish they'd spend some of it on us." Johnny grinned and fed the dispenser another coin. It muttered to itself and slid forth a tray with a glass. "C'mon, drink up, man. It's a long way home, and we've got to fortify ourselves for the trip. A bottle, a battle, and a wench is what I need. Most especially the wench, because I don't think the eminent Dr. McKittrick is gonna be interested in sociability, and it's close quarters aboard the Dog."

Bo kept on sipping slowly. "Johnny," he said, raising his voice to cut through the din, "you're an educated man, I never could figure out why you want to talk like a jumper."

"Because I am one at heart. Look, Bo, why don't you get over that inferiority complex of yours? A man can't run a spaceship without knowing more math and physical science than the average professor on Earth. So you had to work your way through the Academy and never had a chance to fan yourself with a lily white hand while somebody tootled Mozart through a horn. So what?" Johnny's head darted around, bird-like. "If we want some women we'd better make our reservations now."

"I don't, Johnny," said Bo. "I'll just nurse a beer." It wasn't morals so much as fastidiousness; he'd wait till they hit Luna.

"Suit yourself. If you don't want to uphold the honor of the Sirius Transportation Company—"

Bo chuckled. The Company consisted of (a) the *Sirius;* (b) her crew, himself and Johnny; (c) a warehouse, berth, and three other part owners back in Luna City. Not exactly a tramp ship, because you can't normally stop in the middle of an interplanetary voyage and head for somewhere else; but she went wherever there was cargo or people to be moved. Her margin of profit was not great in spite of the charges, for a space trip is expensive; but in a few more years they'd be able to buy another ship or two, and eventually Fireball and Triplanetary would be getting some competition. Even the public lines might have to worry a little.

Johnny put away another couple of shots and rose. Alcohol cost plenty, but it was also more effective in low-gee. "'Scuse me," he said. "I see a target. Sure you don't want me to ask if she has a friend?"

Bo shook his head and watched his partner move off, swift in the puny gravity—the Last Chance didn't centrifuge like some of the tommicker places downtown. It was hard to push through the crowd without weight to help, but Johnny faded along and edged up to the girl with his highest-powered smile. There were several other men standing around her, but Johnny had The Touch. He'd be bringing her back here in a few minutes.

Bo sighed, feeling a bit lonesome. If he wasn't going to make a night of it, there was no point in drinking heavily. He had to make the final inspection of the ship tomorrow, and grudged the cost of anti-hangover tablets. Besides what he was putting back into the business, he was trying to build a private hoard; some day, he'd retire and get married and build a house. He already had the site picked out, on Kullen overlooking the Sound, back on Earth. Man, but it was a long time since he'd been on Earth!

A sharp noise slashed through the haze of talk and music. Bo looked up. There was a tall black haired man, Venusian to judge by his kilts, arguing with Johnny. His face was ugly with anger.

Johnny made some reply. Bo heaved up his form and strode toward the discussion, casually picking up anyone in the way and setting him aside. Johnny liked a fight, but this Venusian was big.

As he neared, he caught words: "—my girl, dammit."

"Like hell I am!" said the girl. "I never saw you before—"

"Run along and play, son," said Johnny. "Or do you want me to change that diaper of yours?"

That was when it happened. Bo saw the little needler spit from the Venusian's fingers. Johnny stood there a moment, looking foolishly at the dart in his stomach. Then his knees buckled and he fell with a nightmare slowness.

The Venusian was already on the move. He sprang straight up, slammed a kick at the wall, and arced out the door into the dome corridor beyond. *A spaceman, that. Knows how to handle himself in low-gee.* It was the only clear thought which ran in the sudden storm of Bo's head.

The girl screamed. A man cursed and tried to follow the Venusian. He tangled with another. "Get outta my way!" A roar lifted, someone slugged, someone else coolly smashed a bottle against the bar and lifted the jagged end. There was the noise of a fist meeting flesh.

Bo had seen death before. That needle wasn't anesthetic, it was poison. He knelt in the riot with Johnny's body in his arms.

-2-

S uddenly the world came to an end.

There was a sheer drop-off onto the next face of the rough cube which was the asteroid. Bo lay on his belly and peered down the cliff, it ran for a couple of miles and beyond it were the deeps of space and the cold stars. He could dimly see the tortured swirl of crystallization patterns in the smooth bareness. No place to hide; his enemy was not there.

He turned the thought over in a mind which seemed stiff and slow. By crossing that little plain he was exposing himself to a shot from one of its edges. On the other hand, he could just as well be bushwhacked from a ravine as he jumped over. And this route was the fastest for completing his search scheme.

The Great Bear slid into sight, down under the world as it turned. He had often stood on winter nights, back in Sweden, and seen its immense sprawl across the weird flicker of aurora; but even then he wanted the spaceman's experience of seeing it from above. Well, now he had his wish, and much good it had done him.

He went over the edge of the cliff, cautiously, for it wouldn't take much of an impetus to throw him off this rock entirely. Then his helpless and soon frozen body would be just another meteor for the next million years. The vague downward sensation of gravity shifted insanely as he moved; he had the feeling that the world was tilting around him. Now it was the precipice which was a scarred black plain underfoot, reaching to a saw-toothed bluff at its farther edge.

He moved with flat low-gee bounds. Besides the danger of springing off the asteroid entirely, there was its low acceleration to keep a man near the ground; jump up a few feet and it would take you a while to fall back. It was utterly silent around him. He had never thought there could be so much stillness.

He was halfway across when the bullet came. He saw no flash, heard no crack, but suddenly the fissured land before him exploded in a soundless shower of chips. The bullet ricocheted flatly, heading off for outer space. No meteor gravel, that!

Bo stood unmoving an instant, fighting the impulse to leap away. He was a spaceman, not a rockhound; he wasn't used to this environment, and if he jumped high he could be riddled as he fell slowly down again. Sweat was cold on his body. He squinted, trying to see where the shot had come from.

Suddenly he was zigzagging off across the plain toward the nearest edge. Another bullet pocked the ground near him. The sun rose, a tiny heatless dazzle blinding in his eyes.

Fire crashed at his back. Thunder and darkness exploded before him. He lurched forward, driven by the impact. Something was roaring, echoes clamorous in his helmet. He grew dimly aware that it was himself. Then he was falling, whirling down into the black between the stars.

There was a knife in his back, it was white-hot and twisting between the ribs. He stumbled over the edge of the plain and fell, waking when his armor bounced a little against stone.

Breath rattled in his throat as he turned his head. There was a white plume standing over his shoulder, air streaming out through the hole and freezing its moisture. The knife in him was not hot, it was cold with an ultimate cold.

Around him, world and stars rippled as if seen through heat, through fever. He hung on the edge of creation by his fingertips, while chaos shouted beneath.

Theoretically, one man can run a spaceship, but in practice two or three are required for non-military craft. This is not only an emergency reserve, but a preventive of emergencies, for one man alone might get too tired at the critical moments. Bo knew he wouldn't be allowed to leave Archilles without a certified partner, and unemployed spacemen available for immediate hiring are found once in a Venusian snowfall.

Bo didn't care the first day. He had taken Johnny out to Helmet Hill and laid him in the barren ground to wait, unchanging now, till Judgment Day. He felt empty then, drained of grief and hope alike, his main thought a dull dread of having to tell Johnny's father when he reached Luna. He was too slow and clumsy with words; his comforting hand would only break the old man's back. Old Malone had given six sons to space, Johnny was the last; from Saturn to the sun, his blood was strewn for nothing.

It hardly seemed to matter that the Guards office reported itself unable to find the murderer. A single Venusian should have been easy to trace on Achilles, but he seemed to have vanished completely.

Bo returned to the transient quarters and dialed Valeria McKittrick. She looked impatiently at him out of the screen. "Well," she said, "what's the matter? I thought we were blasting today."

"Hadn't you heard?" asked Bo. He found it hard to believe she could be ignorant, here where everybody's life was known to everybody else. "Johnny's dead. We can't leave."

"Oh…I'm sorry. He, was such a nice little man—I've been in the lab all the time, packing my things, and didn't know." A frown crossed her clear brow. "But you've got to get me back. I've engaged passage to Luna with you."

"Your ticket will be refunded, of course," said Bo heavily. "But you aren't certified, and the *Sirius* is licensed for no less than two operators."

"Well…damn! There won't be another berth for weeks, and I've *got* to get home. Can't you find somebody?"

Bo shrugged, not caring much, "I'll circulate an ad if you want, but—"

"Do so, please. Let me know." She switched off.

Bo sat for a moment thinking about her. Valeria McKittrick was worth considering. She wasn't beautiful in any conventional sense but she was tall and well built; there were good lines in the strong high boned face, and her hair was a cataract of spectacular red. And brains, too…you didn't get to be a physicist with the Union's radiation labs for nothing. He knew she was still young, and that she had been on Achilles for about a year working on some special project and was now ready to go home.

She was human enough, had been to most of the officers' parties and danced and laughed and flirted mildly, but even the dullest rockhound gossip knew she was too lost in her work to do more. Out here a woman was rare, and a virtuous woman unheard-of; as a result, unknown to herself, Dr. McKittrick's fame had spread through more thousands of people and millions of miles than her professional achievements were ever likely to reach.

Since coming here, on commission from the Lunar lab, to bring her home, Bo Jonsson had given her an occasional wistful thought. He liked intelligent women, and he was getting tired of rootlessness. But of course it would be a catastrophe if he fell in love with her because she wouldn't look twice at a big dumb slob like him. He had sweated out a couple of similar affairs in the past and didn't want to go through another.

He placed his ad on the radinews circuit and then went out to get drunk. It was all he could do for Johnny now, drink him a final wassail. Already his friend was cold under the stars. In the course of the evening he found himself weeping.

He woke up many hours later. Achilles ran on Earth time but did not rotate on it; officially, it was late at night, actually the shrunken sun was high over the domes. The man in the upper bunk said there was a message for him; he was to call one Einar Lundgard at the Comet Hotel soonest.

The Comet! Anyone who could afford a room to himself here, rather than a kip in the public barracks, was well fueled. Bo swallowed a tablet and made his way to the visi and dialed. The robo-clerk summoned Lundgard down to the desk.

It was a lean, muscular face under close cropped brown hair which appeared in the screen. Lundgard was a tall and supple man, somehow neat even without clothes. "Jonsson," said Bo. "Sorry to get you up, but I understood—"

"Oh, yes. Are you looking for a spaceman? I heard your ad and I'm available."

Bo felt his mouth gape open. "Huh? I never thought—"

"We're both lucky, I guess." Lundgard chuckled. His English had only the slightest trace of accent, less than Bo's. "I thought I was stashed here too for the next several months."

"How does a qualified spaceman happen to be marooned?"

"I'm with Fireball, was on the *Drake*—heard of what happened to her?"

Bo nodded, for every spaceman knows exactly what every spaceship is doing at any given time. The *Drake* had come to Achilles to pick up a cargo of refined thorium for Earth; while she lay in orbit, she had somehow lost a few hundred pounds of reaction-mass water from a cracked gasket. Why the accident should have occurred, nobody knew…spacemen were not careless about inspections, and what reason would anyone have for sabotage? The event had taken place about a month ago, when the *Sirius* was already enroute here; Bo had heard of it in the course of shop talk.

"I thought she went back anyway," he said.

Lundgard nodded. "She did. It was the usual question of economics. You know what refined fuel water costs in the Belt; also, the delay while we got it would have carried Earth and Achilles past optimum position, which'd make the trip home that much more expensive. Since we had one more man aboard than really required, it was cheaper to leave him behind; the difference in mass would make up for the fuel loss. I volunteered, even suggested the idea, because...well, it happened during my watch, and even if nobody blamed me I couldn't help feeling guilty." Bo understood that kind of loyalty. You couldn't travel space without men who had it.

"The Company beamed a message: I'd stay here till their schedule permitted an undermanned ship to come by, but that wouldn't be for maybe months," went on Lundgard. "I can't see sitting on this lump that long without so much as a chance at planetfall bonus. If you'll take me on, I'm sure the Company will agree; I'll get a message to them on the beam right away."

"Take us a while to get back," warned Bo. "We're going to stop off at another asteroid to pick up some automatic equipment, and won't go into hyperbolic orbit till after that. About six weeks from here to Earth, all told."

"Against six months here?" Lundgard laughed; it emphasized the bright charm of his manner. "Sunblaze, I'll work for free."

"No need to. Bring your papers over tomorrow, huh?"

The certificate and record were perfectly in order, showing Einar Lundgard to be a Space-tech 1/cl with eight years' experience, qualified as engineer, astronaut, pilot, and any other of the thousand professions which have run into one. They registered articles and shook hands on it. "Call me Bo. It really is my name... Swedish."

"Another squarehead, eh?" grinned Lundgard. "I'm from South America myself."

"Notice a year's gap here," said Bo, pointing to the service record. "On Venus."

"Oh, yes. I had some fool idea about settling but soon learned better. I tried to farm, but when you have to carve your own land out of howling desert—Well, let's start some math, shall we?"

They were lucky, not having to wait their turn at the station computer; no other ship was leaving immediately. They fed it the data and requirements, and got back columns of numbers: fuel requirements, acceleration times, orbital elements. The figures always had to be modified, no trip ever turned out just as predicted, but that could be done when needed with a slipstick and the little ship's calculator.

Bo went at his share of the job doggedly, checking and re-checking before giving the problem to the machine; Lundgard breezed through it and spent his time while waiting for Bo in swapping dirty limericks with the tech. He had some good ones.

The *Sirius* was loaded, inspected, and cleared. A "scooter" brought her three passengers up to her orbit, they embarked, settled down, and waited. At the proper time, acceleration jammed them back in a thunder of rockets.

Bo relaxed against the thrust, thinking of Achilles falling away behind them. "So long," he whispered. "So long, Johnny."

-3-

In another minute, he would be knotted and screaming from the bends, and a couple of minutes later he would be dead.

Bo clamped his teeth together, as if he would grip consciousness in his jaws. His hands felt cold and heavy, the hands of a stranger, as he fumbled for the supply pouch. It seemed to recede from him, down a hollow infinite corridor where echoes talked in a language he did not know.

"Damn," he gasped. "Damn, damn, damn, damn, damn."

He got the pouch open somehow. The stars wheeled around him. There were stars buzzing in his head, like cold white fireflies, buzzing and buzzing in the enormous ringing emptiness of his skull. Pain jagged through him, he felt his eardrums popping as pressure dropped.

The plastic patch stuck to his metal gauntlet. He peeled it off, trying not to howl with the fury ripping in his nerves. His body was slow, inert, a thing to fight. There was no more feeling in his back, was he dead already?

Redness flamed before his eyes, red like Valeria's hair blowing across the stars. It was sheer reflex which brought his arms around to slap the patch over the hole in his suit. The adhesive gripped, drying fast in the sucking vacuum. The patch bellied out from internal air pressure, straining to break loose and kill him.

Bo's mind wavered back toward life. He opened the valves wide on his tanks, and his thermostatic capacitors pumped heat back into him. For a long time he lay there, only lungs and heart had motion. His throat felt withered and flayed, but the rasp of air through it was like being born again.

Born, spewed out of an iron womb into a hollowness of stars and cold, to lie on naked rock while the enemy hunted him. Bo shuddered and wanted to scream again.

Slowly he groped back toward awareness. His frostbitten back tingled as it warmed up again, soon it would be afire. He could feel a hot trickling of blood, but it was along his right side. The bullet must have spent most of its force punching through the armor, caromed off the inside, scratched his ribs, and fallen dead. Next time he probably wouldn't be so lucky. A magnetic-driven .30 slug would go right through a helmet, splashing brains as it passed.

He turned his head, feeling a great weariness, and looked at the gauges. This had cost him a lot of air. There was only about three hours worth left. Lundgard could kill him simply by waiting.

It would be easy to die. He lay on his back, staring up at the stars and the spilling cloudy glory of the Milky Way. A warmth was creeping back into numbed hands and feet; soon he would be warm all over, and sleepy. His eyelids felt heavy, strange that they should be so heavy on an asteroid.

He wanted terribly to sleep.

———

There wasn't much room in the *Sirius,* the only privacy was gained by drawing curtains across your bunk. Men without psych training could get to hate each other on a voyage. Bo wondered if he would reach Luna hating Einar Lundgard.

The man was competent, a willing worker, tempering his cheerfulness with tact, always immaculate in the neat blue and white of the Fireball Line which made Bo feel doubly sloppy in his own old gray coverall. He was a fine conversationalist with an enormous stock of reminiscence and ideas, witty above a certain passion of belief. It seemed as if he and Valeria were always talking, animated voices like a sound of life over the mechanical ship-murmurs, while Bo sat dumbly in a corner wishing he could think of something to say.

The trouble was, in spite of all his efforts, he was doing a cometary dive into another bad case of one-sided love. When she spoke in that husky voice of hers, gray gleam of eyes under hair that floated flaming in nullgee, the beauty he saw in her was like pain. And she was always around. It couldn't be helped. Once they had gone into free fall he could only polish so much metal and tinker with so many appliances; after that they were crowded together in a long waiting.

"—And why were you all alone in the Belt?" asked Lundgard. "In spite of all the romantic stories about the wild free life of the rock-hound, it's the dullest place in the System."

"Not to me," she smiled. "I was working. There were experiments to be done, factors to be measured, away from solar radiation. There are always ions around inside the orbit of Mars to jumble up a delicate apparatus."

Bo sat quiet, trying to keep his eyes off her. She looked good in shorts and half-cape. Too good.

"It's something to do with power beaming, isn't it?" Lundgard's handsome face creased in a frown. "Afraid I don't quite understand. They've been beaming power on the planets for a long time now."

"So they have," she nodded. "What we're after is an interplanetary power beam. And we've got it." She gestured to the baggage rack and a thick trunk full of papers she had put there. "That's it. The basic circuits, factors and constants. Any competent engineer could draw up a design from them."

"Hmmm...precision work, eh?"

"Obviously! It was hard enough to do on, say, Earth—you need a *really* tight beam in just the right frequencies, a feedback signal to direct each beam at the desired outlet, relay stations—oh, yes, it was a ten-year research project before they could even think about building. An interplanetary beam has all those problems plus a number of its own. You have to get the dispersion down to a figure so low it hardly seems possible. You can't use feedback because of the time lag, so the beams have to be aimed *exactly* right—and the planets are always moving, at miles per second. An error of one degree would throw your beam almost two million miles off in crossing one A.U. And besides being so precise, the beam has to carry a begawatt at least to be worth the trouble. The problem looked insoluble till someone in the Order of Planetary Engineers came up with an idea for a trick control circuit hooked into a special computer. My lab's been working together with the Order on it, and I was making certain final determinations for them. It's finished now…twelve years of work and we're done." She laughed. "Except for building the stations and getting the bugs out!"

Lundgard cocked an oddly sardonic brow. "And what do you hope for from it?" he asked. "What have the psychotechs decided to do with this thing?"

"Isn't it obvious?" she cried. "Power! Nuclear fuel is getting scarcer every day, and civilization is finished if we can't find another energy source. The sun is pouring out more than we'll ever need, but sheer distance dilutes it below a useful level by the time it gets to Venus.

"We'll build stations on the hot side of Mercury. Orbital stations can relay. We can get the beams as far out as Mars without too much dispersion. It'll bring down the rising price of atomic energy, which is making all other prices rise, and stretch our supply of fissionables for centuries more. No more fuel worries, no more Martians freezing to death because a converter fails, no more clan feuds on Venus starting over uranium beds—" The excited flush on her cheeks was lovely to look at.

Lundgard shook his head. There was a sadness in his smile. "You're a true child of the New Enlightenment," he said. "Reason will solve everything. Science will find a cure for all our ills. Give man a cheap energy source and leave him forever happy. It won't work, you know."

Something like anger crossed her eyes. "What are you?" she asked. "A Humanist?"

"Yes," said Lundgard quietly.

Bo started. He'd known about the antipsychotechnic movement which was growing on Earth, seen a few of its adherents, but—

"I never thought a spaceman would be a Humanist," he stammered.

Lundgard shrugged wryly. "Don't be afraid, I don't eat babies. I don't even get hysterics in an argument. All I've done is use the scientific method, observing the world without preconceptions, and learned by it that the scientific method doesn't have all the answers."

"Instead," said Valeria scornfully, "we should all go back to church and pray for what we want rather than working for it."

"Not at all," said Lundgard mildly. "The New Enlightenment is—or was, because it's dying—a very natural state of mind. Here Earth had come out of the World Wars, racked and ruined, starving and chaotic, and all because of unbridled ideology. So the physical scientists produced goods and machines and conquered the planets; the biologists found new food sources and new cures for disease; the psychotechs built up their knowledge to a point where the socioeconomic unity could really be planned and the plan worked. Man was unified, war had sunken to an occasional small 'police action,' people were eating and had comfort and security—all through applied, working science. Naturally they came to believe reason would solve their remaining problems. But this faith in reason was itself an emotional reaction from the preceding age of unreason.

"Well, we've had a century of enlightenment now, and it has created its own troubles which it cannot solve. No age can handle the difficulties it raises for itself; that's left to the next era. There are practical problems arising, and no matter how desperately the psychotechs work they aren't succeeding with them."

"What problems?" asked Bo, feeling a little bewildered.

"Man, don't you ever see a newscast?" challenged Lundgard. "The Second Industrial Revolution, millions of people thrown out of work by the new automata. They aren't going hungry, but they are displaced and bitter. The economic center of Earth is shifting to Asia, the political power with it, and hundreds of millions of Asians are skeptical about this antiseptic New Order the West has been bringing them: cultural resistance, and not all the psychotechnic propaganda in the System can shake it off. The men of Mars, Venus, the Belt, the Jovian moons are developing their own civilizations—inevitably, in alien environments; their own ways of living and thinking, which just don't fit into the neat scheme of an Earth-dominated Solar Union. The psychotechs themselves are being driven to oligarchic, unconstitutional acts; they have no choice, but it's making them enemies.

"And then there's the normal human energy and drive. Man can only be safe and sane and secure for so long, then he reacts. This New Enlightenment is really a decadent age, a period where an exhausted civilization has been resting under a holy status quo. It can't last. Man always wants something new."

"You Humanists talk a lot about 'man's right to variability,'" said Valeria. "If you really carry off that revolution your writings advocate you'll just trade one power group for another—and more fanatic, less lawful, than the present one."

"Not necessarily," said Lundgard. "After all, the Union will probably break up. It can't last forever. All we want to do is hasten the day because we feel that it's outlived its usefulness."

Bo shook his head. "I can't see it," he said heavily. "I just can't see it. All those people—the Lunarites, the violent clansmen on Venus, the stiff correct Martians, the asteroid rockhounds, even those mysterious Jovians—they all came from Earth. It was Earth's help that made their planets habitable. We're all men, all one race."

"A fiction," said Lundgard. "The human race is a fiction. There are only small groups with their own conflicting interests."

"And if those conflicts are allowed to break into war—" said Valeria. "Do you know what a lithium bomb can do?"

There was a reckless gleam in Lundgard's eyes. "If a period of interplanetary wars is necessary, let's get it over with," he answered. "Enough men will survive to build something better. This age has gotten stale. It's petrifying. There have been plenty of shake-ups in history—the fall of Rome, the Reformation, the Napoleonic Wars, the World Wars. It's been man's way of progressing."

"I don't know about all those," said Bo slowly. "I just know I wouldn't want to live through such a time."

"You're soft," said Lundgard. "Down underneath you're soft." He laughed disarmingly. "Pardon me. I didn't mean anything personal. I'll never convince you and you'll never convince me, so let's keep it friendly. I hope you'll have some free time on Luna, Valeria. I know a little grill where they serve the best synthosteaks in the System."

"All right," she smiled. "It's a date."

Bo mumbled some excuse and went aft. He was still calling her Dr. McKittrick.

-4-

Y ou can't just lie here and let him come kill you.

There was a picture behind his eyes; he didn't know if it was a dream or a long buried memory. He stood under an aspen which quivered and rustled as if it laughed to itself softly, softly, when the wind embraced it. And the wind was blowing up a red granite slope, wild and salt from the Sound, and there were towering clouds lifting over Denmark to the west. The sunlight rained and streamed through aspen leaves, broken, shaken, falling in spatters against the earth, and he, Bo Jonsson, laughed with the wind and the tree and the far watery glitter of the Sound.

He opened his eyes, wearily, like an old man. Orion was marching past, and there was a blaze on crags five miles off which told of the rising sun. The asteroid spun swiftly; he had been here for many of its days now, and each day burdened him like a year.

Got to get out of here, he knew.

He sat up, pain tearing along his furrowed breast. Somehow he had kept the wrench with him; he stared at it in a dull wonder.

Where to go, where to hide, what to do? Thirst nagged him. Slowly he uncoiled the tube which led from the electrically heated canteen welded to his suit, screwed its end into the helmet nipple, thumbed down the clamp which closed it, and sucked hard. It helped a little.

He dragged himself to his feet and stood swaying, only the near-weightlessness kept him erect. Turning his head in its transparent cage, he saw the sun rise, and bright spots danced before him when he looked away.

His vision cleared, but for a moment he thought the shadow lifting over a nearby ridge was a wisp of unconsciousness. Then he made out the bulky black-painted edge of it, gigantic against the Milky Way, and it was Lundgard, moving unhurriedly up to kill him.

A dark laughter was in his radio earphones. "Take it easy, Bo. I'll be there in a minute."

He backed away, his heart a sudden thunder, looking for a place to hide. Down! Get down and don't stand where he can see you! He crouched as much as the armor would allow and broke into a bounding run.

A slug spat broken stone near his feet. The powdery dust hung for minutes before settling. Breath rattled in his throat. He saw the lip of a meteoric crater and dove.

Crouching there, he heard Lundgard's voice again: "You're somewhere near. Why not come out and finish it now?"

The radio was non-directional, so he snapped back: "A gun against a monkey wrench?"

Lundgard's coolness broke a little; there was almost a puzzled note: "I hate to do this. Why can't you be reasonable? I don't want to kill you."

"The trouble," said Bo harshly, "is that I want to kill you."

"Behold the man of the New Enlightenment!" Bo could imagine Lundgard's grin. It would be tight, and there would be sweat on the lean face, but the amusement was genuine. "Didn't you believe sweet reasonableness could solve everything? This is only the beginning, Bo, just a small preliminary hint that the age of reason is dying. I've already converted you to my way of thinking, by the very fact you're fighting me. Why not admit it?"

Bo shook his head—futile gesture, locked in darkness where he lay. There was a frosty blaze of stars when he looked up.

It was more than himself and Johnny Malone, more even than the principle of the thing and the catastrophe to all men which Lundgard's victory meant. There was something deep and primitive which would not let him surrender, even in the teeth of annihilation. Valeria's image swayed before him.

Lundgard was moving around, peering over the shadowy tumble of blackened rock in search of any trace. There was a magnetic rifle in his hands. Bo strained his helmet to the crater floor, trying to hear ground vibrations, but there was nothing. He didn't know where Lundgard was, only that he was very near.

Blindly, he bunched his legs and sprang out of the pit.

They found the asteroid where Valeria had left her recording instruments. It was a tiny drifting fragment of a world which had never been born, turning endlessly between the constellations; the *Sirius* moored fast with grapples, and Valeria donned a spacesuit and went out to get her apparatus. Lundgard accompanied her. As there was only work for two, Bo stayed behind.

He slumped for a while in the pilot chair, letting his mind pace through a circle of futility. Valeria, Valeria—O strong and fair and never to be forgotten, would he ever see her again after they made Luna?

This won't do, he told himself dully. *I should at least keep busy. Thank God for work.*

He wasn't much of a thinker, he knew that, but he had cleverness in his hands. It was satisfying to watch a machine come right under his tools. Working, he could see the falseness of Lundgard's philosophy. The man could quote history all he wanted; weave a glittering circle of logic around Bo's awkward brain, but it didn't change facts. Maybe this century was headed for trouble; maybe psychotechnic government was only another human self-limitation and should be changed for something else; nevertheless, the truth remained that most men were workers who wished no more than peace in which to create as best they could. All the high ideals in the universe weren't worth breaking the Union for and smashing the work of human hands in a single burst of annihilating flame.

I can feel it, down inside me. But why can't I say it?

He got up and went over to the baggage rack, remembering that Lundgard had dozens of book-reels along and that reading would help him not to think about what he could never have.

On a planet Bo would not have dreamed of helping himself without asking first. But custom is different in space, where there is no privacy and men must be a unit if they are to survive. He was faintly surprised to see that Lundgard's personal suitcase was locked; but it would be hours, probably, before the owner got back: dismantling a recorder setup took time. A long time, in which to talk and laugh with Valeria. In the chill spatial radiance, her hair would be like frosty fire.

Casually, Bo stooped across to Lundgard's sack-hammock and took his key ring off the hook. He opened the suitcase and lifted out some of the reels in search of a promising title.

Underneath them were neatly folded clothes, Fireball uniforms and fancy dress pajamas. A tartan edge stuck out from below, and Bo lifted a coat to see what clan that was. Probably a souvenir of Lundgard's Venusian stay—

Next to the kilt was a box which he recognized. L-masks came in such boxes.

How the idea came to him, he did not know. He stood there for minutes, looking at the box without seeing it. The ship was very quiet around him. He had a sudden feeling that the walls were closing in.

When he opened the box, his hands shook, and there was sweat trickling along his ribs.

The mask was of the latest type, meant to fit over the head, snug around the cheeks and mouth and jaws. It was like a second skin, reflecting expression, not to be told from a real face. Bo saw the craggy nose and the shock of dark hair, limp now, but—

Suddenly he was back on Achilles; with riot roaring around him and Johnny Malone's body in his arms.

No wonder they never found that Venusian. There never was any.

Bo felt a dim shock when he looked at the chronometer. Only five minutes had gone by while he stood there. Only five minutes to turn the cosmos inside out.

Very slowly and carefully he repacked the suitcase and put it in the rack and sat down to think.

What to do?

Accuse Lundgard to his face—no, the man undoubtedly carried that needler. And there was Valeria to think of. A ricocheting dart, a scratch on her, no! It took Bo a long time to decide; his brain seemed viscous. When he looked out of a port to the indifferent stars, he shuddered.

They came back, shedding their spacesuits in the airlock; frost whitened the armor as moisture condensed on chilled surfaces. The metal seemed to breathe cold. Valeria went efficiently to work, stowing the boxed instruments as carefully as if they were her children. There was a laughter on her lips which turned Bo's heart around inside him.

Lundgard leaned over the tiny desk where he sat. "What y' doing?" he asked.

"Recalculating our orbit to Luna," said Bo. "I want to go slow to hyperbolic speed."

"Why? It'll add days to the trip, and the fuel—"

"I...I'm afraid we might barge into Swarm 770. It's supposed to be near here now and, uh, the positions of those things are never known for sure...perturbations..." Bo's mouth felt dry.

"You've got a megamile of safety margin or your orbit would never have been approved," argued Lundgard.

"Hell damn it, I'm the captain!" yelled Bo.

"All right, all right…take it easy, skipper," Lundgard shot a humorous glance at Valeria. "I certainly don't mind a few extra days in…the present company."

She smiled at him. Bo felt ill.

His excuse was thin; if Lundgard thought to check the ephemeris, it would fall to ruin. But he couldn't tell the real reason.

An ion-drive ship does not need to drift along the economical Hohmann. "A" orbit of the big freighters; it can build up such furious speed that the sun will swing it along a hyperbola rather than an ellipse, and can still brake that speed near its destination. But the critical stage of acceleration has to be just right, or there will not be enough fuel to stop completely; the ship will be pulled into a cometary orbit and run helpless, the crew probably starving before a rescue vessel can locate them. Bo dared not risk the trouble exploding at full drive; he would drift along, capture and bind Lundgard at the first chance, and then head for Earth. He could handle the *Sirius* alone even if it was illegal; he could not handle her if he had to fight simultaneously.

His knuckles were white on the controls as he loosed the grapples and nudged away from the asteroid with a whisper of power. After a few minutes of low acceleration, he cut the rockets, checked position and velocity, and nodded. "On orbit," he said mechanically. "It's your turn to cook, Ei…Einar."

Lundgard swooped easily through the air into the cubbyhole which served for a galley. Cooking in free fall is an art which not all spacemen master, but he could—his meals were even good. Bo felt a helpless kind of rage at his own clumsy efforts.

He crouched in midair, dark of mind, a leg hooked around a stanchion to keep from drifting.

When someone touched him, his heart jumped and he whirled around.

"What's the matter, Bo?" asked Valeria. "You look like doomsday."

"I…I…" He gulped noisily and twisted his mouth into a smile. "Just feeling a little off."

"It's more than that, I think." Her eyes were grave. "You've seemed so unhappy the whole trip. Is there anything I can do to help?"

"Thanks…Dr. McKittrick…but—"

"Don't be so formal," she said, almost wistfully. "I don't bite. Too many men think I do. Can't we be friends?"

"With a thick-headed clinker like me?" His whisper was raw.

"Don't be silly. It takes brains to be a spaceman. I like a man who knows when to be quiet." She lowered her eyes, the lashes were long and sooty black. "There's something solid about you, something so few people seem to have these days. I wish you wouldn't go feeling so inferior."

At any other time it would have been a sunburst in him. Now he thought of death, and mumbled something and looked away. A hurt expression crossed her face. "I won't bother you," she said gently, and moved off.

The thing was to fall on Lundgard while he slept—

The radar alarm buzzed during a dinner in which Lundgard's flow of talk had battered vainly against silence and finally given up. Bo vaulted over to the control panel and checked. No red light glowed, and the autopilot wasn't whipping them out of danger, so they weren't on a collision course. But the object was getting close. Bo calculated it was an asteroid on an orbit almost parallel to their own, relative speed only a few feet per second; it would come within ten miles or so. In the magnifying periscope, it showed as a jagged dark cube, turning around itself and flashing hard glints of sunlight off mica beds—perhaps six miles square, all crags and cracks and fracture faces, heatless and lifeless and kindless.

Lundgard yawned elaborately after dinner. "Excuse," he said. "Unless somebody's for chess?" His hopeful glance met the grimness of Bo and the odd sadness of Valeria, and he shrugged. "All right, then. Pleasant dreams."

After ten minutes—*now!*

Bo uncoiled himself. "Valeria," he whispered, as if the name were holy.

"Yes?" She ached her brows expectantly.

"I can't stop to explain now. I've got to do something dangerous. Get back aft of the gyro housing."

"What?"

"Get back!" Command blazed frantically in him. "And stay there, whatever happens."

Something like fear flickered in her eyes. It was a very long way to human help. Then she nodded, puzzled but with an obedience which held gallantry, and slipped out of sight behind the steel pillar.

Bo launched himself across the room in a single null-gee bound. One hand ripped aside Lundgard's curtain, the other got him by the throat.

"What the hell—"

Lundgard exploded into life. His fist crashed against Bo's cheek. Bo held on with one hand and slugged with the other. Knuckles bounced on rubbery muscle. Lundgard's arm snaked for the tunic stretched on his bunk wall; his body came lithely out of the sack. Bo snatched for that wrist. Lundgard's free hand came around, edged out to slam him in the larynx.

Pain ripped through Bo. He let go and sailed across the room. Lundgard was pulling out his needler.

Bo hit the opposite wall and rebounded—not for the armed man, but for the control panel. Lundgard spat a dart at him. It burst on to the viewport over his shoulder, and Bo caught the acrid whiff of poison. Then the converter was roaring to life and whining gyros spun the ship around.

Lundgard was hurled across the room. He collected himself, catlike, grabbed a stanchion, and raised the gun again. "I've got the drop," he said. "Get away from there or you're a dead man."

It was as if someone else had seized Bo's body. Decision was like lightning through him. He had tried to capture Lundgard, and failed, and venom crouched at his back. But the ship was pointed for the asteroid now, where it hung gloomily a dozen miles off, and the rockets were ready to spew.

"If you shoot me," said Bo, "I'll live just long enough to pour on the juice. We'll hit that rock and scatter from hell to breakfast."

Valeria emerged. Lundgard swung the needler to cover her. "Stay where you are!" he rapped.

"What's happening?" she said fearfully.

"I don't know," said Lundgard. "Bo's gone crazy—attacked me—"

Wrath boiled back in the pilot. He snarled, "You killed my partner. You must'a been fixing to kill us too."

"What do you mean?" whispered Valeria.

"How should I know?" said Lundgard. "He's jumped his orbit, that's all. Look, Bo, be reasonable. Get away from that panel—"

"Look in his suitcase, Valeria." Bo forced the words out of a tautened throat. "A Venusian shot my partner. You'll find his face and his clothes in Lundgard's things. I'd know that face in the middle of the sun."

She hung for a long while, not moving. Bo couldn't see her. His eyes were nailed to the asteroid, keeping the ship's nose pointed at it.

"Is that true, Einar?" she asked finally.

"No," he said. "Of course not. I do have Venusian clothes and a mask, but—"

"Then why are you keeping me covered too?"

Lundgard didn't answer at once. The only noise was the murmur of machinery and the dense breathing of three pairs of lungs. Then his laugh jarred forth.

"All right," he said. "I hadn't meant it to come yet, or to come this way, but all right."

"Why did you kill Johnny?" Tears stung Bo's eyes. "He never hurt you."

"It was necessary." Lundgard's mouth twitched. "But you see, we knew you were going to Achilles to pick up Valeria and her data. We needed to get a man aboard your ship, to take over when her orbit brought her close to our asteroid base. You've forced my hand—I wasn't going to capture you for days yet. I sabotaged the *Drake's* fuel tanks to get myself stranded there, and shot your friend to get his berth. I'm sorry."

"Why?" Horror rode Valeria's voice.

"I'm a Humanist. I've never made a secret of that. What our secret is, is that some of us aren't content just to talk revolution. We want to give this rotten, overmechanized society the shove that will bring on its end. We've built up a small force, not much as yet, not enough to accomplish anything lasting. But if we had a solar power beam it would make a big difference. It could be adapted to direct military uses, as well as supplying energy to our machines. A lens effect, a concentration of solar radiation strong enough to burn. Well, it seems worth trying."

"And what do you intend for us?"

"You'll have to be kept prisoners for a while, of course," said Lundgard. "It won't be onerous. We aren't beasts."

"No," said Bo. "Just murderers."

"Save the dramatics," snapped Lundgard. "I have the gun. Get away from those controls."

Bo shook his head. There was a wild hammering in his breast, but his voice surprised him with steadiness: "No. I've got the upper hand. I can kill you if you move. Yell if he tries anything, Valeria."

Lundgard's eyes challenged her. "Do you want to die?" he asked.

Her head lifted. "No," she said, "but I'm not afraid to. Go ahead if you must, Bo. It's all right."

Bo felt cold. He knew he wouldn't. He was bluffing. In the final showdown he could not crash her. He had seen too many withered space drained mummies in his time. But maybe Lundgard didn't realize that.

"Give up," he said. "You can't gain a damn thing. I'm not going to see a billion people burned alive just to save our necks. Make a bargain for your life."

"No," said Lundgard with a curious gentleness. "I have my own brand of honor. I'm not going to surrender to you. You can't sit there forever."

Impasse. The ship floated through eternal silence while they waited.

"All right," said Bo. "I'll fight you for the power beam."

"How's that?"

"I can throw this ship into orbit around the asteroid. We can go down there and settle the thing between us. The winner can jump up here again with the help of a jet of tanked air. The lump hasn't got much gravity."

Lundgard hesitated. "And how do I know you'll keep your end of the bargain?" he asked. "You could let me go through the airlock, then close it and blast off."

Bo had had some such thought, but he might have known it wouldn't work. "What do you suggest?" he countered, never taking his eyes off the planetoid. "Remember, I don't trust you either."

Lundgard laughed suddenly, a hard yelping bark. "I know! Valeria, go aft and remove all the control-rod links and sparcs. Bring them back here, I'll go out first, taking half of them with me, and Bo can follow with the other half. He'll have to."

"I—no! I won't," she whispered. "I can't let you—"

"Go ahead and do it," said Bo. He felt a sudden vast weariness. "It's the only way we can break this deadlock."

She wept as she went toward the engine room.

Lundgard's thought was good. Without linked control-rods, the converter couldn't operate five minutes, it would flare up and melt itself and kill everyone aboard in a flood of radiation. Whoever won the duel could quickly re-install the necessary parts.

There was a waiting silence. At last Lundgard said, almost abstractedly: "Holmgang. Do you know what that means, Bo?"

"No."

"You ought to. It was a custom of our ancestors back in the early Middle Ages—the Viking time. Two men would go off to a little island, a holm, to settle their differences; one would come back. I never thought it could happen out here." He chuckled bleakly. "Valkyries in spacesuits?"

The girl came back with the links tied in two bundles. Lundgard counted them and nodded. "All right." He seemed strangely calm, an easy assurance lay over him like armor. Bo's fear was cold in his belly, and Valeria wept still with a helpless horror.

The pilot used a safe two minutes of low blast to edge up to the asteroid, "I'll go into the airlock and put on my spacesuit," said Lundgard. "Then I'll jump down and you can put the ship in orbit. Don't try anything while I'm changing, because I'll keep this needler handy."

"It—won't work against a spacesuit," said Bo.

Lundgard laughed. "I know," he said. He kissed his hand to Valeria and backed into the lock chamber. The outer valve closed behind him.

"Bo!" Valeria grabbed the pilot by the shoulders, and he looked around into her face. "You can't go out there, I won't let you, I—"

"If I don't," he said tonelessly, "we'll orbit around here till we starve."

"But you could be killed!"

"I hope not. For your sake, mostly, I hope not," he said awkwardly. "But he won't have any more weapons than me, just a monkey wrench." There was a metal tube welded to the leg of each suit for holding tools; wrenches, the most commonly used, were simply left there as a rule. "I'm bigger than he is."

"But—" She laid her head on his breast and shuddered with crying. He tried to comfort her.

"All right," he said at last. "All right. Lundgard must be through. I'd better get started."

"Leave him!" she blazed. "His air won't last many hours. We can wait."

"And when he sees he's been tricked, you think he won't wreck those links? No. There's no way out."

It was as if all his life he had walked on a road which had no turnings, which led inevitably to this moment.

He made some careful calculations from the instrument readings, physical constants of the asteroid, and used another minute's maneuvering to assume orbital velocity. Alarm lights blinked angry, eyes at him, the converter was heating up. No more traveling till the links were restored.

Bo floated from his chair toward the lock. "Good-bye, Valeria," he said, feeling the bloodless weakness of words. "I hope it won't be for long."

She threw her arms about him and kissed him. The taste of tears was still on his lips when he had dogged down his helmet.

Opening the outer valve he moved forth, magnetic boots clamping to the hull. A gulf of stars yawned around him, a cloudy halo about his head. The stillness was smothering.

When he was "over" the asteroid he gauged his position with a practiced eye and jumped free. Falling, he thought mostly of Valeria.

As he landed he looked around. No sign of Lundgard. The man could be anywhere in these square miles of cosmic wreckage. He spoke tentatively into his radio, in case Lundgard should be within the horizon: "Hello, are you there?"

"Yes, I'm coming." There was a sharp cruel note of laughter. "Sorry to play this dirty, but there are bigger issues at stake than you or me. I've kept a rifle in my tooltube all the time…just in case. Good-bye, Bo."

A slug smashed into the pinnacle behind him. Bo turned and ran.

-5-

As he rose over the lip of the crater, his head swung, seeking his enemy. There! It was almost a reflex which brought his arm back and sent the wrench hurtling across the few yards between. Before it had struck, Bo's feet lashed against the pit edge, and the kick arced him toward Lundgard.

Spacemen have to be good at throwing things. The wrench hit the lifted rifle in a soundless shiver of metal, tore it loose from an insecure gauntleted grasp and sent it spinning into shadow. Lundgard yelled, spun on his heel, and dove after it. Then the flying body of Bo Jonsson struck him.

Even in low-gee, matter has all its inertia. The impact rang and boomed within their armor, they swayed and fell to the ground, locking arms and hammering futilely at helmets. Rolling over, Bo got on top, his hands closed on Lundgard's throat—where the throat should have been, but plastic and alloy held fast; instinct had betrayed him.

Lundgard snarled, doubled his legs and kicked. Bo was sent staggering back. Lundgard crawled erect and turned to look for the rifle. Bo couldn't see it either in the near-solid blackness where no light fell, but his wrench lay as a dark gleam. He sprang for that, closed a hand on it, bounced up, and rushed at Lundgard. A swing shocked his own muscles with its force, and Lundgard lurched.

Bo moved in on him. Lundgard reached into his tool-tube and drew out his own wrench. He circled, his panting hoarse in Bo's earphones.

"This…is the way…it was supposed to be," said Bo.

He jumped in, his weapon whirling down to shiver again on the other helmet. Lundgard shook a dazed head and countered. The impact roared and echoed in Bo's helmet, on into his skull. He smashed heavily. Lundgard's lifted wrench parried the blow, it slid off. Like a fencer, Lundgard snaked his shaft in and the reverberations were deafening.

Bo braced himself and smote with all his power. The hit sang back through iron and alloy, into his own bones. Lundgard staggered a little, hunched himself and struck in return.

They stood with feet braced apart, trading fury, a metal rain on shivering plastic. The stuff was almost unbreakable, but not quite, not for long when such violence dinned on it. Bo felt a lifting wild glee, something savage he had never known before leaped up in him and he bellowed. He was stronger, he could hit harder. Lundgard's helmet would break first!

The Humanist retreated, using his wrench like a sword, stopping the force of blows without trying to deal more of his own. His left hand fumbled at his side. Bo hardly noticed. He was pushing in, hewing, hewing. Again the shrunken sun rose, to flash hard light off his club.

Lundgard grinned, his face barely visible as highlight and shadow behind the plastic. His raised tool turned one hit, it slipped along his arm, to rap his flank. Bo twisted his arm around, beat the other wrench aside for a moment, and landed a crack like a thunderbolt.

Then Lundgard had his drinking hose free, pointing in his left hand. He thumbed down the clamp, exposing water at fifty degrees to naked space.

It rushed forth, driven by its own vapor pressure, a stream like a lance in the wan sunshine. When it hit Bo's helmet, most of it boiled off…cooling the rest, which froze instantly.

Blindness clamped down on Bo. He leaped away, cursing, the front of his helmet so frosted he could not see before him. Lundgard bounced around, playing the hose on him. Through the rime-coat, Bo could make out only a grayness.

He pawed at it, trying to wipe it off, knowing that Lundgard was using this captured minute to look for the rifle. As he got some of the ice loose, he heard a sharp yell of victory—found!

Turning, he ran again.

Over that ridge! Down on your belly! A slug pocked the stone above him. Rolling over, he got to his feet and bounded off toward a steep rise, still wiping blindness off his helmet. But he could not wipe the bitter vomit taste of defeat out of his mouth.

His breathing was a file that raked in his throat. Heart and lungs were ready to tear loose, and there was a cold knot in his guts. Fleeing up the high, ragged slope, he sobbed out his rage at himself and his own stupidity.

At the top of the hill he threw himself to the ground and looked down again over a low wall of basalt. It was hard to see if anything moved down in that valley of night. Then the sun threw a broken gleam off polished metal, the rifle barrel, and he saw Einar Lundgard walking around, looking for him.

The voice came dim in his earphones. "Why don't you give up, Bo? I tell you, I don't want to kill you."

"Yeh." Bo panted wearily. "I'm sure."

"Well, you can never tell," said Lundgard mildly. "It would be rather a nuisance to have to keep not only the fair Valeria, but you, tied up all the way to base. Still, if you'll surrender by the time I've counted ten—"

"Look here," said Bo desperately. "I've got half the links. If you don't give up I'll hammer 'em all flat, and let you starve."

"And Valeria?" The voice jeered at him. He knew his secret was read. "I shouldn't have let you bluff me in the first place. It won't happen a second time. All right: one, two, three—"

Bo could get off this asteroid with no more than the power of his own legs; a few jets from the emergency blow valve at the bottom of an air tank would correct his flight as needed to bring him back to the *Sirius*. He wanted to get up there, and inside warm walls, and take Valeria in his hands and never let her go again. He wanted to live.

"—six, seven, eight—"

He looked at his gauges. A lot of oxyhelium mixture was gone from the tanks, but they were big and there was still several atmospheres' pressure in each. A couple of hours life. If he didn't exert himself too much. They screwed directly into valves in the back of his armor, and—

"—ten. All right, Bo." Lundgard started moving up the slope, light and graceful as a bird. It was wide and open, no place to hide and sneak up behind him.

Figures reeled through Bo's mind, senselessly. Mass of the asteroid, effective radius, escape velocity only a few feet per second, and he was already on one of the highest points. *Brains!* he thought with a shattering sorrow. *A lot of good mine have done me!*

He prepared to back down the other side of the hill, run as well as he could, as long as he could, until a bullet splashed his blood or suffocation thickened it. *But I want to fight!* he thought through a gulp of tears. *I want to stand up and fight!*

Orbital velocity equals escape velocity divided by the square root of two.

For a moment he lay there, rigid, and his eyes stared at death walking up the slope but did not see it.

Then, in a crazy blur of motion, he brought his wrench around, closed it on a nut at one side, and turned.

The right hand air tank unscrewed easily. He held it in his hands, a three foot cylinder, blind while calculation raced through his head. What would the centrifugal and Coriolis forces be? It was the roughest sort of estimate. He had neither time nor data, but—

Lundgard was taking it easy, stopping to examine each patch of shadow thrown by some gaunt crag, each meteor scar where a man might hide. It would take him several minutes to reach the hilltop.

Bo clutched the loosened tank in his arms, throwing one leg around it to make sure, and faced away from Lundgard. He hefted himself, as if his body were a machine he must use. Then, carefully, he jumped off the top of the hill.

It was birdlike, dreamlike, thus to soar noiseless over iron desolation. Then sun fell behind him. A spearhead pinnacle clawed after his feet. The Southern Cross flamed in his eyes.

Downward—get rid of that downward component of velocity. He twisted the tank, pointing it toward the surface, and cautiously opened the blow valve with his free hand. Only a moment's exhaust, everything gauged by eye. Did he have an orbit now?

The ground dropped sharply off to infinity, and he saw stars under the keel of the world. He was still going out, away. Maybe he had miscalculated his jump, exceeded escape velocity after all, and was headed for a long cold spin toward Jupiter. It would take all his compressed air to correct such a mistake.

Sweat prickled in his armpits. He locked his teeth and refused to open the valve again.

It was like endless falling, but he couldn't yet be sure if the fall was toward the asteroid or the stars. The rock spun past him. Another face came into view. Yes, by all idiot gods, its gravity was pulling him around!

He skimmed low over the bleakness of it, seeing darkness and starlit death sliding beneath him. Another crag loomed suddenly in his path, and he wondered in a harsh clutch of fear if he was going to crash. Then it ghosted by, a foot from his flying body. He thought he could almost sense the chill of it.

He was a moon now, a satellite skimming low above the airless surface of his own midget world. The fracture plain where Lundgard had shot at him went by, and he braced himself. Up around the tiny planet, and there was the hill he had left, stark against Sagittarius. He saw Lundgard, standing on its heights and looking the way he had gone. Carefully, he aimed the tank and gave himself another small blast to correct his path. There was no noise to betray him, the asteroid was a grave where all sound was long buried and frozen.

He flattened, holding his body parallel to the tank in his arms. One hand still gripped the wrench, the other reached to open the blow valve wide.

The surge almost tore him loose. He had a careening lunatic moment of flight in which the roar of escaping gas boiled through his armor and he clung like a troll to a runaway witch's broom. The sun was blinding on one side of him.

He struck Lundgard with an impact of velocity and inertia which sent him spinning down the hill. Bo hit the ground, recoiled, and sprang after his enemy. Lundgard was still rolling. As Bo approached, he came to a halt, lifted his rifle dazedly, and had it knocked loose with a single blow of the wrench.

Lundgard crawled to his feet while Bo picked up the rifle and threw it off the asteroid. "Why did you do that?"

"I don't know," said Bo. "I should just shoot you down, but I want you to surrender."

Lundgard drew his wrench. "No," he said.

"All right," said Bo. "It won't take long."

When he got up to the *Sirius,* using a tank Lundgard would never need, Valeria had armed herself with a kitchen knife. "It wouldn't have done much good," he said when he came through the airlock. She fell into his arms, sobbing, and he tried to comfort her. "It's all over. All taken care of. We can go home now."

He himself was badly in need of consolation. The inquiry on Earth would clear him, of course, but he would always have to live with the memory of a man stretched dead under a wintery sky. He went aft and replaced the links. When he came back, Valeria had recovered herself, but as she watched his methodical preparations and listened to what he had to tell, there was that in her eyes which he hardly dared believe.

Not him. Not a big dumb slob like him.

GOAT SONG

Three women: one is dead; one is alive; One is both and neither, and will never live and never die, being immortal in SUM.

On a hill above that valley through which runs the highroad, I await Her passage. Frost came early this year, and the grasses have paled. Otherwise the slope is begrown with blackberry bushes that have been harvested by men and birds, leaving only briars, and with certain apple trees. They are very old, those trees, survivors of an orchard raised by generations which none but SUM now remembers (I can see a few fragments of wall thrusting above the brambles)— scattered crazily over the hillside and as crazily gnarled. A little fruit remains on them. Chill across my skin, a gust shakes loose an apple. I hear it knock on the earth, another stroke of some eternal clock. The shrubs whisper to the wind.

Elsewhere the ridges around me are wooded, afire with scarlets and brasses and bronzes. The sky is huge, the westering sun wan-bright. The valley is filling with a deeper blue, a haze whose slight smokiness touches my nostrils. This is Indian summer, the funeral pyre of the year.

There have been other seasons. There have been other lifetimes, before mine and hers; and in those days they had words to sing with. We still allow ourselves music, though, and I have spent much time planting melodies around my rediscovered words. *"In the greenest growth of the Maytime—"* I unsling the harp on my back, and tune it afresh, and sing to her, straight into autumn and the waning day.

> *—You came, and the sun came after,*
> *And the green grew golden above:*
> *And the flag-flowers lightened with laughter,*
> *And the meadowsweet shook with love.*

A footfall stirs the grasses, quite gently, and the woman says, trying to chuckle, "Why, thank you."

Once, so soon after my one's death that I was still dazed by it, I stood in the home that had been ours. This was on the hundred and first floor of a most desirable building. After dark the city flamed for us, blinked, glittered, flung immense sheets of radiance forth like banners. Nothing but SUM could have controlled the firefly dance of a million aircars among the towers: or, for that matter, have

maintained the entire city, from nuclear powerplants through automated factories, physical and economic distribution networks, sanitation, repair, services,
education, culture, order, everything as one immune immortal organism. We had
gloried in belonging to this as well as to each other.

But that night I told the kitchen to throw the dinner it had made for me down
the waste chute, and ground under my heel the chemical consolations which the
medicine cabinet extended to me, and kicked the cleaner as it picked up the mess,
and ordered the lights not to go on, anywhere in our suite. I stood by the viewall,
looking out across megalopolis, and it was tawdry. In my hands I had a little clay
figure she had fashioned herself. I turned it over and over and over.

But I had forgotten to forbid the door to admit visitors. It recognized this
woman and opened for her. She had come with the kindly intention of teasing
me out of a mood that seemed to her unnatural. I heard her enter, and looked
around through the gloom. She had almost the same height as my girl did, and
her hair chanced to be bound in a way that my girl often favored, and the figurine
dropped from my grasp and shattered, because for an instant I thought she was
my girl. Since then I have been hard put not to hate Thrakia.

This evening, even without so much sundown light, I would not make that
mistake. Nothing but the silvery bracelet about her left wrist bespeaks the past we
share. She is in wildcountry garb: boots, kilt of true fur and belt of true leather,
knife at hip and rifle slung on shoulder. Her locks are matted and snarled, her
skin brown from weeks of weather; scratches and smudges show beneath the
fantastic zigzags she has painted in many colors on herself. She wears a necklace
of bird skulls.

Now that one who is dead was, in her own way, more a child of trees and horizons than Thrakia's followers. She was so much at home in the open that she had
no need to put off clothes or cleanliness, reason or gentleness, when we sickened
of the cities and went forth beyond them. From this trait I got many of the names
I bestowed on her, such as Wood's Colt or Fallow Hind or, from my prowlings
among ancient books, Dryad and Elven. (She liked me to choose her names, and
this pleasure had no end, because she was inexhaustible.)

I let my harpstring ring into silence. Turning about, I say to Thrakia, "I wasn't
singing for you. Not for anyone. Leave me alone."

She draws a breath. The wind ruffles her hair and brings me an odor of her:
not female sweetness, but fear. She clenches her fists and says, "You're crazy."

"Wherever did you find a meaningful word like that?" I gibe; for my own pain
and—to be truthful—my own fear must strike out at something, and here she
stands. "Aren't you content any longer with 'untranquil' or 'disequilibrated'?"

"I got it from you," she says defiantly, "you and your damned archaic songs.
There's another word, 'damned.' And how it suits you! When are you going to
stop this morbidity?"

"And commit myself to a clinic and have my brain laundered nice and sani-
tary? Not soon, darling." I use *that* last word aforethought, but she cannot know
what scorn and sadness are in it for me, who know that once it could also have
been a name for my girl. The official grammar and pronunciation of language is

as frozen as every other aspect of our civilization, thanks to electronic recording and neuronic teaching; but meanings shift and glide about like subtle serpents. (O adder that stung my Foalfoot!)

I shrug and say in my driest, most city-technological voice, "Actually, I'm the practical, nonmorbid one. Instead of running away from my emotions—via drugs, or neuroadjustment, or playing at savagery like you, for that matter—I'm about to implement a concrete plan for getting back the person who made me happy."

"By disturbing Her on Her way home?"

"Anyone has the right to petition the Dark Queen while She's abroad on earth."

"But this is past the proper time—"

"No law's involved, just custom. People are afraid to meet Her outside a crowd, a town, bright flat lights. They won't admit it, but they are. So I came here precisely not to be part of a queue. I don't want to speak into a recorder for subsequent computer analysis of my words. How could I be sure She was listening? I want to meet Her as myself, a unique being, and look in Her eyes while I make my prayer."

Thrakia chokes a little. "She'll be angry."

"Is She able to be angry, anymore?"

"I...I don't know. What you mean to ask for is so impossible, though. So absurd. That SUM should give you back your girl. You know It never makes exceptions."

"Isn't She Herself an exception?"

"That's different. You're being silly. SUM has to have a, well, a direct human liaison. Emotional and cultural feedback, as well as statistics. How else can It govern rationally? And She must have been chosen out of the whole world. Your girl, what was she? Nobody!"

"To me, she was everybody."

"You—" Thrakia catches her lip in her teeth. One hand reaches out and closes on my bare forearm, a hard hot touch, the grimy fingernails biting. When I make no response, she lets go and stares at the ground. A V of outbound geese passes overhead. Their cries come shrill through the wind, which is loudening in the forest.

"Well," she says "you are special. You always were. You went to space and came back, with the Great Captain. You're maybe the only man alive who understands about the ancients. And your singing, yes, you don't really entertain, your songs trouble people and can't be forgotten. So maybe She will listen to you. But SUM won't. It can't give special resurrections. Once that was done, a single time, wouldn't it have to be done for everybody? The dead would overrun the living."

"Not necessarily," I say. "In any event, I mean to try."

"Why can't you wait for the promised time? Surely, then, SUM will recreate you two in the same generation."

"I'd have to live out this life, at least, without her," I say, looking away also, down to the highroad which shines through shadow like death's snake, the length of the valley. "Besides, how do you know there ever will be any resurrections? We have only a promise. No, less than that. An announced policy."

She gasps, steps back, raises her hands as if to fend me off. Her soul bracelet casts light into my eyes. I recognize an embryo exorcism. She lacks ritual; every "superstition" was patiently scrubbed out of our metal-and-energy world, long ago. But if she has no word for it, no concept, nevertheless she recoils from blasphemy.

So I say, wearily, not wanting an argument, wanting only to wait here alone: "Never mind. There could be some natural catastrophe, like a giant asteroid striking, that wiped out the system before conditions had become right for resurrections to commence."

"That's impossible," she says, almost frantic. "The homeostats, the repair functions—"

"All right, call it a vanishingly unlikely theoretical contingency. Let's declare that I'm so selfish I want Swallow Wing back now, in this life of mine, and don't give a curse whether that'll be fair to the rest of you."

You won't care either, anyway, I think. None of you. You don't grieve. It is your own precious private consciousnesses that you wish to preserve; no one else is close enough to you to matter very much. Would you believe me if I told you I am quite prepared to offer SUM my own death in exchange for It releasing Blossom-in-the-Sun?

I don't speak that thought, which would be cruel, nor repeat what is crueller: my fear that SUM lies, that the dead never will be disgorged. For (I am not the All-Controller, I think not with vacuum and negative energy levels but with ordinary earth-begotten molecules; yet I can reason somewhat dispassionately, being disillusioned) consider—

The object of the game is to maintain a society stable, just, and sane. This requires satisfaction not only of somatic, but of symbolic and instinctual needs. Thus children must be allowed to come into being. The minimum number per generation is equal to the maximum: that number which will maintain a constant population.

It is also desirable to remove the fear of death from men. Hence the promise: At such time as it is socially feasible, SUM will begin to refashion us, with our complete memories but in the pride of our youth. This can be done over and over, life after life across the millennia. So death is, indeed, a sleep.

—in that sleep of death, what dreams may come—No. I myself dare not dwell on this. I ask merely, privately: Just when and how does SUM expect conditions (in a stabilized society, mind you) to have become so different from today's that the reborn can, in their millions, safely be welcomed back?

I see no reason why SUM should not lie to us. We, too, are objects in the world that It manipulates.

"We've quarreled about this before, Thrakia," I sigh. "Often. Why do you bother?"

"I wish I knew," she answers low. Half to herself, she goes on: "Of course I want to copulate with you. You must be good, the way that girl used to follow you about with her eyes, and smile when she touched your hand, and—But you can't be better than everyone else. That's unreasonable. There are only so many possible ways. So why do I care if you wrap yourself up in silence and go off alone? Is it that that makes you a challenge?"

"You think too much," I say. "Even here. You're a pretend primitive. You visit wildcountry to 'slake inborn atavistic impulses'…but you can't dismantle that computer inside yourself and simply feel, simply be."

She bristles. I touched a nerve there. Looking past her, along the ridge of fiery maple and sumac, brassy elm and great dun oak, I see others emerge from beneath the trees. Women exclusively, her followers, as unkempt as she; one has a brace of ducks lashed to her waist, and their blood has trickled down her thigh and dried black. For this movement, this unadmitted mystique has become Thrakia's by now: that not only men should forsake the easy routine and the easy pleasure of the cities, and become again, for a few weeks each year, the carnivores who begot our species; women too should seek out starkness, the better to appreciate civilization when they return.

I feel a moment's unease. We are in no park, with laid-out trails and campground services. We are in wildcountry. Not many men come here, ever, and still fewer women; for the region is, literally, beyond the law. No deed done here is punishable. We are told that this helps consolidate society, as the most violent among us may thus vent their passions. But I have spent much time in wildcountry since my Morning Star went out—myself in quest of nothing but solitude—and I have watched what happens through eyes that have also read anthropology and history. Institutions are developing; ceremonies, tribalisms, acts of blood and cruelty and acts elsewhere called unnatural are becoming more elaborate and more expected every year. Then the practitioners go home to their cities and honestly believe they have been enjoying fresh air, exercise, and good tension-releasing fun.

Let her get angry enough and Thrakia can call knives to her aid. Wherefore I make myself lay both hands on her shoulders, and meet the tormented gaze, and say most gently, "I'm sorry. I know you mean well. You're afraid She will be annoyed and bring misfortune on your people."

Thrakia gulps. "No," she whispers. "That wouldn't be logical. But I'm afraid of what might happen to you. And then—" Suddenly she throws herself against me. I feel arms, breasts, belly press through my tunic, and smell meadows in her hair and musk in her mouth. "You'd be gone!" she wails. "Then who'd sing to us?"

"Why, the planet's crawling with entertainers," I stammer.

"You're more than that," she says. "So much more. I don't like what you sing, not really—and what you've sung since that stupid girl died, oh, meaningless, horrible!—but, I don't know why, I *want* you to trouble me."

Awkward, I pat her back. The sun now stands very little above the treetops.

Its rays slant interminably through the booming, frosting air. I shiver in my tunic and buskins and wonder what to do.

A sound rescues me. It comes from one end of the valley below us, where further view is blocked off by two cliffs; it thunders deep in our ears and rolls through the earth into our bones. We have heard that sound in the cities, and been glad to have walls and lights and multitudes around us. Now we are alone with it, the noise of Her chariot.

The women shriek, I hear them faintly across wind and rumble and my own pulse, and they vanish into the woods. They will seek their camp, dress warmly, build enormous fires; presently they will eat their ecstatics, and rumors are uneasy about what they do after that.

Thrakia seizes my left wrist, above the soul bracelet, and hauls. "Harper, come with me!" she pleads. I break loose from her and stride down the hill toward the road. A scream follows me for a moment.

Light still dwells in the sky and on the ridges, but as I descend into that narrow valley I enter dusk, and it thickens. Indistinct bramblebushes whicker where I brush them, and claw back at me. I feel the occasional scratch on my legs, the tug as my garment is snagged, the chill that I breathe, but dimly. My perceived-outer-reality is overpowered by the rushing of Her chariot and my blood. My inner-universe is fear, yes, but exaltation too, a drunkenness which sharpens instead of dulling the senses, a psychedelia which opens the reasoning mind as well as the emotions; I have gone beyond myself, I am embodied purpose. Not out of need for comfort, but to voice what Is, I return to words whose speaker rests centuries dust, and lend them my own music. I sing:

> —*Gold is my heart, and the world's golden,*
> *And one peak tipped with light;*
> *And the air lies still about the hill*
> *With the first fear of night;*
>
> *Till mystery down the soundless valley*
> *Thunders, and dark is here;*
> *And the wind blows, and the light goes,*
> *And the night is full of fear.*
>
> *And I know one night, on some far height,*
> *In the tongue I never knew,*
> *I yet shall hear the tidings clear*
> *From them that were friends of you.*
>
> *They'll call the news from hill to hill,*
> *Dark and uncomforted,*
> *Earth and sky and the winds; and I*
> *Shall know that you are dead.—*

But I have reached the valley floor, and She has come in sight.

Her chariot is unlit, for radar eyes and inertial guides need no lamps, nor sun nor stars. Wheel-less, the steel tear rides on its own roar and thrust of air. The pace is not great, far less than any of our mortals' vehicles are wont to take. Men say the Dark Queen rides thus slowly in order that She may perceive with Her own senses and so be the better prepared to counsel SUM. But now Her annual round is finished; She is homeward bound; until spring She will dwell with It which is our lord. Why does She not hasten tonight?

Because Death has never a need of haste? I wonder. And as I step into the middle of the road, certain lines from the yet more ancient past rise tremendous within me, and I strike my harp and chant them louder than the approaching car:

> *I that in heill was and gladness*
> *Am trublit now with great sickness*
> *And feblit with infirmitie:—*
> Timor mortis conturbat me.

The car detects me and howls a warning. I hold my ground. The car could swing around, the road is wide and in any event a smooth surface is not absolutely necessary. But I hope, I believe that She will be aware of an obstacle in Her path, and tune in Her various amplifiers, and find me abnormal enough to stop for. Who, in SUM's world—who, even among the explorers that It has sent beyond in Its unappeasable hunger for data—would stand in a cold wildcountry dusk and shout while his harp snarls

> *Our pleasance here is all vain glory,*
> *This fals world is but transitory,*
> *The flesh is bruckle, the Feynd is slee:—*
> Timor mortis conturbat me.

> *The state of man does change and vary,*
> *Now sound, now sick, now blyth, now sary,*
> *Now dansand mirry, now like to die:—*
> Timor mortis conturbat me.

> *No state in Erd here standis sicker;*
> *As with the wynd wavis the wicker*
> *So wannis this world's vanitie:—*
> Timor mortis conturbat me.—?

The car draws alongside and sinks to the ground. I let my strings die away into the wind. The sky overhead and in the west is gray-purple; eastward it is quite dark and a few early stars peer forth. Here, down in the valley, shadows are heavy and I cannot see very well.

The canopy slides back. She stands erect in the chariot, thus looming over me. Her robe and cloak are black, fluttering like restless wings; beneath the cowl Her face is a white blur. I have seen it before, under full light, and in how many thousands of pictures; but at this hour I cannot call it back to my mind, not entirely. I list sharp-sculptured profile and pale lips, sable hair and long green eyes, but these are nothing more than words.

"What are you doing?" She has a lovely low voice; but is it, as oh, how rarely since SUM took Her to Itself, is it the least shaken? "What is that you were singing?"

My answer comes so strong that my skull resonates; for I am borne higher and higher on my tide. "Lady of Ours, I have a petition."

"Why did you not bring it before Me when I walked among men? Tonight I am homebound. You must wait till I ride forth with the new year."

"Lady of Ours, neither You nor I would wish living ears to hear what I have to say."

She regards me for a long while. Do I indeed sense fear also in Her? (Surely not of me. Her chariot is armed and armored, and would react with machine speed to protect Her should I offer violence. And should I somehow, incredibly, kill Her, or wound Her beyond chemosurgical repair, She of all beings has no need to doubt death. The ordinary bracelet cries with quite sufficient radio loudness to be heard by more than one thanatic station, when we die; and in that shielding the soul can scarcely be damaged before the Winged Heels arrive to bear it off to SUM. Surely the Dark Queen's circlet can call still further, and is still better insulated, than any mortal's. And She will most absolutely be re-created. She has been, again and again; death and rebirth every seven years keep Her eternally young in the service of SUM. I have never been able to find out when She was first born.)

Fear, perhaps, of what I have sung and what I might speak?

At last She says—I can scarcely hear through the gusts and creakings in the trees—"Give me the Ring, then."

The dwarf robot which stands by Her throne when She sits among men appears beside Her and extends the massive dull-silver circle to me. I place my left arm within, so that my soul is enclosed. The tablet on the upper surface of the Ring, which looks so much like a jewel, slants away from me; I cannot read what flashes onto the bezel. But the faint glow picks Her features out of murk as She bends to look.

Of course, I tell myself, the actual soul is not scanned. That would take too long. Probably the bracelet which contains the soul has an identification code built in. The Ring sends this to an appropriate part of SUM, Which instantly sends back what is recorded under that code. I hope there is nothing more to it. SUM has not seen fit to tell us.

"What do you call yourself at the moment?" She asks.

A current of bitterness crosses my tide. "Lady of Ours, why should You care? Is not my real name the number I got when I was allowed to be born?"

Calm descends once more upon Her. "If I am to evaluate properly what you say, I must know more about you than these few official data. Name indicates mood."

I too feel unshaken again, my tide running so strong and smooth that I might not know I was moving did I not see time recede behind me. "Lady of Ours, I cannot give You a fair answer. In this past year I have not troubled with names, or with much of anything else. But some people who knew me from earlier days call me Harper."

"What do you do besides make that sinister music?"

"These days, nothing, Lady of Ours. I've money to live out my life, if I eat sparingly and keep no home. Often I am fed and housed for the sake of my songs."

"What you sang is unlike anything I have heard since—" Anew, briefly, that robot serenity is shaken. "Since before the world was stabilized. You should not wake dead symbols, Harper. They walk through men's dreams."

"Is that bad?"

"Yes. The dreams become nightmares. Remember: Mankind, every man who ever lived, was insane before SUM brought order, reason, and peace."

"Well, then," I say, "I will cease and desist if I may have my own dead wakened for me."

She stiffens. The tablet goes out. I withdraw my arm and the Ring is stored away by Her servant. So again She is faceless, beneath flickering stars, here at the bottom of this shadowed valley. Her voice falls cold as the air: "No one can be brought back to life before Resurrection Time is ripe."

I do not say, "What about You?" for that would be vicious. What did She think, how did She weep, when SUM chose Her of all the young on earth? What does She endure in Her centuries? I dare not imagine.

Instead, I smite my harp and sing, quietly this time:

> *Strew on her roses, roses,*
> *And never a spray of yew.*
> *In quiet she reposes:*
> *Ah! would that I did too.*

The Dark Queen cries, "What are you doing? Are you really insane?" I go straight to the last stanza.

> *Her cabin'd, ample Spirit*
> *It flutter'd and fail'd for breath.*
> *To-night it doth inherit*
> *The vasty hall of Death.*

I know why my songs strike so hard: because they bear dreads and passions that no one is used to—that most of us hardly know could exist—in SUM's ordered universe. But I had not the courage to hope She would be as torn by them as I see. Has She not lived with more darkness and terror than the ancients themselves could conceive? She calls, "Who has died?"

"She had many names, Lady of Ours," I say. "None was beautiful enough. I can tell You her number, though."

"Your daughter? I…sometimes I am asked if a dead child cannot be brought back. Not often, anymore, when they go so soon to the creche. But sometimes. I tell the mother she may have a new one; but if ever We started re-creating dead infants, at what age level could We stop?"

"No, this was my woman."

"Impossible!" Her tone seeks to be not unkindly but is, instead, well-nigh frantic. "You will have no trouble finding others. You are handsome, and your psyche is, is, is extraordinary. It burns like Lucifer."

"Do You remember the name Lucifer, Lady of Ours?" I pounce. "Then You are old indeed. So old that You must also remember how a man might desire only one woman, but her above the whole world and heaven."

She tries to defend Herself with a jeer: "Was that mutual, Harper? I know more of mankind than you do, and surely I am the last chaste woman in existence."

"Now that she is gone, Lady, yes, perhaps You are. But we—Do You know how she died? We had gone to a wildcountry area. A man saw her, alone, while I was off hunting gem rocks to make her a necklace. He approached her. She refused him. He threatened force. She fled. This was desert land, viper land, and she was barefoot. One of them bit her. I did not find her till hours later. By then the poison and the unshaded sun—She died quite soon after she told me what had happened and that she loved me. I could not get her body to chemosurgery in time for normal revival procedures. I had to let them cremate her and take her soul away to SUM."

"What right have you to demand her back, when no one else can be given their own?"

"The right that I love her, and she loves me. We are more necessary to each other than sun or moon. I do not think You could find another two people of whom this is so, Lady. And is not everyone entitled to claim what is necessary to his life? How else can society be kept whole?"

"You are being fantastic," She says thinly. "Let me go."

"No, Lady, I am speaking sober truth. But poor plain words won't serve me. I sing to You because then maybe You will understand." And I strike my harp anew; but it is more to her than Her that I sing.

> *If I had thought thou couldst have died,*
> *I might not weep for thee:*
> *But I forgot, when by thy side,*
> *That thou couldst mortal be:*
> *It never through my mind had past*
> *The time would e'er be o'er,*
> *And I on thee should look my last,*
> *And thou shouldst smile no more!*

"I cannot—" She falters. "I did not know—any such feelings—so strong—existed any longer."

"Now You do, Lady of Ours. And is that not an important datum for SUM?"

"Yes. If true." Abruptly She leans toward me. I see Her shudder in the murk, under the flapping cloak, and hear Her jaws clatter with cold. "I cannot linger here. But ride with Me. Sing to Me. I think I can bear it."

So much have I scarcely expected. But my destiny is upon me. I mount into the chariot. The canopy slides shut and we proceed.

The main cabin encloses us. Bchind its rear door must be facilities for Her living on earth; this is a big vehicle. But here is little except curved panels. They are true wood of different comely grains: so She also needs periodic escape from our machine existence, does She? Furnishing is scant and austere. The only sound is our passage, muffled to a murmur for us; and, because their photomultipliers are not activated, the scanners show nothing outside but night. We huddle close to a glower, hands extended toward its fieriness. Our shoulders brush, our bare arms, Her skin is soft and Her hair falls loose over the thrownback cowl, smelling of the summer which is dead. What, is She still human?

After a timeless time, She says, not yet looking at me: "The thing you sang, there on the highroad as I came near—I do not remember it. Not even from the years before I became what I am."

"It is older than SUM," I answer, "and its truth will outlive It."

"Truth?" I see Her tense Herself. "Sing Me the rest."

My fingers are no longer too numb to call forth chords.

> —*Unto the Death gois all Estatis,*
> *Princis, Prelattis, and Potestatis,*
> *Baith rich and poor of all degree:—*
> Timor mortis conturbat me.
>
> *He takis the knichtis in to the field*
> *Enarmit under helm and scheild;*
> *Victor he is at all mellie:—*
> Timor mortis conturbat me.
>
> *That strong unmerciful tyrand*
> *Takis, on the motheris breast sowkand,*
> *The babe full of benignitie:—*
> Timor mortis conturbat me.
>
> *He takis the campion in the stour,*
> *The captain closit in the tour,*
> *The ladie in bour full of bewtie:—*

(There I must stop a moment.)

> Timor mortis conturbat me.

> *He sparis no lord for his piscence,*
> *Na clerk for his intelligence;*
> *His awful straik may no man flee:—*
> Timor mortis conturbat me.

She breaks me off, clapping hands to ears and half shrieking, "No!"

I, grown unmerciful, pursue Her: "You understand now, do You not? You are not eternal either. SUM isn't. Not Earth, not sun, not stars. We hid from the truth. Everyone of us. I too, until I lost the one thing which made everything make sense. Then I had nothing left to lose, and could look with clear eyes. And what I saw was Death."

"Get out! Let Me alone!"

"I will not let the whole world alone, Queen, until I get her back. Give me her again, and I'll believe in SUM again. I'll praise It till men dance for joy to hear Its name."

She challenges me with wildcat eyes. "Do you think such matters to It?"

"Well," I shrug, "songs could be useful. They could help achieve the great objective sooner. Whatever that is. 'Optimization of total human activity'—wasn't that the program? I don't know if it still is. SUM has been adding to Itself so long. I doubt if You Yourself understand Its purposes, Lady of Ours."

"Don't speak as if It were alive," She says harshly. "It is a computer-effector complex. Nothing more."

"Are You certain?"

"I—yes. It thinks, more widely and deeply than any human ever did or could; but It is not alive, not aware, It has no consciousness. That is one reason why It decided It needed Me."

"Be that as it may, Lady," I tell Her, "the ultimate result, whatever It finally does with us, lies far in the future. At present I care about that; I worry; I resent our loss of self-determination. But that's because only such abstractions are left to me. Give me back my Lightfoot, and she, not the distant future, will be my concern. I'll be grateful, honestly grateful, and You Two will know it from the songs I then choose to sing. Which, as I said, might be helpful to It."

"You are unbelievably insolent," She says without force.

"No, Lady, just desperate," I say.

The ghost of a smile touches Her lips. She leans back, eyes hooded, and murmurs, "Well, I'll take you there. What happens then, you realize, lies outside My power. My observations, My recommendations, are nothing but a few items to take into account, among billions. However…we have a long way to travel this night. Give me what data you think will help you, Harper."

I do not finish the Lament. Nor do I dwell in any other fashion on grief. Instead, as the hours pass, I call upon those who dealt with the joy (not the fun, not the short delirium, but the joy) that man and woman might once have of each other.

Knowing where we are bound, I too need such comfort.

And the night deepens, and the leagues fall behind us, and finally we are beyond habitation, beyond wildcountry, in the land where life never comes. By crooked moon and waning starlight I see the plain of concrete and iron, the missiles and energy projectors crouched like beasts, the robot aircraft wheeling aloft: and the lines, the relay towers, the scuttling beetle-shaped carriers, that whole transcendent nerve-blood-sinew by which SUM knows and orders the world. For all the flitting about, for all the forces which seethe, here is altogether still. The wind itself seems to have frozen to death. Hoarfrost is gray on the steel shapes. Ahead of us, tiered and mountainous, begins to appear the castle of SUM.

She Who rides with me does not give sign of noticing that my songs have died in my throat. What humanness She showed is departing; Her face is cold and shut, Her voice bears a ring of metal. She looks straight ahead. But She does speak to me for a little while yet:

"Do you understand what is going to happen? For the next half year I will be linked with SUM, integral, another component of It. I suppose you will see Me, but that will merely be My flesh. What speaks to you will be SUM."

"I know." The words must be forced forth. My coming this far is more triumph than any man in creation before me has won; and I am here to do battle for my Dancer-on-Moonglades; but nonetheless my heart shakes me, and is loud in my skull, and my sweat stinks.

I manage, though, to add: "You *will* be a part of It, Lady of Ours. That gives me hope."

For an instant She turns to me, and lays Her hand across mine, and something makes Her again so young and untaken that I almost forget the girl who died; and she whispers, "If you knew how I hope!"

The instant is gone, and I am alone among machines.

We must stop before the castle gate. The wall looms sheer above, so high and high that it seems to be toppling upon me against the westward march of the stars, so black and black that it does not only drink down every light, it radiates blindness. Challenge and response quiver on electronic bands I cannot sense. The outer-guardian parts of It have perceived a mortal aboard this craft. A missile launcher swings about to aim its three serpents at me. But the Dark Queen answers—She does not trouble to be peremptory—and the castle opens its jaws for us.

We descend. Once, I think, we cross a river. I hear a rushing and hollow echoing and see droplets glitter where they are cast onto the viewports and outlined against dark. They vanish at once: liquid hydrogen, perhaps, to keep certain parts near absolute zero?

Much later we stop and the canopy slides back. I rise with Her. We are in a room, or cavern, of which I can see nothing, for there is no light except a dull bluish phosphorescence which streams from every solid object, also from Her flesh and mine. But I judge the chamber is enormous, for a sound of great machines at work comes very remotely, as if heard through dream, while our own voices are swallowed up by distance. Air is pumped through, neither warm nor cold, totally without odor, a dead wind.

We descend to the floor. She stands before me, hands crossed on breast, eyes half shut beneath the cowl and not looking at me nor away from me. "Do what you are told, Harper," She says in a voice that has never an overtone, "precisely as you are told." She turns and departs at an even pace. I watch Her go until I can no longer tell Her luminosity from the formless swirlings within my own eyeballs.

A claw plucks my tunic. I look down and am surprised to see that the dwarf robot has been waiting for me this whole time. How long a time that was, I cannot tell.

Its squat form leads me in another direction. Weariness crawls upward through me, my feet stumble, my lips tingle, lids are weighted and muscles have each their separate aches. Now and then I feel a jag of fear, but dully. When the robot indicates *Lie down here,* I am grateful.

The box fits me well. I let various wires be attached to me, various needles be injected which lead into tubes. I pay little attention to the machines which cluster and murmur around me. The robot goes away. I sink into blessed darkness.

I wake renewed in body. A kind of shell seems to have grown between my forebrain and the old animal parts. Far away I can feel the horror and hear the screaming and thrashing of my instincts; but awareness is chill, calm, logical. I have also a feeling that I slept for weeks, months, while leaves blew loose and snow fell on the upper world. But this may be wrong, and in no case does it matter. I am about to be judged by SUM.

The little faceless robot leads me off, through murmurous black corridors where the dead wind blows. I unsling my harp and clutch it to me, my sole friend and weapon. So the tranquility of the reasoning mind which has been decreed for me cannot be absolute. I decide that It simply does not want to be bothered by anguish. (No; wrong; nothing so humanlike; It has no desires; beneath that power to reason is nullity.)

At length a wall opens for us and we enter a room where She sits enthroned. The self-radiation of metal and flesh is not apparent here, for light is provided, a featureless white radiance with no apparent source. White, too, is the muted sound of the machines which encompass Her throne. White are Her robe and face. I look away from the multitudinous unwinking scanner eyes, into Hers, but She does not appear to recognize me. Does She even see me? SUM has reached out with invisible fingers of electromagnetic induction and taken Her back into Itself. I do not tremble or sweat—I cannot—but I square my shoulders, strike one plangent chord, and wait for It to speak.

It does, from some invisible place. I recognize the voice It has chosen to use: my own. The overtones, the inflections are true, normal, what I myself would use in talking as one reasonable man to another. Why not? In computing what to do about me, and in programming Itself accordingly, SUM must have used so many billion bits of information that adequate accent is a negligible sub-problem.

No…there I am mistaken again…SUM does not do things on the basis that It might as well do them as not. This talk with myself is intended to have some effect on me. I do not know what.

"Well," It says pleasantly, "you made quite a journey, didn't you? I'm glad. Welcome."

My instincts bare teeth to hear those words of humanity used by the unfeeling unalive. My logical mind considers replying with an ironic "Thank you," decides against it, and holds me silent.

"You see," SUM continues after a moment that whirrs, "you are unique. Pardon Me if I speak a little bluntly. Your sexual monomania is just one aspect of a generally atavistic, superstition-oriented personality. And yet, unlike the ordinary misfit, you're both strong and realistic enough to cope with the world. This chance to meet you, to analyze you while you rested, has opened new insights for Me on human psychophysiology. Which may lead to improved techniques for governing it and its evolution."

"That being so," I reply, "give me my reward."

"Now look here," SUM says in a mild tone, "you if anyone should know I'm not omnipotent. I was built originally to help govern a civilization grown too complex. Gradually, as My program of self-expansion progressed, I took over more and more decision-making functions. They were *given* to Me. People were happy to be relieved of responsibility, and they could see for themselves how much better I was running things than any mortal could. But to this day, My authority depends on a substantial consensus. If I started playing favorites, as by re-creating your girl, well, I'd have troubles."

"The consensus depends more on awe than on reason," I say. "You haven't abolished the gods, You've simply absorbed them into Yourself. If You choose to pass a miracle for me, your prophet singer—and I will be Your prophet if You do this—why, that strengthens the faith of the rest."

"So you think. But your opinions aren't based on any exact data. The historical and anthropological records from the past before Me are unquantitative. I've already phased them out of the curriculum. Eventually, when the culture's ready for such a move, I'll order them destroyed. They're too misleading. Look what they've done to you."

I grin into the scanner eyes. "Instead," I say, "people will be encouraged to think that before the world was, was SUM. All right. I don't care, as long as I get my girl back. Pass me a miracle, SUM, and I'll guarantee You a good payment."

"But I have no miracles. Not in your sense. You know how the soul works. The metal bracelet encloses a pseudo-virus, a set of giant protein molecules with taps directly to the bloodstream and nervous system. They record the chromosome pattern, the synapse flash, the permanent changes, everything. At the owner's death, the bracelet is dissected out. The Winged Heels bring it here, and the information contained is transferred to one of My memory banks. I can use such a record to guide the growing of a new body in the vats: a young body, on which the former habits and recollections are imprinted. But you don't understand the complexity of the process, Harper. It takes Me weeks, every seven years, and every available biochemical facility, to re-create My human liaison. And the process isn't perfect, either. The pattern is affected by storage. You might say that this body and brain you see before you remembers each death. And those are short deaths. A longer one—man, use your sense. Imagine."

I can; and the shield between reason and feeling begins to crack. I had sung, of my darling dead,

> *No motion has she now, no force;*
> *She neither hears nor sees;*
> *Roll'd round in earth's diurnal course,*
> *With rocks, and stones, and trees.*

Peace, at least. But if the memory-storage is not permanent but circulating; if, within those gloomy caverns of tubes and wire and outerspace cold, some remnant of her psyche must flit and flicker, alone, unremembering, aware of nothing but having lost life—No!

I smite the harp and shout so the room rings: "Give her back! Or I'll kill you!"

SUM finds it expedient to chuckle; and, horribly, the smile is reflected for a moment on the Dark Queen's lips, though otherwise She never stirs. "And how do you propose to do that?" It asks me.

It knows, I know, what I have in mind, so I counter: "How do You propose to stop me?"

"No need. You'll be considered a nuisance. Finally someone will decide you ought to have psychiatric treatment. They'll query My diagnostic outlet. I'll recommend certain excisions."

"On the other hand, since You've sifted my mind by now, and since You know how I've affected people with my songs—even the Lady yonder, even Her— wouldn't you rather have me working for You? With words like, *'O taste, and see, how gracious the Lord is; blessed is the man that trusteth in him. O fear the Lord, ye that are his saints: for they that fear him lack nothing.'* I can make You into God."

"In a sense, I already am God."

"And in another sense not. Not yet." I can endure no more. "Why are we arguing? You made Your decision before I woke. Tell me and let me go!"

With an odd carefulness, SUM responds: "I'm still studying you. No harm in admitting to you, My knowledge of the human psyche is as yet imperfect. Certain areas won't yield to computation. I don't know precisely what you'd do, Harper. If to that uncertainty I added a potentially dangerous precedent—"

"Kill me, then." Let my ghost wander forever with hers, down in Your cryogenic dreams.

"No, that's also inexpedient. You've made yourself too conspicuous and controversial. Too many people know by now that you went off with the Lady." Is it possible that, behind steel and energy, a nonexistent hand brushes across a shadow face in puzzlement? My heartbeat is thick in the silence.

Suddenly It shakes me with decision: "The calculated probabilities do favor your keeping your promises and making yourself useful. Therefore I shall grant your request. However—"

I am on my knees. My forehead knocks on the floor until blood runs into my eyes. I hear through storm winds:

"—testing must continue. Your faith in Me is not absolute; in fact, you're very skeptical of what you call My goodness. Without additional proof of your willingness to trust Me, I can't let you have the kind of importance which your getting your dead back from Me would give you. Do you understand?"

The question does not sound rhetorical. "Yes," I sob.

"Well, then," says my civilized, almost amiable voice, "I computed that you'd react much as you have done, and prepared for the likelihood. Your woman's body was re-created while you lay under study. The data which make personality are now being fed back into her neurones. She'll be ready to leave this place by the time you do.

"I repeat, though, there has to be a testing. The procedure is also necessary for its effect on you. If you're to be My prophet, you'll have to work pretty closely with Me; you'll have to undergo a great deal of reconditioning; this night we begin the process. Are you willing?"

"Yes, yes, yes, what must I do?"

"Only this: Follow the robot out. At some point, she, your woman, will join you. She'll be conditioned to walk so quietly you can't hear her. Don't look back. Not once, until you're in the upper world. A single glance behind you will be an act of rebellion against Me, and a datum indicating you can't really be trusted... and that ends everything. Do you understand?"

"Is that all?" I cry. "Nothing more?"

"It will prove more difficult than you think," SUM tells me. My voice fades, as if into illimitable distances: "Farewell, worshiper."

The robot raises me to my feet. I stretch out my arms to the Dark Queen. Half blinded with tears, I nonetheless see that She does not see me. "Goodbye," I mumble, and let the robot lead me away.

Our walking is long through those mirk miles. At first I am in too much of a turmoil, and later too stunned, to know where or how we are bound. But later still, slowly, I become aware of my flesh and clothes and the robot's alloy, glimmering blue in blackness. Sounds and smells are muffled; rarely does another machine pass by, unheeding of us. (What work does SUM have for them?) I am so careful not to look behind me that my neck grows stiff.

Though it is not prohibited, is it, to lift my harp past my shoulder, in the course of strumming a few melodies to keep up my courage, and see if perchance a following illumination is reflected in this polished wood?

Nothing. Well, her second birth must take time—O SUM, be careful of her!—and then she must be led through many tunnels, no doubt, before she makes rendezvous with my back. Be patient, Harper.

Sing. Welcome her home. No, these hollow spaces swallow all music; and she is as yet in that trance of death from which only the sun and my kiss can wake her; if, indeed, she has joined me yet. I listen for other footfalls than my own.

Surely we haven't much farther to go. I ask the robot, but of course I get no reply. Make an estimate. I know about how fast the chariot traveled coming down…The trouble is, time does not exist here. I have no day, no stars, no clock but my heartbeat and I have lost the count of that. Nevertheless, we must come to the end soon. What purpose would be served by walking me through this labyrinth till I die?

Well, if I am totally exhausted at the outer gate, I won't make undue trouble when I find no Rose-in-Hand behind me.

No, now that's ridiculous. If SUM didn't want to heed my plea, It need merely say so. I have no power to inflict physical damage on Its parts.

Of course, It might have plans for me. It did speak of reconditioning. A series of shocks, culminating in that last one, could make me ready for whatever kind of gelding It intends to do.

Or It might have changed Its mind. Why not? It was quite frank about an uncertainty factor in the human psyche. It may have re-evaluated the probabilities and decided: better not to serve my desire.

Or It may have tried, and failed. It admitted the recording process is imperfect. I must not expect quite the Gladness I knew; she will always be a little haunted. At best. But suppose the tank spawned a body with no awareness behind the eyes? Or a monster? Suppose, at this instant, I am being followed by a half-rotten corpse?

No! Stop that! SUM would know, and take corrective measures. Would It? *Can It?*

I comprehend how this passage through night, where I never look to see what follows me, how this is an act of submission and confession. I am saying, with my whole existent being, that SUM is all-powerful, all-wise, all-good. To SUM I offer the love I came to win back. Oh, It looked more deeply into me than ever I did myself.

But I shall not fail.

Will SUM, though? If there has indeed been some grisly error…let me not find it out under the sky. Let her, my only, not. For what then shall we do? Could I lead her here again, knock on the iron gate, and cry, "Master, You have given me a thing unfit to exist. Destroy it and start over."—? For what might the wrongness be? Something so subtle, so pervasive, that it does not show in any way save my slow, resisted discovery that I embrace a zombie? Doesn't it make better sense to look—make certain while she is yet drowsy with death—use the whole power of SUM to correct what may be awry?

No, SUM wants me to believe that It makes no mistakes. I agreed to that price. And to much else…I don't know how much else, I am daunted to imagine, but that word "recondition" is ugly…Does not my woman have some rights in the matter too? Shall we not at least ask her if she wants to be the wife of a prophet; shall we not, hand in hand, ask SUM what the price of her life is to her?

Was that a footfall? Almost, I whirl about. I check myself and stand shaking; names of hers break from my lips. The robot urges me on.

Imagination. It wasn't her step. I am alone. I will always be alone.

The halls wind upward. Or so I think; I have grown too weary for much kinesthetic sense. We cross the sounding river and I am bitten to the bone by the cold which blows upward around the bridge, and I may not turn about to offer the naked newborn woman my garment. I lurch through endless chambers where machines do meaningless things. She hasn't seen them before. Into what nightmare has she risen; and why don't I, who wept into her dying senses that I loved her, why don't I look at her, why don't I speak?

Well, I could talk to her. I could assure the puzzled mute dead that I have come to lead her back into sunlight. Could I not? I ask the robot. It does not reply. I cannot remember if I may speak to her. If indeed I was ever told. I stumble forward.

I crash into a wall and fall bruised. The robot's claw closes on my shoulder.

Another arm gestures. I see a passageway, very long and narrow, through the stone. I will have to crawl through. At the end, at the end, the door is swinging wide. The dear real dusk of Earth pours through into this darkness. I am blinded and deafened.

Do I hear her cry out? Was that the final testing; or was my own sick, shaken mind betraying me; or is there a destiny which, like SUM with us, makes tools of suns and SUM? I don't know. I know only that I turned, and there she stood. Her hair flowed long, loose, past the remembered face from which the trance was just departing, on which the knowing and the love of me had just awakened—flowed down over the body that reached forth arms, that took one step to meet me and was halted.

The great grim robot at her own back takes her to it. I think it sends lightning through her brain. She falls. It bears her away.

My guide ignores my screaming. Irresistible, it thrusts me out through the tunnel. The door clangs in my face. I stand before the wall which is like a mountain. Dry snow hisses across concrete. The sky is bloody with dawn; stars still gleam in the west, and arc lights are scattered over the twilit plain of the machines.

Presently I go dumb. I become almost calm. What is there left to have feelings about? The door is iron, the wall is stone fused into one basaltic mass. I walk some distance off into the wind, turn around, lower my head, and charge. Let my brains be smeared across Its gate; the pattern will be my hieroglyphic for hatred.

I am seized from behind. The force that stops me must needs be bruisingly great. Released, I crumple to the ground before a machine with talons and wings. My voice from it says, "Not here. I'll carry you to a safe place."

"What more can You do to me?" I croak.

"Release you. You won't be restrained or molested on any orders of Mine."

"Why not?"

"Obviously you're going to appoint yourself My enemy forever. This is an unprecedented situation, a valuable chance to collect data."

"You tell me this, You warn me, deliberately?"

"Of course. My computation is that these words will have the effect of provoking your utmost effort."

"You won't give her again? You don't want my love?"

"Not under the circumstances. Too uncontrollable. But your hatred should, as I say, be a useful experimental tool."

"I'll destroy You," I say.

It does not deign to speak further. Its machine picks me up and flies off with me. I am left on the fringes of a small town farther south. Then I go insane.

I do not much know what happens during that winter, nor care. The blizzards are too loud in my head. I walk the ways of Earth, among lordly towers, under neatly groomed trees, into careful gardens, over bland, bland campuses. I am unwashed, uncombed, unbarbered; my tatters flap about me and my bones are near thrusting through the skin; folk do not like to meet these eyes sunken so far into this skull, and perhaps for that reason they give me to eat. I sing to them.

> *From the hag and hungry goblin*
> *That into rags would rend ye*
> *And the spirit that stan' by the naked man*
> *In the Book of Moons defend ye!*
> *That of your five sound senses*
> *You never be forsaken*
> *Nor travel from yourselves with Tom*
> *Abroad to beg your bacon.*

Such things perturb them, do not belong in their chrome-edged universe. So I am often driven away with curses, and sometimes I must flee those who would arrest me and scrub my brain smooth. An alley is a good hiding place, if I can find one in the oldest part of a city; I crouch there and yowl with the cats. A forest is also good. My pursuers dislike to enter any place where any wildness lingers.

But some feel otherwise. They have visited parklands, preserves, actual wild-country. Their purpose was overconscious—measured, planned savagery, and a clock to tell them when they must go home—but at least they are not afraid of silences and unlighted nights. As spring returns, certain among them begin to follow me. They are merely curious, at first. But slowly, month by month, especially among the younger ones, my madness begins to call to something in them.

> *With an host of furious fancies*
> *Whereof I am commander*
> *With a burning spear, and a horse of air,*
> *To the wilderness I wander.*
> *By a knight of ghosts and shadows*
> *I summoned am to tourney*

Ten leagues beyond the wide world's edge.
Me thinks it is no journey.

They sit at my feet and listen to me sing. They dance, crazily, to my harp. The girls bend close, tell me how I fascinate them, invite me to copulate. This I refuse, and when I tell them why they are puzzled, a little frightened maybe, but often they strive to understand.

For my rationality is renewed with the hawthorn blossoms. I bathe, have my hair and beard shorn, find clean raiment, and take care to eat what my body needs. Less and less do I rave before anyone who will listen; more and more do I seek solitude, quietness, under the vast wheel of the stars, and think.

What is man? Why is man? We have buried such questions; we have sworn they are dead—that they never really existed, being devoid of empirical meaning—and we have dreaded that they might raise the stones we heaped on them, rise and walk the world again of nights. Alone, I summon them to me. They cannot hurt their fellow dead, among whom I now number myself.

I sing to her who is gone. The young people hear and wonder. Sometimes they weep.

Fear no more the heat o' the sun,
Nor the furious winter's rages;
Thou thy worldly task hast done,
Home art gone, and ta' en thy wages:
Golden lads and girls all must
As chimney-sweepers, come to dust.

"But this is not so!" they protest. "We will die and sleep awhile, and then we will live forever in SUM."

I answer as gently as may be: "No. Remember I went there. So I know you are wrong. And even if you were right, it would not be right that you should be right."

"What?"

"Don't you see, it is not right that a thing should be the lord of man. It is not right that we should huddle through our whole lives in fear of finally losing them. You are not parts in a machine, and you have better ends than helping the machine run smoothly."

I dismiss them and stride off, solitary again, into a canyon where a river clangs, or onto some gaunt mountain peak. No revelation is given me. I climb and creep toward the truth.

Which is that SUM must be destroyed, not in revenge, not in hate, not in fear, simply because the human spirit cannot exist in the same reality as It.

But what, then, is our proper reality? And how shall we attain to it?

I return with my songs to the lowlands. Word about me has gone widely. They are a large crowd who follow me down the highroad until it has changed into a street.

"The Dark Queen will soon come to these parts," they tell me. "Abide till She does. Let Her answer those questions you put to us, which make us sleep so badly."

"Let me retire to prepare myself," I say. I go up a long flight of steps. The people watch from below, dumb with awe, till I vanish. Such few as were in the building depart. I walk down vaulted halls, through hushed high-ceilinged rooms full of tables, among shelves made massive by books. Sunlight slants dusty through the windows.

The half memory has plagued me of late: once before, I know not when, this year of mine also took place. Perhaps in this library I can find the tale that—casually, I suppose, in my abnormal childhood—I read. For man is older than SUM: wiser, I swear; his myths hold more truth than Its mathematics. I spend three days and most of three nights in my search. There is scant sound but the rustling of leaves between my hands. Folk place offerings of food and drink at the door. They tell themselves they do so out of pity, or curiosity, or to avoid the nuisance of having me die in an unconventional fashion. But I know better.

At the end of the three days I am little further along. I have too much material; I keep going off on sidetracks of beauty and fascination. (Which SUM means to eliminate.) My education was like everyone else's, science, rationality, good sane adjustment. (SUM writes our curricula, and the teaching machines have direct connections to It.) Well, I can make some of my lopsided training work for me. My reading has given me sufficient clues to prepare a search program. I sit down before an information retrieval console and run my fingers across its keys. They make a clattery music.

Electron beams are swift hounds. Within seconds the screen lights up with words, and I read who I am.

It is fortunate that I am a fast reader. Before I can press the Clear button, the unreeling words are wiped out. For an instant the screen quivers with formlessness, then appears

I HAD NOT CORRELATED THESE DATA WITH THE FACTS CONCERNING YOU. THIS INTRODUCES A NEW AND INDETERMINATE QUANTITY INTO THE COMPUTATIONS.

The nirvana which has come upon me (yes, I found that word among the old books, and how portentous it is) is not passiveness, it is a tide more full and strong than that which bore me down to the Dark Queen those ages apast in wildcountry. I say, as coolly as may be, "An interesting coincidence. If it is a coincidence." Surely sonic receptors are emplaced hereabouts.

EITHER THAT, OR A CERTAIN NECESSARY CONSEQUENCE OF THE LOGIC OF EVENT.

The vision dawning within me is so blinding bright that I cannot refrain from answering, "Or a destiny, SUM?"

MEANINGLESS. MEANINGLESS. MEANINGLESS.

"Now why did You repeat Yourself in that way? Once would have sufficed. Thrice, though, makes an incantation. Are You by any chance hoping Your words will make me stop existing?"

I DO NOT HOPE. YOU ARE AN EXPERIMENT. IF I COMPUTE A SIGNIFICANT PROBABILITY OF YOUR CAUSING SERIOUS DISTURBANCE, I WILL HAVE YOU TERMINATED.

I smile. "SUM," I say, "I am going to terminate You." I lean over and switch off the screen. I walk out into the evening.

Not everything is clear to me yet, that I must say and do. But enough is that I can start preaching at once to those who have been waiting for me. As I talk, others come down the street, and hear, and stay to listen. Soon they number in the hundreds.

I have no immense new truth to offer them: nothing that I have not said before, although piecemeal and unsystematically; nothing they have not felt themselves, in the innermost darknesses of their beings. Today, however, knowing who I am and therefore why I am, I can put these things in words. Speaking quietly, now and then drawing on some forgotten song to show my meaning, I tell them how sick and starved their lives are; how they have made themselves slaves; how the enslavement is not even to a conscious mind, but to an insensate inanimate thing which their own ancestors began; how that thing is not the centrum of existence, but a few scraps of metal and bleats of energy, a few sad stupid patterns, adrift in unbounded space—time. Put not your faith in SUM, I tell them. SUM is doomed, even as you and I. Seek out mystery; what else is the whole cosmos but mystery? Live bravely, die and be done, and you will be more than any machine. You may perhaps be God.

They grow tumultuous. They shout replies, some of which are animal howls. A few are for me, most are opposed. That doesn't matter. I have reached into them, my music is being played on their nerve-strings, and this is my entire purpose.

The sun goes down behind the buildings. Dusk gathers. The city remains unilluminated. I soon realize why. She is coming, the Dark Queen Whom they wanted me to debate with. From afar we hear Her chariot thunder. Folk wail in terror. They are not wont to do that either. They used to disguise their feelings from Her and themselves by receiving Her with grave sparse ceremony. Now they would flee if they dared. I have lifted the masks.

The chariot halts in the street. She dismounts, tall and shadowy cowled. The people make way before Her like water before a shark. She climbs the stairs to face me. I see for the least instant that Her lips are not quite firm and Her eyes abrim with tears. She whispers, too low for anyone else to hear, "Oh, Harper, I'm sorry."

"Come join me," I invite. "Help me set the world free."

"No. I cannot. I have been too long with It." She straightens. Imperium descends upon Her. Her voice rises for everyone to hear. The little television robots flit close, bat shapes in the twilight, that the whole planet may witness my defeat. "What is this freedom you rant about?" She demands.

"To feel," I say. "To venture. To wonder. To become men again."

"To become beasts, you mean. Would you demolish the machines that keep us alive?"

"Yes. We must. Once they were good and useful, but we let them grow upon us like a cancer, and now nothing but destruction and a new beginning can save us."

"Have you considered the chaos?"

"Yes. It too is necessary. We will not be men without the freedom to know suffering. In it is also enlightenment. Through it we travel beyond ourselves, beyond earth and stars, space and time, to Mystery."

"So you maintain that there is some undefined ultimate vagueness behind the measurable universe?" She smiles into the bat eyes. We have each been taught, as children, to laugh on hearing sarcasms of this kind. "Please offer me a little proof."

"No," I say. "Prove to me instead, beyond any doubt, that there is *not* something we cannot understand with words and equations. Prove to me likewise that I have no right to seek for it."

"The burden of proof is on You Two, so often have You lied to us. In the name of rationality, You resurrected myth. The better to control us! In the name of liberation, You chained our inner lives and castrated our souls. In the name of service, You bound and blinkered us. In the name of achievement, You held us to a narrower round than any swine in its pen. In the name of beneficence, You created pain, and horror, and darkness beyond darkness." I turn to the people. "I went there. I descended into the cellars. I know!"

"He found that SUM would not pander to his special wishes, at the expense of everyone else," cries the Dark Queen. Do I hear shrillness in Her voice? "Therefore he claims SUM is cruel."

"I saw my dead," I tell them. "She will not rise again. Nor yours, nor you. Not ever. SUM will not, cannot raise us. In Its house is death indeed. We must seek life and rebirth elsewhere, among the mysteries."

She laughs aloud and points to my soul bracelet, glimmering faintly in the gray-blue thickening twilight. Need She say anything?

"Will someone give me a knife and an ax?" I ask.

The crowd stirs and mumbles. I smell their fear. Streetlamps go on, as if they could scatter more than this corner of the night which is rolling upon us. I fold my arms and wait. The Dark Queen says something to me. I ignore Her.

The tools pass from hand to hand. He who brings them up the stairs comes like a flame. He kneels at my feet and lifts what I have desired. The tools are good ones, a broad-bladed hunting knife and a long double-bitted ax.

Before the world, I take the knife in my right hand and slash beneath the bracelet on my left wrist. The connections to my inner body are cut. Blood flows, impossibly brilliant under the lamps. It does not hurt; I am too exalted.

The Dark Queen shrieks. "You meant it! Harper, Harper!"

"There is no life in SUM," I say. I pull my hand through the circle and cast the bracelet down so it rings.

A voice of brass: *"Arrest that maniac for correction. He is deadly dangerous."*

The monitors who have stood on the fringes of the crowd try to push through. They are resisted. Those who seek to help them encounter fists and fingernails.

I take the ax and smash downward. The bracelet crumples. The organic material within, starved of my secretions, exposed to the night air, withers.

I raise the tools, ax in right hand, knife in bleeding left. "I seek eternity where it is to be found," I call. "Who goes with me?"

A score or better break loose from the riot, which is already calling forth weapons and claiming lives. They surround me with their bodies. Their eyes are the eyes of prophets. We make haste to seek a hiding place, for one military robot has appeared and others will not be long in coming. The tall engine strides to stand guard over Our Lady, and this is my last glimpse of Her.

My followers do not reproach me for having cost them all they were. They are mine. In me is the godhead which can do no wrong.

And the war is open, between me and SUM. My friends are few, my enemies many and mighty. I go about the world as a fugitive. But always I sing. And always I find someone who will listen, will join us, embracing pain and death like a lover.

With the Knife and the Ax I take their souls. Afterward we hold for them the ritual of rebirth. Some go thence to become outlaw missionaries; most put on facsimile bracelets and return home, to whisper my word. It makes little difference to me. I have no haste, who own eternity.

For my word is of what lies beyond time. My enemies say I call forth ancient bestialities and lunacies; that I would bring civilization down in ruin; that it matters not a madman's giggle to me whether war, famine, and pestilence will again scour the earth. With these accusations I am satisfied. The language of them shows me that here, too, I have reawakened anger. And that emotion belongs to us as much as any other. More than the others, maybe, in this autumn of mankind. We need a gale, to strike down SUM and everything It stands for. Afterward will come the winter of barbarism.

And after that the springtime of a new and (perhaps) more human civilization. My friends seem to believe this will come in their very lifetimes: peace, brotherhood, enlightenment, sanctity. I know otherwise. I have been in the depths. The wholeness of mankind, which I am bringing back, has its horrors.

> *When one day*
> *the Eater of the Gods returns*
> *the Wolf breaks his chain*
> *the Horsemen ride forth*
> *the Age ends*
> *the Beast is reborn*

then SUM will be destroyed; and you, strong and fair, may go back to earth and rain.

I shall await you.

My aloneness is nearly ended, Daybright. Just one task remains. The god must die, that his followers may believe he is raised from the dead and lives forever. Then they will go on to conquer the world.

There are those who say I have spurned and offended them. They too, borne on the tide which I raised, have torn out their machine souls and seek in music and ecstasy to find a meaning for existence. But their creed is a savage one, which has taken them into wildcountry, where they ambush the monitors sent against them and practice cruel rites. They believe that the final reality is female. Nevertheless, messengers of theirs have approached me with the suggestion of a mystic marriage. This I refused; my wedding was long ago, and will be celebrated again when this cycle of the world has closed.

Therefore they hate me. But I have said I will come and talk to them.

I leave the road at the bottom of the valley and walk singing up the hill. Those few I let come this far with me have been told to abide my return. They shiver in the sunset; the vernal equinox is three days away. I feel no cold myself. I stride exultant among briars and twisted ancient apple trees. If my bare feet leave a little blood in the snow, that is good. The ridges around are dark with forest, which waits like the skeleton dead for leaves to be breathed across it again. The eastern sky is purple, where stands the evening star. Overhead, against blue, cruises an early flight of homebound geese. Their calls drift faintly down to me. Westward, above me and before me, smolders redness. Etched black against it are the women.

THE BARRIER MOMENT

When he heard the footsteps, Cohen turned on his heel and growled, "Now what the devil is it?" The jaggedness of the movement and of his voice told him how thin his nerves were worn.

A guard in the door saluted. "I was told to escort this gentleman to see you, colonel. Being as how the project is so near, uh, well, the next phase, sir, General Sanchez thought he'd better see you right away."

He stood aside. Cohen laid down the voltmeter he had been about to plug into a testing circuit. He was a large blond man, still fairly young, who had played football for his technical college before going on to a Ph.D. in physics and an officer's commission. "So?"

A stooped gray figure entered from the hall, leaning on a cane and peering through thick-lensed glasses that sat uneasy on a great beak of nose. "Good Lord!" exploded Cohen. "McMurtrie!"

"Surprised?" The old man advanced, one wisp of a hand outstretched. "Don't see what a professor of philosophy is doing in the precious heart of your Project Robinson, eh?" As they shook, his beady gaze swept the apparatus-packed great room. "Biggest mystery to me is how it gets so drab a name. I suppose you ran out of the romantic ones. Eh? To be expected when every two-bit undertaking, to shoot off this rocket or index that file cabinet, has to be called Project Thus and Operation So. Waste not, want not, say the Gods of the Copybook Headings."

His grumble died out and he took a cheroot from his shabby coat.

Cohen jerked his head at the guard, who departed. The colonel sat down on a lab bench, swinging one leg, and indicated a swivel chair. "Well, make yourself at home, professor," he said. "I wish General Sanchez had told me—"

"Too busy, perhaps. Or more likely, didn't want you raising advance objections. He's as intelligent a man as the government allows him to be." McMurtrie lowered himself, focusing attention on the fifty-foot cylinder which gleamed in a cradle near the center of the room. One panel had been removed so that Cohen could probe its electronic guts. "And that is the time machine."

"Please." Cohen winced. "The Tempotron."

McMurtrie stamped his cane on the concrete floor. "Do you believe an object becomes more scientific when you name it with a hybrid of bad Latin and worse Greek? I say time machine."

Despite weariness and tension, Cohen smiled. He had been McMurtrie's neighbor for some two years now; the Army research project was undertaken in collaboration with the University physics department, and on University grounds. They didn't have much in common. Cohen's wife, a shy gentle girl with a degree in arts, was the only one who could even try to talk McMurtrie's kind of shop. But the professor played a slashing game of chess, which had often brought him together with Cohen.

"All right, have it your way," said the colonel. "I suppose mainly we're afraid of the headlines, if and when this is finally made public. Tempotron sounds less sensational."

McMurtrie held a wooden match to his cheroot. "Word magic! But how did this project ever start? How long ago?"

"Not quite three years. Certain phenomena were noticed by Gundestrup when he bombarded lithium with super-high-energy mesons in the big accelerator. He's never understood just what happened, for the same experiment had been performed before without such anomalous results." Cohen shrugged. "However, nuclear physics is at least as much an art as a science. Gundestrup's an imaginative fellow, and saw he could explain his data quite simply by assuming that the *xi* particles formed were thrown backward in time a few microseconds. He devised a special experiment to test his hypothesis, a very simple breadboard circuit. And it worked! I suppose I'd better not go into detail, even if you must have a Q clearance to get in here."

"I wouldn't understand, anyhow," said McMurtrie. "My job is to analyze statements made by men, not squiggles made by electrons." He drew hard on his cigar. "Go on, please. General Sanchez gave me only the barest outline and then referred me to you. This is all so new to me, such a stunning thing—"

"I know," said Cohen. "Even now, two years after I was co-opted, I often catch myself wondering if it can be true."

"Oh, I don't boggle at the idea itself," said McMurtrie. "Philosophers are always coming up with odder ones than time travel. It's adjusting to the fact which is difficult. Continue."

"Gundestrup was getting data for...another project. So everything he did was under security from the start. Thank God for that, or we'd be racing the Russians in still another field!"

"Are you certain that you aren't?"

Cohen winced again. "The basic circuits are astonishingly simple," he hurried on, "and not much energy is required. In some ways, the strangest part of this whole affair is that no one ever stumbled on the phenomenon before. In a matter of months, once the project had been set up, we were sending mice hours back. Eeriest sensation: suddenly the cage would appear, maybe right next to itself. Later we'd take the other cage, or the original one, or whatever you call it, strap it on the projector board, throw a switch—and have only one cage again."

"Ever tried not sending the first cage back?"

"Once. For several days. Until one of the boys needed to test a new hookup, absent-mindedly grabbed the extra cage, and projected it back just far enough. Oh, the theory is well worked out by now. If you really have mulled over time travel, I need only summarize by saying that there are no paradoxes, except for the theoretical possibility of circular causation. And no, we have not yet figured out how to travel into the future. And yes, we have considered the military potentialities, which is why the project has suddenly become so big and urgent."

"I see." McMurtrie scowled. "And yet your longer-range machines have never returned, eh?"

"Exactly," said Cohen. "The longest backward leap we've ever made, successfully, was thirty months. We projected a shell, containing a camera and so on, not into this same laboratory—I told you paradoxes can't happen—but up the hill, in that wooded area where no one ever goes. It stayed for twenty-four hours, photographed certain places in the city beneath it through a telescopic lens—including a house torn down two years ago—and returned on schedule. That was just a few months back."

"But the return trip *is* travel into the future!"

"Not exactly. When a world line doubles back into the past, it reverses direction once more as the projected object rejoins the normal time-flow. This sets up what we call, very loosely, a stress in the continuum. A sort of linkage. The trouble with travel into our future is that we have no, well, no anchor point."

"Your anchor points in the farther past don't seem very helpful."

"No. Which is driving us crazy, inch by inch. There's no reason why we should not send a machine back a billion years. The extra energy required is negligible. The jump-span is determined by the vibration frequency set up in the drive unit. And yet—

"We sent an object back a thousand years. It was to photograph the stars and return, so our astronomers could check the exact date it reached. It never did return, though. We sent others. No luck. We wondered if maybe some Indians weren't destroying them, so we went back a million years. No return. We tried a hundred years back, fifty, ten, five—no return" We've spent half a billion dollars on machines that we never saw again."

McMurtrie regarded his cigar ash. "It's as if you could go no farther back than the date when Gundestrup made his discovery," he mused.

"Yes. But that's absurd! It...it...no, I won't believe it."

"The human psyche does not feel comfortable with any form of philosophical idealism," said McMurtrie. "I mean, you barbarian, any belief that mind is somehow supreme over matter." He puffed for a moment before adding: "I suppose the responsibility seems too great. Eh?"

"Well, I'm not going to believe the world is all in my head without more data," said Cohen grimly. "I know what *I* think our trouble is."

He left the bench and paced, restless as a bird dog. "You still haven't told me what you're doing here, professor," he said.

"Well," McMurtrie answered, "you can partly blame your wife. Security or not, she can't help knowing you are involved with something enormous and more than a little sinister. She's frightened for you. She blurted some of her fears out to me, one evening when you were working late and I'd come over. It happens I know General Sanchez. We often argue history, a hobby of both of us. I told him it might be a good idea to let someone with philosophical training take a look at his project. Not intending myself, d'you understand. I didn't want any of your classified information. I only thought that somebody with some familiarity with the larger issues should consider the implications of whatever was being done, not from the scientific viewpoint alone."

"We have sociologists in the project."

"Nor the pseudoscientific viewpoint. Well, Sanchez asked me if I would. I demurred, but he pressed me, and I remembered the look on your wife's face, and here I am. Of course, this all happened a year ago. My clearance came through only yesterday. I have traveled, and corresponded abroad, so of course it took a year to prove I wasn't about to plant a bomb in your lavatory. How many man-years have you spent in that time, sending machines on one-way trips?"

Cohen raised a brow. "So you have the answer?"

McMurtrie spread his hands wide. "I might. As I said before, in my line of work we've been over this ground again and again. Free will versus determinism. The prediction paradox. Physical impossibilities compared to logical impossibilities. Somewhere in all that literature, the answer may lie ready made."

Cohen suppressed a snort. "General Sanchez actually took that seriously? Uh…I don't want to hurt your feelings, but you know as well as I do, science is quantitative and philosophy is at best only qualitative. Unless you can prove to me that God or the World Soul or whatever doesn't want time travel beyond a certain date—Huh? What's wrong?"

McMurtrie's waspishness dissolved. All at once he was a very old man, huddled in a chair, and Cohen had never seen anything so bleak as his eyes.

The colonel stepped close, wondering whether to call a doctor. He was waved back. Another moment dragged by before McMurtrie whispered: "Something has occurred to me."

"Not a divine prohibition, I hope?" Cohen had hoped his mockery might put life back in the air, but it fell flat.

"No," said McMurtrie. "Worse. Much more final."

Cohen stood rigid.

"You should send machines to the earliest possible date," said McMurtrie in a slow and rusty voice. "If that barrier moment can be repeatedly verified—"

"Then our project is washed up," said Cohen. "What use is a time machine that won't put you any further back than August, 1959?"

"Oh, I can still think of applications," said McMurtrie. His mouth twisted into something that might have been a grin. "It's the discovery itself, the fact, which will end an era."

Cohen knotted his fists. The weariness of labor and tension and underlying fear snapped for him: "If you won't come to the point, professor, then tell me about it when I return."

"Eh?" McMurtrie looked up, blinking.

"I'm on my way. After lunch. I was just making a final check."

"You can't!" The words were gasped.

Cohen shrugged. "I should send another man? The piloted Tempotron is my own idea. I pushed it through, persuaded my superiors, oversaw the job. I'm responsible for this baby here, fifty million dollars' worth."

McMurtrie licked his lips. "You're going back…a year? Two years?"

"I've been back two years, up on the hill. I stood in a grove of trees and looked down across these buildings and knew myself was working inside one of them. Now it's the long jump. A thousand years."

"But—"

"My guess," said Cohen, and anger doubled in him that his tone should be so hoarse, "is that the high vibration frequency needed to go back so far changes the characteristics of the crystals used. I'm taking a complete set of tools, meters, and spare parts."

McMurtrie struggled to his feet. "No," he said. "Please. You must listen."

"Sure. But whatever you say, I'm going."

"You won't come back. I never thought you were a suicidal type."

Cohen shrugged again.

"Your wife—" said the professor in a beggar's voice.

"I told her last night. That I'd be taking a risk. I don't want to talk any more about that."

McMurtrie nodded with slow care. "Ironic," he said. "What the first human traveler through time needs, is time."

"What?"

"Time to think. Suppose an accident occurred, damage was done, which delayed this expedition even a week. You would have time to contemplate my suggestion, and see that it isn't so wild a notion that you will stake your existence on my being wrong. Eh? Sanchez will also have time to digest the concept and inform Washington. The government will order a delay while a more cautious probing program is undertaken. Eventually, my friend, you will be ordered to cease and desist, and thus released from this compulsion to demonstrate your courage."

Cohen stood aside, for McMurtrie was shuffling toward the machine, head thrust forward like an old and wrinkled tortoise. "So?" he clipped.

McMurtrie's cane jabbed forward, slashing across the exposed circuits. Cohen heard glass shatter and saw wires yanked loose.

"So you just had an accident," said McMurtrie, "Very clumsy of me. My foot slipped. I apologize."

"You—"

Cohen picked up a monkey wrench and beat it, most softly and methodically, against a table top. After a long while, keeping his back turned to McMurtrie, he said, "O.K. What is it ?"

"If you had only had a man with proper philosophical training from the start," sighed the other. "Your glorious, expensive, half-cocked Project Robinson would never—Well. Let me explain."

"You'd better."

"I presume nothing can exist prior to existence itself."

"That sounds…reasonable…yes."

"Have you never encountered that philosophical question? Even in own ignorance? It's the oldest chestnut in the book…Oldest!" McMurtrie laughed with so startling a tone that Cohen whirled. He looked into a rather terrible grimace.

"The conundrum is this," said McMurtrie. "How can you prove that the entire cosmos did not appear, or was not created, complete with all evidences of a long past history, at some arbitrary date in the past? Such as, say, August, 1959?"

"What?" shouted Cohen.

"Yes," said McMurtrie. "Damn you for answering the question. When will you scientists leave well enough alone?"

THE STAR BEAST

Therapy for Paradise

The rebirth technician thought he had heard everything in the course of some three centuries. But he was astonished now

"My dear fellow—" he said. "Did you say a tiger—"

"That's right," said Harol. "You can do it, can't you?"

"Well—I suppose so. I'd have to study the problem first of course. Nobody has ever wanted a rebirth that far from human. But offhand I'd say it was possible." The technician's eyes lit with a gleam which had not been there for many decades. "It would at least be—interesting!"

"I think you already have a record of a tiger," said Harol.

"Oh, we must have. We have records of every animal still extant when the technique was invented, and I'm sure there must still have been a few tigers around then. But it's a problem of modification. A human mind just can't exist in a nervous system that different. We'd have to change the record enough—larger brain with more convolutions, of course, and so on…Even then it'd be far from perfect, but your basic mentality should be stable for a year or two, barring accidents. That's all the time you'd want anyway, isn't it?"

"I suppose so," said Harol.

"Rebirth in animal forms is getting fashionable these days," admitted the technician. "But so far they've only wanted animals with easily modified systems. Anthropoid apes, now—you don't even have to change a chimpanzee's brain at all for it to hold a stable human mentality for years. Elephants are good too. But—a tiger—" He shook his head. "I suppose it can be done, after a fashion. But why not a gorilla?"

"I want a carnivore," said Harol.

"Your psychiatrist, I suppose—" hinted the technician. Harol nodded curtly. The technician sighed and gave up the hope of juicy confessions. A worker at Rebirth Station heard a lot of strange stories, but this fellow wasn't giving. Oh, well, the mere fact of his demand would furnish gossip for days.

"When can it be ready?" asked Harol.

The technician scratched his head thoughtfully. "It'll take a while," he said. "We have to get the record scanned, you know, and work out a basic neural pattern that'll hold the human mind. It's more than a simple memory-superimposition. The genes control an organism all through its lifespan, dictating, within the limits of environment, even the time and speed of aging. You can't have an animal with an ontogeny entirely opposed to its basic phylogeny—it wouldn't be viable. So we'll have to modify the very molecules of the cells, as well as the gross anatomy of the nervous system."

"In short," smiled Harol, "this intelligent tiger will breed true."

"If it found a similar tigress," answered the technician. "Not a real one—there aren't any left, and besides, the heredity would be too different. But maybe you want a female body for someone?"

"No, I only want a body for myself." Briefly, Harol thought of Avi and tried to imagine her incarnated in the supple, deadly grace of the huge cat. But no, she wasn't the type. And solitude was part of the therapy anyway.

"Once we have the modified record, of course, there's nothing to superimposing your memory patterns on it," said the technician. "That'll be just the usual process, like any human rebirth. But to make up that record—well, I can put the special scanning and computing units over at Research on the problem. Nobody's working there. Say a week. Will that do?"

"Fine," said Harol. "I'll be back in a week."

He turned with a brief good-by and went down the long slideway toward the nearest transmitter. It was almost deserted now save for the unhuman forms of mobile robots gliding on their errands. The faint, deep hum of activity which filled Rebirth Station was almost entirely that of machines, of electronic flows whispering through vacuum, the silent cerebration of artificial intellects so far surpassing those of their human creators that men could no longer follow their thoughts. A human brain simply couldn't operate with that many simultaneous factors.

The machines were the latter-day oracles. And the life-giving gods. *We're parasites on our machines,* thought Harol. *We're little fleas hopping around on the giants we created once. There are no real human scientists any more. How can there be, when the electronic brains and the great machines which are their bodies can do it all so much quicker and better—can do things we would never even have dreamed of, things of which man's highest geniuses have only the faintest glimmer of an understanding? That has paralyzed us, that and the rebirth immortality. Now there's nothing left but a life of idleness and a round of pleasure—and how much fun is anything after centuries?*

It was no wonder that animal rebirth was all the rage. It offered some prospect of novelty—for a while.

He passed a mirror and paused to look at himself. There was nothing unusual about him; he had the tall body and handsome features that were uniform today. There was a little gray at his temples and he was getting a bit bald on top, though this body was only thirty-five. But then it always had aged early. In the old days he'd hardly have reached a hundred.

I am—let me see—four hundred and sixty-three years old. At least, my memory is—and what am I, the essential I, but a memory track?

Unlike most of the people in the building, he wore clothes, a light tunic and cloak. He was a little sensitive about the flabbiness of his body. He really should keep himself in better shape. But what was the point of it, really, when his twenty-year-old record was so superb a specimen?

He reached the transmitter booth and hesitated a moment, wondering where to go. He could go home—have to get his affairs in order before undertaking the tiger phase—or he could drop in on Avi or—His mind wandered away until he came to himself with an angry start. After four and a half centuries, it was getting hard to coordinate all his memories; he was becoming increasingly absent-minded. Have to get the psychostaff at Rebirth to go over his record, one of these generations, and eliminate some of that useless clutter from his synapses.

He decided to visit Avi. As he spoke her name to the transmitter and waited for it to hunt through the electronic files at Central for her current residence, the thought came that in all his lifetime he had only twice seen Rebirth Station from the outside. The place was immense, a featureless pile rearing skyward above the almost-empty European forests—as impressive a sight, in its way, as Tycho Crater or the rings of Saturn. But when the transmitter sent you directly from booth to booth, inside the buildings, you rarely had occasion to look at their exteriors.

For a moment he toyed with the thought of having himself transmitted to some nearby house just to see the Station. But—oh, well, any time in the next few millennia. The Station would last forever, and so would he.

The transmitter field was generated. At the speed of light, Harol flashed around the world to Avi's dwelling.

The occasion was ceremonial enough for Ramacan to put on his best clothes, a red cloak over his tunic and the many jeweled ornaments prescribed for formal wear. Then he sat down by his transmitter and waited.

The booth stood just inside the colonnaded verandah. From his seat, Ramacan could look through the open doors to the great slopes and peaks of the Caucasus, green now with returning summer save where the everlasting snows flashed under a bright sky. He had lived here for many centuries, contrary to the restlessness of most Earthlings. But he liked the place. It had a quiet immensity; it never changed. Most humans these days sought variety, a feverish quest for the new and untasted, old minds in young bodies trying to recapture a lost freshness. Ramacan was—they called him stodgy, probably. Stable or steady might be closer to the truth. Which made him ideal for his work. Most of what government remained on Earth was left to him.

Felgi was late. Ramacan didn't worry about it; he was never in a hurry himself. But when the Procyonite did arrive, the manner of it brought an amazed oath even from the Earthling.

He didn't come through the transmitter. He came in a boat from his ship, a lean metal shark drifting out of the sky and sighing to the lawn. Ramacan noticed the flat turrets and the ominous muzzles of guns projecting from them. Anachronism—Sol hadn't seen a warship for more centuries than he could remember. But—

Felgi came out of the airlock. He was followed by a squad of armed guards, who grounded their blasters and stood to stiff attention. The Procyonite captain walked alone up to the house.

Ramacan had met him before, but he studied the man with a new attention. Like most in his fleet, Felgi was a little undersized by Earthly standards, and the rigidity of his face and posture were almost shocking. His severe, form-fitting black uniform differed little from those of his subordinates except for insignia of his rank. His features were gaunt, dark with the protective pigmentation necessary under the terrible blaze of Procyon, and there was something in his eyes which Ramacan had never seen before.

The Procyonites looked human enough. But Ramacan wondered if there was any truth to those rumors which had been flying about Earth since their arrival, that mutation and selection during their long and cruel stay had changed the colonists into something that could never have been at home.

Certainly their social setup and their basic psychology seemed to be—foreign.

Felgi came up the short escalator to the verandah and bowed stiffly. The psychographs had taught him modern Terrestrial, but his voice still held an echo of the harsh colonial tongue and his phrasing was strange: "Greeting to you, Commander."

Ramacan returned the bow, but his was the elaborate sweeping gesture of Earth. "Be welcome, Gen—ah—General Felgi." Then, informally: "Please come in."

"Thank you." The other man walked into the house. "Your companions—?"

"My *men* will remain outside." Felgi sat down without being invited, a serious breach of etiquette—but after all, the mores of his home were different.

"As you wish." Ramacan dialed for drinks on the room creator.

"No," said Felgi.

"Pardon me?"

"We don't drink at Procyon. I thought you knew that."

"Pardon me. I had forgotten." Regretfully, Ramacan let the wine and glasses return to the matter bank and sat down.

Felgi sat with steely erectness, making the efforts of the seat to mold itself to his contours futile. Slowly, Ramacan recognized the emotion that crackled and smoldered behind the dark lean visage.

Anger.

"I trust you are finding your stay on Earth pleasant," he said into the silence.

"Let us not make meaningless words," snapped Felgi. "I am here on business."

"As you wish." Ramacan tried to relax, but he couldn't; his nerves and muscles were suddenly tight.

"As far as I can gather," said Felgi, "you head the government of Sol."

"I suppose you could say that. I have the title of Coordinator. But there isn't much to coordinate these days. Our social system practically runs itself."

"Insofar as you have one. But actually you are completely disorganized. Every individual seems to be sufficient to himself."

"Naturally. When everyone owns a matter creator which can supply all his ordinary needs, there is bound to be economic and thus a large degree of social independence. We have public services, of course—Rebirth Station, Power Station, Transmitter Central, and a few others. But there aren't many."

"I cannot see why you aren't overwhelmed by crime." The last word was necessarily Procyonian, and Ramacan raised his eyebrows puzzledly. "Anti-social behavior," explained Felgi irritably. "Theft, murder, destruction."

"What possible need has anyone to steal?" asked Ramacan, surprised. "And the present degree of independence virtually eliminates social friction. Actual psychoses have been removed from the neural components of the rebirth records long ago."

"At any rate, I assume you speak for Sol."

"How can I speak for almost a billion different people? I have little authority, you know. So little is needed. However, I'll do all I can if you'll only tell me—"

"The decadence of Sol is incredible," snapped Felgi.

"You may be right." Ramacan's tone was mild, but he bristled under the urbane surface. "I've sometimes thought so myself. However, what has that to do with the present subject of discussion—whatever it may be?"

"You left us in exile," said Felgi, and now the wrath and hate were edging his voice, glittering out of his eyes. "For nine hundred years, Earth lived in luxury while the humans on Procyon fought and suffered and died in the worst kind of hell."

"What reason was there for us to go to Procyon?" asked Ramacan. "After the first few ships had established a colony there—well, we had a whole galaxy before us. When no colonial ships came from your star, I suppose it was assumed the people there had died off. Somebody should perhaps have gone there to check up, but it took twenty years to get there and it was an inhospitable and unrewarding system and there were so many other stars. Then the matter creator came along and Sol no longer had a government to look after such things. Space travel became an individual business, and no individual was interested in Procyon." He shrugged. "I'm sorry!"

"You're *sorry!*" Felgi spat the words out. "For nine hundred years our ancestors fought the bitterness of their planets, starved and died in misery, sank back almost to barbarism and had to slug their way every step back upwards, waged the cruelest war of history with the Czernigi—unending centuries of war until one race or the other should be exterminated. We died of old age, generation after generation of us—we wrung our needs out of planets never meant for humans—my ship spent twenty years getting back here, twenty years of short human lives—and you're sorry!"

He sprang up and paced the floor, his bitter voice lashing out. "You've had the stars, you've had immortality, you've had everything which can be made of matter. And *we* spent twenty years cramped up in metal walls to get here—wondering if perhaps Sol hadn't fallen on evil times and needed our help!"

"What would you have us do now?" demanded Ramacan. "All Earth has made you welcome—"

"We're a novelty!"

"—all Earth is ready to offer you all it can. What more do you want of us?"

For a moment the rage was still in Felgi's strange eyes. Then it faded, blinked out as if he had drawn a curtain across them, and he stood still and spoke with sudden quietness. "True. I—I should apologize, I suppose. The nervous strain—"

"Don't mention it," said Ramacan. But inwardly he wondered. Just how far could he trust the Procyonites? All those hard centuries of war and intrigue— and then they weren't really human any more, not the way Earth's dwellers were human—but what else could he do? "It's quite all right. I understand."

"Thank you." Felgi sat down again. "May I ask what you offer?"

"Duplicate matter creators, of course. And robots duplicated, to administer the more complex Rebirth techniques. Certain of the processes involved are beyond the understanding of the human mind."

"I'm not sure it would be a good thing for us," said Felgi. "Sol has gotten stagnant. There doesn't seem to have been any significant change in the last half millennium. Why, our spaceship drives are better than yours."

"What do you expect?" shrugged Ramacan. "What possible incentive have we for change? Progress, to use an archaic term, is a means to an end, and we have reached its goal."

"I still don't know—" Felgi rubbed his chin. "I'm not even sure how your duplicators work."

"I can't tell you much about them. But the greatest technical mind on Earth can't tell you everything. As I told you before, the whole thing is just too immense for real knowledge. Only the electronic brains can handle so much at once."

"Maybe you could give me a short resume of it, and tell me just what your setup is. I'm especially interested in the actual means by which it's put to use."

"Well, let me see." Ramacan searched his memory. "The ultrawave was discovered—oh, it must be a good seven or eight hundred years ago now. It carries energy, but it's not electromagnetic. The theory of it, as far as any human can follow it, ties in with wave mechanics.

"The first great application came with the discovery that ultrawaves transmit over distances of many astronomical units, unhindered by intervening matter, and with *no energy loss*. The theory of that has been interpreted as meaning that the wave is, well, I suppose you could say it's 'aware' of the receiver and only goes to it. There must be a receiver as well as a transmitter to generate the wave. Naturally, that led to a perfectly efficient power transmitter. Today all the Solar System gets its energy from the Sun—transmitted by the Power Station on the day side of Mercury. Everything from interplanetary spaceships to televisors and clocks runs from that power source."

"Sounds dangerous to me," said Felgi. "Suppose the station fails?"

"It won't," said Ramacan confidently. "The Station has its own robots, no human technicians at all. Everything is recorded. If any one part goes wrong, it is automatically dissolved into the nearest matter bank and recreated. There are other safeguards too. The Station has never given trouble since it was first built."

"I see—" Felgi's tone was thoughtful.

"Soon thereafter," said Ramacan, "it was found that the ultrawave could also transmit matter. Circuits could be built which would scan any body atom by atom, dissolve it to energy, and transmit this energy on the ultrawave along with the scanning signal. At the receiver, of course, the process is reversed. I'm grossly oversimplifying, naturally. It's not a mere signal which is involved, but a fantastic complex of signals such as only the ultrawave could carry. However, you get the general idea. Just about all transportation today is by this technique. Vehicles for air or space exist only for very special purposes and for pleasure trips."

"You have some kind of controlling center for this too, don't you?"

"Yes. Transmitter Station, on Earth, is in Brazil. It holds all the records of such things as addresses, and it coordinates the millions of units all over the planet. It's a huge, complicated affair, of course, but perfectly efficient. Since distance no longer means anything, it's most practical to centralize the public-service units.

"Well, from transmission it was but a step to recording the signal and reproducing it out of a bank of any other matter. So—the duplicator. The matter creator. You can imagine what that did to Sol's economy! Today everybody owns one, and if he doesn't have a record of what he wants he can have one duplicated and transmitted from Creator Station's great 'library'. Anything whatsoever in the way of material goods is his for the turning of a dial and the flicking of a switch.

"And this, in turn, soon led to the Rebirth technique. It's but an extension of all that has gone before. Your body is recorded at its prime of life, say around twenty years of age. Then you live for as much longer as you care to, say to thirty-five or forty or whenever you begin to get a little old. Then your neural pattern is recorded alone by special scanning units. Memory, as you surely know, is a matter of neural synapses and altered protein molecules, not too difficult to scan and record. This added pattern is superimposed electronically on the record of your twenty-year-old body. Then your own body is used as the matter bank for materializing the pattern in the altered record and—virtually instantaneously—your young body is created—but with all the memories of the old! You're immortal!"

"In a way," said Felgi. "But it still doesn't seem right to me. The ego, the soul, whatever you want to call it—it seems as if you lose that. You create simply a perfect copy."

"When the copy is so perfect it cannot be told from the original," said Ramacan, "then what *is* the difference? The ego is essentially a matter of continuity. You, your essential self, are a constantly changing pattern of synapses bearing only a temporary relationship to the molecules that happen to carry the pattern at the moment. It is the design, not the structural material, that is important; And it is the design that we preserve."

"Do you?" asked Felgi. "I seemed to notice a strong likeness among Earthlings."

"Well, since the records can be altered there was no reason for us to carry around crippled or diseased or deformed bodies," said Ramacan. "Records could be made of perfect specimens and *all* ego-patterns wiped from them; then someone else's neural pattern could be superimposed. Rebirth—in a new body! Naturally, everyone would want to match the prevailing beauty standard, and so a certain uniformity has appeared. A different body would of course lead in time to a different personality, man being a psychosomatic unit. But the continuity which is the essential attribute of the ego would still be there."

"Ummm—I see. May I ask how old you are?"

"About seven hundred and fifty. I was middle-aged when Rebirth was established, but I had myself put into a young body."

Felgi's eyes went from Ramacan's smooth, youthful face to his own hands, with the knobby joints and prominent veins of his sixty years. Briefly, the fingers tightened, but his voice remained soft. "Don't you have trouble keeping your memories straight?"

"Yes, but every so often I have some of the useless and repetitious ones taken out of the record, and that helps. The robots know exactly what part of the pattern corresponds to a given memory and can erase it. After, say, another thousand years, I'll probably have big gaps. But they won't be important."

"How about the apparent acceleration of time with age?"

"That was bad after the first couple of centuries, but then it seemed to flatten out, the nervous system adapted to it. I must say, though," admitted Ramacan, "that it as well as lack of incentive is probably responsible for our present static society and general unproductiveness. There's a terrible tendency to procrastination, and a day seems too short a time to get anything done."

"The end of progress, then—of science, or art, of striving, of all which has made man human."

"Not so. We still have our arts and handicrafts and—hobbies, I suppose you could call them. Maybe we don't do so much any more, but—why should we?"

"I'm surprised at finding so much of Earth gone back to wilderness. I should think you'd be badly overcrowded."

"Not so. The creator and the transmitter make it possible for men to live far apart, in physical distance, and still be in as close touch as necessary. Communities are obsolete. As for the population problem, there isn't any. After a few children, not many people want more. It's sort of, well, unfashionable anyway."

"That's right," said Felgi quietly, "I've hardly seen a child on Earth."

"And of course there's a slow drift out to the stars as people seek novelty. You can send your recording in a robot ship, and a journey of centuries becomes nothing. I suppose that's another reason for the tranquility of Earth. The more restless and adventurous elements have moved away."

"Have you any communication with them?"

"None. Not when spaceships can only go at half the speed of light. Once in a while curious wanderers will drop in on us, but it's very rare. They seem to be developing some strange cultures out in the galaxy."

"Don't you do *any* work on Earth?"

"Oh, some public services must be maintained—psychiatry, human technicians to oversee various stations, and so on. And then there are any number of personal-service enterprises—entertainment, especially, and the creation of intricate handicrafts for the creators to duplicate. But there are enough people willing to work a few hours a month or week, if only to fill in their time or to get the credit-balance which will enable them to purchase such services for themselves if they desire.

"It's a perfectly stable culture, General Felgi. It's perhaps the only really stable society in all human history."

"I wonder—haven't you any precautions at all? Any military forces, any defenses against invaders—*anything?*"

"Why in the cosmos should we fear that?" exclaimed Ramacan. "Who would come invading over light-years—at half the speed of light? Or if they did, *why?*"

"Plunder—"

Ramacan laughed. "We could duplicate anything they asked for and give it to them."

"Could you, now?" Suddenly Felgi stood up. "Could you?"

Ramacan rose too, with his nerves and muscles tightening again. There was a hard triumph in the Procyonite's face, vindictive, threatening.

Felgi signaled to his men through the door. They trotted up on the double, and their blasters were raised and something hard and ugly was in their eyes.

"Coordinator Ramacan," said Felgi, "you are under arrest."

"What—what—" The Earthling felt as if someone had struck him a physical blow. He clutched for support. Vaguely he heard the iron tones:

"You've confirmed what I thought. Earth is unarmed, unprepared, helplessly dependent on a few undefended key spots. And I captain a warship of space filled with soldiers.

"We're taking over!"

-2-

"Tiger, Tiger"

Avi's current house lay in North America, on the middle Atlantic seaboard. Like most private homes these days, it was small and low-ceilinged, with adjustable interior walls and furnishings for easy variegation. She loved flowers, and great brilliant gardens bloomed around her dwelling, down toward the sea and landward to the edge of the immense forest which had returned with the end of agriculture.

They walked between the shrubs and trees and blossoms, she and Harol. Her unbound hair was long and bright in the sea breeze, her eighteen-year-old form was slim and graceful as a young deer's. Suddenly he hated the thought of leaving her.

"I'll miss you, Harol," she said.

He smiled lopsidedly. "You'll get over that," he said. "There are others. I suppose you'll be looking up some of those spacemen they say arrived from Procyon a few days ago."

"Of course," she said innocently. "I'm surprised you don't stay around and try for some of the women they had along. It would be a change."

"Not much of a change," he answered. "Frankly, I'm at a loss to understand the modern passion for variety. One person seems very much the same as another in that regard."

"It's a matter of companionship," she said. "After not too many years of living with someone, you get to know him too well. You can tell exactly what he's going to do, what he'll say to you, what he'll have for dinner and what sort of show he'll want to go to in the evening. These colonists will be—new! They'll have other ways from ours, they'll be able to tell of a new, different planetary system, they'll—" She broke off. "But now so many women will be after the strangers, I doubt if I'll have a chance."

"But if it's conversation you want—oh, well." Harol shrugged. "Anyway, I understand the Procyonites still have family relationships. They'll be quite jealous of their women. And I need this change."

"A carnivore—!" Avi laughed, and Harol thought again what music it was. "You have an original mind, at least." Suddenly she was earnest. She held both his hands and looked close into his eyes. "That's always been what I liked about you, Harol. You've always been a thinker and adventurer, you've never let yourself grow mentally lazy like most of us. After we've been apart for a few years, you're always new again, you've gotten out of your rut and done something strange, you've learned something different, you've grown young again. We've always come back to each other, dear, and I've always been glad of it."

"And I," he said quietly. "Though I've regretted the separations too." He smiled, a wry smile with a tinge of sorrow behind it. "We could have been very happy in the old days, Avi. We would have been married and together for life."

"A few years, and then age and feebleness and death." She shuddered. "Death! Nothingness! Not even the world can exist when one is dead. Not when you've no brain left to know about it. Just—nothing. As if you had never been! Haven't you ever been afraid of the thought?"

"No," he said, and kissed her.

"That's another way you're different," she murmured. "I wonder why you never went out to the stars, Harol. All your children did."

"I asked you to go with me, once."

"Not I. I like it here. Life is fun, Harol. I don't seem to get bored as easily as most people. But that isn't answering my question."

"Yes, it is," he said, and then clamped his mouth shut.

He stood looking at her, wondering if he was the last man on Earth who loved a woman, wondering how she really felt about him. Perhaps, in her way, she loved him—they always came back to each other. But not in the way he cared for her, not so that being apart was a gnawing pain and reunion was—No matter.

"I'll still be around," he said. "I'll be wandering through the woods here; I'll have the Rebirth men transmit me back to your house and then I'll be in the neighborhood."

"My pet tiger," she smiled. "Come around to see me once in a while, Harol. Come with me to some of the parties."

A nice spectacular ornament—"No, thanks. But you can scratch my head and feed me big bloody steaks, and I'll arch my back and purr."

They walked hand in hand toward the beach. "What made you decide to be a tiger?" she asked.

"My psychiatrist recommended an animal rebirth," he replied. "I'm getting terribly neurotic, Avi. I can't sit still five minutes and I get gloomy spells where nothing seems worthwhile any more, life is a dreadful farce and—well, it seems to be becoming a rather common disorder these days. Essentially it's boredom. When you have everything without working for it, life can become horribly flat. When you've lived for centuries, tried it all hundreds of times—no change, no real excitement, nothing to call forth all that's in you—Anyway, the doctor suggested I go to the stars. When I refused that, he suggested I change to animal for a while. But I didn't want to be like everyone else. Not an ape or an elephant."

"Same old contrary Harol," she murmured, and kissed him. He responded with unexpected violence.

"A year or two of wild life, in a new and unhuman body, will make all the difference," he said after a while. They lay on the sand, feeling the sunlight wash over them, hearing the lullaby of waves and smelling the clean, harsh tang of sea and salt and many windy kilometers. High overhead a gull circled, white against the blue.

"Won't you change?" she asked.

"Oh, yes. I won't even be able to remember a lot of things I now know. I doubt if even the most intelligent tiger could understand vector analysis. But that won't matter, I'll get it back when they restore my human form. When I feel the personality change has gone as far as is safe, I'll come here and you can send me back to Rebirth. The important thing is the therapy—a change of viewpoint, a new and challenging environment—Avi!" He sat up, on one elbow and looked down at her. "Avi, why don't you come along? Why don't we both become tigers?"

"And have lots of little tigers?" she smiled drowsily. "No, thanks, Harol. Maybe some day, but not now. I'm really not an adventurous person at all." She stretched, and snuggled back against the warm white dune. "I like it the way it is."

And there are those starmen—Sunfire, what's the matter with me? Next thing you know I'll commit an inurbanity against one of her lovers. I need that therapy, all right.

"And then you'll come back and tell me about it," said Avi.

"Maybe not," he teased her. "Maybe I'll find a beautiful tigress somewhere and become so enamored of her I'll never want to change back to human."

"There won't be any tigresses unless you persuade someone else to go along," she answered. "But will you like a human body after having had such a lovely striped skin? Will we poor hairless people still look good to you?"

"Darling," he smiled, "to me you'll always look good enough to eat."

Presently they went back into the house. The sea gull still dipped and soared, high in the sky.

The forest was great and green and mysterious, with sunlight dappling the shadows and a riot of ferns and flowers under the huge old trees. There were brooks tinkling their darkling way between cool, mossy banks, fish leaping like silver streaks in the bright shallows, lonely pools where quiet hung like a mantle, open meadows of wind-rippled grass, space and solitude and an unending pulse of life.

Tiger eyes saw less than human; the world seemed dim and flat and colorless until he got used to it. After that he had increasing difficulty remembering what color and perspective were like. And his other senses came alive, he realized what a captive within his own skull he had been—looking out at a world of which he had never been so real a part as now.

He heard sounds and tones no man had ever perceived, the faint hum and chirr of insects, the rustling of leaves in a light, warm breeze, the vague whisper of an owl's wings, the scurrying of small, frightened creatures through the long grass—it all blended into a rich symphony, the heartbeat and breath of the forest. And his nostrils quivered to the infinite variety of smells, the heady fragrance of crushed grass, the pungency of fungus and decay, the sharp, wild odor of fur, the hot drunkenness of newly spilled blood. And he felt with every hair, his whiskers quivered to the smallest stirrings, he gloried in the deep, strong play of his muscles—he had come alive, he thought; a man was half dead compared to the vitality that throbbed in the tiger.

At night, at night—there was no darkness for him now. Moonlight was a white, cold blaze through which he stole on feathery feet; the blackest gloom was light to him—shadows, wan patches of luminescence, a shifting, sliding fantasy of gray like an old and suddenly remembered dream.

He laired in a cave he found, and his new body had no discomfort from the damp earth. At night he would stalk out, a huge, dim ghost with only the amber gleam of his eyes for light, and the forest would speak to him with sound and scent and feeling, the taste of game on the wind. He was master then, all the woods shivered and huddled away from him. He was death in black and gold.

Once an ancient poem ran through the human part of his mind. He let the words roll like ominous thunder in his brain and tried to speak them aloud. The forest shivered with the tiger's coughing roar.

> *Tiger, tiger, burning bright*
> *In the forest of the night,*

What immortal hand or eye
Dared frame thy fearful symmetry?

And the arrogant feline soul snarled response: *I did!*

Later he tried to recall the poem, but he couldn't.

At first he was not very successful, too much of his human awkwardness clung to him. He snarled his rage and bafflement when rabbits skittered aside, when a deer scented him lurking and bolted. He went to Avi's house and she fed him big chunks of raw meat and laughed and scratched him under the chin. She was delighted with her pet.

Avi, he thought, and remembered that he loved her. But that was with his human body. To the tiger, she had no esthetic or sexual value. But he liked to let her stroke him, he purred like a mighty engine and rubbed against her slim legs. She was still very dear to him, and when he became human again—

But the tiger's instincts fought their way back; the heritage of a million years was not to be denied no matter how much the technicians had tried to alter him. They had accomplished little more than to increase his intelligence, and the tiger nerves and glands were still there.

The night came when he saw a flock of rabbits dancing in the moonlight and pounced on them. One huge, steely-taloned paw swooped down, he felt the ripping flesh and snapping bone and then he was gulping the sweet, hot blood and peeling the meat from the frail ribs. He went wild, he roared and raged all night, shouting his exultance to the pale frosty moon. At dawn he slunk back to his cave, wearied, his human mind a little ashamed of it all. But the next night he was hunting again.

His first deer! He lay patiently on a branch overhanging a trail; only his nervous tail moved while the slow hours dragged by, and he waited. And when the doe passed underneath he was on her like a tawny lightning bolt. A great slapping paw, jaws like shears, a brief, terrible struggle, and she lay dead at his feet. He gorged himself, he ate till he could hardly crawl back to the cave, and then he slept like a drunken man until hunger woke him and he went back to the carcass. A pack of wild dogs were devouring it, he rushed on them and killed one and scattered the rest. Thereafter he continued his feast until only bones were left.

The forest was full of game; it was an easy life for a tiger. But not too easy. He never knew whether he would go back with full or empty belly, and that was part of the pleasure.

They had not removed all the tiger memories; fragments remained to puzzle him; sometimes he woke up whimpering with a dim wonder as to where he was and what had happened. He seemed to remember misty jungle dawns, a broad brown river shining under the sun, another cave and another striped form beside him. As time went on he grew confused, he thought vaguely that he must once have hunted sambar and seen the white rhinoceros go by like a moving mountain in the twilight. It was growing harder to keep things straight.

That was, of course, only to be expected. His feline brain could not possibly hold all the memories and concepts of the human, and with the passage of weeks and months he lost the earlier clarity of recollection. He still identified himself with a certain sound, "Harol," and he remembered other forms and scenes—but more and more dimly, as if they were the fading shards of a dream. And he kept firmly in mind that he had to go back to Avi and let her send—take?—him somewhere else before he forgot who he was.

Well, there was time for that, thought the human component. He wouldn't lose that memory all at once, he'd know well in advance that the superimposed human personality was disintegrating in its strange house and that he ought to get back. Meanwhile he grew more and deeply into the forest life, his horizons narrowed until it seemed the whole of existence.

Now and then he wandered down to the sea and Avi's home, to get a meal and be made much of. But the visits grew more and more infrequent, the open country made him nervous and—he couldn't stay indoors after dark.

Tiger, tiger—

And summer wore on.

He woke to a raw wet chill in the cave, rain outside and a mordant wind blowing through dripping dark trees. He shivered and growled, unsheathing his claws, but this was not an enemy he could destroy. The day and the night dragged by in misery.

Tigers had been adaptable beasts in the old days, he recalled; they had ranged as far north as Siberia. But his original had been from the tropics. *Hell!* he cursed, and the thunderous roar rattled through the woods.

But then came crisp, clear days with a wild wind hallooing through a high, pale sky, dead leaves whirling on the gusts and laughing in their thin, dry way. Geese honked in the heavens, southward bound, and the bellowing of stags filled the nights. There was a drunkenness in the air; the tiger rolled in the grass and purred like muted thunder and yowled at the huge orange moon as it rose. His fur thickened, he didn't feel the chill except as a keen tingling in his blood. All his senses were sharpened now, he lived with a knife-edged alertness and learned how to go through the fallen leaves like another shadow.

Indian summer, long lazy days like a resurrected springtime, enormous stars, the crisp smell of rotting vegetation, and his human mind remembered that the leaves were like gold and bronze and flame. He fished in the brooks, scooping up his prey with one hooked sweep; he ranged the woods and roared on the high ridges under the moon.

Then the rains returned, gray and cold and sodden, the world drowned in a wet woe. At night there was frost, numbing his feet and glittering in the starlight, and through the chill silence he could hear the distant beat of the sea. It grew harder to stalk game, he was often hungry. By now he didn't mind that too much, but his reason worried about winter. Maybe he'd better get back.

One night the first snow fell, and in the morning the world was white and still. He plowed through it, growling his anger, and wondered about moving south. But cats aren't given to long journeys. He remembered vaguely that Avi could give him food and shelter.

Avi—For a moment, when he tried to think of her, he thought of a golden, dark-striped body and a harsh feline smell filling the cave above the old wide river. He shook his massive head, angry with himself and the world, and tried to call up her image. The face was dim in his mind, but the scent came back to him, and the low, lovely music of her laughter. He would go to Avi.

He went through the bare forest with the haughty gait of its king, and presently he stood on the beach. The sea was gray and cold and enormous, roaring white-maned on the shore; flying spin-drift stung his eyes. He padded along the strand until he saw her house.

It was oddly silent. He went in through the garden. The door stood open, but there was only desertion inside.

Maybe she was away. He curled up on the floor and went to sleep.

He woke much later, hunger gnawing in his guts, and still no one had come. He recalled that she had been wont to go south for the winter. But she wouldn't have forgotten him, she'd have been back from time to time—But the house had little scent of her, she had been away for a long while. And it was disordered. Had she left hastily?

He went over to the creator. He couldn't remember how it worked, but he did recall the process of dialing and switching. He pulled the lever at random with a paw. Nothing happened.

Nothing! The creator was inert.

He roared his disappointment. Slow, puzzled fear came to him. This wasn't as it should be.

But he was hungry. He'd have to try to get his own food, then, and come back later in hopes of finding Avi. He went back into the woods.

Presently he smelled life under the snow. Bear. Previously, he and the bears had been in a state of watchful neutrality. But this one was asleep, unwary, and his belly cried for food. He tore the shelter apart with a few powerful motions and flung himself on the animal.

It is dangerous to wake a hibernating bear. This one came to with a start, his heavy paw lashed out and the tiger sprang back with blood streaming down his muzzle.

Madness came, a berserk rage that sent him leaping forward. The bear snarled and braced himself. They closed, and suddenly the tiger was fighting for his very life.

He never remembered that battle save as a red whirl of shock and fury, tumbling in the snow and spilling blood to steam in the cold air. Strike, bite; rip, thundering blows against his ribs and skull, the taste of blood hot in his mouth and the insanity of death shrieking and gibbering in his head!

In the end, he staggered bloodily and collapsed on the bear's ripped corpse. For a long time he lay there, and the wild dogs hovered near, waiting for him to die.

After a while he stirred weakly and ate of the bear's flesh. But he couldn't leave. His body was one vast pain, his feet wobbled under him, one paw had been crushed by the great jaws. He lay by the dead bear under the tumbled shelter, and snow fell slowly on them.

The battle and the agony and the nearness of death brought his old instincts to the fore. All tiger, he licked his tattered form and gulped hunks of rotting meat as the days went by and waited for a measure of health to return.

In the end, he limped back toward his cave. Dreamlike memories nagged him; there had been a house and someone who was good but—but—

He was cold and lame and hungry. Winter had come.

-3-

Dark Victory

"We have no further use for you," said Felgi, "but in view of the help you've been, you'll be allowed to live at least till we get back to Procyon and the Council decides your case. Also, you probably have more valuable information about the Solar System than our other prisoners. They're mostly women."

Ramacan looked at the hard, exultant face and answered dully, "If I'd known what you were planning, I'd never have helped."

"Oh, yes, you would have," snorted Felgi. "I saw your reactions when we showed you some of our means of persuasion. You Earthlings are all alike. You've been hiding from death so long that the backbone has all gone out of you. That alone makes you unfit to hold your planet."

"You have the plans of the duplicators and the transmitters and power-beams—all our technology. I helped you get them from the Stations. What more do you want?"

"Earth."

"But why? With the creators and transmitters, you can make your planets like all the old dreams of paradise. Earth is more congenial, yes, but what does environment matter to you now?"

"Earth is still the true home of man," said Felgi. There was a fanaticism in his eyes such as Ramacan had never seen even in nightmare. "It should belong to the best race of man. Also—well, our culture couldn't stand that technology. Procyonite civilization grew up in adversity, it's been nothing but struggle and hardship, it's become part of our nature now. With the Czernigi destroyed, we *must* find another enemy."

Oh, yes, thought Ramacan. *It's happened before, in Earth's bloody old past. Nations that knew nothing but war and suffering, became molded by them, glorified the harsh virtues that had enabled them to survive. A militaristic state can't afford peace and leisure and prosperity; its people might begin to think for themselves. So the government looks for conquest outside the borders—Needful or not, there must be war to maintain the control of the military.*

How human are the Procyonites now? What's twisted them in the centuries of their terrible evolution? They're no longer men, they're fighting robots, beasts of prey, they have to have blood.

"You saw us shell the Stations from space," said Felgi. "Rebirth, Creator, Transmitter—they're radioactive craters now. Not a machine is running on Earth, not a tube is alight—nothing! And with the creators on which their lives depended inert, Earthlings will go back to utter savagery."

"Now what?" asked Ramacan wearily.

"We're standing off Mercury, refueling," said Felgi.

"Then it's back to Procyon. We'll use our creator to record most of the crew, they can take turns being briefly recreated during the voyage to maintain the ship and correct the course. We'll be little older when we get home.

"Then, of course, the Council will send out a fleet with recorded crews. They'll take over Sol, eliminate the surviving population, and recolonize Earth. After that—" The mad fires blazed high in his eyes. "The stars! A galactic empire, ultimately."

"Just so you can have war," said Ramacan tonelessly. "Just so you can keep your people stupid slaves."

"That's enough," snapped Felgi. "A decadent culture can't be expected to understand our motives."

Ramacan stood thinking. There would still be humans around when the Procyonites came back. There would be forty years to prepare. Men in space-ships, here and there throughout the System, would come home, would see the ruin of Earth and know who must be guilty. With creators, they could rebuild quickly, they could arm themselves, duplicate vengeance-hungry men by the millions.

Unless Solarian man was so far gone in decay that he was only capable of blind panic. But Ramacan didn't think so. Earth had slipped, but not that far.

Felgi seemed to read his mind. There was cruel satisfaction in his tones: "Earth will have no chance to rearm. We're using the power from Mercury Station to run our own large duplicator, turning rock into osmium fuel for our engines. But when we're finished, we'll blow up the Station too. Spaceships will drift power-less, the colonists on the planets will die as their environmental regulators stop functioning, no wheel will turn in all the Solar System. That, I should think, will be the final touch!"

Indeed, indeed. Without power, without tools, without food or shelter, the final collapse would come. Nothing but a few starveling savages would be left when the Procyonites returned. Ramacan felt an emptiness within himself.

Life had become madness and nightmare. The end…

"You'll stay here till we get around to recording you," said Felgi. He turned on his heel and walked out.

Ramacan slumped back into a seat. His desperate eyes traveled around and around the bare little cabin that was his prison, around and around like the crazy whirl of his thoughts. He looked at the guard who stood in the doorway, leaning on his blaster, contemptuously bored with the captive. If—if—O almighty gods, if *that* was to inherit green Earth!

What to do, what to do? There must be some answer, some way, no problem was altogether without solution. Or was it? What guarantee did he have of cosmic justice? He buried his face in his hands.

I was a coward, he thought. *I was afraid of pain. So I rationalized, I told myself they probably didn't want much, I used my influence to help them get duplicators and plans. And the others were cowards too, they yielded, they were cravenly eager to help the conquerors—and this is our pay!*

What to do, what to do? If somehow the ship were lost, if it never came back—The Procyonites would wonder. They'd send another ship or two—no more—to investigate. And in forty years Sol could be ready to meet those ships—ready to carry the war to an unprepared enemy—if in the meantime they'd had a chance to rebuild, if Mercury Power Station were spared—

But the ship would blow the Station out of existence, and the ship would return with news of Sol's ruin, and the invaders would come swarming in—would go ravening out through an unsuspecting galaxy like a spreading plague—

How to stop the ship—now?

Ramacan grew aware of the thudding of his heart; it seemed to shake his whole body with its violence. And his hands were cold and clumsy, his mouth was parched, he was afraid.

He got up and walked over toward the guard. The Procyonite hefted his blaster, but there was no alertness in him, he had no fear of an unarmed member of the conquered race.

He'll shoot me down, thought Ramacan. *The death I've been running from all my life is on me now. But it's been a long life and a good one, and better to finish it now than drag out a few miserable years as their despised prisoner, and—and—I hate their guts!*

"What do you want?" asked the Procyonite.

"I feel sick," said Ramacan. His voice was almost a whisper in the dryness of his throat. "Let me out."

"Get back."

"It'll be messy. Let me go to the lavatory."

He stumbled, nearly falling. "Go ahead," said the guard curtly. "I'll be along, remember."

Ramacan swayed on his feet as he approached the man. His shaking hands closed on the blaster barrel and yanked the weapon loose. Before the guard could yell, Ramacan drove the butt into his face. A remote corner of his mind was shocked at the savagery that welled up in him when the bones crunched.

The guard toppled. Ramacan eased him to the floor, slugged him again to make sure he would lie quiet, and stripped him of his long outer coat, his boots, and helmet. His hands were really trembling now; he could hardly get the simple garments on.

If he was caught—well, it only made a few minutes' difference. But he was still afraid. Fear screamed inside him.

He forced himself to walk with nightmare slowness down the long corridor. Once he passed another man, but there was no discovery. When he had rounded the corner, he was violently sick.

He went down a ladder to the engine room. Thank the gods he'd been interested enough to inquire about the layout of the ship when they first arrived! The door stood open and he went in.

A couple of engineers were watching the giant creator at work. It pulsed and hummed and throbbed with power, energy from the sun and from dissolving atoms of rocks—atoms recreated as the osmium that would power the ship's engines on the long voyage back. Tons of fuel spilling down into the bins.

Ramacan closed the soundproof door and shot the engineers.

Then he went over to the creator and reset the controls. It began to manufacture plutonium.

He smiled then, with an immense relief, an incredulous realization that he had won. He sat down and cried with sheer joy.

The ship would not get back. Mercury Station would endure. And on that basis, a few determined men in the Solar System could rebuild. There would be horror on Earth, howling chaos, most of its population would plunge into savagery and death. But enough would live, and remain civilized, and get ready for revenge.

Maybe it was for the best, he thought. Maybe Earth really had gone into a twilight of purposeless ease. True it was that there had been none of the old striving and hoping and gallantry which had made man what he was. No art, no science, no adventure—a smug self-satisfaction, an unreal immortality in a synthetic paradise. Maybe this shock and challenge was what Earth needed, to show the starward way again.

As for him, he had had many centuries of life, and he realized now what a deep inward weariness there had been in him. *Death,* he thought, *death is the longest voyage of all. Without death there is no evolution, no real meaning to life, the ultimate adventure has been snatched away.*

There had been a girl once, he remembered, and she had died before the rebirth machines became available. Odd—after all these centuries he could still remember how her hair had rippled in the wind, one day on a high summery hill. He wondered if he would see her.

He never felt the explosion as the plutonium reached critical mass.

Avi's feet were bleeding. Her shoes had finally given out, and rocks and twigs tore at her feet. The snow was dappled with blood.

Weariness clawed at her, she couldn't keep going—but she had to, she had to, she was afraid to stop in the wilderness.

She had never been alone in her life. There had always been the televisors and the transmitters, no place on Earth had been more than an instant away. But the world had expanded into immensity, the machines were dead, there was only cold and gloom and empty white distances. The world of warmth and music and laughter and casual enjoyment was as remote and unreal as a dream.

Was it a dream? Had she always stumbled sick and hungry through a nightmare world of leafless trees and drifting snow and wind that sheathed her in cold through the thin rags of her garments? Or was this the dream, a sudden madness of horror and death?

Death—no, no, no, she couldn't die, she was one of the immortals, she mustn't die!

The wind blew and blew.

Night was falling, winter night. A wild dog bayed, somewhere out in the gloom. She tried to scream, but her throat was raw with shrieking; only a dry croak would come out.

Help me, help me, help me.

Maybe she should have stayed with the man. He had devised traps, had caught an occasional rabbit or squirrel and flung her the leavings. But he looked at her so strangely when several days had gone by without a catch. He would have killed her and eaten her; she had to flee.

Run, run, run—She couldn't run, the forest reached on forever, she was caught in cold and night, hunger and death.

What had happened, what had happened, what had become of the world? What would become of her?

She had liked to pretend she was one of the ancient goddesses, creating what she willed out of nothingness, served by a huge and eternal world whose one purpose was to serve her. Where was that world now?

Hunger twisted in her like a knife. She tripped over a snow-buried log and lay there, trying feebly to rise.

We were too soft, too complacent, she thought dimly. *We lost all our powers, we were just little parasites on our machines. Now we're unfit—*

No! I won't have it! I was a goddess once—

Spoiled brat, jeered the demon in her mind. *Baby crying for its mother. You should be old enough to look after yourself—after all these centuries. You shouldn't be running in circles waiting for a help that will never come, you should be helping yourself, making a shelter, finding nuts and roots, building a trap. But you can't. All the self-reliance has withered out of you.*

No—help, help, help—

Something moved in the gloom. She choked a scream. Yellow eyes glowed like twin fires, and the immense form stepped noiselessly forth.

For an instant she gibbered in a madness of fear, and then sudden realization came and left her gaping with unbelief—then instant eager acceptance.

There could only be one tiger in this forest.

"Harol," she whispered, and climbed to her feet. "Harol."

It was all right. The nightmare was over. Harol would look after her. He would hunt for her, protect her, bring her back to the world of machines that *must* still exist. "Harol," she cried. "Harol, my dear—"

The tiger stood motionless; only his twitching tail had life. Briefly, irrelevantly, remembered sounds trickled through his mind: *"Your basic mentality should be stable for a year or two, barring accidents..."* But the noise was meaningless, it slipped through his brain into oblivion.

He was hungry. The crippled paw hadn't healed well, he couldn't catch game.

Hunger, the most elemental need of all, grinding within him, filling his tiger brain and tiger body until nothing else was left.

He stood looking at the thing that didn't run away. He had killed another a while back—he licked his mouth at the thought.

From somewhere long ago he remembered that the thing had once been—he had been—he couldn't remember—

He stalked forward.

"Harol," said Avi. There was fear rising horribly in her voice.

The tiger stopped. He knew that voice. He remembered—he remembered—

He had known her once. There was something about her that held him back.

But he was hungry. And his instincts were clamoring in him.

But if only he could remember, before it was too late—

Time stretched into a horrible eternity while they stood facing each other—the lady and the tiger.

EUTOPIA

"*Gif thit nafn!*"

The Danska words barked from the car radio as a jet whine cut across the hum of motor and tires. "Identify yourself!" Iason Philippou cast a look skyward through the bubbletop. He saw a strip of blue between two ragged green walls where pine forest lined the road. Sunlight struck off the flanks of the killer machine up there. It wailed, came about, and made a circle over him.

Sweat started cold from his armpits and ran down his ribs. *I must not panic,* he thought in a corner of his brain. *May the God help me now.* But it was his training he invoked. Psychosomatics: control the symptoms, keep the breath steady, command the pulse to slow, and the fear of death becomes something you can handle. He was young, and thus had much to lose. But the philosophers of Eutopia schooled well the children given into their care. You will be a man, they had told him, and the pride of humanity is that we are not bound by instinct and reflex; we are free because we can master ourselves.

He couldn't pass as an ordinary citizen (no, they said mootman here) of Norland. If nothing else, his Hellenic accent was too strong. But he might fool yonder pilot, for just a few minutes, into believing he was from some other domain of this history. He roughened his tone, as a partial disguise, and assumed the expected arrogance.

"Who are you? What do you want?"

"Runolf Einarsson, captain in the hird of Ottar Thorkelsson, the Lawman of Norland. I pursue one who has brought feud on his own head. Give me your name."

Runolf, Iason thought. *Why, yes, I remember you well, dark and erect with the Tyrker side of your heritage, but you have blue eyes that came long ago from Thule.* In that detached part of him which stood aside watching: *No, here I scramble my histories. I would call the autochthons Erythrai, and you call the country of your European ancestors Danarik.*

"I hight Xipec, a trader from Meyaco," he said. He did not slow down. The border was not many stadia away, so furiously had he driven through the night since he escaped from the Lawman's castle. He had small hope of getting that far, but each turn of the wheels brought him nearer. The forest was blurred with his speed.

334

"If so be, of course I am sorry to halt you," Runoff's voice crackled. "Call the Lawman and he will send swift gild for the overtreading of your rights. Yet I must have you stop and leave your car, so I may turn the farseer on your face."

"Why?" Another second or two gained.

"There was a visitor from Homeland"—Europe—"who came to Ernvik. Ottar Thorkellsson guested him freely. In return, he did a thing that only his death can make clean again. Rather than meet Otter on the Valfield, he stole a car, the same make as yours, and fled."

"Would it not serve to call him a nithing before the folk?" *I have learned this much of their barbaric customs, anyhow!*

"Now that is a strange thing for a Meyacan to say. Stop at once and get out, or I open fire."

Iason realized his teeth were clenched till they hurt. How in Hades could a man remember the hundreds of little regions, each with its own ways, into which the continent lay divided? Westfall was a more fantastic jumble than all Earth in that history where they called the place America. *Well,* he thought, *now we discover what the odds are of my hearing it named Eutopia again.*

"Very well," he said. "You leave me no choice. But I shall indeed want compensation for this insult."

He braked as slowly as he dared. The road was a hard black ribbon before him, slashed through an immensity of trees. He didn't know if these woods had ever been logged. Perhaps so, when white men first sailed through the Pentalimne (calling them the Five Seas) to found Ernvik where Duluth stood in America and Lykopolis in Eutopia. In those days Norland had spread mightily across the lake country. But then came wars with Dakotas and Magyars, to set a limit; and the development of trade—more recently of synthetics—enabled the people to use their hinterland for the hunting they so savagely loved. Three hundred years could re-establish a climax forest.

Sharply before him stood the vision of this area as he had known it at home: ordered groves and gardens, villages planned for beauty as well as use, lithe brown bodies on the athletic fields, music under moonlight…Even America the dreadful was more human than a wilderness.

They were gone, lost in the multiple dimensions of space-time, he was alone and death walked the sky. *And no self-pity, you idiot! Spend energy for survival.*

The car stopped, hard by the road edge. Iason gathered his thews, opened the door, and sprang.

Perhaps the radio behind him uttered a curse. The jet slewed around and swooped like a hawk. Bullets sleeted at his heels.

Then he was in among the trees. They roofed him with sun-speckled shadow. Their trunks stood in massive masculine strength, their branches breathed fragrance a woman might envy. Fallen needles softened his foot-thud, a thrush warbled, a light wind cooled his cheeks. He threw himself beneath the shelter of one bole and lay in it gasping with a heartbeat which all but drowned the sinister whistle above.

Presently it went away. Runoff must have called back to his lord. Ottar would fly horses and hounds to this place, the only way of pursuit. But Iason had a few hours' grace.

After that—He rallied his training, sat up and thought. If Socrates, feeling the hemlock's chill, could speak wisdom to the young men of Athens, Iason Philippou could assess his own chances. For he wasn't dead yet.

He numbered his assets. A pistol of the local slug-throwing type; a compass; a pocketful of gold and silver coins; a cloak that might double as a blanket, above the tunic-trousers-boots costume of central Westfall. And himself, the ultimate instrument. His body was tall and broad—together with fair hair and short nose, an inheritance from Gallic ancestors—and had been trained by men who won wreaths at the Olympeion. His mind, his entire nervous system, counted for still more. The pedagogues of Eutopia had made logic, semantic consciousness, perspective as natural to him as breathing; his memory was under such control that he had no need of a map; despite one calamitous mistake, he knew he was trained to deal with the most outlandish manifestations of the human spirit.

And, yes, before all else, he had reason to live. It went beyond any blind wish to continue an identity; that was only something the DNA molecule had elaborated in order to make more DNA molecules. He had his beloved to return to. He had his country: Eutopia, the Good Land, which his people had founded two thousand years ago on a new continent, leaving behind the hatreds and horrors of Europe, taking along the work of Aristotle, and writing at last in their Syntagma, "The national purpose is the attainment of universal sanity."

Iason Philippou was bound home.

He rose and started walking south.

That was on Tetrade, which his hunters called Onsdag. Some thirty-six hours later, he knew he was not in Pentade but near sunset of Thorsdag. For he lurched through the wood, mouth filled with mummy dust, belly a cavern of emptiness, knees shaking beneath him, flies a thundercloud about the sweat dried on his skin, and heard the distant belling of hounds.

A horn responded, long brazen snarl through the leaf arches. They had gotten his scent, he could not outrun horsemen and he would not see the stars again.

One hand dropped to his gun. *I'll take a couple of them with me....No.* He was still a Hellene, who did not kill uselessly, not even barbarians who meant to slay him because he had broken a taboo of theirs. *I will stand under an open sky, take their bullets, and go down into darkness remembering Eutopia and all my friends and Niki whom I love.*

Realization came, dimly, that he had left the pine forest and was in a second growth of beeches. Light gilded their leaves and caressed the slim white trunks. And what was that growl up ahead?

He stopped. A portal might remain. He had driven himself near collapse; but the organism has a reserve which the fully integrated man may call upon. From consciousness he abolished the sound of dogs, every ache and exhaustion. He drew breath after breath of air, noting its calm and purity, visualizing the oxygen atoms that poured through his starved tissues. He made the heartbeat quit racketing, go over to a deep slow pulse; he tensed and relaxed muscles until each functioned smoothly again; pain ceased to feed on itself and died away; despair gave place to calm and calculation. He trod forth.

Plowlands rolled southward before him, their young grain vivid in the light that slanted gold from the west. Not far off stood a cluster of farm buildings, long, low, and peak-roofed. Chimney smoke stained heaven. But his eyes went first to the man closer by. The fellow was cultivating with a tractor. Though the dielectric motor had been invented in this world, its use had not yet spread this far north, and gasoline fumes caught at Iason's nostrils. He had thought that stench one of the worst abominations in America—that hogpen they called Los Angeles!—but now it came to him clean and strong, for it was his hope.

The driver saw him, halted, and unshipped a rifle. Iason approached with palms held forward in token of peace. The driver relaxed. He was a typical Magyar: burly, high in the cheekbones, his beard braided, his tunic colorfully embroidered. *So I did cross the border!* Iason exulted. *I'm out of Norland and into the Voivodate of Dakoty.*

Before they sent him here, the anthropologists of the Parachronic Research Institute had of course given him an electrochemical inculcation in the principal languages of Westfall. (Pity they hadn't been more thorough about teaching him the mores. But then, he had been hastily recruited for the Norland post after Megasthenes' accidental death; and it was assumed that his experience in America gave him special qualifications for this history, which was also non-Alexandrine; and, to be sure, the whole object of missions like his was to learn just how societies on the different Earths did vary.) He formed the Ural-Altaic words with ease: "Greeting to you. I come as a supplicant."

The farmer sat quiet, tense, looking down on him and listening to the dogs far off in the forest. His rifle stayed ready. "Are you an outlaw?" he asked.

"Not in this realm, freeman." (Still another name and concept for "citizen"!) "I was a peaceful trader from Homeland, visiting Lawman Ottar Thorkelsson in Ernvik. His anger fell upon me, so great that he broke sacred hospitality and sought the life of me, his guest. Now his hunters are on my trail. You hear them yonder."

"Norlanders? But this is Dakoty."

Iason nodded. He let his teeth show, in the grime and stubble of his face. "Right. They've entered your country without so much as a by-your-leave. If you stand idle, they'll ride onto your freehold and slay me, who asks your help."

The farmer hefted his gun. "How do I know you speak truth?"

"Take me to the Voivode," Iason said. "Thus you keep both the law and your honor." Very carefully, he unholstered his pistol and offered it butt foremost. "I am forever your debtor."

Doubt, fear and anger pursued each other across the face of the man on the tractor. He did not take the weapon. Iason waited. *If I've read him correctly, I've gained some hours of life. Perhaps more. That will depend on the Voivode. My whole chance lies in using their own barbarism—their division into petty states, their crazy idea of honor, their fetish of property and privacy—to harness them.*

If I fail, then I shall die like a civilized man. That they cannot take away from me.

"The hounds have winded you. They'll be here before we can escape," said the Magyar uneasily.

Relief made Iason dizzy. He fought down the reaction and said: "We can take care of them for a time. Let me have some gasoline."

"Ah...thus!" The other man chuckled and jumped to earth. "Good thinking, stranger. And thanks, by the way. Life has been dull hereabouts for too many years."

He had a spare can of fuel on his machine. They lugged it back along Iason's trail for a considerable distance, dousing soil and trees. If that didn't throw the pack off, nothing would.

"Now, hurry!" The Magyar led the way at a trot.

His farmstead was built around an open courtyard. Sweet scents of hay and livestock came from the barns. Several children ran forth to gape. The wife shooed them back inside, took her husband's rifle, and mounted guard at the door with small change of expression.

Their house was solid, roomy, aesthetically pleasing if you could accept the unrestrained tapestries and painted pillars. Above the fireplace was a niche for a family altar. Though most people in Westfall had left myth long behind them, these peasants still seemed to adore the Triple God Odin-Attila-Manitou. But the man went to a sophisticated radiophone. "I don't have an aircraft myself," he said, "but I can get one."

Iason sat down to wait. A girl neared him shyly with a beaker of beer and a slab of cheese on coarse dark bread. "Be you guest-holy," she said.

"May my blood be yours," Iason answered by rote. He managed to take the refreshment not quite like a wolf.

The farmer came back. "A few more minutes," he said. "I am Arpad, son of Kalman."

"Iason Philippou." It seemed wrong to give a false name. The hand he clasped was hard and warm.

"What made you fall afoul of old Ottar?" Arpad inquired.

"I was lured," Iason said bitterly. "Seeing how free the unwed women were—"

"Ah, indeed. They're a lickerish lot, those Danskar. Nigh as shameless as Tyrkers." Arpad got pipe and tobacco pouch off a shelf. "Smoke?"

"No, thank you." *We don't degrade ourselves with drugs in Eutopia.*

The hounds drew close. Their chant broke into confused yelps. Horns shrilled. Arpad stuffed his pipe as coolly as if this were a show. "How they must be swearing!" he grinned. "I'll give the Danskar credit for being poets, also in their oaths. And brave men, to be sure. I was up that way ten years back, when Voivode Bela sent people to help them after the floods they'd suffered. I saw them laugh as they fought the wild water. And then, their sort gave us a hard time in the old wars."

"Do you think there will ever be wars again?" Iason asked. Mostly he wanted to avoid speaking further of his troubles. He wasn't sure how his host might react.

"Not in Westfall. Too much work to do. If young blood isn't cooled enough by a duel now and then, why, there're wars to hire out for, among the barbarians overseas. Or else the planets. My oldest boy champs to go there."

Iason recalled that several realms further south were pooling their resources for astronautical work. Being approximately at the technological level of the American history, and not required to maintain huge military or social programs, they had put a base on the moon and sent expeditions to Ares. In time, he supposed, they would do what the Hellenes had done a thousand years ago, and make Aphrodite into a new Earth. But would they have a true civilization—be rational men in a rationally planned society—by then? Wearily, he doubted it.

A roar outside brought Arpad to his feet. "There's your wagon," he said. "Best you go. Red Horse will fly you to Varady."

"The Danskar will surely come here soon," Iason worried.

"Let them," Arpad shrugged. "I'll alert the neighborhood, and they're not so stupid that they won't know I have. We'll hold a slanging match, and then I'll order them off my land. Farewell, guest."

"I…I wish I could repay your kindness."

"Bah! Was fun. Also, a chance to be a man before my sons."

Iason went out. The aircraft was a helicopter—they hadn't discovered gravitics here—piloted by a taciturn young autochthon. He explained that he was a stockbreeder, and that he was conveying the stranger less as a favor to Arpad than as an answer to the Norlander impudence of entering Dakoty unbidden. Iason was just as happy to be free of conversation.

The machine whirred aloft. As it drove south he saw clustered hamlets, the occasional hall of some magnate, otherwise only rich undulant plains. They kept the population within bounds in Westfall as in Eutopia. But not because they knew that men need space and clean air, Iason thought. No, they acted from greed on behalf of the reified family. A father did not wish to divide his possessions among many children.

The sun went down and a nearly full moon climbed huge and pumpkin-colored over the eastern rim of the world. Iason sat back, feeling the engine's throb in his bones, almost savoring his fatigue, and watched. No sign of the lunar base was visible. He must return home before he could see the moon glitter with cities.

And home was more than infinitely remote. He could travel to the farthest of those stars which had begun twinkling forth against purple dusk—were it possible to exceed the speed of light—and not find Eutopia. It lay sundered from him by dimensions and destiny. Nothing but the warpfields of a parachronion might take him across the time lines to his own.

He wondered about the why. That was an empty speculation, but his tired brain found relief in childishness. Why had the God willed that time branch and rebranch, enormous, shadowy, bearing universes like the Yggdrasil of Danskar legend? Was it so that man could realize every potentiality there was in him?

Surely not. So many of them were utter horror.

Suppose Alexander the Conqueror had not recovered from the fever that smote him in Babylon. Suppose, instead of being chastened thereby, so that he spent the rest of a long life making firm the foundations of his empire—suppose he had died?

Well, it *did* happen, and probably in more histories than not. There the empire went down in mad-dog wars of succession. Hellas and the Orient broke apart. Nascent science withered away into metaphysics, eventually outright mysticism. A convulsed Mediterranean world was swept up piecemeal by the Romans: cold, cruel, uncreative, claiming to be the heirs of Hellas even as they destroyed Corinth. A heretical Jewish prophet founded a mystery cult which took root everywhere, for men despaired of this life. And that cult knew not the name of tolerance. Its priests denied all but one of the manifold ways in which the God is seen; they cut down the holy groves, took from the house its humble idols, and martyred the last men whose souls were free.

Oh yes, Iason thought, *in time they lost their grip. Science could be born, almost two millennia later than ours. But the poison remained: the idea that men must conform not only in behavior but in belief. Now, in America, they call it totalitarianism. And because of it, the nuclear rockets have had their nightmare hatching.*

I hated that history, its filth, its waste, its ugliness, its restriction, its hypocrisy, its insanity. I will never have a harder task than when I pretended to be an American that I might see from within how they thought they were ordering their lives. But tonight. . . I pity you, poor raped world. I do not know whether to wish you soon dead, as you likeliest will be, or hope that one day your descendants can struggle to what we achieved an age ago.

They were luckier here. I must admit that. Christendom fell before the onslaught of Arab, Viking and Magyar. Afterward the Islamic Empire killed itself in civil wars and the barbarians of Europe could go their own way. When they crossed the Atlantic, a thousand years back, they had not the power to commit genocide on the natives; they must come to terms. They had not the industry, then, to gut the hemisphere; perforce they grew into the land slowly, taking it as a man takes his bride.

But those vast dark forests, mournful plains, unpeopled deserts and mountains where the wild goats run. . .those entered their souls. They will always, inwardly, be savages.

He sighed, settled down, and made himself sleep. Niki haunted his dreams.

Where a waterfall marked the head of navigation on that great river known variously as the Zeus, Mississippi and Longflood, a basically agricultural people who had not developed air transport as far as in Eutopia were sure to build a city. Trade and military power brought with them government, art, science and education. Varady housed a hundred thousand or so—they didn't take censuses in Westfall—whose inward-turning homes surrounded the castle towers of the Voivode. Waking, Iason walked out on his balcony and heard the traffic rumble. Beyond roofs lay the defensive outworks. He wondered if a peace founded on the balance of power between statelets could endure.

But the morning was too cool and bright for such musings. He was here, safe, cleansed and rested. There had been little talk when he arrived. Seeing the condition of the fugitive who sought him, Bela Zsolt's son had given him dinner and sent him to bed.

Soon we'll confer, Iason understood, *and I'll have to be most careful if I'm to live.* But the health which had been restored to him glowed so strong that he felt no need to suppress worry.

A bell chimed within. He re-entered the room, which was spacious and airy however over-ornamented. Recalling that custom disapproved of nudity, he threw on a robe, not without wincing at its zigzag pattern. "Be welcome," he called in Magyar.

The door opened and a young woman wheeled in his breakfast. "Good luck to you, guest," she said with an accent; she was a Tyrker, and even wore the beaded and fringed dress of her people. "Did you sleep well?"

"Like Coyote after a prank," he laughed.

She smiled back, pleased at his reference, and set a table. She joined him too. Guests did not eat alone. He found venison a rather strong dish this early in the day, but the coffee was delicious and the girl chattered charmingly. She was employed as a maid, she told him, and saving her money for a marriage portion when she returned to Cherokee land.

"Will the Voivode see me?" Iason asked after they had finished.

"He awaits your pleasure." Her lashes fluttered. "But we have no haste." She began to untie her belt.

Hospitality so lavish must be the result of customal superimposition, the easy-going Danskar and still freer Tyrker mores influencing the austere Magyars. Iason felt almost as if he were now home, in a world where individuals found delight in each other as they saw fit. He was tempted, too—that broad smooth brow reminded him of Niki. But no. He had little time. Unless he established his position unbreakably firm before Ottar thought to call Bela, he was trapped.

He leaned across the table and patted one small hand. "I thank you, lovely," he said, "but I am under vow."

She took the answer as naturally as she had posed the question. This world, which had the means to unify, chose as if deliberately to remain in shards of separate culture. Something of his alienation came back to him as he watched her sway out the door. For he had only glimpsed a small liberty. Life in Westfall remained a labyrinth of tradition, manner, law and taboo.

Which had well-nigh cost him his life, he reflected; and might yet. Best hurry!

He tumbled into the clothes laid out for him and made his way down long stone halls. Another servant directed him to the Voivode's seat. Several people waited outside to have complaints heard or disputes adjudicated. But when he announced himself, Iason was passed through immediately.

The room beyond was the most ancient part of the building. Age-cracked timber columns, grotesquely carved with gods and heroes, upheld a low roof. A fire pit in the floor curled smoke toward a hole; enough stayed behind for Iason's eyes to sting. They could easily have given their chief magistrate a modern office, he thought—but no, because his ancestors had judged in this kennel, so must he.

Light filtering through slit windows touched the craggy features of Bela and lost itself in shadow. The Voivode was thickset and gray-haired; his features bespoke a considerable admixture of Tyrker chromosomes. He sat a wooden throne, his body wrapped in a blanket, horns and feathers on his head. His left hand bore a horse-tailed staff and a drawn saber was laid across his lap.

"Greeting, Iason Philippou," he said gravely. He gestured at a stool. "Be seated."

"I thank my lord." The Eutopian remembered how his own people had outgrown titles.

"Are you prepared to speak truth?"

"Yes."

"Good." Abruptly the figure relaxed, crossed legs and extracted a cigar from beneath the blanket. "Smoke? No? Well, I will." A smile meshed the leathery face in wrinkles. "You being a foreigner, I needn't keep up this damned ceremony."

Iason tried to reply in kind. "That's a relief. We haven't much in the Peloponnesian Republic."

"Your home country, eh? I hear things aren't going so well there."

"No. Homeland grows old. We look to Westfall for our tomorrows."

"You said last night that you came to Norland as a trader."

"To negotiate a commercial agreement." Iason was staying as near his cover story as possible. You couldn't tell different histories that the Hellenes had invented the parachronion. Besides changing the very conditions that were being studied, it would be too cruel to let men know that other men lived in perfection. "My country is interested in buying lumber and furs."

"Hm. So Ottar invited you to stay with him. I can grasp why. We don't see many Homelanders. But one day he was after your blood. What happened?"

Iason might have claimed privacy, but that wouldn't have sat well. And an outright lie was dangerous; before this throne, one was automatically under oath. "To a degree, no doubt, the fault was mine," he said. "One of his family, almost grown, was attracted to me and—I had been long away from my wife, and everyone had told me the Danskar hold with freedom before marriage, and—well, I meant no harm. I merely encouraged—But Ottar found out, and challenged me."

"Why did you not meet him?"

No use to say that a civilized man did not engage in violence when any alternative existed. "Consider, my lord," Iason said. "If I lost, I'd be dead. If I won, that would be the end of my company's project. The Ottarssons would never have taken weregild, would they? No, at the bare least they'd ban us all from their land. And Peloponnesus needs that timber. I thought I'd do best to escape. Later my associates could disown me before Norland."

"M-m...strange reasoning. But you're loyal, anyhow. What do you ask of me?"

"Only safe conduct to—Steinvik." Iason almost said "Neathenai." He checked his eagerness. "We have a factor there, and a ship."

Bela streamed smoke from his mouth and scowled at the glowing cigar end. "I'd like to know why Ottar grew wrathful. Doesn't sound like him. Though I suppose, when a man's daughter is involved, he doesn't feel so lenient." He hunched forward. "For me," he said harshly, "the important thing is that armed Norlanders crossed my border without asking."

"A grievous violation of your rights, true."

Bela uttered a horseman's obscenity. "You don't understand, you. Borders aren't sacred because Attila wills it, whatever the shamans prate. They're sacred because that's the only way to keep the peace. If I don't openly resent this crossing, and punish Ottar for it, some hothead might well someday be tempted; and now everyone has nuclear weapons."

"I don't want war on my account!" Iason exclaimed, appalled. "Send me back to him first!"

"Oh no, no such nonsense. Ottar's punishment shall be that I deny him his revenge, regardless of the rights and wrongs of your case. He'll swallow that."

Bela rose. He put his cigar in an ashtray, lifted the saber, and all at once he was transfigured. A heathen god might have spoken: "Henceforward, Iason Philippou, you are peace-holy in Dakoty. While you remain beneath our shield, ill done you is ill done me, my house and my people. So help me the Three!"

Self-command broke down. Iason went on his knees and gasped his thanks.

"Enough," Bela grunted. "Let's arrange for your transportation as fast as may be. I'll send you by air, with a military squadron. But of course I'll need permission from the realms you'll cross. That will take time. Go back, relax, I'll have you called when everything's ready."

Iason left, still shivering.

He spent a pleasant couple of hours adrift in the castle and its courtyards. The young men of Bela's retinue were eager to show off before a Homelander. He had to grant the picturesqueness of their riding, wrestling, shooting and riddling contests; something stirred in him as he listened to tales of faring over the plains and into the forests and by river to Unnborg's fabled metropolis; the chant of a bard awakened glories which went deeper than the history told, down to the instincts of man the killer ape.

But these are precisely the bright temptations that we have turned our backs on in Eutopia. For we deny that we are apes. We are men who can reason. In that lies our manhood.

I am going home. I am going home. I am going home.

A servant tapped his arm. "The Voivode wants you." It was a frightened voice.

Iason hastened back. What had gone wrong? He was not taken to the room of the high seat. Instead, Bela awaited him on a parapet. Two men-at-arms stood at attention behind, faces blank under the plumed helmets.

The day and the breeze were mocked by Bela's look. He spat on Iason's feet. "Ottar has called me," he said.

"I— Did he say—"

"And I thought you were only trying to bed a girl! Not seeking to destroy the house that befriended you!"

"My lord—"

"Have no fears. You sucked my oath out of me. Now I must spend years trying to make amends to Ottar for cheating him."

"But—" *Calm! Calm! You might have expected this.*

"You will not ride in a warcraft. You'll have your escort, yes. But the machine that carries you must be burned afterward. Now go wait by the stables, next to the dung heap, till we're ready."

"I meant no harm," Iason protested. "I did not know."

"Take him away before I kill him," Bela ordered.

Steinvik was old. These narrow cobbled streets, these gaunt houses, had seen dragon ships. But the same wind blew off the Atlantic, salt and fresh, to drive from Iason the last hurt of that sullenness which had ridden here with him. He pushed whistling through the crowds.

A man of Westfall, or America, would have slunk back. Had he not failed? Must he not be replaced by someone whose cover story bore no hint of Hellas? But they saw with clear eyes in Eutopia. His failure was due to an honest mistake: a mistake he would not have made had they taught him more carefully before sending him out. One learns by error.

The memory of people in Ernvik and Varady—gusty, generous people whose friendship he would have liked to keep—had nagged him awhile. But he put that aside too. There were other worlds, an endlessness of them.

A signboard creaked in the wind. The Brotherhood of Hunyadi and Ivar, Shipfolk. Good camouflage, that, in a town where every second enterprise was bent seaward. He ran to the second floor. The stairs clattered under his boots.

He spread his palm before a chart on the wall. A hidden scanner identified his fingerpatterns and a hidden door opened. The room beyond was wainscoted in local fashion. But its clean proportions spoke of home; and a Nike statuette spread wings on a shelf.

Nike…Niki…I'm coming back to you! The heart leaped in him.

Daimonax Aristides looked up from his desk. Iason sometimes wondered if anything could rock the calm of that man. "Rejoice!" the deep voice boomed. "What brings you here?"

"Bad news, I'm afraid."

"So? Your attitude suggests the matter isn't catastrophic." Daimonax's big frame left his chair, went to the wine cabinet, filled a pair of chaste and beautiful goblets, and relaxed on a couch. "Come, tell me."

Iason joined him. "Unknowingly," he said, "I violated what appears to be a prime taboo. I was lucky to get away alive."

"Eh." Daimonax stroked his iron-gray beard. "Not the first such turn, or the last. We fumble our way toward knowledge, but reality will always surprise us…. Well, congratulations on your whole skin. I'd have hated to mourn you."

Solemnly, they poured a libation before they drank. The rational man recognizes his own need for ceremony; and why not draw it from otherwise outgrown myth? Besides, the floor was stainproof.

"Do you feel ready to report?" Daimonax asked.

"Yes, I ordered the data in my head on the way here."

Daimonax switched on a recorder, spoke a few cataloguing words and said, "Proceed."

Iason flattered himself that his statement was well arranged: clear, frank and full. But as he spoke, against his will experience came back to him, not in the brain but in the guts. He saw waves sparkle on that greatest of the Pentalimne; he walked the halls of Ernvik castle with eager and wondering young Leif; he faced an Ottar become beast; he stole from the keep and overpowered a guard and by-passed the controls of a car with shaking fingers; he fled down an empty road and stumbled through an empty forest; Bela spat and his triumph was suddenly ashen. At the end, he could not refrain:

"Why wasn't I informed? I'd have taken care. But they said this was a free and healthy folk, before marriage anyway. How could I know?"

"An oversight," Daimonax agreed. "But we haven't been in this business so long that we don't still tend to take too much for granted."

"Why are we here? What have we to learn from these barbarians? With infinity to explore, why are we wasting ourselves on the second most ghastly world we've found?"

Daimonax turned off the recorder. For a time there was silence between the men. Wheels trundled outside, laughter and a snatch of song drifted through the window, the ocean blazed under a low sun.

"You do not know?" Daimonax asked at last, softly.

"Well…scientific interest, of course—" Iason swallowed. "I'm sorry. The Institute works for sound reasons. In the American history we're observing ways that man can go wrong. I suppose here also."

Daimonax shook his head. "No."

"What?"

"We are learning something far too precious to give up," Daimonax said. "The lesson is humbling, but our smug Eutopia will be the better for some humility. You weren't aware of it, because to date we haven't sufficient hard facts to publish any conclusions. And then, you are new in the profession, and your first assignment was elsewhen. But you see, we have excellent reason to believe that Westfall is also the Good Land."

"Impossible," Iason whispered.

Daimonax smiled and took a sip of wine. "Think," he said. "What does man require? First, the biological necessities, food, shelter, medicine, sex, a healthful and reasonably safe environment in which to raise his children. Second, the special human need to strive, learn, create. Well, don't they have these things here?"

"One could say the same for any Stone Age tribe. You can't equate contentment with happiness."

"Of course not. And if anything, is not ordered, unified, planned Eutopia the country of the cows? We have ended every conflict, to the very conflict of man with his own soul; we have mastered the planets; the stars are too distant; were the God not so good as to make possible the parachronion, what would be left for us?"

"Do you mean—" Iason groped after words. He reminded himself that it was not sane to take umbrage at any mere statement, however outrageous. "Without fighting, clannishness, superstition, ritual and taboo…man has nothing?"

"More or less that. Society must have structure and meaning. But nature does not dictate what structure or what meaning. Our rationalism is a non-rational choice. Our leashing of the purely animal within us is simply another taboo. We may love as we please, but not hate as we please. So are we more free than men in Westfall?"

"But surely some cultures are better than others!"

"I do not deny that," Daimonax said. "I only point out that each has its price. For what we enjoy at home, we pay dearly. We do not allow ourselves a single unthinking, merely felt impulse. By excluding danger and hardship, by eliminating distinctions between men, we leave no hopes of victory. Worst, perhaps, is this: that we have become pure individuals. We belong to no one. Our sole obligation is negative, not to compel any other individual. The state—an engineered organization, a faceless undemanding mechanism—takes care of each need and each hurt. Where is loyalty unto death? Where is the intimacy of an entire shared lifetime? We play at ceremonies, but because we know they are arbitrary gestures, what is their value? Because we have made our world one, where are color and contrast, where is pride in being peculiarly ourselves?

"Now these Westfall people, with all their faults, do know who they are, what they are, what they belong to and what belongs to them. Tradition is not buried in books but is part of life; and so their dead remain with them in loving memory. Their problems are real; hence their successes are real. They believe in their rites. The family, the kingdom, the race is something to live and die for. They use their brains less, perhaps—though even that I am not certain of—but they use nerves, glands, muscles more. So they know an aspect of being human which our careful world has denied itself.

"If they have kept this while creating science and machine technology, should we not try to learn from them?"

Iason had no answer.

Eventually Daimonax said he might as well return to Eutopia. After a vacation, he could be reassigned to some history he might find more congenial. They parted in friendly wise.

The parachronion hummed. Energies pulsed between the universes. The gate opened and Iason stepped through.

He entered a glazed colonnade. White Neathenai swept in grace and serenity down to the water. The man who received him was a philosopher. Decent tunic and sandals hung ready to be donned. From somewhere resounded a lyre.

Joy trembled in Iason. Leif Ottarsson fell out of memory. He had only been tempted in his loneliness by a chance resemblance to his beloved. Now he was home. And Niki waited for him, Nikias Demostheneou, most beautiful and enchanting of boys.

Afterward to *Eutopia*

Readers ought to know that writers are not responsible for the opinions and behavior of their characters. But many people don't. In consequence, I, for instance, have been called a fascist to my face. Doubtless the present story will get me accused of worse. And I only wanted to spin a yarn!

Well, perhaps a bit more. That can't be helped. Everybody views the world from his particular philosophical platform. Hence any writer who tries to report what he sees is, inevitably, propagandizing. But as a rule, the propaganda lies below the surface. This is twice true of science fiction, which begins by transmuting reality to frank unreality.

So what have I been advocating here? Not any particular form of society. On the contrary, humankind seems to me so splendidly and ironically variable that there can be no perfect social order. I do suspect that few people are biologically adapted to civilization; consider its repeated collapses. This idea could be wrong, of course. Even if true, it may just be another factor which our planning should take into account. But the mutability of man is hardly open to question.

Thus each arrangement he makes will have its flaws, which in the end bring it to ruin; but each will also have its virtues. I myself don't think here-and-now is such a bad place to live. But others might. In fact, others do. At the same time, we cannot deny that *some* ways of life are, on balance, evil. The worst and most dangerous are those which cannot tolerate anything different from themselves.

So in an age of conflict we need a clear understanding of our own values—and the enemy's. Likewise we have to see with equal clarity the drawbacks of both cultures. This is less a moral than a strategic imperative. Only on such a basis can we know what we ought to do and what is possible for us to do.

For we are not caught in a meaningless nightmare. We are inhabiting a real world where events have understandable causes and causes have effects. We were never given any sacred mission, and it would be fatal to believe otherwise. We do, though, have the right of self-preservation. Let us know what it is we want to preserve. Then common sense and old-fashioned guts will probably get us through.

This is rather a heavy sermon to load on a story which was, after all, meant as entertainment. The point was made far better by Robinson Jeffers:

"Long live freedom and damn the ideologies."

(Editor's note: Normally I prefer to let the stories speak for themselves. There are exceptions to this rule. I was going to comment on this story in my Editor's Introduction but I think that Poul Anderson expressed my thoughts in a manner far superior to what I could do.)

HORSE TRADER

B. *C. 250: The aeolipile of Hero spun in the temple at Alexandria, hissing softly to itself and blowing jets of steam into the fire-lit dimness. It was only for display, an embryonic turbine which would develop no further for lack of the knowledge that it could be put to work. Fifty light-years away, on the planet he called Ruhannoc, Zerwil the Wise had made an ingenious contraption which could have evolved into a pump or a locomotive engine; but it never did, because it had not occurred to anyone that there was any other source of energy than living muscles.*

A. D. 1495: Leonardo da Vinci regarded his airplane model wistfully, and then laid it aside. It could have flown; Man could have risen even as the birds, save that there was no power plant available. He did not know that there was a planet less than nine light-years away on which they were building efficient internal-combustion engines, and that for several reasons—among them the fact that aerial life had never evolved there—they did not think of using this power to give themselves wings.

A. D. 1942: The Allied nations were searching with an intensity approaching desperation for a means of detecting the enemy submarines whose wolf packs were harrowing their convoys and threatening to snap the thin Atlantic lifeline. Supersonics looked promising, but that was a little-known field in which researchers had to start from the very bottom. Not far away, as Galactic distances go, the people of Sumanor on the planet they called Urish could have told the Allied councillors everything about supersonics. It would have been a fair exchange, for on Urish they had never heard of submarines.

A.D. 2275: The rangy blond man with the somewhat improbable name of Auchinleck Welcome stepped off the sidewalk and strode across the springy, semi-living warmth of the floor toward the arched gateway. Suitably dignified flame-letters danced above it to spell out:

BUREAU OF INTERCULTURAL EXCHANGE
Technical Division

But some light-hearted soul had painted a horse on the door and Welcome, not one to stand on dignity, had allowed it to remain. His office was known from Mercury to Minerva as the Horse Traders. He was willing to agree that the description was apt.

The door opened for him and he walked through the outer office, nodding to the clerks and secretaries at the computers, tapefiles, dictoscribes, and the rest of the complex office paraphernalia. A few bars of *Waltzing Matilda* whistled between his teeth as he entered the inner suite. The receptionist smiled at his greeting and he went by her and through the office of his private secretary, Christine Ernenek.

"'Morning," he said, pausing. Despite all the years he had spent in space, there was still a hint of Australian twang in his speech. "How's life?"

"Just fine, Auch," the Greenlander answered. "I think you have a busy day lined up."

"Who's first?"

She glanced at her memotab.

"The little duck from Arcturus. Robotics, you know. Have you seen him yet?"

"No, too busy. He'll have been going through the usual processing first, anyway." Welcome sighed. "When will Health get it through their heads that Man hasn't caught an extraterrestrial disease yet?"

"There's always the first time, Auch. And then the diplomats and so on have to see him. He is a sort of ambassador, after all."

"I know, I know." Welcome nodded impatiently and fumbled out a battered corncob pipe and began stuffing it. Christine had been in the office longer than he; he'd only been given the job a month ago, because of his engineering work on Freyja. A flicker of eagerness kindled in him. "This robotics stuff may turn out to be one of our biggest hauls."

"Maybe so." Christine giggled. "He's cute, that duck." Glancing at the tab again: "Then, of course, you're still negotiating with Vega, Sirius and Procyon. Oh, yes, and a Centaurian."

"What?" Welcome almost dropped his pipe.

"A Centaurian. Alpha A III, from the clan of Brogu, continent of Almerik, name of Helmung. He wants spaceships and atomic energy in exchange for witchcraft."

"Oh, no!"

"The main office said for you to see him, anyway. He seems to have special abilities—Well, you'll find out." Christine grinned with friendly malice. "Good luck."

Welcome shrugged and went on into his own office. You had to take the bad with the good, he supposed. There had been the tentacled monster from Van Maanen's Star who had grown very indignant on learning that Earth didn't care to trade the null-null drive for a system of astrology which, taking Galactic drift into account, was guaranteed infallible. But against that you had to balance the Zarbadian selective-killing process; with a little more work, that device should be able to annihilate any disease germ just by putting the patient under a force generator. And at the present moment, the envoys from Procyon and Vega—possibly the one from Arcturus, too—were carrying portfolios which meant revolutionary technological advances for Earth.

When it took more than four years objective time to reach even the nearest star—however short the interval was subjectively for those on board the spaceship—the traditional cargoes became valueless. No mineral, no material treasure whatever, was worth the cost of such hauling. Nor was there any special reason these days for humans to emigrate. But the intangibles of knowledge—that was another matter. You could well afford to spend a few megacredits and decades, if it meant learning a technology your race might not otherwise master for a thousand years.

And Earth had the only intercultural clearing house in the Galaxy. *They still have to come to us, even if we are the ones who haul them here and back. I just park myself and wait.*

Welcome sat down, feeling the sensuous flow of the chair as it modeled itself to his angular contours, and let his eyes rove the office. It was a big room, tastefully decorated in the Neoflamboyant style, a broad window opening on the jagged view of Luna beyond the dome. It was near dawn, there was a glare on the highest peaks shouldering above the horizon, but Earth still dominated a heaven full of stars. He glanced at the planet, thinking of his family in Sydney. They were visiting there. It wasn't fair to children, keeping them on Luna all the time; they ought to have some sea and open sky.

Well, work to do.

Arcturus—Two planets with intelligent natives, of which only one group had more than a primitive technology, Welcome recalled. Those were a friendly race, anxious to please, and the three expeditions there had all returned quite excited about the cybernetic advances of the leading nation. So now the Arcturian ducks had come to swap horses. Welcome decided that he would get some rather low-pressure salesmanship; after all, the Arcturians couldn't be sure how much humanity already knew, and they were not an aggressive breed.

Still, when you met a people who weren't human to begin with, and had a different cultural pattern to boot, you never knew what to expect. That was the reason for the informal basis on which the Horse Traders were allowed to operate, and their chief's nearly absolute power to drive bargains. But God help him if he made a mistake!

Christine's voice came over the intercom, jarring him to full awareness: "The envoy Rappapa of Kwillitch, planet Arcturus V, to see you, Freeman Welcome." There was a confused noise in the background, and he thought her voice held an uncontrollable laughter.

"Send him in, please." Welcome stood up as the door opened. Since notions of courtesy varied fantastically from world to world, he had decided to stick by Terrestrial conventions.

"HUP-two-three-four! HUP-two-three-four! HUP-two-three-four!"

Welcome thought briefly and wildly that he must be dreaming. A small regiment of dolls was entering his office.

No, not dolls—robots, shiny humanoid robots five inches high. They goosestepped on perfect marching order, swinging their arms in unison, accompanied by tanks and helicopters built to scale. Behind them, quacking his shrill commands, was the Arcturian. He was of ostrichlike shape, some four feet tall, blue-feathered and crested; instead of wings, he had skinny four-fingered arms carrying a large box, and his head was big and round, pop-eyed, with a flexible bill.

"HUP-two-three-four! HUP-two-three-four! Com-pan-ee—HALT! Ri-iight-FACE! Present—ARMS!"

The toy soldiers halted, wheeled, and snapped to attention. A helicopter buzzed watchfully over Welcome's head. It was about the size of a pigeon.

"How do you do, how do you do, noble sir?" The Arcturian bowed, touching the floor with his beak. "I trust that you in splendid health find yourself?"

"Yes," said Welcome faintly. "Excuse me while I pick up my jaw."

"If I your excellency's magnificent jaw have caused to fall, it is to be of the most apologetic," said the Arcturian unhappily.

"Never mind," said Welcome. "Please sit down, Freeman Rappapa. If you wish to," he added hastily; he couldn't remember whether this particular species sat or not.

"If you will it of indifference find, I will stand in the luminous presence of your excellency," said Rappapa. "Among my greetings-to-you-conveying folk, only nesting females sit."

"I—well, do you smoke?" Welcome extended a box of cigars.

"You are to be magnificently thanked," said Rappapa, accepting one. *"Whichuwaki!"* One of the helicopters swooped down and shot out a flame to light it for him.

Welcome seated himself. "I take it those are robots."

"Of a most humble sort, for demonstration purposes alone," said Rappapa. "They are powered by radiation from this control box here, as your excellency is undoubtedly aware. The brain circuits are also herein contained. Each machine has its individual brain, controlling the external body, or any number of brains can be joined in series to produce higher effectiveness."

Welcome forced himself to be impassive. Inwardly, his heart leaped. If the Arcturians could make a cybernetic setup that compact, what *couldn't* they do?

"May I add they can act at individual discretion, within the limits of their basic directives?" said Rappapa eagerly. "Possibly toys or household servants for your superb people?"

"It seems to me that a house could be built to do everything itself, without needing a special robot," said Welcome.

"Of a most suredly! These, as I say, are illustrative only. It has insignificantly occurred to me that your splendid spaceships could be given brains of their own, eliminating necessity for crews on those so-long voyages."

"To be sure, Freeman Rappapa. And control and communications in general—you can doubtless show us a great deal we don't know."

"It is of a strangeness that you, who so daringly bridged the stars, have not surpassed us in this humble endeavor."

"Well, it's not so odd, really." Welcome rekindled his pipe. "Many things determine the technological progress of a culture: social need and demand, the general background of knowledge and tradition, the ability of individual researchers within a given field—sheer accident, too, I suppose. My race has gone furthest in developing transportation and energy sources. Your people stayed on their planet, but instead have gone in primarily for robots, automata, computers—cybernetics. On Procyon A III, they're super-biologists, especially in the line of controlled genetics, but lack atomic energy. And so on throughout the Galaxy. It would be strange if the history of any one race had caused it to excel in everything."

"I am blinded by the clarity of your explanation. Sir, dare I hope that you will find our little skill worthy of consideration?"

"Indeed you may," said Welcome. "Was there anything in particular you would like to have from us, or do you first want to see what we can offer?"

"Your incredible process for obtaining atomic energy from the disintegration of any matter whatsoever would prostrate us of Kwillitch with joy."

The human rubbed his chin. That was certainly a reasonable enough asking price. In fact, his conscience hurt him a bit.

"I think that can be agreed on," he said blandly. "You have, of course, brought specialized assistants, and plans and textbooks and so on, from which our people can learn what you have to teach them? Good. Then you should designate some of your people to study our energy-conversion techniques. The new hypnopedic system will make it possible for both sides to learn these things rather fast. Of course, it isn't quite that simple. One can't introduce a new science into a vacuum. For example, being told all about nuclear disintegration isn't going to help you unless you already know something about magnetronics. I'll give you a general outline of the course, and would like you to prepare a similar outline dealing with cybernetics, just so each side can know exactly what it is the other has to offer. Then the final agreement can be made and we can proceed to teach each other."

"That is a scheme of the slyest magnanimity," said Rappapa with innocent enthusiasm.

"Excellent." Welcome slouched farther back in his chair and went on to social matters. How did the Arcturian party like the quarters which had been prepared for them here in the dome? The food and gravity and air-conditioning were satisfactory? They were enjoying themselves? Tours of Earth would be arranged for them—everything to make the guests from afar feel at home.

And to disarm them, make them more receptive to our suggestions. Well, why not? When the future of entire planets is involved, naiveté would be criminal.

Rappapa was charmed and quacked eloquent praises. His party had already seen a good deal of the dome, met the other extraterrestrials currently there, been lavishly entertained.

Welcome nodded. There was certainly no rule against the different embassies having contact and perhaps driving their own bargains independently of Earth.

As a matter of fact, such a deal was going on right now. The Sirian knowledge of nucleonics had turned out to be inferior to Earth's, but the Vegan representative—who had come alone—was willing to trade some of his high-pressure chemistry for it.

Welcome didn't care very much: since he could always get the chemistry from Vega in exchange for something else—or even from Sirius, perhaps. Once a planet—or nation, tribe, clan, individual—had bought a technology, it was their own business what they did with it. A Horse Trader operated between all parties, playing both ends against the middle.

"On a lower plane than your excellency, I think—"

Rappapa was interrupted by the buzzing of the intercom. Welcome flipped the switch and Christine shouted half hysterically: "No, you can't go in there. He's busy—Auch, look out! The Sirian—"

There was a thunderous crash on the door. Rappapa squawked and made a Lunar-gravity leap to cower behind his regiment. The door flew open and Thevorakz of Dzuga, Dominator from Sirius A IV, stalked in, waving his arms and roaring.

He was a centauroid, with a quadrupedal gray body and a lashing tail. The upper torso, swathed in a black robe and cowl, was almost human; a bristling white walrus mustache concealed the fact that he had no chin. Under a forest of brow, his ruby eyes glared fire, and his ears twitched and his hoofs stamped ominously.

"You!" he bellowed. "You low thiefing monthter! You thcum! You dominated! I do not like you!"

Welcome got up, grateful for the expanse of desk between him and the newcomer. "What's the matter, Dominator Thevorakz?" He tried hard to keep his voice level.

"I thpit my cud on you!" roared Thevorakz. "I foul your floor! I go home to Thiriuth and come back with an army!"

Christine squeaked in the doorway and sprang aside for the envoy from Vega VII. The gleaming six-foot sphere rolled slowly in on its wheels, laying a mechanical hand on Thevorakz's rump, and the viewer swiveled toward Welcome. It looked uncomfortably like a gun.

Inside, breathing hydrogen and ammonia at a pressure of incalculable atmospheres, the monster known only as George was staring at the human. His force-field generator hummed in a sudden crackling silence: if it ever quit, the vehicle would blow up like a gigantic bomb and scatter the dome from here to Copernicus.

It had been a long, difficult, and expensive proposition to contact the natives of New Jupiter and get one of them to make the trip, but living under such conditions, they had learned things about high-pressure chemistry which men had never imagined. They wanted atomic energy and control circuits in exchange.

The first they had gotten from Sirius, the second they had intended to get from Earth.

Only—

Welcome swallowed uneasily and put indignation into his voice. "May I ask the meaning of this intrusion? You know very well that I am in conference with the freeman from Arcturus."

"That *amorakz!*" shouted the Sirian. "Dithmith him!"

"Help!" wailed Rappapa. His robots formed a hollow square about him.

"Calmness, please." George's Voder voice was flat. "I think, Freeman Welcome, you know very well why we have come."

"No, I don't."

"You do tho!" roared Thevorakz.

"I shall detail the matter," said George. "The Sirian group and I reached a bargain, and I educated them as agreed. Naturally, there were many technical data which it would be pointless to memorize, formulas and constants and the like, and I gave them a book of tables. Those tables are the main thing of value which I had to offer, since the basic theory of high-pressure chemistry is already known to you and to Sirius. Dominator Thevorakz put this book in his strongbox last night. This morning the box was open and the book was gone."

"You don't—no!" gasped Christine.

"I'm sorry to hear of this." Welcome forced calmness on himself. "The matter will be investigated at once."

"By you!" bellowed Thevorakz. "And you are the mithbegotten dominated who thtole it!"

Welcome loosed a calculated anger. "You're insulting not only my personal integrity, but the honor of Earth. You have violated the sacred obligation of a guest to his host. I demand an immediate apology." He stalked forward, swinging his clenched fists at his sides.

"I will help your excellency," quacked Rappapa. "Company forward! On the double! Hup-hup-hup-hup-hup!" The robots goosestepped after the man.

Thevorakz suddenly looked worried. "If I am mithtaken, I will apologize," he mumbled sullenly. "But the book had better be found, and you had better prove you did not take it."

Welcome turned to George, preferring the chill sanity of the monster. "Do you really think we'd stoop to theft?"

"I have no opinion in the matter," said the toneless voice. "It would be to your advantage to steal Vega's knowledge and buy something else that we know; thus you would have two technologies in exchange for one. However, the possibility remains that some other of the parties rifled the box. Everyone knew about it."

"Or that the Sirians did it to blackmail us," said Welcome gauntly. "Or that you did it yourself, George."

He took an uneasy turn about the room, the tiny robots scampering to avoid his feet.

"I'm terribly sorry this has happened," he said. "I'll get the dome police on the case immediately. Meanwhile, I wish you would just return to your quarters. I'll notify you as soon as anything happens."

"I will be waiting," said George, and rolled ponderously out of the office. Thevorakz snorted and stalked after him. Rappapa crawled out from under the desk.

"A pretty mess!" Welcome realized that he was shaking. "Just what I need to start my job off right!"

"I am with humble firmness assured that your excellency will on the instant penetrate the depths of all dastardliness," said Rappapa.

"Um, yes, thanks." Welcome looked sharply at the Arcturian. *At least, I suppose I mean thanks.* "Sorry you were bothered this way, Freeman Rappapa. If you don't mind, I'll be rather busy now—"

"Of course. I shall not obtrude." Rappapa lifted his voice. "Compan-ee, ten-SHUN! Form ranks! Right face! Forwaard—MARCH! *Hup*-two-three-four, *hup*-two-three-four, *hup*-two-three-four—" He marched out of the office trailing his army behind him.

Christine leaned against the door and looked helplessly at Welcome.

"Now what?"

"Now we get to work. Get me Captain M'Gamba."

When the police chief's dark face was on the screen, Welcome explained the situation.

M'Gamba frowned. "Bad business, huh?"

"This is not a Good Thing," quoted Welcome. "You can see the spot we're in. If that book isn't recovered fast, we're going to lose face everywhere in the whole Galaxy. Earth will be branded as a planet of thieves and nobody will care to come here to do his Horse Trading. Sirius could take the lead away from us on that, and you know what an arrogant, opinionated lot they are. Nice people to have as the leading race of our new interstellar culture!"

"Maybe they did this job themselves, just to discredit us?"

"I wouldn't put it past 'em. But get busy, will you? You know the line—be tactful, but just as firm as you dare. And, Captain M'Gamba, if we don't settle this affair quick, you and I are both going to be looking for new jobs."

"And good jobs aren't easy to find these days. All right, Freeman Welcome, we'll blast off on it right away. I'll call you as soon as I have a report."

Welcome gave Christine a haggard look. She ran a hand through her blue-black hair and regarded him sympathetically. "Tough luck, Auch."

"For me or for Earth?'" he asked bitterly.

"You, mostly." Her eyes widened. "You don't think this could—lead to war, do you?"

"Oh, no. The logistics of interstellar warfare and conquest are ridiculous. But it could lead to bad relations with our Galactic neighbors." Welcome knocked the dottle from his pipe and began recharging it. "And you know, Chris, this new culture developing with the null-null drive is an abstract thing, an exchange of information and sympathy, ideas, philosophies—abstracts, not tangibles. Ill feeling now could poison it at the source. I don't know. I just don't know."

He stared moodily out at Earth.

M'Gamba's report came in a couple of hours later, and Welcome frowned as he fitted it into the pattern of knowledge he already had.

There were a dozen adjoining suites on the fourth sub-level of the dome, adjustable to the conditions of other planets, and the same level held three large clubrooms for the use of guests. Currently, the apartments housed the envoys of five stars: Sirius, Vega, Arcturus, Procyon, and Alpha Centauri. All these groups had been on Luna for periods ranging from several days to three weeks, and had mingled freely in mutual curiosity. Last night the dome's chief, Carlos Petersen, had thrown one of his periodic parties for the guests, and all had attended. The Sirians had come home late and gone directly to sleep, not noticing that their place was robbed until they woke up the next "morning."

Whoever did the burglary had been confoundedly clever. There was an electronic lock, supposedly burglar-proof, on the outer door of the suite, wired to sound an alarm if anyone tried to break it. It had been opened with no trouble at all. The thief had entered, cut into the strongbox with an energy torch, taken the book, and walked out again, locking the door behind him.

Welcome scowled. The technique of fooling an electronic lock was something beyond the science of Earth.

Of course, Thevorakz himself, or one of his underlings, might have raided the box and hidden the book.

"The torch could have been taken from any of the workshops on the fifth sub-level," said M'Gamba over the screen. "They're open all the time, you know, for the use of anyone who has to build a model or something. The thief need only have taken the torch, used it, and returned it when nobody was around. But what gadget did he have to unlock that door?"

"A key, maybe," suggested Welcome.

"But Thevorakz has the only key to it, except for Petersen's."

"I know. How about the suspects?"

"Well, the company was wandering in and out of the clubrooms all the while the party went on; and everybody was pretty looped, too, except that George creature. In short, nobody we've talked to can swear that any other being was there all evening."

"Hm-hm. Have you searched for the book?"

"We're still looking. We've requested permission to search all the apartments of our guests. So far, only the Arcturians have waived diplomatic immunity and invited us to do so."

"Well, keep plugging, Captain, and let me know what turns up."

"Will do."

———

A few minutes later, Carlos Petersen was on the screen, demanding to know what the trouble was. Welcome sighed and broke the news as gently as possible.

"Oh, Lord!" said Petersen.

"And little blue devils," agreed the Australian.

"I'd have your seat in a sling this moment, Welcome, if it weren't that I have to go to Earth immediately," said Petersen. "I'll be gone a couple of days. When I come back, I'll expect to see this mess straightened out."

"We'll try." Welcome was feeling too harried by now to care for manners. But the fact that he wouldn't have Petersen breathing down his neck was a minor mercy. "M'Gamba's a good man."

"He'd better be. I like you, Welcome, and think you were the right choice for your job. But this can develop into something too big and nasty for ethics to count. If it shows signs of doing so, Earth is going to need a scapegoat and you may very well be it." Petersen grimaced. "If they don't pick me, instead—Or both of us." He glanced at his wrist chrono. "Got to run now. Earth rocket leaves in ten minutes."

"Have fun," said Welcome moodily.

He paced once around the office, and threw himself into his chair. For a minute he exercised the more picturesque parts of his vocabulary.

The intercom interrupted him:

"The envoy Orazuni of Inyahuna, planet Procyon A III, to see you, Freeman Welcome."

The man blinked. "Oh, yes. He did have an appointment, didn't he? Send him in, please."

He stood up, composing himself as the Procyonite entered.

Orazuni looked rather like someone's idea of a medieval demon. His slim graceful body sloped forward, stalking on clawed feet and counterbalanced by the long thick tail. The six-fingered hands were also clawed, and the pointed ears were almost winglike in their size. But the head, though bald, was handsome by human standards, in a high-cheeked, sharp-chinned, flat-nosed way, and the golden eyes were large and luminous and beautiful. He wore a light tunic and a brilliant scarlet cloak, and carried a portfolio under one arm.

"Good day, Freeman Welcome," he said, bowing. He had taken better to the hypnopedic teaching of English than most non-humans, his accent being a nearly perfect Bostonian. "I trust you are in good health and spirits?"

"More or less," said Welcome wryly. He liked the Procyonite, despite the sharp battle of wits which had been going on between them for days now. "And yourself?"

"Quite well, thank you." Orazuni sat down on his tail, bracing himself with his rigidly straight legs, and accepted the proffered cigar. "There seems to have been an unfortunate incident last night."

"Yes, rather. Have you any notion—?"

Orazuni shrugged delicately. "One prefers not to become involved in such matters. I would not throw baseless accusations about. My group has, however, decided to show good faith by permitting the searching of our quarters. I shall so notify the police."

"Thank you. The more cooperation we get, the sooner we'll be able to clear this up." Welcome grinned. "I wish you were as easy to deal with in the line of business, Freeman Orazuni."

"I regret the impression," smiled Orazuni, "but I have my own planet to think of." He opened the portfolio and took out a sheet covered with an elaborate diagram. "Here, sir, is the structural formula—on a genetic rather than a chemical basis—of the human X chromosome, as determined by our technicians since we arrived on Luna. We have found conclusively that the tendency to certain types of cancer in your race—mammary, for instance—is linked here and here." He indicated a point where several lines diverged. That was a cluster of formulas in the alphabet of Inyahuna. "By proper treatment, it should be possible to modify the linkage without otherwise altering heredity in the zygote. The long-range prospect is the total elimination of any possibility of cancer from the heredity of your race."

Welcome nodded, unsurprised. What he wanted was the knowledge of theoretical and applied genetics which made such studies possible in the first place.

Biological engineering—designing any life-form whatsoever, and creating it by controlled mutation! Perhaps Man himself becoming superman—at the very least, losing the inherited weaknesses which dragged him down and shadowed his life and ultimately killed him. This could mean more than the scientific revolution that began with Galileo had yet offered.

Only it hardly seemed fair of the Inyahunans to demand everything Earth knew in exchange. They were welcome to the null-null drive, the energy converter, and the magnetronic tube. When they also asked for instruction in such things as mathematical sociology, supercomputer theory and practice and industrial catalysis, it was going too far. Their culture didn't need all that information. They could only want it for purposes of selling to someone else—underselling Earth, maybe. Welcome and Orazuni had been bargaining for a whole week now.

"We'd have to send a good-sized technical mission to Procyon to teach you all this," said the Australian. "It would be hard to find enough top-rank men in all those fields who'd want to be gone so many years on an alien planet; we'd have to pay them fantastic salaries. And the equipment they'd need! Really, Freeman Orazuni, you must be reasonable. I think I could add a course in advanced metal crystallography to what I've already offered you. That would help you with a good many construction problems. But then, naturally, we'd want you to give us your chemical-probe technique in return."

"In addition to the genetic theory and the tables of constants?" protested Orazuni. "Do you wish to ruin us, Freeman Welcome? What will our poor race be able to trade for further information?"

"Your own biological technology. You can't have worked out genetics as thoroughly as you have without a good background in biochemistry, histology, and I don't know what else." The human put the tips of his fingers together and peered over the bridge they formed. "After all, we do have some good biologists on Earth, too, you know. We could work all this out for ourselves in time. The very knowledge that such things are possible is a long step forward."

"As for that," shrugged Orazuni gracefully, "we could send students to Earth who could consult your books and journals—"

"It would be of limited value without the help of men who've had practical experience," said Welcome. "I'm afraid your people wouldn't even know what to look for."

He left the rest of it unspoken, though it was plain to both of them: Now that the civilized planets had gotten on to the idea of Horse Trading, they weren't going to be particularly cooperative toward casual students from outside. It wasn't a question of censorship; an effective barrier was imposed by the fact that there was no material trade to speak of between the stars. How could a visitor pay for his stay and education? He *had* to be financed by his hosts. And he could only earn such a scholarship as a reward for his planet's having offered a similar one to the other world.

They bargained in a gentlemanly fashion for a while longer, Orazuni dipping into his portfolio from time to time—he never released it, and there were rumors that he slept with it—for some tantalizing sample of information. Welcome in turn threw out remarks concerning the value of nuclear energy and high-strength alloys. The human found himself wishing that he knew more about Inyahuna's culture. They were a polite but reserved people—one might almost say secretive.

It went well today, though. Orazuni seemed much more amenable than he had been yesterday, and at the close of the discussion there was almost complete agreement.

"I think we can wind this up tomorrow," said Welcome. "I repeat my offer of throwing in a course in quantum theory of resonance bonds as applied to alloys. Think it over."

"I must discuss it with my group," replied Orazuni, "but I think they will consider the terms fair. Frankly, I would like to return soon with my wives. Our children will be nearly grown by the time we get home. If you would make arrangements to have the *Messenger* depart in a week or so—"

"Well, all right." Welcome balanced the factors in his mind. He'd have to round up all the instructors and other experts he had on tap to go to Procyon, alert the ship's people, arrange clearance. But a week should be enough. The other Inyahunans would remain to take posts at one of Earth's universities. "Wouldn't you like to visit around in the Solar System for a few months first, though? It seems a shame for you to come all this way without seeing much more than Luna."

"No, thank you. My people are not given to tourism." Orazuni got up to go. "Oh, by the way, if you will pardon my returning to a painful subject—I am curious. What is so unusual about this robbery, apart from the circumstances?"

"Well, the fact that an electronic lock was opened. It's not supposed to be possible without a key." As Orazuni arched his hairless brows, Welcome explained:

"The lock has no keyhole. It's held by a magnetronic field clamping two plates together with a force of several thousand tons, the field being generated by the circulation of an electronic current in several Cheval tubes. The whole thing is also wired in to an alarm circuit which goes off at any attempt to tamper. The key is actually a self-powered tube creating a heterodyning field. Since a literal infinity of wave-combinations is possible, there should be no chance of anyone's using a variable key to fumble the lock open."

"I see. I thought it was something on that order." Orazuni nodded and stroked his chin. "Do you know, if the crime was not committed by the Sirians themselves—or, if you will pardon me, by a human—then it seems logical that the guilty party should have a very advanced knowledge of electronics."

"I'd say so."

"Cybernetics?" murmured Orazuni. He bowed. "Well, I will not intrude further on your time. Good day, Freeman Welcome."

He left.

When he was gone, the human stood thinking for a long while. Small complicated circuits—Arcturus? Rappapa seemed like a pleasant little chap, but you never knew.

He sighed and looked out the window. The slow Lunar dawn was breaking incandescently over the jagged airless horizon and blazing into his eyes.

"Nice day," he muttered bitterly.

M'Gamba called up a few minutes later. "We found the book," he said.

"Eh?" Welcome's long body jerked forward.

"Lying in a corner of Shop Number Seven. Anybody could have left it there. We gave it back to the Sirians, but they weren't very polite about it."

Welcome shrugged. "I don't blame them. Obviously the thief took photomicrographs of the book and got rid of the thing itself away after he was done with it. Now all we have to find is a packet consisting of a few one-inch-square films. Hell, he could have swallowed 'em."

"And grabbed himself a whole technology without paying Vega for it. I guess George is hopping mad too, though you can't tell. He gives me the crawlies."

"The devil with that. We've got to find the burglar to clear ourselves. Been through the apartments?"

"All but the Sirians and George. The Sirians wouldn't hear of it, and it'd be impossible to make a decent search in a place conditioned to New Jupiter. Nothing. Not a thing."

Welcome bit his lip, then blurted out his suspicions of Arcturus.

The police captain nodded. "Sounds pretty reasonable."

"I took Rappapa for a dinkum cobber, but—well, we can't trust anybody, can we? Rig some traps. Try to fluoro him and his bunch without their knowing it. Go through their suite again with an electronic probe. Try anything."

"All jets," said M'Gamba glumly, and clicked off.

The intercom buzzed. "The envoy Helmung dur Brogu-Almerik, planet Alpha Centauri A III, to see you, Freeman Welcome," said Christine in a mechanical voice.

"On top of everything else," groaned the Australian. "All right, send him in." The door flew open. A nine-foot giant stamped in, thumping the butt of his spear on the floor, his chain mail jangling and his sword clanking. He was fairly humanoid, except for a blue skin, a tail, and antennae above his small slant eyes, but the battered face was tattooed in a ferocious pattern of red and yellow. If it hadn't been for several exploration parties from Earth, which had maintained a more or less permanent liaison with the clan chief of Brogu, this visit—or visitation—would never have happened. But the barbarians had heard news of the Horse Traders and insisted on getting into the game, and in the interests of peace, the last expedition had brought this delegate back. *And sloughed him off on me!* thought Welcome with resentment.

"How do you do, Freeman Helmung?" the Earthman said very softly. The Centaurian's head looked immensely high above him.

"Quiet, I will speak!" The walls rattled.

"Just as you wish." Welcome extended the customary box of cigars. Health hadn't reported this race as allergic to tobacco, but he hoped maliciously that Helmung would be.

The giant grabbed a handful, popped them into his mouth, and chewed noisily. "Not bad," he said, sprawling into a chair. He swallowed, spat on the floor, and cocked his spurred feet up on the desk. "I am Helmung dur Brogu-Almerik. Look on me and be afraid." It seemed a ritual greeting, for he added in a more friendly tone: "You may call me Skull-smasher."

"Ah, yes, to be sure." Welcome sat down on the other side of the desk. "I trust you have been enjoying your stay?"

"Not enough fights. No females big enough. That Orazuni, he is good sort and gives me much drink, otherwise you can *hialamar* them all." Welcome did not inquire what it was to *hialamar*, though he could make a shrewd guess. "I am great sorcerer. I have much *vingutyr*."

"You have much everything," agreed Welcome hastily.

"*Vingutyr* is—is what I have much of. That is why I am great sorcerer." The gravelly bass paused for a thunderous belch. "I shall show you how to wish your enemies dead. You shall show me how make ships-that-fly. Then we shall sack many worlds."

"Well, really, I say now—" Welcome had a sudden sense of futility. "There just isn't much witchcraft on Earth these days."

"I knew you was backward peoples!" cried Helmung triumphantly. "Look, dance of death, begins this way." He jumped up, waving his spear, and began to prance around, chanting.

"Isn't there something about making a doll and sticking pins in it?" asked Welcome weakly.

"Old-fashioned. Brogu is modern peoples. My father, top witch in Almerik, study from Earthmen. Learn about laws of science. He go on to figure laws of witchcraft." Helmung ticked off the points on his fingers, and Welcome realized that he must, after all, be his race's equivalent of an intellectual. "Law of likes-make-likes. Law of luck. Law of—"

"Now hold on, please do."

Welcome riffled through his papers till he found the memo on Alpha Centauri submitted by the preliminary investigators, which, in the madhouse today, he hadn't had time to read. Confound it, the barbarian must have something worth the time of a division chief! He skimmed rapidly down, the sheet and stopped at a paragraph referring to a limited degree of telekinesis as a congenital talent. The phenomenon was almost nonexistent among humans, and the parapsychology boys wanted Helmung humored so they could study him in detail.

Welcome thought of the Centaurian tossing boulders through the air by pure will-power, and shuddered.

"I understand," he began cautiously, "that you can move things merely by wishing them to move."

"Well, little things," said Helmung deprecatingly. "Not very big. Powerful wish-mover back home was showed game called dice by Earthmen. He won much treasure from them. But he had be much powerful to move dice."

"I see."

Welcome suppressed an impulse to mop his brow. He wasn't very well briefed on modern parapsych theory, but he remembered vaguely that telekinesis was attributed to a linkage between the neural field and the local sub-electronic fluxes. If that was so, you wouldn't expect the nervous system to have enough energy output to lift anything massive. Still, it would be interesting to watch.

"Do you mind if I try you?" he asked. "I've never seen this before."

"Is little thing," 'said Helmung scornfully. "Why not ask me wish-kill somebody for you?"

"Some other time," said Welcome. He went over to a cabinet in which he kept testing equipment and took out an oscilloscope. When he had a steady sine wave on it, he gestured with one hand. "Can you change that wiggly shape there?" he asked.

"Easy," grunted Helmung. "Orazuni told me about little things, too small to see."

"Yes. As a biologist, he'd naturally be interested in TK, too. Never mind, go ahead, if you please."

Helmung scowled in concentration. The electron trace jerked wildly, slithered across the screen, and began shaping itself into obscene drawings. Welcome hastily shut off the scope.

"That's fine," he said. "That's just beautiful."

Helmung rubbed his hands with a businesslike air. "Now how you build ships-that-fly?"

"I don't think you would be really interested in that," said Welcome as tactfully as possible.

Helmung's tail lashed against his ankles. He leaned across the desk, grabbed the human by the scruff of the neck, lifted him up, and shook him.

"So Brogu witchcraft not good enough for you, hah?"

"Yowp!" Welcome was near choking when Helmung set him down.

"I am patient man," rumbled the barbarian, "but you show me how build ships, or—"

"Now look, Skull-smasher," said Welcome shakily. "Really, I'd like to, you know, but I'm not the boss here. I can't tell you myself. You see—uh—well, on Earth our witches still believe in the dolls-and-pins theory. Also, to build space-ships you'd need tools you don't have, even if you knew how. Why don't you think it over for a while? We could show you lots of other things. For instance, you know what an alloy is? Well, we can tell you how to make better alloys than you now have. Unbreakable swords and so on. Why not start with that and work up?"

"Might be," grumbled Helmung, taking a thoughtful bite off another cigar.

"Oh, and ways to brew firewater, perhaps," added Welcome.

He winked, and Helmung guffawed, and presently the interview ended in a spirit of good fellowship. When the broad mailed back had gone out the door, Welcome made a dash for a three-starred bottle.

He thumbed the intercom switch.

"Come on in, Chris," he said. "I think we both need a drink."

Two hours later, Welcome was pretty sure he had tracked down the thief.

The time had been devoted to hard thinking and to study of the files on the four possible planets, sent up from the Division of Biopoliticology. Four planets, because you could eliminate Helmung immediately, and Welcome was sure enough of his own staff to feel certain that no human, even in a fit of greed or planetarism, had snaffled the book. Furthermore, you had to bear in mind that none of the delegates could have known in advance that a theft would be possible. They could not have made elaborate preparations beforehand for the job, but must have used whatever means were available to them, more or less on impulse. That argued for the burglar's having the technology to pick an electronic lock even if he had never seen one before.

That also ruled out Procyon at once. Enough was known of their science to make it quite certain that they lagged behind Earth in such matters as control circuits. Vega—you couldn't be sure just what George did or did not have at his disposal, but the fact that he had come here in the first place to get some of mankind's electronic and magnetronic knowledge pretty well proved that he couldn't have done the crime. Why should he steal his own book, anyway? New Jupiter wasn't much interested in interstellar intercourse or in setting up its own Horse Traders.

It was also a safe bet that Sirius did not know how to open the lock without a key. To be sure, Thevorakz did have such an instrument, and he might well have faked the crime to discredit Earth in the eyes of other races. But the psychology reports, while not conclusive, did make that line of thought seem improbable. The Dominators weren't that subtle.

By elimination—Arcturus. Welcome sighed and called M'Gamba's office. "Anything new?"

"We're working along," said the policeman. "We've had every human who was on the fourth sub-level last night, at the party or on duty elsewhere, under deep hypnosis—total recall. By piecing together all their accounts, we've shown that every member of the Procyonite and the Arcturian delegations was seen by somebody all the time until the party broke up and the Sirians went home. In other words; there's not a chance that any of them could have done it. There are blank spots as far as the rest are concerned, though."

"Arcturus, eh?" Welcome frowned. "Do you have anything else on them?"

"Well, we have been snapping fluoros at the Arcturian ducks on the sly, as you suggested. You know those little pouches they wear around their necks, to carry things in? One of their party—Srnapopoi, the name is—is carrying around a packet of microfilms. But it can't be the film, can it?"

"Can't it?" Welcome showed his teeth in a humorless grin. "Look, Captain, a circuit technology as highly developed as theirs should be able to crack the electronic lock."

"I tell you, they were under observation all evening!"

"But were their robots?"

M'Gamba paused. "Never thought of that."

"Well, it seems plausible, doesn't it? Trouble is, this is a delicate matter. We can't just arrest them on suspicion; we'll need mighty good proof."

M'Gamba rubbed his chin. "I think a look at this Arcturian's neck pouch could be arranged. He's down in the shop now, working up a demonstration model. I'll have one of my skilled operators go down and talk to him and—ah—accidentally cut the thongs of the pouch with a beam-slicer. Cut the pouch itself open, too. The contents will spill out and—"

"It's your problem. Just make sure you have a cover-up in case he turns out not to be carrying the stuff, after all. Call me as soon as you know, will you?" Welcome clicked off and sat for a moody while, considering his own next move. Finally he sighed and called Christine. "Get hold of Rappapa and have him come here, please. Diplomatically, of course."

"Auch, you don't think—"

"I'm afraid I do."

Welcome stuffed his pipe and looked out at the savage dawn-glare. Damn and blast, how did you accuse an accredited envoy of theft, especially when you liked him?

Rappapa came bustling in accompanied by no more than a midget helicopter.

"Twice in one arbitrary diurnal period?" he quacked. "Believe me, your excellency, I am flattered by such hyper-attention on the part of your doubtless busy-with-vast-problems-of-interstellar-negotiations self."

"I need your help," said the human awkwardly. "Would you like a cigar?"

"Gratitude erupts from me," said Rappapa. "If there is even of-the-most-micrometric way can assist in—"

"It's this business of the theft."

Welcome drew heavily on his pipe. "It puts my whole planet in a deucedly bad light. We have to catch the burglar to save our own reputation. At the same time, he is somebody's diplomat, which could lead to an unholy row if we arrested him."

"Anyone who would ponder the violation of your excellency's so lavish hospitality should be dedignified," said Rappapa indignantly.

"It's not that simple, I'm afraid," Welcome explained. "His planet would react with a great show of injury, one harsh word would lead to another, the seeds of mutual suspicion would be sown. Don't you think, Freeman Rappapa, it would be best for the thief's own planet, too, if he merely surrendered his loot? Then no one need ever know what has happened. The whole thing could be discreetly hushed up and forgotten."

"First the much-to-be-pondered question of locating the pilferish ambassador arises," said Rappapa. "Does your excellency the assistance of my abject self in such detection work desire?"

So he's going to stall, after all.

"If the thief confessed," said Welcome desperately, "I would understand that he committed the act only from the highest motives of planetarism. I would not look down on him for it, or discriminate against him in any way."

Rappapa waved his cigar reverently. "Behold the magnanimity of the magnanimous!"

"If he doesn't confess, though, if we have to find him for ourselves, we may have to be rather stern about it afterward."

"Of course. Your excellency burrows to the very foundation of justice."

The visor buzzed. *Here goes,* thought Welcome. He clicked it on, and M'Gamba's features looked bleakly out at him.

"Well?"

"It worked," said the captain. "My agent got his hands on the films, shoved them under the nearest reader. They're the ones, sure enough."

"And how about the—one who carried them?"

"He insists he didn't know he had them. Says someone must have planted them on him. That wouldn't be hard to do, of course, so I haven't put him under formal arrest yet. What do you suggest?"

"I'll call you back." Welcome clicked off and turned to Rappapa. "Well, we've located our thief. Finally," he said.

"So I g-gathered." The Arcturian jittered about on the floor, stuttering in his excitement. "Who is it? Who is the low, vile, not-to-be-mentioned-without-expectoration creature?"

"His name," said Welcome heavily, "is Srnapopoi."

"Srna—"

"Yes."

"B-but—*donnabi whichu krx killuwi*—it is not of the possible! Believe me, excellent excellency, w-we are p-pure as distilled water!" Rappapa began trembling.

"Your people should be able to figure out an electronic lock and have your robots pick it," said Welcome tonelessly. "And Srnapopoi was carrying the films."

"Copies? Copies m-made by the th-thief to divert suspicion!"

Welcome came around from behind the desk. "Don't take it so hard," he said kindly. "If you like, we'll claim that Srnapopoi did it on his own initiative, without your knowledge. We'll hush it all up."

"But he couldn't have!" wailed Rappapa. "The robots can only my orders obey!"

Welcome leaned back against the desk, scowling. His pipe had gone out and he made an elaborate ritual of relighting it to hide his uneasiness. He had given Rappapa an out and the duck hadn't taken it. Nor would you expect anyone cool enough to pull that job to blow his jets this way when discovered—or, for that matter, to hide his loot so clumsily, though of course there was no accounting for non-human psychology.

Rappapa began to cry. "We are besmirched with accusations and have lost confidence. You think I am a not-fit-to-wipe-the-feet-on-egg-eater. What will my nestmates say?"

"Now, after all—"

"They will say, *'Twiutiuk poipoi tu spung Rappapa.'*"

Welcome scratched his head helplessly. "All right, all right, you didn't do it. You've been the victim of a fraud. But then who is guilty?"

Rappapa rubbed the tears from his bulging eyes. "It is necessary to protect the Kwillitchian self by the true monster finding," he said with some return of his old perkiness. "Will you give me out of your polychromatic mercy a chance?"

"Certainly. Because if you're not guilty, then we've still got to find the one who is." Welcome sat down on a corner of the desk. Inwardly, he groaned at the thought of starting over again, just when he had thought the business was settled—but, damn it, you couldn't simply call an official delegate a liar, however much you might want to. "Let us assume that you did not do it. That leaves two possibilities, Sirius and Vega."

"Would you from the scintillant heights of intellect descend to explain the omission of Procyon and Alpha Centauri?"

"Well, the Centaurian is obvious. He's too stupid even to think of such a job. And Orazuni and his people were never out of sight of a human last night." Fairness forced Welcome to admit: "Neither were you Arcturians, for that matter. But you had the robots."

"Could not Orazuni have had hidden-away robots?"

"Not with his technical background. They're biologists, biochemists, not electronicians, except on an elementary level. Unless Orazuni stole the key, which he did not, he just had no means of opening that lock."

"That leaves only some elaborate and improbable-on-the-face-of-it plot by Sirius or Vega."

"And I don't think it could have been Vega. They're backward in electronics. With the atmospheric pressure of New Jupiter, they never even developed a vacuum tube. And as for Sirius—"

"No, wait! Robot delegate sent to do foul deeds while the weaver of intricate plots sits at his ease in public view." Rappapa's eyes bulged until they seemed in danger of falling out.

Welcome looked at him, and he looked at Welcome.

"Killuweetchungu!" squawked Rappapa. "Let us go!"

"Hold on. We have to think this out."

"No time to think! Come!"

Rappapa bounded from the office. Welcome cursed and charged after him. If that impulsive featherhead accused the wrong being—

Christine saw four feet of squawking Arcturian, followed by six feet of cursing human, followed by seven inches of valiantly laboring helicopter, shoot through her office. She got up and raced after them. The receptionist saw the parade go by and excitedly joined it. A passing janitor saw them streaking through the hall and took out after the receptionist.

Rappapa went down the ramp to the fourth sub-level, screeching and whistling. Thevorakz came out of his quarters to see what the fuss was about, just in time for Rappapa to unbalance him by darting under his legs, Welcome to bowl him over, and Christine, the receptionist, the janitor, and a few odd specimens picked up along the way to trample across him. As he rose, howling his fury, the helicopter collided with his head. He snarled and galloped after the rest.

"Where is the Centaurian?" clacked Rappapa at George, who was rolling down the corridor. "Where is he lurking?"

"In the clubroom," said the Vegan, pointing.

Rappapa vaulted the metal shell. Welcome and Christine leapfrogged over him. The others drew up, until Thevorakz took a flying broad jump above the whole group. George stared after them, shrugged, and rolled imperturbably on his way.

The clubroom was almost deserted: a stray Arcturian was reading a murder mystery, Helmung was draped over the bar clutching a bottle, and Orazuni sat chatting with the warrior.

"There they are!" yammered Rappapa. "There abide the overly diabolical thieves!"

"Shut up, you bloody fool—" Welcome tripped on a chair and went flat on the floor. When he crawled up, Rappapa was grabbing Helmung by the baldric and chattering a stream of questions.

"What is, little one?" rumbled the barbarian. "And why?"

"We want to know how much Orazuni offered you to turn thief!"

"I?" Orazuni smiled tolerantly. "Our colleague seems a trifle excited, Freeman Welcome."

Thevorakz clumped up to the bar, brushing assorted humans aside.

"I demand an apology!" he roared. "I did not come nine light-yearth to be walked on!"

"Let me go," growled Helmung uneasily. He batted Rappapa away.

"Help!" squealed the Arcturian. "Com-pan-ee—HELP!"

"Really, now," said Orazuni reproachfully, "I must say this is a most undignified scene."

"Will you apologize to me?" bellowed Thevorakz.

"I go my place," said Helmung. "Do not follow." He shoved his way through the crowd.

"Stop, thief!" yelled Rappapa. His robots marched in the door. "The Centaurian!" he added.

"Now, see here—" began Orazuni.

"Stop him, too!" cried Rappapa. "He the films has!"

"I shall also demand an apology," said the Procyonite with stiff dignity.

Thevorakz reached out and gathered in a handful of his cloak. "Maybe you better wait a little," he said.

Helmung had just noticed the robots deploying before him.

"I see little men!" he gasped. He waved his arms and started an incantation.

A detachment of robots swarmed up some curtains, took them down, and began to hobble the Centaurian with them. Helmung looked suddenly crushed.

"My witchcraft not works here on Luna," he mumbled. "I want go home."

Welcome decided it was time for him to do something.

"Helmung," he asked, "did you open the door to the Sirian quarters for Orazuni?"

"I promise him I not tell anyone that," said Helmung in a self-righteous voice. "You torture me, do anything, I not confess I was one who open door."

Suddenly Orazuni broke into a laugh.

"Never mind," he said. "Here is the other copy of the book." He fished in his portfolio and tossed a packet over to Welcome. "And now, freemen, if you will excuse me—"

Thevorakz's bellow cut through a sudden quiet. "When do I get my apology?"

"It should have been obvious, I suppose," said Welcome to Christine and M'Gamba. "That attempt to frame the Arcturians by making an extra copy of the book and planting it on one of them couldn't have thrown us off very long. But Orazuni only needed to have us baying along his false trail for a few days; then he'd be safely on his way home, bearing the films. We did know, though, that he had been cultivating Helmung's friendship ever since he learned that the Centaurians are telekinetic. His interest was scientific to start with, but it soon occurred to him that if Helmung could control electron streams easily enough to make pictures on an oscilloscope, he could surely open an electronic lock. And the Vegan data is valuable."

"Did he hope to get more out of it than just the tables themselves?" asked M'Gamba.

"Yes. I was talking to him just now, and he was quite frank and cheerful. Procyon has entertained notions of taking the job of Horse Trading—ultimately the scientific leadership in all respects—away from Earth. This theft would not only have discredited us, but given them a nice chunk of knowledge to trade with, besides what they learned from us through legitimate channels. Orazuni got Helmung to steal the book from him by the bribe of a love potion—A hormone mixture adapted to Centaurian biochemistry. Helmung's received that payment, by the way, and is eager to get home and try it out; so that's one more nuisance off our necks."

"And what are we going to do about Orazuni?" asked Christine worriedly.

Welcome shrugged. "Keep an eye on him. What else can we do? We need the knowledge and the good will of his planet. We'll go on just as if nothing had happened. Horse Traders can't be very prim, you know."

He looked out the office window. The Sun was visible now, its blinding glare filtered to a soft radiance, and the sterile land of crags and craters had an eerie beauty over it.

"Hard to believe this affair only took one working day," he said. "And what a day! Can we have some nice peaceful routine for a while, Chris?"

"Not for long," she told him. "The *Quest* is due in from Tau Ceti soon. The previous expedition there reported the natives were quite anxious to learn from us and readying a delegation. I think their proudest achievement to date is an ingenious method of chipping flint."

MURPHY'S HALL

This is a lie, but I wish so much it were not.

Pain struck through like lightning. For an instant that went on and on, there was nothing but the fire which hollowed him out and the body's animal terror. Then as he whirled downward he knew:

> Oh, no! Must I   Only a month,
> leave them already?   a month.
> *Weltall, verweile doch, du bist so schön.*

The monstrous thunders and whistles became a tone, like a bell struck once which would not stop singing. It filled the jagged darkness, it drowned all else, until it began to die out, or to vanish into the endless, century after century, and meanwhile the night deepened and softened, until he had peace.

But he opened himself again and was in a place long and high. With his not-eyes he saw that five hundred and forty doors gave onto black immensities wherein dwelt clouds of light. Some of the clouds were bringing suns to birth. Others, greater and more distant, were made of suns already created, and turned in majestic Catherine wheels. The nearest stars cast out streamers of flame, lances of radiance; and they were diamond, amethyst, emerald, topaz, ruby; and around them swung glints which he knew with his not-brain were planets. His not-ears heard the thin violence of cosmic-ray sleet, the rumble of solar storms, the slow patient multiplex pulses of gravitational tides. His not-flesh shared the warmth, the blood-beat, the megayears of marvelous life on uncountable worlds.

Seven stood waiting. He rose. "But you—" he stammered without a voice.

"Welcome," Ed greeted him. "Don't be surprised. You were always one of us."

They talked quietly, until at last Gus reminded them that even here they were not masters of time. Eternity, yes, but not time. "Best we move on," he suggested.

"Uh-huh," Roger said. "Especially after Murphy took this much trouble on our account."

"He does not appear to be a bad fellow," Vladimir said.

"I am not certain," Robert answered. "Nor am I certain that we ever will find out. But come, friends. The hour is near."

Eight, they departed the hall and hastened down the star paths. Often the newcomer was tempted to look more closely at something he glimpsed. But he recalled that, while the universe was inexhaustible of wonders, it would have only the single moment to which he was being guided.

They stood after a while on a great ashen plain. The outlook was as eerily beautiful as he had hoped—no, more, when Earth, a blue serenity swirled white with weather, shone overhead: Earth, whence had come the shape that now climbed down a ladder of fire.

Yuri took Konstantin by the hand in the Russian way. "Thank you," he said through tears.

But Konstantin bowed in turn, very deeply, to Willy.

And they stood in the long Lunar shadows, under the high Lunar heaven, and saw the awkward thing come to rest and heard: "Houston, Tranquillity Base here. The Eagle has landed."

Stars are small and dim on Earth. Oh, I guess they're pretty bright still on a winter mountaintop. I remember when I was little, we'd saved till we had the admission fees and went to Grand Canyon Reserve and camped out. Never saw that many stars. And it was like you could see up and up between them—like, you know, you could *feel* how they weren't the same distance off, and the spaces between were more huge than you could imagine. Earth and its people were just lost, just a speck of nothing among those cold sharp stars. Dad said they weren't too different from what you saw in space, except for being a lot fewer. The air was chilly too, and had a kind of pureness, and a sweet smell from the pines around. Way off I heard a coyote yip. The sound had plenty of room to travel in.

But I'm back where people live. The smog's not bad on this rooftop lookout, though I wish I didn't have to breathe what's gone through a couple million pairs of lungs before it reaches me. Thick and greasy. The city noise isn't too bad either, the usual growling and screeching, a jet-blast or a burst of gunfire. And since the power shortage brought on the brownout, you can generally see stars after dark, sort of.

My main wish is that we lived in the southern hemisphere, where you can see Alpha Centauri.

Dad, what are you doing tonight in Murphy's Hall?

A joke. I know. Murphy's Law: "Anything that can go wrong, will." Only I think it's a true joke. I mean, I've read every book and watched every tape I could lay hands on, the history, how the discoverers went out, farther and farther, lifetime after lifetime. I used to tell myself stories about the parts that nobody lived to put into a book.

The crater wall had fangs. They stood sharp and grayish white in the cruel sunlight, against the shadow which brimmed the bowl. And they grew and grew.

Tumbling while it fell, the spacecraft had none of the restfulness of zero weight. Forces caught nauseatingly at gullet and gut. An unidentified loose object clattered behind the pilot chairs. The ventilators had stopped their whickering and the two men breathed stench. No matter. This wasn't an Apollo 13 mishap. They wouldn't have time to smother in their own exhalations.

Jack Bredon croaked into the transmitter: "Hello, Mission Control…Lunar Relay Satellite…anybody. Do you read us? Is the radio out too? Or just our receiver? God damn it, can't we even say goodbye to our wives?"

"Tell 'em quick," Sam Washburn ordered. "Maybe they'll hear."

Jack dabbed futilely at the sweat that broke from his face and danced in glittering droplets before him. "Listen," he said. "This is Moseley Expedition One. Our motors stopped functioning simultaneously, about two minutes after we commenced deceleration. The trouble must be in the fuel feed integrator. I suspect a magnetic surge, possibly due to a short circuit in the power supply. The meters registered a surge before we lost thrust. Get that system redesigned! Tell our wives and kids we love them."

He stopped. The teeth of the crater filled the entire forward window. Sam's teeth filled his countenance, a stretched-out grin. "How do you like that?" he said. "And me the only black astronaut."

They struck.

When they opened themselves again, in the hall, and knew where they were, he said, "Wonder if he'll let us go out exploring."

Murphy's Halt? Is that the real name?

Dad used to shout, "Murphy take it!" when he blew his temper. The rest is in a few of the old tapes, fiction plays about spacemen, back when people liked to watch that kind of story. They'd say when a man had died, "He's drinking in Murphy's Hall." Or he's dancing or sleeping or frying or freezing or whatever it was. But did they really say "Hall"? The tapes are old. Nobody's been interested to copy them off on fresh plastic, not for a hundred years, I guess, maybe two hundred. The holographs are blurred and streaky, the sounds are mushed and full of random buzzes. Murphy's Law has sure been working on those tapes.

I wish I'd asked Dad what the astronauts said and believed, way back when they were conquering the planets. Or pretended to believe, I should say. Of course they never thought there was a Murphy who kept a place where the spacefolk went that he'd called to him. But they might have kidded around about it. Only was the idea, for sure, about a hall? Or was that only the way I heard? I wish I'd asked Dad. But he wasn't home often, those last years, what with helping build and test his ship. And when he did come, I could see how he mainly wanted to be with Mother. And when he and I were together, well, that was always too exciting for me to remember those yarns I'd tell myself before I slept, after he was gone again.

Murphy's Haul?

By the time Moshe Silverman had finished writing his report, the temperature in the dome was about seventy, and rising fast enough that it should reach a hundred inside another Earth day. Of course, waters wouldn't then boil at once; extra energy is needed for vaporization. But the staff would no longer be able to cool some down to drinking temperature by the crude evaporation apparatus they had rigged. They'd dehydrate fast. Moshe sat naked in a running river of sweat.

At least he had electric light. The fuel cells, insufficient to operate the air conditioning system, would at least keep Sofia from dying in the dark.

His head ached and his ears buzzed. Occasional dizziness seized him. He gagged on the warm fluid he must continually drink. *And no more salt,* he thought. *Maybe that will kill us before the heat does, the simmering, still, stifling heat.* His bones felt heavy, though Venus has in fact a somewhat lesser pull than Earth; his muscles sagged and he smelled the reek of his own disintegration.

Forcing himself to concentrate, he checked what he had written, a dry factual account of the breakdown of the reactor. The next expedition would read what this thick, poisonous inferno of an atmosphere did to graphite in combination with free neutrons; and the engineers could work out proper precautions.

In sudden fury, Moshe seized his brush and scrawled at the bottom of the metal sheet: "Don't give up! Don't let this hellhole whip you! We have too much to learn here."

A touch on his shoulder brought him jerkily around and onto his feet. Sofia Chiappellone had entered the office. Even now, with physical desire roasted out of him and she wetly agleam, puffy-faced, sunken-eyed, hair plastered lank to drooping head, he found her lovely.

"Aren't you through, darling?" Her tone was dull but her hand sought his. "We're better off in the main room. Mohandas' punkah arrangement does help."

"Yes, I'm coming."

"Kiss me first. Share the salt on me."

Afterward she looked over his report. "Do you believe they will try any further?" she asked. "Materials so scarce and expensive since the war—"

"If they don't," he answered, "I have a feeling—oh, crazy, I know, but why should we not be crazy?—I think if they don't, more than our bones will stay here. Our souls will, waiting for the ships that never come."

She actually shivered, and urged him toward their comrades.

Maybe I should go back inside. Mother might need me. She cries a lot, still. Crying, all alone in our little apartment. But maybe she'd rather not have me around. What can a gawky, pimply-faced fourteen-year-old boy do?

What can he do when he grows up?

O Dad, big brave Dad, I want to follow you. Even to Murphy's…Hold?

Director Saburo Murakami had stood behind the table in the commons and met their eyes, pair by pair. For a while silence had pressed inward. The bright colors and amateurish figures in the mural that Georgios Efthimakis had painted for pleasure—beings that never were, nymphs and fauns and centaurs frolicking beneath an unsmoky sky, beside a bright river, among grasses and laurel trees and daisies of an Earth that no longer was—became suddenly grotesque, infinitely alien. He heard his heart knocking. Twice he must swallow before he had enough moisture in his mouth to move his wooden tongue.

But when he began his speech, the words came forth steadily, if a trifle flat and cold. That was no surprise. He had lain awake the whole night rehearsing them.

"Yousouf Yacoub reports that he has definitely succeeded in checking the pseudovirus. This is not a cure; such must await laboratory research. Our algae will remain scant and sickly until the next supply ship brings us a new stock. I will radio Cosmocontrol, explaining the need. They will have ample time on Earth to prepare. You remember the ship is scheduled to leave at…at a date to bring it here in about nine months. Meanwhile we are guaranteed a rate of oxygen renewal sufficient to keep us alive, though weak, if we do not exert ourselves. Have I stated the matter correctly, Yousouf?"

The Arab nodded. His own Spanish had taken on a denser accent, and a tic played puppet master with his right eye. "Will you not request a special ship?" he demanded.

"No," Saburo told them. "You are aware how expensive anything but an optimum Hohmann orbit is. That alone would wipe out the profit from this station—permanently, I fear, because of financing costs. Likewise would our idleness for nine months."

He leaned forward, supporting his weight easily on fingertips in the low Martian gravity. "That is what I wish to discuss today," he said. "Interest rates represent competition for money. Money represents human labor and natural resources. This is true regardless of socioeconomic arrangements. You know how desperately short they are of both labor and resources on Earth. Yes, many billions of hands—but because of massive poverty, too few educated brains. Think back to what a political struggle the Foundation had before this base could be established.

"We know what we are here for. To explore. To learn. To make man's first permanent home outside Earth and Luna. In the end, in the persons of our great-grandchildren, to give Mars air men can breathe, water they can drink, green fields and forests where their souls will have room to grow." He gestured at the mural, though it seemed more than ever jeering. "We can't expect starvelings on Earth, or those who speak for them, to believe this is good. Not when each ship bears away metal and fuel and engineering skill that might have gone to keep *their* children alive a while longer. We justify our continued presence here solely by mining the fissionables. The energy this gives back to the tottering economy, over and above what we take out, is the profit."

He drew a breath of stale, metallic-smelling air. Anoxia made his head whirl. Somehow he stayed erect and continued:

"I believe we, in this tiny solitary settlement, are the last hope for man remaining in space. If we are maintained until we have become fully self-supporting, Syrtis Harbor will be the seedbed of the future. If not—"

He had planned more of an exhortation before reaching the climax, but his lungs were too starved, his pulse too fluttery. He gripped the table edge and said through flying rags of darkness: "There will be oxygen for half of us to keep on after a fashion. By suspending their other projects and working exclusively in the mines, they can produce enough uranium and thorium that the books at least show no net economic loss. The sacrifice will...will be...of propaganda value. I call for male volunteers, or we can cast lots, or—Naturally, I myself am the first."

—That had been yesterday.

Saburo was among those who elected to go alone, rather than in a group. He didn't care for hymns about human solidarity; his dream was that someday those who bore some of his and Alice's chromosomes would not need solidarity. It was perhaps well she had already died in a cinderslip. The scene with their children had been as much as he could endure.

He crossed Weinbaum Ridge but stopped when the domecluster was out of sight. He must not make the searchers come too far. If nothing else, a quick dust storm might cover his tracks, and he might never be found. Someone could make good use of his airsuit. Almost as good use as the algae tanks could of his body.

For a time, then, he stood looking. The mountainside ran in dark scars and fantastically carved pinnacles, down to the softly red-gold-ocher-black-dappled plain. A crater on the near horizon rose out of its own blue shadow like a challenge to the ruddy sky. In this thin air—he could just hear the wind's ghostly whistle—Mars gave to his gaze every aspect of itself, diamond sharp, a beauty strong, subtle, and abstract as a torii gate before a rock garden. When he glanced away from the shrunken but dazzling-bright sun, he could see stars.

He felt at peace, almost happy. Perhaps the cause was simply that now, after weeks, he had a full ration of oxygen.

I oughtn't to waste it, though, he thought. He was pleased by the steadiness of his fingers when he closed the valve.

Then he was surprised that his unbelieving self bowed over both hands to the Lodestar and said, "*Namu Amida Butsu.*"

He opened his faceplate.

That is a gentle death. You are unconscious within thirty seconds.

—He opened himself and did not know where he was. An enormous room whose doorways framed a night heaven riotous with suns, galaxies, the green mysterious shimmer of nebulae? Or a still more huge ship, outward bound so fast that it was as if the Milky Way foamed along the bow and swirled aft in a wake of silver and planets?

Others were here, gathered about a high seat at the far end of where-he-was, vague in the twilight cast by sheer distance. Saburo rose and moved in their direction. Maybe, maybe Alice was among them.

But was he right to leave Mother that much alone?

I remember her when we got the news. On a Wednesday, when I was free, and I'd been out by the dump playing ball. I may as well admit to myself, I don't like some of the guys. But you have to take whoever the school staggering throws up for you. Or do you want to run around by yourself (remember, no, don't remember what the Hurricane Gang did to Danny) or stay always by yourself in the patrolled areas? So Jake-Jake does throw his weight around, so he does set the dues too high, his drill and leadership sure paid off when the Weasels jumped us last year. They won't try that again—we killed three, count 'em, three!—and I sort of think no other bunch will either.

She used to be real pretty, Mother did. I've seen pictures. She'd gotten kind of scrawny, worrying about Dad, I guess, and about how to get along after that last pay cut they screwed the spacefolk with. But when I came in and saw her sitting, not on the sofa but on the carpet, the dingy gray carpet, crying—She hung onto that sofa the way she'd hung on Dad.

But why did she have to be so angry at him too? I mean, what happened wasn't his fault.

"Fifty billion munits!" she screamed when we'd got trying to talk about the thing. "That's a hundred, two hundred billion meals for hungry children! But what did they spend it on? Killing twelve men!"

"Aw, now, wait," I was saying, "Dad explained that. The resources involved, uh, aren't identical," when she slapped me and yelled:

"You'd like to go the same way, wouldn't you? Thank God, it almost makes his death worthwhile that you won't!"

I shouldn't have got mad. I shouldn't have said, "Y-y-you want me to become…a desk pilot, a food engineer, a doctor…something nice and safe and in demand…and keep you the way you wanted he should keep you?"

I better stop beating this rail. My fist'll be no good if I don't. Oh, someday I'll find how to make up those words to her.

I'd better not go in just yet.

But the trouble *wasn't* Dad's fault. If things had worked out right, why, we'd be headed for Alpha Centauri in a couple of years. Her and him and me—The planets yonderward, sure, they're the real treasure. But the ship itself! I remember Jake-Jake telling me I'd have been dead of boredom inside six months. "Bored aboard, haw, haw, haw!" He really is a lardbrain. A good leader, I guess, but a lardbrain at heart—hey, once Mother would have laughed to hear me say that— How could you get tired of Dad's ship? A million books and tapes, a hundred of the brightest and most alive people who ever walked a deck—

Why, the trip would be like the revels in Elf Hill that Mother used to read me about when I was small, those old, old stories, the flutes and fiddles, bright clothes, food, drink, dancing, girls sweet in the moonlight…

Murphy's Hill?

From Ganymede, Jupiter shows fifteen times as broad as Luna seen from Earth; and however far away the sun, the king planet reflects so brilliantly that it casts more than fifty times the radiance that the brightest night of man's home will ever know.

"*Here* is man's home," Catalina Sanchez murmured.

Arne Jensen cast her a look which lingered. She was fair to see in the golden-ness streaming through the conservatory's clear walls. He ventured to put an arm about her waist. She sighed and leaned against him. They were scantily clad—the colony favored brief though colorful indoor garments—and he felt the warmth and silkiness of her. Among the manifold perfumes of blossoms (on plants every-where to right and left and behind, extravagantly tall stalks and big flowers of every possible hue and some you would swear were impossible, dreamlike catena-ries of vines and labyrinths of creepers) he caught her summery odor.

The sun was down and Jupiter close to full. While the terraforming project was going rapidly ahead, as yet the moon had too little air to blur vision. Tawny shone that shield, emblazoned with slowly moving cloud bands that were green, blue, orange, umber and with the jewel-like Red Spot. To know that a single one of the storms raging there could swallow Earth whole added majesty to beauty and serenity; to know that, without the magnetohydronamic satellites men had orbited around this globe, its surface would be drowned in lethal radiation, added triumph. A few stars had the brilliance to pierce the luminousness, down by the rugged horizon. The gold poured soft across crags, cliffs, craters, glaciers, and the machinery of the conquest.

Outside lay a great quietness, but here music lilted from the ballroom. Folk had reason to celebrate. The newest electrolysis plant had gone into operation and was releasing oxygen at a rate 15 percent above estimate. However, low-weight or no, you got tired dancing—since Ganymedean steps took advantage, soaring and bounding aloft—mirth bubbled like champagne and the girl you admired said yes, she was in a mood for Jupiter watching—

"I hope you're right," Arne said. "Less on our account—we have a good, happy life, fascinating work, the best of company—than on our children's." He squeezed a trifle harder.

She didn't object. "How can we fail?" she answered. "We've become better than self-sufficient. We produce a surplus, to trade to Earth, Luna, Mars, or plow directly back into development. The growth is exponential." She smiled. "You must think I'm awfully professorish. Still, really, what can go wrong?"

"I don't know," he said. "War, overpopulation, environmental degradation—"

"Don't be a gloomy," Catalina chided him. The lambent light struck rainbows from the tiara of native crystal that she wore in her hair. "People can learn. They needn't make the same mistakes forever. We'll build paradise here. A strange sort of paradise, yes, where trees soar into a sky full of Jupiter, and waterfalls tumble slowly, slowly down into deep-blue lakes, and birds fly like tiny bright-colored bullets, and deer cross the meadows in ten-meter leaps…but paradise."

"Not perfect," he said. "Nothing is."

"No, and we wouldn't wish that," she agreed. "We want some discontent left to keep minds active, keep them hankering for the stars." She chuckled. "I'm sure history will find ways to make them believe things could be better elsewhere. Or nature will—Oh!"

Her eyes widened. A hand went to her mouth. And then, frantically, she was kissing him, and he her, and they were clasping and feeling each other while the waltz melody sparkled and the flowers breathed and Jupiter's glory cataracted over them uncaring whether they existed.

He tasted tears on her mouth. "Let's go dancing," she begged. "Let's dance till we drop."

"Surely," he promised, and led her back to the ballroom.

It would help them once more forget the giant meteoroid, among the many which the planet sucked in from the Belt, that had plowed into grim and marginal Outpost Ganymede precisely half a decade before the Martian colony was discontinued.

Well, I guess people don't learn. They breed, and fight, and devour, and pollute, till:

Mother: "We can't afford it."

Dad: "We can't not afford it."

Mother: "Those children—like goblins, like ghosts, from starvation. If Tad were one of them, and somebody said never mind him, we have to build an interstellar ship…I wonder how you would react."

Dad: "I don't know. But I do know this is our last chance. We'll be operating on a broken shoestring as is, compared to what we need to do the thing right. If they hadn't made that breakthrough at Lunar Hydromagnetics Lab, when the government was on the point of closing it down—Anyway, darling, that's why I'll have to put in plenty of time aboard myself, while the ship is built and tested. My entire gang will be on triple duty,"

Mother: "Suppose you succeed. Suppose you do get your precious spacecraft that can travel almost as fast as light. Do you imagine for an instant it can—an armada can ease life an atom's worth for mankind?"

Dad: "Well, several score atoms' worth. Starting with you and Tad and me."

Mother: "I'd feel a monster, safe and comfortable en route to a new world while behind me they huddled in poverty by the billions."

Dad: "My first duty is to you two. However, let's leave that aside. Let's think about man as a whole. What is he? A beast that is born, grubs around, copulates, quarrels, and dies. Uh-huh. But sometimes something more in addition. He does breed his occasional Jesus, Leonardo, Bach, Jefferson, Einstein, Armstrong, Olveida—whoever you think best justifies our being here—doesn't he? Well, when you huddle people together like rats, they soon behave like rats. What then of the spirit? I tell you, if we don't make a fresh start, a bare handful of us but free folk whose descendants may in the end come back and teach—if we don't, why, who cares whether the two-legged animal goes on for another million years or becomes extinct in a hundred? Humanness will be dead."

Me: "And gosh, Mother, the fun!"

Mother: "You don't understand, dear."

Dad: "Quiet. The man-child speaks. He understands better than you."

Quarrel: till I run from them crying. Well, eight or nine years old. That night, was that the first night I started telling myself stories about Murphy's Hall?

It *is* Murphy's Hall. I say that's the right place for Dad to be.

When Hoo Fong, chief engineer, brought the news to the captain's cabin, the captain sat still for minutes. The ship thrummed around them; they felt it faintly, a song in their bones. And the light fell from the overhead, into a spacious and gracious room, furnishings, books, a stunning photograph of the Andromeda galaxy, an animation of Mary and Tad: and weight was steady underfoot, a full gee of acceleration, one light-year per year per year, though this would become more in shipboard time as you started to harvest the rewards of relativity…a mere two decades to the center of this galaxy, three to the neighbor whose portrait you adored…How hard to grasp that you were dead!

"But the ramscoop is obviously functional," said the captain, hearing his pedantic phrasing.

Hoo Fong shrugged. "It will not be, after the radiation has affected electronic parts. We have no prospect of decelerating and returning home at low velocity before both we and the ship have taken a destructive dose."

Interstellar hydrogen, an atom or so in a cubic centimeter, raw vacuum to Earth-dwellers at the bottom of their ocean of gas and smoke and stench and carcinogens. To spacefolk, fuel, reaction mass, a way to the stars, once you're up to the modest pace at which you meet enough of those atoms per second. However, your force screens must protect you from them, else they strike the hull and spit gamma rays like a witch's curse.

"We've hardly reached one-fourth *c*," the captain protested. "Unmanned probes had no trouble at better than 99 percent."

"Evidently the system is inadequate for the larger mass of this ship," the engineer answered. "We should have made its first complete test flight unmanned too."

"You know we didn't have funds to develop the robots for that."

"We can send our data back. The next expedition—"

"I doubt there'll be any. Yes, yes, we'll beam the word home. And then, I suppose, keep going. Four weeks, did you say, till the radiation sickness gets bad? The problem is not how to tell Earth, but how to tell the rest of the men."

Afterward, alone with the pictures of Andromeda, Mary, and Tad, the captain thought: *I've lost more than the years ahead, I've lost the year behind, that we might have had together.*

What shall I say to you? That I tried and failed and am sorry? But am I? At this hour I don't want to lie, most especially not to you three.

Did I do right?

Yes.

No.

O God, oh, shit, how can I tell? The Moon is rising above the soot-clouds. I might make it that far. Commissioner Wenig was talking about how we should maintain the last Lunar base another few years, till industry can find a substitute for those giant molecules they make there. But wasn't the Premier of United Africa saying those industries ought to be forbidden, they're too wasteful, and any country that keeps them going is an enemy of the human race?

Gunfire rattles in the streets. Some female voice somewhere is screaming.

I've got to get Mother out of here. That's the last thing I can do for Dad.

After ten years of studying to be a food engineer or a doctor, I'll probably feel too tired to care about the Moon. After another ten years of being a desk pilot and getting fat, I'll probably be outraged at any proposal to spend my tax money—

—except maybe for defense. In Siberia they're preaching that strange new missionary religion. And the President of Europe has said that if necessary, his government will denounce the ban on nuclear weapons.

The ship passed among the stars bearing a crew of dead bones. After a hundred billion years it crossed the Edge—not the edge of space or time, which does not exist, but the Edge—and came to harbor at Murphy's Hall.

And the dust which the cosmic rays had made began to stir, and gathered itself back into bones; and from the radiation-corroded skeleton of the ship crept atoms which formed into flesh; and the captain and his men awoke. They opened themselves and looked upon the suns that went blazing and streaming overhead.

"We're home," said the captain.

Proud at the head of his men, he strode uphill from the dock, toward the hall of the five hundred and forty doors. Comets flitted past him, novae exploded in dreadful glory, planets turned and querned, the clinker of a once-living world drifted by, new life screamed its outrage at being born.

The roofs of the house lifted like mountains against night and the light-clouds. The ends of rafters jutted beyond the eaves, carved into dragon heads. Through the doorway toward which the captain led his crew, eight hundred men could have marched abreast. But a single form waited to greet them; and beyond him was darkness.

When the captain saw who that was, he bowed very deeply.

The other took his hand. "We have been waiting," he said.

The captain's heart sprang. "Mary too?"

"Yes, of course. Everyone."

Me. And you. And you. And you in the future, if you exist. In the end, Murphy's Law gets us all. But we, my friends, must go to him the hard way. Our luck didn't run out. Instead, the decision that could be made was made. It was decided for us that our race—among the trillions which must be out there wondering what lies beyond their skies—is not supposed to have either discipline or dreams. No, our job is to make everybody nice and safe and equal, and if this happens to be impossible, then nothing else matters.

If I went to that place—and I'm glad that this is a lie—I'd keep remembering what we might have done and seen and known and been and loved.

Murphy's Hell.

Sister Planet

Long afterward they found a dead man in shabby clothes adrift near San Francisco. The police decided he must have jumped from the Golden Gate Bridge one misty day. That was an oddly clean and lonesome place for some obscure wino to die, but no one was very much interested. Beneath his shirt he carried a Bible with a bookmark indicating a certain passage which had been underlined. Idly curious, a member of the Homicide Squad studied the waterlogged pulp until he deduced the section: Ezekiel vii, 3-4.

-1-

A squall hit when Shorty McClellan had almost set down. He yanked back the stick; jets snorted and the ferry stood on her tail and reached for heaven. An eyeblink later she was whipping about like a wind-tossed leaf. The viewports showed blackness. Above the wind there was a bongo beat of rain. Then lightning blazed and thunder followed and Nat Hawthorne closed off smitten sense channels.

Welcome back! he thought. Or did he say it aloud? The thunder rolled off, monster wheels if it was not laughter. He felt the vessel steady around him. When the dazzle had cleared from his eyes, he saw clouds and calm. A smoky blueness in the air told him that it was near sunset. What answered to sunset on Venus, he reminded himself. The daylight would linger on for hours, and the night never got truly dark.

"That was a near one," said Shorty McClellan.

"I thought these craft were designed to ride out storms," said Hawthorne.

"Sure. But not to double as submarines. We were pretty close to the surface when that one sneaked up on us. We could'a got dunked, and then—" McClellan shrugged.

"No real danger," Hawthorne answered. "We could get out the airlock, I'm sure, with masks, and stay afloat till they picked us up from the station. If Oscar and company didn't rescue us first. You realize there's no trouble from any native life-form. They find us every bit as poisonous as we find them."

"No danger, he says," groaned McClellan. "Well, you wouldn't have to account for five million bucks' worth of boat!"

He began whistling tunelessly as he spiraled down for another approach. He was a small, heavy-set, quick-moving man with a freckled face and sandy hair. For years Hawthorne had only known him casually, as one of the pilots who took cargo between orbiting spaceships and Venus Station: a cocky sort, given to bawdy limericks and improbable narratives about himself and what he called the female race. But on the voyage from Earth, he had ended with shyly passing around stereos of his children and describing plans for opening a little resort on Great Bear Lake when he reached retirement age.

I thank the nonexistent Lord that I am a biologist, thought Hawthorne. *The farcical choice of quitting or accepting a desk job at thirty-five has not yet reached my line of work. I hope I'll still be tracing ecological chains and watching auroras over the Phosphor Sea at eighty.*

As the boat tilted forward, he saw Venus below him; One would never have expected a landless, planet-wide ocean to be so alive. But there were climatic zones, each with its own million restless hues—the color of light, the quality of living organisms, nowhere the same, so that a sea on Venus was not an arbitrary section of water but an iridescent belt around the world. And then there was the angle of the sun, night-lighting, breezes and gales and typhoons, seasons, solar tides which had no barrier to their 20,000 mile march, and the great biological rhythms which men did not yet understand. No, you could sit for a hundred years in one place, watching, and never see the same thing twice. And all that you saw would be beautiful.

"The Phosphor sea girdled the planet between 55 and 63 degrees north latitude. Now from above, at evening, it had grown indigo, streaked with white; but on the world's very edge it shaded to black in the north and an infinitely clear green in the south. Here and there beneath the surface twined scarlet veins. A floating island, a jungle twisted over giant bladderweeds, upbore flame yellows, and a private mistiness. Eastward walked the squall, blue-black and lightning, the water roaring in its track. The lower western clouds were tinged rose and copper. The permanent sky-layer above ranged from pearl gray in the east to a still blinding white in the west, where the invisible sun burned. A double rainbow arched the horizon.

Hawthorne sighed. It was good to be back.

Air whistled under the ferry's glider wings. Then it touched pontoons to water, bounced, came down again, and taxied for the station. A bow wave broke among those caissons and spouted toward the upper deck and the buildings which, gyro-stabilized, ignored such disturbances. As usual, the whole station crew had turned out to greet the vessel. Spaceship arrivals were months apart.

"End of the line." McClellan came to a halt, unbuckled himself, stood up and struggled into his air harness. "You know," he remarked, "I've never felt easy in one of these gizmos."

"Why not?" Hawthorne, hanging the tank on his own shoulders, looked in surprise at the pilot.

McClellan adjusted his mask. It covered nose and mouth with a tight airseal of celluplastic gasketing. Both men had already slipped ultraviolet-filtering contact lenses over their eyeballs. "I keep remembering that there isn't any oxygen molecule that's not man-made for twenty-five million miles!" he confessed. The airhose muffled his voice, giving it for Hawthorne a homelike accent. "I'd feel safer with a space suit."

"De gustibus non disputandum est," said Hawthorne, "which has been translated as, 'There is no disputing that Gus is in the east.' Me, I was never yet in a space suit that didn't squeak and smell of somebody else's garlic."

Through the port he saw a long blue back swirl in the water and thresh impatient foam. A grin tugged at his lips, "Why, I'll bet Oscar knows I'm here," he said.

"Yeah. Soul mates," grunted McClellan.

They went out the airlock. Ears popped, adjusting to a slight pressure difference. The masks strained out some water vapor for reasons of comfort, and virtually all the carbon dioxide, for there was enough to kill a man in three gulps. Nitrogen, argon, and trace gases passed on, to be blent with oxygen from the harness tank and breathed. Units existed which electrolyzed the Earth-vital element directly from water, but so far they were cumbersome.

A man on Venus did, best to keep such an engine handy in his boat or on the dock; for recharging the bottle on his back every few hours. Newcomers from Earth always found that an infernal nuisance, but after a while at Venus Station you fell into a calmer pattern.

A saner one? Hawthorne had often wondered. His latest visit to Earth had about convinced him.

The heat struck like a fist. He had already donned the local costume: loose, flowing garments of synthetic, designed to ward ultraviolet radiation off his skin and not absorb water. Now he paused for a moment, reminded himself that Man was a mammal able to get along quite well at even higher temperatures, and, relaxed. The sea lapped his bare feet where he stood on a pontoon. It felt cool. Suddenly he stopped minding the heat; he forgot it entirely.

Oscar frisked up. Yes, of course it was Oscar. The other cetoids, a dozen or so, were more interested in the ferry, nosing it, rubbing their sleek flanks against the metal, holding their calves up in their foreflippers for a good look.

Oscar paid attention only to Hawthorne. He lifted his blunt bulky head, nuzzled the biologist's toes, and slapped flukes on water twenty feet away.

Hawthorne squatted. "Hi, Oscar," he said. "Didn't think I'd make it back, did you?" He chucked the beast under the chin. Be damned if the cetoids didn't have true chins. Oscar rolled belly-up and snorted.

"Thought I'd pick up some dame Earthside and forget all about you, huh?" murmured Hawthorne. "Why, bless your ugly puss, I wouldn't dream of it! Certainly not. I wouldn't waste Earthside time dreaming of abandoning you for a woman. I'd do it! C'mere, creature."

He scratched the rubbery skin just behind the blow-hole. Oscar bumped against the pontoon and wriggled.

"Cut that out, will you?" asked McClellan. "I don't want a bath just yet." He threw a hawser. When Dykstra caught it, snubbed it around a bollard, and began to haul. The ferry moved slowly to the dock.

"Okay, Oscar, okay, okay," said Hawthorne. "I'm home. Let's not get sickening about it." He was a tall, rather bony man, with dark-blond hair and a prematurely creased face. "Yes, I've got a present for you too; same as the rest of the station, but let me get unpacked first. I got you a celluloid dock. Leggo there!"

The cetoid sounded. Hawthorne was about to step off onto the dock ladder when Oscar came back. With great care, the swimmer nudged the mans ankles and then, awkwardly, because this was not the regular trading pier, pushed something out of his mouth to lay at Hawthorne's feet. After which Oscar sounded again and Hawthorne muttered total, profane astonishment and felt his eyes sting a little.

He had just been presented with one of the finest fire-gems on record.

-2-

After dark, the aurora became visible. The sun was so close, and the Venusian magnetic field so weak, that even in the equator the sky became criss-crossed at times with great banners of light. Here in the Phosphor sea, the night was royal blue, with rosy curtains and silent white shuddering streamers. And the water itself shone, bioluminescence, each wave laced by cold fires. Where droplets struck the station deck, they glowed for minutes before evaporating, as if gold coals had been strewn at random over its gleaming circumference.

Hawthorne looked out the transparent wall of the wardroom. "It's good to be back," he said.

"Get that," said Shorty McClellan. "From wine and women competing in droves for the company of a glamorous interplanetary explorer, it is good to be back. This man is crazy."

The geophysicist, Wim Dykstra, nodded with seriousness. He was the tall swarthy breed of Dutchman, whose ancestral memories are of Castilian uplands. Perhaps that is why so many of them feel forever homeless.

"I think I understand, Nat," he said. "I read between the lines of my mail. Is it that bad on Earth?"

"In some ways." Hawthorne leaned against the wall, staring into Venus night.

The cetoids were playing about the station. Joyous torpedo shapes would hurtle from the water, streaming liquid, radiance, arch over and come down in a fountain that burned. And then they threshed the sea and were off around a mile-wide circle, rolling and tumbling. The cannon-crack of bodies and flukes could be heard this far up.

"I was afraid of that. I do not know if I want to take my next furlough when it comes," said Dykstra.

McClellan looked· bewildered. "What're you fellows talking about?" he asked. "What's wrong?"

Hawthorne sighed. "I don't know where to begin," he said. "The trouble is, Shorty, you see Earth continually. Get back from a voyage and you're there for weeks or months before taking off again. But we…we're gone three, four, five years at a stretch. We notice the changes."

"Oh, sure." McClellan shifted his weight uneasily in his chair. "Sure, I suppose you aren't used to—well, the gangs, or the corvées, or the fact that they've begun to ration dwelling space in America since the last time you were there. But still, you guys are well paid, and your job has prestige. You rate special privileges. What arc *you* complaining about?"

"Call it the atmosphere," said Hawthorne. He sketched a smile. "If God existed, which thank God He doesn't, I'd say He has forgotten Earth."

Dykstra flushed. "God does not forget," he said. "Men do."

"Sorry, Wim," said Hawthorne. "But I've seen—not just Earth. Earth is too big to be anything but statistics. I visited my own country, the place where I grew up. And the lake where I went fishing as a kid is an alga farm and my mother has to share one miserable room with a yattering old biddy she can't stand the sight of.

"What's worse, they've cut down Bobolink Grove to put up still another slum mislabeled a housing project, and the gangs are operating in open daylight now. Armed escort has become a major industry. I walk into a bar and not a face is happy. They're just staring stupefied at a telescreen, and—" He pulled up short. "Never mind. I probably exaggerate."

"I'll say you do," said McClellan. "Why, I can show you places where no man has been since the Indians left—if it's nature you want. You've never been to San Francisco, have you? Well, come with me to a pub I know in North Beach, and I'll show you the time of your life."

"Sure," said Hawthorne. "What I wonder is, how much longer will those fragments survive?"

"Some of them, indefinitely," said McClellan. "They're corporate property. These days C. P. means private estates."

Wim Dykstra nodded. "The rich get richer," he said, "and the poor get poorer, and the middle class vanishes. Eventually there is the fossilized Empire. I have read history."

He regarded Hawthorne out of dark, thoughtful eyes. "Medieval feudalism and monasticism evolved *within* the Roman domain: they were there when it fell apart. I wonder if a parallel development may not already be taking place. The feudalism of the large organizations on Earth; the monasticism of planetary stations like this."

"Complete with celibacy," grimaced McClellan. "Me, I'll take the feudalism!"

Hawthorne sighed again. There was always a price. Sex-suppressive pills, and the memory of fervent lips and clinging arms on Earth were often poor comfort.

"We're not a very good analogy, Wim," he argued. "In the first place, we live entirely off the jewel trade. Because it's profitable, we're allowed to carry on the scientific work which interests us personally: that's part of our wage, in effect. But if the cetoids stopped bringing gems, we'd be hauled home so fast we'd meet ourselves coming back. You know nobody will pay the fabulous cost of interplanetary freight for knowledge—only for luxuries."

Dykstra shrugged. "What of it? The economics is irrelevant to our monasticism. Have you ever drunk Benedictine?"

"Uh…yeah, I get it. But also, we're only celibate by necessity. Our big hope is that eventually we have our own women."

Dykstra smiled. "I am not pressing the analogy too close," he said. "My point is that we feel ourselves serving a larger purpose, a cultural purpose. Science, in our case, rather than religion, but still a purpose worth all the isolation and other sacrifice; If, in our hearts, we really consider the isolation a sacrifice."

Hawthorne winced. Sometimes Dykstra was too analytical. *Indeed,* thought Hawthorne, *the station personnel were monks.* Wim himself—but he was a passionate man, fortunate enough to be single-minded. Hawthorne, less lucky, had spent fifteen years shaking off a Puritan upbringing, and finally realized that he never would. He had killed his fathers unmerciful God, but the ghost would always haunt him.

He could now try to make up for long self-denial by an Earthside leave which was one continuous orgy, but the sense of sin plagued him notwithstanding, disguised as bitterness. I have been iniquitous upon Terra. Ergo, Terra is a sink of evil.

Dykstra continued, with a sudden unwonted tension in his voice. "The analogy with medieval monasteries holds good in another respect too. They thought they were retreating from the world. Instead, they became the nucleus of its next stage. And we too, unwittingly until now, may have changed history."

"Uh-uh," denied McClellan. "You can't have a history without a next generation, can you? And there's not a woman on all Venus."

Hawthorne said, quickly, to get away from his own thoughts: "There was talk in the Company offices about that. They'd like to arrange it, if they can, to give all of us more incentive to, stay. They think maybe it'll be possible. If trade continues to expand, the Station will have to be enlarged, and the new people could just as well be female technicians and scientists."

"That could lead to trouble," said McClellan.

"Not if there were enough to go around," said Hawthorne.

"And nobody signs on here who hasn't long ago given up any hope of enriching their lives with romantic love, or fatherhood."

"They could have that," murmured Dykstra. "Fatherhood, I mean."

"Kids?" Hawthorne was startled. "On Venus?"

A look of exultant triumph flickered across Dykstra's face. Hawthorne, reverting to the sensitivity of intimate years, knew that Dykstra had a secret; which he wanted to shout to the universe, but could not yet. Dykstra had discovered something wonderful.

To give him a lead, Hawthorne said: "I've been so busy swapping gossip, I've had no time for shop talk. What have you learned about this planet since I left?"

"Some promising things," said Dykstra, evasively. His tone was still not altogether steady.

"Found how the firegems are created?"

"Heavens, no. That would scuttle us, wouldn't it—if they could be synthesized? No…you can talk to Chris, if you wish. But I know he has only established that they are a biological product, like pearls. Apparently several strains of bacteroids are involved, which exist only under Venusian deep-sea conditions."

"Learn more about the life cycle?" asked McClellan. He had a spaceman's somewhat morbid fascination with any organisms that got along without oxygen.

"Yes, Chris and Mamoru and their co-workers have developed quite a lot of the detailed chemistry," said Dykstra. "It is over my head, Nat. But you will want to study it, and they have been anxious for your help as an ecologist. You know this business of the plants, if one may call them that, using solar energy to build up unsaturated compounds, which the creatures we call animals then oxidize? Oxidation need not involve oxygen, Shorty."

"I know that much chemistry," said McClellan, looking hurt.

"Well, in a general way the reactions involved did not seem energetic enough to power animals the size of Oscar" No enzymes could be identified which—" He paused, frowning a little. "Anyhow, Mamoru got to thinking about fermentation, the closest Terrestrial analogy. And it seems that micro-organisms really *are* involved. The Venusian enzymes are indistinguishable from…shall we call them viruses, for lack of a better name? Certain forms even seem to function like genes. How is that for a symbiosis, eh? Puts the classical examples in the shade."

Hawthorne whistled.

"I daresay it's a very fascinating new concept," said McClellan. "As for myself, I wish you'd hurry up and give us our cargo, so we can go home. Not that I don't like you guys, but you're not exactly my type."

"It will take a few days," said Dykstra. "It always does."

"Well, just so they're Earth days, not Venusian."

I may have a most important letter for you to deliver," said Dykstra. "I have not yet gathered the crucial data, but you must wait for that if nothing else."

Suddenly he shivered with excitement.

-3-

The long nights were devoted to study of material gathered in the daytime. When Hawthorne emerged into sunrise, where mists smoked along purple wafers under a sky like nacre," the whole station seemed to explode outward around him; Wim Dykstra had already scooted off with his new assistant, little Jimmy Cheng-tung of the hopeful grin, and their two-man sub was over the horizon, picking up data-recording, units off the sea bottom. Now boats left the wharf in every direction: Diehl and Matsumoto to gather pseudo-plankton, Vassiliev after some of the beautiful coralite on Erebus Bank, Lafarge continuing his mapping of the currents, Glass heading straight up to investigate the clouds a bit more…

The space ferry had been given its first loading during the night. Shorty McClellan walked across a bare deck with Hawthorne and Captain Jevons. "Expect me back again about local sundown," he said. "No use coming before then, with everyone out fossicking?"

"I imagine not." Jevons, white-haired and dignified, looked wistfully at Lafarge's retreating craft.

Five cetoids frisked in its wake, leaping and spouting and gaily swimming rings around it. Nobody had invited them, but by now few men would have ventured out of station view without such an escort.

More than once, when accidents happened—and they happened often on an entire planet as big and varied as Earth—the cetoids had saved lives. A man could ride on the back of one, if worst came to worst, but more often several would labor to keep a damaged vessel afloat, as if they knew the cost of hauling even a rowboat across space.

"I'd like to go fossicking myself," said Jevons. He chuckled. "But someone has to mind the store."

"Uh, how did the Veenies go for that last lot of stuff?" asked McClellan. "The plastic jewelry?"

"They didn't," said Jevons. "They simply ignored it. Proving, at least, that they have good taste. Do you want the beads back?"

"Lord, no! Chuck 'em in the ocean. Can you recommend any other novelties? Anything you think they might like?"

"Well," said Hawthorne, "I've speculated about tools such as they could use, designed to be held in the mouth. And—"

"We'd better experiment with that right here, before getting samples from Earth," said Jevons. "I'm skeptical, myself. What use would a hammer or a knife be to a cetoid?"

"Actually," said Hawthorne, "I was thinking about a saw. To cut coralite blocks and make shelters on the sea bottom."

"Whatever for?" asked McClellan, astonished.

"I don't know," said Hawthorne. "There's so little we know. Probably not shelters against undersea weather—" though that might not be absolutely fantastic, either. "There are cold currents in the depths, I'm sure. What I had in mind, was—I've seen scars on many cetoids, like teeth marks, but left by something gigantic."

"It's an idea." Jevons smiled. "It's good to have you back ideating, Nat. And it's decent of you to volunteer to take your station watch the first thing, right after our return. That wasn't expected of you."

"Ah, he's got memories to soften the moment," said McClellan. "I saw him in a hostess joint in Chicago. Brother, was he making time!"

The air masks hid most expression, but Hawthorne felt his ears redden. Jevons minded his own business, but he was old-fashioned, and more like a father than the implacable man in black whom Hawthorne dimly remembered. One did not boast of Earthside escapades in Jevons' presence.

"I want to mull over the new biochemical data and sketch out a research program in the light of it," said the ecologist hastily. "And, too, renew my acquaintance with Oscar. I was really touched when he gave me that gem. I felt like a louse, handing it over to the Company."

"At the price it'll command, I'd feel lousy too," said McClellan.

"No, I don't mean that. I mean—Oh, run along jetboy!"

Hawthorne and Jevons stood watching the spacecraft taxi off across the water. Its rise was slow at first—much fire and noise, then a gradual acceleration. But by the time it had pierced the clouds, it was a meteor in reverse flight. And still it moved faster, streaking through the planet's thick permanent overcast until it was high in the sky and the clouds to the man inside did not show as gray but as blinding white.

So many miles high, even the air of Venus grew thin and piercingly cold, and water vapor was frozen out. Thus absorption spectra had not revealed to Earthbound astronomers that this planet was one vast ocean. The first explorers had expected desert and instead they had found water. But still McClellan rode his lightning horse, faster and higher, into a blaze of constellations.

When the rocket noise had faded, Hawthorne came out of his reverie and said: "At least we've created one beautiful thing with all our ingenuity—just one, space travel. I'm not sure how much destruction and ugliness that makes up for."

"Don't be so cynical," said Jevons. "We've also done Beethoven sonatas, Rembrandt portraits. Shakespearean drama…and you, of all people, should be able to rhapsodize on the beauty of science itself."

"But not of technology," said Hawthorne. "Science, pure ordered knowledge, yes. I'll rank that beside anything your Beethovens and Rembrandts ever made. But this machinery business, gouging a planet so that more people can pullulate—" *It was good to be back with Jevons,* he thought. *You could dare be serious talking to the captain.*

"You've been saddened by your furlough," said the old man. "It should be the other way around. You're too young for sadness."

"New England ancestors." Hawthorne tried to grin. "My chromosomes insist that I disapprove of something."

"I am luckier," said Jevons. "Like Pastor Grundtvig, a couple of centuries back, I have made a marvelous discovery. God is *good.*"

"If one can believe in God. You know I can't. The concept just doesn't square with the mess humanity has made of things on Earth."

"God has to leave us free, Nat. Would you rather be an efficient, will-less puppet?"

"Or He may not care," said Hawthorne. "Assuming He does exist, have we any strong empirical grounds for thinking we're His particular favorites? Man may be just another discarded experiment, like the dinosaurs, set aside to gather dust and die. How do you know Oscar's breed don't have souls? And how do you know we do?"

"It's unwise to romanticize the cetoids," said Jevons. "They show a degree of intelligence, I'll concede. But—"

"I know. But they don't build spaceships. They haven't got hands, and of course fire is impossible for-them: I've heard all that before, Cap. I've argued it a hundred times, here and on Earth. But how can we tell what the cetoids do and don't do on the sea floor? They can stay underwater for days at a time, remember. And even here, I've watched those games of 'tag' they play. They are very remarkable games in some respects.

"I swear I can see a pattern, too intricate to make much sense to me, but a distant pattern notwithstanding. An art form, like our ballet, but using the wind and currents and waves to dance to. And how do you account for their display of taste and discrimination in music, individual taste; so that Oscar goes for those old jazz numbers, and Sambo won't come near them but will pay you carat for carat if you give him some Buxtehude? Why trade at all?"

"Pack rats trade on Earth," said Jevons.

"Now you're being unfair. The first expedition rafting here thought it was pack rat psychology, too—-cetoids snatching oddments off the lower deck and leaving bits of shell, coralite, finally jewels. Sure, I know all that. But by now it's developed into too intricate a price system. The cetoids are shrewd about it—honest, but shrewd. They've got our scale of values figured to an inch: everything from a conchoidal shell to a firegem. Completely to the inch—keep that in mind.

"And why should mere animals go for music tapes, sealed in plastic and run off a thermionic cell? Or for waterproof reproductions of our great art? As for tools? They're often seen helped by schools of specialized fish, rounding up sea creatures, slaughtering and flensing, harvesting pseudo-kelp. They don't need hands, Cap! They use *live* tools!"

"I have been here a good many years," said Jevons dryly.

Hawthorne flushed. "Sorry. I gave that lecture so often Earthside, to people who didn't even have the data, that it's become a reflex."

"I don't mean to down-grade our damp friends," said the captain. "But you know as well as I do that all the years of trying to establish communication with them symbols, signals—everything has failed."

"Are you sure?" asked Hawthorne.

"What?"

"How do you know the cetoids have not learned our alphabet off those slates?"

"Well…after all—"

"They might have good reasons for not wanting to take a grease pencil in their jaws and scribble messages back to us. A degree of wariness, perhaps. Let's face it, Cap. We're the aliens here, the monsters. Or maybe they simply aren't interested: our vessels are fun to play with, our goods amusing enough to be worth trading for, but we ourselves seem drab. Or, of course—and I think this is the most probable explanation—our minds are too strange. Consider the two planets, how different they are. How alike would you expect the thinking of two wholly different races to be?"

"An interesting speculation," said Jevons. "Not new, of course."

"Well, I'll go set out the latest gadgets for them," said Hawthorne. He walked a few paces, then stopped and turned around.

"You know," he said, "I'm being a fool. Oscar did communicate with us, only last evening. A perfectly unambiguous message, in the form of a firegem."

-4-

Hawthorne went past a heavy machine gun, loaded with explosive slugs. He despised the rule that an entire arsenal must always be kept ready. When had Venus ever threatened men with anything but the impersonal consequences of ignorance?

He continued on along the trading pier. Its metal gleamed, nearly awash. Basketlike containers had been lowered overnight, with standard goods. These included recordings and pictures the cetoids already knew, but always seemed to want more of. Did each individual desire some, or did they distribute these things around their world, in the undersea equivalent of museums or libraries?

Then there were the little plastic containers of sodium chloride, aqua ammonia, and other materials, whose taste the cetoids apparently enjoyed. Lacking continents to leach out, the Venusian ocean was less mineralized than Earth's, and these chemicals were exotic. Nevertheless the cetoids had refused plastibulbs of certain compounds, such as the permanganates—and later biochemical research had shown that these were poisonous to Venusian life.

But how had the cetoids known that, without ever crushing a bulb between teeth? They just knew, that was all. Human senses and human science didn't exhaust all the information in the cosmos. The standard list of goods had come to include a few toys, like floating balls, which the cetoids used for some appallingly rough games; and specially devised dressings, to put on injuries…

Oh, nobody doubted that Oscar was much more intelligent than a chimpanzee, thought Hawthorne. *The problem had always been, was he as highly intelligent as a man?*

He pulled up the baskets and took out the equally standardized payments which had been left in them. There were firegems, small and perfect or large and flawed. One was both big and faultless, like a round drop of rainbow. There were particularly beautiful specimens of coralite, which would be made into ornaments on Earth, and several kinds of exquisite shell.

There were specimens of marine life for study, most of them never before seen by Man. How many million species would an entire planet hold? There were a few tools, lost overboard, and only now freed of ooze by shifting currents; a lump of something unidentifiable, light and yellow and greasy to the touch, perhaps a biological product like ambergris, possibly only of slight interest and possibly offering a clue to an entire new field of chemistry. The plunder of a world rattled into Hawthorne's collection boxes.

All novelties had a fixed, rather small value. If the humans took the next such offering, its price would go up, and so on until a stable fee was reached, not too steep for the Earthmen or too low to be worth the cetoids' trouble. It was amazing how detailed a bargain you could strike without language.

Hawthorne looked down at Oscar. The big fellow had nosed up close to the pier and now lay idly swinging his tail. The blue sheen along his upcurved back was lovely to watch.

"You know," murmured Hawthorne, "for years all Earth has been chortling over your giving us such nearly priceless stuff for a few cheaply made geegaws. But I've begun to wonder if it isn't reciprocal. Just how rare are firegems on Venus?"

Oscar spouted a little and rolled a wickedly gleaming eye. A curious expression crossed his face. Doubtless one would be very unscientific to call it a grin. But Hawthorne felt sure that a grin was what Oscar intended.

"Okay," he said. "Okay. Now let's see what you think of our gr-r-reat new products, brought to you after years of research for better living. Each and every one of these products, ladies and gentle-cetoids, has been tested in our spotless laboratories, and don't think it was easy to test the patent spot remover in particular. Now—"

The music bubbles of Schonberg had been rejected. Perhaps other atonalists would be liked, but with spaceship mass ratios what they were, the experiment wasn't going to be done for a long time. On the other hand, a tape of traditional Japanese songs was gone and a two-carat gem had been left, twice the standard price for a novelty: in effect, some cetoid was asking for more of the same.

As usual, every contemporary pictorial artist was refused, but then, Hawthorne agreed they were not to his taste either. Nor did any cetoid want Picasso (middle period), but Mondrian and Matisse had gone well. A doll had been accepted at low valuation, a mere bit of mineral: "Okay, we (I?) will take just this one sample, but don't bother bringing any more."

Once again, the waterproof illustrated books had been rejected; the cetoids had never bought books, after the first few. It was an idiosyncrasy, among others, which had led many researchers to doubt their essential basic intelligence and perception.

That doesn't follow, thought Hawthorne. *They haven't got hands, so a printed text isn't natural for them. Because of sheer beauty—or interest, or humor, or whatever they get out of it—some of our best art is worth the trouble of carrying underwater and preserving. But if they're looking for a factual record, they may well have more suitable methods. Such as what? God knows. Maybe they have perfect memories. Maybe, by sheer telepathy or something, they build their messages into the crystal structure of stones on the ocean bed.*

Oscar bustled along the pier, following the man. Hawthorne squatted down and rubbed the cetoid's smooth wet brow. "Hey, what do you think about me?" he asked aloud. "Do you wonder if *I* think? All right. All right. My breed came down from the sky and built floating metal settlements and brought all sorts of curious goodies. But ants and termites have pretty intricate behavior patterns, and you've got similar things on Venus."

Oscar snorted and nosed Hawthorne's ankles. Out in the water, his people were playing, and foam burned white against purple where they arched skyward and came down again. Still further out, on the hazy edge of vision, a few adults were at work, rounding up a school of "fish" with the help of three tame (?) species. They seemed to be enjoying the task.

"You have no right to be as smart as you are, Oscar," said Hawthorne. "Intelligence is supposed to evolve in response to a rapidly changing environment, and the sea isn't supposed to be changeable enough. Well, maybe the Terrestrial sea isn't. But this is Venus, and what do we know about Venus? Tell me, Oscar, are your dog-type and cattle-type fish just dull-witted animal slaves like the aphids kept by ants, or are they real domestic animals, consciously trained? It's got to be the latter. I'll continue to insist it is, until ants develop a fondness for van Gogh and Beiderbecke."

Oscar sounded, drenching Hawthorne with carbonated sea water. It foamed spectacularly, and tingled on his skin. A small wind crossed the world, puffing the wetness out of his garments. He sighed. The cetoids were like children, never staying put—another reason why so many psychologists rated them only a cut above Terrestrial apes.

A logically unwarranted conclusion, to say the least. At the quick pace of Venusian life, urgent business might well arise on a second's notice. Or, even if the cetoids were merely being capricious, were they stupid on that account? Man was a heavy-footed beast, who forgot how to play if he was not always being reminded. Here on Venus there might just naturally be more joy in living.

I shouldn't run down my own species the way I do, thought Hawthorne. *"All centuries but this and every country but his own." We're different from Oscar, that's all. But by the same token, is he any worse than us?*

He turned his mind to the problem of designing a saw which a cetoid could handle. Handle? Manipulate? Not when a mouth was all you had! If the species accepted such tools in trade, it would go a long way toward proving them comparable to man. And if they didn't, it would only show that they had other desires, not necessarily inferior ones.

Quite conceivably, Oscar's race was more intellectual than mankind. Why not? Their bodies and their environment debarred them from such material helps as fire, chipped stone, forged metal, or pictograms. But might this not force their minds into subtler channels? A race of philosophers, unable to talk to Man because it had long ago forgotten baby talk…

Sure, it was a far-fetched hypothesis. But the indisputable fact remained, Oscar was far more than a clever animal, even if he was not on a level with Man.

Yet, if Oscar's people had evolved to, say, the equivalent of Pithecanthropus, they had done so because something in Venusian conditions had put a premium on intelligence. The same factor should continue to operate. In another half-million years or so, almost certainly, the cetoids would have as much brain and soul as Man today. (And Man himself might be extinct, or degraded.) Maybe more soul—more sense of beauty and mercy and laughter—if you extrapolated their present behavior.

In short, Oscar was (a) already equal to Man, or (b) already beyond Man, or (c) on the way up, and his descendants would in time achieve (a) and then (b). Welcome, my brother!

The pier quivered. Hawthorne glanced down again. Oscar had returned. He was nosing the metal impatiently and making gestures with his foreflipper. Hawthorne went over and looked at him. Oscar curved up his tail and whacked his own back, all the time beckoning.

"Hey, wait!" Hawthorne got the idea. He hoped. "Wait, do you want me to come for a ride?" he asked.

The cetoid blinked both eyes. Was the blink the counterpart of a nod? And if so, had Oscar actually understood the English words?

Hawthorne hurried off to the oxygen electrolyzer. Skindiving equipment was stored in the locker beside it. He wriggled into the flexible, heat-retaining Long John. Holding his breath, he unclipped his mask from the tank and air mixer he wore, and put on a couple of oxynitro flasks instead, thus converting it to an aqualung.

For a moment he hesitated. Should he inform Jevons, or at least take the collection boxes inside? No, to hell with it! This wasn't Earth, where you couldn't leave an empty beer bottle unwatched without having it stolen. Oscar might lose patience. The Venusian—damn it, he *would* call them that, and the devil take scientific caution!—had rescued distressed humans, but never before had offered a ride without utilitarian purpose. Hawthorne's pulse beat loudly.

He ran back. Oscar lay level with the pier. Hawthorne straddled him, grasping a small cervical fin and leaning back against the muscular dorsal. The long body glided from the station. Water rippled sensuously around Hawthorne's bare feet. Where his face was not masked, the wind was fresh upon it. Oscar's flukes churned up foam like a snowstorm.

Low overhead there scudded rain clouds, and lightning veined the west. A small polypoid went by, its keel fin submerged, its iridescent membrane-sail driving it on a broad reach. A nearby cetoid slapped the water with his tail in a greeting.

The motion was so smooth that Hawthorne was finally startled to glance behind and see the station five miles off. Then Oscar submerged.

Hawthorne had done a lot of skin-diving, as well as more extensive work in submarines or armor. He was not surprised by the violet clarity of the first yards, nor the rich darkening as he went on down. The glowfish which passed him like rainbow comets were familiar. But he had never before felt the living play of muscles between his thighs; suddenly he knew why a few wealthy men on Earth still kept horses.

When he was in cool, silent, absolute blackness, he felt Oscar begin to travel. Almost, he was tom off by the stream; he lost himself in the sheer exhilaration of hanging on. With other senses than vision he was aware how they twisted through caves and canyons in buried mountains. An hour had passed when light glowed before him, a spark. It took another half hour to reach its source.

He had often seen luminous coralite banks. But never this one. It lay not far from the station as Venusian distances went, but even a twenty-mile radius sweeps out a big territory and men had not chanced by here. And the usual reef was a good bit like its Terrestrial counterpart, a ragged jumble of spires, bluffs, and grottos, eerie but unorganized beauty.

Here, the coralite was shaped. A city of merfolk opened up before Hawthorne.

Afterward he did not remember just how it looked. The patterns were so strange that his mind was not trained to register them. He knew there were delicate fluted columns, arched chambers with arabesque walls, a piling of clean masses at one spot and a Gothic humoresque elsewhere. He saw towers enspiraled like a narwhal's tusk, arches and buttresses of fragile filigree, an overall unity of pattern at once as light as spindrift and as strong as the world-circling tide, immense, complex, and serene.

A hundred species of coralite, each with its own distinctive glow, were blended to make the place, so that there was a subtle play of color, hot reds and icy blues and living greens and yellows, against ocean black. And from some source, he never knew what, came a thin crystal sound, a continuous contrapuntal symphony which he did not understand but which recalled to him frost flowers on the windows of his childhood home.

Oscar let him swim about freely and look. He saw a few other cetoids, also drifting along, often accompanied by young. But plainly, they didn't live here. Was this a memorial, an art gallery, or—Hawthorne didn't know. The place was huge, it reached farther downward than he could see, farther than he could go before pressure killed him, at least half a mile straight down to the sea bottom. Yet this miraculous place had never been fashioned for any "practical" reason. Or had it? Perhaps the Venusians recognized what Earth had forgotten, though the ancient Greeks had known it—that the contemplation of beauty is essential to thinking life.

The underwater blending of so much that was constructively beautiful could not be a freak of nature. But neither had it been carved out of some pre-existing mountain. No matter how closely he looked, and the flameless fire was adequate to see by, Hawthorne found no trace of chisel or mould. He could only decide that in some unknown way, Oscar's people had grown this thing.

He lost himself. It was Oscar who finally nudged him—a reminder that he had better go back before he ran out of air. When they reached the pier and Hawthorne had stepped off, Oscar nuzzled the man's foot, very briefly, like a kiss, and then he sounded in a tremendous splash.

-5-

Toward the close of the forty-three-hour daylight period, the boats came straggling in. For most it had been a routine shift, a few dozen discoveries, books and instruments filled with data to be wrestled with and perhaps understood. The men landed wearily, unloaded their craft, stashed their findings and went off for food and rest. Later would come the bull sessions.

Wim Dykstra and Jimmy Cheng-tung had returned earlier than most, with armfuls of recording meters. Hawthorne knew in a general way what they were doing. By seismographs, sonic probes, core studies, mineral analyses, measurements of temperature and radioactivity and a hundred other facets, they tried to understand the planet's inner structure. It was part of an old enigma. Venus had 80% of Earth's mass, and the chemical composition was nearly identical.

The two planets should have been sisters. Instead, the Venusian magnetic field was so weak that iron compasses were useless; the surface was so nearly smooth that no land rose above the water; volcanic and seismic activity were not only less, but showed unaccountably different patterns, lava flows and shock waves here had their own laws; the rocks were of odd types and distributions. And there was a galaxy of other technicalities which Hawthorne did not pretend to follow.

Jevons had remarked that in the past weeks Dykstra had been getting more and more excited about something. The Dutchman was the cautious type of scientist, who said never a word about his results until they were nailed down past argument. He had been spending Earthdays on end in calculations. When someone finally insisted on a turn at the computer, Dykstra often continued figuring with a pencil. One gathered he was well on the way to solving the geological problem of Venus.

"Or aphroditological?" Jevons had murmured. "But I know Wim. There's more behind this than curiosity, or a chance at glory. Wim has something very big afoot, and very close to his heart. I hope it won't take him too long!"

Today Dykstra had rushed downstairs and sworn nobody would get at the computer until he was through. Cheng-tung hung around for a while, brought him sandwiches, and finally wandered up on deck with the rest of the station to watch Shorty McClellan come in again.

Hawthorne sought him out. "Hey, Jimmy," he said. "You don't have to keep up that mysterious act. You're among friends."

The Chinese grinned. "I have not the right to speak," he said. "I am only the apprentice. When I have my own doctorate, then you will hear me chatter till you wish I'd learn some Oriental inscrutability."

"Yes, but hell, it's obvious what you're doing in general outline," said Hawthorne. "I understand Wim has been calculating in advance what sort of data he ought to get if his theory is sound. Now he's reducing those speculative assumptions for comparison. So okay, what *is* his theory?"

"There is nothing secret about its essence," said Cheng-tung. "It is only a confirmation of a hypothesis made more than a hundred years ago, before anyone had even left Earth. The idea is that Venus has a core unlike our planet's, and that this accounts for the gross differences we've observed.

"Dr. Dykstra has been elaborating it, and data so far have confirmed his beliefs. Today we brought in what may be the crucial measurements—chiefly seismic echoes from depth bombs exploded in undersea wells."

"M-m-m, yeah, I do know something about it." Hawthorne stared across the ocean. No cetoids were in sight. Had they gone down to their beautiful city? And if so, why? *It's a good thing the questions aren't answered,* he thought. *If there were no more riddles on Venus, I don't know what I'd do with my life.*

"The core here is supposed to be considerably smaller and less dense than Earth's, isn't it?" he went on. His curiosity was actually no more than mild, but he wanted to make conversation while they waited for the spacecraft.

The young Chinese had arrived on the same ship which had taken Hawthorne home to furlough. Now they would be together for a long time, and it was well to show quick friendliness. He seemed a likeable little fellow anyhow.

"True," nodded Cheng-tung. "Though 'supposed' is the wrong word. The general assertion was proven quite satisfactorily quite some time ago. Since then Dr. Dykstra has been studying the details."

"I seem to have read somewhere that Venus ought by rights not to have a core at all," said Hawthorne. "Not enough mass to make enough pressure, or something of the sort. The planet ought to have a continuous rocky character right to the center, like Mars."

"Your memory is not quite correct," said Cheng-tung. His sarcasm was gentle and inoffensive. "But then, the situation is a trifle complex. You see, if you use quantum laws to calculate the curve of pressure at a planet's center, versus the planet's mass, you do not get a simple figure.

"Up to about eight-tenths of an Earth-mass it rises smoothly, but there is a change at what is called the Y-point. The curve doubles back, as if mass were decreasing with added pressure, and only after it has thus jogged back a certain amount—equivalent to about two percent of Earth's mass—does the curve resume a steady rise."

"What happens at this Y-point?" asked Hawthorne rather absently.

"The force becomes great enough to start collapsing the central matter. First crystals, which had already assumed their densest possible form, break down completely. Then, as more mass is added to the plant, the atoms themselves collapse. Not their nuclei, of course. That requires mass on the order of a star's.

"But the electron shells are squeezed into the smallest possible compass. Only when this stage of quantum degeneracy has been reached—when the atoms will not yield any further, and there is a true core, with a specific gravity of better than ten—only thereafter will increased mass again mean a steady rise in internal pressure."

"Uh…yes. I do remember Wim speaking of it, quite some time ago. But he never did like to talk shop, either, except to fellow specialists. Otherwise he'd rather debate history. I take it, then, that Venus has a core which is not collapsed as much as it might be?"

"Yes. At its present internal temperature, Venus is just past the Y-point. If more mass should somehow be added to this planet, its radius would actually decrease. This, not very incidentally, accounts rather well for the observed peculiarities. You can see how the accretion of material in the beginning, when the planets were formed, reached a point where Venus began to shrink—and then, as it happened, stopped, not going on to produce maximum core density and thereafter a steadily increasing size like Earth.

"This means a smooth planet, with no upthrust masses to reach above the hydrosphere and form continents. With no exposed rocks, there was nothing to take nearly all the CO_2 from the air. So life evolved for a different atmosphere. The relatively large mantle, as well as the low-density core, lead to a non-Terrestrial seismology, vulcanology, and mineralogy. The Venusian core is less conductive than Earth's—conductivity tends to increase with degeneracy—so the currents circulating in it are much smaller. Hence, the weak planetary magnetism."

"Very interesting," said Hawthorne. "But why the big secret? I mean, it's a good job of work, but all you've shown is that Venusian atoms obey quantum laws. That's hardly a surprise to spring on the universe."

Cheng-tung's small body shivered a bare trifle. "It has been more difficult than one might suspect," he said. "But yes, it is true. Our data now reveal unequivocally that Venus has just the type of core which it could have under present conditions."

Since Cheng-tung had during the night hours asked Hawthorne to correct any mistakes in his excellent English, the American said, "You mean the type of core it should have."

"I mean precisely what I said, and it is not a tautology." The grin was dazzling. Cheng-tung, hugged himself and did a few dance steps. "But it is Dr. Dykstra's brain child. Let him midwife it." Abruptly he changed the conversation.

Hawthorne felt puzzled, but dismissed the emotion. And presently McClellan's ferry blazed out of the clouds and came to rest. It was a rather splendid sight, but Hawthorne found himself watching it with only half an eye. Mostly he was still down under the ocean, in the living temple of the Venusians.

Several hours past nightfall, Hawthorne laid the sheaf of reports down on his desk. Chris Diehl and Mamoru Matsumoto had done a superb task. Even in this earliest pioneering stage, their concept of enzymatic symbiosis offered possibilities beyond imagination. Here there was work far a century of science to come. And out of that work would be gotten a deeper insight into living processes, including those of Earth, than men had yet hoped for.

And who could tell practical benefits? The prospect was heartcatching. Hawthorne had already realized a little of what he himself could do, and yes, in a hazy fashion he could even begin to see, if not understand, how the Venusians had created that lovely thing beneath the water…But a person can only concentrate so long at a time. Hawthorne left his cubbyhole office and wandered down a passageway toward the wardroom.

The station murmured around him. He saw a number of its fifty men at work. Some did their turn at routine chores, maintenance of apparatus, sorting and baling of trade goods, and the rest. Others puttered happily with test tubes, microscopes, spectroscopes, and less understandable equipment. Or they perched on lab benches, brewing coffee over a Bunsen burner while they argued, or sat feet on desk, pipe in mouth, hands behind head, and labored. Those who noticed Hawthorne hailed him as he passed. The station itself muttered familiarly, engines, ventilators, a faint quiver from the surrounding forever unrestful waters.

It was good to be home again.

Hawthorne went up a companionway, down another corridor, and into the wardroom. Jevons sat in a corner with his beloved Montaigne. McClellan and Cheng-tung were shooting dice. Otherwise the long room was deserted. Its transparent wall opened on seas which tonight were almost black, roiled and laced with gold luminosity.

The sky seemed made from infinite layerings of blue and gray, a low haze diffusing the aurora, and a rain-storm was approaching from the west with its blackness and lightning. The only sign of life was a forty-foot sea snake, quickly writhing from one horizon to another, its created jaws dripping phosphorescence.

McClellan looked up. "Hi, Nat," he said. "Want to sit in?"

"Right after Earth leave?" said Hawthorne. "What would I use for money?" He went over to the samovar and tapped himself a cup.

"Eighter from Decatur," chanted Jimmy Cheng-tung.

"Come on, boys, let's see that good old Maxwell distribution."

Hawthorne sat down at the table. He was still wondering how to break his news about Oscar and the holy place. He should have reported it immediately to Jevons, but for hours after returning he had been dazed, and then the inadequacy of words had reared a barrier. He was too conditioned against showing emotion to want to speak about it at all.

He had, though, prepared some logical conclusions. The Venusians were at least as intelligent as the builders of the Taj Mahal; they had finally decided the biped strangers were fit to be shown something and would presumably have a whole planet's riches and mysteries to show on later occasions. Hawthorne scalded his tongue on red bitterness.

"Cap," he said.

"Yes?" Jevons lowered his dog-eared volume, patient as always at the interruption.

"Something happened today," said Hawthorne.

Jevons looked at him keenly. Cheng-tung finished a throw but did not move further, nor did McClellan. Outside there could be heard the heavy tread of waves and a rising wind.

"Go ahead," invited Jevons finally.

"I was on the trading pier and while I was standing there—"

Wim Dykstra entered. His shoes rang on the metal floor. Hawthorne's voice stumbled into silence. The Dutchman dropped fifty clipped-together sheets of paper on the table. It seemed they should have clashed, like a sword thrown in challenge, but only the wind spoke.

Dykstra's eyes blazed. "I have it," he said.

"By God!" exploded Cheng-tung.

"What on Earth?" said Jevons' mild old voice.

"You mean off Earth," said McClellan. But tightness grew in him as he regarded Dykstra.

The geophysicist looked at them all for several seconds.

He laughed curtly. "I was trying to think of a suitable dramatic phrase," he said. "None came to mind. So much for historic moments."

McClellan picked up the papers, shuddered, and dropped them again. "Look, math is okay, but let's keep it within reason," he said. "What do those squiggles mean?"

Dykstra took out a cigarette and made a ceremony of lighting it. When smoke was in his lungs, he said shakily: "I have spent the past weeks working out the details of an old and little-known hypothesis, first made by Ramsey in nineteen fifty-one, and applying it to Venusian conditions. The data obtained here have just revealed themselves as final proof of my beliefs."

"There isn't a man on this planet who doesn't hope for a Nobel Prize," said Jevons.

His trick of soothing dryness didn't work this time. Dykstra pointed the glowing cigarette like a weapon and answered: "I do not care about that. I am interested in the largest and most significant engineering project of history."

They waited. Hawthorne began for no good reason to feel cold.

"The colonization of Venus," said Dykstra.

-6-

Dykstra's words fell into silence as if into a well. And then, like the splash, Shorty McClellan said, "Huh? Isn't the Mindanao Deep closer to home?"

But Hawthorne spilled hot tea over his own fingers.

Dykstra began to pace, up and down, smoking in short nervous drags. His words rattled out: "The basic reason for the steady decay of Terrestrial civilization is what one may call crampedness. Every day we have more people and fewer resources. There are no longer any exotic foreigners to challenge and stimulate any frontier…no, we can only sit and brew an eventual, inevitable atomic civil war.

"If we had some place to go, what a difference! Oh, one could not relieve much population pressure by emigration to another planet—though an increased demand for such transportation would surely lead to better, more economical spaceships. But the fact that men could go, somehow, perhaps to hardship but surely to freedom and opportunity, that fact would make a difference even to the stay-at-homes. At worst, if civilization on Earth must die, its best elements would be on Venus, carrying forward what was good, forgetting what was evil. A second chance for humankind—do you see?"

"It's a pleasant theory, at least," said Jevons slowly, "but as for Venus. No, I don't believe a permanent colony forced to live on elaborated rafts and to wear masks every minute outdoors could be successful."

"Of course not," said Dykstra. "That is why I spoke of an engineering project. The transformation of Venus to another Earth."

"Now wait a minute!" cried Hawthorne, springing up. No one noticed him. For them, in that moment, only the dark man who spoke like a prophet had reality. Hawthorne clenched his fists together and sat down, muscle by muscle, forcing himself.

Dykstra said through a veil of smoke: "Do you know the structure of this planet? Its mass puts it just beyond the Y-point—"

Even then, McClellan had to say, "No, I don't know. Tell me w'y point?"

But that was automatic, and ignored. Dykstra was watching Jevons, who nodded.

The geophysicist went on, rapidly, "Now in the region where the mass-pressure curve jogs back, it is not a single-valued function. A planet with the mass of Venus has three possible central pressures. There is the one it does actually have, corresponding to a small core of comparatively low density and a large rocky mantle. But there is also a higher-pressure situation, where the planet has a large degenerate core, hence a greater overall density and smaller radius. And, on the other side of the Y-point, there is the situation of lower central pressure. This means that the planet has no true core but, like Mars, is merely built in layers of rock and magma.

"Now such an ambiguous condition is unstable. It is possible for the small core which exists to change phase. This would not be true on Earth, which has too much mass, or on Mars, which does not have enough. But Venus is very near the critical point. If the lower mantle collapsed, to make a larger core and smaller total radius, the released energy would appear as vibrations and ultimately as heat."

He paused an instant, as if to give weight to his words.

"If, on the other hand, the at-present collapsed atoms of the small core were to revert to a higher energy level, there would be blast waves traveling to the surface, disruption on a truly astronomical scale—and, when things had quieted down, Venus would be larger and less dense than at present, *without any core at all.*"

McClellan said, "Wait a bit, pal! Do you mean this damn golf ball is liable to explode under us at any minute?"

"Oh, no," said Dykstra more calmly. "Venus does have a mass somewhat above the critical for existing temperatures. Its core is in a metastable rather than unstable condition, and there would be no reason to worry for billions of years. Also, if temperature did increase enough to cause an expansion, it would not be quite as violent as Ramsey believed, because the Venusian mass *is* greater than his Y-point value. The explosion would not actually throw much material into space. But it would, of course, raise continents."

"Hey!" That was from Jevons. He jumped up. (Hawthorne sat slumped into nightmare. Outside the wind lifted, and the storm moved closer across the sea.) "You mean…increased planetary radius, magnifying surface irregularities—"

"And the upthrust of lighter rocks," added Dykstra, nodding. "It is all here in my calculations. I can even predict the approximate area of dry land resulting—about equal to that on Earth. The newly exposed rocks will consume carbon dioxide in huge amounts, to form carbonates. At the same time, specially developed strains of Terrestrial photosynthetic life—very like those now used to maintain the air on spaceship –can be sown.

"They will thrive, liberating oxygen in quantity, until a balance is struck. I can show that this balance can be made identical with the balance which now exists in Earth's atmosphere. The oxygen will form an ozone layer, thus blocking the now dangerous level of ultraviolet radiation. Eventually, another Earth. Warmer, of course—a milder climate, nowhere too hot for man—cloudy still, because of the closer sun—but nevertheless, New Earth!"

Hawthorne shook himself, trying to find a strength which seemed drained from him. He thought dully that one good practical objection would end it all, and then he could wake up.

"Hold on, there," he said in a stranger's voice. "It's a clever idea, but these processes you speak of—I mean, all right, perhaps continents could be raised in hours or days, but changing the atmosphere, that would take millions of years. Too long to do humans any good."

"Ah, no," said Dykstra. "This also I have investigated. There are such things as catalysts. Also, the growth of micro-organisms under favorable conditions, without any natural enemies, presents no difficulties. Using only known techniques, I calculate that Venus could be made so a man can safely walk naked on its surface in fifty years.

"In fact, if we wanted to invest more effort, money, and research, it could be done faster. To be sure, then must come the grinding of stone into soil, the fertilizing and planting, the slow painful establishment of an ecology. But that, again, needs only to be started. The first settlers on Venus could make oases for themselves, miles wide, and thereafter expand these at their leisure. By using specialized plants, agriculture can even be practiced in the original desert.

"Oceanic life would expand much more rapidly, of course, without any human attentions. Hence the Venusians could soon carry on fishing and pelagiculture. I have good estimates to show that the development of the planet could even exceed the population growth. The firstcomers would have hope—their grandchildren will have wealth!"

Hawthorne sat back. "There are already Venusians," he mumbled.

Nobody heard him. "Say," objected McClellan, "how do you propose to blow up this balloon in the first place?"

"Is it not obvious?" said Dykstra. "Increased core temperature can supply the energy to push a few tons of matter into a higher quantum state. This would lower the pressure enough to trigger the rest. A single large hydrogen bomb at the very center of the planet would do it. Since this is unfortunately not attainable, we must tap several thousand deep wells in the ocean floor, and touch off a major nuclear explosion in all simultaneously.

"That would be no trick at all. Very little fallout would result, and what did get into the atmosphere would be gone again in a few years. The bombs are available. In fact, they exist already in far larger amounts than would be needed for this project. Would this not be a better use for them than using them as a stockpile to destroy human life?"

"Who would pay the bill?" asked Cheng-tung unexpectedly.

"Whatever government has the foresight—if all the governments on Earth cannot get together on it. I am not greatly concerned about that. Regimes and policies go, nations die, cultures are forgotten. But I want to be sure that *Man* will survive. The cost would not be great—comparable, at most, to one military satellite, and the rewards are enormous even on the crassest immediate terms. Consider what a wealth of uranium and other materials, now in short supply on Earth, would become accessible."

Dykstra turned to the transparent wall. The storm had reached them. Under the station caissons, the sea raged and struck and shattered in radiant foam. The deep, strong force of those blows traveled up through steel and concrete like the play of muscles in a giant's shoulders. Rain began to smash in great sheets on the deck. A continuous lightning flickered across Dykstra's lean countenance, and thunder toned.

"A world," he whispered.

Hawthorne stood up again. He leaned forward, his fingertips resting on the table. They were cold. His voice still came to him like someone else's. "No," he said. "Absolutely not."

"Eh?" Dykstra turned almost reluctantly from watching the storm. "What is wrong. Nat?"

"You'd sterilize a living planet," said Hawthorne.

"Well…true," admitted Dykstra. "Yes. Humanely, though. The first shock wave would destroy all organisms before they even had time to feel it."

"But that's murder!" cried Hawthorne.

"Come, now," said Dykstra. "Let us not get sentimental. I admit it will be a pity to destroy life so interesting, but when children starve and one nation after another is driven to despotism—" He shrugged and smiled.

Jevons, still seated, stroked a thin hand across his book, as if he wanted to recall a friend five hundred years dead. There was trouble on his face. "This is too sudden to digest, Wim," he said. "You must give us time."

"Oh, there will be time enough, years of it," said Dykstra. He laughed. "First my report must go to Earth, and be published, and debated and publicized, and wrangled about, and then they will send elaborate expeditions to do my work all over again, and then they will haggle and—have no fears, it will be at least a decade before anything is actually done. And thereafter we of the station, with our experience, will be quite vital to the project."

"Shucks," said McClellan, speaking lightly to conceal the way he felt, "I wanted to take a picnic lunch and watch the planet go up next Fourth of July."

"I don't know." Jevons stared into emptiness. "There's a question of…prudence? Call it what you will, but Venus can teach us so much as it is. A thousand years is not too long to study everything here. We may gain a few more continents at the price of understanding what life is all about, or the means for immortality—if that's a goal to be desired—or perhaps a philosophy. I don't know."

"Well, it is debatable," conceded Dykstra. "But let all mankind debate it, then."

Jimmy Cheng-tung smiled at Hawthorne. "I believe the captain is right," he said. "And I can see your standpoint, as a scientist. It is not fair to take your lifework away from you. I shall certainly argue in favor of waiting at least a hundred years."

"That may be too long," warned Dykstra. "Without some safety valve, technological civilization on Earth may not last another century."

"You don't understand!"

Hawthorne shouted it at them, as he looked into their eyes. Dykstra's gaze in particular caught the light in such a way that it seemed blank, Dykstra was a skull with two white circles for eyes. Hawthorne had the feeling that he was talking to deaf men. Or men already dead.

"You don't understand," he repeated. "It isn't my job, or science, or any such thing I'm worried about. It's the brutal fact of murder. The murder of an entire intelligent race. How would you like it if beings came from Jupiter and proposed to give Earth a hydrogen atmosphere? My God, what kind of monsters are we, that we can even think seriously about such a thing?"

"Oh, no!" muttered McClellan. "Here we go again. Lecture Twenty-eight-B. I listened to it all the way from Earth."

"Please," said Cheng-tung. "The issue is important."

"The cetoids do pose an embarrassing problem," conceded Jevons. "Though I don't believe any scientist has ever objected to vivisection—even the use of close cousins like the apes—for human benefit."

"The cetoids aren't apes!" protested Hawthorne, his lips whitening. "They're more human than you are!"

"Wait a minute," said Dykstra. He moved from his vision of lightning, toward Hawthorne. His face had lost its glory. It was concerned. "I realize you have opinions about this, Nat. But after all, you have no more evidence—"

"I do!" gasped Hawthorne. "I've got it at last. I've been wondering all day how to tell you, but now I must."

What Oscar had shown him came out in words, between peals of thunder.

At the end, even the gale seemed to pause, and for a while only rain, and the *brroom-brroom* of waves far below, continued to speak. McClellan stared at his hands, which twisted a die between the fingers. Cheng-tung rubbed his chin and smiled with scant mirth. Jevons, however, became serenely resolute. Dykstra was harder to read, his face flickered from one expression to the next. Finally he got very busy lighting a new cigarette.

When the silence had become too much, Hawthorne said, "Well?" in a cracked tone.

"This does indeed put another complexion on the matter," said Cheng-tung.

"It isn't proof," snapped Dykstra. "Look at what bees and bower birds do on Earth."

"Hey," said McClellan. "Be careful, Wim, or you'll prove that we're just glorified ants ourselves."

"Exactly," said Hawthorne. "I'll take you out in a submarine tomorrow and show you, if Oscar himself won't guide us. Add this discovery to all the other hints we've had, and damn it, you can no longer deny that the cetoids are intelligent. They don't think precisely as we do, but they think at least as well."

"And could doubtless teach us a great deal, " said Cheng-tung. "Consider how much your people and mine learned from each other: and they were of the same species."

Jevons nodded. "I wish you had told me this earlier, Nat," he said. "Of course there would have been no argument."

"Oh, well," said McClellan, "guess I'll have to go back to blowing up squibs on the Fourth."

The rain, wind-flung, hissed against the wall. Lightning still flickered, blue-white, but the thunder wagon was rolling off. The sea ran with wild frosty fires.

Hawthorne looked at Dykstra. The Dutchman was tense as a wire. Hawthorne felt his own briefly relaxing sinews grow taut again.

"Well, Wim?" he said.

"Certainly, certainly!" said Dykstra. He had grown pale. The cigarette fell unnoticed from his lips. "I am still not absolutely convinced, but that may be only my own disappointment. The chance of genocide is too great to take."

"Good boy," smiled Jevons.

Dykstra smote a fist into his palm. "But my report," he said. "What shall I do with my report?"

So much pain was in his voice that Hawthorne felt shock, even though the ecologist had known this question must arise.

McClellan said, startled: "Well, it's still a nice piece of research, isn't it?"

Then Cheng-tung voiced the horror they all felt.

"I am afraid we must suppress the report, Dr. Dykstra," he said. "Regrettably, our species cannot be trusted with the information."

Jevons bit his lip. "I hate to believe that," he said.

"We wouldn't deliberately and cold-bloodedly exterminate a billion or more sentient beings for our own…convenience."

"We have done similar things often enough in the past," said Dykstra woodenly.

I've read enough history myself, Wim, to give a very partial roll call, thought Hawthorne. And he began to tick off on his fingers. *Troy. Jericho. Cartharge. Jerusalem. The Albigensians. Buchenwald.*

That's enough for now, he thought, feeling a wish to vomit.

"But surely—" began Jevons. "By now, at least—"

"It is barely possible that humane considerations may stay Earth's hand for a decade or two," said Dykstra. "The rate at which brutality is increasing gives me little hope even of that, but let us assume so. However, a century? A millennium? How long can we live in our growing poverty with such a temptation? I do not think forever."

"If it came to a choice between taking over Venus and watching our civilization go under," said McClellan, "frankly, I myself would say too bad for Venus. I've got a wife and kids."

"Be glad, then, that the choice will not be so clear-cut in your lifetime," said Cheng-tung.

Jevons nodded. He had suddenly become an old man, whose work neared an end. "You have to destroy that report, Wim," he said. "Totally. None of us here can ever speak a word about it."

And now Hawthorne wanted to weep, but could not. There was a barrier in him, like fingers closing on his throat.

Dykstra drew a long breath. "Fortunately," he said, "I have been close-mouthed. No hint escaped me. I only trust the Company will not sack me for having been lazy and produced nothing all these months."

"I'll see to it that they don't, Wim," said Jevons. His tone was immensely gentle beneath the rain.

Dykstra's hands shook a little, but he tore the first sheet off his report and crumpled it in an ashtray and set fire to it.

Hawthorne flung out of the room.

-7-

The air was cool outside, at least by contrast with daytime. The squall had passed and only a mild rain fell, sluicing over his bare skin. In the absence of the sun he could go about with no more than shorts and mask. That was a strangely light sensation, like being a boy again in a summer forest which men had since cut down. Rain washed on the decks and into the water, two distinct kinds of noise, marvelously clear.

The waves themselves still ran strong, swish and boom and a dark swirling. Through the air shone a very faint auroral trace, barely enough to tinge the sky with a haze of rose. But mostly, when Nat Hawthorne had left lighted windows behind him, the luminance came from the ocean, where combers glowed green along their backs and utter white when they foamed. Here and there a knife of blackness cut the water, as some quick animal surged.

Hawthorne went down past the machine gun to the trading pier. Heavy seas broke over it, reaching to his knees and spattering him with phosphor glow. He clung to the rail and peered into rain, hoping Oscar would come.

"The worst of it is," he said aloud, "they all mean so well."

A winged being passed overhead, only a shadow and whisper.

"The proverb is wrong," babbled Hawthorne. He gripped the rail, though he knew a certain hope that a wave would sweep him loose…and afterward the Venusians would retrieve his bones and take no payment.

"Who shall watch the watchmen? Simple. The watchmen themselves who are of no use anyway, if they aren't honorable. But what about the thing watched? It's on the enemy's side. Wim and Cap and Jimmy and Shorty—and I. We can keep a secret. But nature can't. How long before someone else repeats this work? We hope to expand the station. There'll be more than one geophysicist here, and—and—Oscar! Oscar, where the hell are you, Oscar?"

The ocean gave him reply, but in no language he knew.

He shivered, teeth clapping in his jaws. There was no reason to hang around here. It was perfectly obvious what had to be done. The sight of Oscar's ugly, friendly face wouldn't necessarily make the job easier. It might even make it harder. Impossible, perhaps.

Oscar might make me sane, thought Hawthorne. *Ghosts of Sinaic thunder walked in his skull. I can't have that. Not yet, Lord God of Hosts, why must I be this fanatical? Why not register my protest when the issue arises, like any normal decent crusader, organize pressure groups, struggle by all the legal proper means. Or, if the secret lasts out my lifetime, why should I care what may happen afterward? I won't be aware of it.*

No. That isn't enough. I require certainty, not that justice will be done, for that is impossible, but that injustice will not be done. For I am possessed.

No man, he thought in the wet blowing night, no man could foresee everything. But he could make estimates, and act on them. His brain was as clear as glass, and about as alive, when he contemplated purely empirical data.

If Venus Station stopped paying off, Venus would not be visited again. Not for a very long time, during which many things could happen…a Venusian race better able to defend itself, or even a human race that had learned self-control. Perhaps men would never return. Technological civilization might well crumble and not be rebuilt. Maybe that was best, each planet working out its own lonely destiny. But all this was speculation. There were immediate facts at hand.

Item: If Venus Station was maintained, not to speak of its possible expansion, Dykstra's discovery was sure to be repeated. If one man had found the secret, once in a few years of curiosity, another man or two or three would hardly need more than a decade to grope their way to the same knowledge.

Item: Venus Station was at present economically dependent on the cooperation of the cetoids.

Item: If Venus Station suffered ruin due to the reported hostile action of the cetoids, the Company was unlikely to try rebuilding it.

Item: Even if the Company did make such an attempt, it would soon be abandoned again if the cetoids really did shun it.

Item: Venus would then be left alone.

Item: If you believed in God and sin and so forth which Hawthorne did not, you could argue that the real benefactor would be humankind, saved from the grisliest burden of deeds since a certain momentous day on Golgotha.

The worst of this for me, Hawthorne came to realize, *is that I don't care very much about humankind. It's Oscar I want to save. And how much hate for one race can hide under love for another?*

He felt dimly that there might be some way to flee nightmare. But the only path down which a man, flipperless and breathing oxygen, could escape, was back through the station.

He hurried along a quiet, brightly-lit corridor to a stairwell sloping down toward the bowel of the station and down. No one else was about. He might have been the last life in a universe turned ashen.

But when he entered the stockroom, it was a blow that another human figure stood there. Ghosts, ghosts…what right had the ghost of a man not yet dead to walk at this moment?

The man turned about. It was Chris Diehl, the biochemist. "Why, hi, Nat," he said. "What are you doing at this hour?"

Hawthorne wet his lips. The Earthlike air seemed to wither him. "I need a tool," he said. "A drill, yes—a small electric drill."

"Help yourself," said Diehl.

Hawthorne lifted a drill off the rack. His hands began to shake so much that he dropped it. Diehl stared at him.

"What's wrong, Nat?" he asked softly. "You look like second-hand custard."

"I'm all right," whispered Hawthorne. "Quite all right."

Hawthorne picked up the drill and went out.

The locked arsenal was low in the station hull. Hawthorne could feel Venus' ocean surge below the deckplates. That gave him the strength to drill the lock open and enter, to break the cases of explosive and lay a fuse. But he never remembered having set a time cap on the fuse. He only knew he had done so.

His next recollection was of standing in a boathouse, loading oceanographic depth bombs' into one of the little submarines, Again, no one stirred. No one was there to question him. What had the brothers of Venus Station to fear?

Hawthorne slipped into the submarine and guided it out the sea gate. Minutes later he felt the shock of an explosion. It was not large, but it made so much noise in him that he was stunned and did not see Venus Station go to the bottom. Only afterward did he observe that the place was gone. The waters swirled wildfire above it, a few scraps of wreckage bobbing in sheeting spindrift.

He took a compass bearing and submerged. Before long, the coralite city glowed before him. For a long moment he looked at its spires and grottos and lovelinesses, until fear warned him that he might make himself incapable of doing what was necessary. So he dropped his bombs, hastily, and felt his vessel shudder with their force, and saw the temple become a ruin.

And next he remembered surfacing. He went out on deck and his skin tasted rain. The cetoids were gathering. He could not see them, except in glimpses, a fluke or a back, phosphor streaming off into great waves, with once a face glimpsed just under the low rail, almost like a human baby's in that uncertain light.

He crouched by the machine gun, screaming, but they couldn't understand and anyway the wind made a rag of his voice. "I have to do this! I have no choice, don't you see? How else can I explain to you what my people are like when their greed dominates them? How else can I make you avoid them, which you've got to do if you want to live? Can you realize that? Can you? But no, you can't, you mustn't. You have to learn hate from us, since you've never learned it from each other—"

And he fired into the bewildered mass of them.

The machine gun raved for a long time, even after no more living Venusians were around. Hawthorne didn't stop shouting until he ran out of ammunition. Then he regained consciousness. His mind felt quiet and very clear, as if a fever had possessed him and departed. He remembered summer mornings when he was a boy, and early sunlight slanting in his bedroom window and across his eyes. He re-entered the turret and radioed the spaceship with total rationality.

"Yes, Captain, it was the cetoids, beyond any possibility of doubt. I don't know how they did it. Maybe they disarmed some of our probe bombs, brought them back and exploded them. But anyhow the station has been destroyed. I got away in a submarine. I glimpsed two other men in an open boat, but before I could reach them the cetoids had attacked. They stove in the boat, and killed the men as I watched…God, no, I can't imagine why! Never mind why! Let's just get away from here!"

He heard the promise of rescue by ferry, set an automatic location signal, and lay down on the bunk. It was over now, he thought in a huge grateful weariness. No human would ever learn the truth. Given time, he himself might forget it.

The space vessel descended at dawn, when the sky was turning to mother-of-pearl. Hawthorne came out on deck. Some dozen Venusian corpses rolled alongside the hull. He didn't want to see them, but there they were, and suddenly he recognized Oscar.

Oscar gaped blindly into the sky. Small pincered crustaceans were eating him. His blood was green.

Oh, God, thought Hawthorne, *please exist. Please make a hell for me.*

AMONG THIEVES

His Excellency M'Katze Unduma, Ambassador of the Terrestrial Federation to the Double Kingdom, was not accustomed to being kept waiting. But as the minutes dragged into an hour, anger faded before a chill deduction.

In this bleakly clock-bound society a short delay was bad manners, even if it were unintentional. But if you kept a man of rank cooling his heels for an entire sixty minutes, you offered him an unforgivable insult. Rusch was a barbarian, but he was too canny to humiliate Earth's representative without reason.

Which bore out everything that Terrestrial Intelligence had discovered. From a drunken junior officer, weeping in his cups because Old Earth, Civilization, was going to be attacked and the campus where he had once learned and loved would be scorched to ruin by *his* fire guns—to the battle plans and annotations thereon, which six men had died to smuggle out of the Royal War College—and now, this degradation of the ambassador himself—everything fitted.

The Margrave of Drakenstane had sold out Civilization.

Unduma shuddered, beneath the iridescent cloak, embroidered robe, and ostrich-plume headdress of his rank. He swept the antechamber with the eyes of a trapped animal.

This castle was ancient, dating back some eight hundred years to the first settlement of Norstad. The grim square massiveness of it, fused stone piled into a turreted mountain, was not much relieved by modern fittings. Tableservs, loungers, drapes, jewel mosaics, and biomurals only clashed with those fortress walls and ringing flagstones; fluorosheets did not light up all the dark corners, there was perpetual dusk up among the rafters where the old battle banners hung.

A dozen guards were posted around the room, in breastplate and plumed helmet but with very modern blast rifles. They were identical seven-foot blonds, and none of them moved at all, you couldn't even see them breathe. It was an unnerving sight for a Civilized man.

Unduma snubbed out his cigar, swore miserably to himself, and wished he had at least brought along a book.

The inner door opened on noiseless hinges and a shavepate officer emerged. He clicked his heels and bowed at Unduma. "His Lordship will be honored to receive you now, excellency."

The ambassador throttled his anger, nodded, and stood up. He was a tall thin man, the relatively light skin and sharp features of Bantu stock predominant in him. Earth's emissaries were normally chosen to approximate a local ideal of beauty—hard to do for some of those weird little cultures scattered through the galaxy—and Norstad-Ostarik had been settled by a rather extreme Caucasoid type which had almost entirely emigrated from the home planet.

The aide showed him through the door and disappeared. Hans von Thoma Rusch, Margrave of Drakenstane, Lawman of the Western Folkmote, Hereditary Guardian of the White River Gates, et cetera, et cetera, et cetera, sat waiting behind a desk at the end of an enormous black-and-red tile floor. He had a book in his hands, and didn't close it till Unduma, sandals whispering on the great chessboard squares, had come near. Then he stood up and made a short ironic bow.

"How do you do, your excellency," he said. "I am sorry to be so late. Please sit." Such curtness was no apology at all, and both of them knew it.

Unduma lowered himself to a chair in front of the desk. He would *not* show temper, he thought, he was here for a greater purpose. His teeth clamped together.

"Thank you, your lordship," he said tonelessly. "I hope you will have time to talk with me in some detail. I have come on a matter of grave importance."

Rusch's right eyebrow tilted up, so that the archaic monocle he affected beneath it seemed in danger of falling out. He was a big man, stiffly and solidly built, yellow hair cropped to a wiry brush around the long skull, a scar puckering his left cheek. He wore Army uniform, the gray high-collared tunic and old-fashioned breeches and shiny boots of his planet; the trident and suns of a primary general; a sidearm, its handle worn smooth from much use. If ever the iron barbarian with the iron brain had an epitome, thought Unduma, here he sat!

"Well, your excellency," murmured Rusch—though the harsh Norron language did not lend itself to murmurs—"of course I'll be glad to hear you out. But after all, I've no standing in the Ministry, except as unofficial advisor, and—"

"Please." Unduma lifted a hand. "Must we keep up the fable? You not only speak for all the landed warlords—and the Nor-Samurai are still the most powerful single class in the Double Kingdom—but you have the General Staff in your pouch and, ah, you are well thought of by the royal family. I think I can talk directly to you."

Rusch did not smile, but neither did he trouble to deny what everyone knew, that he was the leader of the fighting aristocracy, friend of the widowed Queen Regent, virtual step-father of her eight-year-old son King Hjalmar—in a word, that he was the dictator. If he preferred to keep a small title and not have his name unnecessarily before the public, what difference did that make?

"I'll be glad to pass on whatever you wish to say to the proper authorities," he answered slowly. "Pipe." That was an order to his chair, which produced a lit briar for him.

Unduma felt appalled. This series of—informalities—was like one savage blow after another. Till now, in the three-hundred-year history of relations between Earth and the Double Kingdom, the Terrestrial ambassador had ranked everyone but God and the royal family.

No human planet, no matter how long sundered from the mainstream, no matter what strange ways it had wandered, failed to remember that Earth was Earth, the home of man and the heart of Civilization. No *human* planet—had Norstad-Ostarik, then, gone the way of Kolresh?

Biologically, no, thought Unduma with an inward shudder. Nor culturally—yet. But it shrieked at him, from every insolent movement and twist of words, that Rusch had made a political deal.

"Well?" said the Margrave.

Unduma cleared his throat, desperately, and leaned forward. "Your lordship," he said, "my embassy cannot help taking notice of certain public statements, as well as certain military preparations and other matters of common knowledge—"

"And items your spies have dug up," drawled Rusch. Unduma started. "My lord!"

"My good ambassador," grinned Rusch, "it was you who suggested a straightforward talk. I know Earth has spies here. In any event, it's impossible to hide so large a business as the mobilization of two planets for war."

Unduma felt sweat trickle down his ribs.

"There is…you…your Ministry has only announced it is a…a defense measure," he stammered. "I had hoped…frankly, yes, till the last minute I hoped you…your people might see fit to join us against Kolresh."

There was a moment's quiet. *So* quiet, thought Unduma. A redness crept up Rusch's cheeks, the scar stood livid and his pale eyes were the coldest thing Unduma had ever seen.

Then, slowly, the Margrave got it out through his teeth:

"For a number of centuries, your excellency, our people hoped Earth might join them."

"What do you mean?" Unduma forgot all polished inanities. Rusch didn't seem to notice. He stood up and went to the window.

"Come here," he said. "Let me show you something."

The window was a modern inset of clear, invisible plastic, a broad sheet high in the castle's infamous Witch Tower. It looked out on a black sky, the sun was down and the glacial forty-hour darkness of northern Norstad was crawling toward midnight.

Stars glittered mercilessly keen in an emptiness which seemed like crystal, which seemed about to ring thinly in contracting anguish under the cold. Ostarik, the companion planet, stood low to the south, a gibbous moon of steely blue; it never moved in that sky, the two worlds forever faced each other, the windy white peaks of one glaring at the warm lazy seas of the other. Northward, a great curtain of aurora flapped halfway around the cragged horizon.

From this dizzy height, Unduma could see little of the town Drakenstane: a few high-peaked roofs and small glowing windows, lamps lonesome above frozen streets. There wasn't much to see anyhow—no big cities on either planet, only the small towns which had grown from scattered thorps, each clustered humbly about the manor of its lord. Beyond lay winter fields, climbing up the valley walls to the hard green blink of glaciers. It must be blowing out there, he saw snow-devils chase ghostly across the blue-tinged desolation.

Rusch spoke roughly: "Not much of a planet we've got here, is it? Out on the far end of nowhere, a thousand light-years from your precious Earth, and right in the middle of a glacial epoch. Have you ever wondered why we don't set up weather-control stations and give this world a decent climate?"

"Well," began Unduma, "of course, the exigencies of—"

"Of war." Rusch sent his hand upward in a chopping motion, to sweep around the alien constellations. Among them burned Polaris, less than thirty parsecs away, huge and cruelly bright. "We never had a chance. Every time we thought we could begin, there would be war, usually with Kolresh, and the labor and materials would have to go for that. Once, about two centuries back, we did actually get stations established, it was even beginning to warm up a little. Kolresh blasted them off the map.

"Norstad was settled eight hundred years ago. For seven of those centuries, we've had Kolresh at our throats. Do you wonder if we've grown tired?"

"My lord, I...I can sympathize," said Unduma awkwardly. "I am not ignorant of your heroic history. But it would seem to me...after all, Earth has also fought—"

"At a range of a thousand light-years!" jeered Rusch. "The forgotten war. A few underpaid patrolmen in obsolete rustbucket ships to defend unimportant outposts from sporadic Kolreshite raids. We live on their borders!"

"It would certainly appear, your lordship, that Kolresh is your natural enemy," said Unduma. "As indeed it is of all Civilization, of Homo sapiens himself. What I cannot credit are the, ah, the rumors of an, er, alliance—"

"And why shouldn't we?" snarled Rusch. "For seven hundred years we've held them at bay, while your precious so-called Civilization grew fat behind a wall of our dead young men. The temptation to recoup some of our losses by helping Kolresh conquer Earth is very strong!"

"You don't mean it!" The breath rushed from Unduma's lungs.

The other man's face was like carved bone. "Don't jump to conclusions," he answered. "I merely point out that from our side there's a good deal to be said for such a policy. Now if Earth is prepared to make a different policy worth our while—do you understand? Nothing is going to happen in the immediate future. You have time to think about it."

"I would have to...communicate with my government," whispered Unduma.

"Of course," said Rusch. His bootheels clacked on the floor as he went back to his desk. "I've had a memorandum prepared for you, an unofficial informal sort of protocol, points which his majesty's government would like to make the basis of negotiations with the Terrestrial Federation. Ah, here!" He picked up a bulky folio. "I suggest you take a leave of absence, your excellency, go home and show your superiors this, ah—"

"Ultimatum," said Unduma in a sick voice.

Rusch shrugged. "Call it what you will." His tone was empty and remote, as if he had already cut himself and his people out of Civilization.

As he accepted the folio, Unduma noticed the book beside it, the one Rusch had been reading: a local edition of Schakspier, badly printed on sleazy paper, but in the original Old Anglic. Odd thing for a barbarian dictator to read. But then, Rusch was a bit of an historical scholar, as well as an enthusiastic kayak racer, meteor polo player, chess champion, mountain climber, and…and all-around scoundrel!

Norstad lay in the grip of a ten-thousand-year winter, while Ostarik was a heaven of blue seas breaking on warm island sands. Nevertheless, because Ostarik harbored a peculiarly nasty plague virus, it remained an unattainable paradise in the sky till a bare two hundred fifty years ago. Then a research team from Earth got to work, found an effective vaccine, and saw a mountain carved into their likeness by the Norron folk.

It was through such means—and the sheer weight of example, the liberty and wealth and happiness of its people—that the Civilization centered on Earth had been propagating itself among colonies isolated for centuries. There were none which lacked reverence for Earth the Mother, Earth the Wise, Earth the Kindly: none but Kolresh, which had long ceased to be human.

Rusch's private speedster whipped him from the icicle walls of Festning Drakenstane to the rose gardens of Sorgenlos in an hour of hell-bat haste across vacuum. But it was several hours more until he and the queen could get away from their courtiers and be alone.

They walked through geometric beds of smoldering blooms, under songbirds and fronded trees, while the copper spires of the little palace reached up to the evening star and the hours-long sunset of Ostarik blazed gold across great quiet waters. The island was no more than a royal retreat, but lately it had known agonies.

Queen Ingra stooped over a mutant rose, tiger-striped and a foot across; she plucked the petals from it and said, close to weeping: "But I liked Unduma. I don't want him to hate us."

"He's not a bad sort," agreed Rusch. He stood behind her in a black dress uniform with silver insignia, like a formal version of death.

"He's more than that, Hans. He stands for decency—Norstad froze our souls, and Ostarik hasn't thawed them. I thought Earth might—" Her voice trailed off. She was slender and dark, still young, and her folk came from the rainy dales of Norstad's equator, a farm race with gentler ways than the miners and fishermen and hunters of the red-haired ice ape who had bred Rusch. In her throat, the Norron language softened to a burring music; the Drakenstane men spat their words out rough-edged.

"Earth might what?" Rusch turned a moody gaze to the west. "Lavish more gifts on us? We were always proud of paying our own way."

"Oh, no," said Ingra wearily. "After all, we could trade with them, furs and minerals and so on, if ninety per cent of our production didn't have to go into defense. I only thought they might teach us how to be human."

"I had assumed we were still classified Homo sapiens," said Rusch in a parched tone.

"Oh, you know what I mean!" She turned on him, violet eyes suddenly aflare. "Sometimes I wonder if *you're* human, Margrave Hans von Thoma Rusch. I mean free, free to be something more than a robot, free to raise children knowing they won't have their lungs shoved out their mouths when a Kolreshite cruiser hulls one of our spaceships. What is our whole culture, Hans? A layer of brutalized farmhands and factory workers—serfs! A top crust of heel-clattering aristocrats who live for nothing but war. A little folk art, folk music, folk saga, full of blood and treachery. Where are our symphonies, novels, cathedrals, research laboratories…where are people who can say what they wish and make what they will of their lives and be happy?"

Rusch didn't answer for a moment. He looked at her, unblinking behind his monocle, till she dropped her gaze and twisted her hands together. Then he said only: "You exaggerate."

"Perhaps. It's still the basic truth." Rebellion rode in her voice. "It's what all the other worlds think of us."

"Even if the democratic assumption—that the eternal verities can be discovered by counting enough noses—were true," said Rusch, "you cannot repeal eight hundred years of history by decree."

"No. But you could work toward it," she said. "I think you're wrong in despising the common man, Hans…when was he ever given a chance, in this kingdom? We could make a beginning now, and Earth could send psychotechnic advisors, and in two or three generations—"

"What would Kolresh be doing while we experimented with forms of government?" he laughed.

"Always Kolresh." Her shoulders, slim behind the burning-red cloak, slumped. "Kolresh turned a hundred hopeful towns into radioactive craters and left the gnawed bones of children in the fields. If Kolresh killed my husband, like a score of kings before him, Kolresh blasted your family to ash, Hans, and scarred your face and your soul—" She whirled back on him, fists aloft, and almost screamed: "Do you want to make an ally of Kolresh?"

The Margrave took out his pipe and began filling it. The saffron sundown, reflected off the ocean to his face, gave him a metal look.

"Well," he said, "we've been at peace with them for all of ten years now. Almost a record."

"Can't we find allies? Real ones? I'm sick of being a figurehead! I'd befriend Ahuramazda, New Mars, Lagrange—We could raise a crusade against Kolresh, wipe every last filthy one of them out of the universe!"

"Now who's a heel-clattering aristocrat?" grinned Rusch.

He lit his pipe and strolled toward the beach. She stood for an angry moment, then sighed and followed him.

"Do you think it hasn't been tried?" he said patiently. "For generations we've tried to build up a permanent alliance directed at Kolresh. What temporary ones we achieved have always fallen apart. Nobody loves us enough—and, since we've always taken the heaviest blows, nobody hates Kolresh enough."

He found a bench on the glistening edge of the strand, and sat down and looked across a steady march of surf, turned to molten gold by the low sun and the incandescent western clouds. Ingra joined him.

"I can't really blame the others for not liking us," she said in a small voice. "We are overmechanized and undercultured, arrogant, tactless, undemocratic, hardboiled…oh, yes. But their own self-interest—"

"They don't imagine it can happen to them," replied Rusch contemptuously. "And there are even pro-Kolresh elements, here and there." He raised his voice an octave: "Oh, my dear sir, my dear Margrave, what are you *saying?* Why, of *course* Kolresh would never attack us! They made a *treaty* never to attack us!"

Ingra sighed, forlornly. Rusch laid an arm across her shoulders. They sat for a while without speaking.

"Anyway," said the man finally, "Kolresh is too strong for any combination of powers in this part of the galaxy. We and they are the only ones with a military strength worth mentioning. Even Earth would have a hard time defeating them, and Earth, of course, will lean backward before undertaking a major war. She has too much to lose; it's so much more comfortable to regard the Kolreshite raids as mere piracies, the skirmishes as 'police actions.' She just plain will not pay the stiff price of an army and a navy able to whip Kolresh and occupy the Kolreshite planets."

"And so it is to be war again." Ingra looked out in desolation across the sea.

"Maybe not," said Rusch. "Maybe a different kind of war, at least—no more black ships coming out of *our* sky."

He blew smoke for a while, as if gathering courage, then spoke in a quick, impersonal manner: "Look here. We Norrons are not a naval power. It's not in our tradition. Our navy has always been inadequate and always will be. But we can breed the toughest soldiers in the known galaxy, in unlimited numbers; we can condition them into fighting machines, and equip them with the most lethal weapons living flesh can wield.

"Kolresh, of course, is just the opposite. Space nomads, small population, able to destroy anything their guns can reach but not able to dig in and hold it against us. For seven hundred years, we and they have been the elephant and the whale. Neither could ever win a real victory over the other; war became the normal state of affairs, peace a breathing spell. Because of the mutation, there will always be war, as long as one single Kolreshite lives. We can't kill them, we can't befriend them—all we can do is to be bled white to stop them."

A wind sighed over the slow thunder on the beach. A line of sea birds crossed the sky, thin and black against glowing bronze.

"I know," said Ingra. "I know the history, and I know what you're leading up to. Kolresh will furnish transportation and naval escort; Norstad-Ostarik will furnish men. Between us, we may be able to take Earth."

"We will," said Rusch flatly. "Earth has grown plump and lazy. She can't possibly rearm enough in a few months to stop such a combination."

"And all the galaxy will spit on our name."

"All the galaxy will lie open to conquest, once Earth has fallen."

"How long do you think we would last, riding the Kolresh tiger?"

"I have no illusions about them, my dear. But neither can I see any way to break this eternal deadlock. In a fluid situation, such as the collapse of Earth would produce, we might be able to create a navy as good as theirs. They've never yet given us a chance to build one, but perhaps—"

"Perhaps not! I doubt very much it was a meteor which wrecked my husband's ship, five years ago. I think Kolresh knew of his hopes, of the shipyard he wanted to start, and murdered him."

"It's probable," said Rusch.

"And you would league us with them." Ingra turned a colorless face on him. "I'm still the queen. I forbid any further consideration of this…this obscene alliance!"

Rusch sighed. "I was afraid of that, your highness."

For a moment he looked gray, tired. "You have a veto power, of course. But I don't think the Ministry would continue in office a regent who used it against the best interests of—"

She leaped to her feet. "You wouldn't!"

"Oh, you'd not be harmed," said Rusch with a crooked smile. "Not even deposed. You'd be in protective custody, shall we say. Of course, his majesty, your son, would have to be educated elsewhere, but if you wish—"

Her palm cracked on his face. He made no motion. "I…won't veto—" Ingra shook her head. Then her back grew stiff. "Your ship will be ready to take you home, my lord. I do not think we shall require your presence here again."

"As you will, your highness," mumbled the dictator of the Double Kingdom.

Though he returned with a bitter word in his mouth, Unduma felt the joy, the biological rightness of being home, rise warm within him. He sat on a terrace under the mild sky of Earth, with the dear bright flow of the Zambezi River at his feet and the slim towers of Capital City rearing as far as he could see, each gracious, in its own green park. The people on the clean quiet streets wore airy blouses and colorful kilts—not the trousers for men, ankle-length skirts for women, which muffled the sad folk of Norstad. And there was educated conversation in the gentle Tierrans language, music from an open window, laughter on the verandas and children playing in the parks: freedom, law, and leisure.

The thought that this might be rubbed out of history, that the robots of Norstad and the snake-souled monsters of Kolresh might tramp between broken spires where starved Earthmen hid, was a tearing in Unduma.

He managed to lift his drink and lean back with the proper casual elegance. "No, sir," he said, "they are not bluffing."

Ngu Chilongo, Premier of the Federation Parliament, blinked unhappy eyes. He was a small grizzled man, and a wise man, but this lay beyond everything he had known in a long lifetime and he was slow to grasp it.

"But surely—" he began. "Surely this…this Rusch person is not insane. He cannot think that his two planets, with a population of, what is it, perhaps one billion, can overcome four billion Terrestrials!"

"There would also be several million Kolreshites to help," reminded Unduma. "However, they would handle the naval end of it entirely—and their navy *is* considerably stronger than ours. The Norron forces would be the ones which actually landed, to fight the air and ground battles. And out of those paltry one billion, Rusch can raise approximately one hundred million soldiers."

Chilongo's glass crashed to the terrace. "What!"

"It's true, sir." The third man present, Mustafa Lefarge, Minister of Defense, spoke in a miserable tone. "It's a question of every able-bodied citizen, male and female, being a trained member of the armed forces. In time of war, virtually everyone not in actual combat is directly contributing to some phase of the effort—a civilian economy virtually ceases to exist. They're used to getting along for years at a stretch with no comforts and a bare minimum of necessities." His voice grew sardonic. "By necessities, they mean things like food and ammunition—not, say, entertainment or cultural activity, as we assume."

"A hundred million," whispered Chilongo. He stared at his hands. "Why, that's ten times our *total* forces!"

"Which are ill-trained, ill-equipped, and ill-regarded by our own civilians," pointed out Lefarge bitterly.

"In short, sir," said Unduma, "while we could defeat either Kolresh or Norstad-Ostarikin in all-out war—though with considerable difficulty—between them they can defeat us."

Chilongo shivered. Unduma felt a certain pity for him.

You had to get used to it in small doses, this fact which Civilization screened from Earth: that the depths of hell are found in the human soul. That no law of nature guards the upright innocent from malice.

"But they wouldn't dare!" protested the Premier. "Our friends…everywhere—"

"All the human-colonized galaxy will wring its hands and send stiff notes of protest," said Lefarge. "Then they'll pull the blankets back over their heads and assure themselves that now the big bad aggressor has been sated."

"This note—of Rusch's." Chilongo seemed to be grabbing out after support while the world dropped from beneath his feet. Sweat glistened on his wrinkled brown forehead. "Their terms…surely we can make some agreement?"

"Their terms are impossible, as you'll see for yourself when you read," said Unduma flatly. "They want us to declare war on Kolresh, accept a joint command under Norron leadership, foot the bill and—No!"

"But if we have to fight anyway," began Chilongo, "it would seem better to have at least one ally—"

"Has Earth changed that much since I was gone?" asked Unduma in astonishment. "Would our people really consent to this…this extortion…letting those hairy barbarians write our foreign policy for us—Why, jumping into war, making the first declaration ourselves, it's unconstitutional! It's *un-Civilized!*"

Chilongo seemed to shrink a little. "No," he said. "No, I don't mean that. Of course it's impossible; better to be honestly defeated in battle. I only thought, perhaps we could bargain—"

"We can try," said Unduma skeptically, "but I never heard of Hans Rusch yielding an ångström without a pistol at his head."

Lefarge struck a cigar, inhaled deeply, and took another sip from his glass. "I hardly imagine an alliance with Kolresh would please his own people," he, mused.

"Scarcely!" said Unduma. "But they'll accept it if they must."

"Oh? No chance for us to get him overthrown—assassinated, even?"

"Not to speak of. Let me explain. He's only a petty aristocrat by birth, but during the last war with Kolresh he gained high rank and a personal following of fanatically loyal young officers. For the past few years, since the king died, he's been the dictator. He's filled the key posts with his men: hard, able, and unquestioning. Everyone else is either admiring or cowed. Give him credit, he's no megalomaniac—he shuns publicity—but that simply divorces his power all the more from responsibility. You can measure it by pointing out that everyone knows he will probably ally with Kolresh, and everyone has a nearly physical loathing of the idea—but there is not a word of criticism for Rusch himself, and when he orders it they will embark on Kolreshite ships to ruin the Earth they love."

"It could almost make you believe in the old myths," whispered Chilongo. "About the Devil incarnate."

"Well," said Unduma, "this sort of thing has happened before, you know."

"Hm-m-m?" Lefarge sat up.

Unduma smiled sadly. "Historical examples," he said. "They're of no practical value today, except for giving the cold consolation that we're not uniquely betrayed."

"What do you mean?" asked Chilongo.

"Well," said Unduma, "consider the astropolitics of the situation. Around Polaris and beyond lies Kolresh territory, where for a long time they sharpened their teeth preying on backward autochthones. At last they started expanding toward the richer human-settled planets. Norstad happened to lie directly on their path, so Norstad took the first blow—and stopped them.

"Since then, it's been seven hundred years of stalemated war. Oh, naturally Kolresh outflanks Norstad from time to time, seizes this planet in the galactic west and raids that one to the north, fights a war with one to the south and makes an alliance with one to the east. But it has never amounted to anything important. It can't, with Norstad astride the most direct line between the heart of Kolresh and the heart of Civilization. If Kolresh made a serious effort to by-pass Norstad, the Norrons could—and would—disrupt everything with an attack in the rear.

"In short, despite the fact that interstellar space is three-dimensional and enormous, Norstad guards the northern marches of Civilization."

He paused for another sip. It was cool and subtle on his tongue, a benediction after the outworld rotgut.

"Hm-m-m, I never thought of it just that way," said Lefarge. "I assumed it was just a matter of barbarians fighting each other for the usual barbarian reasons."

"Oh, it is, I imagine," said Unduma, "but the result is that Norstad acts as the shield of Earth.

"Now if you examine early Terrestrial history—and Rusch, who has a remarkable knowledge of it, stimulated me to do so—you'll find that this is a common thing. A small semicivilized state, out on the marches, holds off the enemy while the true civilization prospers behind it. Assyria warded Mesopotamia, Rome defended Greece, the Welsh border lords kept England safe, the Transoxanian Tartars were the shield of Persia, Prussia blocked the approaches to western Europe…oh, I could add a good many examples. In every instance, a somewhat backward people on the distant frontier of a civilization, receive the worst hammer-blows of the really alien races beyond, the wild men who would leave nothing standing if they could get at the protected cities of the inner society."

He paused for breath. "And so?" asked Chilongo.

"Well, of course suffering isn't good for people," shrugged Unduma. "It tends to make them rather nasty. The marchmen react to incessant war by becoming a warrior race, uncouth peasants with an absolute government of ruthless militarists. Nobody loves them, neither the outer savages nor the inner polite nations.

"And in the end, they're all too apt to turn inward. Their military skill and vigor need a more promising outlet than this grim business of always fighting off an enemy who always comes back and who has even less to steal than the sentry culture.

"So Assyria sacks Babylon; Rome conquers Greece; Percy rises against King Henry; Tamerlane overthrows Bajazet; Prussia clanks into France—"

"And Norstad-Ostarik falls on Earth," finished Lefarge.

"Exactly," said Unduma. "It's not even unprecedented for the border state to join hands with the very tribes it fought so long. Percy and Owen Glendower, for instance…though in that case, I imagine both parties were considerably more attractive than Hans Rusch or Klerak Belug."

"What are we going to do?" Chilongo whispered it toward the blue sky of Earth, from which no bombs had fallen for a thousand years.

Then he shook himself, jumped to his feet, and faced the other two. "I'm sorry, gentlemen. This has taken me rather by surprise, and I'll naturally require time to look at this Norron protocol and evaluate the other data. But if it turns out you're right"—he bowed urbanely—"as I'm sure it will—"

"Yes?" said Unduma in a tautening voice.

"Why, then, we appear to have some months, at least, before anything drastic happens. We can try to gain more time by negotiation. We do have the largest industrial complex in the known universe, and four billion people who have surely not had courage bred out of them. We'll build up our armed forces, and if those barbarians attack we'll whip them back into their own kennels and kick them through the rear walls thereof!"

"I hoped you'd say that," breathed Unduma.

"*I* hope we'll be granted time," Lefarge scowled. "I assume Rusch is not a fool. We cannot rearm in anything less than a glare of publicity. When he learns of it, what's to prevent him from cementing the Kolresh alliance and attacking at once, before we're ready?"

"Their mutual suspiciousness ought to help," said Unduma. "I'll go back there, of course, and do what I can to stir up trouble between them."

He sat still for a moment, then added as if to himself: "Till we do finish preparing, we have no resources but hope."

The Kolreshite mutation was a subtle thing. It did not show on the surface: physically, they were a handsome people, running to white skin and orange hair. Over the centuries, thousands of Norron spies had infiltrated them, and frequently gotten back alive; what made such work unusually difficult was not the normal hazards of impersonation, but an ingrained reluctance to practice cannibalism and worse.

The mutation was a psychic twist, probably originating in some obscure gene related to the endocrine system. It was extraordinarily hard to describe—every categorical statement about it had the usual quota of exceptions and qualifications. But one might, to a first approximation, call it extreme xenophobia. It is normal for Homo sapiens to be somewhat wary of outsiders till he has established their bona fides; it was normal for Homo Kolreshi to *hate* all outsiders, from first glimpse to final destruction.

Naturally, such an instinct produced a tendency to inbreeding, which lowered fertility, but systematic execution of the unfit had so far kept the stock vigorous. The instinct also led to strongarm rule within the nation; to nomadism, where a planet was only a base like the oasis of the ancient Bedouin, essential to life but rarely seen; to a cult of secrecy and cruelty, a religion of abominations; to an ultimate goal of conquering the accessible universe and wiping out all other races.

Of course, it was not so simple, nor so blatant. Among themselves, the Kolreshites doubtless found a degree of tenderness and fidelity. Visiting on neutral planets—i.e., planets which it was not yet expedient to attack—they were very courteous and had an account of defending themselves against one unprovoked aggression after another, which some found plausible. Even their enemies stood in awe of their personal heroism.

Nevertheless, few in the galaxy would have wept if the Kolreshites all died one rainy night.

Hans von Thoma Rusch brought his speedster to the great whaleback of the battleship. It lay a light-year from his sun, hidden by cold emptiness; the co-ordinates had been given him secretly, together with an invitation which was more like a summons.

He glided into the landing cradle, under the turrets of guns that could pound a moon apart, and let the mechanism suck him down below decks. When he stepped out into the high, coldly lit debarkation chamber, an honor guard in red presented arms and pipes twittered for him.

He walked slowly forward, a big man in black and silver, to meet his counterpart, Klerak Belug, the Overman of Kolresh, who waited rigid in a blood-colored tunic. The cabin bristled around him with secret police and guns.

Rusch clicked heels. "Good day, your dominance," he said. A faint echo followed his voice. For some unknown reason, this folk liked echoes and always built walls to resonate.

Belug, an aging giant who topped him by a head, raised shaggy brows. "Are you alone, your lordship?" he asked in atrociously accented Norron. "It was understood that you could bring a personal bodyguard."

Rusch shrugged. "I would have needed a personal dreadnought to be quite safe," he replied in fluent Kolra, "so I decided to trust your safe conduct. I assume you realize that any harm done to me means instant war with my kingdom."

The broad, winkled lion-face before him split into a grin. "My representatives did not misjudge you, your lordship. I think we can indeed do business. Come."

The Overman turned and led the way down a ramp toward the guts of the ship. Rusch followed, enclosed by guards and bayonets. He kept a hand on his own sidearm—not that it would do him much good, if matters came to that.

Events were approaching their climax, he thought in a cold layer of his brain. For more than a year now, negotiations had dragged on, hemmed in by the requirement of secrecy, weighted down by mutual suspicion. There were only two points of disagreement remaining, but discussion had been so thoroughly snagged on those that the two absolute rulers must meet to settle it personally. It was Belug who had issued the contemptuous invitation.

And he, Rusch, had come. Tonight the old kings of Norstad wept worms in their graves.

The party entered a small, luxuriously chaired room.

There were the usual robots, for transcription and reference purposes, and there were guards, but Overman and Margrave were essentially alone.

Belug wheezed his bulk into a seat. "Smoke? Drink?"

"I have my own, thank you." Rusch took out his pipe and a hip flask.

"That is scarcely diplomatic," rumbled Belug.

Rusch laughed. "I'd always understood that your dominance had no use for the mannerisms of Civilization. I daresay we'd both like to finish our business as quickly as possible."

The Overman snapped his fingers. Someone glided up with wine in a glass. He sipped for a while before answering: "Yes. By all means. Let us reach an executive agreement now and wait for our hirelings to draw up a formal treaty. But it seems odd, sir, that after all these months of delay, you are suddenly so eager to complete the work."

"Not odd," said Rusch. "Earth is rearming at a considerable rate. She's had almost a year now. We can still whip her, but in another six months we'll no longer be able to; give her automated factories half a year beyond *that,* and she'll destroy us!"

"It must have been clear to you, sir, that after the Earth Ambassador—what's his name, Unduma—after he returned to your planets last year, he was doing all he could to gain time."

"Oh, yes," said Rusch. "Making offers to me, and then haggling over them—brewing trouble elsewhere to divert our attention—a gallant effort. But it didn't work. Frankly, your dominance, you've only yourself to blame for the delays. For example, your insisting that Earth be administered as Kolreshite territory—"

"My dear sir!" exploded Belug. "It was a talking point. Only a talking point. Any diplomatist would have understood. But you took six weeks to study it, then offered that preposterous counter-proposal that everything should revert to *you,* loot and territory both—Why, if you had been truly willing to co-operate, we could have settled the terms in a month!"

"As you like, your dominance," said Rusch carelessly.

"It's all past now. There are only these questions of troop transport and prisoners, then we're in total agreement."

Klerak Belug narrowed his eyes and rubbed his chin with one outsize hand. "I do not comprehend," he said, "and neither do my naval officers. We have regular transports for your men, nothing extraordinary in the way of comfort, to be sure, but infinitely more suitable for so long a voyage than…than the naval units you insist we use. Don't you understand? A transport is for carrying men or cargo; a ship of the line is to fight or convoy. You do *not* mix the functions!"

"I do, your dominance," said Rusch. "As many of my soldiers as possible are going to travel on regular warships furnished by Kolresh, and there are going to be Double Kingdom naval personnel with them for liaison."

"But—" Belug's fist closed on his wineglass as if to splinter it. "Why?" he roared.

"My representatives have explained it a hundred times," said Rusch wearily. "In blunt language, I don't trust you. If…oh, let us say there should be disagreement between us while the armada is en route…well, a transport ship is easily replaced, after its convoy vessels have blown it up. The fighting craft of Kolresh are a better hostage for your good behavior." He struck a light to his pipe. "Naturally, you can't take our whole fifty-million-man expeditionary force on your battle wagons; but I want soldiers on every warship as well as in the transports."

Belug shook his ginger head. "No."

"Come now," said Rusch. "Your spies have been active enough on Norstad and Ostarik. Have you found any reason to doubt my intentions? Bearing in mind that an army the size of ours cannot be alerted for a given operation without a great many people knowing the fact—"

"Yes, yes," grumbled Belug. "Granted." He smiled, a sharp flash of teeth. "But the upper hand is mine, your lordship. I can wait indefinitely to attack Earth. You can't."

"Eh?" Rusch drew hard on his pipe.

"In the last analysis, even dictators rely on popular support. My Intelligence tells me you are rapidly losing yours. The queen has not spoken to you for a year, has she? And there are many Norrons whose first loyalty is to the Crown. As the thought of war with Earth seeps in, as men have time to comprehend how little they like the idea, time to see through your present anti-Terrestrial propaganda—they grow angry. Already they mutter about you in the beer halls and the officers' clubs, they whisper in ministry cloakrooms. My agents have heard.

"Your personal cadre of young key officers are the only ones left with unquestioning loyalty to you. Let discontent grow just a little more, let open revolt break out, and your followers will be hanged from the lamp posts.

"You can't delay much longer."

Rusch made no reply for a while. Then he sat up, his monocle glittering like a cold round window on winter.

"I can always call off this plan and resume the normal state of affairs," he snapped.

Belug flushed red. "War with Kolresh again? It would take you too long to shift gears—to reorganize."

"It would not. Our war college, like any other, has prepared military plans for all foreseeable combinations of circumstances. If I cannot come to terms with you, Plan No. So-and-So goes into effect. And obviously *it* will have popular enthusiasm behind it!"

He nailed the Overman with a fish-pale eye and continued in frozen tones: "After all, your dominance, I would prefer to fight you. The only thing I would enjoy more would be to hunt you with hounds. Seven hundred years have shown this to be impossible. I opened negotiations to make the best of an evil bargain—since you cannot be conquered, it will pay better to join with you on a course of mutually profitable imperialism.

"But if your stubbornness prevents an agreement, I can declare war on you in the usual manner and be no worse off than I was. The choice is, therefore, yours."

Belug swallowed. Even his guards lost some of their blankness. One does not speak in that fashion across the negotiators' table.

Finally, only his lips stirring, he said: "Your frankness is appreciated, my lord. Some day I would like to discuss that aspect further. As for now, though…yes, I can see your point. I am prepared to admit some of your troops to our ships of the line." After another moment, still sitting like a stone idol: "But this question of returning prisoners of war. We have never done it. I do not propose to begin."

"*I* do not propose to let poor devils of Norrons rot any longer in your camps," said Rusch. "I have a pretty good idea of what goes on there. If we're to be allies, I'll want back such of my countrymen as are still alive."

"Not many are still sane," Belug told him deliberately. Rusch puffed smoke and made no reply.

"If I give in on the one item," said Belug, "I have a right to test your sincerity by the other. We keep our prisoners."

Rusch's own face had gone quite pale and still. It grew altogether silent in the room.

"Very well," he said after a long time. "Let it be so."

Without a word, Major Othkar Graaborg led his company into the black cruiser. The words came from the spaceport, where police held off a hooting, hissing, rock-throwing mob. It was the first time in history that Norron folk had stoned their own soldiers.

His men tramped stolidly behind him, up the gangway and through the corridors. Among the helmets and packs and weapons, racketing boots and clashing body armor, their faces were lost, they were an army without faces.

Graaborg followed a Kolreshite ensign, who kept looking back nervously at these hereditary foes, till they reached the bunkroom. It had been hastily converted from a storage hold, and was scant cramped comfort for a thousand men.

"All right, boys," he said when the door had closed on his guide. "Make yourselves at home."

They got busy, opening packs, spreading bedrolls on bunks. Immediately thereafter, they started to assemble heavy machine guns, howitzers, even a nuclear blaster.

"You, there!" The accented voice squawked indignantly from a loudspeaker in the wall. "I see that. I got video. You not put guns together here."

Graaborg looked up from his inspection of a live fission shell. "Obscenity you," he said pleasantly. "Who are you, anyway?"

"I executive officer. I tell captain."

"Go right ahead. My orders say that according to treaty, as long as we stay in our assigned part of the ship, we're under our own discipline. If your captain doesn't like it, let him come down here and talk to us." Graaborg ran a thumb along the edge of his bayonet. A wolfish chorus from his men underlined the invitation.

No one pressed the point. The cruiser lumbered into space, rendezvoused with her task force, and went into nonspatial drive. For several days, the Norron army contingent remained in its den, more patient with such stinking quarters than the Kolreshites could imagine anyone being. Nevertheless, no spaceman ventured in there; meals were fetched at the galley by Norron squads.

Graaborg alone wandered freely about the ship. He was joined by Commander von Brecca of Ostarik, the head of the Double Kingdom's naval liaison on this ship: a small band of officers and ratings, housed elsewhere. They conferred with the Kolreshite officers as the necessity arose, on routine problems, rehearsal of various operations to be performed when Earth was reached a month hence—but they did not mingle socially. This suited their hosts.

The fact is, the Kolreshites were rather frightened of them. A spaceman does not lack courage, but he is a gentleman among warriors. His ship either functions well, keeping him clean and comfortable, or it does not function at all and he dies quickly and mercifully. He fights with machines, at enormous ranges.

The ground soldier, muscle in mud, whose ultimate weapon is whetted steel in bare hands, has a different kind of toughness.

Two weeks after departure, Graaborg's wrist chronometer showed a certain hour. He was drilling his men in full combat rig, as he had been doing every "day" in spite of the narrow quarters.

"Ten-SHUN!" The order flowed through captains, lieutenants, and sergeants; the bulky mass of men crashed to stillness.

Major Graaborg put a small pocket amplifier to his lips. "All right, lads," he said casually, "assume gas masks, radiation shields, all gun squads to weapons. Now let's clean up this ship."

He himself blew down the wall with a grenade.

Being perhaps the most thoroughly trained soldiers in the universe, the Norron men paused for only one amazed second. Then they cheered, with death and hell in their voices, and crowded at his heels.

Little resistance was met until Graaborg had picked up von Brecca's naval command, the crucial ones, who could sail and fight the ship. The Kolreshites were too dumfounded. Thereafter the nomads rallied and fought gamely. Graaborg was handicapped by not having been able to give his men a battle plan. He split up his forces and trusted to the intelligence of the noncoms.

His faith was not misplaced, though the ship was in poor condition by the time the last Kolreshite had been machine-gunned.

Graaborg himself had used a bayonet, with vast satisfaction.

M'Katze Unduma entered the office in the Witch Tower. "You sent for me, your lordship?" he asked. His voice was as cold and bitter as the gale outside.

"Yes. Please be seated." Margrave Hans von Thoma Rusch looked tired. "I have some news for you."

"What news? You declared war on Earth two weeks ago. Your army can't have reached her yet." Unduma leaned over the desk. "Is it that you've found transportation to send me home?"

"Somewhat better news, your excellency." Rusch leaned over and tuned a telescreen. A background of clattering robots and frantically busy junior officers came into view.

Then a face entered the screen, young, and with more life in it than Unduma had ever before seen on this sullen planet. "Central Data headquarters—Oh, yes, your lordship." Boyishly, against all rules: "We've got her! The *Bheoka* just called in…she's ours!"

"Hm-m-m. Good." Rusch glanced at Unduma. "The *Bheoka* is the super-dreadnought accompanying Task Force Two. Carry on with the news."

"Yes, sir. She's already reducing the units we failed to capture. Admiral Sorrens estimates he'll control Force Two entirely in another hour. Bulletin just came in from Force Three. Admiral Gundrup killed in fighting, but Vice Admiral Smitt has assumed command and reports three-fourths of the ships in our hands. He's delaying fire until he sees how it goes aboard the rest. Also—"

"Never mind," said Rusch. "I'll get the comprehensive report later. Remind Staff that for the next few hours all command decisions had better be made by officers on the spot. After that, when we see what we've got, broader tactics can be prepared. If some extreme emergency doesn't arise, it'll be a few hours before I can get over to HQ."

"Yes, sir. Sir, I…may I say—" So might the young Norron have addressed a god.

"All right, son, you've said it." Rusch turned off the screen and looked at Unduma. "Do you realize what's happening?"

The ambassador sat down; his knees seemed all at once to have melted. "What have you done?" It was like a stranger speaking.

"What I planned quite a few years ago," said the Margrave.

He reached into his desk and brought forth a bottle. "Here, your excellency. I think we could both use a swig. Authentic Terrestrial Scotch. I've saved it for this day."

But there was no glory leaping in him. It is often thus, you reach a dream and you only feel how tired you are.

Unduma let the liquid fire slide down his throat.

"You understand, don't you?" said Rusch. "For seven centuries, the Elephant and the Whale fought, without being able to get at each other's vitals. I made this alliance against Earth solely to get our men aboard their ships. But a really large operation like that can't be faked. It has to be genuine—the agreements, the preparations, the propaganda, everything. Only a handful of officers, men who could be trusted to…to infinity"—his voice cracked over, and Unduma thought of war prisoners sacrificed, hideous casualties in the steel corridors of spaceships, Norron gunners destroying Kolreshite vessels and the survivors of Norron detachments which failed to capture them—"only a few could be told, and then only at the last instant. For the rest, I relied on the quality of our troops. They're good lads, every one of them, and therefore adaptable. They're especially adaptable when suddenly told to fall on the men they'd most like to kill."

He tilted the bottle afresh. "It's proving expensive," he said in a slurred, hurried tone. "It will cost us as many casualties, no doubt, as ten years of ordinary war. But if I hadn't done this, there could easily have been another seven hundred years of war. Couldn't there? Couldn't there have been? As it is, we've already broken the spine of the Kolreshite fleet. She has plenty of ships yet, to be sure, still a menace, but crippled. I hope Earth will see fit to join us. Between them, Earth and Norstad-Ostarik can finish off Kolresh in a hurry. And after all, Kolresh *did* declare war on you, had every intention of destroying you. If you won't help, well, we can end it by ourselves, now that the fleet is broken. But I hope you'll join us."

"I don't know," said Unduma. He was still wobbling in a new cosmos. "We're not a…a hard people."

"You ought to be," said Rusch. "Hard enough, anyway, to win a voice for yourselves in what's going to happen around Polaris. Important frontier, Polaris."

"Yes," said Unduma slowly. "There is that. It won't cause any hosannahs in our streets, but...yes, I think we will continue the war, as your allies, if only to prevent you from massacring the Kolreshites. They can be rehabilitated, you know."

"I doubt that," grunted Rusch. "But it's a detail. At the very least, they'll never be allowed weapons again." He raised a sardonic brow. "I suppose we, too, can be rehabilitated, once you get your peace groups and psychotechs out here. No doubt you'll manage to demilitarize us and turn us into good plump democrats. All right, Unduma, send your Civilizing missionaries. But permit me to give thanks that I won't live to see their work completed!"

The Earthman nodded, rather coldly. You couldn't blame Rusch for treachery, callousness, and arrogance—he was what his history had made him—but he remained unpleasant company for a Civilized man. "I shall communicate with my government at once, your lordship, and recommend a provisional alliance, the terms to be settled later," he said. "I will report back to you as soon as...ah, where will you be?"

"How should I know?" Rusch got out of his chair.

The winter night howled at his back. "I have to convene the Ministry, and make a public telecast, and get over to Staff, and—No. The devil with it! If you need me inside the next few hours, I'll be at Sorgenlos on Ostarik. But the matter had better be urgent!"

Operation Changeling

And then a nurse led me to the bed where my darling lay. Always fair-hued, she was white after her battle, and the beautiful bones stood sharply in her face. But her hair was fire across the pillow, and though the lids drooped on her eyes, that green had never shone brighter.

I bent and kissed her, as gently as I could. "Hi, there," she whispered.

"How are you?" was the foolish single thing that came to me to say.

"Fine." She regarded me for a moment before, abruptly, she grinned. "But you look as if couvade might be a good idea."

As a matter of fact, some obstetricians do put the father to bed when a child is being born. Our doctor followed majority opinion in claiming that I'd give my wife the maximum possible sympathetic help by just sweating it out in the waiting room. I'd studied the subject frantically enough, these past months, to become somewhat of an authority. A first birth for a tall slim girl like Ginny was bound to be difficult. She took the prospect with her usual coolness, unbending only to the extent of casting runes to foretell the sex of the child, and that only so we wouldn't be caught flat-footed for a name.

"How do you like your daughter?" she asked me.

"Gorgeous," I said.

"Liar," she chuckled. "The man never lived who wasn't horrified when they told him he'd sired that wrinkled blob of red protoplasm." Her hand reached for mine. "But she will be lovely, Steve. She can't help being. It's so lovely between us."

I told myself that I would not bawl right in front of the mothers in this room. The nurse saved me with a crisp: "I think we had better let your wife rest, Mr. Matuchek. And Dr. Ashman would like to finish things so he can go home."

He was waiting for me in the naming office. When I had passed through the soundproof door, the nurse, sealed it behind me with wax and a davidstar. This was an up-to-date hospital where they took every care. Thomas Ashman was a grizzled, craggy six-footer with a relaxed manner, at present a bit droopy from weariness. I saw that beneath the impressive zodiacal traceries on his surgical gown, he'd been wearing white duck pants and a tee shirt—besides his amulet, of course.

431

We shook hands. "Everything's good," he assured me. "I've gotten the lab report. You understand that, with no therianthropes on the maternal side, none of your children will ever be a natural werewolf. But since this one has inherited the complete recessive gene complex from you, she'll take transformation spells quite easily. A definite advantage, especially if she goes in for a thaumaturgic career like her mother. It does mean, however, that certain things should be guarded against. She'll be more subject to paranatural influences than most people are."

I nodded. Ginny and I had certainly had an undue share of adventures we didn't want.

"Marry her off right," Ashman joked, "and you'll have werewolf grandchildren."

"If she takes after her old lady," I said, "Lord help any poor boy we tried to force on her!" I felt as idiotic as I sounded. "Look, Doctor, we're both tired. Let's make out the birth certificates and turn in."

"Sure." He sat down at the desk. The parchments were already inscribed with parental names, place and date, and the file number they bore in common. "What're you calling her?"

"Valeria."

"Yes, I suppose your wife would pick something like that. Her idea, wasn't it? Any middle name?"

"Uh…Mary. My decision—for my own mother—" I realized I was babbling again.

"Good thought. She can take refuge in it if she doesn't like the fancy monicker. Though I suspect she will." He typed out the information, signed, gave me the document, and dropped the carbon in an out-box. Rather more ceremoniously, he laid down the primary certificate that bore her fingerprints. "And the true name?"

"Victrix."

"Hm?"

"Ginny always liked it. Valeria Victrix. The last Roman legion in Britain." The last that stood against Chaos, she had said in one of her rare wholly serious moments.

Ashman shrugged. "Well, it isn't as if the kid's going to use it."

"I hope she never has to!"

"That'd imply a bad emergency," he agreed. "But don't fret. I see too many young husbands, shaken up by what they've undergone, be knocked for a loop at the grim possibilities they have to face now. Really, though, this is nothing more than another sensible precaution, like a vaccination, only against criminal name spells."

"I know," I said. "Wish they'd had the idea when I was born." Medical science is one of the few areas where I'll admit that genuine progress gets made.

Ashman dipped an eagle quill in a well of oak-gall ink. "By the bird of thy homeland and the tree of the lightning," he intoned, "under their protection and God's, child of this day, be thy true name, known on this earth but to thy parents, thy physician, and thee when thou shalt come of age: Victrix; and may thou bear it in honor and happiness while thy years endure. Amen." He wrote, dusted sand from Galilee across the words, and stood up again. "This one I'll file personally," he said. Yawning. "Okay, that's all."

We repeated our handshake. "I'm sorry you had to deliver her at such an unsanctified hour," I said.

"We GP's get used to that," he answered. The sleepiness left him. He regarded me very steadily. "Besides, in this case I expected it."

"Huh?"

"I'd heard something about you and your wife already," Ashman said. "I looked up more. Cast a few runes of my own. Maybe you don't know it yourself, but that kid was begotten on the winter solstice. And, quite apart from her unusual heredity, there's something else about her. I can't identify it. But I felt pretty sure she'd be born this night—because a full moon was due on Matthewsmas. I'm going to watch her with a great deal of interest, Mr. Matuchek, and I suggest you take extra special care of her…Good night, now."

Nothing spectacular happened to us in the following three years. Or so you would have thought; but you are somebody else. For our little circle, it was when the world opened up for our taking and, at the same time, buckled beneath our feet.

To start with, Valeria was unexpected. We found out later that Svartalf had been chasing the Brownie again and, in revenge, the Good Folk had turned Ginny's pills to aspirin. Afterward I've wondered if more didn't lie behind the incident than that. The Powers have Their ways of steering us toward situations that will sense Their ends.

At first Ginny intended to go ahead according to our original plan, as soon as the youngster was far enough along that a babysitter could handle things by day. And she did take her Ph.D. in Arcana, and had some excellent job offers. But once our daughter was part of our home, well, mama's emancipation kept getting postponed. We weren't about to let any hireling do slobwork on Valeria! Not yet, when she was learning to smile, when she was crawling everywhere around, when her noises of brook and bird were changing into language—later, later.

I quite agreed. But this meant giving up, for a while if not forever, the condition we'd looked forward to: of a smart young couple with a plump double income, doing glamorous things in glamorous places among glamorous people. I did propose trying to take up my Hollywood career again, but would have been astounded if Ginny had been willing to hear word one of that idea. "Do you imagine for half a second," she said, "that I'd want a mediocre player of Silver Chief and Lassie, when I could have a damn good engineer?" Personally, I don't think the pictures I made were that all bad; but on the whole, her answer relieved me.

A newly created B.Sc. doesn't step right into the kind of challenging project he hopes for, especially when he's older than the average graduate. I had to start out with what I could get. By luck—we believed then—that was unexpectedly good.

The Nornwell Scryotronics Corporation was among the new outfits in the booming postwar communications and instrument business. Though small, it was upward bound on an exponential curve. Besides manufacture, it did R & D, and I was invited to work on the latter. This was not simply fascinating in itself, it was a long step toward my ultimate professional goal. That pay wasn't bad, either. And before long, Barney Sturlason was my friend as much as he was my boss.

The chief drawback was that we had to stay in this otherwise dull city and endure its ghastly Upper Midwestern winters. But we rented a comfortable suburban house, which helped. And we had each other, and little Valeria. Those were good years. It's just that nobody else would find an account of them especially thrilling.

That's twice true when you consider what went on meanwhile at large. I suppose mankind has always been going to perdition in a roller coaster and always will be. Still, certain eras remind you of the old Chinese curse: "May you live in interesting times!"

Neither Ginny nor I had swallowed the propaganda guff about how peace and happiness would prevail forevermore once the wicked Caliphate had been defeated. We knew what a legacy of wretchedness all wars must leave. Besides, we knew this conflict was more a symptom than a cause of the world's illness. The enemy wouldn't have been able to overrun most of the Eastern Hemisphere and a chunk of the United States if Christendom hadn't been divided against itself. For that matter, the Caliphate was nothing but the secular arm of a Moslem heresy; we had plenty of good Allah allies.

It did seem reasonable, though, to expect that afterward people would have learned their lesson, put their religious quarrels aside, and settled down to reconstruction. In particular, we looked for the Johannine Church to be generally discredited and fade away. True, its adherents had fought the Caliph too, had in fact taken a leading role in the resistance movements in the occupied countries. But wasn't its challenge to the older creeds—to the whole basis of Western Society—what had split and weakened our civilization in the first place? Wasn't its example what had stimulated the rise of the lunatic Caliphist ideology in the Middle East?

I now know better than to expect reasonableness in human affairs.

Contrary to popular impression, the threat didn't appear suddenly. A few men warned against it from the beginning. They pointed out how the Johnnies had become dominant in the politics of more than one nation, which thereupon stopped being especially friendly to us, and how in spite of this they were making converts throughout America. But most of us hardly listened. We were too busy repairing war damage, public and personal. We considered those who sounded the alarm to be reactionaries and would-be tyrants—which some, perhaps, were. The Johannine theology might be nuts, we said, but didn't the First Amendment guarantee its right to be preached? The Petrine churches might be in trouble, but wasn't that their problem? And really, in our scientific day and age, to talk about subtle, pervasive dangers in a religious-philosophical system...a system which emphasized peacefulness almost as strongly as the Quakers, which exalted the commandment to love thy neighbor above every other—well, it just might be that our materialistic secular society and our ritualistic faiths would benefit from a touch of what the Johnnies advocated.

So the movement and its influence grew. And then the activist phase began: and somehow orderly demonstrations were oftener and oftener turning into riots, and wildcat strikes were becoming more and more common over issues that made less and less sense, and student agitation was paralyzing campus after campus, and person after otherwise intelligent person was talking about the need to tear down a hopelessly corrupt order of things so that the Paradise of Love could be built on the ruins…and the majority of us, that eternal majority which wants nothing except to be left alone to cultivate its individual gardens, wondered how the country could have started to disintegrate overnight.

Brother, it did not happen overnight. Not even over Walpurgis Night.

I came home early that June day. Our street was quiet, walled in between big old elms, lawns, and houses basking in sunlight. The few broomsticks in view were ridden by local women, carrying groceries in the saddlebags and an infant or two strapped in the kiddie seat. This was a district populated chiefly by young men on the way up. Such tend to have pretty wives, and in warm weather these tend to wear shorts and halters. The scenery lightened my mood no end.

I'd been full of anger when I left the turbulence around the plant. But here was peace. My roof was in sight. Ginny and Val were beneath it. Barney and I had a plan for dealing with our troubles, come this eventide. The prospect of action cheered me. Meanwhile, I was home!

I passed into the open garage, dismounted, and racked my Chevvy alongside Ginny's Volksbesen. As I came out again, aimed at the front door, a cannonball whizzed through the air and hit me. "Daddy! Daddy!"

I hugged my offspring close, curly yellow hair, enormous blue eyes, the whole works. She was wearing her cherub suit, and I had to be careful not to break the wings. Before, when she flew, it had been at the end of a tether secured to a post, and under Ginny's eye. What the deuce was she doing free—?

Oh—Svartalf zoomed around the corner of the house on a whisk broom. His back was arched, his tail was raised, and he used bad language. Evidently Ginny had gotten him to supervise. He could control the chit fairly well, no doubt, keep her in the yard and out of trouble…until she saw Daddy arrive.

"Okay!" I laughed. "Enough. Let's go in and say boo to Mother."

"Wide piggyback?"

For Val's birthday last fall I'd gotten the stuff for an expensive spell and had Ginny change me. The kid was used to playing with me in my wolf form, I'd thought; but how about a piggyback ride, the pig being fat and white and spotted with flowers? The local small fry were still talking about it. "Sorry, no," I had to tell her. "After that performance of yours, you get the Air Force treatment." And I carried her by her ankles, squealing and wiggling, while I sang,

Up in the air, junior birdman,
Up in the air, upside down—

Ginny came into the living room, from the work-room, as we did. Looking behind her, I saw why she'd deputized the supervision of Val's flytime. Washday. A three-year-old goes through a lot of clothes, and we couldn't afford self-cleaning fabrics. She had to animate each garment singly, and make sure they didn't tie themselves in knots or something while they soaped and rinsed and marched around to dry off and so forth. And, since a parade like that is irresistible to a child, she had to get Val elsewhere.

Nonetheless, I wondered if she wasn't being a tad reckless, putting her familiar in charge. Hitherto, she'd done the laundry when Val was asleep. Svartalf had often shown himself to be reliable in the clutch. But for all the paranatural force in him, he remained a big black tomcat, which meant he was not especially dependable in dull everyday matters…Then I thought, what the blazes, since Ginny stopped being a practicing witch, the poor beast hasn't had much excitement; he hasn't even got left a dog or another cat in the whole neighborhood that dares fight him; this assignment was probably welcome; Ginny always knows what she's doing; and—

"—and I'm an idiot for just standing here gawping," I said, and gathered her in. She was dressed like the other wives I'd seen, but if she'd been out there too I wouldn't have seen them.

She responded. She knew how.

"What's a Nidiot?" Val asked from the floor. She pondered the matter. "Well, Daddy's a *good* Nidiot."

Svartalf switched his tail.

I relaxed my hold on Ginny a trifle. She ran her fingers through my hair. "Wow," she murmured. "What brought that on, tiger?"

"Daddy's a woof," Val corrected her.

"You can call me tiger today," I said, feeling happier by the minute.

Ginny leered. "Okay, pussycat."

"Wait a bit—"

She shrugged. The red tresses moved along her shoulders. "Well, if you insist, okay, Lame Thief of the Waingunga."

Val regarded us sternly. "When you fwoo wif you' heads," she directed, "put 'em outside to melt."

The logic of this, and the business of getting the cherub rig off her, took time to unravel. Not until our offspring was bottoms up on the living-room floor, watching cartoons on the crystal ball, and I was in the kitchen watching Ginny start supper, did we get the chance to talk.

"How come you're home so early?" she asked.

"How'd you like to reactivate the old outfit tonight?" I replied.

"Which?"

"Matuchek and Graylock—no, Matuchek and Matuchek—Troubleshooters Extraordinary, Licensed Confounders of the Ungodly."

She put down her work and gave me a long look. "What are you getting at, Steve?"

"You'll see it on the ball, come news time," I answered. "We aren't simply being picketed any more. They've moved onto the grounds. They're blocking every doorway. Our personnel had to leave by skylight, and rocks got thrown at some of them."

She was surprised and indignant, but kept the coolness she showed to the world outside this house. "You didn't call the police?"

"Sure, we did. I listened in, along with Barney, since Roberts thought a combat veteran might have some useful ideas. We can get police help if we want it. The demonstrators have turned into trespassers; and windows are broken, walls defaced with obscene slogans, that sort of thing. Our legal case is plenty clear. Only the opposition is out for trouble. Trouble for us, as much as possible, but mainly they're after martyrs. They'll resist any attempt to disperse them. Just like the fracas in New York last month. A lot of these characters are students too. Imagine the headlines: Police Brutality Against Idealistic Youths. Peaceful Protesters Set On With Clubs and Geas Casters.

"Remember, this is a gut issue. Nornwell manufactures a lot of police and defense equipment, like witchmark fluorescers and basilisk goggles. We're under contract to develop more kinds. The police and the armed forces serve the Establishment. The Establishment is evil. Therefore Nornwell must be shut down."

"*Quod erat demonstrandum* about," she sighed.

The chief told us that an official move to break up the invasion would mean bloodshed, which might touch off riots at the University, along Merlin Avenue—Lord knows where it could lead. He asked us to stop work for the rest of the week, to see if this affair won't blow over. We'd probably have to, anyway. Quite a few of our men told their supervisors they're frankly scared to come back, the way things are."

The contained fury sparked in her eyes. "If you knuckle under," she said, "they'll proceed to the next on their list."

"You know it," I said. "We all do. But there is that martyrdom effect. There are those Johnny priests ready to deliver yet another sanctimonious sermon about innocent blood equals the blood of the Lamb. There's a country full of well-intentioned bewildered people who'll wonder if maybe the Petrine churches aren't really on the way out, when the society that grew from them has to use violence against members of the Church of Love. Besides, let's face the fact, darling, violence has never worked against civil disobedience."

"Come back and tell me that after the machine guns have talked," she said.

"Yeah, sure. But who'd want to preserve a government that resorts to massacre? I'd sooner turn Johnny myself. The upshot is, Nornwell can't ask the police to clear its property for it."

Ginny cocked her head at me. "You don't look too miserable about this."

I laughed. "No. Barney and I brooded over the problem for a while and hatched us quite an egg; I'm actually enjoying myself by now, sort of. Life's too tame of late. Which is why I asked if you'd like get in on the fun."

"Tonight?"

"Yes. The sooner the better. I'll give you the details after our young hopeful's gone to bed."

Ginny's own growing smile faded. "I'm not sure I can get a sitter on notice that short. This is final exam week at the high school."

"Well, if you can't, what about Svartalf?" I suggested. "You won't be needing a familiar, and he can see to the elementary things, keep guard, dash next door and yowl a neighbor awake if she gets collywobbles—Normally she sleeps fine."

Ginny agreed. I could see the eagerness build up in her. Though she'd accepted a housewife's role for the time being, no race horse really belongs on a plowing team.

In this fashion did we prepare the way for hell to break loose, literally.

The night fell moonless, a slight haze dulling the stars. We left soon after, clad alike in black sweaters and slacks, headlights off. Having maintained the witch-sight given us in the army, we made a flight that was safe, if illegal, high over the city's constelled windows and lamps until our stick swung downward again toward the industrial section. It lay still darker and emptier than was normal at this hour.

But Nornwell's grounds shone forth, an uneasy auroral glow in the air. As we neared, the wind that slid past, stroking and whispering to me, bore odors—flesh and sweat, incense and electric acridity of paranatural energies. The hair stood erect along my spine. I was content not to be in wolf-shape to get the full impact of that last.

The paved area around the main building was packed close to solid with bodies. So was the garden that made our workers' warm-weather lunches pleasant, nothing remained of it except mud and cigarette stubs. I estimated five hundred persons altogether, blocking any except aerial access. Their mass was not restless, but the movement of individuals created an endless rippling through it, and the talk and foot-shuffle gave those waves a voice.

Near the sheds, our lot was less crowded. Scattered people there were taking a break from the vigil to fix a snack or flake out in a sleeping bag. They kept a respectful distance from a portable altar at the far end, though from time to time, someone would kneel in its direction.

I whistled, long and low. "That's arrived since I left." Ginny's arms caught tighter around my waist.

A Johannine priest was holding service. Altitude or no, we couldn't mistake his white robe, high-pitched minor-key chanting, spread-eagle stance which he could maintain for hours, the tau crucifix that gleamed tall and gaunt behind the altar, the four talismans—Cup, Wand, Sword, and Disc—upon it. Two acolytes swung censers whence came the smoke that sweetened and, somehow, chilled the air.

"What's he up to?" I muttered. I'd never troubled to learn much about the new church. Or the old ones, for that matter. Not that Ginny and I were igno-rant of modern scientific discoveries proving the reality of the Divine and things like absolute evil, atonement, and an afterlife. But it seemed to us that so little is known beyond these bare hints, and that God can have so infinitely many partial manifestations to limited human understanding, that we might as well call ourselves Unitarians.

"I don't know," she answered. Her tone was bleak. "I studied what's public about their rites and doctrines, but that's just the top part of the iceberg, and it was years ago for me. Anyhow, you'd have to be a communicant—no, a lot more, an initiate, ultimately an adept, before you were told what a given procedure really means."

I stiffened. "Could he be hexing our side?"

Whetted by alarm, my vision swept past the uneasy sourceless illumination and across the wider scene. About a score of burly blue policemen were posted around the block. No doubt they were mighty sick of being jeered at. Also, probably most of them belonged to traditional churches. They wouldn't exactly mind arresting the agent of a creed which said that their own creeds were finished.

"No," I replied to myself, "he can't be, or the cops'd have him in the cooler this minute. Maybe he's anathematizing us. He could do that under freedom of religion, I suppose. But actually casting a spell, bringing goetic forces in to work harm—"

Ginny interrupted my thinking aloud. "The trouble is," she said, "when you deal with these Gnostics, you don't know where their prayers leave off and their spells begin. Let's get cracking before something happens. I don't like the smell of the time-stream tonight."

I nodded and steered for the principal building. The Johnny didn't fret me too much. Chances were he was just holding one of his esoteric masses to encourage the demonstrators. Didn't the claim go that his church was the church of universal benevolence? That it actually had no need of violence, being above the things of this earth? "The day of the Old Testament, of the Father, was the day of power and fear; the day of the New Testament, of the Son, has been the day of expiation; the day of the Johannine Gospel, of the Holy Spirit, will be the day of love and unveiled mysteries." No matter now.

The police were interdicting airborne traffic in the immediate vicinity except for whoever chose to leave it. That was a commonsense move. None but a minority of the mob were Johnnies. To a number of them, the idea of despising and renouncing a sinful material world suggested nothing more than that it was fashionable to wreck that world. The temptation to flit overhead and drop a few Molotov cocktails could get excessive.

Naturally, Ginny and I might have insisted on our right to come here, with an escort if need be. But that could provoke the explosion we wanted to avoid. Altogether, the best idea was to slip in, unnoticed by friend and foe alike. Our commando-type skills were somewhat rusty, though; the maneuver demanded our full attention.

We succeeded. Our stick ghosted through a skylight left open, into the garage. To help ventilate the rest of the place, this was actually a well from roof to ground floor. Normally our employees came and went by the doors. Tonight, however, those were barred on two sides—by the bodies of the opposition, and by protective force-fields of our own which it would take an expert wizard to break.

The Pinkerton technician hadn't conjured quite fast enough for us. Every first-story window was shattered. Through the holes drifted mumbled talk, background chant. Racking the broom, I murmured in Ginny's ear—her hair tickled my lips and was fragrant—"You know, I'm glad they did get a priest. During the day, they had folk singers."

"Poor darling." She squeezed my hand. "Watch out for busted glass." We picked our way in the murk to a hall and upstairs to the R & D section. It was defiantly lighted. But our footfalls rang too loud in its emptiness. It was a relief to enter Barney Sturlason's office.

His huge form rose behind the desk. "Virginia!" he rumbled. "What an unexpected pleasure." Hesitating: "But, uh, the hazard—"

"Shouldn't be noticeable, Steve tells me," she said. "And I gather you could use an extra thaumaturgist."

"Sure could." I saw how his homely features sagged with exhaustion. He'd insisted that I go home and rest. This was for the practical reason that, if things went sour and we found ourselves attacked, I'd have to turn wolf and be the main line of defense until the police could act. But he'd stayed on, helping his few volunteers make ready.

"Steve's explained our scheme?" he went on. His decision to accept her offer had been instantaneous. "Well, we need to make sure the most delicate and expensive equipment doesn't suffer. Quite apart from stuff being ruined, imagine the time and cost of recalibrating every instrument we've got, from dowsers to tarots! I think everything's adequately shielded, but I'd certainly appreciate an independent check by a fresh mind."

"Okay." She'd visited sufficiently often to be familiar with the layout. "I expect you two'll be busy for a while."

"Yes, I'm going to give them one last chance out there," Barney said, "and in case somebody gets overexcited, I'd better have Steve along for a bodyguard."

"And *I* still believe you might as well save your breath," I snorted.

"No doubt you're right, as far as you go," Barney said, "but don't forget the legal aspect. I don't own this place, I only head up a department. We're acting on our personal initiative after the directors agreed to suspend operations. Jack Roberts' approval of our plan was strictly *sub rosa*. Besides, ownership or not, we can no more use spells offensively against trespassers than we could use shotguns. I have to make it perfectly clear before plenty of witnesses that we intend to stay within the law."

I shed my outer garments. Underneath was the elastic knit one-piecer that would keep me from arrest for indecent exposure as a human, yet not hamper me as a wolf. The moonflash already hung around my neck like a thick round amulet. Ginny kissed me hard. "Take care of yourself, tiger," she whispered.

She had no strong cause to worry. The besiegers were unarmed, except for fists and feet and possibly some smuggled billies or the like—nothing I need fear after Skinturning. Even knives and bullets and fangs could only inflict permanent harm under rare and special conditions, like those which had cost me my tail during the war. Besides, the likelihood of a fight was very small. Why should the opposition set on us? Nonetheless, Ginny's tone was not completely level, and she watched us go down the hall till we had rounded a corner.

At that time, Barney said, "Wait a tick," opened a closet, and extracted a blanket that he hung on his arm. "If you should have to change shape," he said, "I'll throw this over you."

"Whatever for?" I exclaimed. "That's not sunlight outside, it's elflight. It won't inhibit transformation."

"It's changed character since that priest set up shop. I used a spectroscope to make certain. The glow's acquired enough ultraviolet—3500 angstroms to be exact—that you'd have trouble. Byproduct of a guard against any that we might try to use offensively."

"But we *won't*!"

"Of course not. It's pure ostentation on his part. Clever, though. When they saw a shield-field established around them, the fanatics and naive children in the mob leaped to the conclusion that it was necessary; and thus Nornwell gets reconfirmed as the Enemy." He shook his head. "Believe me, Steve, these demonstrators are being operated like gloves, by some mighty shrewd characters."

"You sure the priest himself raised the field?"

"Yeah. They're all Magi in that clergy, remember—part of their training—and I wonder what else they learn in those lonesome seminaries. Let's try talking with him."

"Is he in charge?" I wondered. "The Johannine hierarchy does claim that when its members mix in politics, they do it strictly as private citizens."

"I know," Barney said. "And I am the Emperor Norton."

"No, really," I persisted. "These conspiracy theories are too bloody simple to be true. What you've got is a, uh, a general movement, something in the air, people, disaffected—"

But then, walking, we'd reached one of the ornamental glass panels that flanked the main entrance. It was smashed like the windows, but no one had thought to barricade it, and our protective spell forestalled entry. Of course, that did not affect us. We stepped through, onto the landing, right alongside the line of bodies that was supposed to keep us in.

We couldn't go farther. The stairs down to ground were packed solid. For a moment we weren't noticed. Barney tapped one straggle-bearded adolescent on the shoulder. "Excuse me," he said from his towering height. "May I?" He plucked a sign out of the unwashed hand, hung the blanket over the placard, and waved his improvised flag of truce aloft. The color was bilious green.

A kind of gasp like the puff of wind before a storm, went through the crowd. I saw faces and faces and faces next to me, below me, dwindling off into the dusk beyond the flickering elflight. I don't think it was only my haste and my prejudice that made them look eerily alike.

You hear a lot about long-haired men and short-haired women, bathless bodies and raggedy clothes. Those were certainly present in force. Likewise I identified the usual graybeard radicals and campus hangers-on, hoodlums, unemployables, vandals, True Believers, and the rest. But there were plenty of clean, well-dressed, terribly earnest boys and girls. There were the merely curious, too, who had somehow suddenly found themselves involved. And everyone was tall, short, or medium, fat, thin, or average, rich, poor, or middleclass, bright, dull, or normal, heterosexual, homosexual, or I know not what, able in some fields, inept in others, interested in some things, bored by others, each with an infinite set of memories, dreams, hopes, terrors, loves—each with a soul.

No, the sameness appeared first in the signs they carried. I didn't count how many displayed St. John 13:34 or I John 2:9-11 or another of those passages; how many more carried the texts, or some variation like Love thy neighbor or plain Love: quite a few, anyway, repeating and repeating. Others were less amiable:

Dematerialize the materialists!

Weaponmakers, weep!

Stop giving police devils horns!

Kill the killers, Hate the haters, Destroy the destroyers!

Shut down this shop!

And so it was as if the faces—worse, the brains behind them—had become nothing but placards with slogans written across.

The indrawn breath returned as a guttural sigh that edged toward a growl. The nearest males took a step or two in our direction. Barney waved his flag. "Wait!" he called, a thunderous basso overriding any other sound. "Truce! Let's talk this over! Take your leader to me!"

"Nothing *to* talk about, you murderers!" screamed a pimply girl. She swung her sign at me. I glimpsed upon it PEACE AND BROTHERHOOD before I had to get busy protecting my scalp. Someone began a chant that was quickly taken up by more and more: "Down with Diotrephes, down with Diotrephes, down with Diotrephes—"

Alarm stabbed through me. Those words had hypnotized other crowds into destructive frenzy.

I took her sign away from the girl, defended my eyes from her fingernails, and reached for my flash. But abruptly everything changed. A bell sounded. A voice cried. Both were low, both somehow penetrated the rising racket.

"Peace. Hold love in your hearts, children. Be still in the presence of the Holy Spirit."

My attacker retreated. The others who hemmed us in withdrew. Individuals started falling on their knees. A moan went through the mob, growing almost orgasmic before it died away into silence. Looking up, I saw the priest approach.

He traveled with bell in one hand, holding onto the upright of his tau crucifix while standing on its pedestal. Thus Christ nailed to the Cross of Mystery went before him. Nothing strange about that, I thought wildly, except that other churches would call it sacrilegious to give the central sign of their faith yonder shape, put an antigrav spell on it and use it like any broomstick. Yet the spectacle was weirdly impressive. It was like an embodiment of that Something Else on which Gnosticism is focused.

As the priest landed in front of us, though, he looked entirely human. He was short and skinny, his robe didn't fit too well, glasses perched precariously on his button nose, his graying hair was so thin I could hardly follow the course of his tonsure—the strip shaven from ear to ear, across the top of the head, that was said to have originated with Simon Magus.

He turned to the crowd first. "Let me speak with these gentlemen out of love, not hatred, and righteousness may prevail," he said in his oddly carrying tone. "'He that loveth not knoweth not God; for God is love.'"

"Amen," mumbled across the grounds.

As the little man faced back toward us, I had a sudden belief that he really meant that dear quotation. It didn't drive away the miasma. The Adversary knows well how to use single-minded sincerity. But I felt less hostile to this priest as a person.

He smiled at us and bobbed his head. "Good evening," he said. "I am Initiate Fifth Class Marmiadon, at your service."

"Your, uh, ecclesiastical name?" Barney asked.

"Why, of course. The old name is the first of the things of this world that must be left behind at the Gate of Passage. I'm not afraid of a hex, if that is what you mean, sir."

"No, I suppose not." Barney introduced us, a cheap token of amity since we were both easily identifiable. "We came out hoping to negotiate a settlement."

Marmiadon beamed. "Wonderful! Blessings! I'm not an official spokesman, you realize. The Committee for National Righteousness called for this demonstration. However, I'll be glad to use my good offices."

"The trouble is," Barney said, "we can't do much about their basic demands. We're not against world peace and universal disarmament ourselves, you understand; but those are matters for international diplomacy. In the same way, the President and Congress have to decide whether to end the occupation of formerly hostile countries and spend the money on social uplift at home. Amnesty for rioters is up to our city governments. School courses in Gnostic philosophy and history have to be decided on by elected authorities. As for total income-equalization and phasing out of materialism, hypocrisy, injustice—" He shrugged. "That needs a Constitutional amendment at least."

"You can, however, lend your not inconsiderable influence to forwarding those ends," Marmiadon said. "For example, you can contribute to the Committee's public education fund. You can urge the election of the proper candidates and help finance their campaigns. You can allow proselytizers to circulate among your employees. You can stop doing business with merchants who remain obstinate." He spread his arms. "In the course of so doing, my children, you can rescue yourselves from eternal damnation!"

"Well, maybe; though Pastor Karlslund over at St. Olaf's Lutheran might give me a different opinion on that," Barney said. "In any case, it's too big a list to check off in one day."

"Granted, granted." Marmiadon quivered with eagerness. "We reach our ends a step at a time. The present dispute is over a single issue."

"The trouble is," Barney said, "you want us to cancel contracts we've signed and taken money for. You want us to break our word and let down those who trust us."

His joy dropped from Marmiadon. He drew himself to his full meager height, looked hard and straight at us, and stated: "These soldiers of the Holy Spirit demand that you stop making equipment for the armed forces, oppressors abroad, and for the police, oppressors at home. Nothing more is asked of you at this time, and nothing less. The question is not negotiable."

"I see. I didn't expect anything else," Barney said. "But I wanted to put the situation in plain language before witnesses. Now I'm going to warn you."

Those who heard whispered to the rest, a hissing from mouth to mouth. I saw tension mount anew.

"If you employ violence upon those who came simply to remonstrate," Marmiadon declared, "they will either have the law upon you, or see final proof that the law is a creature of the vested interests…which I tell you in turn are the creatures of Satan."

"Oh, no, no," Barney answered. "We're mild sorts, whether you believe it or not. But you are trespassing. We're about to run an experiment. You could be endangered. Please clear the grounds for your own safety."

Marmiadon grew rigid. "If you think you can get away with a deadly spell—"

"Nothing like. I'll tell you precisely what we have in mind. We're thinking about a new method of transporting liquid freight. Before going further, we have to run a safety check on it. If the system fails, unprotected persons could be hurt." Barney raised his volume, though we knew some of the police officers would have owls' ears tuned in. "I order you, I warn you, I beg you to stop trespassing, and get off company properly. You have half an hour."

We wheeled and were back inside before the noise broke loose. Curses, taunts, obscenities, and animal howls followed us down the halls until we reached the blessed isolation of the main alchemy lab.

The dozen scientists, technicians, and blue-collar men whom Barney had picked out of the volunteers to stay with him, were gathered there. They sat smoking, drinking coffee, talking in low voices. When we entered, a small cheer came from them. They'd watched the confrontation on a closed-loop ball. I sought out Ike Abrams, the warehouse foreman. "All in order?" I asked.

He made a swab-O sign. "By me, she's clear and on green. I can't wait."

I considered him for a second. "You really have it in for those characters, don't you?"

"In my position, wouldn't you?" He looked as if he were about to spit.

In your position, I thought, or in any of a lot of other positions, such as my own rationalism, but, especially in yours, Ike—yes. The Gnostics do more than pervert the Gospel According to St. John, perhaps the most beautiful and gentle if the most mystical book in Holy Writ. They pluck out of context passages like

"For many deceivers are entered into the world, who confess not that Jesus Christ is come in the flesh. This is a deceiver and an antichrist." You would see reviving around you the ancient nightmare of anti-Semitism.

A little embarrassed, I turned to Bill Hardy, our chief paracelsus, who sat swinging his legs from a lab bench. "How much stuff did you produce?" I asked.

"About fifty gallons," he said, pointing.

"Wow! With no alchemy?"

"Absolutely not. Pure, honest-to-Berzelius molecular interaction. I admit we were lucky to have a large supply of the basic ingredients on hand."

I winced, recalling the awful sample he'd whipped up when our scheme was first discussed. "How on Midgard did that happen?"

"Well, the production department is—was—filling some big orders," he said. "For instance, a dairy chain wanted a lot of rancidity preventers. You know the process, inhibit the reaction you don't want in a test tube, and cast a sympathetic spell to get the same effect in ton-lots of your product. Then the government is trying to control the skunk population in the Western states, and—" He broke off as Ginny came in.

Her eyes glistened. She held her wand like a Valkyrie's sword. "We're set, boys." The words clanged.

"Let's go." Barney heaved his bulk erect. We followed him to the containers. They were ordinary flat one-gallon cans such as you buy paint thinner in, but Solomon's seal marked the wax that closed each screw top and I could subliminally feel the paranatural forces straining around them. It seemed out of keeping for the scientists to load them on a cart and trundle them off.

Ike and his gang went with me to my section. The apparatus I'd thrown together didn't look especially impressive either. In fact, it was a haywire monstrosity, coils and wires enclosing a big gasoline-driven electric generator. Sometimes you need more juice for an experiment than the carefully screened public power lines can deliver.

To cobble that stuff on, I'd have to remove the generator's own magnetic screens. Therefore, what we had was a mass of cold free iron; no spell would work in its immediate vicinity. Ike had been in his element this afternoon, mounting the huge weight and awkward bulk on wheels for me. He was again, now, as he directed it along the halls and skidded it over the stairs.

No doubt he sometimes wished people had never found how to degauss the influences that had held paranatural forces in check since the Bronze Age ended. He wasn't Orthodox; his faith didn't prohibit him having anything whatsoever to do with goetics. But neither was he Reform or Neo-Chassidic. He was a Conservative Jew, who could make use of objects that others had put under obedience but who mustn't originate any cantrips himself. It's a tribute to him that he was nonetheless a successful and popular foreman.

He'd rigged a husky block-and-tackle arrangement in the garage. The others had already flitted to the flat roof. Ginny had launched the canisters from there.

They bobbed about in the air, out of range of the magnetic distortions caused by the generator when we hoisted its iron to their level. Barney swung the machine around until we could ease it down beside the skylight. That made it impossible for us to rise on brooms or a word. We joined our friends via rope ladder.

"Ready?" Barney asked. In the restless pale glow, I saw sweat gleam on his face. If this failed, he'd be responsible for unforeseeable consequences.

I checked the connections. "Yeah, nothing's come loose. But let me first have a look around."

I joined Ginny at the parapet. Beneath us roiled the mob, faces and placards turned upward to hate us. They had spied the floating containers and knew a climax was at hand. Behind his altar, Initiate Marmiadon worked at what I took to be reinforcement of his defensive field. Unknown phrases drifted to me: "…*Heliphomar Mabon Saruth Gefutha Enunnas Sacinos…*" above the sullen mumble of our besiegers. The elflight flickered brighter. The air seethed and crackled with energies. I caught a thunderstorm whiff of ozone.

My darling wore a slight, wistful smile. "How Svartalf would love this," she said.

Barney lumbered to our side. "I'll give them one last chance." He shouted the same warning as before. Yells drowned him out. Rocks and offal flew against our walls. "Okay," he growled. "Let 'er rip!"

I went back to the generator and started the motor, leaving the circuits open. It stuttered and shivered. The vile fumes made me glad we'd escaped depending on internal combustion engines. I've seen automobiles, as they were called, built around 1900, shortly before the first broomstick flights. Believe me, museums are where they belong—a chamber of horrors, to be exact.

Ginny's clear call snapped my attention back. She'd directed the canisters into position. I could no longer see them, for they floated ten feet over the heads of the crowd, evenly spaced. She made a chopping gesture with her wand. I threw the main switch.

No, we didn't use spells to clear Nornwell's property. We used the absence of spells. The surge of current through the coils on the generator threw out enough magnetism to cancel every charm, ours and theirs alike, within a hundred-yard radius.

We'd stowed whatever gear might be damaged in safe conductive-shell rooms. We'd repeatedly cautioned the mob that we were about to experiment with the transportation of possibly dangerous liquids. No law required us to add that these liquids were in super-pressurized cans which were bound to explode and spray their contents the moment that the wall-strengthening force was annulled.

We'd actually exaggerated the hazard…in an attempt to avoid any slightest harm to trespassers. Nothing vicious was in those containers. Whatever might be slightly toxic was present in concentrations too small to matter, although a normal sense of smell would give ample warning regardless. Just a harmless mixture of materials like butyl mercaptan, butyric acid, methanethiol, skatole, cadaverine, putrescine…well, yes, the organic binder did have penetrative properties; if you got a few drops on your skin, the odor wouldn't disappear for a week or two…

The screams reached me first. I had a moment to gloat. Then the stench arrived. I'd forgotten to don my gas mask, and even when I'm human my nose is quite sensitive. The slight whiff I got sent me gasping and retching backward across the roof. It was skunk, it was spoiled butter, it was used asparagus, it was corruption and doom and the wheels of juggernaut lubricated with Limburger cheese, it was beyond imagining. I barely got my protection on in time.

"Poor dear. Poor Steve." Ginny held me close.

"Are they gone?" I sputtered.

"Yes. Along with the policemen and, if we don't get busy, half this postal district."

I relaxed. We need hardly expect a return visit, I thought in rising glee. If you suffer arrest or a broken head for the Cause, you're a hero who inspires others. But if you merely acquire for a while a condition your best friends won't tell you about because they can't come within earshot of you—hasn't the Cause taken a setback?

I grabbed Ginny to me and started to kiss her. Damn, I'd forgotten my gas mask again! She disentangled our snouts. "I'd better help Barney and the rest hex away those molecules before they spread," she told me. "Switch off your machine and screen it."

"Uh, yes," I must agree. "We want our staff returning to work in the morning."

What with one thing and another, we were busy for a couple of hours. After we finished, Barney produced some bottles, and the celebration lasted till well nigh dawn. The eastern sky blushed pink when Ginny and I wobbled aboard our broom and hiccoughed, "Home, James."

The air blew cool, heaven reached high. "Know something?" I said over my shoulder. "I love you."

"Purr-rr-rr." She leaned forward to rub her cheek against mine. Her hands wandered.

"Shameless hussy," I said.

"You prefer some other kind?" she asked.

"Well, no," I said, "but you might wait a while. Here I am in front of you, feeling more lecherous every minute but without any way to lech."

"Oh, there are ways," she murmured dreamily. "On a broomstick yet. Have you forgotten?"

"No. But dammit, the local airlanes are going to be crowded with commuter traffic pretty soon, and I'd rather not fly several miles looking for solitude when we've got a perfectly good bedroom nearby."

"Right. I like that thought. Pour on the coal, James."

The stick accelerated.

I was full of glory and the glory that was her. She caught the paranatural traces first. My indication was that her head lifted from between my shoulder blades, her arms loosened around my waist while the fingernails bit through my shirt. "What the Moloch?" I exclaimed.

"*Hsh!*" she breathed. We flew in silence through the thin chill dawn wind. The city spread darkling beneath us. Her voice came at last, tense, but somehow dwindled and lost: "I said I didn't like the feel of the time-stream. In the excitement, I forgot."

My guts crawled, as if I were about to turn wolf. Senses and extrasenses strained forth. I've scant thaumaturgic skill—the standard cantrips, plus a few from the Army and more from engineering training—but a lycanthrope has inborn instincts and awarenesses. Presently I also knew.

Dreadfulness was about.

As we flitted downward, we knew that it was in our house.

We left the broomstick on the front lawn. I turned my key in the door and hurled myself through. "Val!" I yelled into the dim rooms. "Svartalf!"

Chairs lay tumbled, vases smashed where they had fallen off shaken tables, blood was spattered over walls, floors, carpets, from end to end of the building.

We stormed into Valeria's room. When we saw that little shape quietly asleep in her crib, we held each other and wept.

Finally Ginny could ask, "Where's Svartalf? What happened?"

"I'll look around," I said. "He gave an epic account of himself, at least."

"Yes—" She wiped her eyes. As she looked around the wreckage in the nursery, that green gaze hardened. She stared down into the crib. "Why didn't you wake up?" she said in a tone I'd never heard before.

I was already on my way to search. I found Svartalf in the kitchen. His blood had about covered the linoleum. In spite of broken bones, tattered hide, belly gashed open, the breath rattled faintly in and out of him. Before I could examine the damage further, a shriek brought me galloping back to Ginny.

She held the child. Blue eyes gazed dully at me from under tangled gold curls. Ginny's face, above, was drawn so tight it seemed the skin must rip on the cheekbones. "Something's wrong with her," she told me. "I can't tell what, but something's wrong."

I stood for an instant feeling my universe break apart. Then I went into the closet. Dusk was giving place to day, and I needed darkness. I shucked my outer clothes and used my flash. Emerging, I went to those two female figures. My wolf nose drank their odors.

I sat on my haunches and howled.

Ginny laid down what she was holding. She stayed completely motionless by the crib while I changed back.

"I'll call the police," I heard my voice, say to her. "That thing isn't Val. It isn't even human."

I take care not to remember the next several hours in detail.

At noon we were in my study. Our local chief had seen almost at once that the matter was beyond him and urged us to call in the FBI. Their technicians were still busy checking the house and grounds, inch by inch. Our best service was to stay out of their way. I sat on the day bed, Ginny on the edge of my swivel chair. From time to time one of us jumped up, paced around, made an inane remark, and slumped back down. The air was fogged with smoke from ashtray-overflowing cigarettes. My skull felt scooped out. Her eyes had retreated far back into her head. Sunlight, grass, trees were unreal in the windows.

"You really ought to eat," I said for the -?-th time. "Keep your strength."

"Same to you," she answered, not looking at me or at anything I could tell.

"I'm not hungry."

"Nor I."

We returned to the horror.

The extension phone yanked us erect. "A call from Dr. Ashman," it said. "Do you wish to answer?"

"For God's sake yes!" ripped from me. "Visual." The sympathetic connection was made.

Ashman's face looked well-nigh as exhausted as Ginny's. "We have the report," he said.

I tried to respond and couldn't.

"You were right," he went on. "It's a homunculus."

"What took you so long?" Ginny asked. Her voice wasn't husky any more, just hoarse and harsh.

"Unprecedented case," Ashman said. "Fairy changelings have always been considered a legend. Nothing in our data suggests any motive for nonhuman intelligences to steal a child…nor any method by which they could if they wanted to, assuming the parents take normal care…and certainly no reason for such hypothetical kidnappers to leave a sort of golem in its place." He sighed. "Apparently we know less than we believed."

"What are your findings?" The restored determination in Ginny's words brought my gaze to her.

"The police chirurgeon, the crime lab staff, and later a pathologist from the University hospital worked with me," Ashman told us. "Or I with them. I was merely the family doctor. We lost hours on the assumption Valerie was bewitched. The simulacrum is excellent, understand. It's mindless—the EEG is practically flat—but it resembles your daughter down to fingerprints. Not till she…it…had failed to respond to every therapeutic spell we commanded between us, did we think the body might be an imitation. You told us so at the outset, Steve, but we discounted that as hysteria. I'm sorry. Proof required a whole battery of tests. For instance, the saline content and PBI suggest the makers of the homunculus had no access to oceans. We clinched the matter when we injected some radioactivated holy water; that metabolism is not remotely human."

His dry tone was valuable. The horror began to have some shadowy outline; my brain creaked into motion, searching for ways to grapple with it. "What'll they do with the changeling?" I asked.

"I suppose the authorities will keep it in the hope of—of learning something, doing something through it," Ashman said. "In the end, if nothing else happens, it'll doubtless be institutionalized. Don't hate the poor thing. That's all it is, manufactured for some evil reason but not to blame."

"Not to waste time on, you mean," Ginny rasped. "Doctor, have you any ideas about rescuing Val?"

"No. It hurts me." He looked it. "I'm only a medicine man, though. What further can I do? Tell me and I'll come flying."

"You can start right away," Ginny said. "You've heard, haven't you, my familiar was critically wounded defending her? He's at the vet's, but I want you to take over."

Ashman was startled. "What?"

"Look, Svartalf will get well. But vets don't have the expensive training and equipment used on people. I want him rammed back to health overnight. What runes and potions you don't have, you'll know how to obtain. Money's no object."

"Wait," I started to say, recalling what leechcraft costs are like.

She cut me off short. "Nornwell will foot the bill, unless a government agency does. They'd better. This isn't like anything else they've encountered. Could be a major emergency shaping up." She stood straight. Despite the sooted eyes, hair hanging lank, unchanged black garb of last night, she was once more Captain Graylock of the 14th United States Cavalry. "I am not being silly, Doctor. Consider the implications of your discoveries. Svartalf may or may not able to convey a little information to me about what he encountered. He certainly can't when he's unconscious. At the least, he's always been a good helper, and we need whatever help we can get."

Ashman reflected a minute. "All right," he said.

He was about to sign off when the study door opened. "Hold it," a voice ordered. I turned on my heel, jerkily, uselessly fast.

The hard brown face and hard, rangy frame of Robert Shining Knife confronted me. The head of the local FBI office had discarded the conservative business suit of his organization for working clothes. His feather bonnet seemed to brush the ceiling; a gourd stuck into his breechclout rattled dryly to his steps, the blanket around his shoulders and the paint on his skin were patterned in thunderbirds, sun discs, and I know not what else.

"You listened in," I accused.

He nodded. "Couldn't take chances, Mr. Matuchek. Dr. Ashman, you'll observe absolute secrecy. No running off to any blabbermouth shaman or goodwife you think should be brought in consultation.'

Ginny blazed up. "See here—"

"Your cat'll be repaired for you," Shining Knife promised in the same blunt tone. "I doubt he'll prove of assistance, but we can't pass by the smallest possibility. Uncle Sam will pick up the tab and Dr. Ashman may as well head the team. But I want to clear it with the other members, and make damn sure they aren't told more than necessary. Wait in your office, Doctor. An operative will join you inside an hour."

The physician bristled. "And how long will he then take to certify that each specialist I may propose is an All-American Boy?"

"Very little time. You'll be surprised how much he'll know about them already. You'd also be surprised how much trouble someone would have who stood on his rights to tell the press or even his friends what's been going on." Shining Knife smiled sardonically. "I'm certain that's a superfluous warning, sir. You're a man of patriotism and discretion. Good-bye."

The phone understood him and broke the spell.

"Mind if I close the windows?" Shining Knife asked as he did. "Eavesdroppers have sophisticated gadgets these days." He had left the door ajar; we heard his men move around in the house, caught faint pungencies and mutterings. "Please sit down." He leaned back against a bookshelf and watched us.

Ginny controlled herself with an effort I could feel. "Aren't you acting rather high-handed?"

"The circumstances require it, Mrs. Matuchek," he said.

She bit her lip and nodded.

"What's this about?" I begged.

The hardness departed from Shining Knife. "We're confirming what your wife evidently suspects," he said with a compassion that made me wonder if he had a daughter of his own. "She's a witch and would know, but wouldn't care to admit it till every hope of a less terrible answer was gone. This is no ordinary kidnapping."

"Well, of course—!"

"Wait. I doubt if it's technically any kind of kidnapping. My bureau may have no jurisdiction. However, as your wife said, the case may well involve the national security. I'll have to communicate with Washington and let them decide. In the last analysis, the President will. Meanwhile, we don't dare rock the boat."

I looked from him to Ginny to the horror that was again without form, not a thing to be fought but a condition of nightmare. "Please," I whispered.

Shining Knife spoke flatly and fast:

"We've ascertained the blood is entirely the cat's. There are some faint indications of ichor, chemical stains which may have been caused by it, but none of the stuff itself. We got better clues from scratches and gouges in floor and furnishings. Those marks weren't left by anything we can identify, natural or paranatural; and believe me, our gang is good at identifications."

"The biggest fact is that the house was never entered. Not any way we can check for—and, again, we know a lot of different ones. Nothing was broken, forced, or picked. Nothing had affected the guardian signs and objects; their fields were at full strength, properly meshed and aligned, completely undisturbed. Therefore nothing flew down the chimney, or oozed through a crack, or dematerialized past the walls, or compelled the babysitter to let it in.

"The fact that no one in the neighborhood was alerted is equally significant. Remember how common hex alarms and second-sighted watchdogs are. Something paranatural and hostile in the street would've touched off a racket to wake everybody for three blocks around. Instead, we've only got the Delacortes next door, who heard what they thought was a catfight."

He paused. "Sure," he finished, "we don't know everything about goetics. But we do know enough about its felonious uses to be sure this was no forced entry."

"What, then?" I cried.

Ginny said it for him: "It came in from the hell universe."

"Theoretically, could have been an entity from Heaven." Shining Knife's grin was brief and stiff. "But that's psychologically—spiritually—impossible. The M.O. is diabolic."

Ginny sat forward. Her features were emptied of expression, her chin rested on a fist, her eyes were half shut, the other hand drooped loosely over a knee. She murmured as if in a dream:

"The changeling fits your theory quite well, doesn't it? To the best of our knowledge, matter can't be transferred from one space-time plenum to another in violation of the conservation laws of physics. Psychic influences can go, yes. Visions, temptations, inspirations, that sort of thing. The uncertainty principle allows them. But not an actual object. If you want to take it from its proper universe to your own, you have to replace it with an identical amount of matter, whose configuration has to be fairly similar to preserve momentum. You may remember Villegas suggested this was the reason angels take more or less anthropomorphic shapes on earth."

Shining Knife looked uneasy. "This is no time to be unfriends with the Most High," he muttered.

"I've no such intention," Ginny said in her sleep-walker's tone. "He can do all things. But His servants are finite. They must often find it easier to let transferred matter fall into the shape it naturally wants to, rather than solve a problem involving the velocities of ten to the umpteenth atoms in order to give it another form. And the inhabitants of the Low Continuum probably can't. They aren't creative. Or so the Petrine churches claim. I understand the Johannine doctrine includes Manichaean elements.

"A demon could go from his universe to a point in ours that was inside this house. Because his own natural form is chaotic, he wouldn't have to countertransfer anything but dirt, dust, trash, rubbish, stuff in a high-entropy condition. After he finished his task, he'd presumably return that material in the course of returning himself. It'd presumably show effects. I know things got generally upset in the fight, Mr. Shining Knife, but you might run a lab check on what was in the garbage can, the catbox, and so forth."

The FBI man bowed. "We thought of that, and noticed its homogenized condition," he said. "If *you* could think of it, under these circumstances—"

Her eyes opened fully. Her speech became like slowly drawn steel: "Our daughter is in hell, sir. We mean to get her back."

I thought of Valeria, alone amidst cruelty and clamor and unnamable distortions, screaming for a Daddy and a Mother who did not come. I sat there on the day bed, in the night which has no ending, and heard my lady speak as if she were across a light-years-wide abyss:

"Let's not waste time on emotions. I'll continue outlining the event as I reconstruct it; check me out. The demon—could have been more than one, but I'll assume a singleton—entered our cosmos as a scattered mass of material but pulled it together at once. By simple transformation, he assumed the shape he wanted. The fact that neither the Adversary nor any of his minions can create—if the Petrine tradition is correct—wouldn't handicap him. He could borrow any existing shape. The fact that you can't identify it means nothing. It could be a creature of some obscure human mythology, or some imaginative drawing somewhere, or even another planet.

"This is not a devout household. It'd be hypocrisy, and therefore useless, for us to keep religious symbols around that we don't love. Besides, in spite of previous experience with a demon or two, we didn't expect one to invade a middle-class suburban home. No authenticated case of that was on record. So the final possible barrier to his appearance was absent.

"He had only a few pounds of mass available to him. Any human who kept his or her head could have coped with him—if nothing else, kept him on the run, too busy to do his dirty work, while phoning for an exorcist. But on this one night, no human was here. Svartalf can't talk, and he obviously never got the chance to call in help by different means. He may have outweighed the demon, but not by enough to prevail against a thing all teeth, claws, spines, and armor plate. In the end, when Svartalf lay beaten, the demon took our Val to the Low Continuum. The counter-transferred mass was necessarily in her form.

"Am I right?"

Shining Knife nodded. "I expect you are."

"What do you plan to do about it?"

"Frankly, at the moment there's little or nothing we can do. We haven't so much as a clue to motive."

"You've been told about last night. We made bad enemies. I'd say the Johnny cathedral is the place to start investigating."

Behind his mask of paint, Shining Knife registered unhappiness. "I explained to you before, Mrs. Matuchek, when we first inquired who might be responsible, that's an extremely serious charge to make on no genuine evidence. The public situation is delicately balanced. Who realizes that better than you? We can't afford fresh riots. Besides, more to the point, this invasion could be the start of something far bigger, far worse than a kidnapping."

I stirred. "Nothing's worse," I mumbled.

He ignored me, sensing that at present Ginny was more formidable.

"We know practically zero about the hell universe. I'll stretch a point of security, because I suspect you've figured the truth out already on the basis of unclassified information; quite a few civilian wizards have. The Army's made several attempts to probe it, with no better success than the Faustus Institute had thirty years ago. Men returned in states of acute psychic shock, after mere minutes there, unable to describe what'd happened. Instruments recorded data that didn't make sense."

"Unless you adopt Nickelsohn's hypothesis," she said.

"What's it?"

"That space-time in that cosmos is non-Euclidean, violently so compared to ours, and the geometry changes from place to place."

"Well, yes, I'm told the Army researchers did decide—" He saw the triumph in her eyes. "Damn! What a neat trap you set for me!" With renewed starkness: "Okay. You'll understand we dare not go blundering around when forces we can't calculate are involved for reasons we can scarcely guess. The consequences could be disastrous. I'm going to report straight to the Director, who I'm sure will report straight to the President, who I'm equally sure will have us keep alert but sit tight till we've learned more."

"What about Steve and me?"

"You too. You might get contacted, remember."

"I doubt it. What ransom could a demon want?"

"The demon's master—"

"I told you to check on the Johnnies."

"We will. We'll check on everything in sight, reasonable or not. But it'll take time."

"Meanwhile Valeria is in hell. We want a chance to go after our daughter."

My heart sprang. The numbness tingled out of me. I rose.

Shining Knife braced himself. "I can't permit that. Sure, you've both accomplished remarkable things in the past, but the stakes are too high now for amateurs to play. Hate me all you want. If it's any consolation, that'll pain me. But I can't let you jeopardize yourselves and the public interest. You'll stay put. Under guard."

"You—" I nearly jumped him. Ginny drew me back.

"Hold on, Steve," she said crisply. "Don't make trouble. What we'll do, you and I, if it won't interfere with the investigation, is choke down some food and a sleeping potion and cork off till we're fit to think again."

Shining Knife smiled. "Thanks," he said. "I was certain you'd be sensible. I'll go hurry 'em along in the kitchen so you can get that meal soon."

I closed the door behind him. Rage shivered me. "What the blue deuce is this farce?" I stormed. "If he thinks we'll sit and wait on a gaggle of bureaucrats—"

"Whoa." She pulled my ear down to her lips. "What he thinks," she whispered, "is that his wretched guard will make any particular difference to us."

"Oh-ho!" For the first time I laughed. It wasn't a merry or musical noise, but it was a laugh of sorts.

We weren't exactly under house arrest. The well-behaved young man who stayed with us was to give us what protection and assistance we might need. He made it clear, though, that if we tried to leave home or pass word outside, he'd suddenly and regretfully discover reason to hold us for investigation of conspiracy to overthrow the Interstate Commerce Commission.

He was a good warlock, too. An FBI agent must have a degree in either sorcery or accounting; and his boss wanted to be sure we didn't try anything desperate. But at supper Ginny magicked out of him the information she required. How she did that, I'll never understand. I don't mean she cast a spell in the technical sense. Rather, the charm she employed is the kind against which the only male protection is defective glands. What still seems impossible to me is that she could sit talking, smiling, flashing sparks of wit a across a surface of controlled feminine sorrow, and leading him on to relate his past exploits…when each corner of the place screamed that Valeria was gone.

We retired early, pleading exhaustion. Actually we were well rested and wiretaut. "He's sharp on thaumaturgy," my sweetheart murmured in the darkness of our bedroom, "but out of practice on mantics. A smoothly wrought Seeming ought to sucker him. Use the cape."

I saw her intent. A cold joy, after these past hours in chains, beat through me. I scrambled out of my regular clothes, into my wolf suit, and put the civvies back on top. As I reached for the tarnkappe—unused for years, little more than a war souvenir—she came to me and pressed herself close. "Darling, be careful!" Her voice was not steady and I tasted salt on her lips.

She had to stay, allaying possible suspicion, ready to take the ransom demand that *might* come. Hers was the hard part.

I donned the cloak. The hood smelled musty across my face, and small patches of visibility showed where moths had gotten at the fabric. But what the nuts, it was merely to escape and later (we hoped) return here in. There are too many counter-agents these days for tarnkappen to be effective for serious work, ranging from infrared detectors to spray cans of paint triggered by an unwary foot. Our friendly Fed no doubt had instruments ready to buzz him if an invisibilizing field moved in his vicinity.

Ginny went into her passes, *sotto voce* incantations, and the rest. She'd brought what was necessary into this room during the day. Her excuse was that she wanted to give us both as strong a protection against hostile influences as she was able. She'd done it, too, with the FBI man's admiring approval. In particular, while the spell lasted, I'd be nearly impossible to locate by paranatural means alone.

The next stage of her scheme was equally straightforward. While terrestrial magnetism is too weak to cancel paranatural forces, it does of course affect them, and so do its fluctuations. Therefore ordinary goetic sensor devices aren't designed to register minor quantitative changes. Ginny would establish a Seeming. The feeble tarnkappe field would appear gradually to double in intensity, then, as I departed, oscillate back to its former value. On my return, she'd phase out the deception.

Simple in theory. In practice it took greater skill to pull off without triggering an alarm than her record showed she could possess. What the poor old FBI didn't know was that she had what went beyond training and equipment, she had a Gift.

At her signal, I slipped through the window. The night air was chill and moist; dew glistened on the lawn in the goblin glow of street lamps; I heard a dog howl. It had probably caught a whiff of my cloak. And no doubt the grounds were under surveillance…yes, my witch-sight picked out a man in the shadows beneath the elms across the way…I padded fast and softly down the middle of the pavement, where I'd be least likely to affect some watchbeast or sentry field. When it comes to that sort business, I'm pretty good myself.

After several blocks, safely distant, I reached the local grade school and stowed my tarnkappe in a playground trash can. Thereafter I walked openly, an unremarkable citizen on his lawful occasions. At the first phone booth I called Barney Sturlason's home. He said to come right on over. Rather than a taxi, I took a crosstown carpet, reasoning I'd be more anonymous as one of a crowd of passengers. I was.

Barney opened the door. Hallway light that got past his shoulders spilled yellow across me. He let out a soft whistle. "I figured you'd be too bushed to work today, Steve, but not that you'd look like Monday after Ragnarok. What's wrong?"

"Your family mustn't hear," I said.

He turned immediately and led me to his study. Waving me to one of the leather armchairs, he relocked the door, poured two hefty Scotches, and settled down opposite me. "Okay," he invited.

I told him. Never before had I seen anguish on those features. "Oh no," he whispered.

Shaking himself, like a bear making ready to charge, he asked: "What can I do?"

"First off, lend me a broom," I answered.

"Hold on," he said. "I do feel you've been rash already. Tell me your next move."

"I'm going to Siloam and learn what I can."

"I thought so." The chair screaked under Barney's shifting weight. "Steve, it won't wash. Burgling the Johnny cathedral, maybe trying to beat an admission out of some priest—No. You'd only make trouble for yourself and Ginny at a time when she needs every bit of your resources. The FBI will investigate, with professionals. You could wreck the very clues you're after, assuming they exist. Face it, you are jumping to conclusions." He considered me. "A moral point in addition. You didn't agree that mob yesterday had the right to make its own laws. Are you claiming the right for yourself?"

I took a sip and let the whisky burn its loving way down my gullet. "Ginny and I've had a while to think," I said. "We expected you'd raise the objections you do. Let me take them in order. I don't want to sound dramatic, but how can we be in worse trouble? Add anything to infinity and, and, and"—I must stop for another belt of booze—"you've got the same infinity.

"About the FBI being more capable. We don't aim to bull around just to be doing something; give us credit for some brains. Sure, the Bureau must've had agents in the Johannine Church for a long while, dossiers on its leaders, the standard stuff. But you'll remember how at the HUAC hearings a few years back, no evidence could be produced to warrant putting the Church on the Attorney General's list, in spite of its disavowal of American traditions."

"The Johnnies are entitled to their opinions," Barney said. "Shucks, I'll agree with certain claims of theirs. This society has gotten too worldly, too busy chasing dollars and fun, too preoccupied with sex and not enough with love, too callous about the unfortunate—"

"Barney," I snapped, "you're trying to sidetrack me and cool me off, but it's no go. Either I get your help soon or I take my marbles elsewhere."

He sighed, fumbled a pipe from his tweed jacket and began stuffing it. "Okay, continue. If the Feds can't find proof that the Johannine hierarchy is engaged in activities illegal or subversive, does that prove the hierarchy is diabolically clever...or simply innocent?"

"Well, the Gnostics brag of having information and powers that nobody else does," I said, "and they do get involved one way or another in more and more of the social unrest going on—and mainly, who else, what else might be connected with this thing that's happened? Maybe even unwittingly; that's imaginable; but connected."

I leaned forward. "Look, Barney," I went on, "Shining Knife admits he'll have to move slow. And Washington's bound to keep him on a tighter leash than he wants personally. Tomorrow, no doubt, he'll have agents interviewing various Johnnies. In the nature of the case, they'll learn nothing. You'd need mighty strong presumptive evidence to get a search warrant against a church, especially one that so many people are convinced bears the final Word of God, and most especially when the temple's a labyrinth of places that none but initiates in the various degrees are supposed to enter."

"What could you learn?" Barney replied.

"Perhaps nothing either," I said. "But I mean to act now, not a week from now; and I won't be handicapped by legal rules and public opinion; and I do have special abilities and experience in dark matters; and they won't expect me, and in short, if anything's there to find, I've the best chance in sight of finding it."

He scowled past me.

"As for the moral issue," I said, "you may be right. On the other hand, I'm not about to commit brutalities like some imaginary Special Agent Vee Eye Eye. And in spite of Shining Knife's fear, I honestly don't see what could provoke a major invasion from the Low World. That'd bring in the Highest, and the Adversary can't afford such a confrontation.

"Which is worse, Barney, an invasion of property and privacy, maybe a profanation of a few shrines...or a child in hell?"

He thunked his glass down on an end table. "You win!" exploded from him.

We rose together. "How about a weapon?" he offered.

I shook my head. "Let's not compound the felony. Whatever I meet, probably a gun won't handle." It seemed needless to add that I carried a hunting knife under my civvies and, in wolf-shape, a whole mouthful of armament.

"I suggest you take the Plymouth," he said "It's not as fast as either sports job, but the spell runs quieter and the besom was tuned only the other day." He stood for a bit, thinking. Stillness and blackness pressed on the windowpanes. "Meanwhile I'll start research on the matter. Bill Hardy...Janice Wenzel from our library staff...hm, we could co-opt your Dr. Ashman, and how about Prof Griswold from the University?...and more, able close-mouthed people, who'll be glad to help and hang any consequences. If nothing else, we can assemble all unclassified data regarding the Low Continuum, and maybe some that aren't. We can set up equations delimiting various conceivable approaches to the rescue problem, and crank 'em through the computator, and eliminate unworkable ideas. Yeah, I'll get busy right off."

What can you say to a guy like that except thanks?

It seemed in character for the Johannine Church to put its cathedral for the whole Upper Midwest not in Chicago, Milwaukee, or any other city, but off alone, a hundred miles even from our modest town. The location symbolized and emphasized the Gnostic rejection of this world as evil, the idea of salvation through secret rites and occult knowledge. Unlike Petrine Christianity, this kind didn't come to you; aside from dismal little chapels here and there, scarcely more than recruiting stations, you came to it.

Obvious, yes. And therefore, I thought, probably false. Nothing about Gnosticism was ever quite what it seemed. That lay in its very nature.

Perhaps its enigmas, veils behind veils and mazes within mazes, were one thing that drew so many people these days. The regular churches made their theologies plain. They clearly described and delimited the mysteries as such, with the commonsense remark that we mortals aren't able to understand every aspect of the Highest. They declared that this world was given us by the Creator, and hence must be fundamentally good. Was that overly unromantic? Did the Johannines appeal to the daydream, childish but always alive in us, of becoming omnipotent by learning a secret denied the common herd? No doubt that was partially true. But the more I thought, the less it felt like the whole explanation.

I had plenty of time and chance and need for thought, flitting above the night land, where scattered lights of farms and villages looked nearly as remote as the stars overhead and the air slid cold around me. Grimly, as I traveled, I set myself to review what I could about the Johannine Church, from the ground up.

Was it merely a nut cult of the past two or three generations? Or was it in truth as old as it maintained—founded by Christ himself?

The other churches said no. Doubtless Catholic, Orthodox, and Protestant should not be lumped together as Petrine. But the popular word made a rough kind of sense. They did have a mutual interpretation of Jesus' charge to his apostles. They agreed on the special importance of Peter. No matter what differences had arisen since, including the question of apostolic succession, they all derived from the Twelve in a perfectly straightforward way.

And yet...and yet...there is that strange passage at the close of the Gospel According to St. John. "If I will that he tarry till I come, what is that to thee?" Certainly it gave rise to a fugitive tradition that here Our Lord was creating something more than any of them but John ever knew—some unproclaimed other Church, within or parallel to the Church of Peter, which would at the end manifest itself and guide man to a new dispensation.

The association of such a claim with other-worldliness was almost inevitable. Under many labels, Gnosticism has been a recurring heresy. The original form, or rather forms, were an attempt to fuse Christianity with a mishmash of Oriental mystery cults, Neoplatonism, and sorcery. Legend traced it back to the Simon Magus who appears in the eighth chapter of Acts. Modern Johanninism was doubly bold in reviving that dawn-age movement by name, in proclaiming it not error but a higher truth and Simon Magus not a corrupter but a prophet.

So you've got communities of ascetics, ecstatics and mysteries. They drew pilgrims, who needed housing, food, services. The priests, priestesses, acolytes, and lay associates did too. A temple—more accurate than "cathedral," but the Johnnies insisted on the latter word to emphasize that they were Christians—grew up, and often a community around it—like Siloam, where I was headed.

Simple. Banal. Why did I rehearse it? Merely to escape thinking about Valeria?—No. To get as much as possible straight in my head, when most was tangled and ghostly.

The Something Else, the Thing Beyond…was it no illusion, but a deeper insight? And if so, an insight into what? I recalled the Johannines' intolerance and troublemaking. I recalled the frank assertion that their adepts held powers no one else imagined, and that more was revealed to them every year. I recalled stories told by certain apostates, who hadn't advanced far in their degrees when they experienced that which scared them off: nothing illegal, immoral, or otherwise titillating; merely ugly, hateful, sorrowful, and hence not very newsworthy; deniable or ignorable by those who didn't want to believe them. I recalled the Gnostic theology, what part of it was made public: terrible amidst every twist of revelation and logic, the identification of their Demiurge with the God of the Old Testament with Satan.

I thought of Antichrist.

But there I shied off, being agnostic about such matters, as I've said. I took my stand on the simple feeling that it didn't make sense that the Almighty would operate in any such fashion.

Light glimmered into view, far off across the prairie. I was glad of journey's end, no matter what happened next. I didn't care to ride further with those reflections of mine.

Siloam was ordinary frame houses in ordinary yards along ordinary streets. A sign beneath the main airlane, as you neared, said Pop. 5240; another announced that the Lions Club met every Thursday at the Kobold Kettle Restaurant. There were a couple of small manufacturing enterprises, a city hall, an elementary school, a high school, a firehouse, a bedraggled park, a hotel, more service stations than needed. The business district held stores, a cafe or two, a bank, chirurgeon's and dentist's offices above a Rexall apothecary…the American works.

That homeliness made the rest freezingly alien. Though the hour lacked of midnight, downtown was a tomb. The residential streets were nearly as deserted—nobody out for a stroll, no teenagers holding hands, scarcely a stick or a wagon moving, beneath the rare lamps—once in a while a robed and hooded figure slowly pacing. Each home lay drawn into itself, behind drawn shades. Where the inhabitants weren't asleep, they were probably not watching crystal or playing cards or having a drink or making love, they were most likely at the devotions and studies they hoped would qualify them for a higher religious degree, more knowledge and power and surety of salvation.

And everything centered on the cathedral. It soared above the complex of box-like ancillary buildings that surrounded it, above town and plain. The pictures I'd seen of it had not conveyed the enormity. Those flat, bone-white walls went up and up and up, till the roof climbed farther yet to make the vast central cupola. From afar, the windows looked like nailheads, one row to a story; but then I saw the stained glass pair, each filling half the facade it occupied with murky colors and bewildering patterns, Mandala at the west end and Eye of God at the east.

From the west, also, rose the single tower, which in a photograph only looked austere, but now became one leap into the stars.

Light played across the outside of the cathedral and shone dimly from its glass. I heard a chant, men's voices marching deep beneath the wild icy sweepings and soarings of women who sang on no scale I could identify, in no language of earth.

> —*Helfioth Alaritha arbar Neniotho Melitho Tarasunt*
> *Chanados Umia Theirura Marada Seliso*—

The music was so amplified as to be audible to the very outskirts of town. And it never ended. This was a perpetual choir. Priests, acolytes, pilgrims were always on hand to step in when any of the six hundred and one wearied. I failed to imagine how it must be to live in that day-and-night haze of canticle. If you were a dweller in Siloam, you'd soon stop noticing on a conscious level. But wouldn't the sound weave into your thoughts, dreams, bones, finally into your soul?

And yet the attendant at the gate was a pleasant young man, his tow hair and blue eyes right out of the folk who'd been hereabouts for more than a hundred years, his friendliness out of Walt Whitman's own America. Although I was obviously a heathen by his lights, he didn't seem to think I was damned. Probably he wasn't a lay brother, just an employee, one of the decent majority you find in all organizations, all countries. He greeted me cordially and remarked on the lateness of my visit. I explained I was traveling in ankhs, had gotten hung up and must start again early tomorrow, but wanted to hear the choir. He showed me where to leave my stick on the parking lot, gave me a leaflet, and waved me in.

The auxiliary buildings formed a square around a paved yard centered on the cathedral. Walls had been raised between them, making the only entrances three portals closable by wire gates. The offices, storerooms, living quarters were plain, in fact drab. A few cenobites moved about, male scarcely distinguishable from female in their robes and overshadowing cowls. I remembered the complete absence of any scandals, anywhere in the world, though the Johannines mingled the sexes in celibacy. Well, of course their monks and nuns weren't simply consecrated; they were initiates. They had gone beyond baptism, beyond the elementary mystery rites and name-changing (with the old public name retained for secular use) that corresponded to a Petrine confirmation. For years they had mortified the flesh, disciplined the soul, bent the mind to mastering what their holy books called divine revelation, and unbelievers called pretentious nonsense, and some believers in a different faith called unrecognized diabolism...

Blast it, I thought, I've got to concentrate on my job. Never mind those silent sad figures rustling past. Ignore, if you can, the overwhelmingness of the cathedral you are nearing and the chant that now swells from it to fill the whole night. Deny that your werewolf heritage senses things it fears to a degree that is making you ill. Sweat prickles forth on your skin, runs cold down your ribs and reeks in your nostrils. You see the world through a haze of dream and relentless music. But Valeria is in hell.

I stopped where the vague, shifty light was and read the leaflet. It bade me a courteous welcome and listed the regulations for tourists. On the flip side was a floor plan of the basilica section of the main building. The rest was left blank. Everybody realized that an abundance of rooms existed on the levels of the north and south sides, the tower, and even the cupola. It was no secret that great crypts lay beneath. They were used for certain ceremonies—parts of them, anyhow. Beyond this information: nothing. The higher in degree you advanced, the more you were shown. Only adepts might enter the final sanctums, and only they knew what went on there.

I mounted the cathedral steps. A couple of husky monks stood on either side of the immense, open door. They didn't move, but their eyes frisked me. The vestibule was long, low-ceilinged, whitewashed, bare except for a holy water font. Here was no cheerful clutter of bulletin board, parish newsletter, crayon drawings from the Sunday school. A nun standing at the middle pointed me to a left entrance. Another one at that position looked from me to a box marked offerings and back until I had to stuff in a couple of dollars. It might have been funny except for the singing, the incense, the gazes, the awareness of impalpable forces which drew my belly muscles taut.

I entered an aisle and found myself alone in a roped-off section of pews, obviously for outsiders. It took me a minute to get over the impact of the stupendous interior and sit down. Then I spent several more minutes trying to comprehend it, and failing.

The effect went beyond size. When everything was undecorated, naked white geometry of walls and pillars and vaulting, you had nothing to scale by; you were in a cavern that reached endlessly on. God's Eye above the altar, Mandala above the choir loft, dominated a thick dusk. But they were unreal too, like candles glimmering from place to place. Proportions, curves, intersections, all helped create the illusion of illimitable labyrinthine spaces. Half a dozen worshipers, scattered along the edge of the nave, were lost. But so would any possible congregation be. This church was *meant* to diminish its people.

A priest stood at the altar with two attendants. I recognized them by their white robes as initiates. At their distance they were dwarfed nearly to nothing. Somehow the priest was not. In the midnight-blue drapery and white beard of an adept, he stood tall, arms outspread, and I feared him. Yet he wasn't moving, praying, anything…Smoke from the hanging censers drugged my lungs. The choir droned and shrilled above me. I had never felt more daunted.

Hauling my glance away, I forced myself to study the layout as if this were an enemy fortress to be penetrated: which it was, for me tonight, whether or not it bore any guilt for what had happened to my little girl. The thought of her started a rage brewing that soon got strong enough to serve for courage. My witch-sight didn't operate here; counterspells against such things must have been laid. Normal night vision was adapting, though, stretched to the same ultimate as every other faculty I had.

The noncommunicants' section was as far as could be from the altar, at the end of the extreme left side aisle. So on my right hand were pews reaching to the nave, on my left a passage along the north wall. The choir loft hung over me like a thundercloud. This isn't helping me figure out how to burgle the joint, I thought.

A monk went past me on soft-sandaled feet. Over his robe he wore a long surplice embroidered with cabalistic symbols. Halfway to the transept he halted before a many-branched sconce, lit a candle, and prostrated himself for minutes. Rising, bowing, and backing off seven steps, he returned in my direction.

From pictures, I recognized his outer garment as the one donned by choristers. Evidently he'd been spelled and, instead of taking straight off to shuck the uniform, had acquired a bit of merit first. When he had gone by, I twisted around to follow his course. The pews left some clear space at the rear end. The choral balcony threw it into such gloom that I could barely see the monk pass through a door in the corner nearest me.

The idea burst forth like a pistol from the holster. I sat outwardly still, inwardly crouched, and probed from side to side of the basilica. Nobody was paying attention to me. Probably I wasn't even visible to celebrants or worshipers; this placement was designed to minimize the obtrusiveness of infidels. My ears, which beneath the clamant song picked out the monk's footfalls, had detected no snick of key in lock. I could follow him.

Then what? I didn't know and didn't greatly care. If they nailed me at once, I'd be a Nosy Parker. They'd scold me and kick me out, and I'd try some different approach. If I got caught deeper in the building—well, that was the risk I'd come courting.

I waited another three hundred million microseconds, feeling each one. The monk needed ample time to get out of this area. During the interval I knelt, gradually hunching lower and lower until I'd sunk out of sight. It drew no stares or inquiries. Finally I was on all fours.

Now! I scuttled, not too fast, across to that shadowy corner. Risen, I looked behind me. The adept stood like a gaunt eidolon, the initiates handled the four sacred objects in complicated ways, the choir sang, a man signed himself and left via the south aisle. I waited till he had exited before gripping the doorknob. It felt odd. I turned it most slowly and drew the door open a crack. Nothing happened. Peering in, I saw dim blue lights.

I went through.

Beyond was an anteroom. A drapery separated it from a larger chamber, which was also deserted. That condition wouldn't last long. The second of the three curtained openings gave on a spiral staircase down which the hymn came pouring. The third led to a corridor. Most of the space was occupied by racks on which hung surplices. Obviously you borrowed one after receiving your instructions elsewhere, and proceeded to the choir loft. At the end of your period, you came back this way. Given six hundred and one singers, reliefs must show quite often. Maybe they weren't so frequent at night, when the personnel were mostly clergy with more training and endurance than eager-beaver laymen. But I'd best not stick around.

I unsnapped the sheath from my inner belt and stuffed my knife in a jacket pocket before stepping into the hall. Lined with doors for the length of the building, the corridor might have been occupied by any set of prosaic offices. Mostly they were closed, and the light overhead was turned low. A few panels glowed yellow. Passing by one, I heard a typewriter. Within the endless chant, that startled me as if it'd been the click of a skeleton's jaws.

My plans were vague. Presumably Marmiadon, the priest at the Nornwell demonstration, operated out of this centrum. He'd have returned and asked his brethren to get the stench off him. An elaborate spell, too expensive for the average person, would clean him up sooner than nature was able. At least, he was my only lead. Otherwise I could ransack this warren for a fruitless decade.

Where staircases ran up and down, a directory was posted on the wall. I'd expected that. A lot of civilians and outside clergy had business here. Marmiadon's office was listed as 413. Because an initiate in the fifth degree ranked fairly high—two more and he'd be a candidate for first-degree adept status—I'd assumed he was based in the cathedral rather than serving as a mere chaplain or missionary. But it occurred to me that I didn't know what his regular job was.

I took the steps quietly, by twos. At the third-floor landing, a locked wrought-iron gate barred further passage. Not surprising, I thought; I'm getting into officer country. It wasn't too big for an agile man to climb over. What I glimpsed of that hall looked no different from below, but my skin prickled at a strengthened sense of abnormal energies.

The fourth floor didn't try for any resemblances to Madison Avenue. Its corridor was brick, barrel-vaulted, lit by Grail-shaped oil lamps hung in chains from above, so that shadows flickered huge. The chant echoed from wall to wall. The atmosphere smelled of curious, acrid musks and smokes. Rooms must be large, for the pointed-arch doors stood well apart.

One door stood open between me and my goal. Incongruously bright light spilled forth. I halted and stared in slantwise at shelves upon shelves of books. Some few appeared ancient, but mostly they were modern—yes, that squat one must be the *Handbook of Alchemy and Metaphysics*, and yonder set the *Encyclopaedia Arcanorum*, and there was a bound file of *Mind*—well, scientists need reference libraries, and surely very strange research was conducted here. It was my hard luck that someone kept busy this late at night.

I glided to the jamb and risked a closer peek. One man sat alone. He was huge, bigger than Barney Sturlason, but old, old; hair and beard were gone, the face might have belonged to Rameses' mummy. An adept's robe swathed him. He had a book open on his table, but wasn't looking at it. Deep-sunken, his eyes stared before him while a hand walked across the pages. I realized he was blind. That book, though, was not in Braille.

The lights could be automatic, or for another worker in the stacks. I slipped on by.

Marmiadon's place lay several yards further. Beneath his name and rank, the brass plate read "Fourth Assistant Toller." Not a bell ringer, for God's sake, that runt…was he? The door was locked. I should be able to unscrew the latch or push out the hinge pins with my knife. Better wait till I was quite alone, however. Meanwhile I could snoop—

"What walks?"

I whipped about. The adept stood in the hall at the library entrance. He leaned on a pastoral staff; but his voice reverberated so terribly that I didn't believe he needed support. Dismay poured through me. I'd forgotten how strong a Magus he must be.

"Stranger, what are you?" the bass cry bayed.

I tried to wet my sandpapery lips. "Sir—your Enlightenment—"

The staff lifted to point at me. It bore a Johannine capital, the crook crossed by a tau. I knew it was more than a badge, it was a wand. "Menace encircles you," the adept called. "I felt you in my darkness. Declare yourself."

I reached for the knife in my pocket, the wereflash under my shirt. Forlorn things; but when my fingers closed on them, they became talismans. Will and reason woke again in me. I thought beneath the hammering:

It'd have been more luck than I could count on, not to get accosted. I meant to try and use the circumstance if it happened. Okay, it has. That's a scary old son of a bitch, but he's mortal. Whatever his powers are, they don't reach to seeing me as I see him, or he'd do so.

Nonetheless I must clear my throat a time or two before speaking, and the words rang odd in my ears. "I—I beg your Enlightenment's pardon. He took me by surprise. Would he please tell me…where Initiate Marmiadon is?"

The adept lowered his staff. Otherwise he didn't move. The dead eyes almost rested on me, unwavering: which was worse than if they actually had. "What have you with him to do?"

"I'm sorry, your Enlightenment. Secret and urgent. As your Enlightenment recognizes, I'm a, uh, rather unusual messenger. I can tell him I'm supposed to get together with Initiate Marmiadon in connection with the, uh, trouble at the Nornwell company. It turns out to be a lot more important than it looks."

"That I know, and knew from the hour when he came back. I summoned—I learned—enough. It is the falling stone that may loose an avalanche."

I had the eldritch feeling his words weren't for me but for someone else. And what was this about the affair worrying him also? I dared not stop to ponder. "Your Enlightenment will understand, then, why I'm in a hurry and why I can't break my oath of secrecy, even to him. If he'd let me know where Marmiadon's cell is—"

"The failed one sleeps not with his brothers. The anger of the Light-Bearer is upon him for his mismanagement, and he does penance alone. You may not seek him before he has been purified." An abrupt snap: "Answer me! Whence came you, what will you, how can it be that your presence shrills to me of danger?"

"I…I don't know either," I stammered.

"You are no consecrate—"

"Look, your Enlightenment, if you, if he would—Well, maybe there's been a misunderstanding. My, uh, superior ordered me to get in touch with Marmiadon. They said at the entrance I might find him here, and lent me a gate key." That unobtrusive sentence was the most glorious whopper I ever hope to tell. Consider its implications. Let them ramify. Extrapolate, extrapolate. Sit back in wonder. "I guess they were mistaken."

"Yes. The lower clerics have naturally not been told. However—" The Magus brooded.

"If your Enlightenment'd tell me where to go, who to see, I could stop bothering him."

Decision. "The night abbot's secretariat, Room 107. Ask for Initiate-Six Hesathouba. Of those on duty at the present hour, he alone has been given sufficient facts about the Matuchek case to advise you."

Matuchek case?

I mumbled my thanks and got away at just short of a run, feeling the sightless gaze between my shoulder blades the whole distance to the stairs. Before climbing back over the gate, I stopped to indulge in the shakes.

I knew I'd scant time for that. The adept might suffer from a touch of senility, but only a touch. He could well fret about me until he decided to set inquiries afoot, which might not end with a phone call to Brother Hesathouba. If I was to have any chance of learning something real, I must keep moving.

Where to, though in this Gormenghast house? How? What hope? I ought to admit my venture was sheer quixotry and slink home.

No! While the possibility remained, I'd go after the biggest windmills in sight. My mind got into gear. No doubt the heights as well as the depths of the cathedral were reserved for the ranking priests. But the ancient mystery religions had held their major rites underground. Weren't the crypts my best bet for locating Marmiadon?

I felt a grin jerk of itself across my face. They wouldn't lighten his ordeal by spelling the smell off him. Which was another reason to suppose he was tucked away below, out of nose range.

Human noses, that is.

I retraced my steps to the first level. From there I hastened downward. No one happened by. The night was far along; sorcerers might be at work, but few people else.

I descended past a couple of sublevels. In one I glimpsed a sister hand-scrubbing the hall floor. Duty? Expiation? Self-abasement? It was a lonely sight. She didn't spy me.

A ways beyond, I encountered another locked gate. On its far side the stairway steepened, concrete no longer but rough-hewn stone. I was down into bedrock. The wall was chilly and wet to touch, the air to breathe. Modern illumination fell behind. My sole lights were candles, set in iron sconces far apart. They guttered in the draft from below. My shadow flapped misshapen around them. Finally I could not hear the mass. And still the path led downward.

And downward, until after some part of eternity it ended.

I stepped onto the floor of a natural cave. Widely spaced flames picked stalactites and stalagmites out of dense, unrestful murk. Hands of Glory burned over the mouths of several tunnels leading away into the dark. Quickly I peeled off suit, socks, shoes, and hid behind a boulder. The knife I clipped back onto my elastic shorts. I turned the Polaroid lens on myself and pressed the switch.

Transformation seized me. I dropped to the ground as hands and feet became paws. For a minute bones, muscles, organs, nerves were fluid, then they reached their wolf shapes and firmed. Instead I held tight in my diminished cerebral cortex the purpose I had, to use animal senses and sinews for my human end.

The feeble illumination ceased being a handicap. Wolves don't depend on their eyes the way men do. Ears, feet, tongue, every hair on my body, before all else my nose, drank a flood of data. The cave was not now a hole to stumble in, it was a place that I understood.

And…yes, faint but unmistakable from one tunnel came a gust of unforgettable nastiness. I checked a hunter's yelp barely in time and trotted off in that direction.

The passage was lengthy, twisting, intersected by many others. Without my sense of smell for a guide, I'd soon have been lost. The lighting was from Hands, above the cells dug out of the rock at rare intervals. It was public knowledge that every candidate for primary initiation spent a day and night alone here, and the devout went back on occasion. Allegedly the soul benefited from undisturbed prayers and meditations. But I wasn't sure what extra influences crept in subliminally as well. Certain odors, at the edge of my lupine perception, raised the fur on my neck.

After a while they were drowned out by the one I was tracing. Wolves have stronger stomachs than people, but I began to gag. When finally I reached the source, I held my breath while looking in.

The dull blue glow from the fingers over the entrance picked out little more than highlights in the cubicle. Marmiadon was asleep on a straw pallet. He wore his robe for warmth; it was grubby as his skin. Otherwise he had some hardtack, a jerry can of water, a cup, a Johannine Bible, and a candle to read it by. He must only have been leaving his cell to visit an oubliette down the tunnel. Not that it would have made any large difference if he didn't. Phew!

I backed off and humanized. The effluvium didn't strike me too hard in that shape, especially after my restored reasoning powers took charge. No doubt Marmiadon wasn't even noticing it any more.

I entered his quarters, hunkered, and shook him. My free hand drew the knife. "Wake up, you."

He floundered to awareness, saw me, and gasped. I must have been a pretty grim sight, black-clothed where I wasn't nude and with no mercy in my face. He looked as bad, hollow-eyed in that corpse-light. Before he could yell, I clapped my palm over his mouth. The unshaved bristles felt scratchy, the flesh dough-like. "Be quiet," I said without emphasis, "or I'll cut your guts out."

He gestured agreement and I let go. "M-m-mister Matuchek," he whispered, huddling away from me till the wall stopped him.

I nodded. "Want to talk with you."

"I—How—In God's name, what about?"

"Getting my daughter home unharmed."

Marmiadon traced crosses and other symbols in the air. "Are you possessed?" He became able to look at me and answer his own question. "No. I could tell—"

"I'm not being puppeted by a demon," I grunted, "and I haven't got a psychosis. Talk."

"Bu—bu—but I haven't anything to say. Your daughter? What's wrong? I didn't know you had one."

That rocked me back. He wasn't lying, not in his state. "Huh?" I could only say. He grew a trifle calmer, fumbled around after his glasses and put them on, settled down on the pallet and watched me.

"It's holy truth," he insisted. "Why should I have information about your family? Why should anyone here?"

"Because you've appointed yourselves my enemies," I said in renewed rage.

He shook his head. "We're no man's foe. How can we be? We hold to the Gospel of Love." I sneered. His glance dropped from mine. "Well," he faltered, "we're sons of Adam. We can sin like everybody else. I admit I was furious when you pulled that…that trick on us…on those innocents—"

My blade gleamed through an arc. "Stow the crap, Marmiadon. The solitary innocent in this whole miserable business is a three-year-old girl, and she's been snatched into hell."

His mouth fell wide. His eyes frogged.

"Start blabbing," I said.

For a while he couldn't get words out. Then, in complete horror: "No. Impossible. I would never, never—"

"How about your fellow priests? Which of them?"

"None. I swear it. Can't be." I pricked his throat with the knife point. He shuddered. "Please. Let me know what happened. Let me help."

I lowered the blade, shifted to a sitting position, rubbed my brow, and scowled. This wasn't according, to formula. "See here," I accused him, "you did your best to disrupt my livelihood. When my life itself is busted apart, what am I supposed to think? If you're not responsible, you'd better give me a lot of convincing."

The initiate gulped. "I…yes, surely. I meant no harm. What you were doing, arc doing—it's sinful. You're damning yourselves and aiding others to do likewise. The Church can't stand idle. More of its ministers volunteer to help than don't."

"Skip the sermon," I ordered. Apart from everything else, I didn't want him working up enough to stop being dominated by me. "Stick to events. You were sent to abet that mob."

"No. Not—well, I was on the list of volunteers. When this occasion arose, I was the one allowed to go. But not to…do what you say…instead to give aid, counsel, spiritual guidance—and, well, yes, defend against possible spells—Nothing else! You were the ones who attacked."

"Sure, sure. We began by picketing, and when that didn't work we started on trespass, vandalism, blockade, terrorizing—uh-huh. And you were so strictly acting as a private citizen that when you failed, your superiors comforted you and you're back at your regular work already."

"My penance is for the sin of anger," he said.

A tiny thrill ran along my spine. We'd reached a significant item. "You aren't down here simply because you got irritated with us," I said. "What'd you actually do?'

Fear seized him afresh. He raised strengthless hands. "Please. I can't have—No." I brought my knife close again. He shut his eyes and said fast: "In my wrath when you were so obdurate, I laid a curse on your group. The Curse of Mabon. My reverend superiors—I don't know how they knew what I'd done, but adepts have abilities—When I returned here, I was taxed with my sin. They told me the consequences could be grave. No more. I wasn't told there…there'd been any. Were there really?"

"Depends," I said. "What is this curse?"

"No spell. You do understand the distinction, don't you? A spell brings paranatural forces to—to bear, by using the laws of goetics. Or it summons nonhuman beings or—It's the same principle as using a gun, any tool, or whistling up a dog, Mr. Matuchek. A prayer is different. It's an appeal to the Highest or His cohorts. A curse is nothing except a formula for asking Them to, well, punish somebody. They do it if They see fit—it's Them alone—"

"Recite it."

"*Absit omen!* The danger!"

"You just got through saying it's harmless in itself."

"Don't you know? Johannine prayers are different from Petrine. We're the new dispensation, we've been given special knowledge and divine favor, the words we use have a potency of their own. I can't tell what would happen if I said them, even without intent, under uncontrolled conditions like these."

That was very possibly right, I thought. The essence of Gnosticism in the ancient world had been a search for power through hidden knowledge, ultimately power, over God Himself. Doubtless Marmiadon was sincere in denying his church had revived that particular concept. But he hadn't progressed to adept status; the final secrets had not been revealed to him. I thought reluctantly, that he wasn't likely to make it, either, being at heart not a bad little guy.

My mind leaped forward. Let's carry on that idea, I thought in the space of half a second. Let's assume the founders of modern Gnosticism did make some discoveries that gave them capabilities not known before, results that convinced them they were exerting direct influence on the Divine. Let's further suppose they were mistaken—deceived—because, hang it, the notion that mortals can budge Omnipotence is unreasonable. What conclusion does this lead us to? This: that whether they know it or not, the blessings and curses of the Johannines are in fact not prayers, but peculiarly subtle and powerful spells.

"I can show you the text," Marmiadon chattered, "you can read for yourself. It's not among the forbidden chapters."

"Okay," I agreed.

He lit his candle and opened the book. I'd glanced at Johannine Bibles but never gotten up the steam to get through one. They replaced the Old Testament with something that even a gentile like me considered blasphemous, and followed the standard parts of the New with a lot of the Apocrypha, plus other stuff whose source never has been identified by reputable scholars. Marmiadon's shaky finger touched a passage in that last section. I squinted, trying to make out the fine print. The Greek was paralleled with an English translation, and itself purported to render the meaning of a string of words like those in the canticles upstairs.

Holy, holy, holy. In the name of the seven thunders. O Mabon of righteousness, exceeding great, angel of the Spirit, who watcheth over the vials of wrath and the mystery of the bottomless pit, come thou to mine aid, wreak sorrow upon them that have done evil to me, that they may know contrition and afflict no longer the servants of the hidden truth and the Reign that is to come. By these words be thou summoned, Heliphomar Mabon Saruth Gefutha Enunnas Sacinos. Amen. Amen. Amen.

I closed the book. "I don't go for that kind of invocation," I said slowly.

"Oh, you could recite it aloud," Marmiadon blurted. "In fact, an ordinary communicant of the Church could, and get no response. But I'm a toller. A summoner, you'd call it. Not too high-ranking or skillful; nevertheless, certain masteries have been conferred."

"Ah, s-s-so!" The sickening explanation grew upon me. "You raise and control demons in your regular line of work—"

"Not demons. No, no, no. Ordinary paranatural beings for the most part. Occasionally a minor angel."

"You mean a thing that tells you it's an angel."

"But it is!"

"Never mind. Here's what happened. You say you got mad and spoke this curse, a black prayer, against us. I say that knowingly or not, you were casting a spell. Since nothing registered on detectors, it must've been a kind of spell unknown to science. A summons to something from out of this universe. Well, you Johnnies do seem to've acquired a pipeline to another world. You believe, most of you, that world is Heaven. I'm convinced you're fooled; it's actually hell."

"No," he groaned.

"The demon answered your call. It happened that of the Nornwell people around, my wife and I had the one household exposed that night to his action. So the revenge was worked on us."

Marmiadon squared his puny shoulders. "Sir, I don't deny your child is missing. But if she was taken…as an unintended result of my action…well, you needn't fear."

"When she's in hell? Supposing I got her back this minute, what'll that place have done to her?"

"No, honestly, don't be afraid." Marmiadon ventured to pat my hand where it clenched white-knuckled around the knife. "If she were in the Low Continuum, retrieval operations would involve temporal phasing. Do you know what I mean? I'm not learned in such matters myself, but our adepts are, and a portion of their findings is taught to initiates, beginning at the fourth degree. The mathematics is beyond me. But as I recall, the hell universe has a peculiar, complex space-time geometry. It would be as easy to recover your daughter from the exact instant when she arrived there as from any other moment."

The weapon clattered out of my grasp. A roar went through my head. "Is that the truth?"

"Yes. More than I'm canonically allowed to tell you—"

I covered my face. The tears ran out between my fingers.

"—but I want to help you, Mr. Matuchek. I repent my anger." Looking up, I saw him cry too.

After a while we were able to get to business. "Of course, I must not mislead you," he declared. "When I said it would be as easy to enter hell at one point of time as another, I did not mean it would not be difficult. Insuperably so, indeed, except for our highest adepts. No geometers are alive with the genius to find their way independently through those dimensions.

"Fortunately, however, the question doesn't arise. I just wanted to reassure you enough so you'd listen to the real case. It may be that your daughter was removed in answer to my curse. That would account for the displeasure of my superiors with me. But if so, she's under angelic care."

"Prove it," I challenged.

"I can try. Again, I'm breaking the rules, especially since I'm under penance and you're an unbeliever. Still, I can try to summon an angel." He smiled timidly at me. "Who knows? If you recant, your girl could be restored to you on the spot."

I didn't like the idea of a Calling. In fact, I was bloody well chilled by it. But I was prepared to face worse than devils on this trip. "Go ahead."

He turned his Bible to another passage I didn't recognize. Kneeling, he started to chant, a high-pitched rise and fall which sawed at my nerves.

A wind blew down the tunnel. The lights didn't go out, but a dimness came over my eyes, deepening each second, as if I were dying, until I stood alone in a whistling dark. And the night was infinite and eternal; and the fear left me, but in its place there fell absolute despair. Never had I known a grief like this—not when Valeria was taken, not when my mother died—for now I had reached the final end of every hope and looked upon the ultimate emptiness of all things; love, joy, honor were less than ash, they had never been, and I stood hollow as the only existence in hollow creation.

Far, far away a light was kindled. It moved toward me, a spark, a star, a sun. I looked upon the vast mask of a face, into the lifeless eyes; and the measured voice beat through me:

"The hour is here. Despite everything, your destiny has endured, Steven. It was not my will or my planning. I foresaw the danger that you would wreck my newest great enterprise. But I could not know what would bring you to confront my works: the thoughtless call of one fool, the rash obedience of another. Now you would seek to storm my inner keep.

"Be afraid, Steven. I may not touch you myself, but I have mightier agents to send than those you met before. If you go further against me, you go to your destruction. Return home; accept your loss as humbly as befits a son of Adam;

beget other children, cease meddling in public matters, attend solely to what is your own. Then you shall have pleasure and wealth, and success in abundance, and your days shall be long in the land. But this is if you make your peace with me. If not, you will be brought down, and likewise those you care for. Fear me."

The sight, the sound, the blindness ended. I sagged, wet and areek with sweat looking stupidly at Marmiadon in the candlelight. He beamed and rubbed his hands. I could scarcely comprehend him:

"There! Wasn't I right? Aren't you glad? Wasn't he glorious? I'd be down on my knees if I were you, praising God for His mercy."

"Hu-u-uh?" dragged out of me.

"The angel, the angel!"

I shook myself. My heart was still drained. The world felt remote, fragile. But my brain functioned, in a mechanical fashion. It made my lips move. "I could have seen a different aspect of the being. What happened to you?"

"The crowned head, the shining wings," he crooned. "Your child is safe. She will be given back to you when your penitence is complete. And because of having been among the blessed in her mortal life, she will become a saint of the true Church."

Well, trickled through my head, this doubtless isn't the first time the Adversary's made an instrument of people who honestly believe they're serving God.

"What did you experience?" Marmiadon asked.

I might or might not have told him my revelation. Probably not; what good would that have done? A sound distracted us both—nearing footsteps, words.

"What if he hasn't been here?"

"We'll wait for some hours."

"In this thin garb?"

"The cause of the Lord, brother."

I stiffened. Two men coming: monks, from the noise of their sandals; big, from its volume on the stone. The adept I met upstairs must have grown suspicious; or Marmiadon's invocation and its effect had registered elsewhere; or both. If I got caught—I'd been warned. And my existence was beyond price, until I could get home the information that might help rescue Val.

I turned the flash on myself. Marmiadon whimpered as I changed shape. I went out in a single gray streak.

The pair of monks didn't see me through the gloom until I was almost on them. They were beefy for sure. One carried a stick, the other a forty-five automatic. I darted between the legs of the latter, bowling him over. His buddy got a crack across my ribs with his cudgel. Pain slowed me for a moment. A bone may have been broken. It knitted with the speed of the werewolf condition and I dashed on. The pistol barked. Slugs whanged nastily past. If they included argent rounds, a hit would stop me. I had to move!

Up the stairs I fled. The friars dropped from sight. But an alarm started ahead of me, bells crashing through the hymns. Did my pursuers have a walkie-talkie ball with them? Produced at Nornwell? I burst into the first-floor hallway. There must be other exits than the main door, but I didn't know them. A wolf can travel like bad news. I was through the curtain which screened off the choir vestry before any nightshifter had glanced out of an office or any sleepy monk arrived from another section.

The church was in a boil. I cracked the door to the aisle sufficiently for a look. The chant went on. But folk ran about in the nave, shouting. More to the point, a couple of them were closing doors to the vestibule. I couldn't get out.

Feet slapped floor in the corridor. The Johnnies weren't certain which way I'd skittered, and were confused anyhow by this sudden unexplained emergency. Nevertheless, I'd scant time until someone thought to check here.

A possible tactic occurred to me. I didn't consider the wherefores of it, which a wolf isn't equipped to do. Trusting instinct, I slapped the switch on my flash with a forepaw. The blue entry-room lights didn't interfere with my reverting to human. Darting back to the vestry, I grabbed a surplice and threw it over my head. It fell nearly to my feet. They stayed bare, but maybe no one would notice.

Ascending to the choir loft in record time, I stopped in the archway entrance and studied the situation. Men and women stood grouped according to vocal range. They held hymnals. Spare books lay on a table. The view from here, down to the altar and up to the cupola, was breathtaking. But I'd no breath to spend. I picked my spot, helped myself to a book, and moved solemnly forward.

I wouldn't have gotten away with it under normal conditions. Conditions not being normal, the choir was agitated too, its attention continually pulled down to the excitement on the floor. The song kept wandering off key. I found a place on the edge of the baritones and opened my hymnal to the same page as my neighbor.

"*Mephnounos Chemiath Aroura Maridon Elison*," he chanted. I'd better make noises likewise. The trouble was, I'd not had the rehearsals they gave to laymen who wanted to participate. I couldn't even pronounce most of those words, let alone carry the tune.

My neighbor glanced at me. He was a portly, officious-looking priest. I oughtn't to stand around with my teeth in my mouth, he must be thinking. I gave him a weak smile. "*Thatis Etelelam Tetheo Abocia Rusar,*" he intoned in a marked manner.

I grabbed at the first melody I recalled which had some general resemblance to the one he was using. Mushing it up as much as I dared, I studied my book and commenced:

> *A sailor told me before he died—*
> *I don't know whether the bastard lied—*

In the general counterpoint, not to mention the uproar below, it passed. The cleric took his eyes off me. He continued with the canticle and I with *The Big Red Wheel.*

I trust I may be forgiven for some of the other expedients I found necessary in the hour that followed. An hour, I guessed, was an unsuspicious time for a lay singer to stay. Meanwhile, by eye and ear, I'd followed roughly the progress of the hunt for me. The size and complexity of the cathedral worked in my favor for once; I could be anywhere. Unquestionably spells were being used in the search. But the wizard had little to go on except what Marmiadon could tell. And I had everything protective that Ginny, who's one of the best witches in the Guild, was able to give me before I left. Tracing me, identifying me, would be no simple matter, even for those beings that the most potent of the adepts might raise.

Not that I could hold out long. If I didn't scramble soon I was dead, or worse. A part of me actually rejoiced at that. You see, the danger, the calling up of every resource I had to meet it, wiped away the despair at the core of hell which I had met in the crypts. I was alive, and it mattered, and I'd do my best to kill whatever stood between me and my loves!

After a while I'd figured out a plan. Leaving the choir and disrobing, I turned wolf. The north corridor was again deserted, which was lucky for any Johnnies I might have encountered. Having doubtless posted a guard at every door, they were cooling their chase. It went on, but quietly, systematically, no longer disruptive of religious atmosphere. Lupine senses helped me avoid patrols while I looked for a window.

On the lower levels, these were in rooms that were occupied or whose doors were locked. I had to go to the sixth floor—where the scent of wrongness was almost more than I could bear—before finding a window in the corridor wall. It took resolution, or desperation, to jump through. The pain as the glass broke and slashed me was as nothing to the pain when I hit the concrete beneath.

But I was Lyco. My injuries were not fatal or permanently crippling. The red rag of me stirred, grew together, and became whole. Sufficient of my blood was smeared around, unrecoverable, that I felt a bit weak and dizzy; but a meal would fix that.

The stars still glittered overhead. Vision was uncertain. And I doubted the outer gatekeepers had been told much, if anything. The hierarchy would be anxious to hush this trouble as far as might be. I stripped off what remained of my clothes with my teeth, leaving the wereflash fairly well covered by my ruff, and trotted off to the same place where I'd entered. "Why, hullo, pooch," said my young friend. "Where'd you come from?" I submitted to having my ears rumpled before I left.

In Siloam's darkened downtown I committed a fresh crime, shoving through another window, this time in the rear of a grocery store. Besides the several pounds of hamburger I found and ate, I needed transportation; and after humanizing I was more than penniless, I was naked. I phoned Barney. "Come and get me," I said. "I'll be wolf at one of these spots." I gave him half a dozen possibilities, in case the pursuit of me spilled beyond cathedral boundaries.

"What happened to my broom?" he demanded.

"I had to leave it parked," I said. "You can claim it tomorrow."

"I'm eager to hear the story."

"Well, it was quite a night, I can tell you."

My detailed relation I gave to Ginny after sneaking back into our house. I was numb with exhaustion, but she insisted on hearing everything at once, whispered as we lay side by side. Her questions drew each last detail from me, including a lot that had slipped my mind or that I hadn't especially noticed at the time. The sun was up before she fixed my breakfast and allowed me to rest. With a few pauses for nourishment and drowsy staring, I slept a full twenty-four hours.

Ginny explained this to our FBI man as the result of nervous prostration, which wasn't too mendacious. She also persuaded him and his immediate boss (Shining Knife had gone to Washington) that if they wanted to keep matters under wraps, they'd better not hold us incommunicado. Our neighbors already knew something was afoot. They could be stalled for but a short while, our close friends and business associates for a shorter while yet. If the latter got worried, they could bring more to bear in the way of sortileges than the average person.

The upshot was that we kept our guest. When Mrs. Delacorte dropped around to borrow a gill of brimstone, we introduced him as my cousin Louis and mentioned that we'd sent Val on an out-of-town visit while our burglary was being investigated. It didn't rate more than a paragraph on an inside page of the daily paper. I was allowed to work again, Ginny to go shopping. We were told what number to call if we received any demands. Nothing was said about the men who shadowed us. They were good; without our special skills, we'd never have known about them.

On the third morning, therefore, I showed at Nornwell. Barney Sturlason was primed. He found a do-not-disturb job for me to do in my office—rather, to fake doing while I paced, chain-smoked my tongue to leather, drank coffee till it gurgled in my ears—until time for an after-lunch conference with some outside businessmen. I knew what that conference was really to be about. When the intercom asked me to go there, I damn near snapped my head off accelerating before I remembered to walk the distance and say hello to those I passed.

The meeting room was upstairs. Its hex against industrial espionage operated equally well against official surveillance. Barney bulked at the end of the table, collar open, cigar fuming. The assembled team comprised eleven, to help assure we'd harbor no Judas. I knew Griswold, Hardy, Janice Wenzel, and, slightly, Dr. Nobu, a metaphysicist we had sometimes consulted. Another man turned out to be a retired admiral, Hugh Charles, who'd specialized in intelligence; another was a mathematician named Falkenberg; a third was Pastor Karlslund from Barney's church. All of these looked weary. They'd worked like galley slaves, practically up to this minute. The last pair seemed fresh, and totally undistinguished except that one had a large sample case which he'd put on the table.

Before he got to their names, Barney made a pass and spoke a phrase. "Okay," he said, "the security field is back at full strength. Come on out and join the coven."

Their figures blurred, went smoky, and firmed again as the Seeming passed. Ginny's hair gleamed copper in the sunlight from the windows. Dr. Ashman opened his case. Svartalf poured out, restored to health, big, black, and arrogant as ever. "Mee-owr-r-r," he scolded us. The pastor offered the cat a soothing hand. I didn't have time to warn him. Luckily, Ashman was in the habit of carrying Band-Aids. Svartalf sat down by Ginny and washed himself.

"How'd you manage it?" the admiral asked with professional interest.

Ginny shrugged. "Simple. Barney told the doctor on the QT what to do and when. He fetched Svartalf at the hospital. We'd already verified there was no tail on him." Svartalf switched his in a smug fashion. "Meanwhile I'd gone downtown. They're having a sale at Perlman's. Easiest crowd in the world to disappear into, and who'll notice a bit of sorcery? Having changed my looks, I rendezvoused with Dr. Ashman and altered him." Svartalf threw the man a speculative look. "We proceeded here. Barney knew exactly when we'd arrive, and had the field low enough that it didn't whiff our disguises."

She opened her purse, which hadn't needed much work to resemble a briefcase, got out her vanity, and inspected her appearance. In demure makeup and demure little dress, she hardly suggested a top-flight witch, till you noticed what else she was packing along.

"To business," Barney said. "We informed this team at once of what you'd discovered, Steve. It was a scientific as well as religious and political jolt. I think that we better review that second aspect before we go on to discuss what can maybe be done about it."

"If the Johannine Church is indeed of diabolic origin—" Griswold grimaced. "I hate to believe that. Not that I agree with its tenets, but—well, are you sure, Mr. Matuchek, that the vision you had in the cell was not actually an illusion?"

"If the Johnnies are legit," my wife clipped, "why are they keeping quiet? They ought to have filed a complaint or something. But never a peep, not even when Barney's man fetched back his broomstick. I say they can't risk an investigation."

"They might be trying to get your daughter returned to you through their paranatural contacts," Hardy suggested without conviction.

Admiral Charles snorted. "Big chance! I don't doubt the Adversary would like to cancel the whole episode. But how? He can return her with zero time-lapse in hell, you say, Mr. Matuchek—quite astounding, that. Nevertheless, I don't imagine he can change the past: the days we've lived without her, the things we've learned as a consequence."

"Our silence could be her ransom," Hardy said.

"What man would feel bound by that kind of bargain?" the admiral replied.

Karlslund added: "No contracts can be made with the Low Ones anyhow. Being incapable of probity, a devil is unable to believe humans won't try to cheat him."

"So," Charles said, "he'd gain nothing by releasing her, and lose whatever hostage value she has."

Ashman said painfully: "He's already succeeded in dividing the forces of good. I get the impression this meeting is in defiance of the government, an actual conspiracy. Is that wise?"

"Let me handle that question," Barney said. "I've got connections in Washington, and Admiral Charles, who has more, confirms my guess as to what's going on there. The facts of the kidnapping are being officially suppressed. The reason is mainly fear—of the consequences; there *are* a lot of Johnny voters—though ordinary bureaucratic inertia enters in, too. If no further outrages take place, the government won't move. And we know that's to be the case. The kidnapping was a bad mistake by someone on the Adversary's side."

He halted to rekindle his cigar. The room had become very still as we listened. Smoke filled the sunbeams with blue strata and our nostrils with staleness. Ginny and I exchanged a forlorn look across the table. Yesterday I'd gone into the basement to replace a blown fuse. She'd come along, because these days we stayed together when we could. Some things of Valeria's stood on a shelf, lately outgrown and not yet discarded. The ever-filled bottle, the Ouroboros teething ring, the winged training spoon, the little pot with a rainbow at the end—We went upstairs and asked our guard to change the fuse.

Her fists clenched before her. Svartalf rubbed his head on her arm, slowly, demanding no attention in return.

"Therefore," Barney said, "as of today, we, this bunch of us, have the right and duty to take what action we can.

"You see, Doctor, we've done nothing technically illegal. Steve was not under arrest. He was free to go where he chose, in any manner he wished. At most he committed a civil tort, invading private sections of the cathedral. Let the hierarchy sue him for damages if it wants. It won't; its monks committed a felonious assault on him!

"Likewise, we aren't contemplating any crime and thus we aren't conspiring. I grant you, soon the National Defense Act is likely to be invoked against us. That's one reason we have to move fast. But at present we are still legally free to do what we have in mind."

"Also," said Falkenberg, "as I understand the situation, the, ah, enemy are off balance at present. Mr. Matuchek took them by surprise. Evidently the, ah, Adversary is debarred from giving them direct help, counsel, or information. Or else he considers it inadvisable, as it might provoke intervention by the Highest. The, ah, Johannine Magi can do extraordinary things, but they are not omniscient or omnipotent. They can't be sure what we have learned and what we will attempt. Give them time, however, in this universe, and they will, ah, recover their equilibrium, quite possibly make some countermove."

Ginny said out of her Medusa mask: "Whatever the rest of you decide, Steve and I won't sit waiting."

"Blazes, no!" exploded from me. Svartalf laid back his ears, fangs gleamed amidst his whiskers and the fur stood up on him.

"This group is already resolved to help you," Barney said.

Eyes went from us to Ashman. He flushed and said: "I'm not going henhouse on you. Remember, all this has just been sprung on me without warning. I'm bound to raise the arguments that occur to me. I don't believe that encouraging Valeria's parents to commit suicide will do her any good."

"What do you mean?' Barney asked.

"Do I misunderstand? Isn't your intention to send Steven and Virginia—my patients—into the hell universe?"

That brought me up cold. I'd been ready and raging for action; but now the heart slammed in me. I stared at Ginny. She nodded.

The whole group registered various degrees of dismay. I scarcely noticed the babble that lifted or Barney's quelling of it. Finally we all sat in a taut-strung silence.

"I must apologize to this committee," Barney said. His tone was deep and measured as a vesper bell's. "I set you onto various aspects of a study of the Low Continuum. You did magnificently, especially after you got Steve's findings to work with. But you were too busy to think beyond the assignment, or to imagine that it was more than a long-range, rather hypothetical study: something that might eventually give us capabilities against further troubles of this nature.

"I saw no alternative to handling it that way. But Ginny Matuchek reached me meanwhile, surreptitiously. I gave her the whole picture, we discussed it at length and evolved a plan of campaign." He bowed slightly toward Ashman. "Congratulations on your astuteness, Doctor."

She knew, I thought in the shards of thinking, and yet no one could have told it on her, not even me.

She raised her hand. "The case is this," she said with the same military crispness as when first I'd met her. "A small, skilled team has a chance of success. A large, unskilled bunch has none. It'd doubtless suffer catastrophe."

"Death, insanity, or imprisonment in hell with everything that that implies—" Ashman whispered. "You assume Steven will go."

"I know better than to try stopping him," she said.

That gave me a measure of self-control again. I was not unconscious of admiring glances. But mainly I listened to her:

"He and I and Svartalf are as good a squad as you'll find. If anybody has a hope of pulling the stunt off, we do. The rest of you can help with preparations and with recovering us. If we don't return, you'll be the repositories of what has already been learned. Because these discoveries are vitally important in themselves—just like anything else we may find out."

Ashman hesitated before saying, with a kind of smile, "All right, I apologize. You must admit my reaction was natural and I'm still afraid for you. But you have my support. May I ask what your scheme is?"

Barney relaxed a trifle. "You may," he said. "Especially since we've got to explain it to some of the others."

He stubbed out his cigar and began on a fresh one. "Let me put the proposition in nickel words first," he said, "then the experts can correct and amplify according to their specialties. Our universe has a straightforward space-time geometry. Hell doesn't. Demons know how to move around through those wildly contorted and variable dimensions. Men don't. They can get there, but then are practically helpless. Or were, until today.

"You see, Steve's information that we could reach any point in hell time opened a door or broke a logjam or something. Suddenly there was a definite basic fact to go on, a relationship between the Low Continuum and ours that could be mathematically described. Dr. Falkenberg set up the equations and started solving them for different conditions. Professor Griswold and Bill Hardy helped by suggesting how the laws of nature would be affected. Oh, we've barely begun, and our conclusions haven't been subjected to experimental test. But at least they've enabled Dr. Nobu and me to design some spells. We completed them this morning. They should protect the expedition, give it some guardianship when it arrives, and haul it back fast. That's more than anybody previous had going for them."

"Insufficient." Charles was the new objector. "You can't have a full description of the hell universe—why, we don't have that even for this cosmos—and you absolutely can't predict what crazy ways the metric there varies from point to point."

"True," Barney said.

"So protection which is adequate at one place will be useless elsewhere."

"Not if the space-time configuration can be described mathematically as one travels. Then the spells can be adjusted accordingly."

"What? But that's an impossible job. No mortal man—"

"Right," Ginny said.

We gaped at her.

"A passing thing Steve heard, down in the crypts, was the clue," Ginny said. "Same as your remark, actually, Admiral. No mortal man could do it. But the greatest geometers are dead."

A gasp went around the table.

With appropriate Seemings laid on, and Svartalf indignantly back in the sample case, our community left the plant on a company carpet. It was now close to four. If my FBI shadow didn't see me start home around five or six o'clock, he'd get suspicious. But there wasn't a lot I could do about that.

We landed first at St. Olaf's while Pastor Karlslund went in to fetch some articles. Janice Wenzel, seated behind us, leaned forward and murmured: "I guess I'm ignorant, but isn't this appealing to the saints a Catholic rather than a Lutheran thing?"

The question hadn't been raised at the conference. Karlslund was satisfied with making clear the distinction between a prayer—a petition to the Highest, with any spells we cast intended merely to ease a way for whoever might freely respond—and an illegitimate attempt at necromancy.

"I doubt if the sect makes any difference," Ginny said. "What is the soul? Nobody knows. The observations that prove it exists are valid, but scattered and not repeatable under controlled conditions. As tends to be the case for many paranatural phenomena."

"Which, however," Dr. Nobu put in, "is the reason in turn why practical progress in goetics is so rapid once a correct insight is available. For example, three days after learning about the time variability of hell, we feel some confidence that our new spells will work. The numerical details just aren't as important as in physics technology…But as for the soul, I incline towards the belief that its character is supernatural rather than paranatural."

"Not me," Ginny said. "I'd call it an energy structure that's formed by the body but outlives that matrix. Once free, it can easily move between universes. If it hangs around here for some reason, like remorse, isn't that a ghost? If the Highest allows it to come nearer His presence, isn't that Heaven? If the Lowest has more attraction for it, isn't that damnation? If it enters a newly fertilized ovum, isn't that reincarnation?"

"Dear me," Janice said. Ginny uttered a brittle laugh.

Barney turned around in the pilot's seat. "About your question that started this seminar, Janice," he said, "it's true we Lutherans don't make a habit of calling on the saints. But neither do we deny that sometimes they intervene. And I've known Jim Karlslund for years, I know he's trustworthy…and here he comes, too, with an armful of ecclesiastical gear."

We took off again and proceeded to Trismegistus University. Sunlight slanted gold across remembered lawns, groves, buildings. Few persons were about in this pause between spring and summer sessions; a hush lay over the campus, distantly backgrounded by the city's whirr. I glanced at Ginny, but her face had gone unreadable.

We landed and entered the physical sciences hall. Griswold had keys to every lab and stockroom there. Karlslund would have preferred the chapel, but that was too public. Besides, probably the religious part of our undertaking was secondary.

The pastor's appeal ought to have the elements of unselfishness and devotion, without which no saint was apt to respond. But they seldom do anyway. The Highest expects us to solve our own problems. What we relied on—what gave us a degree of confidence we would get some kind of reaction—was the progress we'd made, the direct access we believed we had to the Adversary's realm and our stiff resolve to use it. The implications were too enormous for Heaven to ignore…we hoped.

I thought, in the floating lightheadedness to which stress had brought me: Perhaps we'll be forbidden to try.

Our site was the Berkeley Philosophical Laboratory. It was large, new, and splendidly outfitted. Light fell cool through gray-green glass in the Gothic windows. Zodiacal symbols encircled a golden Bohr atom on the ceiling. You'd never find a place further in spirit from that cathedral at Siloam. My kind of people had raised this.

Griswold locked the door. Ginny took off the Seemings and let Svartalf out. He padded into a corner, tail going like a metronome. Karlslund set up his sacred objects, improvising an altar on a bench. The rest of us worked under Barney. We established a shield-field and an anti-spy hex in the usual way. Next we prepared to open the gates between universes.

You can look up in the manuals what we used to help our hope-for saint to reach us. Bible and Poimanderes opened to the right passages, menorah with seven tall candles lit by flint and steel, vial of pure air, chest of consecrated earth, horn of Jordan water, Pythagorean harp. According to Petrine doctrine, the effect was symbolic more than physical, just as our prayer would simply be an earnest of the appeal which God had already read in our hearts.

Hell is another case entirely. In physical terms, it's on a lower energy level than our universe. In spiritual terms, the Adversary and his minions aren't interested in assisting us to anything except our destruction. We could definitely force our way in and overpower them—if we swung enough power!

I am not going to reveal what our new spells were by which we meant to attempt that. You might guess they involved an inversion of the prayer ritual, so I'll state we employed these articles: a certain one of the Apocrypha, a *Liber Veneficarum*, a torch, a globe of wind from a hurricane, some mummy dust, thirteen drops of blood, and a sword. I don't swear to the truthfulness of my list.

We didn't expect we'd require that stuff right away, but it was another demonstration of intent. Besides, Ginny needed a chance to study it and use her trained intuition to optimize the layout.

Karlslund's bell called us. He was ready. We assembled before his altar. "I must first consecrate this and hold as full a service as possible," he announced. I looked at my watch—damn near five—but dared not object. His feeling of respect for the process was vital.

Curiously, though, as that simple rite proceeded, I began to enjoy a measure of peace and a sense of wordless wonder.

"Our Father, Who art in Heaven—"

There was a knock on the door.

I didn't notice at first. But it came again, and again, and a voice trickled through the heavy panels: "Dr. Griswold! Are you in there? Phone call for you. A Mr. Shining Knife from the FBI. Says it's urgent."

That rocked me. My mood went smash. Ginny's nostrils dilated and she clutched her book as if it were a weapon. Karlslund's tones faltered.

Griswold pattered to the door and said to the janitor or whoever it was: "Tell him I've a delicate experiment under way. It can't be interrupted. Get his number, and I'll call back in an hour or so."

Good for you! half of me wanted to shout. The rest was tangled in cold coils of wondering about God's mercy.

Somehow we had struggled through with our service. At the end, Karlslund said, troubled: "I'm not sure we're going to get anywhere now. The proper reverence seems to be lost. But I suppose we may as well try. What exact help do you wish?"

Barney, Ginny, and the rest exchanged blank looks. I realized that in the rush, they'd forgotten to specify that. It probably hadn't seemed urgent, since Heaven is not as narrowly literal-minded as hell.

Barney cleared his throat. "Uh, the idea is," he said, "that a first-rank mathematician would go on learning, improving, gaining knowledge and power we can't guess at, after passing on. We want a man who pioneered in non-Euclidean geometry."

"Riemann is considered definitive," Falkenberg told us, "but he did build on the work of others. I'd suggest, well Lobachevsky. He was the first to prove a geometry can be self-consistent that denies the axiom of parallels. Around 1830 or 1840 as I recall, though the history of mathematics isn't my long suit. Everything in that branch of it stems from him."

"That'll do," Barney decided, "considering we don't know if we can get any particular soul for an ally. Any whatsoever, for that matter," he added raggedly. To Falkenberg: "You and the pastor work out the words while we establish the spell."

That took time also, but kept us busy enough that we didn't worry about what Shining Knife might be up to. We made the motions, spoke the phrases, directed the will, felt the indescribable stress of energies build toward breaking point. This was no everyday hex, it was heap big medicine.

Shadows thickened. The seven candle flames burned unnaturally tall. The symbols overhead glowed with their own radiance and began slowly turning. The harp played itself, strings plangent with the music of the spheres. Weaving my way across the unseen as one of the seven who trod the slow measures of the *bransle grave*, I heard a voice cry "Aleph!" and long afterward: "Zain."

At that we halted, the harp ceased, the eternal silence of the infinite spaces fell upon us, and the pastor made his appeal.

"—we beg that Thou allow them a guide and counselor through the wilderness of hell. We ask that Thou commend unto them Thy departed servant Nikolai Ivanovitch Lobachevsky, or whoever else may have knowledge in these matters as having been on earth a discoverer of them. This do we pray in the name of the Father, and of the Son, and of the Holy Ghost. Amen."

There was another stillness.

Then the cross on the altar shone forth, momentarily sun-bright, and we heard one piercing, exquisite note, and I felt within me a rush of joy I can only vaguely compare to the first winning of first love. But another noise followed, as of a huge wind. The candles went out, the panes went black, we staggered when the floor shook beneath us. Svantalf screamed.

"Ginny!" I heard myself yell. Simultaneously I was whirled down a vortex of images, memories, a bulbous-towered church on an illimitable plain, a dirt track between rows of low thatch-roofed cottages and a horseman squeaking and jingling along it with saber at belt, an iron winter that ended in thaw and watery gleams and returning bird-flocks and shy breath of green across the beechwoods, a disordered stack of books, faces, faces, hands, a woman who was my wife, a son who died too young, half of Kazan in one red blaze, the year of the cholera, the letter from Gottingen, loves, failures, blindness closing in day by slow day; *and none of it was me.*

A thunderclap rattled our teeth. The wind stopped, the light came back, the sense of poised forces was no more. We stood bewildered in our ordinary lives. Ginny cast herself into my arms.

"*Lyubimyets,*" I croaked to her, "no, darling—*Gospodny pomiluie*—" while the kaleidoscope gyred within me. Svartalf stood on a workbench, back arched, tail bottled, not in rage but in panic. His lips, throat, tongue writhed through a ghastly fight with sounds no cat can make. He was trying to talk.

"What's gone wrong?" Barney roared.

Ginny took over. She beckoned to the closest men. "Karlslund, Hardy, help Steve," she rapped. "Check him, Doc." I heard her fragmentarily through the chaos. My friends supported me. I reached a chair, collapsed, and fought for breath.

My derangement was short. The recollections of another land, another time, stopped rocketing forth at random. They had been terrifying because they were strange and out of my control. *Poko'y* sounded in my awareness, together with *Peace*, and I knew they meant the same. Courage lifted. I sensed myself thinking, with overtones of both formalism and compassion:

—I beg your pardon, sir. This re-embodiment confused me likewise. I had not paused to reflect what a difference would be made by more than a hundred years in the far realms where I have been. A few minutes will suffice, I believe, for pre-liminary studies providing the informational basis for a *modus vivendi* that shall be tolerable to you. Rest assured that I regret any intrusion and will minimize the same. I may add, with due respect, that what I chance to learn about your private affairs will doubtless be of no special significance to one who has left the flesh behind him.

Lobachevsky! I realized.

—Your servant, sir. Ah, yes, Steven Anton Matuchek. Will you graciously excuse me for the necessary brief interval?

This, and the indescribable stirring of two memory sets that followed, went on at the back of my consciousness. The rest of me was again alert: uncannily so. I waved Ashman aside with an "I'm okay" and scanned the scene before me.

In Svartalf's hysterical condition, he was dangerous to approach. Ginny tapped a basin of water at a work-bench sink and threw it over him. He squalled, sprang to the floor, dashed to a corner, crouched and glowered. "Poor puss," she consoled. "I had to do that." She found a towel. "Come here to mama and we'll dry you off." He made her come to him. She squatted and rubbed his fur.

"What got into him?" Charles asked.

Ginny looked up. Against the red hair her face was doubly pale. "Good phrase, Admiral," she said. "Something did. I shocked his body with a drenching. The natural cat reflexes took over, and the invading spirit lost its dominance. But it's still there. As soon as it learns its psychosomatic way around, it'll try to assume control and do what it's come for."

"Which is?"

"I don't know. We'd better secure him."

I rose. "No, wait," I said. "I can find out." Their eyes swiveled toward me. "You see, uh, I've got Lobachevsky."

"What?" Karlslund protested. "His soul in your—Can't be! The saints never—"

I brushed past, knelt by Ginny, took Svartalf's head between my hands, and said, "Relax. Nobody wants to hurt you. My guest thinks he understands what's happened. Savvy? Nikolai Ivanovitch Lobachevsky is his name. Who are you?"

The muscles bunched, the fangs appeared, a growing ululation swept the room. Svartalf was about to have another fit.

—Sir, by your leave, the thought went in me. He is not hostile. I would know if he wcrc. Hc is disconcerted at what has occurred, and has merely a feline brain to think with. Evidently he is unacquainted with your language. May I endeavor to calm him?

Russian purled and fizzled from my lips. Svartalf started, then I felt him ease a bit in my grasp. He looked and listened as intently as if I were a mousehole. When I stopped, he shook his head and mewed.

—So he was not of my nationality either. But he appears to have grasped our intent.

Look, I thought, you can follow English, using my knowledge. Svartalf knows it too. Why can't his...inhabitant...do like you?

—I told you, sir, the feline brain is inadequate. It has nothing like a human speech-handling structure. The visiting soul must use every available cortical cell to maintain bare reason. But it can freely draw upon its terrestrial experience, thanks to the immense data storage capacity of even a diminutive mammalian body. Hence we can use what languages it knew before.

I thought: I see. Don't underrate Svartalf. He's pure-bred from a long line of witch familiars, more intelligent than an ordinary cat. And the spells that've surrounded him through his life must've had effects.

—Excellent. *"Sprechen Sie Deutsch?"*

Svartalf nodded eagerly. "Meeöh," he said with an umlaut.

"Guten Tag, gnädiger Herr. Ich bin der Mathematiker Nikolai Iwanowitsch Lobatschewski, quondam Oberpfarrer zu der Kasans Universilat in Russland. Je suis votre tres humble serviteur, Monsieur." That last was in French, as politeness called for in the earlier nineteenth century.

"W-r-r-rar-r." Claws gestured across the floor.

Ginny said, wide-eyed with awe: "He wants to write...Svartalf, listen. Don't be angry. Don't be afraid. Don't fight, help him. There's a good cat." She rubbed him under the chin. It didn't seem quite the proper treatment for a visiting savant, but it worked, because at last he purred.

While she and Griswold made preparations, I concentrated on meshing with Lobachevsky. The rest stood around, shaken by what had happened and the sudden complete unknownness of the next hour. A fraction of me hearkened to their low voices.

Charles: "Damnedest apparition of saints I ever heard of."

Karlslund: "Admiral, please!"

Janice: "Well, it's true. They shouldn't have intruded in bodies like, like demons taking possession."

Griswold: "Maybe they had to. We did neglect to provide counter-transferral mass for inter-continuum crossing."

Karlslund: "They aren't devils. They never required it in the past."

Barney: "Whoa. Let's think about that. A spirit or a thought can travel free between universes. Maybe that's what returned saints always were—visions, not solid bodies."

Karlslund: "Some were positively substantial."

Nobu: "I would guess that a saint can utilize any mass to form a body. Air, for instance, and a few pounds of dust for minerals, would provide the necessary atoms. Don't forget what he or she is, as far as we know: a soul in Heaven, which is to say one near God. How can he fail to gain remarkable abilities as well as spiritual eminence—from the Source of power and creativity?"

Charles: "What ails these characters, then?"

"Messieurs," my body said, stepping toward them, "I beg your indulgence. As yet I have not entirely accustomed myself to thinking in this corporeal manifold. Do me the honor to remember that it is unlike the one I originally inhabited. Nor have I assimilated the details of the problem which led to your request for help. Finally, while confined to human form, I have no better means than you for discovering the identity of the gentleman in the cat. I do believe I know his purpose, but let us wait, if you will, for more exact knowledge before drawing conclusions."

"Wow!" Barney breathed. "How's it feel, Steve?"

"Not bad," I said. "Better by the minute." That was an ultimate understatement. As Lobachevsky and I got acquainted, I felt in myself, coexistent with my own thoughts and emotions, those of a being grown good and wise beyond imagining.

Of course, I couldn't share his afterlife, nor the holiness thereof. My mortal brain and grimy soul didn't reach to it. At most, there sang at the edge of perception a peace and joy which were not static but a high eternal adventure. I did, though, have the presence of Lobachevsky the man to savor. Think of your oldest and best friend and you'll have a rough idea what that was like.

"We should be ready now," Ginny said.

She and Griswold had set a Ouija board on a bench, the easiest implement for a paw to use. Svartalf took position at the gadget while I leaned across the opposite side to interrogate.

The planchette moved in a silence broken only by breathing. It was sympathetic with a piece of chalk under a broomstick spell, that wrote large on a blackboard where everyone could see.

ICH BIN JANOS BOLYAI VON UNGARN

"Bolyai!" gasped Falkenberg. "God, I forgot about him! No wonder he—but how—?"

"Enchanté, Monsieur," Lobachevsky said with a low bow. *"Dies ist für mich eine grosse Ehre. Ihrer Werke sint eine Inspiration für alles."* He meant it.

Neither Bolyai nor Svartalf were to be outdone in courtliness. They stood up on his hind legs, made a reverence with paw on heart, followed with a military salute, took the planchette again and launched into a string of flowery French compliments.

"Who is he, anyhow?" Charles hissed behind me.

"I…I don't know his biography," Falkenberg answered likewise. "But I recall now, he was the morning star of the new geometry."

"I'll check the library," Griswold offered. "These courtesies look as if they'll go on for some time."

"Yes," Ginny said in my ear, "can't you hurry things along a bit? We're way overdue at home, you and I. And that phone call could be trouble."

I put it to Lobachevsky, who put it to Bolyai, who wrote ABER NATÜRLICH and gave us his assurances—at considerable length—that as an Imperial officer he had learned how to act with the decisiveness that became a soldier when need existed, as it clearly did in the present instance, especially when two such charming young ladies in distress laid claim upon his honor, which honor he would maintain upon any field without flinching, as he trusted he had done in life…

I don't intend to mock a great man. Among us, he was a soul trying to think with the brain and feel with the nerves and glands of a tomcat. It magnified human failings and made well-nigh impossible the expression of his intellect and knightliness. We found these hinted at in the notes on him that Griswold located in encyclopedias and mathematical histories, which we read while he did his gallant best to communicate with Lobachevsky.

Janos Bolyai was born in Hungary in 1802, when it was hardly more than a province of the Austrian Empire. His father was also a noted mathematician. Twenty years old, he became an officer of engineers, well known as a violinist and a swordsman dangerous to meet in a duel. In 1823 he sent to his father a draft of his *Absolute Science of Space*. This was the first rigorous proof that space doesn't logically need to obey axioms like the one about parallel lines.

Unfortunately, it wasn't published till 1833, and just as an appendix to a two-volume work of the old man's. By then Lobachevsky had independently announced similar results. Bolyai remained obscure. He died there in 1860.

We found more on the Russian. In his life, which ran from 1793 to 1856, he showed more than genius. He showed patience, dedication, compassion, practical helpfulness toward all, in the face of poverty, tyrannical jealousy, humiliation, epidemic, danger, sorrow, and ultimate blindness. Of course he became a saint!

—No, Steven Pavlovitch, you should not raise me above my worth. I stumbled and sinned more than most, I am sure. But the mercy of God has no bounds. I have been…it is impossible to explain. Let us say I have been allowed to progress.

The blackboard filled. Janice wielded an eraser and the chalk squeaked on. To those who knew French—to which the Russian and the Hungarian had switched as being more elegant than German—it gradually became clear what had happened. But I alone shared Lobachevsky's degree of comprehension. As this grew, I fretted over ways to convey it in American. Time was shrinking on us fast.

—Indeed, Lobachevsky answered. Brusque though contemporary manners have become *(pardoranez-moi, je vous en prie)*, haste is needed, for I agree that the hour is late and the peril dire.

Therefore I called the group to me when at last the questioning was done. Except for Ginny, who couldn't help being spectacular, and Svartalf, who sat at her feet with a human soul in his eyes, they were an unimpressive lot to see, tired, sweaty, haggard, neckties loosened or discarded, hair unkempt, cigarettes in most hands. I was probably less glamorous, perched on a stool facing them. My voice grated and I'd developed a tic in one cheek. The fact that a blessed saint had joint tenancy of my body didn't much affect pain, scared, fallible me.

"Things have got straightened out," I said. "We made a mistake. God doesn't issue personal orders to His angels and saints, at least not on our behalf. Consciously or not, we assumed we're more important than we are." Lobachevsky corrected me. "No, everybody's important to Him. But there must be freedom, even for evil. And furthermore, there are considerations of—well, I guess you can't say *Realpolitik*. I don't know if it has earthly analogues. Roughly speaking, though, neither God nor the Adversary want to provoke an early Armageddon. For two thousand years, they've avoided direct incursions into each other's, uh, home territories, Heaven or hell. That policy's not about to be changed.

"Our appeal was heard. Lobachevsky's a full-fledged saint. He couldn't resist coming down, and he wasn't forbidden to. But he's not allowed to aid us in hell. If he goes along, it has to be strictly as an observer, inside a mortal frame. He's sorry, but that's the way the elixir elides. The result was, he entered this continuum, with me as his logical target.

"Bolyai's different. He heard too, especially since the prayer was so loosely phrased it could well have referred to him. Now, he hasn't made sainthood. He says he's been in Purgatory. I suspect most of us'd think of it as a condition where you haven't got what it takes to know God directly but you can improve your-self. At any rate, while he wasn't in Heaven, he wasn't damned either. And so he's under no prohibition as regards taking an active part in a fight. This looked like a chance to do a good deed. He assessed the content of our appeal, including the parts we didn't speak, and likewise chose me. Lobachevsky, who's more powerful by virtue of sanctity, and wasn't aware of his intent, arrived a split second ahead of him."

I stopped to bum a cigarette. What I really wanted was a gallon of hard cider. My throat felt like a washboard road in summer. "Evidently these cases are governed by rules," I said. "In part, I guess, it's to protect mortal flesh from undue shock and strain. Only one extra identity per customer. Bolyai hasn't the capability of a saint, to create a temporary real body out of whatever's handy, as you suggested a while back, Dr. Nobu. His way to manifest himself was to enter a live corpus. Another rule: such a returned soul can't switch from person to person. It must stay with whom it's at for the duration of the affair.

"Bolyai had to make a snap decision. I was pre-empted. His sense of propriety wouldn't let him, uh, enter a woman. It wouldn't do a lot of good if he hooked up with one of you others, who aren't going. Though our prayer hadn't mentioned it, he'd gathered from the overtones that the expedition did have a third member who was male. He willed himself there. He always was rash. Too late, he discovered he'd landed in Svartalf."

Barney's brick-house shoulders drooped. "Our project's gone for nothing?"

"No," I said. "With Ginny's witchcraft to help—boost his feline brain power—Bolyai thinks he can operate. He's spent a sizable chunk of afterlife studying the geometry of the continua, exploring planes of existence too weird for him to hint at. He loves the idea of a filibuster into hell."

Svartalf's tail swung, his ears stood erect, his whiskers dithered.

"Then it worked!" Ginny shouted. "Whoopee!"

"So far and to this extent, yeah." My determination was unchanged but my enthusiasm less. Lobachevsky's knowledge darkened me:—I sense a crisis. The Adversary can ill afford to let you succeed.

"Well," Karlslund said blankly. "Well, well."

Ginny stopped her war dance when I said: "Maybe you better make that phone call, Dr. Griswold."

The little scientist nodded. "I'll do it from my office. We can plug in an extension here, audio-visual reception."

We had a few minutes' wait. I held Ginny close by my side. Our troops muttered aimlessly or slumped exhausted. Bolyai was alone in his cheerfulness. He used Svartalf to tour the lab with eager curiosity. By now he knew more math and science than living men will acquire before world's end; but it intrigued him to see how we were going about things.

The phone awoke. We saw what Griswold did. The breath sucked in between my teeth.

"I'm sorry to keep you waiting," the professor said. "It was impossible for me to come earlier. What can I do for you?"

Shining Knife identified himself and showed his sigil. "I'm trying to get in touch with Mr. and Mrs. Steven Matuchek. You know them, don't you?"

"Well, ah, yes…haven't seen them lately—" Griswold was a lousy liar.

Shining Knife's countenance hardened. "Please listen, sir. I returned this afternoon from a trip to Washington on their account. The matter they're involved in is that big. I checked with my subordinates. Mrs. Matuchek had disappeared. Her husband had spent time in a spy-proof conference room. He'd not been seen to leave his place of work at quitting time. I sent a man in to ask for him, and he wasn't to be found. Our people had taken pictures of those who went into the plant. A crime lab worker here recognized you among the members of the conference. Are you sure the Matucheks aren't with you?"

"Y-yes. Yes. Why do you want them? Not a criminal charge?"

"No, unless they misbehave. I've a special order enjoining them from certain actions they may undertake. Whoever abetted them would be equally subject to arrest."

Griswold was game. He overcame his shyness and sputtered: "Frankly, Mr. Shining Knife, I resent your implication. And in any event, the writ must be served to have force. Until such time, they are not bound by it, nor are their associates."

"True. Mind if I come look around your place? They might happen to be there…without your knowledge."

"Yes, sir, I do mind. You may not."

"Be reasonable, Dr. Griswold. Among other things, the purpose is to protect them from themselves."

"That attitude is a major part of what I dislike about the present Administration. Good day to you, sir."

"Uh, hold." Shining Knife's tone remained soft, but nobody could mistake his expression. "You don't own the building you're in."

"I'm responsible for it. Trismegistus is a private foundation. I can exercise discretionary authority and forbid access to your…your myrmidons."

"Not when they arrive with a warrant, Professor."

"Then I suggest you obtain one." Griswold broke the spell.

In the lab, we regarded each other. "How long?" I asked.

Barney shrugged. "Under thirty minutes. The FBI has ways."

"Can we scram out of here?" Ginny inquired of him.

"I wouldn't try it. The area probably went under surveillance before Shining Knife tried to call. I expect he stayed his hand simply because he doesn't know what we're doing and his directive is to proceed with extreme caution."

She straightened. "Okay. Then we go to hell." Her mouth twitched faintly upward. "Go directly to hell. Do not pass Go. Do not collect two hundred dollars."

"Huh?" Barney grunted, as if he'd been kicked in the stomach. "No! You're as crazy as the Feds think you are! No preparation, no proper equipment—"

"We can cobble together a lot with what's around here," Ginny said. "Bolyai can advise us and Lobachevsky till we leave. We'll win an advantage of surprise. The demonic forces won't have had time to organize against our foray. Once we're out of American jurisdiction, can Shining Knife legally recall us? And he won't keep you from operating our lifeline. That'd be murder. Besides, I suspect he's on our side, not glad of his duty. He may well offer you help." She went to Barney, took one of his hands between both of hers, and looked up into his craggy face. "Don't hinder us, old friend," she pleaded. "We've got to have you on our side."

His torment was hurtful to see. But he started ripping out commands. Our team plunged into work.

Griswold entered. "Did you—Oh! You can't leave now."

"We can't not," I said.

"But you haven't…haven't had dinner! You'll be weak and—Well, I know I can't stop you. We keep a fridge with food in the research lab, for when a project runs late. I'll see what it holds."

So that's how we went to storm the fastness of hell: Janice's borrowed shoulder purse on Ginny, and the pockets of Barney's outsize jacket (sleeves haggled short) on me, abulge with peanut butter sandwiches, tinned kipper for Svartalf-Bolyai, and four cans of beer.

We had some equipment, notably Ginny's kit. This included Valeria's primary birth certificate, which Ashman had brought. The directions he could give us for using it were the main reason he'd been recruited. She put it in her own bag, clipped to her waist, for the time being.

Nobody, including our geometers, knew exactly what would and would not work in hell. Lobachevsky was able to tell us that high-religious symbols had no power there as they do here. Their virtue comes from their orientation to the Highest, and the fundamental thing about hell is that no dweller in it can love. However, we might gain something from paganism. Its element of honor and justice meant nothing where we were bound, but its element of power and pro-pitiation did, and although centuries have passed since anyone served those gods, the mana has not wholly vanished from their emblems.

Ginny habitually wore on her dress the Moon Goddess pin that showed she was a licensed witch. Griswold found a miniature jade plaque, Aztec, carved with a grotesque grinning feathered serpent, that could be secured to the wereflash beneath my shirt. A bit sheepish under Pastor Karlslund's eye, Barney fished out a silver hammer pendant, copy of a Viking era original. It belonged to his wife, but he'd carried it himself "for a rabbit's foot" since this trouble broke, and now passed the chain around Svartalf's neck.

Projectile weapons weren't apt to be worth lugging. Ginny and I are pretty good shots in the nearly Euclidean space of this plenum. But when the trajectory is through unpredictable distortions that affect the very gravity, forget it, chum. We buckled on swords. She had a slender modern Solingen blade, meant for ritual use but whetted to a sharp point and edge. Mine was heavier and older, likewise kept for its goetic potency, but that stemmed from its being a cutlass which had once sailed with Decatur.

Air might be a problem. Hell was notoriously foul. Scuba rigs were in stock, being used for underwater investigations. When this gets you involved with nix-ies or other tricky creatures, you need a wizard or witch along, whose familiar won't be a convenient beast like a seal unless you have the luck to engage one of the few specialists. Accordingly there are miniature oxygen bottles and adjustable masks for a wide variety of animals. We could outfit Svartalf, and I tied another pint-size unit to the tank on my back—for Val, in case. That completed the list.

While we busked ourselves with several helpers, Barney and Nobu made the final preparations to transmit us. Or almost final. At the last minute I asked them to do an additional job as soon as might be.

At the center of the Nexus drawn on the door, whose shape I won't reveal, they'd put a regular confining pentacle set about with blessed candles. A giant bell jar hung from a block and tackle above, ready to be lowered. This was for the counter-mass from the hell universe, which might be alive, gaseous, or other-wise troublesome. "After we've gone," I said, "lay a few hundred extra pounds of mate-rial in there, if the area's not too dangerous to enter."

"What?" Barney said, astonished. "But that'd allow, uh, anything—a pur-suer—to make the transition with no difficulty."

"Having arrived here, it can't leave the diagram," I pointed out. "We can and will, in a mighty quick jump. Have spells ready to prevent its return home. Thing is, I don't know what we'll find. Could be an item, oh, of scientific value; and the race needs more data about hell. Probably we won't collect any loot. But let's keep the option."

"Okay. Sound thinking, for a lunatic." Barney wiped his eyes. "Damn, I must be allergic to something here."

Janice didn't weep alone when we bade good-bye. And within me paced the grave thought:

—No more may I aid you, Steven Pavlovitch, Virginia Williamovna, Janos Farkasovitch, and cat who surely has a soul of his own. Now must I become a mere watcher and recorder, for the sake of nothing except my curiosity. I will not burden you with the grief this causes me. You will not be further aware of my presence. May you fare with God's blessing.

I felt him depart from the conscious part of my mind like a dream that fades as you wake and try to remember. Soon he was only something good that had happened to me for a couple of hours. Or no, not entirely. I suspect what calm I kept in the time that followed was due to his unsensed companionship. He couldn't help being what he was.

Holding our brooms, Ginny and I walked hand in hand to the Nexus. Svartalf paced ahead. At the midpoint of the figure, we halted for a kiss and a whisper before we slipped the masks on. Our people cast the spell. Again the chamber filled with night. Energies gathered. Thunder and earthquake brawled. I hung onto my fellows lest we get separated. Through the rising racket, I heard my witch read from the parchment whereon stood the name Victrix, urging us toward her through diabolic space-time.

The room, the world, the stars and universes began to rotate about the storm's eye where we stood. Swifter and swifter they turned until they were sheer spinning, the Grotte quern itself. Then was only a roar as of great waters. We were drawn down the maelstrom. The final glimpse of light dwindled with horrible speed, and when we reached infinity, it was snuffed out. Afterward came such twistings and terrors that nothing would have sent us through them except our Valeria Victrix.

I must have blanked out for a minute or a millennium. At least, I became aware with ax-chop abruptness that the passage was over and we had arrived.

Wherever it was.

I clutched Ginny to me. We searched each other with a touch that quivered and found no injuries. Svartalf was hale too. He didn't insist on attention as he normally would. Bolyai made him pad in widening spirals, feeling out our environment.

With caution I slipped off my mask and tried the air. It was bitterly cold, driving in a wind that sought to the bones, but seemed clean—sterile, in fact.

Sterility. That was the whole of this place. The sky was absolute and endless black, though in some fashion we could see stars and ugly cindered planets, visibly moving in chaotic paths; they were pieces of still deeper darkness, not an absence but a negation of light. We stood on a bare plain, hard and gray and flat as concrete, relieved by nothing except scattered boulders whose shapes were never alike and always hideous. The illumination came from the ground, wan, shadowless, colorless. Vision faded at last into utter distance. For that plain had no horizon, no interruptions; it went on. The sole direction, sound, movement, came from the drearily whistling wind.

Ginny removed her mask too, letting it hang over the closed bottle like mine. She shuddered and hugged herself. The dress whipped around her. "I w-w-was ready to guard against flames," she said. It was as appropriate a remark as most that are made on historic occasions.

"Dante described the seventh circle of the Inferno as frozen," I answered slowly. "There's reason to believe he knew something. Where are we?"

"I can't tell. If the name spell worked, along with the rest, we're on the same planet—if 'planet' means a lot here—as Val will be, and not too far away." We'd naturally tried for a before-hand arrival."

"This isn't like what the previous expeditions reported."

"No. Nor was our transition. We used different rituals, and slanted across time to boot. Return should be easier."

Svartalf disappeared behind a rock. I didn't approve of that. *"Kommen Sie züriick!"* I shouted into the wind. *"Retournez-vous!"* I realized that, without making a fuss about it, Lobachevsky had prior to our departure impressed on me fluent French and German. By golly, Russian too!

"Meeowr-r," blew back. I turned. The cat was headed our way from opposite to where he'd been. "What the dickens?" I exclaimed.

"Warped space," Ginny said. "Look." While he trotted steadily, Svartalf's path wove as if he were drunk. "A line where he is must answer to a curve elsewhere. And he's within a few yards. What about miles off?"

I squinted around. "Everything appears straight."

"It would, while you're stationary. Br-r-r! We've got to get warmer."

She drew the telescoping wand from her purse. The star at its tip didn't coruscate here; it was an ember. But it made a lighted match held under our signatures and Svartalf's paw-print generate welcome heat in our bodies. A bit too much, to be frank; we started sweating. I decided the hell universe was at such high entropy—so deep into thermodynamic decay—that a little potential went very far.

Svartalf arrived. Staring uneasily over the plain, I muttered, "We haven't met enough troubles. What're we being set up for?"

"We've two items in our favor," Ginny said. "First, a really effective transfer spell. Its influence is still perceptible here, warding us, tending to smooth out fluctuations and similarize nature to home. Second, the demons must have known well in advance where and when the earlier expeditions would come through. They'd ample time to fix up some nasty tricks. We, though, we've stolen a march." She brushed an elflock from her brow and added starkly: "I expect we'll get our fill of problems as we travel."

"We have to?"

"Yes. Why should the kidnaper make re-entry at this desert spot? We can't have landed at the exact point we want. Be quiet while I get a bearing."

Held over the Victrix parchment, the proper words sung, her dowser pointed out an unequivocal direction. The scryer globe remained cloudy, giving us no hint of distance or look at what lay ahead. Space-time in between was too alien.

We ate, drank, rested what minutes we dared, and took off. Ginny had the lead with Svartalf on her saddlebow, I flew on her right in echelon. The sticks were cranky and sluggish, the screenfields kaput, leaving us exposed to the wind from starboard. But we did loft and level off before the going got tough.

At first it was visual distortion. What I saw—my grasp on the controls, Svartalf, Ginny's splendid figure, the stones underneath—rippled, wavered, widened, narrowed, flowed from one obscene caricature of itself to a worse. Gobs of flesh seemed to slough off, hang in drops, stretch thin, break free and disappear. Sound altered too; the skirl turned into a cacophony of yells, buzzes, drones, fleetingly like words almost understandable and threatening, pulses too deep to hear except with the body's automatic terror reaction. "Don't pay heed!" I called. "Optical effects, Doppler—" but no message could get through that gibbering.

Suddenly my love receded. She whirled from me like a blown leaf. I tried to follow, straight into the blast that lashed tears from my eyes. The more rudder I gave the broom, the faster our courses split apart. "Bolyai, help!" I cried into the aloneness. It swallowed me.

I slid down a long wild curve. The stick would not pull out of it. Well, flashed through my fear, I'm not in a crash dive, it'll flatten a short ways above—

And the line of rocks athwart my path were not rocks, they were a mountain range toward which I catapulted. The gale laughed in my skull and shivered the broom beneath me. I hauled on controls, I bellowed the spells, but any change I could make would dash me on the ground before I hit those cliffs.

Somehow I'd traveled thousands of miles—had to be that much, or I'd have seen these peaks on the limitless plain, wouldn't I have?—and Ginny was lost, Val was lost, I could brace myself for death but not for the end of hope.

"Yeee-ow-w-w!" cut through the clamor. I twisted in my seat. And there came Ginny. Her hair blew in fire. The star on her wand burned anew like Sirius. Bolyai was using Svartalf's paws to steer; yellow eyes and white fangs flared in the panther countenance.

They pulled alongside. Ginny leaned over till our fingers met. Her sensations ran down the circuit to me. I saw with her what the cat was doing. I imitated. It would have wrecked us at home. But here we slewed sideways and started gaining altitude.

How to explain? Suppose you were a Flatlander, a mythical creature (if any creature is mythical) of two space dimensions, no more. You live in a surface. That's right, *in.* If this is a plane, its geometry obeys the Euclidean rules we learn in high school: parallel lines don't meet, the shortest distance between two points is a straight line, the angles of a triangle total 180 degrees, et cetera. But now imagine that some three-dimensional giant plucks you out and drops you into a surface of different shape. It might be a sphere, for example. You'll find space fantastically changed. In a sphere, you must think of lines in terms of meridians and parallels, which means they have finite length; in general, distance between points is minimized by following a great circle; triangles have a variable number of degrees, but always more than 180—You might well go mad. Now imagine cones, hyperboloids, rotated trigonometric and logarithmic curves, Mobius bands, whatever you can.

And now imagine a planet which is all water, churned by storms and not constrained by the ordinary laws of physics. At any point its surface can have any form, which won't even stay constant in time. Expand the two dimensions into three; make it four for the temporal axis, unless this requires more than one, as many philosophers believe; add the hyperspace in which paranatural forces act; put it under the rule of chaos and hatred: and you've got some analogy to the hell universe.

We'd hit a saddle point back yonder, Ginny passing to one side of it, I to the other. Our courses diverged because the curvatures of space did. My attempt to intercept her was worse than useless; in the region where I found myself, a line aimed her way quickly bent in a different direction. I blundered from geometry to geometry, through a tuck in space that bypassed enormous reaches, toward my doom.

No mortal could have avoided it. But Bolyai was mortal no longer. To his genius had been added the knowledge and skill of more than a century's liberation from the dear but confining flesh. Svartalf's body had changed from a trap to a tool, once his rapport with Ginny enabled the mathematician to draw on her resources also. He could make lightning-quick observations of a domain, mentally write and solve the equations that described it, calculate what its properties would be, get an excellent notion of what the contour would shade into next—in fractional seconds. He wove through the dimensional storms of hell like a quarterback bound for a touchdown.

He gloried. For lack of other voice, he sang the songs of a black tomcat out after fornication and battle. We clawed over the mountains and streaked toward our goal.

It was no milk run. We must keep aware and reacting each instant. Often we made an error that well-nigh brought us to grief. I'd lose contact with Ginny and wander off again; or a lurch would nearly make us collide; or the intense gravitational field where space was sharply warped hurled our sticks groundward and tried to yank out guts and eyeballs; or a quick drop in weight sent us spinning; or we shot through folds in space instead of going around and were immediately elsewhere—I don't recall every incident. I was too busy to notice a lot of them.

We traveled, though, and faster than we'd hoped, once Bolyai discovered what tricks we could play when the time dimension was buckled. The deafening racket and disgusting illusions plagued us less as we got the hang of passing smoothly from metric to metric. Moreover, the world around us grew steadier. Somebody or something wanted to lair in a region where disturbances tended to cancel out—surely our goal.

I became able to study the landscape. It changed behind us, though its desolation was constant. The plain gave way to crags, to miles of jumbled bones, to a pit that seemed without bottom, to a lava sea across which sleeted flames and from which rose fumes that made us don our masks, to a swamp of dead trees where thin black mantis-like figures danced around a steeple-high bonfire where other figures writhed shrieking…and on to worse things. We plowed through. Each time Ginny lifted her globe, a pale but waxing glow from inside it showed we were nearer our destination.

We couldn't hope to be unobserved, that whole long route. And doubtless word would flash ahead. We pushed the hardest we could.

We crossed a forest of gallows and a river that flowed with a noise like sobbing and whose spray, cast up by a gust, was warm and salt. We suffered the heat and poisonous vapors from a system of roads where motor vehicles of some kind crawled nose to tail across miles. We traversed hills gouged with trenches and the craters of explosions, rusted cannon the last sign of life except for one flag, raised as in victory, whose colors had faded to gray. The hills climbed till we met another range so high we needed our masks; flitting through its canyons, we dodged stones that fell upward.

But past those mountains the land swooped down anew. Another plain of boulders reached beyond sight. Far off upon it, toylike at their remove, we spied gaunt black towers. The globe flared brilliant, the wand leaped to point in Ginny's fingers. "By Hecate," she cried, "that's it!"

I drew alongside. The air was still cold and blowing, a wail in our ears, a streaming past our ribs, a smell akin to burning sulfur and wet iron. At hover, the broomsticks rocked and pitched. Her foot against mine was a very precious contact.

We peered into the globe she held. Svartalf-Bolyai craned around her arm to see. This close, the intervening space not too different from home geometry, the scrying functioned well. Ginny zoomed in on the castle. It was sable in hue, monstrous in size and shape. Or had it a shape? It sprawled, it soared, it burrowed with no unity except ugliness. Here a thin spire lifted crookedly from a cubical donjon, there a dome swelled pustular, yonder a stone beard overhung a misproportioned gate…square miles of planless deformity, aswarm with the maggoty traffic of devils.

We tried to look through the walls, but didn't penetrate far. Behind and beneath the cavernous chambers and twisted labyrinths that we discerned, too much evil force roiled. It was just as well, considering what we did vaguely make out. At the limit, a thought came from just beyond, for an instant—no, not a thought, a wave of such agony that Ginny cried aloud and I bit blood out of my lip. We blanked the globe and embraced till we could stop shuddering.

"Can't afford this," she said, drawing free. "Time's gotten in short supply."

She reactivated the scryer, with a foreseer spell. Those rarely work in our universe, but Lobachevsky had theorized that the fluid dimensions of the Low Continuum might give us a better chance. The view in the globe panned, steadied on one spot, and moved close. Slab-like buildings and contorted towers enclosed a certain courtyard in an irregular septagon. At the middle of this was a small, lumpy stone house, windowless and with a single doorway. A steeple climbed from it, suggestive of a malformed ebon toadstool, that overtopped the surrounding structures and overshadowed the pavement.

We couldn't view the inside of this either, for the same reason as before. It seemed to be untenanted, though. I had the creepy feeling that it corresponded in some perverted way to a chapel.

"Unambiguous and sharp," Ginny said. "That means she'll arrive there, and soon. We'll have to lay our plans fast."

"And move fast, too," I said. "Give me an overall scan, will you, with spot closeups?"

She nodded. The scene changed to one from on high. I noted afresh how it pullulated in the crowds. Were they always this frantic? Not quite, surely. We focused on a single band of demons. No two looked alike; vanity runs high in hell. A body covered with spines, a tentacled dinosaur, a fat slattern whose nipples were tiny grinning heads, a flying swine, a changeable blob, a nude man with a snake for a phallus, a face in a belly, a dwarf on ten-foot pencil-thin legs, and less describable sights— What held my attention was that most of them were armed. They didn't go for projectiles either, evidently. However, those medievalish weapons would be bad to encounter.

Sweeping around, our vision caught similar groups. The confusion was unbelievable. There was no discipline, no consideration, everybody dashed about like a decapitated chicken yelling at everybody else, they jostled and snarled and broke into fights. But more arms were being fetched each minute from inside, more grotesque flyers lumbered into the air and circled.

"They've been alerted, all right," I said.

"I don't suppose they know what to expect," Ginny said in a low, tight voice. "They aren't especially guarding the site we're after. Didn't the Adversary pass word about us?"

"He seems to be debarred from taking a personal hand in this matter, same as Lobachevsky and for analogous reasons, I guess. At most, he may've tipped his underlings to watch out for trouble from us. But they can't know we've acquired the capability to do what we did. Especially since we've made an end run in time."

"And the diabolic forces are stupid," Ginny said. "Evil is never intelligent or creative. They receive word a raid is possible, and look at that mess!"

"Don't underrate them. An idiot can kill you just as dead." I pondered. "Here's what we'll do, if you agree. Rush straight in. We can't prevent them seeing us, so we have to be quick. Good thing our sticks function close to normal in this neighborhood. We won't make directly for the yard or they might block us off. See that palace, I assume it is, over to the left—the one with the columns in front that look like bowels? Must belong to the big cheese, which makes it a logical spot for enemies to drop a bomb on. At the last moment we'll swerve toward our real mark. You get inside, establish our paranatural defenses, and ready the return spell. I'll keep the door. The instant Val appears, you skewer the kidnaper and grab her. Got it?"

"Yes. Oh, Steve." The tears ran silently from her eyes. "I love you."

We kissed a final time, there in the sky of hell. Then we attacked.

The wind of our passage shouted around us. The dreary landscape reeled away beneath. I heard Svartalf's challenge and answered with my own whoop. Fear blew out of me. Gangway, you legions of darkness, we're coming to fetch our girl!

They began to see us. Croaks and yammers reached our ears, answered by shrieks from below. The flying devils milled in the air. Others joined them till several hundred wings beat in a swarm across the sooty stars. They couldn't make up the minds they scarcely had what to do about us. Nearer we came and nearer. The castle rose in our vision like the ranges we had crossed.

Ginny must spend her entire force warding off sorceries. Lightning bolts spattered blue on the shield-field, yards off, followed by thunder and ozone. Lethal clouds boiled from smokestacks, englobed our volume of air and dissipated. I had no doubt that, unperceived by us, curses, hoodoos, illusions, temptations, and screaming meemies rained upward and rebounded.

The effort was draining her. I glimpsed the white, strained countenance, hair plastered to brow and cheek by sweat, wand darting while the free hand gestured and the lips talked spells. Svartalf snarled in front of her; Bolyai piloted the broom. None of them could keep it up for many minutes.

But that conjure wave made it impossible for anything to get at us physically. The creature in charge must have realized this at the end, for the assault stopped. An eagle the size of a horse, wearing a crocodile's head, swooped upon us.

My cutlass was drawn. I rose in the stirrups. "Not one cent for tribute!" I bayed, and struck. The old power awoke in the blade. It smote home with a force I felt through my bones. Blood spurted from a sheared-off wing. The devil bawled and dropped.

A batsnake threw a loop around my right arm. I grabbed its neck with my left hand before it could sink fangs in me. Human, I remain wolf; I bit it in two. Barely in time, I cut at a twin-tailed manta coming for Ginny. It fell aft, spilling guts. An aerial hound sought to intercept us. I held my weapon straight and got him with the point.

Horns hooted their discord. The flapping, cawing, stinking flock retreated in its regular disorder. Our stratagem had worked. Their entire outfit, infantry, air corps, and all, was being summoned to defend the palace.

We pursued to within a hundred yards. The manor was no longer visible for wings and feculent bodies. I lifted my blade as signal. We swung right and whizzed downward. Babel erupted behind us.

We landed jarringly hard. Surrounded by walls, brooded over by the cap of its tower, the building huddled in twilight. I bounced from my seat to the door and tried its ill-feeling handle. It creaked open and we ran in.

A single room, dank jagged stone, lay before us. It wasn't large in area, but opened above on the measureless dark of the tower. The room was bare except for an altar where a Glory Hand cast dull blue light. The arrangement of objects and the pattern on the floor were similar to those we'd employed for transit.

The heart cracked in me. "Val!" I sobbed. Ginny wrestled me to a halt. She couldn't have done so without Svartalf getting between my ankles.

"Hold it," she gasped. "Don't move. That's the changeling."

I drew a lungful of air and regained my sanity. Of course, of course. But it was more than I could endure to look at that chubby shape before the altar, gold curls and empty, empty eyes. Strange, also, to see next to the half-alive thing the mass already exchanged from our house: dust flug, sandbox contents, coffee grounds, soggy paper towels, a Campbell's Soup can—

The devil garrison was boiling over the walls and through the portals into this courtyard. I slammed the door and dropped the bolt. It was good and heavy: might buy us a few minutes.

How many did we need? I tried to reconstruct events. The kidnaper was doubtless moronic even by hell's standards. He'd heard Marmiadon's curse. A lot of them must have, but didn't see anything they could do to fulfill it. This one noticed our vulnerability. "Duh," he said, and flashed off to collect some kudos, without consulting any of the few demons that are able to think. Such a higher-up could have told him to lay off. His action would give a clue to the link between hell and the Johannine Church, and thus imperil the whole scheme for the sabotage of religion and society that the Adversary had been working on since he deluded the first of the neo-Gnostics.

Being the dimbulb he was, this creature could not solve the momentum problem of transferring a body other than his own between universes, unless the exchange mass was nearly identical in configuration. His plan would have been to appear in our home, scan Valeria as she slept, return here, 'chant a hunk of meat into her semblance, and go back after her. The first part would only have taken seconds, though it got the wind up Svartalf. The snatch ought to have gone quickly too, but the cat was waiting and attacked.

At this moment, if simultaneity had meaning between universes, the fight ramped and Svartalf's blood was riven from him. My throat tightened. I stooped over him. "We'd have arrived too late here except for you," I whispered. "They don't make thanks for that sort of help." Infinitely gently, I stroked the sleek head. He twitched his ears, annoyed. In these surroundings, he'd no patience with fine sentiments. Besides, currently they were Janos Bolyai's ears too.

Ginny was chalking a diagram around the room for a passive defense against demonurgy. It took care, because she mustn't disturb altar, emblem, or objects elsewhere. They were the fiend's return ticket. Given them, he need simply cast the appropriate spell in our cosmos, just as we'd use the things and symbols in Griswold's lab for a lifeline. If the kidnaper found himself unable to make it back with his victim, God alone knew what would happen. They'd certainly both leave our home and a changeling replace them. But we'd have no inkling of how this came about or where they'd gone. It might provide the exact chance the enemy needed to get his project back on the rails.

Outside, noise swelled—stamp, howl, whistle, grunt, gibber, bubble, hiss, yelp, whine, squawk, moan, bellow. The door reverberated under fists, feet, hoofs. I might well have to transform. I dropped the scuba gear and my outer garments, except for wrapping Barney's jacket around my left forearm.

A mouth, six feet wide and full of clashing teeth, floated through a wall. I yelled, Svartalf spat. Ginny grabbed her wand and cried dismissal. The thing vanished. But thereafter she was continually interrupted to fight off such attacks.

She had to erect fortifications against them before she could begin the spell that would send us home. The latter ritual must not be broken off till at least a weak field had been established between this point and the lab on earth, or it became worthless. Having made initial contact, Ginny could feel out at leisure what balance of forces was required, and bring them up to the strength necessary for carrying us. Now she wasn't getting leisure. In consequence, her defensive construction went jaggedly and slowly.

The hullabaloo outside dwindled somewhat. I heard orders barked. Thuds and yammers suggested they were enforced with clubs. A galloping grew. The door rocked under a battering ram.

I stood aside. At the third blow, the door splintered and its hinges tore loose. The lead devil on the log stumbled through. He was rather like a man-sized cockroach. I cut him apart with a brisk sweep. The halves threshed and clawed for a while after they fell. They entangled the stag-horned being that came next, enabling me to take him with ease.

The others hauled back the log, which blocked the narrow entrance. But my kills remained as a partial barrier in front of me. The murk outside turned most of the garrison into shadows, though their noise stayed deafening and their odors revolting.

One trod forward in the shape of a gorilla on man's legs. He wielded an ax in proportion to his size. It hewed. Poised in karate stance, I shifted to let it go by. Chips sleeted where it hit stone. My cutlass sang. Fingers came off him. He dropped the ax. Bawling his pain, he cuffed at me. I did the fastest squat on record. While that skull-cracker of a hand boomed above, I got an Achilles tendon. He fell. I didn't try for a death, because he barred access while he dragged himself away. My pulse seethed in my ears.

A thing with sword and shield was next. We traded blows for a couple of minutes. He was good. I parried, except for slashes that the jacket absorbed; but I couldn't get past that shield. Metal clashed above the bedlam as sparks showered in twilight. My breath started coming hard. He pressed close. A notion flashed in me. As he cut over the top of his shield, I dropped down again. My weapon turned his, barely. My left hand grabbed the ax, stuck the helve between his legs, and shoved. He toppled, exposing his neck. I smote.

Rising, I threw the ax at the monster behind, who reeled back. A spear-wielder poked at me. I got the shaft and chopped it over.

No further candidates advanced right away. The mass churned around, arguing with itself. Through the hammering of my heart, I realized I couldn't hold out much longer. As human, that is. Here was a chance to assume the less vulnerable Lyco state. I tossed my blade aside and turned the flash on myself.

At once I discovered that transformation was slow and agonizing amidst these influences. For a space I writhed helpless between shapes. A rooster-headed fiend cackled his glee and rushed forward, snickersnee on high. Werewolf or no, I couldn't survive bisection. Svartalf bolted past me, walked up the enemy's abdomen, and clawed his eyes out.

Wolf, I resumed my post. The cat went back inside. We were just in time. The garrison finally got the idea of throwing stuff. Space grew thick with rocks, weapons, and assorted impedimenta. Most missed. Hell is no place to develop your throwing arm. Those that hit knocked me about, briefly in pain, but couldn't do any real damage.

The barrage ended when, in sheer hysteria, they tried to storm us. That was turmoil, slice, hack, rip, tumbling about in their vile welter. They might have overrun me by numbers had Ginny not finished her paranatural defenses and come to my aid. Her weapon disposed of the demons that crawled over the pile of struggling bodies.

When at last they withdrew, their dead and wounded were heaped high. I sat down amidst the ichor, the fragments, the lamentations, unreeled my tongue and gulped air. Ginny rumpled my fur, half laughing, half crying. Some claws had reached her; blood trickled from scratches and her dress was tattered into battle banners. Svartalf's aid had prevented her opponents from inflicting serious wounds, though. I glanced within and saw him playing mousey with a devil's tail.

More important was the soft luminosity from the lines woven across the floor. We were accessible as ever to physical force, but goetics couldn't touch us now. To break down her impalpable walls would take longer than we'd possibly stay.

"Steve, Steve, Steve—" Ginny straightened. "I'd better prepare for our return."

"*Halt!*" called a voice from the dusk. It was hoarse, with an eerie hypnotic rhythm, not calming, but, rather, invoking wrath and blind energy. "*Waffenstillstand. Parlamentieren Sie mit uns.*"

The devils, even the strewn wounded, fell quiet. Their noise sibilated away until the silence was nearly total, and those who could, withdrew until they merged in vision with the blackness behind them. I knew their master had spoken, the lord of this castle...who stood high in the Adversary's councils, if he commanded obedience from these mad creatures.

Boots clacked over flagstones. The demon chief came before us. The shape he had adopted startled me. Like his voice, it was human; but it was completely unmemorable. He was of medium height or less, narrow-shouldered, face homely and a bit puffy, ornamented with nothing but a small toothbrush mustache and a lock of dark hair slanting across the brow. He wore some kind of plain brown military uniform. But why did he add a red armband with the ancient and honorable sign of the fylfot?

Svartalf quit his game and bristled. Through diabolic stench, I caught the smell of Ginny's fear. When you looked into the eyes in that face, it stopped being ordinary. She braced herself, made a point of staring down along the couple of inches she overtopped him, and said in her haughtiest tone, *"Was willst du?"*

It was the *du* of insult. Her personal German was limited, but while Bolyai was in Svartalf she could tap his fluency by rapport with her familiar. (Why did the devil prince insist on German? There's a mystery here that I've never solved.) I retained sufficient human—type capabilities to follow along.

"I ask you the same," the enemy replied. Though he kept to the formal pronoun, his manner was peremptory. "You have encroached on our fatherland. You have flouted our laws. You have killed and maimed our gallant warriors when they sought to defend themselves. You desecrate our House of Sendings with your odious presence. What is your excuse?"

"We have come to gain back what is ours."

"Well? Say on."

I growled a warning, which Ginny didn't need. "If I told you, you might find ways to thwart us," she said. "Be assured, however, we don't intend to stay. We'll soon have completed our mission." Sweat glistened forth on her brow. "I...I suggest it will be to the advantage of both parties if you let us alone meanwhile."

He stamped a boot. "I must know! I demand to know! It is my right!"

"Diseases have no rights," Ginny said. "Think. You cannot pierce our spell-wall nor break through by violence in the time that is left. You can only lose troops. I do not believe your ultimate master would be pleased at such squandering of resources."

He waved his arms. His tone loudened. "I do not admit defeat. For me, defeat has no existence. If I suffer a reverse, it is because I have been stabbed in the back by traitors." He was heading off into half a trance. His words became a harsh, compelling chant. "We shall break the iron ring. We shall crush the vermin that infest the universes. We shall go on to victory. No surrender! No compromise! Destiny calls us onward!"

The mob of monsters picked up a cue and cried hail to him. Ginny said: "If you want to make an offer, make it. Otherwise go away. I've work to do."

His features writhed, but he got back the self-control to say: "I prefer not to demolish the building. Much effort and wizardry is in these stones. Yield yourselves and I promise fair treatment."

"What are your promises worth?"

"We might discuss, for example, the worldly gains rewarding those who serve the cause of the rightful—"

Svartalf mewed. Ginny spun about. I threw a look behind, as a new odor came to me. The kidnaper had materialized. Valeria lay in his grasp.

She was just coming awake, lashes aflutter, head turning, one fist to her lips. "Daddy?" the sleepy little voice murmured. "Mothuh?"

The thing that held her was actually of less weight. It wore an armor-plated spiky-backed body on two clawed feet, a pair of gibbon-like arms ending in similarly murderous talons, and a tiny head with blob features. Blood dripped off it here and there. The loose lips bubbled with an imbecilic grin, till it saw what was waiting.

It yowled in English, "Boss, help!" as it let Val go and tried to scuttle aside. Svartalf blocked the way. It raked at him. He dodged. Ginny got there. She stamped down. I heard a crunch. The demon ululated.

I'd stuck at my post. The lord of the castle tried to get past me. I removed a chunk of his calf. It tasted human, too, sort of. He retreated, into the shadow chaos of his appalled followers. Through their din I followed his screams: "I shall have revenge for this! I shall unleash a secret weapon! Let the House be destroyed! Our pride demands satisfaction! *My patience is exhausted!*"

I braced myself for a fresh combat. For a minute, I almost got one. But the baron managed to control his horde; the haranguing voice overrode theirs. As Ginny said, he couldn't afford more futile casualties.

I thought, as well as a wolf can: Good thing he doesn't know they might not have been futile this time.

For Ginny could not have aided me. After the briefest possible enfolding of her daughter, she'd given the kid to Svartalf. The familiar—and no doubt the mathematician—busied himself with dances, pounces, patty-cake, and wurra-wurra, to keep her out of her mother's hair. I heard the delighted laughter, like silver bells and springtime rain. But I heard, likewise, Ginny's incantation.

She must have about five unbroken minutes to establish initial contact with home, before she could stop and rest. Then she'd need an additional period to determine the precise configuration of vectors and gather the required paranatural energies. And then we'd go!

It clamored in the dark. An occasional missile flew at me, for no reason except hatred. I stood in the door and wondered if we had time.

A rumbling went through the air. The ground shuddered underfoot. The devils keened among shadows. I heard them retreating. Fear gripped me by the gullet. I have never done anything harder than to keep that guardian post.

The castle groaned at its foundations. Dislodged blocks slid from the battlements and crashed. Flamelight flickered out of cracks opened in gates and shutters. Smoke tried to strangle me. It passed, and was followed by the smell of ancient mold.

"*...in nomine Potestatis, fiat janua...*" the witch's hurried verses ran at my back.

The giant upheaved himself.

Higher he stood than the highest spire of this stronghold beside which he had lain buried. The blackness of him blotted out the stars of hell. His tottering feet knocked a curtain wall down in a grinding roar; dust whirled up, earthquake ran. Nearly as loud was the rain of dirt, mud, gravel from the wrinkled skin. Fungi grew there, pallidly phosphorescent, and worms dripped from his eye sockets. The corruption of him seized the breath. The heat of his decay smoldered and radiated. He was dead; but the power of the demon was in him.

"*—saeculi aeternitatis.*" Ginny had kept going till she could pause without danger to the spell. She was that kind of girl. But now she came to kneel by me. "Oh, darling," she wept, "we almost won through!"

I fumbled at my flash. The giant wove his head from side to side as if he still had vision. The faceless visage came to a stop, pointed our way. I shoved the switch and underwent the Skin-turning back to human. The giant raised a foot. He who operated him was trying to minimize damage to the castle. Slowly, carefully, he set it down inside the fortifications.

I held my girl to me. My other girl laughed and romped with the cat. Why trouble them? "We've no chance?"

"I…no time…first-stage field ready, b-b-but flesh can't cross before I…complete—I love you, I love you."

I reached for Decatur's sword where it gleamed in the Handlight. We've come to the end of creation, I thought, and we'll die here. Let's go out fighting. Maybe our souls can escape.

Souls!

I grabbed Ginny by the shoulder and thrust her back to look at. "We can send for help," burst from me. "Not mortals, and angels're forbidden, but, but you do have contact established and…the energy state of this universe—it doesn't take a lot to—There's bound to be many c-creatures, not of Heaven but still no friends of hell—"Her eyes kindled. She sprang erect, seized wand and sword, swung them aloft and shouted.

The giant stepped into our courtyard. The crippled devils gibbered their terror, those he did not crush underfoot. His fingers closed around the tower.

I couldn't tell what language Ginny's formula was in, but she ended her cry in English: "Ye who knew man and were enemies of Chaos, by the mana of the signs we bear I call on you and tell you that the way from earth stands open!"

The chapel rocked. Stones fell, inside and outside. The tower came off. It broke apart in the giant's clutch, a torrent that buried the last of hell's wounded. We looked into lightless constellations. The giant groped to scoop us out.

Our rescuers arrived.

I don't know who or what they were. Perhaps their looks were illusion. I'll admit that the quarters of the compass were from whence they came, because these are nonsense in hell. Perhaps what answered Ginny's call was simply a group of beings, from our universe or yet another, who were glad of a chance to raid the realm of the Adversary that is theirs too. She had built a bridge that was, as yet, too frail to bear mortal bodies. However, as I'd guessed, the entropy of the Low Continuum made paranatural forces able to accomplish what was impossible elsewhere.

Explain it as you like. This is what I saw:

From the West, the figure of a woman, queenly in blue-bordered white robe. Her eyes were gray, her features of icicle beauty. The dark tresses bore a crested helmet. Her right hand carried a spear whose head shimmered midnight azure with glitters as of earthly stars; and upon that shoulder sat an owl. On her left arm was a long shield, which for boss had the agonized face of another woman whose locks were serpents.

From the South, the greatest serpent of them all. His orbs were like suns, his teeth like white knives. Plumes of rainbow color grew on his head, nodding in the wind he brought with him, shining with droplets of the rain that walked beneath. More feathers made a glory down his back. His scales were coral, the scutes upon his belly shone golden. The coils of him lashed about as does the lightning.

From the North, a man in a chariot drawn by two goats. He stood burly, red-bearded, clad in helmet and ring-mail, iron gloves and an iron belt. Driving with his left hand, he gripped a short-handled hammer in his right. The cloak blew behind him on mighty gales. The rumble of his car wheels went down and down the sky. He laughed, swung the hammer and threw it. Where it struck, fire blasted and the air roared; it returned to him.

Each of these loomed so tall that the firmament would hardly contain them. Hell trembled at their passage. The devils fled in a cloud. When his master left, the giant's animation ceased. He fell with an impact that knocked me off my feet. It demolished a large part of the castle. The newcomers didn't stop to level the rest right away, but took off after the fiends. I don't imagine that many escaped.

We didn't watch. Ginny completed the transfer spell and seized Valeria in both her arms. I tucked Decatur's sword under one of mine—damn if it'd be left here!—and offered Svartalf the crook of that elbow. From the floor I plucked up the kidnaper demon. It had a broken leg. "Boss, don't hurt me, I'll be good, I'll talk, I'll tell ya ever't'ing ya want," he kept whining. Evil has no honor.

Ginny spoke the final word, made the final pass. We crossed.

It was nothing like the outbound trip. We were headed back where we belonged. The cosmic forces didn't buck us, they worked for us. We knew a moment of whirling, and were there.

Barney's gang waited in the lab. They sprang back with a cry, a sob, a prayer of thanks as we whoofed into sight under the bell jar. It turned out that we'd only been absent a couple of hours from this continuum. And maybe no more in hell? We couldn't be sure, our watches having stopped during the first transition. It felt like centuries. I looked upon Valeria and Ginny, and it felt like no time.

The child was blinking those big heaven-colored eyes around in astonishment. It struck me that the terrible things she'd witnessed might have scarred her for life. Shakily, I bent over her. "Are you okay, sweetheart?"

"Ooh, Daddy," she beamed. " 'At was fun. Do it again?"

Ginny set her down. I bent and swept the little one to me. She was restless. "I'm hungry," she complained.

I'd let the prisoner go. After the bell jar was raised, it tried to creep off. But it couldn't leave the pentacle, and Barney had laid the spell I asked for that prevented it from returning to the Low Continuum without our leave. Shining Knife had gotten his warrant. He waited too, with a number of his men. He strode in among us and lifted the demon by its sound leg. The grotesque figure sprattled in his grasp. "Boss, gimme a break, boss," it begged. "I'll squeal."

The changeling, of course, vanished from the juvenile home when Valeria was restored. Poor flesh, I hope it was allowed to die.

I didn't think of these matters immediately. Being sure our daughter was well, Ginny and I sought each other. What broke our kiss was a Joy greater yet, a happiness whose echo will never stop chiming in us: *"Free! O Father!"* And when we could look at this world again, Svartalf was only Svartalf.

The gracious presence within me said:—Yes, for this deed Janos Bolyai is made a saint and admitted to the nearness of God. How glad I am. And how glad you won your cause, dear friends, and Valeria Stevenovna is safe and the enemies of the Highest confounded! (Shyly) I have a selfish reason for additional pleasure, be it confessed. What I observed on this journey has given me some fascinating new ideas. A rigorous theoretical treatment—

I sensed the wish that Lobachevsky could not bring himself to think overtly, and uttered it for him: You'd like to stick around awhile?

—Frankly, yes. A few days, after which I must indeed return. It would be marvelous to explore these discoveries, not as a soul, but once again as a mortal. It is like a game, Steven Pavlovitch. One would like to see how far it is possible to go within the constraints of humanity. (In haste) But I beg you, esteemed friend, do not consider this a request. Your lady and yourself have endured perils, hardships, and fear of losing more than your lives. You wish to celebrate your triumph. Believe me, I would never be so indelicate as to—

I looked fondly, a trifle wistfully, at Ginny and thought back: I know what you mean, Nick, and I've every intention of celebrating with her, at frequent intervals, till we reach an implausibly ripe old age. But you've forgotten that the flesh has physical as well as mental limits. She needs a good rest. I need a better one. You might as well stay for a bit. Besides, I want to see that what you write goes to the proper journals. It'll be quite a boost for our side.

And this is how it happened that, although Bolyai led our expedition, Lobachevsky published first.

There is no such thing as living happily ever after.

You'd like to be famous? You can have it, buster: every last reporter, crystal interview, daily ton of mail, pitch for Worthy Causes, autograph hound, belligerent drunk, crank phone call, uninvited visitor, sycophant, and you name it. Luckily, we followed sound advice and played loose. I ended up with a better position than I probably rate, Ginny with the freelance studio she'd always wanted, and we're no longer especially newsworthy. Meanwhile Valeria's gotten to the boy-friend stage, and none of them seem worthy of her. They tell me every father of a girl goes through that. The other children keep me too busy to fret much.

It was quite a story. The demon's public confession brought the Johannine Church down in spectacular style. We've got its diehards around yet, but they're harmless. Then there's the reformed sect of it—where my old sparring partner Marmiadon is prominent—that tries to promulgate the Gospel of Love as merely another creed. Since the Gnosticism and the secret diabolism are out, I don't expect that either St. Peter or gentle St. John greatly mind.

Before he left me for Heaven, Lobachevsky proved some theorems I don't understand. I'm told they've doubled the effectiveness of the spells that Barney's people worked out in those long-ago terrible hours. Our buddy Shining Knife had a lot to do with arranging sensible dissemination of the new knowledge. It has to be classified; you can't trust any old nut with the capabilities conferred. However, the United States government is not the only one that knows how to invade hell if provoked. The armies of Earth couldn't hope to conquer it, but they could make big trouble, and Heaven would probably intervene. As a result, we've no cause to fear other direct assaults from the Adversary's dominion. From men, yes—because he still tempts, corrupts, seduces, tricks, and betrays. But I think if we keep our honor clean and our powder dry we won't suffer more than we can bear.

Looking back, I often can't believe it happened: that this was done by a red-haired witch, a bobtailed werewolf, and a snooty black tomcat. Then I remember it's the Adversary who is humorless. I'm sure God likes to laugh.

Acknowledgments

The following people helped make this book possible.

Technical help was provided by Dave Grubbs and Alice Lewis.

Proofreading was done by David Anderson, Ann Broomhead, Jim Burton, Lis Carey, Gay Ellen Dennett, Lisa Hertel, Suford Lewis, Tony Lewis, Paula Lieberman, Mark Olson, Priscilla Olson, Joe Ross, Jean Rossner, Sharon Sbarsky, and Tim Szczesuil.

A further round of proofing was then done by Jean Rossner and Sharon Sbarsky.

Dave Grubbs then did the final proofing of the book

Alice Lewis did her magic in producing the dust jacket.

Special thanks to David G. Hartwell for his introduction to the book and Karen Anderson who provided another nifty picture of Poul Anderson—

—And to the New England Science Fiction Association (NESFA) Inc. for its support in bringing classic science fiction back in print. The NESFA Choice Books are proposed by a member of NESFA, and all of them remain in print. See the following page for a sample list of some of our books with information on how to look at our web site which contains the full list of books.

Rick Katze, editor
October 1, 2010

Superlative SF Available from NESFA Press

Call Me Joe (volume 1) by Poul Anderson $29

The Queen of Air and Darkness (volume 2) by Poul Anderson $29

The Saturn Game (volume 3) by Poul Anderson $29

Major Ingredients by Eric Frank Russell $29

Entities by Eric Frank Russell $29

Flights of Eagles by James Blish $29

Brothers in Arms by Lois McMaster Bujold $25

Robots and Magic by Lester Del Rey $29

The Masque of Mañana by Robert Sheckley $29

Magic Mirrors by John Bellairs $25

Transfinite: The Essential A. E. van Vogt $29

This Mortal Mountain (volume 3) by Roger Zelazny $29

Last Exit to Babylon (volume 4) by Roger Zelazny $29

Nine Black Doves (volume 5) by Roger Zelazny $29

The Road to Amber (volume 6) by Roger Zelazny $29

Details on these books and many others are available online at: www.nesfa.
org/press/. Books may be ordered online or by writing to:

NESFA Press, PO Box 809, Framingham MA 01701

We accept checks (in US $), most major credit cards, and PayPal. Please add
$4 P&H for one book, $8 for an order of two to five books, and $2/book for
orders of six or more. For foreign orders, $12/book for one or two books,
$36 for three to five books, and $6/book for 6 or more books. Please allow
3-4 weeks. for delivery. (Overseas, allow 2 months or more. Massachusetts
residents please add 6.25% sales tax. Fax orders (include credit card or PayPal
information): (617) 776-3243.

NESFA Press

Post Office Box 809
Framingham, MA 01701
www.nesfa.org/press
2011